Blood on the Stage, 1975–2000

Milestone Plays of Crime, Mystery, and Detection: An Annotated Repertoire

Amnon Kabatchnik

THE SCARECROW PRESS, INC.
Lanham • Toronto • Plymouth, UK
2012

Published by Scarecrow Press, Inc.
A wholly owned subsidiary of The Rowman & Littlefield Publishing Group, Inc.
4501 Forbes Boulevard, Suite 200, Lanham, Maryland 20706
www.rowman.com

10 Thornbury Road, Plymouth PL6 7PP, United Kingdom

British Library Cataloguing in Publication Information Available

Library of Congress Cataloging-in-Publication Data
Kabatchnik, Amnon, 1929–
  Blood on the stage, 1975–2000 : milestone plays of crime, mystery, and
detection: an annotated repertoire / Amnon Kabatchnik.
      p. cm.
  Includes bibliographical references and index.
  ISBN 978-0-8108-8354-3 (cloth : alk. paper) — ISBN 978-0-8108-8355-0 (ebook)
  1. Detective and mystery plays—History and criticism. 2. Detective and
mystery plays—Stories, plots, etc. I. Title.
  PN1952.K36 2012
  809.2'527—dc23   2012020471

♾ ™ The paper used in this publication meets the minimum requirements of
American National Standard for Information Sciences—Permanence of Paper
for Printed Library Materials, ANSI/NISO Z39.48-1992.

Printed in the United States of America

To the memory of my beloved parents,
Hanita and Alexander

Contents

Acknowledgments

I would like to express my gratitude to a number of friends and scholars who were extremely helpful in various ways and made this project possible.

To Marv Lachman who, several decades ago, invited me to a series of literary parties at his Bronx apartment where he, Bob Aucott, Jon Breen, Lianne Carlin, Pat Erhardt, Allen J. Hubin, Francis Nevins Jr., Otto Penzler, Charles Shibuk, and Chris Steinbrunner suggested that I not only read and collect detective literature but also study its sources, history, and trends. These gifted ladies and gentlemen have since edited journals, penned books, and launched a wave of scholarship in the field. Their influence on the development of this resource book is highly appreciated.

I am greatly indebted to the late publisher Ted Dikty, who planted the seed of *Blood on the Stage* in my mind, and to Professor Robert Reginald of California State University at San Bernardino for encouraging me to develop an annotated checklist of suspense plays into a book-length endeavor.

A special note of thanks to Bryan Reddick, academic dean of Elmira College, and professors Jerome Whalen and Leonard Criminale, who offered valuable suggestions regarding classic crime plays.

In my pursuit of old, out-of-print manuscripts and yesteryear's newspapers and magazines, I traveled to a number of libraries near and far. My gratitude in particular to the librarians of the Steele Memorial Library of Elmira, New York (notably Owen Frank); the Corning, New York, Public Library; the Olin and Uris Libraries at Cornell University in Ithaca, New York; the New York Public Library of the Performing Arts at Lincoln Center, Manhattan (especially Rod Bladel, Christopher Frith, Christine Karatnytsky, Jeremy McGraw, curator Karen Nickeson, and the three little witches of the photocopy room). Thanks also to Howard Prouty, acquisition archivist at the Center for Motion Picture Study, Beverly Hills,

California, and Shimon Lev-Ari, director of the Israeli Documentation Center for the Performing Arts in Tel-Aviv, Israel.

My appreciation goes to past and present staffers of the national office of the Mystery Writers of America in New York City; Eleanor Bader of Brooklyn; Alexa Kelly, Brian Richardson, Andrew Charity, and Alvin and Myra Chanin of Manhattan; George Koch of Queens; Michele Slung of Woodstock, New York; Nancy McCaig of Corning, New York; Lindsay Bajo of San Diego, California; Helga Schier of Santa Monica, California; Lauren Holingsworth of Culver City, California; Bill Waters of Burbank, California; Diana James, publicist, of Pasadena, California; and Regina Miller of the Geffen Theatre, Westwood, California.

Finally, salutation to Peter E. Blau of Washington, D.C., and Andrew Joffe of New York City for their input on Sherlock Holmes and the collecting of Sherlockiana.

Introduction

The first stage crime was committed in ancient Greece. The amphitheatres of Athens were awash in blood. In one of the earliest plays on record, *Prometheus Bound* (479 BC), the upstart playwright Aeschylus had the gumption to paint Zeus, the king of Olympus, as a mass murderer. To protect his turf, Zeus utilizes his instrument of death, a bolt of lightning, to dispatch the rabble-rouser Prometheus and his loyal nymphs to Hades, because he has "stolen fire from the gods and given it to man."

Aeschylus continued to center his plots on treachery and homicide. In *The Danaid Tetralogy* (463 BC), the fifty daughters of Daneus attempt to flee Egypt to avoid marriage with their cousins. When their escape is foiled, the daughters murder the bridegrooms on the wedding night, thus keeping their virginity and avoiding incestuous relationships. *The Oresteia* (458 BC), Aeschylus's masterpiece, depicts a succession of crimes and their retribution in the House of Atreus. Clytemnestra, Queen of Argos, is furious at her husband, Agamemnon, leader of the Greek forces in the Trojan War, for bringing the Trojan princess Cassandra into the palace as a slave. The jealous Clytemnestra murders Cassandra, and then throws a robe, like a fish net, around Agamemnon, strikes him three times with an axe, and rejoices as his blood spurts. A feud inherited from generation to generation culminates in the revenge murder of Clytemnestra by her son, Orestes, and his sister, Electra. Orestes also attacks Clytemnestra's lover, Aegisthus, and slashes him with his sword. The bloody events lead to an early stage trial: the goddess Athena assembles a jury of twelve Athenian citizens. Their vote is a tie and Orestes is acquitted.

The playwright Sophocles was not far behind in matters of intrigue and suspense. The title character of *Ajax* (c. 444 BC) loses a debate with Odysseus over who should inherit the recently deceased Achilles's armor. Incensed, Ajax plans to kill Agamemnon and Menelaus for assigning the armor to Odysseus. However, the goddess Athena drives

Ajax temporarily insane and he instead slaughters cattle and sheep that the Greeks had captured in raids. In *Oedipus Rex* (c. 430 BC), Sophocles penned the first play to recount the step-by-step investigation of a murder through the interrogation of witnesses. Ironically, the first detective was also the unwitting murderer.

The third great Greek tragedian, Euripides, created the anti-heroine *Medea* (431 BC), a princess scorned; her jealousy and wrath led her into the compulsive killings of a rival, with a robe smeared with poison, and her own two children, leaving their father, Jason, in hopeless despair. In *Hecuba* (425 BC), the MacGuffin that causes a series of murders is a bag of gold. The god Dionysus manipulates the women of Thebes to tear their king apart with their bare hands in *The Bacchae* (405 BC).

On a lighter note, Aristophanes throws satirical darts at corrupt judges in *The Knights* (424 BC) and ridicules the trial courts in *The Wasps* (422 BC).

The Roman man-of-letters Seneca incorporated many motifs of Greek mythology into his plays. However, while the Greek dramatists were mostly concerned with the relationship of man and god, Seneca emphasized the human hero's merits and faults, pangs of conscience, and final resolution to accept his appointed place in the universe. Still, Seneca's plays contain Grand Guignol elements: in *Medea* (first century AD), the blood-curdling events caused by the vengeful title character are pictured graphically. She instructs her children to deliver to Jason's new bride a robe and a necklace cursed with witchcraft powers. Upon donning the robe, flames engulf the princess and she burns to death. Medea then stabs one of her sons on the roof of the palace. Horrified, Jason watches from the courtyard as Medea stabs her other son and throws both bodies down to him. With an aura of exaltation, Medea flies away in her dragon-drawn chariot. In Seneca's *Thystes* (first century AD), the brothers Thystes and Atreus are to share the throne of their late father. However, Thystes seduces Atreus's wife, steals the "Golden Lamb," a symbol of sovereignty, and usurps the throne. Atreus wins back the kingdom in battle, but still nurtures revenge. He captures his nephews and sacrifices them on the altar, chopping their bodies into pieces. All but their heads become part of a banquet menu. The last course is hidden beneath the cover of a silver platter. After Thystes has eaten his meal, the heads of his two sons are revealed and presented to him. When the mourning father requests a proper burial for his sons, Atreus informs him that he has just eaten them. Now Thystes starts planning his payback, illustrating Seneca's theme that crime perpetuates crime.

* * *

Crime continues to take center stage in mid-fifteenth century Passion plays. Anonymous playwrights dramatized the biblical stories of Cain and Abel, Abraham's sacrifice of Isaac, and Daniel in the lion's den. *The Second Shepherd's Play* is a masterwork of medieval farce concerning theft and its consequences.

The Lytell Peste of Robyn Hoode (latter half of the fifteenth century) is a long dramatic narrative that fuses old and popular ballads about Robin Hood. It preceded numerous plays about the admired rebel of Sherwood Forest. Lighthearted milestones in the art of farcical roguery were *Pierre Patelin* (1469), about a clever conman, written by an unknown playwright; *Gammer Gurton's Needle* (1575), also written anonymously, in which old Gurton suspects various people of having stolen her precious needle; and *Three Ladies of London* (1584) by Robert Wilson, wherein the leading character is a hustler, a cheat, and a thief.

Arguably the most popular play of the sixteenth century, *The Spanish Tragedy* (1587) by Thomas Kyd depicts a sensational story of murder and revenge. Christopher Marlowe dipped his pen in blood to create *Tamburlaine the Great* (c. 1587), in which a barbarian conqueror leads his savage hordes across Central Asia, leaving behind a grisly trail of violence and torture; *The Tragical History of Doctor Faustus* (1588–1589), wherein the title character pledges his soul to the super-human villain, Mephistopheles; and *Edward II* (1591), the violent tragedy of a young king whose homosexual love leads to wars, purges, royal intrigue, and ultimately to his own hideous murder at the hands of a professional assassin.

Arden of Feversham (1592, anonymous), based on the real case of a husband murdered by his wife and her lover in 1551, is the earliest known example of domestic tragedy. After repeated attempts, the lovers succeed in committing the crime but are soon caught and brought to justice.

William Shakespeare wrote a series of plays drenched with treachery, bloodshed, and horror, such as *Titus Andronicus* (1594), an account of torture, rape, and a succession of murders taking place at a Roman palace; *Julius Caesar* (c. 1599), a tale of political conspiracy, assassination, and its aftermath; and *Hamlet* (c. 1600) with its "mouse-trap," set by the melancholy prince to draw a confession out of a murderer. *The Merchant of Venice* (1595) is highlighted by a memorable courtroom scene. *Othello* (c. 1604) introduces the supreme hypocritical villain, Iago. *Macbeth* (c. 1605) is arguably the greatest play ever written about murder-motivated-by-ambition and the exploration of human guilt. *King Lear* (c. 1606) tells the story of an old king who divides his kingdom between two of his three daughters, who prove to be monsters of ingratitude, bringing destruction to them all. The title character of *Coriolanus* (c. 1608) is a Roman patrician whose pride and arrogance lead to his downfall; a lynch mob stabs and tramples him to death. In *Pericles* (1610), the jealous, ambitious wife of a governor orders an attendant to murder the fourteen-year-old daughter of the Prince of Tyre, a plan that backfires. *Cymbeline* (1611) contains wheels within wheels of seemingly unrelated motifs—court intrigue, an idyllic romance shattered by a con man, an attempted murder with a poisonous phial, long-lost sons, masquerades, British-Roman wars—all meshed ingeniously by the master.

Ben Jonson's *Volpone; or, The Fox* (1606), the classic comedy of greed, cunning, and chicanery, was followed by a succession of Jacobean horror plays. The most nightmarish were *The Revenger's Tragedy* (1607) by Cyril Tourneur, *The White Devil* (c.1608) by John Webster, *The Maid's Tragedy* (1611) by Francis Beaumont and John Fletcher, *The Duchess of Malfi* (c. 1612), by John Webster, and *The Changeling* (1622) by Thomas Middleton.

The French entered the fray with Moliere's *Tartuffe* (1664), featuring the famous con man who takes control of an entire bourgeois household, and more somberly with Jean Racine's tragedies *Phaedra* (1677), based on Greek mythology, *Esther* (1689), and *Athaliah* (1691), both inspired by stories from the Old Testament.

* * *

The eighteenth century boasted several criminous masterpieces on both sides of the Atlantic. *The Beggar's Opera* (1728) by John Gay is a witty and colorful expose of London's underworld. *The London Merchant* (1731) by George Lilo, based on an actual murder, is the story of an apprentice who is led astray by a prostitute, kills his kind uncle, and ends on the gallows despite his repentance. America joined the scene in *Prince of Parthia* (c. 1759) by Thomas Godfrey, a drama of political intrigue, treachery, suicide, and murder—the first play ever written by an American and performed by professional American actors. In 1790, William Dunlop, "The Father of the American Theatre," presented *The Fatal Deception; or, The Progress of Guilt*, which he based on a real-life incident, a narrative of adultery, mistaken identity, murder, revenge, and madness.

The Count of Narbone (1781) by Robert Jephson is a dramatization of Horace Walpole's *The Castle of Otranto*, the first of the Gothic novels. A year later, Germany's Friedrich Schiller wrote *The Robbers*, one of the finest "storm and stress" plays, about a young man who, disenchanted with society's law and order, leads a group of bandits to found a ruthless, bloodthirsty republic. Schiller's compatriot Johann Wolfgang von Goethe based his poetic, supernatural *Faust* (1808) on the German legend of an actual sixteenth-century mountebank—an arch-magician and wayward scholar notorious for his alchemistic exploits and unethical swindles. Rumored to have reached a pact with the devil, he died in 1540 under mysterious circumstances.

In 1802, Englishman Thomas Holcroft adapted *Coelina Ou L'Enfant Du Mystere* (1880) by the prolific French playwright Rene-Charles Guilbert de Pixerecourt as *A Tale of Mystery*, the first English play to be labeled a "melo-drame." The characters are entirely good or bad, virtuous or dastardly; the hero is handsome, romantic, and stalwart; the villain is completely ruthless; the heroine, a helpless orphan, discovers the "secret of her birth"; virtue is triumphant in a happy ending—features that were imitated in the flood of melodramas to come.

* * *

The nineteenth century was rich with criminous plays of a wide variety. *Bertram; or, The Castle of St. Aldobrand* (1816) by Charles R. Maturin illustrated almost every trait typical of the era's Gothicism: seduction, adultery, robbery, murder, cowardly assassination, madness, and suicide. Thomas Dibdin penned the first of many adaptations based on Sir Walter Scott's novel, *The Heart of Midlothian* (1819), which in turn was influenced by a true case of infanticide: a mother is accused of killing her child and is brought to trial. Based on Hungarian legends, *Le Vampire* by Charles Nodier was first performed in Paris in 1820, and was translated into English as *The Bride of the Isles* by J. R. Planche later that same year. It is the first known vampire play. Richard Brinsley Peake's *Presumption; or, The Fate of Frankenstein* (1823) was the first dramatization of Mary Shelley's 1818 novel about a manmade monster. The play influenced a growing trend toward spectacular and terrifying stage fare. Three years later came *Frankenstein; or, The Man and the Monster* by H. M. Milner, in which the creature falls in love with Dr. Frankenstein's wife, kidnaps her, stabs his creator to death, and finally leaps into a boiling volcano.

Lord Byron (George Gordon) paralleled his incestuous relationship with his half-sister in the poetic drama *Manfred* (written, 1817; first performed, 1852), dabbled in political intrigue in *Marino Faliero* (1821), and drew upon the Old Testament in *Cain* (1924), depicting the title character as a willing student of Lucifer when killing his brother Abel.

Perhaps the most prolific playwright of the nineteenth century was Edward Fitzball (1793–1873), who specialized in nautical melodramas. In *The Floating Beacon* (1824) he introduced assorted characters aboard a boat: a shipwrecked juvenile; smugglers who hold him at bay; a low comedian who attempts to rescue him; a young girl who falls in love with him; a weird, wild captive woman whose husband has been murdered and who now recognizes the juvenile as her long lost son. *The Flying Dutchman; or, The Phantom Ship* (1827) is a spectacular melodrama in which the Flying Dutchman, armed with supernatural powers, attempts to abduct a beautiful woman, while *The Red Rover; or, The Mutiny of the Dolphin* (1828) was a phenomenally successful "skull-and-crossbones" play wherein the protagonist is a cutthroat pirate who is gentle with the ladies. The climax features a burning ship sinking with its entire crew.

Another prolific writer of melodrama was Douglas Jerrold, whose *Fifteen Years a Drunkard's Life* (1828) was the first play to utilize alcoholism as its central theme. In the final stages of degradation, the drunkard robs and murders his own wife. *Black-Ey'd Susan; or, All in the Downs* (1829) revolves around a sailor who strikes his captain for kissing his wife and is condemned to hang. *Vidocq; or, The French Police Spy* (1829) is based on the colorful exploits of the famous criminal turned police informer, who later established the French detective police force, the Brigade de la Suret. *Vidocq* anticipated a flood of detective melodramas that flourished later in the century.

Also inspired by real-life events was *Maria Marten; or, The Murder in the Red Barn* (1828) by Montague Slater, in which the victim had a child with the lover who killed her. *Jack Shepard* (1839) by W. T. Moncrieff, featuring the popular actor Newton Treen Hicks in the role of a highwayman, was the first play that caused the audience to hiss at a villain.

The Inspector General (1836) by Nikolai Gogol is a devastating Russian satire on bureaucratic corruption, the torchbearer of later plays that dealt with communal greed—*Enemy of the People* by Henrik Ibsen, *The Treasure* by David Pinski, and *The Visit* by Friedrich Dürrenmatt.

Fashion; or, Life in New York (1845) by Anna Cora Mowatt, considered by many America's finest nineteenth-century comedy, savagely satirizes affected manners and speech adopted by a rising idle wealthy class. A visiting no-nonsense Yankee farmer, Adam Trueman, skewers the hypocritical household of Mrs. Tiffany, scares away a blackmailing clerk, and unmasks the monocled French "Count" Jolimaitre as an impostor.

The String of Pearls; or, Sweeney Todd (1847) by George Dibdin Pitt is a horror play about a barber who cuts his customers' throats and consigns them to a pastry cook, who then bakes them in her pies.

Dion Boucicault proved to be the foremost melodramatist of his time with such plays as *The Poor of New York* (1857), depicting embezzlement, arson, and false arrest; *The Octoroon; or, Life in Louisiana* (1859), wherein a villainous plantation owner commits a murder and is convicted when a photographic plate proves his crime; *The Colleen Bawn; or, The Brides of Garryowen* (1860), which features breath-taking action sequences, including a dastardly attempt to drown the heroine in a lake, followed by a spectacular dive to rescue her; and *After Dark* (1868), which is peppered with lurid scenes in London's criminal underworld.

* * *

Three of the era's most popular novels were adapted to the stage: *East Lynne* (1862) by Clifton W. Tayleure, from the book by Mrs. Henry Wood, a tear-jerking melodrama about a peaceful household destroyed by the manipulations of a heartless aristocrat; *Lady Audley's Secret* (1863) by William E. Suter, based on the pioneering novel of detection by M. E. Braddon; and *The Woman in White* (1871), dramatized by Wilkie Collins from his own novel, picturing the relentless persecution of a wealthy wife by her opportunistic husband and his henchman, Count Fosco, one of the most amoral villains in literature. Wilkie Collins also adapted to the stage his novel *The Moonstone* (1877), described by T. S. Eliot as "the first, the longest, and the best of modern detective novels." Its serpentine plot involves a stolen Indian diamond, sleepwalking, and other curious events. The investigator, Sergeant Richard Cuff, who has a passion for roses and would rather till his garden than work on a case, is a character based on an actual Scotland Yard inspector.

In 1863 France, *L'Aieule* by Adolphe D'ennery and Charles Edmond was the first murder-mystery melodrama to conceal the identity of the criminal until the concluding moments. In that same year England's *The Ticket-of-Leave Man* by Tom Taylor introduced Hawkshaw, the first official detective on stage, a master of disguise.

The Black Crook (1866) by Charles M. Barras, America's first musical comedy, spotlights villainy, sorcery, and a pact with the devil. Augustin Daly's *Under the Gaslight* (1867), a post–Civil War melodrama, was the first to feature the hero tied to a railway track, with a climactic last-minute rescue.

In 1873, Émile Zola adapted to the stage his novel *Thérèse Raquin*, in which an adulterous relationship culminates in the murder of a husband by the lovers. Four years later, Thomas Russell Sullivan was the first to dramatize Robert Louis Stevenson's novella, *Dr. Jekyll and Mr. Hyde*, the classic horror tale about the dual nature of man. Stevenson collaborated with W. E. Henley on *Deacon Brodie; or, The Double Life* (1884), wherein a Bow Street runner unmasks a rogue who lives a double life—an honest carpenter by day, a leader of an underworld gang by night. The 1880s were also enriched with criminous plays penned by poet Percy Bysshe Shelley (*The Cenci*, 1886) and novelists Victorien Sardou (*La Tosca*, 1887), and Leo Tolstoy (*The Power of Darkness*, 1888).

The Grand Guignol, a theatre genre that started in 1898 in a seamy hall near the Place Pigalle in Paris, presented short grisly horror plays blending sex, sadism, and macabre humor, often ending with an ironic twist or a physical atrocity.

The nineteenth century ended on a high note with *Sherlock Holmes* (1899) by and starring William Gillette, an adaptation that combined several Arthur Conan Doyle stories about the world's foremost consulting detective.

* * *

As discussed in the first volume of this series, *Blood on the Stage, 1900–1925*, the twentieth century began its theatrical offerings with plays of transgression that continued the trend of blood-and-thunder melodrama—urban, Western, nautical, or war-oriented—earmarked by wild plots with little logic, stock characters, broad comedy, a spread of cliff-hangers, and special effects galore. Among the melodramatists who had the knack to whip full-length sensational fare within a week or two, thus becoming the first playwright-millionaires, were Owen Davis (whose 1906 mega-hit *Nellie, the Beautiful Cloak Model*, was only one of Davis's 150 plays), Theodore Kremer, James Halleck Reid, Charles E. Blaney, Lincoln J. Carter, Charles A. Taylor, Langdon McCormick, and Max Marcin.

A more subdued approach began to emerge in the writings of Henry Bernstein (*The Thief*, 1906), Paul Armstrong (*Alias Jimmy Valentine*, 1910), and Willard Mack (*Kick In*, 1914). August Strindberg (*There Are Crimes and Crimes*, 1900), Maxim Gorky (*The Lower Depths*, 1902), and Eden Phillpotts (*The Shadow*, 1913), provided psychological insight into their characters' motivation. Tragic overtones enveloped works by John Masefield (*The Tragedy of Nan*, 1908) and Eugene O'Neill (*Desire under the Elms*, 1924). Social criticism crept into the dramas of John Galsworthy (*Justice*, 1910) and Bayard Veiller (*Within the Law*, 1912). Police brutality, shady business manipulations, and underhanded political shenanigans were exposed by George Broadhurst (*The Man of the Hour*, 1906), Charles Klein (*The Third Degree*, 1909), and Clyde Fitch (*The City*, 1909). Early, innovative courtroom dramas included *Madame X* (1908) by Alexandre Bisson, highlighted by a climactic scene in which a mother charged with murder is unknowingly defended by her son, making it perhaps the most wrenching trial in the annals of theatre; Elmer Rice's *On Trial* (1914) introduced to the stage a novelty borrowed from the silent cinema—the flashback; *The Ware Case* (1915) by George Pleydell broke through the fourth wall and for the first time assigned the audience to become the jury in a murder case; in *The Woman on the Jury* (1923) by Bernard K. Burns, the title character persuaded eleven jurors that the accused, a woman charged with the fatal shooting of her lover, was innocent.

From France came *Arsène Lupin* (1908), featuring Maurice Leblanc's flamboyant rogue, a master of disguise who employs numerous aliases, and *The Mystery of the Yellow Room* (1912) by Gaston Leroux, in which young journalist Joseph Rouletabille, a disciple of Edgar Allan Poe's C. Auguste Dupin and Arthur Conan Doyle's Sherlock Holmes, solves an "impossible" murder case: the victim is found in a room bolted from the inside with its windows barred. There is no sign of entry on the walls, in the floor, or in the ceiling. How could the culprit enter the room and, for that matter, how could he exit unseen with witnesses stationed outside the door?

* * *

Among the most successful plays produced in the first quarter of the twentieth century were *The Girl of the Golden West* (1905) by David Belasco, a colorful saga of saloon brawls, gunplay, lynch mobs, bandits versus lawmen, and love that conquers all during California's gold rush era; *The Argyle Case* (1912) by Harriet Ford and Harvey J. O'Higgins, presenting a new approach in the formulating of the theatre's murder mystery: the crime has been committed before the curtain goes up, and the identity of the culprit is concealed until the second act; *Seven Keys to Baldpate* (1913) by George M. Cohan, a medley of mystery and farce, loaded with surprising twists; *The Thirteenth Chair* (1916) by Bayard Veiller, which included a breathtaking trick knife and atmospheric séance sequences before the criminal is unmasked by a clever medium; *The Green Goddess* (1920) by William Archer, produced when the vogue for anti-Asian "yellow peril" plays was in fashion, set in an Himalayan temple where a persecuted heroine is saved from the clutches of a lascivious raja by the last-minute arrival of the Royal Air Force; *The Bat* (1920) by Mary Roberts Rinehart and Avery Hopwood, pitting an elderly spinster against an arch-criminal and providing a wallop of a surprise ending; *The Cat and the Canary* (1922) by John Willard, famed for its ingenious use of secret panels and sliding doors; *The Gorilla* (1925), with a pair of hick detectives furnishing the fun, a mystery-burlesque that began a trend of spilling frantic action into the auditorium; and *The Ghost Train* (1925), picturing dirty work afoot in a haunted railway station.

From 1900 to 1925, the masterpieces were few and far between—*The Lower Depths* (1902) by Maxim Gorky, *The Playboy of the Western World* (1907) by John Millington Synge, *The Tragedy of Nan* (1908) by John Masefield, *The Passion Flower* (1913) by Jacinto Benavente, *The Adding Machine* (1923) by Elmer Rice, *Desire under the Elms* (1924) by Eugene O'Neill, and *The Golem* (1925) by H. Leivick. But for sheer adventure, excitement, and heart-pounding thrills, while slowly developing toward the realistic theatre as we know it today, this period may have been the genre's golden age.

* * *

The second volume of *Blood on the Stage* studies plays of crime, mystery, and detection mounted between 1925 and 1950. Old-fashioned melodrama became a dying breed and only a few plays of this category were produced on Broadway: *Wooden Kimono* (1926) by John Floyd, *The Call of the Banshee* (1927) by W. D. Hepenstall and Ralph Cullinan, *The Clutching Claw* (1928) by Ralph Thomas Kettering, and *The Skull* (1928) by Bernard J. McOwen and Harry E. Humphrey.

Edgar Wallace, the prolific English writer of hundreds of crime novels and short stories, was the first to make a specialty of detective drama. His *The Ringer* (1926), *On the Spot* (1930), and *The Case of the Frightened Lady* aka *Criminal at Large* (1931) thrilled audiences on both shores of the Atlantic. Dorothy L. Sayers was not far behind, and brought her famous amateur sleuth, Lord Peter Wimsey, to the stage in *Busman's Honeymoon* (1936). Agatha Christie, unhappy with several dramatizations of her early novels, jumped into the cauldron with a dozen or so plays of her own, of which the best known are *Ten Little Indians* (1943), *The Mousetrap* (1952), and *Witness for the Prosecution* (1953). Christie's beloved Hercule Poirot and Jane Marple made the transformation from the printed page to the stage in a number of adaptations that became fixtures of summer stock and community theatres. Charlie Chan, Philo Vance, Ellery Queen, Mr. and Mrs. North, and Jack "Flashgun" Casey—heroes of novels, radio, screen, and television—also took to the stage, albeit rarely. And Sherlock Holmes continued to scratch on his Stradivarius and solve baffling cases in dramatizations of many an Arthur Conan Doyle story.

Mainstream playwrights also entered the fold. Among the Broadway contributors who dabbled in theft, kidnapping, and murder were Sidney Howard, Paul Green, Elmer Rice, Philip Barry, George S. Kaufman, Robert E. Sherwood, Maxwell Anderson, Sidney Kingsley, Irwin Shaw, and Lillian Hellman—the Who's Who of the era's American theatre. In England, W. Somerset Maugham, A. A. Milne, Emlyn Williams, J. B. Priestley, Daphne du Maurier, and Terrence Rattigan wrote plays of crime and detection. Betrayal and violence are key elements in the dramas of Hungarian Laszlo Fodor, German Ernst Toller, Spanish Federico Garcia Lorca, Italian Ugo Betti, and French Jean Genet.

Also plunging into the world of greasepaint and papier-mâché were famed novelists and poets Wilbur Daniel Steele, Damon Runyon, Robert Penn Warren, Aldous Huxley, and Herman Wouk. Nobel Prize winners who spilled blood on the stage included Eugene O'Neill, John Steinbeck, Ernest Hemingway, Albert Camus, and Jean-Paul Sartre. Other names on this unique roster were Mae West, Clare Boothe (Luce), Ayn Rand, and James M. Cain.

Presented in English during 1925–1950 were adaptations of Emile Zola's *Thérèse Raquin* and Fyodor Dostoyevsky's *Crime and Punishment*. Also dramatized were such important novels as Theodore Dreiser's *An American Tragedy*, Hugh Walpole's *The Man with Red Hair*, and Henry James's *The Turn of the Screw*. Adaptations of Mary Shelley's *Frankenstein* and Bram Stoker's *Dracula*, both in 1927, kept spectators glued to their seats. Musicals tinged with elements of crime included Guy Bolton and Fred Thompson's *Rio Rita* (1926), Bertolt Brecht and Kurt Weill's *The Threepenny Opera* (1928), Earl Carroll and Rufus King's *Murder at the Vanities* (1933), and Maxwell Anderson and Kurt Weill's *Lost in the Stars* (1949).

Popular courtroom dramas were Bayard Veiller's *The Trial of Mary Dugan* (1927), *The Bellamy Trial* (1928) by Frances Noyes Hart and Frank E. Carstarphen, *Ladies of the Jury* (1929) by Fred Ballard, and Edward Wooll's *Libel!* (1934). Prison cells were designed for Maurine Watkins's *Chicago*,

(1926), *The Criminal Code* (1929) by Martin Flavin, *Children of Darkness* (1930) by Edwin Justus Mayer, *The Last Mile* (1930) by John Wexley, and *Chalked Out* (1937) by Warden Lewis E. Lawes. Murders were committed in such singular settings as a nunnery, a monastery, a radio station, a Broadway theatre, an underground subway, and a remote island.

As the twentieth century unfolded, dark psychological thrillers became the vogue with such plays as *Jealousy* (1928) by Eugene Walter; Patrick Hamilton's *Rope* (1929) and *Gas Light* (1938); Jeffrey Dell's *Payment Deferred* (1931); *Night Must Fall* (1935) by Emlyn Williams; *The Two Mrs. Carrolls* (1935) by Martin Vale; James Warwick's *Blind Alley* (1935); *Ladies in Retirement* (1940) by Edward Percy and Reginald Denham; *Guest in the House* (1942) by Hagar Wilde and Dale Eunson; *Black Chiffon* (1949) by Lesley Storm; and *The Man* (1950) by Mel Dinelli.

Pure whodunits, often ornamented with surprise endings, were the hallmark of Agatha Christie. Other writers who expertly handled the unmasking of clever criminals are Elmer Rice and Philip Barry (*Cock Robin*, 1927); Fulton Oursler and Lowell Brentano (*The Spider*, 1927); Jack de Leon and Jack Celestin (*The Man at Six*, 1928); Basil Ring (*The Leavenworth Case*, 1936); Mignon G. Eberhart and Fred Ballard (*320 College Avenue*, 1938); and Charlotte Hastings (*Bonaventure*, 1949). "Impossible" murder cases baffled the viewers in *The Locked Room* (1933) by Herbert Ashton Jr. and *The Speckled Band* (1937) by Ruth Fenisong, an adaptation of a Conan Doyle story. *I Killed the Count* (1937) by Alec Coppel had three suspects come forth and confess to the same murder, while A. A. Milne's *The Fourth Wall* aka *The Perfect Alibi* (1928) introduced the inverted form of the detective story to the stage: the murderer is shown committing the crime, and the chief concern is the method by which he will be apprehended.

Dirty politics found an outlet in *Wings over Europe* (1928) by Robert M. B. Nichols and Maurice Brown, and in *All the King's Men* (1948) by Robert Penn Warren. Espionage maneuvers play dirty in *The Fifth Column* (1940) by Ernest Hemingway, and *Incognito* (1941) by N. Richard Nusbaum.

* * *

Amid the violence and blood-letting, comic relief and sly satire were furnished in *Murder on the Second Floor* (1929) by Frank Vosper; *Jewel Robbery* (1932) by Laszlo (Ladislaus) Fodor; *Whistling in the Dark* (1932) by Laurence Gross and Edward Childs Carpenter; *The Bishop Misbehaves* (1934) by Frederick Jackson; *A Slight Case of Murder* (1935) by Damon Runyon and Howard Lindsay; *Margin for Error* (1939) by Clare Booth; and *Arsenic and Old Lace* (1941) by Joseph Kesselring.

The highlights of the genre during 1925–1950 included Mae West's *Diamond Lil* (1928), a lurid affair of dope smuggling and white slavery taking place in a Chinatown saloon in the 1890s; Elmer Rice's *Street Scene*

(1929), a harsh, hard-knuckled slice of tenement life on the West Side of New York; Eugene O'Neill's *Mourning Becomes Electra* (1931), tracing the rise and fall of a New England family afflicted with conflict, hatred, suicide, and murder, paralleling *The Oresteia* by Aeschylus; *Night Must Fall* (1935) by Emlyn Williams, the often-revived play about a psychotic and charismatic serial killer, who carries with him a hat box containing the gruesome relic of a horrible crime; Maxwell Anderson's *Winterset* (1935), a prize-winning drama loosely based on the Sacco-Vanzetti case; Lillian Hellman's *The Little Foxes* (1939), arguably the supreme play about human greed, picturing the vulturous members of the Hubbard family as they scorn, hate, and out-maneuver one another; J. B. Priestley's *An Inspector Calls* (1945), unfolding during a society engagement party, with the title character drawing from each guest a confession about his share of responsibility for the recent suicide of a working girl; *The Winslow Boy* (1946) by Terence Rattigan, wherein the incident of a youngster being expelled from an English school for an alleged theft grows into a "cause célèbre" that nearly shakes the foundation of the government; and *Detective Story* (1949) by Sidney Kingsley, a realistic picture of routine cases brought to a metropolitan police precinct in the course of a day.

* * *

The third installment of *Blood on the Stage* covers milestone plays in the genre produced during 1950–1975. Frederick Knott scored big with *Dial "M" for Murder* (1952), in which a cold-blooded husband commissions the murder of his wife, but his plans go awry. That same year, Agatha Christie came up with *The Mousetrap*, a whodunit still performing in London today, the longest-running play in world theatre history. A typical Christie yarn, it features a group of strangers stranded in an isolated inn during a snowstorm, a murderer stalking his prey while whistling "Three Blind Mice," and an unexpected solution. In 1953, Christie's *Witness for the Prosecution* won both the New York Critics Circle Award and the Antoinette Perry Award as the best foreign play of the year. The plot revolves around a likable young man accused of killing a wealthy spinster, culminating in a triple surprise. The Queen of Crime struck a hat trick with *Spider's Web* (1954), a comedy-thriller written especially for English star Margaret Lockwood. Lockwood portrayed the ditzy wife of a government official who discovers a dead body in her drawing room and goes through manifold efforts to dispose of it. However, ensuing plays by Christie—*Towards Zero* (1956), *Verdict* (1958), *The Unexpected Guest* (1958), *Go Back for Murder* (1960), and *Rule of Three*, a trio of one-acts (1962)—were less successful.

While Christie's *Witness for the Prosecution* highlights the pomp and ceremony of London's Old Bailey, Herman Wouk's *The Caine Mutiny Court-Martial* (1953) unfolds in a gray room of the Twelfth Naval District in San Francisco, where Lt. Stephen Maryk is accused of wartime mutiny for "willfully, without proper authority and without justifiable cause" relieving from duty Lieutenant Commander Philip Francis Queeg, the captain of the SS *Caine*. In a grueling cross-examination, Captain Queeg goes through a rambling account of stolen strawberries, a missing key, and incomplete officers' logs. The outwardly self-assured captain gradually disintegrates and ends up trembling and sobbing, a broken man. Another court-martial drama followed three years later—*Time Limit!* by Henry Denker, in which an Army Major is accused of betraying his fellow Americans in a North Korean prison camp by cooperating with the enemy, making propaganda broadcasts, and falsely confessing that the United States has unleashed germ warfare.

It was a banner era for pulsating courtroom dramas, some fictional, others based on real-life cases. *Inherit the Wind* (1955) by Jerome Lawrence and Robert E. Lee followed the outline of the historic "monkey trial" of Tennessee high school teacher John T. Scopes, accused of teaching Charles Darwin's theory of evolution in defiance of state law. *Compulsion* (1957) by Meyer Levin dramatized the 1924 cause célèbre case of Nathan Leopold, age nineteen, and Richard Loeb, age eighteen, spoiled sons of Chicago millionaires, who conspired to kill a fourteen-year-old boy for the thrill of it. When caught and brought to trial, the counsel for the defense, Clarence Darrow, convinced the judge that the heinous act was rooted in a pathologically compulsive, uncontrollable urge; instead of the chair, Leopold and Loeb got away with life imprisonment. In Fay and Michael Kanin's *Rashomon* (1959), a samurai warrior of a thousand years ago had been killed with a sword, and his frightened wife is found lost in the woods. The culprit, a wandering bandit, is arrested, accused of rape and murder. In a police court, several contradictory versions of the event are shown in flashback.

The Andersonville Trial (1959) was freely adapted by Saul Levitt from the official record of the actual military trial of Henry Wirz, the commander of the notorious Confederate prison at Andersonville during the Civil War. The play raises the issue of passive moral conviction among soldiers who blindly obey the inhumane orders of their superiors. *The Deadly Game* (1960), adapted by James Yaffe from a radio play by Swiss playwright Friedrich Duerrenmatt, takes place in a secluded Alpine retreat, where three retired men of law—a judge, a prosecutor, and a defense attorney—relive their glory days by playing legal charades with stranded strangers. A fourth elderly gentleman, who hovers in the background, has served the municipality as its official hangman. William Saroyan, the American Pulitzer Prize–winner playwright, joined Henry Cecil, a British county court judge and a prolific detective-story writer, in adapting to the stage Cecil's novel, *Settled out of Court* (1960). The proceedings unfold in the study of a High Court Judge, where an escaped convict conducts a trial, complete with an array of witnesses, to prove his innocence of the murder charge that sent him to prison for life. In Marcel Achard's *A Shot in the Dark* (1961), a young, idealistic examining magistrate, who has just been promoted to a post in Paris, is assigned his first case—a seemingly cut-and-dried murder. The prime suspect is a sexy parlormaid who was found unconscious, nude, and clutching a gun alongside her dead lover, the chauffeur. As the investigation progresses, the magistrate concludes that the earthy, guileless, babbling girl could not have committed the crime and the pendulum of suspicion moves in the direction of her employers. Philip Dunning's *Sequel to a Verdict* (1962) takes place in an imaginary 1920s Connecticut town, where a German immigrant, a carpenter by trade, is on trial for the kidnapping and murder of an infant girl. The circumstances of the case are reminiscent of the Charles Lindbergh tragedy. Despite flimsy proof, the accused is sentenced to death in the electric chair. The play is a protest against capital punishment.

Additional courtroom dramas included Henry Denker's *A Case of Libel* (1963), about a war correspondent's litigation for slander against a widely syndicated columnist who, in a barrage of poisonous articles, questioned the correspondent's patriotism, accused him of being a war profiteer, and branded him a "drunken, immoral, yellow-bellied degenerate" who engages in sexual vulgarities. Jack Roffey's *Hostile Witness* (1964) rewarded its viewers with colorful glimpses of the pomp and ceremony of the British judicial system, the unusual dilemma of a famous barrister finding himself accused of murder, and a last-minute surprise resolution. Robert Shaw's *The Man in the Glass Booth* (1967) is based on the case of Adolf Eichmann, a Nazi colonel known as "the architect of the Holocaust." After World War II, Eichmann fled to Argentina and lived there under a false identity. In 1960 he was captured by Mossad agents and abducted to Israel, where he was tried for war crimes and crimes against humanity. He was found guilty and executed in 1962. Playwright Barry England goes to 1800s India in *Conduct Unbecoming* (1969), depicting a kangaroo court-martial of a British second lieutenant accused of attempted rape.

* * *

The volatile 1960s—the aftermath of the McCarthy hearings, the Vietnam War, the demand for civil rights, the women's movement—influenced the theatre. A new format, the docudrama, exhibiting material from court transcripts, became popular. Germany's Heinar Kipphardt sifted through 3,000 pages of official documents before penning *In the Matter of J. Robert Oppenheimer* (1964), "the father of the atomic bomb," who was interrogated by a Congressional committee regarding his security clearance. In *Inquest* (1970), Donald Freed covers the controversial trial and execution of Julius and Ethel Rosenberg as Soviet spies, while in *The Trial of the Catonsville Nine* (1971), Daniel Berrigan describes how, at the height of the Vietnam War protests, he, his brother Philip, and seven other Catholic activists were found guilty of entering the draft board of Catonsville, Maryland, taking 378 recruitment files to a parking lot, and setting them on fire.

Basil Rathbone, the quintessential Sherlock Holmes of the movies, returned to 221B Baker Street in a disastrous 1953 stage play penned by his wife. Ouida Rathbone based her *Sherlock Holmes* on Conan Doyle's "The Adventure of the Bruce-Partington Plans" and "The Adventure of the Second Stain" with cuttings from "A Scandal in Bohemia," "The Final Problem," "The Empty House," and "His Last Bow." A cast of twenty-five populated a series of elaborate sets, and the serpentine plot was difficult to follow. The climax pitted the consulting detective against arch-criminal Professor Moriarty, with both men toppling into Reichenbach Falls. The critics greeted *Sherlock Holmes* with disdain and the play closed its doors after three performances. However, Holmes proved his staying power in several successive productions: the musical *Baker Street* (1965), book by Jerome Coopersmith, in which "The Woman," Irene Adler, plays an important role; a revival by the Royal Shakespeare Company in 1974 in both London and New York of William Gillette's turn-of-the-twentieth-century *Sherlock Holmes*; *Sherlock's Last Case* (1974) by Charles Marowitz, an astounding concoction wherein Dr. Watson, the ever-devoted sidekick, lures the master detective to a dark cellar, cleverly clamps down his arms and legs in a dentist's chair, rasps, "You arrogant, supercilious, egocentric, narcissistic, smug and self-congratulatory bastard," and proceeds to spray the bound sleuth with an acid-filled canister; and *Sherlock Holmes and the Curse of the Sign of the Four* (1975) by Dennis Rosa, who added a few wrinkles of his own to the original Conan Doyle novel.

In addition to *Baker Street*, other musicals of the era integrated elements of crime. *Guys and Dolls* (1950), with book by Jo Swerling and Abe Burrows, music and lyrics by Frank Loesser, brought to the Broadway stage Damon Runyon's sleazy New York City characters—grifters, hustlers, molls, and petty mobsters. *West Side Story* (1957), book by Arthur Laurents, music by Leonard Bernstein, and lyrics by Stephen Sondheim, followed the composition of *Romeo and Juliet* but transferred Shakespeare's tragedy to New York's West Side, where the feuding houses of Montague and Capulet became two rival street gangs claiming the same turf. *Redhead* (1959), with book and lyrics by Herbert and Dorothy Fields, and music by Albert Hague, is an atmospheric murder mystery unfolding in a waxworks museum of turn-of-the-twentieth-century London. *Oliver* (1960), with book, lyrics, and music by Lionel Bart, kept intact the key plot turns of Charles Dickens's *Oliver Twist*, the story of an orphan who gets entangled with such underworld figures as Fagin, Nancy, Sikes, and the Artful Dodger. With shades of Raffles and *To Catch a Thief* by Alfred Hitchcock, *Drat! The Cat!* (1965), book and lyrics by Ira Levin, music by Milton Schafer, is a musical spoof about a female cat burglar who has all of New York in a state of panic. *It's a Bird. . . . It's a Plane. . . . It's Superman*, book by David Newman and Robert Benton, music by Charles Strouse, lyrics by Lee Adams, flew the comics superstar to Broadway in 1966, singing and dancing in the streets of Metropolis, hiding behind his meek Clark Kent alias, and saving the world from a mad scientist's nuclear threat. *Dracula, Baby* (1970), book by Bruce Ronald, lyrics by John Jakes, music by Claire Strauch, loosely based on the Bram Stoker vampire novel, features Count Dracula, Professor Van Helsing, Dr. Seward, and madman Renfield crooning and hoofing in the plains of Transylvania, the pubs of London, and the catacombs of Carfax. *Something's Afoot* (1972), book, music, and lyrics by James McDonald, David Vos, and Robert Gerlach, is a musical burlesque on the whodunit genre. It borrows from Agatha Christie's *And Then There Were None* for its plot shenanigans and farcical darts.

* * *

Michael Shayne, a hard-boiled, two-fisted hero of more than sixty novels penned by Brett Halliday, made it to the stage in *Murder Is My Business* (1958), adapted by James Reach from a 1945 Halliday novel of the same name, in which Shayne untangles a case of blackmail and murder. Lieutenant Columbo, the rumpled, cigar-stub-chewing police investigator made famous by the long-running television series, was first created by William Link and Richard Levinson in a 1962 play, *Prescription: Murder*, depicting a cat-and-mouse duel of wits between the investigator and a murderous dentist.

Innovative suspense plays produced mid-twentieth century included *Stalag 17* (1951) by Donald Bevan and Edmond Trzcinski, unfolding in a barbwired Nazi prison camp during World War II. It soon becomes clear that one of the American POWs is a traitor. Who is he? Maxwell Anderson's *Bad Seed* (1954) introduces Rhoda Penmark, a neat, quaint, and pretty girl of eight. She is also a triple murderess. *The Desperate Hours* (1955) by Joseph Hayes, the story of a peaceful Indianapolis home invaded by three escaped criminals, spotlights the theme of civilized people being driven to violence. *A Hatful of Rain* (1955), developed at the Actors Studio by Michael V. Gazzo, is a pioneering play about drug addiction. Also exploring the lonely world of the drug addict is Jack Gelber's *The Connection* (1959), first performed by the Living Theatre. Gore Vidal's *The Best Man* (1960) is a political melodrama about character assassination and high-pressure chicanery on the eve of the balloting at a presidential convention. *Catch Me If You Can* (1965), adapted by Jack Weinstock and

Willie Gilbert from the French of Robert Thomas, begins with the kidnapping of a young wife from a summer lodge and ends with one of the most
surprising denouements in the annals of stage mysteries. *Frankenstein*
(1965) by Judith Malina and Julian Beck is an unorthodox, physical, and
thoroughly theatrical adaptation of Mary Shelley's novel, in which the
Living Theatre founders theorize that our society was conceived in violence and thrives upon it to survive. The heroine of Frederick Knott's *Wait
until Dark* (1966) is a blind wife who is terrorized by a trio of dangerous
criminals—and wins the day.

   Loot (1966) by Joe Orton, the enfant terrible of the British theatre, is an
unruly black comedy lambasting detective fiction, police investigative
methods, and the Roman Catholic Church. It is the story of a bank robbery that ends with the thieves and the lawmen agreeing to share the loot.
Also satirizing the old formulas of suspense literature is Tom Stoppard's
The Real Inspector Hound (1968), a play-within-a-play that also takes on the
drama critics, and Anthony Shaffer's *Sleuth* (1970), a tour-de-force of diabolical games and surprising twists. Lucille Fletcher, the author of *Sorry,
Wrong Number*, defended the genre with an ingeniously plotted mystery,
Night Watch (1972). An unhappy and disturbed heiress, who lives in a
plush East Side townhouse in Manhattan, sees a dead body through the
window in an empty tenement house across the street. Did she imagine
it? Was there really a corpse? Is somebody playing a cruel hoax on her?

* * *

   The topic of good versus evil is at the heart of several allegories produced by mid-century Broadway. Herman Melville's *Billy Budd*, dramatized in 1951 by Louis O. Coxe and Robert Chapman, unfolds aboard
the British naval vessel *Indomitable* during the Napoleonic war. The title
character, a handsome, guileless sailor, is accused by the malevolent,
sadist master-at-arms John Claggart of spreading unrest and rebellion in
the crew, urging the men to mutiny. After agonized gesturing and stam-
mering, the shocked Billy hits Claggart, who staggers, falls, then lies still,
dead. Since this is a wartime cruise, according to the Admiralty code, Billy
is sentenced to be hanged. Arthur Miller's *The Crucible* (1953) is a poetic
yet political drama using the 1692 Salem witch trials as a parable about
the 1940–1950s House Un-American Activities Committee that held hearings and conducted wide-range investigations of suspected Communists.
Written in 1940 but first produced in 1958, Bertolt Brecht's *The Resistible
Rise of Arturo Ui* is a satiric analogy comparing Adolf Hitler and the National Socialist Party's rise to power to organized crime in Chicago.

   Courageous individuals taking a stand against totalitarian regimes
are the subject of *Darkness at Noon* (1951), which Sidney Kingsley
adapted from Arthur Koestler's masterpiece, confining the grim action

to a Russian prison, where one of the inmates, a former member of the Central Committee, prefers to go to his death rather than confess to falsehoods as demanded by the government. In *The Prisoner* (1954) by Bridget Boland, inspired by the plight of Hungarian Catholic Cardinal József Mindszenty, the action unfolds in a gloomy cell, spotlighting a tense confrontation between a prisoner and his interrogator representing two diametrically opposed beliefs.

Racial animosities exploded in *The Blacks* (1959) by Jean Genet, *Blues for Mr. Charlie* (1964) by James Baldwin, and *Dutchman* (1964) by LeRoi Jones. An earthy, realistic, and savage picture of life in prison was captured in John Herbert's *Fortune and Men's Eyes* (1967) and in *Short Eyes* (1974) by Miguel Piñero, a former inmate of Sing Sing.

The era's spine-tingling plays included *Speaking of Murder* (1956) by Kelley Roos, pseudonym for husband-and-wife writers Audrey (Kelley) Roos and William Roos, in which a wicked, jealous governess locks her mistress in a suffocating, soundproof vault; *Frankenstein: The Gift of Fire*, a lurid 1959 adaptation of the Mary Shelley novel by David Campton; *The Spiral Staircase* (1962), dramatized by F. Andrew Leslie from the 1933 novel *Some Must Watch* by Ethel Lina White and the 1946 screenplay by Mel Dinelli, confining the action to a gloomy mansion located on the outskirts of a small Massachusetts city during a violent storm. A serial killer has been murdering girls afflicted with imperfections and his next victim may be the live-in maid, who is deaf. *We Have Always Lived in the Castle* (1966), adapted by Hugh Wheeler from Shirley Jackson's 1962 novel, is the story of two sisters who live in an isolated Vermont home, surrounded by the spirits of their dead father, mother, and aunt, who died after sugar mixed with arsenic was sprinkled on their blackberries. What evil lurks within the walls of St. Charles School for Boys is the query of *Child's Play* (1970) by Robert Marasco. An accident in the chemistry lab, a brawl in the dormitory, and a growing number of kids hurt between classes seem to indicate that some of the students have become malevolent. The violence escalates into frenzied sadism, but the final curtain falls without ever spelling out the mystical secrets at St. Charles. *Count Dracula* (1971) by Ted Tiller emphasizes the unholy relationship between the vampire and madman Renfield, whose corpse is found dangling across a balcony rail, his bloody face upside down toward the audience, while in *Dracula* (1973) playwright Crane Johnson changed genders: vampire hunter Professor Van Helsing is a whip-carrying, cigar-smoking woman. In 1975, John Osborne adapted Oscar Wilde's 1890 novel, *The Picture of Dorian Gray*, faithfully transforming to the stage the gradual moral deterioration and depraved behavior of the society man who preserves his youth and handsome looks while his portrait changes into a shriveled, wrinkled reflection.

Comic relief is provided by *My 3 Angels* (1953), a Sam and Bella Spewack adaptation from the French, where murder is amusing, even palatable, in a Christmas fable about three rogues—an embezzler and two assassins—who have been banished to a penal colony in Cayenne, French Guyana. *Meet a Body* (1954), "An Improbable Adventure in Three Acts" by Frank Launder and Sidney Gilliat, is a rollicking thriller about a vacuum-cleaner salesman who inadvertently gets entangled in a series of life-and-death escapades. *The Ponder Heart* (1956), adapted by Joseph Fields and Jerome Chodorov from a story by Eudora Welty, focuses on Uncle Daniel Ponder, who inherited a fortune from his father, which he keeps distributing among the villagers of a small Southern town. The man "with the sweetest disposition in the world" finds himself tried for the murder of his child bride during a thunderstorm. On the witness stand, Uncle Daniel gives away all his assets but manages to turn the tables on an ambitious district attorney and is found not guilty. Brendan Behan's bawdy and wild comedy-drama *The Hostage* (1958) unfolds in a sleazy Dublin brothel. Amid songs, dances, vaudeville gags, and winking asides to the audience, a skeletal plot emerges: a young member of the Irish Republican Army is to be hanged in a Belfast jail the next morning. Armed officers of the IRA sneak into the brothel a nineteen-year-old English soldier whom they have captured against the threatened Belfast execution. In the morning, the brothel is surrounded by English Secret Police and the hostage is cut down by a volley of bullets. However, before the final curtain, the playwright emphasizes that it is all just playacting, only a theatrical game, by having the "dead" man jump to his feet and sing lustily, warning the audience that "the bells of hell go ting-a-ling-a-ling" not for him but for them. *The Gazebo* (1958) by Alec Coppel is a lightly amusing crime escapade about a writer of television whodunits who decides to silence a blackmailer with his six-shooter and conceal the body in the fresh concrete foundation of a new garden gazebo. The next morning, the writer is horrified when the corpse turns up in his Long Island living room. In desperation, he calls Alfred Hitchcock for advice, asking how to get rid of a dead body that keeps coming back. The farcical premise of Lorenzo Semple Jr.'s *Golden Fleecing* (1959) sends three naval personnel to Venice, Italy, where they hatch a scheme to hit the jackpot at the local casino. Woody Allen contributed a comedy of Cold War intrigue in *Don't Drink the Water* (1966), setting some zany, improbable happenings in the American embassy of an unnamed country behind the Iron Curtain. In 1975, theatrical agent Bob Barry concocted a frothy comedy-thriller, *Murder Among Friends*, revolving around a Broadway matinee idol and his rich wife as they scheme to kill one another. That same year, Graham Greene came up with *The Return of A. J. Raffles*, resurrecting E. W. Hornung's gentleman-burglar in a graceful, albeit mischievous, pastiche that involves Oscar Wilde, Lord Alfred Douglas, and Harry "Bunny" Manders, Raffles's valet, in bisexual flirtations.

* * *

The present volume, covering plays of mayhem and murder produced between 1975 and 2000, begins with a bang when Roxie Hart, a beautiful chorus girl, shoots her sugar daddy with a pearl-handed .32 revolver. Roxie is the unorthodox heroine of the musical *Chicago* (1975), adapted from Maurine Watkins's 1926 play of the same name by Fred Ebb (book and lyrics) and John Kander (music). Much of the action takes place in the women's ward of the Cook County jail amid tabloid hoopla.

While the theatre in 1900–1925 was awash with sensational melodramas, in 1925–1950 with psychological thrillers, and in 1950–1975 with courtroom dramas, the last quarter of the twentieth century boasted a series of plush, highly budgeted criminous musicals. After *Chicago* came *Sweeney Todd, The Demon Barber of Fleet Street* (1979), book by Hugh Wheeler, music by Stephen Sondheim. It is the story of a vengeful barber who cuts the throats of his customers and sends the bodies down a chute to a meat-pie proprietress with whom he has an entrepreneurial partnership. *The Mystery of Edwin Drood* (1985), book, music, and lyrics by Rupert Holmes, offers half a dozen potential solutions to the puzzlement inherent in Charles Dickens's last and unfinished novel: is young Edwin Drood dead, and if so, who killed him? *Sherlock Holmes—The Musical* aka *The Revenge of Sherlock Holmes* (1988), book, music, and lyrics by Leslie Bricusse, adds new wrinkles to the saga of the Great Detective, notably the introduction of young Bella Spellgrove, who turns out to be Professor Moriarty's daughter, bent on avenging her father's death at the Reichenbach Falls. *The Phantom of the Opera* (1988), book by Richard Stilgoe and Andrew Lloyd Webber, music by Webber, lyrics by Charles Hart, goes back to Gaston Leroux's 1910 novel about Erik, the half-crazed, murderous musician who resides in the catacombs of the Paris Opera House. Still sending its chandelier toward the stage above a gasping audience, *Phantom* is the longest running play in Broadway history. *City of Angels* (1989), book by Larry Gelbart, music by Cy Coleman, lyrics by David Zippel, treads upon the hardboiled territory of Dashiell Hammett, Raymond Chandler, and Ross Macdonald in a double-decker spoof about a screenwriter and his creation, a tough private eye. As the writer punches the keys of his Smith Corona, the shamus comes to life, walking through the mean streets of Sam Spade, Philip Marlowe, and Lew Archer. *Assassins* (1990), book by John Weidman, music and lyrics by Stephen Sondheim, begins and ends with a chorus of gun-slingers—seven men and two women who have entered the underbelly of American history as the killers or would-be killers of the president. *The Scarlet Pimpernel* (1997), book and lyrics by Nan Knighton, music by Frank Wildhorn, recaptures the adventures of the enigmatic British Lord and his men (initially created by Baroness Orczy in a 1903 non-musical production), who help Parisian aristocrats escape the guillotine during the French Revolution. Wildhorn also composed the score for *Jekyll & Hyde*, based on the 1886 novella by Robert Louis Stevenson.

* * *

Sherlock Holmes, who first appeared on stage in 1893 in a one-act musical satire, *Under the Clock*, continued to solve cases throughout the twentieth century and beyond. A 1976 adaptation of *The Hound of the Baskervilles* by Tim Kelly confines the action to a single set, the sitting room in Baskerville Hall, shifts the proceedings to "the present," and tampers with the dramatis personae of Conan Doyle's novel. Paul Giovanni's *The Crucifer of Blood* (1978) is a distorted version of *The Sign of Four* in which one-legged Jonathan Small and his pygmy ally, Tonga, are not the blowpipe murderers; in a sharp departure from the novel, a victim's daughter turns out to be the culprit. Arthur Conan Doyle himself appears at 221B Baker Street in *The Penultimate Problem of Sherlock Holmes* (1978) by John Nassivera, informing the detective that "on May 4, 1891, Mr. Holmes, I shall kill you at Reichenbach Falls and have done with you once and for all." In *The Mask of Moriarty* (1985), Hugh Leonard calls upon Holmes to solve an "impossible" murder: a maid is stabbed to death on Waterloo Bridge but the constable on the beat has not seen anyone else entering or exiting the area. In Jeremy Paul's *The Secret of Sherlock Holmes* (1988), the world's foremost consulting detective reveals to a shocked Dr. Watson that his nemesis, the Napoleon of Crime, Professor Moriarty, does not exist, but was his invention. He now intends to retire to "a life of philosophy, agriculture—and bee-keeping." Conan Doyle's trim and under-appreciated story *The Adventure of the Sussex Vampire*, adapted to the stage by Peter Buckley in 1988, is the only affair in the canon in which the Great Detective potentially confronts a supernatural creature. An old schoolmate of Watson's arrives at 221B Baker Street with a curious, desperate plea. His beloved wife, a beautiful Peruvian, the mother of their one-year-old baby, was seen by the nurse leaning over the infant, seemingly biting his neck, causing a small wound from which a stream of blood has escaped. *Sherlock Holmes—The Last Act!* (1999) by David Stuart Davies is designed as a one-man show that explores the character and career of the sleuth, and places under scrutiny the friendship and feelings he had for his chronicler Dr. Watson.

Agatha Christie, too, remains immortal with posthumous dramatizations of her works. Christie's fiftieth novel, *A Murder Is Announced*, was adapted to the stage by prolific television writer Leslie Darbon in 1977, featuring

Jane Marple in a perplexing case of a double murder. Darbon also dramatized, in 1981, Christie's 1936 novel, *Cards on the Table*, removing Hercule Poirot from his version and letting Mrs. Ariadne Oliver, renowned author of mystery novels (and arguably Agatha Christie's alter ego) solve the fatal stabbing of a London socialite during a bridge game. Another TV contributor, Clive Exton, adapted 1939's *Murder Is Easy* aka *Easy to Kill* in 1993, the tale of a series of murders in a small, sleepy English village.

In addition to Arthur Conan Doyle and Agatha Christie adaptations, the novels of several other well-known authors in the genre were transferred to the stage. *No Orchids for Miss Blandish*, James Hadley Chase's classic 1938 thriller, was dramatized forty years later by Robert David MacDonald. It is a gritty, violent tale of a kidnapped-for-ransom heiress by ruthless gangsters. Also in 1978, Stuart and Carolyn Gordon converted to the stage Raymond Chandler's hard-knuckled narrative of sibling betrayal, *The Little Sister*, dispensing with some sub-plots and secondary characters, keeping most of the action in Philip Marlowe's drab Hollywood office. Two popular thrillers by Edgar Wallace, *The Green Archer* and *The Black Abbot*, were adapted by Tim Kelly in 1980 and 1982, respectively, both taking place in the 1920s in medieval manors complete with sliding panels, secret passageways, and torture chambers, and both populated with ghostly, hooded apparitions. The elderly heroes of Robert L. Fish's Murder League trilogy, members of a London society composed of crime authors, were recruited by adapters Michael Sutton and Anthony Fingleton to appear in the parody *Over My Dead Body* (1984) and solve the case of the Baker Street Bludgeoner, a contemporary Jack the Ripper. William F. Buckley Jr. dramatized his own *Stained Glass* in 1989, pitting his series' CIA agent, Blackford Oakes, against Russian spies during the Cold War. Walter Mosley's *A Red Death* was adapted in 1997 by David Barr, plunging African American private eye Ezekiel "Easy" Rawlins and his homicidal sidekick Raymond "Mouse" Alexander into the political, legal, and moral tar pits of Los Angeles during the early 1950s. Phyllis Nagy's 1998 play adaptation of *The Talented Mr. Ripley* faithfully follows Patricia Highsmith's original novel, introducing Tom Ripley, one of the most amoral rogues in modern literature.

Also adapted to the stage are the plays *Twelve Angry Women* (1977), which Sherman L. Sergel borrowed from Reginald Rose's Studio One teleplay of 1954 with a change of gender—an all-female cast of white jurors debates the case of a black youth from the slums charged with the stabbing death of his father; *To Kill a Mockingbird* (1987), adapted by Christopher Sergel from Harper Lee's Pulitzer Prize–winning novel, depicts the events that rocked imaginary-yet-real Maycomb, Alabama in 1935, where "Scout," an alert six-year-old, sneaks into the local courthouse to watch her lawyer father, Atticus, defend a young black man accused of raping a white woman; and *Travels with My Aunt* (1989), converted to the stage by Giles Havergal from Graham Greene's novel, in which a meek, reclusive, retired bank manager is suddenly thrust into the picaresque world of his flamboyant aunt and finds himself part of a series of nefarious escapades. The protagonist of Richard Condon's political thriller *The Manchurian Candidate*, dramatized by John Lahr in 1991, is Sergeant Raymond Shaw, secretly brainwashed by the enemy during the Korean War and sent back to the United States as a human time bomb to inflict havoc on an unsuspecting nation. That same year, Ken Hill adapted *The Invisible Man*, H. G. Wells's 1869 "Scientific Romance," as a vaudevillian act, complete with a Master of Ceremonies, depicting the havoc created by Griffin, a misguided scientist, in the Village of Iping, West Sussex, England. *Jane Eyre*, Charlotte Brontë's Gothic novel, was dramatized in 1997 by Polly Teale in a revolutionary manner: the plain, frustrated governess of the title, and Bertha, the madwoman trapped in the attic of Thornfield Hall, become the contrasting inner and outer forces of the same woman. *The Collector*, John Fowles's portrait of a psychopath who abducts a young woman out of what he imagines is love, was adapted in 1998 by Mark Healy with the action unfolding entirely in an isolated cellar, where a wrenching battle of wits develops between kidnapper and victim.

* * *

Bram Stoker's Count and Mary Shelley's Monster continued their march on the stage, the first in *Dracula*, adapted by John Mattera in 1980, the other in *Frankenstein*, adapted by Victor Gialanella the following year, each playwright adding a few elements of his own. Supernatural horror is also manifested in Jack Sharkey's 1980 treatment of Oscar Wilde's Faustian *The Picture of Dorian Gray*, Stephen Mallatratt's rendering of Susan Hill's ghostly novel *The Woman in Black* (1987), and Jeffrey Hatcher's 1996 adaptation of Henry James's novella *The Turn of the Screw*, utilizing a cast of two to relate the life-or-death clash between a nameless governess and the evil scepters that have possessed two children in her care.

Ira Levin, who at the age of twenty-two wrote the Edgar-winning *A Kiss Before Dying* (1953) and followed it with such cult novels as *Rosemary's Baby* (1967), *The Stepford Wives* (1972), and *The Boys from Brazil* (1976), took New York by storm with his twisty thriller *Deathtrap* (1978). Two renowned English detective story novelists also became successful playwrights: Francis Durbridge, creator of Paul Temple, a beloved sleuth in print, on radio, television, and screen, penned a number of wheels-within-wheels thrillers, of which *Sweet Revenge* (1993) is a befitting representative. Simon Brett blended his double interest in crime and the theatre into a series of popular whodunits featuring actor-sleuth Charles Paris, and in the mystery-comedy *Murder in Play* (1993).

Mainstream playwrights who joined the genre by experimenting in suspense elements included David Rabe, known for a trilogy of anti-war dramas, the last of which is 1976's *Streamers*. Unfolding in an Army barracks in Virginia, the climax of *Streamers* is devastatingly bloody. Terence Rattigan, author of *The Winslow Boy*, penned another courtroom drama, *Cause Célèbre* (1977), based on a 1935 English case about a thirty-eight-year-old "scarlet woman" who led an adolescent handyman astray, which led to the murder of her husband. Among Sam Shepard's forty-some plays is Pulitzer Prize–winning *Buried Child* (1978), a brew of realistic action and symbolic implications rotating around a bizarre, dysfunctional farming family with a terrible secret. Sidney Michaels, nominated for Tony Awards in three successive seasons during the 1960s, came up with *Tricks of the Trade* (1980), which he dubbed "A Romantic Mystery." A Cold War spy story, the action unfolds in a posh psychiatry office on Central Park South in Manhattan, where an analyst and his female patient are not who they seem to be. Jerome Chodorov and Norman Panama, who contributed light fare to stage and screen, detoured to *A Talent for Murder* (1981), in which Anne Royce McClain, America's foremost writer of thrillers, now old and ailing, finds herself in jeopardy; some unsavory relatives, anxious to lay hands on Anne's fortune, intend to put her away in an institution. Murder follows.

Bernard Slade, who in the 1970s contributed to the Broadway scene several bittersweet plays, notably *Same Time, Next Year*, arguably the most successful romantic comedy ever to grace the stage, penned two fiendishly clever mysteries in the 1980s—*Fatal Attraction* (1984) and *An Act of the Imagination* (1987). Stephen Sondheim and George Furth, who won Tony Awards for their 1970 musical *Company*, collaborated on the whodunit *Getting Away with Murder*, setting the scene in the penthouse suite of a dilapidated building on the upper West Side of Manhattan. Seven patients are waiting for a group session with their therapist but soon they discover the doctor's pulped body. Tennessee Williams wrote *Not About Nightingales* in 1938 but the play, about a sadistic prison warden and the ill-fated inmates of Hall C, didn't make it to Broadway until 1998. Although a young man's effort, the drama has already signposted flashes of poetic writing and memorable characterization. The climax, taking place in a cell where the temperature reaches more than 125 degrees, is not for the squeamish.

* * *

Several young, up-and-coming playwrights dabbled in crime early in their careers. In *American Buffalo* (1975), David Mamet introduced three small-time hoodlums who think of crime as legitimate free enterprise and plan the robbery of a valuable coin collection. John Pielmeier's *Agnes of God* (1980) spotlights a court-appointed psychiatrist who is assigned to determine the sanity of a young nun accused of strangling her own baby. William Mastrosimone tackled the issue of sexual assault in his taut, violent *Extremities* (1980). Charles Fuller addressed racially-motivated murders in *Zooman and the Sign* (1980) and *A Soldier's Play* (1981). John Logan buried himself in trial transcripts, psychiatric reports, police statements, and newspaper accounts before penning *Never the Sinner* (1985), an account of the Nathan Leopold and Richard Loeb homicide case of 1924. Tracy Letts's *Killer Joe* (1993) is a gritty, brutal drama about a dysfunctional rural family and a murderer-for-hire. Romulus Linney's *True Crimes* (1995) also paints a family seeped in greed, revenge, and murder— in the Appalachian Mountains. *Art of Murder* (1999) by Joe DiPietro presents a carousel of betrayals and shifting alliances unfolding one autumn evening in a remote country house in Connecticut.

Courtroom dramas continued to be the bulwark of the genre. Inspired by a 1911 trial in Michigan, Milan Stitt's *The Runner Stumbles* (1976) is the story of a maverick priest who is charged with the murder of a nun. The court action of *Nuts* (1980) by Tom Topor takes place on the seventh floor of Manhattan's Bellevue Hospital where a young inmate is intent on proving herself mentally fit to stand trial for slaughter-in-the-first-degree rather than being institutionalized indefinitely. Emily Mann's *Execution of Justice* (1984) covers the trial of Dan White, a former member of San Francisco's Board of Supervisors, who in 1978 shot and killed Mayor George Moscone and gay City Supervisor Harvey Milk. Jeffrey Archer's *Beyond Reasonable Doubt* (1987) takes place in London's Old Bailey, where the defendant, accused of poisoning his wife, is a member of the Bar. When still a novice playwright, Aaron Sorkin penned *A Few Good Men* (1989), in which a Marine Lance Corporal is charged with Murder in the Second Degree. A memorable military trial pits a neophyte defense lawyer against a formidable, flag-waving Lieutenant Colonel. Moisés Kaufman and the Members of Tectonic Theatre Project traveled to Laramie, Wyoming, interviewed townspeople regarding the hate crime against Matthew Shepard, a gay student, and collated the material into *The Laramie Project* (2000). The docudrama covers the trial of two local men, who were found guilty of kidnapping, robbery, and second-degree murder.

Espionage maneuvers are depicted in several plays produced in the 1980s. Hugh Whitemore's *Pack of Lies* (1983) is inspired by an actual case, in which a married couple living in a suburb of London aid the Secret Service, M15, to capture a pair of Russian agents living across the street, while Tom Stoppard's *Hapgood* (1988) throws satirical darts at M15's cloak-and-dagger activities in a case of double-agents and twin-spies. *M. Butterfly* (1988), by David Henry Hwang, recounts the unique event of a French diplomat passing information to his lover, a Chinese Opera singer, whom he mistakenly believed to be a woman for twenty years.

Tongue-in-cheek crimes occur in *Murder at the Howard Johnson's* (1979) by Ron Clark and Sam Bobrick, a comedy-thriller about a triangular relationship with lots of deadly plans that never come to fruition; *Whodunit* (1982) by Anthony Shaffer, a spoof on the Murder-in-the-Library type of mystery, taking place in an old manor during a stormy night when a dastardly blackmailer is decapitated by a sword; and *Corpse!* (1983) by Gerald Moon, highlighted by preposterous shenanigans unraveling in two London flats inhabited by identical twin brothers. Before the final curtain comes down, a number of bloody cadavers are scattered about. Charles Ludlam's burlesque-spoof *The Mystery of Irma Vep* (1984) combines elements from the 1915 silent serial *Les Vampires* with splices from *Rebecca*, *The Mummy*, and *The Wolf Man*, recycles from Shakespeare and Ibsen, and snatches from Victorian melodrama. John Bishop's *The Musical Comedy Murders of 1940* (1987) transpires in a snowed-in Westchester mansion that serves as the scene of the crime in a parody that laces together *The Cat and the Canary*, *The Mousetrap*, and Hollywood espionage movies of World War II. The game-play of Rupert Holmes's *Accomplice* (1990) begins when the audience peruses the Playbill: characters are not given names, and there are more biographies of understudies than there are roles.

Moose Murders (1983) by Arthur Bickell, a satire on the mystery genre, achieved the dubious distinction of garnering unanimous negative reviews from the New York critics and dropping the curtain after its one and only performance. Conversely, Warren Manzi's *Perfect Crime* (1987), a half-baked psychological thriller, opened off-Broadway in 1987, and, after twenty-five years, is still running, albeit to half-empty houses.

*   *   *

This work aims to provide an overview of milestone plays of crime, mystery, and detection that deal with a wide variety of topics—murder, theft, chicanery, kidnapping, political intrigue, or espionage. It was not my intention to embrace every single crime-and-punishment play ever produced. I have selected manuscripts of enduring importance, pioneering contributions, singular innovations, outstanding commercial or artistic successes, and representative works by prolific playwrights in the genre. And as in the preceding volumes of *Blood on the Stage*, the slate includes some personal favorites.

This volume covers plays produced between 1975 and 2000 that were performed in the English language at least once. The entries are arranged in chronological order, and each consists of a plot synopsis, production data, a look at unique features, and the opinions of critics and scholars.

To gain a historical perspective, I have kept potentially offensive elements intact and did not edit sexism, racial prejudices, anti-Semitic slurs, or other derogatory content. The plays must be seen in their historical context, each a work of art shaped by its era. The opinions set forth in the plays are not necessarily my own.

Please be advised that the entries will often reveal the solution or twist of a play, because each individual plot synopsis aims to be complete. I hope that the selections discussed in this work will kindle interest in neglected playwrights and forgotten plays.

Chicago (1975)

Book by Fred Ebb (United States, 1932–2004) and Bob Fosse (United States, 1927–1987), Lyrics by Fred Ebb, Music by John Kander (United States, 1927–)

Drawing from her experience as a court reporter for the *Chicago Tribune*, Maurine Watkins (1901–1969) wrote the first draft of *Chicago* as a class assignment in a drama course taught by Professor George Pierce Baker at Yale University. An embellished version was optioned by veteran producer Sam Harris, who engaged George Abbott to stage the "satirical comedy" for a December 30, 1926, opening at New York's Music Box Theatre. Overnight, the twenty-five-year-old novice playwright became the toast of Broadway with a hit show that ran for 172 performances.

Chicago begins with a bang when Roxie Hart, a beautiful married chorus girl, described as a Raphael angel with a touch of Medusa, accuses her sugar daddy of betraying her with another woman and promptly shoots him to death with her pearl-handled .32 revolver.

Roxie is held in the women's ward of the Cook County Jail amid tabloid hoopla coining her "the prettiest woman ever charged with murder in Chicago." The play is peppered with biting satirical darts aimed at media mongers, opportunistic lawyers, and corrupt politicians. "God, if I can only hang that woman!" prays an ambitious assistant state attorney as he poses for the press.

In prison, Roxie meets various inmates on the so-called Murderess Row, including Velma Kelly, a dark, quiet woman in her late thirties, who denies that she killed her husband for insurance money. Soon the two women launch a fierce competition for the media spotlight. Jealous of the attention that Velma gets when her trial commences, Roxie pretends to faint and, upon recovery, claims, sobbing, that she is pregnant. Of course, this is fodder for front-page news. *Chicago*'s edge is sharpest when Roxie's counsel for the defense, Billy Flynn, a short man with a Napoleon complex, coaches his client in how to behave in court. He instructs her to throw her head back, nobly, never to look at the jury, and instead seek the eyes of her husband. Flynn hopes that the jury will want to play Cupid and reunite the young couple.

Chicago toured successfully in Detroit, Boston, Chicago, and Los Angeles. It was filmed in 1927, deviating from the original concept by focusing on the plight of Roxie's husband, Amos Hart. In a 1942 remake more akin to the stage play, Ginger Rogers portrayed the title role in *Roxie Hart*, costarring Adolphe Menjou as her manipulative attorney.

Chicago got a new lease on life when converted into "a musical vaudeville" in 1975. The action unfolds in the late 1920s. The curtain rises on a Master of Ceremonies who addresses the audience and introduces "a story of murder, greed, corruption, violence, exploitation, adultery, and treachery—all those things we hold near and dear to our hearts." Velma Kelly, one of six "Merry Murderesses" in the Cook County jail, leads the chorus, singing "All That Jazz." In another part of the stage, an elevator comes up carrying the dancer Roxie Hart and Fred Casely, her sugar daddy. Roxie, very drunk, hiccups, and loses her shoe. She assures Fred that her husband is not at home. They go into the apartment and the door closes.

The Center Winch rolls in. We are in the Hart bedroom. Roxie is sprawled on the bed wearing a teddy. Fred takes off his pants. She holds the sheet back for him and he jumps into bed. The lovemaking is mechanical and businesslike. When it's over, Fred pulls on his trousers, puts on his jacket, and straightens his tie. Roxie gets a gun from under the pillow. "So that's final, huh Fred?" she asks. "Yeah, I'm afraid so, Roxie," he answers. Roxie declares, "Nobody walks out on me," and shoots him twice.

In jail, Velma and five other female prisoners belt out the "Cell Block Tango," in which each of them insists that she murdered her lover because "he had it coming." The Master of Ceremonies introduces the "Keeper of the Keys, the Countess of the Clink, the Mistress of Murderer's Row—Matron Mama Morton." The matron sings "When You're Good to Mama, Mama's Good to You." Morton assures Velma that she'll be acquitted on March 7th, and on March 8th she will go on an already arranged vaudeville tour. For $50.00 she'll make another telephone call to the William Morris Agency that will insure Velma a weekly fee of $2,500. Resigned, Velma hands Morton the money.

Newcomer Roxie hangs nervously onto the jail bars. Matron Morton calmly tells her that "in this town, murder is a form of entertainment," and that "Cook County ain't never hung a woman yet." If Roxie gives her a hundred-dollar bill, she'll make a phone call to Billy Flynn, "the best criminal lawyer in all Chicago."

Flynn, dressed to the teeth, walks down center and relates to the audience that all he cares about is the fee of $5,000 per case, no exceptions. Amos Hart, Roxie's husband, agrees to pay this fee. Flynn coaches Roxie in a sob story: convent, runaway marriage, foolish affair, and then "We both reached for the gun."

Roxie muses that if Flynn gets her off, the ensuing sky-rocketing publicity might lend her a starring role in vaudeville. In the song "Roxie" she conjures lines of autograph seekers and her name on the marquee above that of the era's biggest star, Sophie Tucker. Conversely, Velma bemoans the loss of interest from press and talent agencies. The word is that she's washed up, finished. "I Can't Do It Alone," sings Velma sadly as she asks Roxie to team up with her. The two women burst into "My Own Best Friend," in which each of them decides, "I am my own best friend." At the end of the number, Velma bows and Roxie faints. Billy Flynn, as well as concerned inmates and reporters, surround her. Roxie lifts her head and says, "Oh, don't worry about me. It's just that I'm going to have a baby." Everyone reacts, flashbulbs pop, as the curtain falls.

Billy Flynn concocts a scheme to achieve universal sympathy for Roxie: he will convince her husband, Amos Hart, to sue Roxie for divorce because she's supposedly pregnant. Amos is self-effacing to the point of believing that "nobody ever knows that I'm around; not even my parents noticed me." He stands alone in a dim spotlight and sings "Mister Cellophane," acknowledging that he's "invisible, inconsequential." Flynn easily maneuvers Amos to file for divorce. The enterprising lawyer sketches the forthcoming courtroom scene for Roxie: she'll be knitting on the witness stand and Flynn will reconcile the couple in front of the pitying jury. But Roxie, flushed with her status as a national celebrity, thinks that she's big enough now to manage alone. She calls Flynn "a greasy Mick lawyer" and fires him. Flynn retorts, "You're a phony celebrity, kid. You're a flash-in-the-pan. In a couple of weeks, nobody'll even know who you are. That's Chicago."

After one of the Murderesses is hanged, the first woman to be executed in Cook County in forty-seven years, a frightened Roxie runs back to Flynn, ready to obey any and all of his instructions. He prepares for his big courtroom scene by assuming his "Clarence Darrow look," pulling his shirt out, messing his hair, and exposing some down-home suspenders. "It's all a circus, kid," he tells Roxie, ready to "Razzle Dazzle" the court.

And he does. Flynn calls Amos to the witness stand and convinces him that he is the father of Roxie's unborn child. Flynn summons Roxie and she testifies that because she'd quarreled with her beloved husband, she drifted into an affair with one Fred Casely. On that fateful night, Casely forced his way into her bedroom, ripped off her kimono, and threw her on the bed. Mr. Hart's revolver was layin' there between them. Casely grabbed for the gun. She got it first. She closed her eyes and shot.

The jury finds Roxie not guilty. While the Foreman announces the verdict, a gunshot and a scream are heard off stage. Confusion ensues, and the reporters rush out. Roxie, who still plans to capitalize on her notoriety, attempts to stop them but all are gone. Even Flynn walks off. Only Amos remains loyal, but Roxie brushes him off, telling him that she had feigned the pregnancy.

The set begins to change and the Master of Ceremonies announces a new act: "Not one little lady but two! You've read about them in the papers and now here they are—a double header! Chicago's own killer dillers—those two scintillating sinners—Roxie Hart and Velma Kelly!" Roxie and Velma appear and go through a dancing routine with top hats and canes. At the end of their act, they take their bows and thank the audience for "your faith and your belief in our innocence. It was your letters, telegrams, and words of encouragement that helped us through our terrible ordeal." The orchestra strikes up "The Battle Hymn of the Republic." Roxie and Velma bow again, throw roses to the audience, wave, and smile as the curtain descends.

* * *

Directed and choreographed by Bob Fosse, *Chicago* opened at New York's Forty-Sixth Street Theatre on June 3, 1975. The leading actors-singers-dancers were Gwen Verdon (Roxie Hart), Chita Rivera (Velma Kelly), and Jerry Orbach (Billy Flynn). The critics' reception was mostly enthusiastic. Douglas Watt, in the *Daily News*, called the musical "bold, cynical and stylish as can be."[1] Leonard Probst of NBC-TV found *Chicago* to be "a highly stylized, highly polished razz-ma-tazz musical . . . a bang-up Broadway show."[2] *Cue* magazine's Marilyn Stasio advised her readers that the show "propositions you with forbidden pleasure, dangerous beauty. It's all about evil, and it's irresistible."[3] *Newsweek*'s Jack Kroll admired the direction and choreography—"In a high-pressure stream of brilliantly staged, bitingly funny scenes, Bob Fosse paints a world of grotesquely gay corruption,"[4] while T. E. Kalen of *Time* magazine was taken by "the erotic poetry in motion that uncoils whenever Gwen Verdon (Roxie Hart) and her sister in crime, Chita Rivera (Velma Kelly), do their solos and duets."[5]

There were a few dissenting voices. Clive Barnes, in the *New York Times*, labeled *Chicago* "one of those shows where a great deal has been done with very little . . . never in the history of the Broadway theatre has so much been done by so many for so few final results."[6] The *Christian Science Monitor*'s John Beaufort concluded, "For all of its flamboyance, talent and super-directed energy, *Chicago* wound up seeming hollow, melancholy and abrasively alienating."[7] Kevin Sanders of WABC-TV announced, "The show has no unifying theme. It has no center."[8] Still, *Chicago* became the toast of New York, garnering 936 performances.

Twenty years later (and seventy years after the presentation of the original Maurine Watkins play), the musical *Chicago* was revived—in a concert rendition—at Manhattan's City Center, followed (on November 14, 1996) by a full-scale, enormously successful production at the Richard Rodgers Theatre, starring Ann Reinking (who also choreographed the show in the vaudevillian style of Bob Fosse) as Roxie, Bebe Neuwirth as Velma, and James Naughton as Flynn. As of October 2, 2011, *Chicago* had played 6176 performances. It is still going strong.

A motion picture version, scripted by Bill Condon and directed by Rob Marshall, an energetic concoction enhanced by jump-cut editing and cynical, on-the-mark performances by Renée Zellweger (Roxie), Catherine Zeta-Jones (Velma), Richard Gere (Flynn), and Queen Latifah (the prison matron)—winning Oscars for Best Picture of 2002 and for Supporting Actress (Zeta-Jones), Film Editing, Art Direction, Costume Design, and Sound.

Jerry Springer, the tabloid television host, played Billy Flynn for six weeks in a 2009 London revival of the musical *Chicago*.

* * *

The promise engendered by Maurine Dallas Watkins's original *Chicago* fizzled when her next play, *Revelry*, based on the controversial Samuel Hopkins Adams novel about the corrupt regime of President Warren G. Harding, received mixed reviews while trying out in Philadelphia, and contemptuous ones upon opening in New York's Masque Theatre on September 12, 1927, where it had a short forty-eight-performance run.

Watkins achieved notable success as a screenwriter. *Up the River* (1930), directed by John Ford, featured Spencer Tracy and Warren Hymer as convicts escaping from prison, coming to the aid of a blackmailed couple (Humphrey Bogart and Claire Luce), and returning "up the river" in time to win the prison's annual baseball game. A remake was shot in 1938. *Party Girl* (1932), with Loretta Young, focused on compulsive gambling, while *The Strange Love of Molly Louvain* (1932), based on Watkins' unpublished play *Tinsel Girl* (copyrighted 1931), pictured the travails of a cigar-counter girl, portrayed by Ann Dvorak, who gets in trouble with the police. *Professional Sweetheart* (1933) starred Ginger Rogers as Glory Eden, a radio celebrity, who rebels against the sponsor's insistence that she lead a pristine existence; Glory refuses to sign her new contract until she is allowed "to sin and suffer." *Search for Beauty*, featuring the odd combination of Larry "Buster" Crabbe (the Flash Gordon of the celebrated serials) and Ida Lupino, spotlights the behind-the-scenes shenanigans at a beauty pageant. The romantic comedy *Libeled Lady* (1936), nominated for a Best Picture Oscar, depicts the desperate efforts by the *New York Evening Star* to avoid a $5,000,0000 suit for a false story about an heiress (Myrna Loy). The *Star* people (Spencer Tracy, William Powell, and Jean Harlow) utilize any and all means to change the heiress's mind. The film was remade in 1946 under the title *Easy to Wed*, featuring Esther Williams, Van Johnson, Lucille Ball, and Keenan Wynn. *I Love You Again* (1940), is the story of an amnesic con man (William Powell) who settles in Habersville, Pennsylvania, marries a beautiful socialite (Myrna Loy), and becomes a pillar of the community.

In its issue of May–February, 2012, the *Strand Magazine* published a "lost," never-before-published short story by Watkins, titled "Bound." Andrew Gulli, the Managing Editor of the *Strand*, writes: "'Bound' is perhaps a reminder of Watkins' humble genius—a tangled tale of love and ownership told from the perspective of a deaf farmhand."[9]

* * *

Lyricist Fred Ebb was born in 1928 in Manhattan to a poor Jewish family. He worked during the early 1950s bronzing baby shoes, as a trucker's assistant, and in a department store credit office. He earned a bachelor's degree in English Literature at New York University and a master's degree in English from Columbia University.

Ebb's early collaborators included Phil Springer, Norman Martin, and Paul Klein. Ebb's initial contributions to Broadway were lyrics in the musical revues *Baker's Dozen*, *Isn't America Fun*, and *From A to Z*. In 1962, Ebb met John Kander. Their first Broadway venture, *Flora the Red Menace* (1965), depicting the misadventures of a fashion designer, was directed by George Abbott and won its star, Liza Minnelli, a Tony Award, but the show closed after a brief run of eighty-seven performances. However, their second collaboration, *Cabaret* (1966), based on John Van Druten's play *I Am a Camera* and directed by Harold Prince, won eight Tony Awards, including Best Musical and Best Score, and was a smash hit, running for 1,165 showings. Its action unfolding at a seedy night club in 1930s Berlin against the backdrop of growing Nazi terror, *Cabaret* was adapted into a film by Bob Fosse, won eight Academy Awards (though not Best Picture), and was revived in New York twice, first in 1987 with Joel Grey reprising his original role as the emcee, and again in 1998, featuring Alan Cumming in the part.

The next few works by Ebb and Kander were less successful: *The Happy Time* (1968), relating the travails of a French-Canadian village family, won director-choreographer Gower Champion the Tony, but struggled through 286 sparsely attended performances. *Zorba* (1968), the story of a friendship that evolves between a Greek mine worker and a young

American who has inherited an abandoned mine in Crete, ran for 305 performances. A 1983 revival starring Anthony Quinn played for 362.The play *70, Girls, 70* (1971), about a group of larcenous old folks who steal furs from various New York stores to finance the purchase of an Upper West Side retirement hotel, closed after thirty-five performances. In 1972, Ebb wrote the television special, *Liza with a Z*. Three years later, Ebb and Kander collaborated on the score of both *Funny Lady*, a sequel to *Funny Girl*, and *Chicago*.

In 1977, Ebb and Kander worked with Martin Scorsese and Liza Minnelli twice: on the film *New York, New York*, with its well-known title track, and on the stage musical *The Act*, the story of a fading movie star attempting a comeback as a Las Vegas entertainer. It ran for 233 performances. Ebb and Kander's next team effort was *Woman of the Year* (1981), a hit that won them their second Tony Award for Best Score. With Lauren Bacall in the role of a nationally known television news personality who is torn between family responsibilities and a demanding career, the musical amassed 770 performances. Ebb and Kander paired again with Chita Rivera and Liza Minnelli—for 204 showings—in *The Rink* (1984), about the owner of a dilapidated roller skating rink who attempts to reconcile with her estranged daughter. A transgender window dresser and a Marxist revolutionary are prison cellmates in *Kiss of the Spider Woman* (1992, West End; 1993, Broadway), which in spite of mixed reviews ran for 904 performances and won Ebb and Kander their third Tony Award for Best Score.

Later efforts by Ebb and Kander include *Steel Pier* (1997), wherein the characters interwind during a 1933 Atlantic City dance marathon. Choreographed by Susan Stroman and featuring Kristin Chenoweth, the show was nominated for eleven Tonys but won none and closed after seventy-six performances. *Over and Over*, based on Thornton Wilder's 1943 Pulitzer Prize–winning play *The Skin of Our Teeth*, the story of an Everyfamily's journey across history from the Ice Age to the present, incubated at the Signature Theatre in Arlington, Virginia in 1999 but never made it to New York. *The Visit* (2001), based on the 1956 play by Friedrich Dürrenmatt, focuses on one of the world's richest women who returns to her financially depressed hometown and offers its residents a fortune in exchange for the murder of the man who scorned her years before. The musical adaptation was presented by Chicago's Goodman Theatre in 2001, by the Signature Theatre of Arlington, Virginia, in 2008, and as an Actors Fund benefit concert for one night, on November 30, 2011, at the Ambassador Theatre in Manhattan.

Through the years, Ebb penned the book and lyrics for solo appearances on Broadway by Liza Minnelli, Shirley MacLaine, Barbara Cook, and Chita Rivera. His songs graced the television shows of Lawrence Welk, Carol Burnett, Ed Sullivan, Bob Hope, Dick Cavett, Dinah Shore, Johnny Carson,

Benny Hill, Tony Bennett, Dean Martin, and Larry King as well as *Glee*, *Dancing with the Stars*, and several Academy Awards annuals.

In June 2004, Ebb and Kander gave the New York Public Library for the Performing Arts a gift of their archives—thousands of pages of scripts, songs, and other pieces of stage memorabilia. Later that year, on September 11, Fred Ebb died, at seventy-six, of a heart attack at his home in Manhattan. At the time of his death, he was working on a new musical with Kander, *Curtains*, "A Backstage Murder Mystery Musical Comedy," a spoof about a series of murders committed during the mounting of a show at Boston's Colonial Theatre in 1959. The first victim is a much-disliked star who dies on opening night during the curtain call. Police Lieutenant Frank Cioffi arrives on the scene to conduct the investigation.[10]

In 2010, *The Scottsboro Boys*, a formerly unproduced musical with lyrics by Ebb, music by Kander, and book by David Thompson, premiered at off-Broadway's Vineyard Theatre and later moved to Broadway's Lyceum Theatre. *The Scottsboro Boys* explores the famous case of the 1930s when a group of African American teenagers were unjustly accused of attacking two white women. *The Scottsboro Boys* was nominated for a Drama Desk Award and won the Lucille Lortel Award for Outstanding Musical, proving to be a worthy epitaph for one of the theatre's distinguished lyricists.

John Kander was born in 1927 in Kansas City, Missouri. He attended the Pembroke Country-Day School and Oberlin College before earning, in 1953, his MA at Columbia University where he studied composition with Jack Beeson. Kander began his Broadway career as a substitute pianist for *West Side Story* and an audition pianist for *Gypsy*. His first show as a composer was *A Family Affair* (1962), with book and lyrics by James and William Goldman. It is the story of a young suburban couple who decide to marry, but their families, in their madcap zeal for a large country club affair, almost destroy the wedding. The show was plagued with backstage problems from the very beginning and ran for only sixty-five performances. Later in 1962, Kander's fortunes changed when he met lyricist Fred Ebb, marking the beginning of a songwriting collaboration that lasted for more than four decades.

The son of a vaudevillian, Robert Louis Fosse was born in 1927 in Chicago, Illinois. He attended dance schools as a child and began dancing professionally at the age of thirteen. Though asthmatic, Fosse was a dance prodigy. He teamed up with another young dancer, Charles Grass, and under the name The Riff Brothers they toured throughout the Chicago area. Between 1947 and 1953, Fosse was cast in Broadway musicals and national road companies as a chorus dancer. Spotted by a talent scout, he migrated to Hollywood where he appeared in three film musicals, including *Kiss Me, Kate*. But soon disillusioned with Tinseltown, he returned to New York.

Jerome Robbins gave Fosse his first big Broadway break when engaging him to choreograph 1954's *The Pajama Game*, for which Fosse won the first of eight Tony Awards for choreography. Fosse established his own unique, slinky, sexy style of dancing and clever, angular groupings. He often worked with his third wife, the dancing star Gwen Verdon, and with dancer/choreographer Ann Reinking, who later served as a guardian of the Fosse legacy. Returning to films, Fosse choreographed *How to Succeed in Business Without Really Trying* (1967) and *Sweet Charity* (1969). In 1972, he directed/choreograped *Cabaret*, shooting on location in Germany, and won an Academy Award. He also directed the nonmusical *Lenny* (1974), based on the life of comedian Lenny Bruce, and the autobiographical *All That Jazz* (1979).

Fosse's last assignment on Broadway was directing and choreographing *Big Deal* (1986), based on the hilarious 1958 Italian movie *Big Deal on Madonna Street*, shifting the action to Chicago of the 1930s, relating the misadventures of a group of hapless, unemployed African American men who plan to rob a pawnshop. Fosse died of a heart attack the following year, at the age of sixty, and was cremated, his ashes scattered in the Atlantic Ocean off the shores of Quogue, New York.

Acting Edition: (of the musical version) Samuel French, Inc.

Awards and Honors: The original play was a top-ten selection in *The Best Plays of 1926–1927*. The musical version was a top ten selection in *The Best Plays of 1975–1976* ("The most popular new musical of the season . . . stylishly colorful.")[11] The musical version (1996 revival) won five 1997 Antoinette Perry Awards: Best Revival of a musical; Leading Actor in a musical—James Naughton (Billy Flynn); Leading Actress in a musical—Bebe Neuwirth (Velma Kelly); Lighting Design—Ken Billington; Choreography—Ann Reinking; Direction of a musical—Walter Bobbie. In 1998, *Chicago* also garnered the Laurence Olivier Award, performed at London's Adelphi Theatre, as Outstanding Musical Production of the season, and a Grammy Award for Musical Show Album. Bob Fosse, John Kander, and Fred Ebb were each inducted into the Theatre Hall of Fame for outstanding contributions to the American theatre. Ebb was inducted into the Songwriters Hall of Fame in 1983. John Kander and Fred Ebb were recipients of Kennedy Center Honors, 1998. In 2003, they were named "Living Landmarks" by the New York Landmarks Conservancy. In 2007, the Drama Desk honored Kander and (the late) Ebb with a Special Award for "42 years of excellence in advancing the art of the musical theatre." Kander and Ebb were Tony Award nominees eleven times for best score and lyrics, winning three—for *Cabaret* (1967), *Woman of the Year* (1981), and *Kiss of the Spider Woman* (1993). They were also awarded (with Terence McNally) the 2002 Joseph Jefferson Award for their musical adaptation of *The Visit*, performed at the Goodman Theatre in Chicago. Bob

Fosse won Best Choreography Tony Awards for *The Pajama Game* (1955), *Damn Yankees* (1956), *Redhead* (1959), *Little Me* (1963), *Sweet Charity* (1966), *Pippin* (1973), *Dancin'* (1978), and *Big Deal* (1986). He pulled off a show-business equivalent of the hat trick in 1973, becoming the first director in history to win an Oscar (for the movie version of *Cabaret*), a Tony (for *Pippin*), and an Emmy (for the TV special *Liza With a Z*) in a single season.

NOTES

1. *Daily News*, June 4, 1975.
2. *NBC-TV*, June 4, 1975.
3. *Cue Magazine*, June 16, 1975.
4. *Newsweek*, June 16, 1975.
5. *Time*, June 16, 1975.
6. *New York Times*, June 4, 1975.
7. *Christian Science Monitor*, June 6, 1975.
8. *WABC-TV*, June 3, 1975.
9. *Strand Magazine* XXXVI, February–May 2012, 2.
10. After the death of Fred Ebb in 2004, composer John Kander continued to work on *Curtains* with a new librettist, Rupert Holmes. The musical had its world premiere at the Ahmanson Theatre in Los Angeles in July 2006, was transferred to New York's Al Hirschfeld Theatre in March 2007, garnered mixed reviews, albeit eight Tony Award nominations, and ran for 511 performances.
11. Otis Guernsey Jr., ed., *The Best Plays of 1975–1976* (New York: Dodd, Mead, 1976), 13.

American Buffalo (1975)

David Mamet (United States, 1947–)

"In 1975, I was just out of school, working at the Goodman Theatre in Chicago as assistant to everybody and as the director of Stage 2, when a guy about my age walked in with a play under his arm," writes Gregory Mosher in an introduction to the published edition of *American Buffalo*. "I told him I'd read it over the weekend. 'You don't need to read it; just do it,'" the man said. Mosher read the play and was awed: "Mamet worked iambic pentameter out of the vernacular of the underclass. He made it sound like people talking, and he made it funny. . . . There's more to the play than the words, of course, because there was more on Mamet's mind than a linguistic parlor trick. . . . *American Buffalo* popped out, full grown, as the American drama's funniest, most vicious attack on the ethos of Big Business and the price that it exacts upon the human soul."[1]

American Buffalo premiered at Goodman Theatre's Stage 2 on November 23, 1975 under Mosher's direction. After a twelve-performance showcase, the drama reopened at Chicago's St. Nicholas Theatre. In February 1976, it played at off-off-Broadway's St. Clements in New York, again staged by Mosher. A Broadway production opened a year later, on February 16, 1977, at the Ethel Barrymore Theatre, under the direction of Ulu Grosbard.

The play unfolds at a Chicago junkshop, a cluttered, below-street-level store. It is Friday morning and the proprietor, middle-aged, phlegmatic, cigar-addicted Don Dubrow, is rebuking Bobby, a young, dimwitted junkie he has taken under his wing, for losing sight of a man whose movements he was supposed to track. Don tells Bobby that when he is supposed to do something, he should do it with no excuses. "Action talks and bullshit walks," says Don.

Enter Walter Cole, nicknamed "Teach," tough and aggressive. We learn that a well-dressed man came into the shop a few days earlier, browsed, and bought a supposedly rare buffalo head nickel for ninety dollars.

11

Don, Teach, Bobby, and Fletcher (who does not appear in the play, but is referred to) are conspiring to burglarize the nearby apartment of the coin collector. Bobby leaves and returns to report that he has just spotted the man leaving his building with a suitcase, getting into a car and driving away. It seems that the coast is clear for a break-in that night.

Teach presses Don to remove Bobby from the team because he feels the boy is inexperienced and potentially disloyal. By eleven at night, Fletcher has not shown up and Teach becomes agitated, suspecting that Fletcher may have planned to do the job on his own. Teach wants to go ahead with the plan anyway, but Don, doubtful, asks Teach how he intends to break into the man's house and how he will handle the situation if the coins are stored in a safe. Teach's answers are lame and unconvincing.

Teach takes out a revolver and begins to load it. The sight of the gun upsets Don, who feels that they "don't need a gun." Teach assures him that it is "merely a deterrent." They halt their argument briefly as a police car cruises by.

There is a lot of back-and-forth between the two small-time hoods, but very little action. Toward the end, things escalate when Teach wrongly accuses Bobby of lying, viciously strikes him on the head with a metal object, and proceeds to trash the junkshop.

The play winds up oddly optimistic: as Don and Teach support Bobby on the way to the hospital, a fragile bond develops among the three characters. They never pull off the burglary.

* * *

American Buffalo, featuring Kenneth McMillan (Don), John Savage (Bobby), and Robert Duvall (Teach), received the gamut of critical reactions. Martin Gottfried opined that the play's three characters represent "a working class America whose basic, informal self has been reduced to animal impulses." The reviewer admired Mamet's "street language of the people, a polyglot of curse words, catch-phrases and animal cry."[2] Clive Barnes wrote, "It is a comedy about violence and a play about action that is curiously inactive. Yet it is also one of the foulest-mouthed plays ever staged, at a time when very few writers produce dialogue that actually smells of roses. Yet it holds the attention, is often very funny and is at times exciting."[3] Howard Kissel stated, "Mamet's play is to actors what a jam session is to jazz musicians—it invites the most experienced kind of playfulness and risk taking." Kissel applauded Robert Duvall, who, as Teach, "fills the stage with a wacky, manic energy"; Kenneth McMillan who, "as the crusty shopkeeper, is masterful at suggesting authority in spite of apparent wheeziness"; and John Savage, who "has one of the most expressive, nuanced dead-pans in the business."[4] Christopher Potterfield complimented Ulu Grosbard's "taut direction" and Santo Loquasto's setting—"It depicts a junk shop, a clutter of old furniture, toys and appliances that poignantly reflect the battered grimy souls who cast them off."[5]

Conversely, Douglas Watt found *American Buffalo* "a poor excuse for a play."[6] Edwin Wilson theorized, "Perhaps Mr. Mamet is trying to make some statement about capitalism and the decline of morals in America. If so, his symbols are interesting but they won't stick, and the play is not heavy enough to support the weight of such ideas."[7] John Beaufort scoffed at "a very thin slice of lowlife. . . . The playwright's observations (psychological, sociological, etc.) are too superficial to waste time upon."[8]

The television reviewers were also less than kind. Bob Lape gleaned in *American Buffalo* "three performers in search of a play. . . . Some perfectly reasonable actors got mugged in *American Buffalo,* and the whole play aborts."[9] Leonard Probst remarked that "after ten years in movies such as *The Godfather* and *Network,* Robert Duvall has returned to Broadway—in the wrong play. I kept waiting for all the symbolism to add up to something, but it didn't. The center of the play is missing."[10]

Despite the mixed reactions, *American Buffalo* won the New York Drama Critics Award for best play of the 1977 season, and was nominated for two Tony awards: Best Direction of a Play and Best Scenic Design. The play ran for 135 performances. In 1978 it was produced—for thirty performances—by the Trinity Square Repertory Company in Providence, Rhode Island. Two years later *American Buffalo* was mounted by New Haven's Long Wharf Theatre, directed by Arvin Brown and starring Al Pacino as Teach, a production that was transferred in 1981 to off-Broadway's Circle in the Square, where it ran for 262 performances before moving again, on October 27, 1983, this time to Broadway's Booth Theatre.

Unlike the original 1977 press reception, now almost the entire cadre of critics treated the play with respect. Douglas Watt changed his tune and saluted "a skimpy comedy of menace that has developed into an uproariously funny evening,"[11] and naysayer John Beaufort admitted that the strengths of *American Buffalo* lie in its "word patterns, cadences, and rhythms; its verbal flights, odd turns, and sudden stops."[12] Clive Barnes remained the champion of "a terrific play" and lauded Al Pacino, "a great actor" who "runs through the play like an electric wire."[13] Howard Kissel, too, reiterated his admiration for "the richest, most vital American play of the past decade."[14] Only Frank Rich of the *New York Times* expressed disdain for a production in which "the meat and blood are gone" because of a "mechanical stylization" performance by Al Pacino that "saps the work's raw power."[15] The play ran for 102 performances.

American Buffalo was revived off-Broadway by the Atlantic Theatre Company in 2000, with William H. Macy as Teach, running seventy-eight performances. John Leguizamo played Teach in a 2008 Broadway reincarnation, co-starring with Cedric the Entertainer as Don and Haley Joel Osment as Bobby. Critic Ben Brantley lamented: "The whooshing noise coming from the Belasco Theatre is the sound of the air being let out of David Mamet's dialogue. Robert Fall's deflated revival of Mr. Mamet's *American Buffalo* evokes the woeful image of a souped-up sport car's flat tire, built for speed but going nowhere."[16] David Cote agreed: "This brutally clownish paean to petty criminals and their pretzel morality doesn't deliver the same shock as when it coldcocked Chicago and New York in 1976. . . . For the mountains of old garbage in Donny's shop, there's very little whiff of mothballs on the Belasco's stage."[17] The play lasted for only eight showings.

In April 2012, The Geffen Playhouse of Los Angeles announced that *American Buffalo* will be included in its 2012–2013 season. A motion picture version of the play was made in 1996, directed by Michael Corrente, starring Dustin Hoffman (Teach), Dennis Franz (Don), and Sean Nelson (Bobby).

* * *

David Alan Mamet was born in Chicago, Illinois in 1947 to Jewish parents. His father was an attorney, his mother a teacher. Mamet was educated at the progressive Francis W. Parker School and at Goddard College in Plainfield, Vermont. One of his early jobs was as a waiter at Chicago's Second City.

Mamet's initial plays were produced out of town in the early 1970s: *The Duck Variations*, in which two old men sit on a park bench, watch ducks, and philosophize on mating habits, friendship, and death; *Sexual Perversity in Chicago*, spotlighting nine weeks in the life and loves of two working-class couples; and *American Buffalo*. On his way to becoming one of America's top dramatists, Mamet penned several plays that incorporated criminous elements. *The Water Engine* (originally written as a radio play; staged at off-Broadway's Public Theatre, 1977; Broadway, 1978; television movie, 1992) is the story of a young amateur inventor who designs an engine that runs on water. He plans to patent it, but soon finds himself up against shyster-attorneys who represent Big Business. In *Edmond* (first performed at the Goodman Theatre, Chicago, Illinois, 1982; New York, 1982; London, 2003; filmed, 2006), a white-collar worker in New York City leaves his family on the advice of a fortune teller and embarks on an odyssey through downtown's seedy underbelly. His wandering takes him to several bars, a bordello, and a peep show. He is mugged, robbed, and ends up stabbing a waitress to death. In prison, he is sodomized by his African-American cellmate but eventually forgives him and the play ends as the two say "good night," kiss, and fall asleep side by side on the bed. *Glengarry Glen Ross* (London, 1983; Broadway, 1984; filmed, 1992) is populated with desperate, cutthroat Chicago real estate salesmen who lie, threaten, bribe, and burglarize while competing for buyers. *Oleanna* (Back Bay Theatre, Cambridge, Massachusetts, 1992; London, 1993; filmed, 1994) begins with a college student, Carol, dropping by her professor's office seeking his help with her class work. A few days later the professor, John, finds that Carol has filed a formal complaint, accusing him of sexually harassing her during the meeting. Despite protestations, John loses his job. *Romance* (Atlantic Theatre Company, New York, 2005; London, 2005) is a courtroom farce that lampoons the American judicial system. *The Voysey Inheritance* (2006), adapted from a play by Harley Granville Barker, is a portrait of a wealthy family coming apart when it is revealed that the aging father has amassed his fortune by embezzling from his clients. In *Race* (Broadway, 2009), two lawyers try to decide whether to take on the case of a rich white man accused of raping a black woman.

Notable plays by Mamet include *A Life in the Theatre* (Goodman Theatre, Chicago, 1977; off-Broadway, 1977; television movie, 1993; London, 2005; Broadway, 2010), focusing on the relationship between two actors, one an old stage veteran and the other young and promising, both on and off stage; *Speed-the-Plow* (Broadway, 1988; Los Angeles, 2006; London, 2008), a satirical dissection of the American film industry with emphasis on its shady back-room maneuvers; *Faustus* (San Francisco, 2004), a modern interpretation of the classic tale; *November* (2007), an Oval Office satire picturing one day in the life of a beleaguered commander-in-chief during an election year. Mamet also modernized the Anton Chekhov plays *The Cherry Orchard* (1985), *Uncle Vanya* (1988), and *The Three Sisters* (1991).

Mamet demonstrated his interest in the criminal mind when penning the screenplays of *The Postman Always Rings Twice* (1981), based on the novel by James M. Cain, in which the young, seductive wife of an elderly roadside café owner and an amoral drifter begin a steamy affair and conspire to murder the woman's husband. In *The Verdict* (1982), an alcoholic, down-on-his-luck lawyer undertakes a difficult medical malpractice case in an attempt to salvage his self-respect and get a decent settlement for his clients. *The Untouchables* (1987) is a colorful account of Federal Agent Eliot Ness, who assembles a small, handpicked team to encounter Chicago's crime boss Al Capone. *House of Games* (1997) spotlights a Harvard-educated psychiatrist who is drawn by a smooth-talking grifter into the seedy world of stings, scams, and con men. In *Things Change* (1988), an Italian-American shoe-shiner with a remarkable likeness to a mafia don is paid to take the rap for murder. *Homicide* (1991) is the story of a Jewish detective investigating the murder of an elderly lady in a candy shop. The trail leads him to a Zionist group. The protagonist of *The Spanish Prisoner* (1997) is a young inventor who is conned and finds himself framed for murder. The hero-villains of *Ronin* (1998) are gunmen-for-hire whose mission is to retrieve a suitcase from a man who is about to sell its contents to the Russians. After the mission is completed, everyone backstabs everyone else—with deadly results. *Lansky* (1999) covers the life of Meyer Lansky, a young man growing up in the Jewish ghettos of America's big cities. He becomes a crime boss at the turn of the twentieth century. *The Winslow Boy*, based on a play by Terence Rattigan, depicts the stubborn fight of an adolescent's parents to clear his name after he was expelled from the royal naval academy for stealing five shillings. *Hannibal* (2001) continues the saga of Hannibal Lecter, the psychotic, murderous cannibal created by Thomas Harris, who previously appeared in the 1991 motion picture *The Silence of the Lambs*. No one trusts anyone in the twisty caper movie *Heist* (2001), in which an aging thief, saddled with a beautiful wife, joins a band of shady characters to pull one last job. The hero of *Spartan* (2004) is a maverick government agent who is assigned to find the abducted drug-addicted daughter of a Washington politician. He traces the girl to a bordello, only to realize that the captors have recruited her for a Middle Eastern white slavery market.

In 1985, Mamet co-founded (with William H. Macy) off-Broadway's Atlantic Theatre Company. Mamet's former and present wives, the actresses Lindsay Crouse and Rebecca Pidgeon, starred in many of his plays.

Acting Edition: Samuel French, Inc.

Awards and Honors: A top ten selection in *The Best Plays of 1976–1977*. Winner of the New York Drama Critics for Best Play (1977). David Mamet's *The Water Engine* was nominated for a Drama Desk Award for Outstanding New Play (1978). *Glengarry Glen Ross* won the Laurence Olivier Award for Best New Play (1983), the Pulitzer Prize for Drama (1984), and the New York Drama Critics' Circle Award for Best American Play (1984) as well as the Drama Desk Award and the Tony Award for Best Revival of a Play (2005). *Speed-the-Plow* was nominated for a Tony Award for Best Play (1988). As a screenwriter, Mamet received Oscar nominations for *The Verdict* (1982) and *Wag the Dog* (1997).

NOTES

1. David Mamet, *American Buffalo* (New York: Grove Press, 1996), ix, xi.
2. *New York Post*, February 17, 1977.
3. *New York Times*, February 17, 1977.
4. *Women's Wear Daily*, February 17, 1977.
5. *Time*, February 28, 1977.
6. *Daily News*, February 17, 1977.
7. *Wall Street Journal*, February 23, 1977.
8. *Christian Science Monitor*, February 23, 1977.
9. *WABC-TV7*, February 16, 1977.

10. *NBC-TV*, February 16, 1977.
11. *Daily News*, October 28, 1983.
12. *Christian Science Monitor*, November 8, 1983.
13. *New York Post*, October 27, 1983.
14. *Women's Wear Daily*, October 28, 1983.
15. *New York Times*, October 28, 1983.
16. *New York Times*, November 18, 2008.
17. *Time Out New York*, November 20–26, 2008.

Streamers (1976)

David Rabe (United States, 1940–)

Streamers is the last in a trilogy of plays by David Rabe based upon his experiences in the U.S. military during the Vietnam War. The others include *Sticks and Bones* (1969), an unkind portrait of religious, intolerant middle-class American parents who persuade their son, blinded in Vietnam, to commit suicide; and *The Basic Training of Pavlo Hummel* (1971), depicting the horrors of combat as a mortally wounded soldier looks back on his service career. *Streamers* (1976) concentrates on the psychological effect of basic training and is more realistic and more violent than its predecessors, climaxing with two impulsive fatal stabbings.

The title is a metaphor for a dud parachute, taken from a song concocted by paratroopers from Fort Bragg. A soldier plummets through the air toward his death while the cords of his chute drift slowly down to earth like slow-moving streamers. "Mr. Rabe suggests that many people today are hurtling toward destruction," wrote Edwin Wilson in the *Wall Street Journal*, "cut off from those things which might sustain or save them."[1]

The action of *Streamers* unfolds in an Army barracks in Virginia. There are three bunks and three wall lockers. At the foot of each bunk is a green wooden footlocker. Two hanging lights at the center of the room provide some illumination. Several maps hang in the corner near a trashcan. A door at the back wall opens onto a hallway that runs off to the latrines, showers, and other cadet rooms.

It is dusk as the curtain rises. Martin, black and thin, is pacing back and forth. A white towel stained red with blood is wrapped around his wrist. Richie, suburban, effeminate, is seated wearily on his bunk. The door opens and Carlyle enters. He is "a large black man" wearing filthy fatigues, grease-stained and dark with sweat. A pivotal character, Carlyle will prove to be a hostile recruit, resentful over the lowly treatment by the men in his company. He says he's looking for a black man he heard is bunking in this room. Richie tells him that the person he is looking for is Roger, who isn't here at the moment. Martin displays his wrist to Carlyle and says, "I slit my wrist." Taken aback, Carlyle exits.

Billy, blonde, trim, a Wisconsin straight arrow, enters, carrying a slice of pie on a paper napkin. He sits on his footlocker and takes off his shoes as Martin confides, "I cut my wrist, Billy. . . . I can't stand the army anymore." Billy asks if there's anything he can do to help but Richie tells him that he washed Martin's wound with peroxide and everything is under control. Martin wanders out and Richie rushes after him. Billy scrambles to get his shoes on and follows them into the hall.

Enter Roger, a tall, well-built African-American wearing a long-sleeved Khaki shirt. He starts doing pushups when Billy returns. Roger tells him that he is itching to get "outa this goddamn typin' terrors outfit and into some kinda real army." They are surprised that their alcoholic sergeant, Rooney, "who cannot light his own cigar for shakin'," has just gotten orders to Vietnam where he'll be a demolition expert, "blowing up bridges and shit." It seems likely that they'll be following their sergeant to a war they didn't know of before enlisting. Billy finds it hard to conceive of the idea of other people shooting at him and aiming to kill.

Richie bounds into the room and undresses at his locker. He is in a cheerful mood as he believes his talk with Martin has done the would-be suicide, who "made this rather desperate, pathetic gesture for attention," some good. Flirtatiously, Richie suggests to Billy that they go to a movie together and heads for the showers to get ready.

Roger and Billy speculate on whether Richie is really gay. Billy is certain he is. Roger is doubtful: Richie has a pin-up of a naked woman in his locker. Billy steps out to get mops, buckets, and wax to clean the floor. Alone, Roger opens Richie's locker and looks at the pin-up. Carlyle comes in and stands looking at Roger, then asks if that locker with a picture of a white woman is his. No, replies Roger, "This here is the locker of a faggot." Carlyle pulls a pint of whiskey from his hip pocket and offers Roger a drink. Carlyle complains that from what he has been able to see, he and Roger are two of only a handful of blacks on the base, and "all the officers are always white." Suddenly, without any warning, Carlyle states angrily, "Oh, man, I hate this goddam army. I hate this bastard army." Carlyle leaps on Billy's bed and shouts, "It ain't war, brother . . . it ain't our war no how because it ain't our country and that's what burns my ass."

Richie enters, his hair wet, traces of shaving cream on his face. Billy returns pushing a mop bucket with a wringer attached, and carrying a container of wax. Richie needles Billy with homophobic jokes. Billy, upset, warns Richie to "cut the cute shit." Richie explains that he has been privileged all of his life, used to having whatever he wanted. When Roger and Billy express doubt that Richie is a "screaming goddam faggot," Richie insists, "I know all about it. Everything. All the various positions."

From a distance there is the loud bellowing sound of Sergeant Rooney. Billy leaps into bed, covering his face with a *Playboy* magazine under his blankets. Roger is trying to get the wax put away so that he can get into his own bunk. Sergeants Cokes and Rooney stagger into the room, both very drunk. They are in their fifties, their hair whitish, their bellies inflated. As they pass around their bottle of whiskey, Rooney tells the guys that Sergeant Cokes has recently returned from Vietnam. The proof is in his boots—canvas-topped boots designed for walking in a jungle swamp.

Rooney and Cokes reminisce about the old days when they were in the 101st Airborne Division together. They whoop and holler and mime jumping out of a plane, shouting "Geronimo!" Cokes remembers that one of their comrades, O'Flannigan, was gonna release the parachute lever mid-air, then reach up, grab the lines, and float on down, hanging. He pulled the lever at five hundred feet, reached up to two fistfuls of air, the chute twenty feet above him, started to desperately claw at the sky, and went into the ground like a knife. No, he did not have time to sing "beautiful streamer." Cokes, rocking a little on his feet, begins to hum "Beautiful streamer" to the tune of Stephen Foster's "Beautiful Dreamer." The two old sergeants put their arms around each other and croon:

> "Beautiful Streamer
> Open for me,
> The Sky is above me,
> But no canopy . . .
> Beautiful Streamer,
> This looks like the end,
> The earth is below me,
> My body won't bend.
> Just like a mother,
> Watching o're me.
> Beautiful Streamer
> Ohhhhh, open for me."

Cokes topples forward onto his face and flops limply to his side. They all rush to his aid but the sergeant regains consciousness. During the ensuing conversation it is revealed that he was sent back from Vietnam because the Army suspects that his fainting spells are symptoms of leukemia. Cokes insists that his falling down is due to nothing but chronic drunkenness. Rooney assures him that soon the two of them will return to the war zone in 'Nam and do demolition duty together.

The sergeants decide it's lights-out time and stagger out of the room, their arms around each other, flicking the light switch off as they go.

Roger, Richie, and Billy get into their beds and remain silent for a moment. The door bursts open and Carlyle, inebriated, comes crawling in, imitating the sounds of machine guns and cannons. He mumbles that there's no doubt that the three of them, because they have friends, influence, and special jobs, will remain in the base, while he, Carlyle, will be sent over to be killed. Roger tells him that they'll all end up in the war, and the best thing for Carlyle to do would be to "get cool" and "just hang in there." Carlyle falls asleep on the floor. Roger and Richie cover him with blankets. A distant bugle begins to play Taps as the curtain descends.

Act 2, scene 1 takes place in the late afternoon. Roger and Billy prepare to go to the gym by going through a series of pushups. Richie enters and the three of them begin to toss a basketball around. Roger and Billy leave while Richie takes a pack of cigarettes from his locker, lies on his bed, and reads Pauline Kael's *I Lost It at the Movies*.

Carlyle steps into the room and looks around. He asks Richie, "Where's the black boy?" Richie tells him that he doesn't know where Roger is. They look at each other. Richie rises, walks toward the door, closes it, and returns to his bed. Carlyle stares at Richie, approaches, leans over him, and moves his fingers through Richie's hair. "I bet if I was to hang my boy out in front of you," he says, "my big boy, man, you'd start wanting to touch him." Carlyle slides down on the bed and places his arm over Richie's leg. He taunts Richie by pretending that Richie made advances to him the other night while he was sleeping on the floor—or perhaps he just dreamed it. Richie laughs, "My god, you're outrageous," and Carlyle suddenly becomes angry. "You goddamn face ugly fuckin' queer punk!" he spits out at Richie. Carlyle's outburst is a signpost of things to come.

Confused, Richie marches into the hall. Carlyle lies on Richie's bed, making himself comfortable. He takes a pint bottle from his back pocket and drinks. Billy enters. Carlyle asks him if Richie is the only "punk" in the room. "He's not queer if that's what you're saying," answers Billy. "A little effeminate but that's all, no more." Carlyle pursues the topic and queries if there's a three-way gay scene going on in this room; if so, he wants to get in on the action. Billy denies that any such thing is happening. Roger enters fresh from a shower. The scene ends with Roger, Richie, Billy, and Carlyle going out for an excursion in the city. Carlyle is pleased: "We all goin' to be friends!"

Act 2, scene 2 unfolds later that night. Billy, Carlyle, Roger, and Richie are sprawled about the room. Richie, sitting on the floor and resting against Roger's footlocker, tells the others a dream he'd had about his father. He vaguely remembers that when he was six years old, his father, a big man who apparently was an alcoholic and a gambler, pushed him out of the way, left home, and disappeared with his suitcase.

Carlyle confides that he was illegitimate. He and Richie appear to become friends. They exchange sexual innuendos and it irritates Billy, who feels that Richie is carrying his effeminate poses too far. Richie starts to rub Carlyle's foot and asks Billy and Roger to go out for a walk. Roger exits but Billy insists on staying. Carlyle thinks his presence might be a little "weird," but he's game.

The atmosphere becomes more and more tense. Carlyle snaps out the only light and hurls Richie down onto his knees. Billy lunges to the wall switch, throws it. The overhead lights flash on. Billy then hurls a shoe at Carlyle's feet. Carlyle takes a switchblade out of his pocket, crosses the room, and flashes the knife across Billy's palm; the blood flows. Carlyle, forlorn and angry, says, "Bastard ruin my mood, Richie. . . . Goddamn man threw a shoe at me, a lotta people woulda cut his heart out. . . . But I don't hurt him bad . . ."

Billy wraps a towel around his hurt hand, grabs a straight razor, changes his mind, and flings it into his locker. He rushes at Richie, calls him, "a goddamn faggot-queer," then whirls on Carlyle, yelling, "You are your own goddamn faggot, Sambo! Sambo!" The knife flashes in Carlyle's hand into Billy's stomach. Billy yelps, "Ahhhhhhhhh," staggers, and collapses onto his knees.

Roger rushes in, having heard the commotion. He and Richie go to Billy, who at first pretends he isn't hurt, then doubles over and vomits blood. Richie runs out for help. Billy grabs a blanket, grapples with it, and at last gets it over his face. After a moment of silence, Carlyle crosses slowly and gently lifts the blanket. They look at each other. Billy reaches up, pats Carlyle's hand, and stammers, "I'm cold. . . . My blood . . . is . . ."

Sergeant Rooney staggers into the doorway, very drunk, a beer bottle in hand. Carlyle quickly slips the knife into his pocket. Richie follows Rooney into the room and says, "Carlyle stabbed Billy, he stabbed him." The knife again showing in his hand, Carlyle attempts to bolt for the door, but Rooney is in his way. Carlyle raises the knife and Rooney lifts the beer bottle, waving it threateningly. Carlyle lunges at Rooney and the knife goes into the sergeant's belly. Carlyle keeps stabbing him. Roger grabs Carlyle and pulls him away from Rooney. Carlyle whimpers, wipes the bloody knife on his shirt, and waves the weapon at Roger, who backs away. Carlyle turns and flees out the door.

Roger bends over Billy and whispers, "Oh, Billy, man, Billy." A Military Police lieutenant comes running in, his .45 automatic drawn. The lieutenant immediately assumes that Roger is responsible for the carnage. Two more MPs enter with Carlyle, his hands cuffed behind him. Carlyle tries to float a story that he was attacked by practical jokers who poured chicken blood on him. Richie exclaims, "He did it! Him, him!"

The MPs drag Carlyle away, then return and remove Billy's and Rooney's bodies on stretchers. The lieutenant gives Richie and Roger forms to fill out, orders them to report to his office the next day at 0800, and barks, "Two perfectly trained and primed, strong pieces of U.S. Army property got cut to shit up here. We're going to find out how and why. Is that clear?" He marches out.

Roger and Richie are left alone. Roger, quietly weeping, takes out a mop and begins to clean up the bloodstains. Richie watches him in horror. Sergeant Cokes enters, drunk as usual. He is looking for Rooney, he tells them. They were playing hide-and-seek and he cannot find him. Roger tells Cokes that they don't know the whereabouts of Rooney and whispers to Richie, "Let it be for the night." Richie begins to cry. Cokes ask why, and Roger says, "He's cryin' 'cause he's a queer." Surprisingly, Cokes reacts sympathetically: "There's a lotta worse things in the world than bein' a queer," he says, "I mean, you could have leukemia. That's worse."

Cokes asks if he can doze in their room tonight, as he isn't in shape to walk. Roger and Billy tell him it's OK. Coke sits on Billy's footlocker and begins to sing a makeshift language imitating Korean to the tune of "Beautiful Dreamer / Beautiful Streamer." The lights fade.

* * *

Streamers was first produced by the Long Wharf Theatre in New Haven, Connecticut, on January 30, 1976. Mike Nichols directed. Tony Walton designed the scenery. The cast consisted of mostly unknowns, with the exception of Kenneth McMillan and Dolph Sweet in the roles of Sergeants Rooney and Cokes, respectively. On April 21, the New York Shakespeare Festival sponsored a move to Lincoln Center's Mitzie E. Newhouse Theatre.

The reviews were by and large laudatory. "The play is oddly compelling," wrote Clive Barnes. "It has a dramatic power and, more significant, a dramatic idea that is absolutely a knockout. . . . Mr. Rabe's purpose is to show the face of violence. He takes the interlinking themes of two minorities—homosexuals and blacks—and indicates the sudden awful pressures that can detonate a disaster. . . . We seem to be watching real people rather than stage characters and, as a result—which is helped by Tony Walton's bleak designing—the melodramatic burst of blood at the end becomes as credible as a street accident."[2]

Douglas Watt opined that Streamers "has the cathartic effect of Greek tragedy" and admired the fact that "the play is hard-hitting and extremely funny at the same time. . . . Its very directness and relentless coiling inside give it a quality unlike anything else on our stage at the moment."[3] Martin Gottfried believed that Streamers is "untidy" and its climax is "overlong";

nevertheless, "the play stands. Indeed, it soars. . . . Its tension fills the place tight as a pressure cooker."[4] Edwin Wilson asserted, "*Streamers* is strong stuff—a body blow to the gut. But it will also make you think, and in the theatre that combination is hard to beat."[5]

A sole dissenting view came from John Beaufort of the *Christian Science Monitor*: "What one may regard as Mr. Rabe's concern for the trainees does not compensate for the play's crude sensationalism and lack of any fresh insights."[6]

Streamers ran for 478 performances. In 1983, Robert Altman directed a movie version, scripted by David Rabe, with Matthew Modine as Billy and George Dzundza as Sergeant Cokes. The Hudson Backstage Theatre of Hollywood, California, revived *Streamers* in 1999, and off-Broadway's Roundabout Company mounted the drama at the Laura Pels Theatre in 2008. Reviewer Helen Shaw of *Time Out New York* gleaned in the play "delicacy, craft and humor," while blaming director Scott Ellis and "most of his cast" for "often seeming intent on draining those qualities from the show."[7]

* * *

David William Rabe was born in Dubuque, Iowa in 1940. His father, a high school teacher, and his mother, a department store employee, provided David with a very religious upbringing. He attended Catholic primary and secondary schools, and in 1962 received his bachelor's degree from Loras College, a Catholic liberal arts institution in Dubuque.

Rabe enrolled for his graduate studies at Villanova University in Pennsylvania, but midway, in 1965, was drafted into the United States Army. After serving in Vietnam, he returned to Villanova and earned his MA in theatre in 1968.[8]

Rabe's experiences in Vietnam as a draftee assigned to a hospital-support unit spawned the trilogy *Sticks and Bones, The Basic Training of Pavlo Hummel*, and *Streamers*. Other plays by Rabe include *In the Boom Boom Room* (1973), depicting the downward spiral of a go-go dancer, Chrissy, who is yearning to escape a seedy Philadelphia environment. *The Orphan* (1973) uses Aeschylus's *The Oresteia* as a framework for a plot that makes a connection between Charles Manson's violence and that in Vietnam. *Goose and Tomtom* (1982) is the story of two small-time jewel thieves who are united in a strange, unsettling friendship. The bittersweet dramas *Hurlyburly* (1984) and *Those the River Keeps* (1991) are about drugs and disillusionment in Hollywood. *A Question of Mercy* (1998) is a sensitive exploration of euthanasia. *A Dog Problem* (2001) is a wicked comedy that begins with a presumed scandalous *ménage à trois* when Ray sleeps with Teresa and his dog jumps in bed with them. Teresa's brother, who has Mafia connections, decides to rough Ray up a bit and a Mafia don rules that someone must die for this act—either the man or his dog. In *The Black*

Monk (2003), based on an 1894 Anton Chekhov novella of the same name, Kovrin, a young philosophy student, escapes from the demands of big-city Moscow by going to his rural boyhood village. Kovrin falls in love there and plans to get married, but his hallucinations of an emissary from the unknown—the black monk—threaten his hopes for a happy future. Rabe's latest play, *An Early History of Fire*, revolves around a Midwestern factory worker who finds himself increasingly drawn to a rich young girl from the right side of the tracks. The drama opened at off-Broadway's Acorn Theatre on April 30, 2012 and garnered a tepid review from Ben Brantley of *New York Times*, who found it "a tumultuous work that has been given a surprisingly flat production by the New Group."[9]

For the movies, Rabe penned the screenplays of his plays *Sticks and Bones* (1973) and *Hurlyburly* (1998) as well as *I'm Dancing as Fast as I Can* (1982), the story of a woman's survival in a battle for her sanity. He also scripted *Casualties of War* (1989), in which an American squad kidnaps, rapes, and kills a female villager during the Vietnam War, and *The Firm* (1993), an adaptation from the John Grisham book, about a young lawyer who gets entangled in the machinations of a corrupt and sinister law firm.

Acting Edition: Samuel French, Inc.

Awards and Honors: *Streamers* was a top ten selection in *The Best Plays of 1975–1976*, won the 1976 Drama Desk Award for Outstanding New Play, and was nominated for the 1977 Tony Award for Best Play. David Rabe won the 1971 Drama Desk Award as Most Promising Playwright for *The Basic Training of Pavlo Hummel* and garnered a 1972 Tony Award for Best Play for *Sticks and Bones*. In 1985, Rabe was nominated for a Best Play Tony for *Hurlyburly*.

NOTES

1. *Wall Street Journal*, April 27, 1976.
2. *New York Times*, April 22, 1976.
3. *Daily News*, April 22, 1976.
4. *New York Post*, April 22, 1976.
5. *Wall Street Journal*, April 27, 1976.
6. *Christian Science Monitor*, April 26, 1976.
7. *Time Out New York*, November 13–19, 2008.
8. David Rabe was married to actress Jill Clayburgh from 1978 until her death from leukemia in 2010. One of their three children is Lily Rabe, who has appeared on Broadway in revivals of *Steel Magnolias* (2005) and *Heartbreak House* (2006). Lily also played Portia opposite Al Pacino's Shylock in a 2010 production of *The Merchant of Venice*, performed in Central Park in New York City; she was nominated for a Tony Award for her role.
9. *New York Times*, May 1, 2012.

The Runner Stumbles (1976)

Milan Stitt (United States, 1941–2009)

Milan Stitt fashioned his courtroom drama, the *Runner Stumbles*, on a 1911 trial in Michigan, in which a Roman Catholic priest was accused of murdering a nun. The play was conceived in 1965 at the Yale School of Drama, then developed, tenaciously, during the next decade in a Boston University playwright's workshop at the Berkshire Theatre Festival (1971), a showcase at the Manhattan Theatre Club (1974), and a performance at the Hartman Theatre in Stamford, Connecticut (1975). Finally it opened at Broadway's Little Theatre on May 18, 1976.

On a practically bare stage, the action of *The Runner Stumbles* unfolds in a jail cell, then moves to the courthouse. Flashbacks take place in Father Rivard's home. A similar technique was utilized in other plays based on real-life trials—*Nine Pine Street, Compulsion, A Case of Libel, Time Limit*, and *The Andersonville Trial* but in Stitt's drama the flashback scenes are fleeting and kaleidoscopic, prompting Martin Gottfried of the *New York Post* to complain of "awkward writing and construction."[1]

Father Rivard is a maverick priest relegated to a parish in a rural, predominantly Protestant area of Michigan. The arrival of Sister Rita, a young, vivacious nun, ignites forbidden feelings. The priest lets Sister Rita reside at the rectory, and, to the dismay of his housekeeper Mrs. Shandig, a converted, devout Catholic, priest and nun fall in love.

Unable to curb their emotions, tension builds between Father Rivard and Sister Rita. Frustrated, he treats her harshly. In a moment of deep despair, the priest exclaims, "I hate God. I hate God. I want to kill God. I always wanted to kill," and he commences to choke Sister Rita. When the nun is found dead the next morning, Father Rivard is charged with her murder.

The priest's court-appointed lawyer, Toby Felker, is a novice who has "never argued an actual trial before." But at the end of the play, as aptly described by Douglas Watt in the *Daily News*, the lawyer "pulls a rabbit out of the hat."[2] Felker calls Mrs. Shandig to the stand and elicits from her an unexpected confession. Sister Rita was evil, says Mrs. Shandig. Father Rivard did not strangle the Sister to death but she deserved to die. She found the Sister wiggling on the ground, making noises. She went to get a shovel and hit the snake's head. Then everything was peaceful.

Father Rivard walks free and Mrs. Shandig is arrested, only to commit suicide in jail. "Banged her head against the wall till she died," relates Felker to the priest at the conclusion of a melancholy, dark play about lost souls caught in the web of hierarchical despotism.

* * *

The Runner Stumbles met with mixed reviews. Mel Gusow of the *New York Times* was taken by the play's "strong, emotional impact,"[3] and the *Wall Street Journal's* Edwin Wilson proclaimed that it "offers its own excitement—a mystery story, an exploration of psychological and moral problems, a whirlwind of strong passions, and excellent acting."[4] However, Douglas Watt stamped *The Runner Stumbles* as "a whodunit that exhausts a listener's interest in the outcome long before it arrives."[5]

The play stumbled along for 191 performances. It has had numerous regional productions over the years, notably by the Actors Theatre of Louisville in November 1978, running for seventeen performances. Off-Broadway's The Actors Company Theatre revived *The Runner Stumbles* in the fall of 2007; the Harold Washington College, Chicago, Illinois, in the spring of 2008; and the Port City Playhouse of Muskegon, Michigan in the summer of 2009. In October 2009, Birmingham City University presented the UK premiere of the play.

The Runner Stumbles was transferred to the screen by Stanley Kramer, starring Dick Van Dyke (Father Rivard), Kathleen Quinlan (Sister Rita), Maureen Stapleton (Mrs. Shandig), and Beau Bridges (lawyer Felker). It was Stanley Kramer's last film. It opened to negative reviews and failed to be a commercial success.

* * *

Milan Stitt was born in Detroit, Michigan, in 1941. He studied for the priesthood at Albion College but dropped out, later enrolling at the University of Michigan and earning a bachelor's degree in 1963. Three years later he received an MFA from the Yale School of Drama. He held various writing and publicity jobs before founding Circle Repertory Company, an off-Broadway incubator for playwrights. In charge of Circle Rep's development program, he served as dramaturge to budding playwrights Arthur Kopit, Albert Innaurato, Lanford Wilson, Paul Zindel, and David Mamet. At Circle Rep he wrote for Christopher Reeve the drama *Back in the Race*, in which the descendant of a distinguished

American family returns to his now ramshackle ancestral summer home determined to fathom the unsettling legacy of his forefathers and exorcise ghosts of the past.

Stitt was chair of the playwriting program at Yale University from 1987 to 1993. He also taught dramatic writing at Princeton University, the University of Michigan, and New York University. In 1997 he was appointed head of the dramatic writing program at Carnegie Mellon University. For television, Stitt penned teleplays and miniseries, notably *The Gentleman Bandit* for CBS (1981) and *Long Shadow* for PBS's American Playhouse (1996). He was a member of the Dramatists League, Writers Guild of America, P.E.N., the Eugene O'Neill Society, and the National Academy of Television Arts and Sciences.

Stitt died in 2009 of liver cancer at St. Vincent's Hospital in New York City.

Acting Edition: Dramatists Play Service.

Awards and Honors: A top ten selection in *The Best Plays of 1975–1976* ("The year's outstanding Broadway drama," according to editor Otis L. Guernsey Jr.).[6]

NOTES

1. *New York Post*, May 19, 1976.
2. *Daily News*, May 19, 1976.
3. *New York Times*, May 19, 1976.
4. *Wall Street Journal*, May 19, 1976.
5. *Daily News*, May 19, 1976.
6. Otis L. Guernsey Jr., ed., *The Best Plays of 1975–1976* (New York: Dodd, Mead, 1976), 3.

The Hound of the Baskervilles (1976)

Tim Kelly (United States, 1931–1998)

The Hound of the Baskervilles is Sherlock Holmes's most intriguing and well-known adventure. Serialized in *Strand Magazine* between August 1901 and April 1902, and published in book form in 1902 by Newnes (London) and McClure, Phillips (New York), the story of the spectral hound combines elements of detection with the supernatural.

The narrative begins with the arrival of Dr. James Mortimer at 221B Baker Street, the London dwelling of the world's foremost consulting detective, Sherlock Holmes, and his sidekick Dr. John Watson. Holmes scrutinizes the visitor's walking stick and from it deduces Mortimer's habits and way of life. Mortimer recounts that his friend, old Sir Charles Baskerville, went for an evening walk through the yew trees of his estate in Dartmoor, Devonshire, and was later found dead of a heart attack. There were no signs of violence at the scene, but his face was distorted with terror. Near the body, Mortimer noticed a gigantic footprint of a dog. Mortimer tells Holmes and Watson that the Baskerville family seems to be cursed with a succession of deaths caused by the fangs of a demonic dog prowling the English moor.

Sir Henry Baskerville, the heir, arrives from Canada. He relates to Holmes a curious incident: the theft of one of his boots, not the pair, from his hotel suite. For protection, Holmes sends Watson with him to Baskerville Hall, a gloomy, depressing mansion. Sir Henry and Watson encounter several suspicious characters, including the Hall's servants, John and Eliza Barrymore; Selden, called the Notting Hill Murderer, an escaped convict who roams the swamps; and nearby neighbors Jack and Beryl Stapleton. Much of the action unfolds at the desolate Grimpen Mire, where a misguided step may sink a traveler in fogbound swamps. Distant, blood-curdling howls are heard sporadically; the climax consists of a life-or-death chase between Holmes and the spectral dog.

The cinema has taken full advantage of the atmospheric exteriors of the moors while stage versions have had to contend with verbal accounts of deadly, off-stage events.

Tim Kelly, perhaps the most prolific (albeit little known) American playwright, adapted *The Hound of the Baskervilles* into a one-set thriller, unfolding entirely in the sitting room in Baskerville Hall—"a melancholy room with the scent of age and tradition in every corner."

Kelly updated the proceedings to "the present" and tampered with the dramatis personae of the Conan Doyle novel by converting Dr. James Mortimer into Lady Agatha Mortimer—"ample, 'tweedy,' forceful," and the groom Perkins into a young scullery maid of the same name. There is no apparent reason for the gender change, except, possibly, for casting balance.

With the elimination of 221B Baker Street, Holmes and Watson are invited by Lady Agatha to Baskerville Hall ("When I heard you and Mr. Holmes were on holiday nearby, I wasted no time getting in touch," she tells Watson). In this version, Holmes finds Lady Agatha's walking stick at the excavations of Grimpen Mire and proceeds to dazzle her with his deductions: "The tip is coated with a reddish clay that is found only in that area. . . . Teeth marks on the walking stick . . . this small puff of silver-gray dog fur leads me to surmise—a miniature schnauzer."

"You take my breath away, Holmes," says Lady Agatha and relates to the visitors the circumstances of the recent demise of Sir Charles Baskerville, who, she believes, was frightened to death. She submits for their perusal a document detailing the violent history of the Baskerville family.

Sir Henry—"a good-looking young man"—enters via the French doors and shakes hands with Holmes and Watson. Lady Agatha rebukes him for wandering in the desolate countryside.

The proceedings continue along the narrative of the original work— Holmes departing for London, leaving Watson to snoop around; the suspicious circumstances of the Barrymores and their relative, the escaped convict Selden (here the butler signals through the window with a flashlight instead of a candle, snapping it on and off); Watson sending messages to Holmes—"Every time I call London I get his answering machine," Watson complains; the disappearing shoe from Sir Henry's bedroom (in lieu of the novel's hotel suite), a device used to lure a sniffing, enormous dog, "part mastiff part Great Dane," to attack Sir Henry; Holmes's arrival in the nick of time to save Henry; the young aristocrat's growing attachment to Kathy Stapleton (in the original, Beryl Stapleton); the discovery that Kathy is not Jack Stapleton's sister, but his wife.

The denouement, however, detours sharply from the original by painting Kathy Stapleton as a femme fatale who instigated and planned the murders of both Sir Charles and Sir Henry so that her husband Jack would become heir to the estate. He's the son of Rodger Baskerville, the younger brother of Sir Charles, who fled to South America and allegedly died unmarried.

SIR HENRY: You . . . you and Stapleton plotted all this together!
KATHY: Jack? Don't be a fool. He's weak. Never did a thing that I wasn't right there behind him, pushing, insisting. It was all my idea.

The Stapletons are apprehended by the police. Their dog is shot.

"Kathy had no feeling for me at all," sighs Sir Henry.

"If it's any consolation," says Holmes, "the most winning woman I ever knew was hanged for poisoning three little children for their insurance money."

The Hound of the Baskervilles was first presented by the Valley Players Guild in Cathedral City, California, on October 15, 1976, running for ten performances. The play was directed by Joan Woodbury. Ray Mitchell played Holmes. Subsequent productions were mounted by Queens College, Charlotte, North Carolina (1978); VHS Drama Group, Albuquerque, New Mexico (1978); and Marin Actors Company, San Rafael, California (1979). New Yorkers attended Kelly's version at Off-Broadway's Apple Corps Theatre (1983), with Richard Fancy and Skip Corris portraying Holmes and Watson.

* * *

The indefatigable Tim Kelly, whose credits include many plays featuring Sherlock Holmes, revisited Baskerville Hall in a one-act spoof, *Beast of the Baskervilles* (1984), trumpeted by its publishers as "an off-the-wall comedy, with madcap action, crazy jokes and hilarious thrills."

The "silly serving girl," Cordelia, hears strange growls coming from the attic. Barrymore, the "sinister butler," declares that "the curse of the Baskervilles has returned!" Sherlock Holmes is summoned to the rescue. His emissary, Mrs. Hudson, arrives on the scene, opens the bolted outside door with a hatpin, confides modestly that she is the one who cleared up The Chinese Noodle Mystery, cross-examines the household servants, and soon proclaims, "The case is solved." She has noticed in a wall portrait "a peculiar malformation of Sir Hugo's foot. . . . Webbed toes." She has also perceived Mr. Jack Stapleton's odd foot movements . . . as if he had—webbed toes. . . . Obviously, webbed toes are a Baskerville family trait."

Other one-act plays by Tim Kelly featuring Sherlock Holmes include *Sherlock Holmes Meets the Phantom,* in which the Great Detective pursues a sinister apparition that has been haunting the Virginia City Opera House. *The Adventure of the Clouded Crystal* deals with a stormy relationship between Arthur Conan Doyle and the magician Harry Houdini. *If Sherlock*

Holmes Were a Woman presents a young coed, Shirley Holmes, who is a fanatic admirer of the world's foremost consulting detective. She attempts to step into his shoes when the housemother in her dorm is found prostrate, seemingly dead, in her armchair.

Acting Edition: *The Hound of the Baskervilles*—Samuel French, Inc. *Beast of the Baskervilles*—Pioneer Drama Service.

Twelve Angry Women (1977)

Reginald Rose (United States, 1920–2002)

The twentieth century was awash with numerous courtroom dramas and a dozen or so jury-room plays, of which the most notable are *The Woman on the Jury* (1923) by Bernard K. Burns; *The Jury of Her Peers* (1925) by Edward Harry Peple; *Ladies of the Jury* (1929) by Fred Ballard; and *Ladies and Gentlemen* (1939) by Charles MacArthur and Ben Hecht.

The Woman on the Jury is Betty Brown, who three years earlier was ditched by her lover, George Wayne, after a summer liaison in a Vermont mountain cottage. As he was leaving, she sent a bullet through the door. Summoned to jury duty on a murder case, Betty realizes that the victim was Wayne, and that he was shot by the accused, Grace Pierce, for deceiving her after their child was born. Eleven men on the jury vote for conviction. Betty, sympathizing with Grace and recalling that she herself almost killed Wayne, recommends acquittal. She holds out for two days and nights. Finally, in order to convince her fellow jurors, she confesses her experience with Wayne, risking the loss of both her reputation and husband. The jury agrees to exonerate and Betty's husband forgives her.

The Woman on the Jury opened at Broadway's Eltinge Theatre on August 15, 1923, and ran for seventy-two performances. The *New York Times* had reservations about the play—"quite frankly conceived as melodrama"—but complimented the lead actress, Mary Newcomb, for her "quiet and effective art."[1]

The Jury of Her Peers is a hilarious satire spotlighting the first ever United States jury composed entirely of women. The jurors, members of the Women's Progressive League, are united in condemning the defendant, handsome William Keets, over his broken promise to young, alluring Catherine Carroll. The feisty jurors are unaware that the lawsuit is a setup planned by "victim" Carroll, "rascal" Keets, and their own respective husbands, who have all banded together against them, determined to inflict "a nice little boomerang of ridicule" upon "twelve eager and palpitating juresses and two hair-pulling female attorneyesses." The masculine scheme fails, and the men find themselves spending a night in jail for contempt of court.

The Jury of Her Peers was copyrighted by Samuel French Inc. in 1925.

Most of the action of *Ladies of the Jury* takes place in a Rosedale, New Jersey, jury room, where a panel of twelve men and women deliberates the case of Yvette Gordon, an ex-chorus girl charged with the murder of her rich, elderly husband. When the jurors commence to weigh the evidence, eleven members vote guilty, and there is one holdout—Mrs. Livingston Baldwin Crane, a middle-aged, high-society matron. There is hardly any discussion of the pros and cons of the case. Crane simply swings the other jurors to her side with beguiling charm and disarming bribes: she orders hot food for the sequestered group, distributes silk pajamas and robes for an overnight stay, compliments the artistic merits of a poet and ukulele player, and offers another juror the position of cook in her household. Slyly, she flatters the group—"Who could ask for more charming company than our scintillating friends gathered here." Finally, on the 124th ballot, the twelve members of the jury turn in a unanimous vote of not guilty.

Any misgivings regarding Crane's method of influence were dissipated by the era's First Lady of the American theatre, Minnie Maddern Fiske. When *Ladies of the Jury* opened at Broadway's Erlanger's Theatre on October 21, 1929, the *New York Times* critic praised Fiske's "gay and bubbling performance. . . . She plays with great spirit and zest but she also brings out shadings and nuances of character not to be discerned in the general run of comedy. . . . With this particular First Actress in charge, Mr. Ballard's new comedy becomes a good-natured piece of fooling which last night's audience found hilariously funny."[2]

Ladies of the Jury ran for eighty-eight performances.

On October 17, 1939, Helen Hayes, another First Lady of the American Stage, became a member of the jury in *Ladies and Gentlemen*, adapted by Charles MacArthur and Ben Hecht from a drama by Hungary's Ladislaus Bush-Fekete. The jurors are pondering the fate of a popular novelist accused of causing his wife's death by pushing her off a cliff on Mount Wilson. Miss Scott (Helen Hayes), secretary to a Hollywood movie mogul, and an admirer of the writer's works, insists that he could not have committed the crime. One by one—"Through cajolery, flattery, guile and a dash of sex," according to the *New York World-Telegram*[3]—she wins the opposing jurors over, while romantically succumbing to the charms of the antagonistic foreman.

Ladies and Gentlemen ran for 105 performances at New York's Martin Beck Theatre.

* * *

The best-known jury play is arguably *Twelve Angry Men*, adapted by Sherman L. Sergel from Reginald Rose's Studio One teleplay of 1954. In 1964, Leo Genn appeared in the play version at the Queen's Playhouse, London. The following year, it was presented by The Cleveland Playhouse. Many theatrical productions of *Twelve Angry Men* have popped up around the world, including two in a Hebrew translation, offered by Israel's Habimah National Theatre in 1959 and 1995. Harold Pinter directed a production of the play that opened at the Bristol Old Vic on March 7, 1996. The Roundabout Theatre Company of New York presented *Twelve Angry Men* in 2004 for a run of 228 performances. Richard Thomas starred as Juror No. 8 in a 2007 national tour. That same year, Los Angeles Theatre Works offered a production of the play later recorded as an audiobook. The George Street Playhouse in New Brunswick, New Jersey revived *Twelve Angry Men* from March 13 to April 8, 2012 with Jack Klugman as Juror No. 9.[4]

In the mid-1970s, Sergel adapted the original TV show for an all-female cast and coined it *Twelve Angry Women*. The entire action unfurls in a stuffy jury room where twelve jurors, all white females from varied rungs of society, are debating the case of a black youth from the slums charged with the stabbing death of his father. A failure to reach a unanimous verdict will result in a mistrial. A guilty verdict will be accompanied by a mandatory death sentence.

Sergel provides a character description of the jurors in the published Acting Edition of *Twelve Angry Women*: The Foreman is "a small, pretty woman who is impressed with the authority she has and handles herself quite formally. She is not overly bright, but dogged." Juror No. Two is "a meek, hesitant woman who finds it difficult to maintain any opinion of her own. She is easily swayed." Juror No. Three is "a very strong, forceful, extremely opinionated woman, within whom can be detected a streak of sadism." Juror No. Four "seems to be a woman of wealth and position, and a practiced speaker who presents herself well at all times. Her only concern is with the facts of this case." Juror No. Five is "a naïve, very frightened young woman who finds it difficult to speak up when her elders have the floor." Juror No. Six is "an honest but dull-witted woman who comes upon her decisions slowly and carefully." Juror No. Seven is "a loud, flashy, glad-handing woman who works in a department store and has more important things to do than sit on a jury. She is quick-tempered, a bully and, of course, a coward." Juror

No. Eight is "a quiet, thoughtful, gentle woman—a woman who sees all sides of every question and constantly seeks the truth. She is a woman of strength tempered with compassion." Juror No. Nine is "a mild, gentle old woman, long since defeated by life and now merely waiting to die." Juror No. Ten is "an angry, bitter woman—a woman who antagonizes almost at sight. She is also a bigot who places no value on any human life save her own." Juror No. Eleven is "a refugee from Europe, who came to this country in 1941. She speaks with an accent and is ashamed, humble, almost subservient to the people around her." Juror No. Twelve is "a slick, bright advertising woman who thinks of human beings in terms of percentages, graphs and polls, and has no real understanding of people."

The Guard is a bit part—"She can be a policewoman, of any age."

After a short discussion, eleven jurors vote guilty, but Juror Number Eight is doubtful and insists on reviewing the witnesses' testimonies. Juror Number Three brings up the fact that early on the evening of the murder, an old neighbor heard the kid and his father quarreling. Juror Number Ten reminds all that a woman across the street testified that she saw the actual killing from her window. Juror Number Seven recounts the checkered past of the accused—stealing, mugging, reform school at fifteen. Juror Number Three points out that after the encounter with his father, the kid went to a neighborhood store and bought a switchblade.

Number Eight asks the guard to bring in the murder weapon. It is an oddly designed knife, but Number Eight reaches into her purse and withdraws an identical one. She then goes step by step through the various strands of evidence and one by one the jurors change their minds. Upon illustrating that a five-foot-eight-inch-tall kid could not have stabbed his six-foot-two-father downward, and upon the realization that the woman across the street would not have worn her bifocals when going to bed, the jurors are unanimously convinced that "there is reasonable doubt."

While *Twelve Angry Men* made it to Broadway, played around the world, and was successfully adapted to the silver screen, *Twelve Angry Women* has only been produced by community theatres, high schools, and colleges on both shores of the Atlantic. The Monroe Theatre Guild of Monroe, Wisconsin, presented the female version at the Monroe Junior High Auditorium on February 17, 18, 19, 1977. During the first decade of the twenty-first century, *Twelve Angry Women* was mounted by Texas Christian University, Fort Worth, Texas (2003); Swindon's Old Town Theatre Company, Swindon Wilts, England (2004); The Theatre of Western Springs, Western Springs, Illinois (2005); Branch River Theatre, Marlborough, New Hampshire (2008); Manhattan Theatre Source, New York (2008); Hollywood Fight Club Theatre, Hollywood, California (2009); The University of Hartford, Hartford, Connecticut (2009); Unitarian Universalist Church, Bloomington, Indiana (2009); Convent of the Sacred Heart, Greenwich, Connecticut (2010); McLean High School, McLean, Virginia (2010); Perrysburg Area Arts Council, Perrysburg, Ohio (2011); Newman High School Drama Department, Newman, Georgia (2011); Seattle Pacific University, Seattle, Washington (2011); and Gloucester County Institute of Technology, New Jersey (2012).

An all-black cast played the angry women at the Black Arts & Cultural Center, Kalamazoo, Michigan (2009). A mixed troupe of men and women was recruited for *Twelve Angry Jurors*, produced by the Performing Arts Center at Glendale Community College, Glendale, Arizona (2010).

* * *

Born in Manhattan in 1920, Reginald Rose attended Townsend Harris High School and studied at City College from 1937 to 1938 before serving in the U.S. Army during 1942–1946, attaining the rank of first lieutenant. He sold his first teleplay, *Bus to Nowhere*, in 1950 to the live CBS dramatic anthology program Studio One, for which he wrote his breakaway hit *Twelve Angry Men* four years later. The drama was inspired by a real-life experience: Rose had been a member of the jury on a manslaughter case that involved a furious, eight-hour argument among the jurors.

Rose joined Paddy Chayefsky and Rod Serling in creating thought-provoking dramas during the Golden Age of live television. He wrote for all three major broadcast networks. *Crime in the Streets* was shown on ABC's *Elgin Hour* in 1955. His 1957 pilot *The Defender* launched the series *The Defenders* for CBS.[5] *The Sacco-Vanzetti Story* was presented by NBC's *Sunday Showcase* in 1960.[6] *Dear Friends* made a splash on CBS Playhouse in 1967.[7] He contributed scripts to *Philco Television Playhouse, Alcoa Hour, Playhouse 90, Suspense*, and *The Twilight Zone*.

In the mid-1950s, Rose adapted to the screen his three acclaimed teleplays: *Crime in the Streets*, a drama focused on an alienated teen, played by John Cassavetes, who conspires to commit a murder; *Twelve Angry Men*; and *Dino*, a juvenile delinquent tale featuring Sal Mineo. In 1958, Rose penned the screenplays of *Man of the West*, an epic-scale Western starring Gary Cooper as a reformed outlaw, and *The Man in the Net*, a whodunit with Alan Ladd, which Rose adapted from a novel by Patrick Quentin.[8] *Baxter* (1973) spotlights the relationship between a young, lisping boy and his speech therapist, played by Patricia Neal. *The Wild Geese* (1978) is an action yarn—highlighted by the participation of top British actors Richard Burton, Roger Moore, Richard Harris, and Stewart Granger—about mercenaries who rescue a kidnapped African leader. *Somebody Killed Her Husband* (1978) has Farrah Fawcett entangled in a "tepid comedy-mystery-romance," according to movie maven Leonard Maltin.[9]

In the 1980s, Rose scripted *The Sea Wolves*, based on the true story of a retired British cavalry unit undertaking an espionage mission during World War II; adapted from a play by Brian Clark, *Whose Life Is It Anyway?* is about a sculptor, portrayed by Richard Dreyfuss, who is paralyzed from the neck down and argues for his right to die; *The Final Option* (aka *Who Dares Wins*), an account of a British officer's attempt to infiltrate a terrorist gang; and *Wild Geese II*, an adventure sequel in which a gaggle of mercenaries are recruited to spring arch-Nazi Rudolf Hess from Berlin's Spandau prison.

Married twice and the father of six boys, Rose died in 2002 in Norwalk, Connecticut from heart failure. He was 81.

Acting Edition: The Dramatic Publishing Company.

Awards and Honors: Reginald Rose received an Emmy Award for his teleplay and an Oscar nomination for his screenplay of *Twelve Angry Men*. The 1957 motion picture was also nominated for an Academy Award in the categories of Best Picture and Best Director (Sidney Lumet). It won the Golden Bear Award at the Berlin International Film Festival, and in 2007 the Library of Congress selected *Twelve Angry Men* for preservation in the United States National Film Registry. The Roundabout production of *Twelve Angry Men* garnered a 2005 Drama Desk Award for Best Revival of a Play and was nominated for a Tony Award in the same category.

NOTES

1. *New York Times*, August 16, 1923.
2. *New York Times*, October 22, 1929.
3. *New York World-Telegram*, October 18, 1939.
4. In 1957, Sidney Lumet directed a stellar cast, headed by Henry Fonda and Lee J. Cobb, in a definitive motion picture version of *Twelve Angry Men*. Forty years later, William Friedkin helmed a remake for television that starred Jack Lemmon, George C. Scott, James Gandolfini, William Petersen, Tony Danza, Hume Cronin, and Ossie Davis. In 2007, Russian director Nikita Mikhalkov filmed an updated version, called *12*, featuring Sergei Makovetsky and Sergey Garmash. In *12*, the jury is sequestered in an unused school gymnasium to decide the fate of a Chechen boy accused of murdering his adoptive Russian father. The movie was nominated for an Oscar as best foreign-language film.

5. *The Defenders* ran on CBS-TV from 1961 to 1965. The series starred E. G. Marshall and Robert Reed as a father-son team of lawyers who tackle challenging legal cases. Reginald Rose utilized elements from the show for a two-act stage adaptation also called *The Defenders*.

6. Reginald Rose adapted to the stage his teleplay *The Sacco-Vanzetti Story*, about the trial and execution of Italian immigrants Nicola Sacco and Bartolomeo Vanzetti who were accused of murdering two payroll guards in a daylight robbery in April 1920. Under the title *This Agony, This Triumph*, the play was produced in California in 1972.

7. The teleplay *Dear Friends*, in which three couples meet and discuss their problems only to gradually lash out at each other by exposing closet skeletons, was transferred to the stage by Reginald Rose, produced in Edinburgh, Scotland in 1968, and by the Lakewood Little Theatre, Cleveland, Ohio, the following year.

8. Patrick Quentin, Q. Patrick, and Jonathan Stagge are the pseudonyms of four authors in a complicated collaboration. The main contributor, Hugh Callingham Wheeler, was born in Hampstead, London in 1912 and educated at Clayesmore School in Dorset and at the University of London, where he received a BA with honors in 1933. The following year he moved to the United States, became a naturalized American citizen in 1942, and served in the U.S. Army Medical Corps during World War II. From 1936 to 1957, Wheeler jointly penned more than thirty highly regarded detective novels, a true-crime paperback original (*The Girl on the Gallows*, 1954), and a collection of criminous tales, *The Ordeal of Mrs. Snow and Other Stories*, for which he won the Mystery Writers of America's Edgar Allan Poe Award in 1963. In the 1960s, Wheeler shifted gears to playwriting and had his ups and downs on Broadway. Generally, his dramas and comedies did not fare well: *Big Fish, Little Fish* (ANTA Theatre, March 15, 1961—101 performances), is about a small-press editor surrounded by hangers-on. *Look: We've Come Through* (Hudson Theatre, October 25, 1961—five performances), depicts the developing relationship between a girl-with-a-past and a young man with a homosexual history. *Rich Little Rich Girl*, based on a play by Miguel Mihura and Alvaro de Laiglesia (a pre-Broadway tryout, for two weeks, at the Walnut Street Theatre, Philadelphia, October 26, 1964), is a comedy of murder involving a South American dictator. *Truckload* (Lyceum Theatre, September 6, 1975—closed after a week of previews) tells of hitchhiking across the country in trucks. Wheeler did, however, contribute the libretto for some very successful musicals, winning Tony, Drama Critics Circle, and Drama Desk Awards: *A Little Night Music* (Shubert Theatre, February 25, 1973—600 performances), based on the 1955 Ingmar Bergman film; *Smiles of a Summer Night*, about a weekend of romance and sex at a country estate; *Irene* (Minskoff Theatre, March 13, 1973—604 performances), an adaptation of a 1919 musical focusing on the behind-the-scenes romance between a fashion designer and his female associate; *Candide* (Chelsea Theatre Center of Brooklyn, December 11, 1973—forty-eight performances; transferred to the Broadway Theatre, March 10, 1974—740 performances), a revised book of the 1956 musical based on Voltaire; *Pacific Overtures* (Winter Garden, January 11, 1976—193 performances),

additional material to the book by John Weidman regarding Admiral Perry's arrival in 1853 in isolated Japan; and *Sweeney Todd, the Demon Barber of Fleet Street* (Uris Theatre, March 1, 1979—557 performances), founded on a version of *Sweeney Todd* by Christopher Bond, concerning a London barber who soothes an ire at society by slitting his customers' throats and consigning them to a pastry cook who then sells them baked in her pies. For the cinema, Wheeler co-wrote the screenplays for *Five Miles to Midnight* (1962), *Something for Everyone* (1969), *Cabaret* (1972), and *Travels with My Aunt* (1973).

9. *Leonard Maltin's 2012 Movie Guide* (New York: Plume, 2011), 1282.

Cause Célèbre (1977)

Terence Rattigan (England, 1911–1977)

In 1946, renowned playwright Terence Rattigan wrote *The Winslow Boy*, a drama based on the real-life case of George Archer-Shee, a young cadet at an English naval academy who was accused of stealing and cashing a five-shilling postal order. He was expelled. His parents waged a stubborn campaign to clear George's name in a case that caused a furor in England prior to World War I. Some dismissed it as an idiotic crusade; others hailed the "Cause Célèbre" as a milestone in protecting the honor and rights of the individual.

Three decades later, in 1977, Rattigan penned another courtroom drama based on an actual case—*Cause Célèbre*—re-creating the Alma Rattenbury-George Wood trial of 1935, the first double lawsuit in English history. In it, each defendant tried to exonerate the other by taking complete blame. Alma Rattenbury was an attractive thirty-eight-year-old composer of popular songs who had married an elderly, retired businessman, Francis, and subsequently entered into a sexual liaison with her eighteen-year-old handyman, George Wood. Francis Rattenbury was beaten to death with a wooden mallet, and both Alma and George were charged with the murder.

The case of a "scarlet woman" who had led a young man astray became a 1935 cause célèbre. The jury of the Central Criminal Court at the Old Bailey in London found Rattenbury innocent of the charge of murder, and she was released. Wood, however, was found guilty and was sentenced to be hanged. Convinced that her young lover was to die on the gallows, Alma Rattenbury stabbed herself with a knife. A few weeks later, Wood was reprieved and his sentence commuted to life imprisonment. By the 1950s he was released.

"It had always been pure raw material for a Rattigan drama, and he knew it," writes Geoffrey Wansell in *Terence Rattigan*. "But he did not simply want to re-create the events of the trial. He would use the case as another opportunity to explore the English attitude to sex, to emotions, and the reactions of reticence and fear both regularly prompted."[1]

The setting of *Cause Célèbre* is a composite, with different areas of the stage used to represent different locales during the unfolding action. In general, the central area is furnished as a sitting room used by both the Rattenbury Villa Madeira in Bournemouth, a seashore resort town in South England, and the Davenport apartment in Kensington, an affluent borough of West London. The area down-right represents the Old Bailey, while down-left is a prison cell. The action is juggled between present court proceedings and flashbacks of past events. Changes of locale are achieved through lighting.

When the curtain rises, the stage is in darkness except for spots pinpointing Alma Rattenbury, Edith Davenport, and the Clerk of the Court, who announces that Alma Victoria Rattenbury is charged with the murder of Francis Mawson Rattenbury on March the twenty-eighth, nineteen hundred and thirty-five. Alma pleads "Not Guilty." The spots fade and the lights come up on a Kensington flat, where Mrs. Edith Davenport tells her younger sister Stella that she has just received an official summons for jury service. Alma also confides that she's determined to divorce her husband, John, an employee at the Home Office and a habitual womanizer. Their young son, Tony, who adores his father, will be hurt, but her mind is set.

The lights cross-fade to the Rattenbury villa. George Wood, seventeen, stands by the door, taking off his bicycle clips. He tells Irene Riggs, a maid, that he came about the advertisement for a houseboy. Alma Rattenbury interviews George at length and seems to be taken with him. When her sickly, cantankerous husband, "Ratz," returns from a walk and settles into his usual armchair, Alma vouches for young Wood and he gets the job.

Back at the Davenport flat, Tony rushes in with a newspaper and tells his mother that "Mrs. Rattenbury and Wood battered old Rattenbury on the head so hard they completely mashed his skull." The article conjectures that the defense will maintain that Wood was doped on cocaine and Mrs. Rattenbury was drunk. Edith Davenport expresses her belief that the more mature Mrs. Rattenbury ought to be lynched.

In prison, Alma Rattenbury is allowed to wear her own clothes. Her wardress, Joan Webster, is a gruff-voiced, rather forbidding young woman. O'Connor, Alma's lawyer, arrives for a consultation, accompanied by Montagu, his junior assistant. Alma reaffirms her statement to the police, in which she contended that she was the one who picked up a mallet and hit her husband. O'Connor responds by telling her that Wood told investigators where the mallet would be found, hidden in the garden, and it was found exactly there, with his fingerprints all over it. Alma is taken aback for a moment, but she still insists, her voice firm and unwavering, "I killed Ratz alone and George had nothing to do with it."

Montagu harshly describes the strength and ruthlessness of the three mallet strikes that spilled the brains of the victim, and Alma begins to sob helplessly.

In darkness, we hear mob cries outside the courthouse: "Kill her!" "Hang her!" "Hanging is too good for her!" "Give her the cat!"

In a small cell, Casswell, George Wood's lawyer, dismisses his client's claim that he killed Mr. Rattenbury when under the influence of cocaine. During a quick cross-examination Wood cannot identify the color of the drug and is ignorant of the fact that it is called snow because it is white. Wood's only defense, says Casswell, is to testify that the older Alma Rattenbury made him do it. Wood refuses his lawyer's advice. He wants to live, but he's not going to betray the only woman "I've ever had, and the only one I've ever loved."

In act 2 we learn that Edith Davenport was selected to be a member of the jury in the Rattenbury-Wood murder trial. The jury appoints her forewoman because her father was a judge. Edith's sister, Stella, informs her that the bookmakers are giving three-to-one odds for conviction.

At the Old Bailey, Police Sergeant Bagwell testifies for the prosecution that after receiving a call from the local hospital saying that all attempts to revive the deceased had failed, he presented himself at the Villa Madeira. Time? Two forty-seven a.m. There was a lot of commotion inside. The gramophone was playing full blast and the female prisoner, attired in a nightdress, was imitating bullfighting with her bed jacket. A flashback visualizes the event at the villa: Alma Rattenbury taking a hefty swig from an almost empty bottle, and drunkenly greeting Sergeant Bagwell with a shriek of joy. She approaches him sensually. The Sergeant turns the gramophone off and questions Alma. She says that her husband wanted to die, gave her a mallet, and dared her to kill him. She did.

Back on the witness stand, the Sergeant concludes his testimony by expressing his disgust at the behavior of a woman whose husband had been brutally killed only a few hours earlier. Defense Attorney O'Connor asks the Sergeant if he has ever heard of hysteria and the effect of alcohol on a shocked system.

The only witness for the defense is Alma Rattenbury herself. O'Connor elicits from her the information that prior to her union with Francis Rattenbury ("Ratz"), she was married twice and had a child with her second husband. Francis was her third husband and they were married for eight years and have a son, John, now six. It was not a happy marriage. Francis was—well—stingy. They had constant quarrels about money. For several years they had lived in separate rooms. Yes, for two years she was having "regular sexual intercourse" with John Wood, the houseboy. They often went to hotels, where John "loved being waited on and called sir," and where she gave him such presents as silk pajamas and a new suit.

"Now we come to Sunday, the day of the murder," says O'Connor, and the lights fade up on the Villa Madeira sitting room. Alma, in her dressing gown, helps Rattenbury down the stairs and settles him in his armchair. They make plans to go on a trip and visit their friends, the Jenks. Wood appears at the top of the staircase, in his shirtsleeves. He calls Alma in a commanding tone to come upstairs, "Now!" She climbs up the stairs and Wood, forcefully, grabs her wrist. He demands to know why the bedroom was locked—was she making love to her husband? Alma dismisses the notion. He calls her "you lying bitch," and slaps her face. Alma warns Wood that if he ever does this again, she'll order him out of the house for good, and sends him to the kitchen to help with supper.

In the morning, we dimly see the slumped body of Francis Rattenbury in the armchair. Upstairs, Alma is in bed in pajamas, reading. Wood enters and climbs in beside her. He begins to cry and hesitantly tells her that he "hurt Ratz badly." Alma runs down the stairs, lets out a loud scream, and staggers with shock. Irene, the housekeeper, comes out of her room, and Alma sends her to fetch Dr. O'Donnell. Rattenbury's body suddenly slumps onto the floor. Wood approaches and whispers that he had to do it—"he was stealing you away from me."

Back in court, prosecutor Croom-Johnson pounds Alma with the suggestion that she dominated "a boy of seventeen." A turning point occurs when Alma lets it slip that she and Wood sometimes made love in her bedroom while little John was asleep in the same room. The prosecutor kept emphasizing the point in his summation, calling Alma "a self-confessed liar, self-confessed adultress, self-confessed seducer of a tender youth of seventeen . . . a boy young enough to be her son." In his turn, attorney O'Connor points out to the jury that even though they may feel a "natural disgust" for the defendant, that sense *must not* sway them to convict her of the crime of murder.

Alma and Wood are standing on the dock when jury forewoman Davenport reads Wood's verdict of "Guilty, with a rider to recommendation of mercy," and Alma's verdict of "Not guilty." The court is flooded with a storm of booing, hissing, and shouts of "Shame." The judge announces that Wood will be "taken from this place to a lawful prison, and thence to a place of execution, and that you there be hanged by the neck until you are dead."

George Wood is taken away. Alma Rattenbury is discharged. Her maid, Irene, greets her with enthusiasm, slips on a large pair of horn-rimmed glasses, and they follow a policeman to a side exit.

The lights cross-fade to Edith Davenport's flat. Stella confronts her sister about the verdict. Edith confides that as forewoman she sat at the head of the table. Each person spoke up and she took the votes down. There were initially five for guilty, six for not. Her vote, not guilty, made it seven-five—"Then all the others gave way." Stella asks, "For God's name, why?" Edith pours herself a large neat whiskey and says, "Because she was innocent . . . of murder."

The lights fade up on a coroner—a little man sitting at an insignificant desk, reading aloud from a folder a statement from a parish laborer: Walking across a meadow along a stream, he watched a lady stab herself five or six times before he could get to her and stop her.

The coroner looks up at an unseen court of inquiry and remarks that if Mrs. Rattenbury lived only a few more days, she would have heard of the reprieve accorded to George Wood by the Home Secretary.

* * *

Initially titled "A Woman of Principle," *Cause Célèbre* began as a radio drama broadcast by BBC in October 1975. When premiering in London's Her Majesty's Theatre on July 4, 1977, the program—just as it had done for *The Winslow Boy*—contained a disclaimer: "This play is based on a famous case, but the characters are all fictitious." Rattigan wanted Dorothy Tuttin for the role of the doomed Alma Rattenbury, but Glynis Johns was cast.

Ill with cancer, Terence Rattigan came to London for the July 4, 1977 opening of *Cause Célèbre*, knowing it would be his last first night. The play was still running at the time of Rattigan's death on November 30, 1977, achieving 282 performances. The American debut of *Cause Célèbre* took place at the Ahmanson Theatre in Los Angeles on October 12, 1979. Anne Baxter portrayed Alma Rattenbury for fifty-one performances.

Teamed with Hector Bolitho, Rattigan had previously penned an additional work with criminous elements—*Grey Farm*, depicting a tortured, possessive father, James Grantham, who, afflicted with murderous urges, fights against the impulse to kill both his son and the son's fiancée, finally strangling a blackmailing maid and shooting himself. Oscar Homolka played Grantham in this forgotten Rattigan melodrama that opened in New York's Hudson Theatre on May 3, 1940, and lasted thirty-five performances.

* * *

Terence Mervyn Rattigan began his theatrical career as a member of the Oxford University Dramatic Society. His first play, *First Episode* (1933), co-authored with Philip Heimann, unfolds in the living room of an undergraduate dormitory. Following the incubation of five unproduced efforts, through which young Rattigan learned his craft, came *French without Tears* (1936), a comedy about a flirtatious student who toys with her male classmates. The play scored big and played in London for over 1000 performances. A few successive comedies had hefty runs, and then, in 1946, Rattigan's first serious drama, *The Winslow Boy*, enhanced his reputation as master of the "well-made," neatly constructed play.

Rattigan returned to weighty themes in a series of plays that were first performed in London and then made the New York scene: *The Browning Version* (1948), a one-act about an embittered schoolmaster, Andrew Crocker-Harris, who is feared by his students, despised by his peers, and betrayed by his wife; *The Deep Blue Sea* (1952), in which a middle-aged woman, rejected by her lover and unable to face her husband, attempts to commit suicide before a doctor friend saves her life and restores her courage; *Separate Tables* (1954), a double bill set in a drab seaside residential hotel where the guests are lonely, desperate, and in need of redemption; *Ross* (1960), depicting, in sixteen scenes, the mystical life of T. E. Lawrence (Lawrence of Arabia); *Man and Boy* (1963), the story of a ruthless tycoon who lets nothing stand in his way;[2] *A Bequest to the Nation* (1970), picturing the affair between Admiral Nelson and Lady Hamilton.

Rattigan comedies that came to New York include *First Episode* (1934); *French without Tears* (1937); *While the Sun Shines* (1944); *O Mistress Mine* (1946); *The Sleeping Prince* (1956; musical version, *The Girl Who Came to Supper*, book by Harry Kurnitz, music and lyrics by Noel Coward, 1963); and *In Praise of Love* (1974).

Distinguished directors who tackled Rattigan plays included, in London, Anthony Asquith, Lawrence Olivier, John Gielgud, and John Dexter; in New York, Margaret Webster, George S. Kaufman, Michael Redgrave, and Fred Coe; both in London and New York, Alfred Lunt, Glen Byam Shaw, Peter Glenville, and Michael Benthall.

Rattigan's canon was graced by a Who's Who of the theatre: Charles Boyer, Rex Harrison, Alec Guinness, Trevor Howard, Eric Portman, Stanley Baker, Roland Culver, Francis L. Sullivan, Michael Wilding, Jeremy Brett, Kenneth More, Laurence Olivier, John Mills, Paul Scofield, Maurice Evans, the Lunts, Vivien Leigh, Margaret Leighton, Peggy Ashcroft, Martita Hunt, Margaret Sullavan, Julie Harris, Barbara Bel Geddes, Nancy Kelly, and Jessica Tandy.

For the cinema, Rattigan concocted twenty-one screenplays, often in collaboration, including adaptations of his own *French without Tears* (1939), *The Winslow Boy* (1948), *While the Sun Shines* (1950), *The Browning Version* (1951), *The Deep Blue Sea* (1955), *The Man Who Loved Redheads, Who is Sylvia?* (1955), *The Prince and the Showgirl, The Sleeping Prince* (1957), *Separate Tables* (nominated for an Academy Award, 1958), and *A Bequest to the Nation* (1973), as well as scripting the notable motion pictures *The Avengers* (1942), *The Way to the Stars* (1945), *Brighton Rock* (1948), *Breaking the Sound Barrier* (1952), *The V.I.P.s* (1963), *The Yellow Rolls-Royce* (1964), and *Goodbye Mr. Chips* (1969). Rattigan adapted Dickens' *A Tale of Two Cities* for radio in 1951 and contributed five original plays to television.

In *Great Writers of the English Language*, Leonard R. N. Ashley perceives: "His best works will long be studied as models of playwriting and also as mirrors of the times. Rattigan can capture the social outlook of a whole period in *Cause Célèbre* (or the cause célèbre of *The Winslow Boy*). . . . He can make folly funny and pathos poignant and what some would dismiss as 'a purely theatrical experience' deeply moving and quite unforgettable."[3]

The *London Times* obituary described Rattigan as "an emerging influence on the English theatre" and "one of the leaders of the twentieth century stage in what has come to be known as the Theatre of Entertainment . . . he wrote some of the most enduring narrative plays of his period, designed for a 'commercial' theatre and using traditional techniques Pinero and Henry Arthur Jones would have recognized."[4]

Critic Michael Billington commented in *The Guardian*: "It was often assumed that Rattigan was simply a purveyor of good middlebrow entertainment. . . . Yet his whole world is a sustained assault on English middle-class values: fear of emotional commitment, terror in the face of passion, apprehension about sex. In fact, few dramatists this century have written with more understanding about the human heart than Terence Rattigan."[5]

Acting Edition: Samuel French, Inc.

Awards and Honors: Rattigan's *The Winslow Boy*—Ellen Terry Award, 1947; New York Drama Critics Circle Award as Best Foreign Play, 1947–1948; a top ten selection in *The Best Plays of 1947–1948*. Other Rattigan top ten entries in the *Best Plays* yearbook: *O Mistress Mine*, 1945–1946, and *Separate Tables*, 1956–1957. Rattigan was appointed Commander, Order of the British Empire (CBE) in 1958, and knighted in 1971.

NOTES

1. Geoffrey Wansell, *Terence Rattigan* (London: Fourth Estate, 1995), 383.

2. *Man and Boy* was revived by off-Broadway's Roundabout Theatre Company in October 2011, with Frank Langella as a shadowy, Romanian-born oil magnate who clashes with a son who worships and detests him. While acknowledging "Mr. Langella's personal triumph," critic Ben Brantley called it a "lesser Rattigan work . . . an uneasy mix of daring plot gimmicks and synthetically silky dialogue" (*New York Times*, October 10, 2011).

3. James Vinson, ed., *Great Writers of the English Language: Dramatists* (New York: St. Martin's, 1979), 490.

4. *London Times*, December 1, 1977.

5. *The Guardian*, London, December 1, 1977.

A Murder Is Announced (1977)

Leslie Darbon (England)

London producer Peter Saunders, who put Agatha Christie on the theatrical map by presenting all of her plays since 1951's *The Hollow*, continued to attach himself to the author's works even after her death in 1976.

In 1977, Saunders helmed Leslie Darbon's faithful adaptation of Christie's fiftieth novel, *A Murder Is Announced* (1950), with the action confined to "Little Paddocks," Letitia Blacklock's Victorian house on the edge of Chipping Cleghorn, a typical English village.

One sunny morning, the good people of Chipping Cleghorn have their breakfast spoiled by a disconcerting notice in the "Personal" column of the *Gazette:*

"A murder is announced and will take place on Friday, October the 13th, at Little Paddocks—at 6:30 p.m. Friends please accept this, the only intimation."

Letitia Blacklock, "beyond middle-age, but still a very attractive woman," shares her household with a companion, a vague, scatter-brained school friend named Dora Bunner; two distant cousins, Julian and Patrick Simmons, both in their twenties, good-looking, and highly competitive; and Mitzi, a rather explosive housekeeper.

A few curious neighbors and friends appear at the appointed time. Among them is Miss Jane Marple, described here as "an elderly lady with an over-inquisitive mind which gets her into all sorts of trouble." Miss Marple has recently arrived from St. Mary Mead to be treated for her rheumatism at the local spa.

When the clock chimes half past six, the lights go out, leaving the room in total darkness. The main door bursts open with a crash and a powerful flashlight plays around the room. Two shots are fired—then a tiny pause—followed by a third shot. The unexpected visitor, Rudi Scherz from Switzerland, falls with a heavy thud, dead. Letitia Blacklock is also hurt—blood drips down her cheek and onto her white blouse.

Chief Inspector Dermot Craddock, a man about fifty, is on the case trying to determine who attempted to kill Letitia Blacklock. It is the beginning of a beautiful friendship with Miss Marple.[1] The cousins Simmons come under suspicion because they stand to inherit Miss Blacklock's sizable assets. Complications multiply when Dora Bunner chokes to death on a slice of poisoned cake.

"Some people say I'm like a bad penny," says Miss Marple to Inspector Craddock. Still, her efforts pay off; her dogged snooping and her "knowledge of human nature" solve the case.

And a very complicated case it is, too perplexing for easy viewing. Past information is thrown in thick and fast; crucial events occur offstage and several individuals are not who they appear to be. Sorting through family skeletons and following such elusive verbal clues as the exchange of "Letty" with "Lotty," Miss Marple deduces that Letitia Blacklock is not the intended victim but the culprit, attempting to hide the fact that she previously usurped the identity of her sister, the inheritor of Little Paddocks, as well as a considerable fortune.

* * *

A Murder Is Announced was first presented at the Theatre Royal in Brighton, and subsequently moved to the Vaudeville Theatre in London, on September 21, 1977. Robert Chetwyn directed, and Dulcie Gray was cast as Miss Marple, Dinah Sheridan played the villainess, and James Grout the Inspector.

Reviewer Sheridan Morley wrote in *Punch*, "Dulcie Gray's Miss Marple is a long way from Margaret Rutherford and I suspect in the wrong direction—though Christie purists may prove me wrong."[2] *The Times of London* scowled: "There is no sense of village life, more of suburban dullness. . . . There are enough twists to stir the audience. . . . But the dialogue is stiff . . . and there is almost no mood of mystery."[3] Despite the negative critical reception, *A Murder Is Announced* ran for 429 performances.

In the United States, the play was mounted by the Dallas, Texas, Theatre Center on December 7, 1982, for forty-six showings.

NBC television aired *A Murder Is Announced* on December 30, 1956, as an entry in the *Goodyear TV Playhouse* series. William Templeton adapted the novel as a one-hour whodunit, directed by Paul Stanley. Gracie Fields, a renowned British singer-actress-comedienne, played Jane Marple, supported by Jessica Tandy—who created the role of Blanche DuBois in Tennessee Williams' *A Streetcar Named Desire* on Broadway—as Letitia Blacklock, and Roger Moore—later to play James Bond—as cousin Patrick Simmons.

* * *

Jane Marple, whose innocent china-blue eyes belie her shrewd intellect, began her detective prowls at the approximate age of sixty-five. The character is based on Christie's own grandmother, who, according to the author, "expected the worst of everyone and everything."

Ann Hart, in *The Life and Times of Miss Jane Marple*, pieced together bits and pieces from Christie's novels for an affectionate profile of the amateur sleuth. Miss Marple was born in the small village of St. Mary Mead. It is evident that her Victorian childhood was stamped with many dos and don'ts. "When I was a girl, Inspector," she says, "nobody ever mentioned the word stomach." There were long hours in the schoolroom, visits to Madame Tussaud's, and a finishing school in Florence.[4]

Miss Marple resides in a pretty Victorian house. She lives on a small fixed income that is augmented by her nephew, Raymond West, a successful novelist. Hart describes how, prone to gossip, Marple gets entangled in various unfathomable situations. While the professional investigators are attempting to sort out facts, the mild-mannered maiden, her knitting needles clicking softly, arrives at the right solutions by utilizing past experiences and insisting that human nature is the same everywhere. No matter how complex a case might be, Miss Marple's practice was to hark back to parallel scandals in her village.[5] Author William L. DeAndrea jocularly commented that St. Mary Mead "has put on a pageant of human depravity rivaled only by that of Sodom and Gomorrah."[6]

In Marple's early adventures "she had on black lace mittens, and a black lace cap surmounted the piled-up masses of her snowy hair" (*The Tuesday Club Murders*, 1933). Years later, apparently giving in to changing styles, she is described as "wearing an old-fashioned tweed coat and skirt, a couple of scarves and a small felt hat with a bird's wing" (*A Pocketful of Rye*, 1953).

Miss Marple was a founding member of the Tuesday Club, a group of six friends assembled to tackle unresolved crimes. They take turns recounting mysteries from their own experiences for the others to decipher. Marple would ramble about maids and desserts and country dances until the solution was evident.[7]

Among her more sensational cases were the homicide of an unknown blonde in an evening gown in *The Body in the Library* (1942), the nasty poison pen letters of *The Moving Finger* (1943), the deadly events that take place when visiting an old school friend in *Murder with Mirrors* (1952), the killing of a pathetic parlor maid in *A Pocketful of Rye* (1953), and the strangulation of a woman in the first-class train carriage in *What Mrs. McGillicuddy Saw!* (1957).

Miss Marple continued her snooping and sleuthing in the intricate cases of *The Mirror Crack'd from Side to Side* (1962), *A Caribbean Mystery* (1964), *At Bertram's Hotel* (1965), and *Nemesis* (1971). *Sleeping Murder*, published posthumously in 1977, has the singular old maid solving a macabre strangulation that occurred eighteen years earlier; family skeletons are uncovered, passions awakened, and the murderer strikes again.

* * *

Miss Marple made it to the screen in 1962. *Murder, She Said*—based on Christie's 1957 novel *4:50 From Paddington* (U.S. title, *What Mrs. McGillicuddy Saw!*)—was the first of four British MGM motion pictures featuring Margaret Rutherford as the irrepressible investigator. Here Miss Marple takes a job as a domestic worker in order to solve a strangulation she witnessed on a passing train.

In *The Murder at the Gallop* (1963)—inspired by the 1953 Hercule Poirot novel *After the Funeral* (U.S. title, *Funerals Are Fatal*)—Miss Marple suspects foul play when a wealthy recluse dies and a commotion ensues during the reading of his will. She is the lone jury member to believe the defendant innocent in *Murder Most Foul* (1964), adapted from *Mrs. McGinty's Dead*—a 1952 Poirot case. The last entry in the series, *Murder Ahoy*, is an original screenplay in which Miss Marple investigates a murder on a naval training ship. George Pollock zestfully directed all four films.

Angela Lansbury portrayed Miss Marple in *The Mirror Crack'd* (1980), a star-studded whodunit (Elizabeth Taylor, Kim Novak, Rock Hudson, Tony Curtis) about a murder committed during the filming of a movie in St. Mary Mead, based on Christie's 1962 novel.

Three fine actresses embodied Miss Marple on television: Gracie Fields in a 1956 one-hour episode based on *A Murder Is Announced* for NBC's *Goodyear Playhouse*; Helen Hayes in two made-for-TV movies, both for CBS—*A Caribbean Mystery* (1983) and *Murder with Mirrors* (1984); and Joan Hickson, coined "The definitive Miss Marple," in a series of nine BBC adaptations, all shown in the U.S. on the PBS *Mystery!* program (1986–1989).

Starting in 2004, the UK's ITV presented eleven Jane Marple movies starring Geraldine McEwan, including *The Body in the Library*, *The Murder at the Vicarage*, *4:50 from Paddington*, and *A Murder Is Announced*. Julia McKenzie took over the role in 2008, appearing in *A Pocketful of Rye*, *Murder Is Easy*, and *Why Didn't They Ask Evans?* Some of these were adapted from non-Marple novels, but included her as the sleuth.

* * *

Born in Torquay, Devon, Agatha Mary Clarissa Miller (1890–1976) was raised reading detective stories. Among her treasured literary influences were Gaston Leroux's *The Mystery of the Yellow Room*, a sealed-room classic; Robert Barr's *The Triumphs of Eugene Valmont*, a pioneering volume of humorous sleuthing; and Marie Belloc Lowndes's creation of French investigator Hercules Popeau. During World War I, Agatha married

Archibald Christie, a dashing colonel in the Royal Flying Corps. While working in the Volunteer Aid Detachment Hospital, she gained knowledge of drugs and poisons, information that later came in handy. Agatha had not planned to be a writer. In fact, her first novel was written as a response to a challenge by her sister, Madge. *The Mysterious Affair at Styles* (1920) introduced Hercule Poirot, the diminutive Belgian detective who was destined to rival the popularity of Sherlock Holmes.

In her second novel, *The Secret Adversary* (1922), Christie plotted an adventure tale in which the leading characters, Prudence Cowley, known to her friends as Tuppence, and Thomas Beresford, her beau, pursue an elusive man who plots to overthrow the British government.[8] Successive novels in the early 1920s introduced the recurring characters of Colonel Race and Superintendent Battle of Scotland Yard. In 1926 came the tour de force *The Murder of Roger Ackroyd*, which made Christie a household name.

Following the publication of *The Murder of Roger Ackroyd*, Christie herself became a headline mystery. On December 3, 1926, the celebrated author did not return home. Her frost-covered car, a green Morris, was found alongside a dirt road with the lights on. On the seat were a brown fur coat and a small dressing case that had burst open, scattering clothing and papers, including an out-of-date driver's license in her name. The disappearance caused a sensation. Was Christie the victim of foul play? Did she commit suicide? Or was it merely an audacious publicity stunt? A nationwide search was launched immediately.

Author Gwyn Robyns, in *The Mystery of Agatha Christie* (1978), asserts that in order to understand the circumstances of the bizarre case it is important to learn that "It had been a traumatic year for Agatha Christie." Her mother had died after a severe illness, and her marriage had deteriorated.

Kathleen Tynan, in *Agatha* (1978), provides an imaginary scenario about the author's disappearance: Preoccupied with the painful realization that she was losing her husband to a beautiful rival, the shy, sensitive author withdraws into herself—and drops out of sight. Tynan's speculative narrative attempts to penetrate the psyche of a woman betrayed. How will this accomplished mystery writer, plotter of intrigue, and creator of suspenseful incidents, react? Will she remain passive, or will she direct her talents towards sinister revenge?[9]

Agatha returned home after eleven days, claiming temporary amnesia. Two years later the Christies were divorced. In 1930, Agatha Christie married Max Mallowan, an archeologist. By accompanying him on digs to the Middle East, Christie discovered exotic source material for such books as *Murder in Mesopotamia* (1936), *Death on the Nile* (1937), *Appointment with Death* (1938), *Death Comes as the End* (1945), and *They Came to Baghdad* (1951).

It is widely perceived that only the Bible and the plays of Shakespeare have sold more copies than Agatha Christie's murder mysteries. "In a career that spanned over half a century," writes popular-culture czar Peter Haining, "she published in all 78 crime novels, 19 plays (of which seven are adaptations of her books), six romantic novels under the pen-name Mary Westmacott, and four non-fiction titles . . . it is true to say that Agatha Christie is the most widely published writer of any time and in any language, and the royalties deriving from her books alone now run in excess of two million pounds every year."[10] Haining calls attention to the energetic productivity and high achievements of Dame Christie in the world of entertainment—on stage, in films, and on radio and television: "This contribution amounts to at least 20 major theatrical productions on both sides of the Atlantic (not to mention a vast number of touring productions and repertory performances); two dozen films for the cinema; in excess of 50 radio programs; and an even larger number of individual stories and serials for both British and American television."[11]

Agatha Christie died peacefully at her home in Wallingford, Berkshire, on January 12, 1976, at age eighty-five.

* * *

Leslie Darbon, who in addition to *A Murder Is Announced* dramatized Agatha Christie's *Cards on the Table* (1981), began his writing career as a provincial journalist and then turned to radio and television. Beginning in 1962 and for the next three decades, Darbon contributed episodes of *Suspense, Department S, Shoestring, Bergerac,* and other notable television programs. In the 1970s, he embarked upon fluffy stage comedies. *Who Goes Bare?* and *Two and Two Make Sex,* both co-written with Richard Harris in 1974, and *Correspondents' Course,* with Paul Finney in 1976, are playful he-and-she pieces, in which mistaken identities abound and rebound until they are sorted out just before the final curtain. On his own, Darbon penned *Time to Kill* (1979), a bizarre melodrama picturing a kangaroo court in which the town's lothario, manacled to a wrought-iron chair in a posh living room, is accused by four angry women of causing the death of their friend. A conviction, they tell him, carries the death penalty.

Acting Edition: Samuel French, Inc.

Awards and Honors: Agatha Christie became a Fellow, Royal Society of Literature, in 1950. She was awarded the C.B.E. (Commander, Order of the British Empire) in 1956, and made a D.B.E. (Dame Commander, Order of the British Empire) in 1971. She was president of England's Detection Club (1954) and recipient of the Mystery Writers of America Grand Master Award (1955). The University of Exeter conferred a D.Litt in 1961.

NOTES

1. Miss Marple and Inspector Craddock will combine forces in the story "Sanctuary" from *Double Sin* (1961), and the novels *4.50 from Paddington*, aka *What Mrs. McGillicuddy Saw!* (1957), and *The Mirror Crack'd from Side to Side* (1962).

2. Peter Haining, *Agatha Christie—Murder in Four Acts* (London: Virgin, 1990), 37.

3. Dennis Sanders and Len Lovallo, *The Agatha Christie Companion* (New York: Delacorte, 1984), 424.

4. Anne Hart, *The Life and Times of Miss Jane Marple* (New York: Dodd, Mead, 1985), 27.

5. Hart, *The Life and Times of Miss Jane Marple*, 37.

6. William L. DeAndrea, *Encyclopedia Mysteriosa* (New York: Prentice Hall, 1994), 233.

7. Hart, *The Life and Times of Miss Jane Marple*, 40.

8. Tuppence and Tommy will return in Christie's novels *Partners in Crime* (1929), *N or M?* (1941), *By the Pricking of My Thumbs* (1968), and *The Postern of Fate* (1973).

9. *Agatha* was filmed by director Michael Apted in 1979, featuring Vanessa Redgrave in the title role, Timothy Dalton as the fickle husband, and Dustin Hoffman as an American reporter, Wally Stanton, who tracks Christie down to a seaside hotel.

10. Haining, *Agatha Christie*, 11.

11. Haining, *Agatha Christie*, 11–12.

The Crucifer of Blood (1978)

Paul Giovanni (United States, 1933–1990)

Paul Giovanni's *The Crucifer of Blood* (1978), a distorted version of Arthur Conan Doyle's *The Sign of Four*, begins at the Red Fort of Agra, India, 1857, during the British occupation in the days of the Indian mutiny.

Three British soldiers—Major Alistair Ross, Captain Neville St. Claire, and Private Jonathan Small—come upon a Maharajah's treasure chest containing precious stones, kill its two native guards, and share a blood-oath to divide the spoils equally upon their return to England.

Thirty years later, in 1887, we meet the world's foremost consulting detective, Sherlock Holmes, at 221B Baker Street, London. He wears a silk dressing gown, scratches away on the violin, and—to the concern of companion Dr. Watson—injects his arm with a syringe filled with a 7 percent solution of cocaine.

Irene St. Claire, the daughter of Captain Neville St. Claire, "a young woman of great beauty," rushes into Holmes's flat in obvious distress. She informs the sleuth that her father has received a map by mail and since then has been "cowering in the corner like a frightened child."

Holmes fails to save the life of Neville St. Claire, who is murdered by a blowpipe's poisonous dart. The hunt for the killer takes the detective, disguised as an old Mandarin, to an opium den in Limehouse and to a police launch on the Thames. One-legged Jonathan Small and his pigmy ally, Tonga, are the main suspects, but in a sharp departure from the Conan Doyle novel and all previous stage interpretations, it is Irene St. Claire who turns out to be the cold-blooded murderer. "You are an unnatural creature," says Holmes when slapping cuffs on her wrists. Irene explains that it was an act of revenge: her father had cavorted with an Indian whore and given her mother syphilis. After a great deal of pain, her mother threw herself under the wheels of a train.

Holmes instructs Watson to "file this case away in our archives. Someday, perhaps, the true story can be told."

* * *

The Crucifer of Blood was first produced at the Studio Arena Theatre in Buffalo, New York, on January 6, 1978, and ran for thirty-nine performances. The lead actors were Paxton Whitehead (Sherlock Holmes), Timothy Landfield (Dr. Watson), Christopher Curry (Jonathan Small), and Glenn Close (Irene St. Claire). The quartet reprised their roles in a subsequent Broadway production that opened at the Helen Hayes Theatre on September 28, 1978. Playwright-director Paul Giovanni stated in the program that *The Crucifer of Blood* was based on a document that "has only recently come to light. It was found among the effects of Dr. John Watson." The note quotes Dr. Watson's recollection of the "dreadful" 1887 case that formed "one of the most painful and alarming episodes in my long association with Mr. Sherlock Holmes."

The show garnered mixed reviews. The naysayers included critics Howard Kissel, who wrote, "*The Crucifer of Blood* is a return to cheap thrills. . . . For the most part the dialog is stilted";[1] Walter Kerr, who stated, "In spite of all its thunder and lightning and smuggled jewels, the evening is just plain tedious";[2] and T. E. Kalem, who sniffed, "Giovanni's play is silly, campy and confusing."[3]

Praise came from Bob Lape, who chirped, "A jolly thriller."[4] John Beaufort gushed, "Mr. Giovanni mingles surprises, comedy, stage effects, and a flow of nicely turned Victorian rhetoric."[5] Likewise, Jack Kroll applauded "a captivating entertainment . . . an ingenious pastiche of the actual stories of Conan Doyle."[6]

The cast won unanimous kudos, "with special mention to Glenn Close as the damsel in distress, and to Mr. Paxton Whitehead, who is swift and wicked perfection as Sherlock Holmes."[7] Close was described as "staunch and impassioned," "meltingly distraught and touchingly loyal as the client in the case," "an imperiously beautiful study in scarlet and alabaster."[8]

The Crucifer of Blood ran for 228 performances. The play was revived by the American Conservatory Theatre in San Francisco, California (1980), with Peter Donat (Holmes) and Daniel Davis (Watson); by the Ahmanson Theatre in Los Angeles, California (1981), starring Charlton Heston (Holmes) and Jeremy Brett (Watson); by the Indianapolis Civic Theatre in Indianapolis, Indiana (1997), featuring Kurt Owens (Holmes) and Gus Pearey (Watson); by the Berkshire Theatre Festival in Stockbridge, Massachusetts (1999), marqueeing Stephen Spinella and David Watkins as the youthful Holmes and Watson.

In the 2008–2009 season, *The Crucifer of Blood* was brought back to the stage by the Wayward Actors Company of Louisville, Kentucky, and the Alley Theatre in Houston, Texas.

In 1991, Charlton Heston returned to the role of the Great Detective in a made-for-television movie adapted and directed by his son, Fraser C.

Heston. Richard Johnson played Dr. Watson; Susannah Harker portrayed Irene St. Claire. Filmed in England, the 105-minute *Crucifer of Blood* was broadcast in the United States on November 4, 1991 and June 6, 2002.

Prior to *The Crucifer of Blood*, Paul Giovanni was best known for providing the music for the 1977 British cult horror film *The Wicker Man*. Giovanni died from AIDS on June 20, 1990.

* * *

Arthur Conan Doyle was born on May 22, 1859 in Edinburgh, Scotland. He attended Stonyhurst College, where he pursued his interest in poetry, and Edinburgh University, where he studied medicine. Among his instructors was Professor Rutherford who, "with his Assyrian beard, his prodigious voice, his enormous chest and his singular manner,"[9] became the prototype for Doyle's fictitious character, Professor Challenger. Teacher John Bell—"thin, wiry, dark, with a high-nosed acute face, penetrating grey eyes, angular shoulders," whose "strong point was diagnosis, not only of disease, but of occupation and character"[10]—was Conan Doyle's inspiration for Sherlock Holmes.

Conan Doyle moved to London and began to practice medicine but he soon learned that "shillings might be earned in other ways than by filling phials" and wrote an adventure story called *The Mystery of Sassassa Valley*. To his pleasant surprise, it was accepted by the *Chambers Journal* and published in the September 6, 1879 issue. In 1880, he went as a ship surgeon on the whaler *Hope* to the Arctic Seas and on the steamer *Mayumba* to Africa. The voyages later provided background for his adventure novels.

Influenced by Mayne Reid, Jules Verne, Robert Louis Stevenson, and Henry James, Dr. Conan Doyle continued to moonlight, writing stories for several journals. Attracted to the intricate criminous plots of Emile Gaboriau and the analytical detective stories of Edgar Allan Poe, Doyle wrote *A Study in Scarlet*, the first Sherlock Holmes vehicle (in an early draft, the sleuth was named Sherringford Holmes). Doyle sold the rights to *A Study in Scarlet* for twenty-five pounds and the novel was featured in *Beeton's Xmas Annual* of 1887. "I never at any time received another penny for it," writes Doyle.[11]

Little did he know at the time that his consulting detective would become one of the most famous characters in English literature.

Conan Doyle penned a second Sherlock Holmes novel, *The Sign of Four* (1890), and a series of Holmes stories for the *Strand Magazine*, but he believed that his true calling was writing historical novels. Alas, *Micah Clark* (1889), *The White Company* (1891), *The Refugees* (1893), *Uncle Bernac* (1896), and *Sir Nigel* (1906) are all but forgotten today. Conan Doyle attempted to liberate himself from his Frankenstein monster and devised the demise of Holmes in *The Final Problem* (1893), where the detective and his archenemy,

Professor Moriarty, plunge to their doom at Reichenbach Falls. However, public outcry forced Doyle to resurrect his hero in the novel *The Hound of the Baskervilles* (1902) and ensuing stories. Throughout his career, Doyle wrote fifty-six tales and four novels (the fourth was *The Valley of Fear*, 1915), featuring Holmes and his chronicler, Dr. John H. Watson.

During the 1899–1902 Boer War, Conan Doyle served as a physician at a field hospital in South Africa. He recounted his experience in the highly regarded *The Great Boer War* (1900). In 1902, he was knighted. That year, a dip into politics was unsuccessful when he narrowly lost his run for a seat in Edinburgh.

Stepping into the shoes of Sherlock Holmes, Conan Doyle cajoled Scotland Yard to re-investigate the real-life cases of George Edalji, a mixed-race student convicted of mutilating horses, and Oscar Slater, a German Jew jailed for the murder of an elderly woman. Upon the renewed probe, both Edalji and Slater were exonerated.

Conan Doyle was married twice. When his son Kingsley was mortally wounded during World War I, spiritualism became an important factor in Doyle's life. He zealously advocated and pursued communication with the dead for the rest of his life. Conan Doyle died on July 7, 1930 of angina pectoris. He was seventy-one.

"The Sherlock Holmes stories will be read as long as humanity keeps its love for puzzles," wrote mystery author Julian Symons, " . . . and Conan Doyle's behavior as a man was throughout his life almost wholly admirable. The indignation he felt at official cruelty or neglect, and his struggles to obtain justice for men personally uncongenial to him, show him as a man of an integrity rare in his own or any time."[12]

As a playwright, Conan Doyle had a spotty West End record. In 1893, he collaborated with J. M. Barrie on the libretto of an operetta, *Jane Annie; or, the Good Conduct Prize*, picturing lighthearted shenanigans in a girls' school. It opened on May 13, 1893 at London's Savoy Theatre, was greeted by a testy review from George Bernard Shaw, and struggled for fifty lackluster performances. "After that," commented biographer Hesketh Pearson, "Barrie and Doyle confined their collaboration to cricket."[13]

Still struggling with the craft of playwriting, Doyle concocted a political drama, *Foreign Policy*, which premiered in June 1893, at Terry's Theatre. It closed after only six performances.

Doyle's *The Story of Waterloo* (aka *Waterloo*), a one-hour, one-act performed for the first time at the Prince's Theatre, Bristol, in September 1894, proved to be a triumphant vehicle for famed actor-manager Henry Irving. The role of Corporal Gregory Brewster, late of the Third Life Guards at Waterloo, where he earned a medal for bravery before turning into a shriveled old man, became one of Irving's permanent repertory fixtures. It opened in London later that year and was revived annually for more than a decade. Irving brought *Waterloo* to New York during frequent visits between 1899 and 1903.

The playlet was adapted to the silver screen (as *The Veteran of Waterloo*) in 1933, and for television (as *Waterloo*) in 1937.

Biographer Martin Booth criticizes Conan Doyle's *Halves*, based on a novel by James Payn, for "a hackneyed plot about two young brothers who promise to meet in twenty-one years and share whatever fortunes they have made."[14] The play opened at Aberdeen's Her Majesty's Theatre in April 1899, and moved to London's Garrick Theatre two months later, running for sixty performances.

Conan Doyle's colorful stories about the Napoleonic campaigns, collected in *The Exploits of Brigadier Gerard* (1896) and *The Adventures of Gerard* (1897), were first adapted to the stage for swashbuckling American actor James O'Neill, renowned for *Monte Cristo*. Upon the opening of *The Adventures of Gerard* at Smith's Theatre in Bridgeport, Connecticut in November 1903, the *New York Times* wrote, "It is full of action, adventure and intrigue, but is faulty by too many long dialogues by the leading characters."[15] Conan Doyle's own adaptation, *Brigadier Gerard,* premiered at the Imperial Theatre in London in 1906 and featured Lewis Waller in the title role. It ran for 114 performances. Later that year it crossed the Atlantic. Matinee idol Kyrle Bellew starred in a production that played in Hartford, Connecticut and moved to New York's Savoy Theatre for a run of sixteen performances.[16]

The heroic hussar, loyal to Emperor Napoleon against the betraying Talleyrand, appeared in three motion picture versions: *Brigadier Gerard* (1915), *The Fighting Eagle* (1927), and *The Adventures of Gerard* (1970).

Conan Doyle dramatized his novel, *The Tragedy of Korosko*, into a four-act "modern morality play," *The Fires of Fate*. It opened at London's Lyric Theatre on June 15, 1909. Lewis Waller enacted Colonel Cyril Egerton of the Bengal Lancers, a man suffering from incurable spinal degeneration. Doomed, he plunges into a series of adventures—and romances—in Egypt. The happy ending has Egerton miraculously cured after sustaining a shock. Audiences flocked to the Lyric for 125 performances.

The first American production of *The Fires of Fate* took place in Chicago's Illinois Theatre later in 1909 (with Lionel Barrymore as Abdullah, an Arab guide). The play reached New York's Liberty Theatre in December and ran for twenty-three performances. It was filmed in 1923 and 1932.

The House of Temperley: Melodrama of the Ring, which Doyle dramatized from his prizefighting novel *Rodney Stone*, opened at the Adelphi Theatre in London, on December 27, 1909. Its highlight was a bare-knuckles boxing bout that drew crowds for 167 performances. The play was transferred to the screen in 1913; a 1920 film was based on the novel.

In 1910, Conan Doyle adapted his celebrated short story, "The Adventure of the Speckled Band," into a three-act play. *The Speckled Band* opened at London's Adelphi Theatre on June 4, 1910 and ran for 169 performances.

The Speckled Band was the only Sherlock Holmes play written solely by Conan Doyle. But throughout the twentieth century and to this very day, many admiring disciples have tried their hands at bringing the Great Detective to the stage.

Acting Edition: Samuel French, Inc.

NOTES

1. *Women's Wear Daily*, September 29, 1978.
2. *New York Times*, round-up of plays, November 6, 1978.
3. *Time*, October 9, 1978.
4. *WABC-TV*, October 1, 1978.
5. *Christian Science Monitor*, October 2, 1978.
6. *Newsweek*, October 9, 1978.
7. Dennis Cunningham, *WABC-TV2*, October 1, 1978.
8. Glenn Close would soon arrive in Hollywood and become a major star. Her criminous motion pictures include *Jagged Edge* (1985), *Fatal Attraction* (1987), *Dangerous Liaisons* (1988), *Reversal of Fortune* (1990), *Hamlet* (1990), *Mary Reilly* (1996), *101 Dalmatians* (1996) and *102 Dalmatians* (2000), and *Air Force One* (1997).
9. Arthur Conan Doyle, *Memories and Adventures*, 2nd ed. (London: John Murray, 1930), 32.
10. Doyle, *Memories and Adventures*, 32.
11. Doyle, *Memories and Adventures*, 91.
12. Julian Symons, *Portrait of an Artist: Conan Doyle* (London: Whizzard, 1979), 123.
13. Hesketh Pearson, *Conan Doyle: His Life and Art* (London: Methuen, 1943), 105.
14. Martin Booth, *The Doctor and the Detective: A Biography of Sir Arthur Conan Doyle* (New York: St. Martin's, 1997), 208.
15. *New York Times*, November 10, 1903.
16. Three years earlier, Kyrle Bellew won high praise as *Raffles, the Amateur Cracksman*.

The Hound of the Baskervilles (1978)

F. Andrew Leslie (United States, 1927–)

The 1978 adaptation of *The Hound of the Baskervilles* by F. Andrew Leslie is generally faithful to the original Arthur Conan Doyle novel. The proceedings take place in two sets—Sherlock Holmes's study at 221B Baker Street in London, and Baskerville Hall in Dartmoor, Devonshire. The curtain rises on Holmes's conjectures about the cane left behind by a visitor, Dr. James Mortimer—"there emerges a young fellow under thirty, amiable, unambitious, absent-minded, and the possessor of a favorite dog."

Dr. Mortimer—a tall, thin, youngish man, much in character with Holmes's deductions—enters and exhibits an old parchment that records the strange history of his neighbors, the Baskerville family. It all began in 1742, when the "wild, profane and godless" Hugo Baskerville carried off the daughter of a next-door farmer. The maiden escaped. Enraged, Hugo raced after her on horseback, followed by several drunken friends. In a moonlit clearing they found the bodies of both the young girl and her pursuer. Horrified, they saw "a great, black beast, shaped like a hound," plucking at the throat of Sir Hugo.

Dr. Mortimer recounts that "Since the coming of the hound, others of the Baskerville line have been unhappy in their deaths, which have been sudden, bloody and mysterious." The demise of Sir Charles Baskerville is the most recent example. He was found lifeless at the far end of the garden of his Dartmoor estate. "There were no signs of violence, although the medical report mentions an almost incredible facial distortion." Sir Charles had a long-standing organic disease and may have died of heart failure, but Dr. Mortimer is concerned about traces found upon the ground near the body.

HOLMES: Footprints?
MORTIMER: Footprints.
HOLMES: A man's or a woman's?
MORTIMER (his voice almost a whisper): Mr. Holmes, they were the footprints of a gigantic hound.

Sir Henry Baskerville, the heir—"about thirty years of age, sturdily built, and with a ruddy complexion of man used to the outdoor life"—has just returned from Canada and appears in the doorway.[1] He relates that a curious unsigned letter was delivered to his hotel that morning: "As you value your life or your reason keep away from the moor." Also of interest are his missing boots—one of a new set he has just purchased, the other of an old set put out for cleaning.

Sir Henry proclaims that he is eager to see his ancestral home. Holmes recommends that Dr. Watson accompany Sir Henry to Dartmoor as he himself has urgent business in London. "And bring your revolver with you," he says. "It's an ugly business, Watson, an ugly dangerous business."

The domestic staff at Baskerville Hall consists of butler John Barrymore—"a tall, handsome man with a full, black beard," and his wife Eliza, housekeeper and cook.[2] Late at night, a vigilant Watson notices the Barrymores holding a candle in the window and moving it slowly from side to side, as if giving a signal. When confronted, they confess to beckoning Mrs. Barrymore's younger brother, Selden, the Notting Hill murderer, an escaped convict. "My unhappy brother is starving on the moor," stammers Mrs. Barrymore. "We cannot let him perish at our very gates. The light is a signal to him that we have food and clothing for him. . . . There were some old things of yours, Sir Henry, that you told me to dispose of. I took the liberty."

Wearing a cloak that belonged to Sir Henry turns out to cause Selden's brutal death at the jaws of a huge hound that was turned loose to rip the man whose scent matched that of an old boot.

The culprit proves to be the neighbor John Stapleton ("a rather prim-looking young man, thin and clean shaven"), a naturalist who roams the area with a butterfly net, but clandestinely rears a large dog, training it to become a stalker by scent and killer by mission. Capitalizing on the Baskerville legend, Stapleton dripped phosphorous on the beast's face, engendering a bluish flame that seemed to emerge from its jaw and circle its eyes with rings of fire.

Holmes notices a striking resemblance between Stapleton and a wall portrait of Sir Hugo Baskerville. "He knew that two lives stood between him and the Baskerville estate," says the Great Detective, "Sir Charles and Sir Henry."

Stapleton sends his ferocious dog after Sir Henry, and a violent scene transpires off-stage, complete with shouts, barks, and a series of pistol shots. The hound is killed, Sir Henry, albeit shaken, is saved, and Stapleton escapes into the foggy mire where his fate will remain forever sealed.

A romantic subplot is provided by Stapleton's sister Beryl (who is eventually revealed to be Stapleton's long-suffering wife) and Sir Henry. A happy ending is assured, but just as Holmes, Watson, and the young couple raise glasses to toast "the conclusion of a most baffling case," and the curtain begins a slow descent, the chilling sound of a baying hound is heard from far off on the moor.

The Hound of the Baskervilles was first presented by the Frill and Dagger Players, Geneva College, Geneva, New York, on February 16, 1978, running six performances. The play was directed by Dr. Harry Farra, who cast Jim Miller in the role of Sherlock Holmes.

* * *

Frederick Andrew Leslie (born in 1927) has specialized in stage adaptations from novels and screenplays by other hands. The standout among his plays is *The Spiral Staircase* (1962), based on Mel Dinelli's screenplay, which in turn was inspired by Ethel Lina White's novel, *Some Must Watch*—a gothic thriller, unfolding in a Victorian-style manor during a stormy night, about an elusive serial killer who has been strangling "imperfect" women. A mute maid, Helen, is targeted as the next victim.[3]

In 1964, Leslie dramatized *The Haunting of Hill House,* the classic ghost story by Shirley Jackson, detailing the investigation of a broody, isolated mansion by a team of scientists.[4]

Leslie's bittersweet dramas include *The Boy with Green Hair* (1961), an allegory of a twelve-year-old war orphan, Peter, who becomes a social miscast because his hair changes color, but eventually understands that he is entrusted with a mission to transform all around him for the better;[5] *Splendor in the Grass* (1966) describes how school sweethearts Bud Stamper and Deanie Loomis are plunged into tragic events that dash their plans. In a final, touching scene they gently break old ties and gain the strength to move on to what lies ahead;[6] *Lilies of the Field* (1967) focuses on a relationship between a discharged soldier, Homer, who is heading west, and a Mother Superior, Maria Marthe, who convinces him to stay and help build a chapel;[7]*The People Next Door* (1969) tells of a troubled New York household—the parents of a drug-addicted daughter trying desperately to rehabilitate her.[8]

On a lighter note, Leslie adapted to the stage three motion picture comedies: *The Bachelor and the Bobby-Soxer* (1961), which spotlights the dilemma of playboy Dick Nugent, who is romantically pursued by teenager Susan Turner, while his heart belongs to Susan's older sister Margaret, a severe, no-nonsense judge.[9] *The Farmer's Daughter* (1962) is the story of a Scandinavian immigrant, Katrin Holstrom, a naïve, straight-arrow maid at the home of a powerful senator—who winds up as a candidate of the opposition party.[10] *Mr. Hobbs' Vacation* (1963) pictures the misadventures of a family—father, mother, and college-age daughter—renting a summer cottage on an island off the coast of New England.[11]

Acting Edition: Dramatists Play Service.

NOTES

1. Mrs. Hudson, the lodging's caretaker at 221B Baker Street, who usually shows visitors up, does not appear in this adaptation.

2. A third household member, a scullery maid, is omitted.

3. The superb, suspenseful 1946 picture, directed by Robert Siodmak, starred Dorothy McGuire as Helen, Ethel Barrymore as her bedridden employer, and George Brent as the demented culprit. Less successful was a 1975 British remake, directed by Peter Collinson, featuring Jacqueline Bisset, Mildred Dunnock, and Christopher Plummer.

4. An eerie motion picture based on Jackson's novel, titled *The Haunting* (1963), was directed by Robert Wise. A pale imitation was made in 1999.

5. A 1949 RKO film, on which the play is based, was director Joseph Losey's first Hollywood assignment. Dean Stockwell enacted the title role.

6. William Inge won an Academy Award for his screenplay of *Splendor in the Grass* (1961). Elia Kazan directed; Warren Beatty and Natalie Wood starred.

7. A 1963 film, directed by Ralph Nelson, marqueed Sidney Poitier and Lilia Skala in the leads, winning Poitier an Oscar.

8. J. P. Miller adapted his TV script to the screen. Eli Wallach and Julie Harris portrayed the desperate parents; Deborah Winters was the junkie in this grim 1970s film.

9. A 1947 movie, starring Cary Grant, Myrna Loy, and Shirley Temple, earned Sidney Sheldon an Academy Award for his original screenplay.

10. Loretta Young won an Oscar in the title role. The supporting cast, under H. C. Potter's direction, included Joseph Cotton, Ethel Barrymore, Charles Bickford, and Harry Davenport.

11. James Stewart and Maureen O'Hara starred in the 1962 feature, directed by Henry Koster.

No Orchids for Miss Blandish (1978)

Robert David MacDonald
(Scotland, 1929–2004)

London-born James Hadley Chase (pseudonym for René Barbazon Raymond, 1906–1985) had been a door-to-door encyclopedia salesman and a wholesale bookseller when he wrote his first book, *No Orchids for Miss Blandish*, in the summer of 1938. Chase has not yet been to America, but with the help of a detailed map, a dictionary of American slang, and perhaps inspired by William Faulkner's controversial novel *Sanctuary* (1931), he concocted a gritty, violent tale of a kidnapped-for-ransom Kansas City heiress by a gang of ruthless gangsters, headed by the sadistic Ma Grisson and her neurotic son, Slim.[1]

No Orchids for Miss Blandish was published in London by Jarrolds in 1939 and became the toast of the town. Over the next four decades, Chase wrote seventy-eight additional thrillers, but *No Orchids for Miss Blandish* remains his claim to posterity. The novel was transferred to the screen in 1951 and 1971.

A stage adaptation of *No Orchids for Miss Blandish*, penned by Chase and Robert Nesbitt, was presented at London's Prince of Wales Theatre on July 30, 1942, and ran for 203 performances. The cast was headed by Linda Travers (Miss Blandish), Robert Newton (Slim Grisson), Mary Clare (Ma Grisson), and Hartley Power (Dave Fenner, the detective on the case). A provincial tour ran from 1942 to 1949.

A French adaptation by d'Éliane Charles and Marcel Duhamel was produced in Paris at the Grand Guignol Theatre on January 2, 1950, directed by Alexandre Dundas, featuring Nicole Riche (Miss Blandish), Jean-Marc Tennberg (Slim Grisson), Renée Gardes (Ma Grisson), and Sacha Tarride (Inspector Fenner).[2] A program note described *No Orchids for Miss Blandish* as "a bloody drama, the drama of policemen and gangsters; the beauty, the hysteria and the fear of fear thrive in this effective tragedy in which revolvers fire away and submachine guns have the last word. The author introduces depraved people. The Grand-Guignol theatre made a great decision by presenting to the Parisian public that horrible play, perfect for making us shiver, and quite well constructed."

Critic J. B. Jeener wrote in *Le Figaro*: "The audience feels trapped, embarrassed, and shameful; they hardly dared applaud." René Barjavel of *Carrefour* agreed: "Thanks to *Miss Blandish*, our nerves hurt, our jaws tightened, our hands clenched the armrest. . . . Whether or not you like the hardboiled crime genre, *No Orchids for Miss Blandish* is unquestionably a masterpiece."

Almost three decades later, in 1978, Glasgow's celebrated Citizens Theatre mounted *No Orchids for Miss Blandish*, dramatized and directed by its artistic director, Robert David MacDonald. MacDonald planted the proceedings in the early forties, before U.S. entry into World War II. The central element of his setting was a white cube isolated in the middle of the stage, serving in the first scene as Miss Blandish's room, and in subsequent scenes as the room in which she is held prisoner. Sliding walls masked the front of the cube during the sequences in which Blandish did not appear, allowing fast changes of locale.

The curtain rises on the Blandish home, "decorated with a baleful, frigid luxury like a mortician's office. Mirrors reflect each other in sterile repetition . . . unbecoming light cast by a cut-glass chandelier. No flowers . . . everything money can buy, which does not, of course, include life." This luxurious, albeit sterile, environment will later punctuate Blandish's transformation from a spoiled brat to a woman in touch with her basic instincts.

The center of the room is occupied by a surgical trolley, which in turn is occupied by what momentarily appears to be a female corpse, wrapped in a sheet, the face covered with a gauze mask. Anna Morgenstern enters. In her early thirties, the surgical-style overall she wears does not conceal her good looks. She crosses to the trolley and unwraps the body, revealing a girl "of an improbably perfect beauty"—Miss Blandish. As Anna attends to Miss Blandish with beautician's paraphernalia, the two women converse and we learn that Miss Blandish is the daughter of a successful banker and that she's engaged to a wealthy rancher named Frederick McGowan, "a brainless Adonis." Today is Miss Blandish's twenty-first birthday and a lavish party is planned at the Paradise nightclub.

Enter Mr. Lucie, John Blandish's secretary, "a man of startling saturnine good looks and impeccable address. . . . He has manners beneath which lurks a dangerous potential for violence." Lucie gives Blandish a diamond necklace from her father and a bouquet of orchids from himself. She's surprised, for her relationship with Lucie is strained; she does not let him forget that he's a paid employee.[3] Upon the secretary's departure, Miss Blandish disdainfully tosses the flowers to Anna Morgenstern and says,

"Freddy's probably bought me the Botanic Gardens anyway. No orchids for Miss Blandish."

The room disappears. Miss Blandish stands at the top of a staircase, waving to the crowd at the Paradise. A band plays "Happy Birthday." Two goons, Doyle and Riley, enter and snatch Miss Blandish. Doyle fights with Freddy, killing him with a kick to his head.[4] The elevated railway roars overhead as the lights fade out.

The second scene unfolds in a disused garage. A few oil drums and car wheels inform us of the original use of the building, as does the big sliding metal door upstage. Doyle and Riley enter with Miss Blandish. She is bound and gagged with a strip of duct tape. Her Chanel dress has taken quite a beating.

Doyle states that they have to "knock off" the girl as she "saw everything." Riley rebukes Doyle for already kicking a man to death; they'll hide her and send her father a ransom note. "We stand to pick up a weighty sack of gold," says Riley.

Unexpectedly, three members of the notorious Grisson gang arrive on the scene: Eddie Schultz is "a slightly overweight Casanova, not without a certain sluggish charm"; Doc Williams is "a sad-eyed, buffeted ruined alcoholic"; Chink is "a vicious little reptile." Soon they are joined by the leader of the band, Slim Grisson, described as "mean as a rattler" with a reputation for doing "some terrible things" with his favorite weapon—a knife.

Doyle and Riley say that the girl they brought to the garage is "a stewed little hustler." A heated argument ensues after which Doyle reaches for his gun, but is shot dead by the impassive Chink. They tie Riley. Slim orders the others to take Miss Blandish out. They roll up the garage door. Headlights glare onto the stage from the back, silhouetting Slim with a knife in his hand, and a screaming Riley.

The action shifts to a bar that serves as the Grisson headquarters—"an elaborate old-fashioned altarpiece of engraved glass mirrors and shelves" with a few gingham-clothed tables completing a none-too-attractive picture. Eddie, Chink, and Doc bring in Miss Blandish, and introduce her with a mocking flourish to Ma Grisson. A bulky woman, she is tightly corseted, her hair is "scraped back in a severe bun," her eyes are "little wet stones," and her mouth has been "lipsticked into a tight, mean parody of a cupid's bow." Ma comes out from behind the bar, snaps her account book shut, grinds her cigarette out on the floor, and circles Miss Blandish. Ma sounds like "a hungry tomcat" when she tells the frightened girl that her father better come across but if he "tries to be cute," she'll tear her apart in bits, "such bits to be dispatched daily to your Daddy till he realizes that if blood's thicker than water, gravy's thicker than either." She slaps Miss Blandish and orders Doc to take the girl to an inner room.

Doc says that he feels sorry for Miss Blandish but Ma Grisson counters with, "she's had everything up to now. Let her suffer . . . suffering does people good." Ma whispers to Doc that after the ransom money is paid, the girl will not be sent home—"she knows too much." Ma instructs Doc to write a letter to Mr. John Blandish with a request for "one million dollars in a white suitcase." An ad in the *Tribune*, a day after tomorrow, offering consignment of white paint for sale will mean that the money's ready.

Slim enters and confides to his mother that he wants to keep Miss Blandish. He never had a girl, and she's "like a fairytale." Ma tries to persuade him otherwise and moves toward him. She slides her hand down the front of his shirt and we get the inkling of an incestuous relationship.[5] Again, the elevated train roars overhead as the lights fade.

It is a dark and misty night when a new major character is introduced—Dave Fenner—a middle-aged private detective who wears a raincoat and a battered hat and is described as "merciful, weary, vulnerable and lonely." Fenner is summoned to a meeting with Mr. Lucie, John Blandish's secretary, during which he is hired to locate Miss Blandish and is paid a $3,000 retainer. Lucie explains that a communication from the kidnappers warned against contacting the police.[6]

A harrowing scene unfolds in a room illuminated by a powerful naked light bulb. Miss Blandish, lying in an iron bedstead, is strapped by her arms and legs. Ma Grisson whacks the girl with a corncob and warns her that she must submit to Slim as his birthday present. "You can't make me," says Blandish. "Nothing could ever make me." Ma Grisson drives the corncob between Miss Blandish's legs, and the girl screams.

Eddie, Chink, and Doc sit around in the bar when Ma Grisson enters from the street and triumphantly brandishes a newspaper. She instructs Doc to write another letter to "Big Daddy" to have that "fag secretary" take the money to the Maxwell filling station on Highway 71; a mile further on he'll meet Eddie's car, throw the suitcase out of his vehicle, and speed away. Eddie expresses concern: "The town's crawling with Feds. . . . The bulls are out in force hunting for Riley and Doyle." And, says Eddie, when the girl is released, she'll talk. Ma assures all that Blandish won't be returning home—Doc'll give her a fatal shot when she's asleep.

The lights again come up on the bar. Eddie and Chink enter, lugging a white suitcase filled with a million dollars in hundred-dollar bills. Ma informs the gang that since the money is "hot," instead of squandering it, she arranged to buy the Paradise club; they'll install a few high-class girls and have themselves "a sweet operation." As for Miss Blandish, she has to go. Slim objects: "She belongs to me. No one touches her. . . . Anyone makes a move towards her, I'll cut him in half."

Miss Blandish's hostage room is now quite done-up: a scarf over the light, a Victrola, rugs, a picture of the Virgin and Child. A curtain in the corner covers racks of dresses. Slim comes in carrying several parcels. He tells Miss Blandish that if it weren't for him, "Ma'd have you in a sack in the river by now." He went shopping and brought her some presents—opera records, a blue dress, a statue of the Madonna. When Miss Blandish does not respond, Slim, enraged, drops the Madonna statuette on the floor, where it smashes, snatches the scarf off the lamp, pulls the dress racks down, and turns off the Victrola, dragging the needle across the record. Ma Grisson enters and slaps him. Slim pulls a knife. He tells his mother that he cannot stand the fact that Miss Blandish "don't say anything. She just sits there, and looks at me."

Ma Grisson hands Miss Blandish a lipstick, but the girl smears her face grotesquely. Ma puts out the light, pulls her son's trousers down, and he shuffles over to the bed.

Weeks pass. With the aid of drugs and beatings, Ma forces Miss Blandish to submit to Slim. The Grisson gang has fortified their hiding place with steel shutters and strong firepower. Lucie informs Fenner that it is now assumed that Miss Blandish is dead and his services are no longer required. But the detective says that he intends to see Anna Morgenstern, who was Frank Riley's lover and was known to have been at Miss Blandish's home the day the girl vanished.

Fenner dons horn-rimmed spectacles, a cigarette holder, and a persona to match and meets Anna at a bar. He introduces himself as Peabody of the talent agency Spewack, Anderson, and Hart, representing, he says, "anything from Rin-tin-tin to Theda Bara's moustache." He confides that Mr. Spewack caught her act last night at the Paradise, and offers Anna an exclusive contract for the next five years. The only concern the agency has, he maintains, is her link to an underworld figure, Frank Riley, who seems to be connected to the Blandish kidnapping. When did she last see Riley? "The morning before the snatch," she says. Eddie Schultz enters and without much ado, Fenner fells him with a punch and admits to Anna that he's not a talent agent. "Did Lucie send you?" she asks. Fenner suggests that she "take the back alley out of there fast fast fast, or they'll have to scrape you off the wallpaper."

Various blood-splattered events follow rapidly: Fenner encounters Eddie again in the garage hideout. Slim throws in a bomb. Fenner extricates himself from under the dead Eddie and dusts himself off. Chink places a call to secretary Lucie, strikes a deal, and rushes to Miss Blandish's room. He urges her to hurriedly leave with him and return home. But her mind is foggy due to Doc's daily drug injections, so Miss Blandish does not remember where she came from and tells Chink that she'll stay with Slim for the rest of her life. Chink begins to drag her out when Slim enters. The two men face each other, then Slim presses his knife into Chink's belly. Chink falls against the Victrola, which starts to play a cracked record of

Ave Maria. Miss Blandish giggles and falls back onto the bed. Slim lies on top of her, and they laugh quietly, happily, like children, while Chink drips into death.

In the bar, Doc enters and tells Ma Grisson that the girl's gone and Chink's up there dead. Sirens are heard approaching and a loud speaker barks: "Grisson, come out with your hands in the air." Ma gulps a drink and says, "End of the road, Doc." He wants Ma to join him in coming out and yield to the surrounding police officers. She won't. "It's been a real privilege, Ma'am," says Doc and exits. She shoots him in the back. A rattle of gunfire ensues. She staggers back, her dress drenched with blood. Cops dash in. Fenner enters and holds Ma's hands. Her throat filled with blood, she utters a growling laugh, and dies.

Slim and Miss Blandish are lying asleep in a hideout when Lucie enters with gun in hand. "Why didn't you kill her, Slim?" he asks. "I told Ma to get rid of her." We realize that secretly Lucie had been pulling strings in the background and that he was party to Miss Blandish's kidnapping. Lucie coaxes Slim to throttle Miss Blandish but Slim throws his knife at Lucie, who fires. Slim falls. Fenner raises the shutter door and headlights stream into the room. Anna Morgenstern runs to Miss Blandish but stops when she sees Lucie. Anna retreats toward Fenner as Lucie fires. Anna takes the shot—falls. "You louse," she moans and dies.

Lucie orders Fenner to drop his gun. He tells Fenner that he has engaged him in the first place because of the detective's dubious reputation as "the most fiddle-footed, mud-headed, copper-bottomed, aluminum-plated incompetent dick God ever put breath into." Fenner counters that from the very beginning he wondered why Lucie hadn't gone directly to Pinkerton's, instead of coming to "a slob who can't even shoot straight." No doubt Lucie told Ma Grisson where kidnapper Riley would be and convinced Old Man Blandish to pay the ransom money.

Lucie smirks and assures Fenner that he's the last living man the shamus will see. But Miss Blandish has picked up Fenner's gun and shoots Lucie. She tells Fenner that she shot Lucie because he killed Slim. Fenner puts his raincoat over the girl's shoulders and leads her out. Miss Blandish insists that they take a last look at her imprisonment room. As she looks around, Fenner states, "You're young. You're rich. You're beautiful. You'll learn to be happy." However, Miss Blandish insists that Slim is not dead; he is with her. And no, she does not want to return to her father and her old way of life.

Miss Blandish asks Fenner to leave her alone for a minute to contemplate her situation. Fenner goes out. Miss Blandish looks around the room, shivering and quaking. She totters over to the door and locks it. She stands in the middle of the room, desperate and irresolute. Suddenly she feels Fenner's gun in the raincoat pocket. There is a knock at the door;

it is repeated, louder and louder, more urgent each time. Her eyes on the wall crucifix, Miss Blandish turns the gun to her heart and fires. Blackout.[7]

* * *

Though James Hadley Chase followed *No Orchids for Miss Blandish* with numerous thrillers, private detective Dave Fenner appeared in only one other novel, *Twelve Chinks and a Woman* (1940). Chase penned a tough-as-nails sequel to *No Orchids for Miss Blandish*, *The Flesh of the Orchid*, in 1948.

George Orwell, in his article "Raffles and Miss Blandish," numerates the sordid details of James Hadley Chase's novel: "The book contains eight full-dress murders, an unassessable number of casual killings and woundings, an exhumation (with a careful reminder of the stench), the flogging of Miss Blandish, the torture of another woman with red-hot cigarette-ends, a strip-tease act, a third-degree scene of unheard of cruelty and much else of the same kind." Orwell concludes that the theme "is the struggle for power and the triumph of the strong over the weak. The big gangsters wipe out the little ones as mercilessly as a pike gobbling up the little fish in a pond; the police kill off the criminals as cruelly as the angler kills the pike."[8]

"*No Orchids for Miss Blandish* was one of the most successful books of its decade," wrote scholar D. Streatfeild in his study, *Persephone*.

Not only were several million copies of the book itself sold, but a film was made of the story, and Miss Blandish's name became literally a "household word." . . . Miss Blandish, in fact, became one of the great legendary figures that inhabit the communal mind; she belongs almost to the company of Sherlock Holmes, Tarzan, Alice, and Peter Pan. . . . Miss Blandish is a typical mythological figure, a portrayal, that is to say, of a symbolical destiny expressed in terms of human life. Images of this nature are universal in humanity and are to be found in the myths and legends of all peoples at all times. . . . Miss Blandish's enormous popularity can only be accounted for by elements in her story that have some significance apart from the mere superficial handling of it. It would be foolish to deny that much of the popular appeal of the book did lie in the lewd and gruesome episodes in which it abounds. Sex and horrors have always been popular themes, and today the purveying of such matter has become a prosperous industry, yet no figure from the horror fiction, or indeed from any fiction, of her decade found anything like the same universal acceptance as Miss Blandish. *No Orchids* remains a classic, still to be found on the shelves of respectable libraries, and although its popularity has now faded it can confidently be predicted that in due course it will revive.[9]

"Often referred to in the past as 'the king' of thriller writers by both English and Continental critics, Chase propels the reader through complex, intricate plots with gaudy, explosive characters and a fast-moving, hard-boiled style," opines Mary Ann Grochowski in *Twentieth Century*

Crime and Mystery Writers. Grochowski points out that James Hadley Chase also penned a series of novels under the pen name of Raymond Marshall, "sometimes about Brick-Top Corrigan, an unscrupulous private eye, or Don Micklem, a millionaire playboy—the same hard-boiled, explosive, violent, and fast-paced world of the Chase novels."[10]

Renewed appreciation for James Hadley Chase's contributions to suspense literature was expressed by the magazine *Paperback Parade* in its September 2009 issue, when it dedicated its entire issue 73 to the British author and his works—with emphasis on colorful soft-cover reprints that have become much-desired collector's items.

* * *

Robert David MacDonald's stage version of *No Orchids for Miss Blandish* was written for and first performed by the Citizens Theatre in Glasgow, Scotland, on February 17, 1978. The leading roles were played by Pauline Moran (Miss Blandish), Peter Jonfield (Slim Grisson), Sian Thomas (Ma Grisson), David Hayman (Dave Fenner), Garry Cooper (Mr. Lucie), and Julia Blalock (Anna Morgenstern). Pierce Brosnan, soon to be an international movie star, enacted the goon Eddie Schultz. The American premiere of *No Orchids for Miss Blandish* took place at the Williamstown Theatre Festival, Williamstown, Massachusetts, on June 26, 1990, directed by Rosey Hay, featuring Margaret Klenek (Miss Blandish), John Hickey (Slim Gisson), Molly Regan (Ma Grisson), and Steve Ryan (Dave Fenner).

MacDonald was born in Elgin, Invernesshire, Scotland, in 1929. His father was a tobacco baron and his mother was a doctor. He was educated at Wellington School and at Magdalen, Oxford, and was trained as a musician at London's Royal College of Music and the Munich Conservatory. Abandoning music, MacDonald took a job as a translator for UNESCO, where in 1955 he met renowned theatre director Erwin Piscator. He later translated a stage version of Leo Tolstoy's novel *War and Peace* into English for him. The play was produced in New York and London and televised in the United States. Theatre became MacDonald's calling. In 1960 he was appointed director of Her Majesty's, a repertory theatre in Carlisle City, and in 1967 he moved to America as a freelance director, staging plays in Chicago, Houston, Atlanta, and Minneapolis. Four years later he returned to Scotland and joined Giles Havergal in the position of co-artistic director at the Citizens Theatre in Glasgow. During the next three decades, and prior to his retirement in 2003, MacDonald wrote fourteen plays and translated-adapted seventy works from ten different languages for the company, all while also directing some fifty productions and appearing in a score of others.

MacDonald's original plays include *The De Sade Show* (1975), borrowing from the profane novels of the notorious marquis; *Chinchilla* (1977), dealing with the love affair of dancer Vaslav Nijinski and impresario Sergei Diaghilev; and *Webster* (1983), about the backstage world of the Jacobean playwright John Webster. Among MacDonald's adaptations were *Camille* (1974), from the play by Alexandre Dumas fils; *Don Juan* (1980), from the comedy by Carlo Goldoni; *The Seagull*, from the drama by Anton Chekhov, and *Phaedra*, from the tragedy by Jean Racine (both in 1984); *Intermezzo*, from the play by Arthur Schnitzler, and *Philistines*, from the play by Maxim Gorky (both in 1985); *School for Wives*, from the farce by Moliere; *Anna Karenina*, from the novel by Leo Tolstoy; and *Mary Stuart*, from the poetic drama by Friedrich von Schiller (all three in 1987); *Faust* (1988), from the play by Johann Wolfgang von Goethe; *Enrico IV* (1990), from the play by Luigi Pirandello; *Brand* (1991), from the play by Henrik Ibsen; *Miss Julie*, from the one-act by August Strindberg, and *The Representative*, from the play by Rolf Hochhuth (both in 1997); *Death in Venice* (1999), from the novella by Thomas Mann; *The Threepenny Opera*, from the musical by Bertolt Brecht and Kurt Weill (2000).

For British television, MacDonald translated Federico Garcia Lorca's *The House of Bernarda Alba* (1991). His motion picture appearances included feature roles in David Hare's political melodrama *Paris by Night* (1988), the historical drama *The Scarlet and the Black* (1993), and the dark comedy of murder and betrayal, *Shallow Grave* (1994).

MacDonald's translation of Jean Genet's *The Blacks* was produced posthumously in 2007 at Theatre Royal Stratford East, London.

Acting Edition: Oberon Books, Birmingham, England.

Awards and Honors: Robert David MacDonald and Glasgow's Citizens Theatre were awarded in 1982 a special London Critics' Circle Theatre Award.

NOTES

1. Temple Drake, the kidnapped heroine of William Faulkner's sensational 1931 novel *Sanctuary*, returned twenty years later in Faulkner's play *Requiem for a Nun* (1951). The plot, production data, and critics' reception of *Requiem for a Nun* are covered in Amnon Kabatchnik's *Blood on the Stage, 1950–1975*, published by Scarecrow Press in 2011.

2. Life imitated art when in April 1950 twenty-two-year-old actress Nicole Riche, who portrayed Miss Blandish, was handed a note while changing costume for the third act, turned pale, and ran to the stage door. She was seen talking to a tall blond man, and while the doorman's back was turned, she disappeared. The audience got its money back at the box office and an investigation by the police ensued. The only clue was an unsigned note found on the floor of Riche's dressing room: "You have no right to appear in an immoral production." After two days of anxiety, Riche walked into a Paris police station at 4:00

a.m. She said that her kidnapper had turned her loose in the forest and friendly gypsies helped her find her way back. The Pigalle police commissioner was dubious. "Sheer poppycock," he said.

3. Mr. Lucie, the effeminate secretary of John Blandish, does not appear in James Hadley Chase's original novel. Conversely, John Blandish, father of Miss Blandish, does not appear in this stage version and is represented by Mr. Lucie. The reason for the juxtaposition becomes clear at the climax of the play.

4. In the original novel, Freddy McGowan goes to Miss Blandish's aid and is shot to death.

5. Somewhat obscure in this stage adaptation, James Hadley Chase's novel openly states that though Slim Grisson takes a fancy to Miss Blandish, he is sexually impotent. Slim's mother sees in this the chance of curing Slim's malady and instigates—by drugs and torture—the rape of their captive by her son.

6. In the original novel, it is Miss Blandish's father, John Blandish, who meets private eye Dave Fenner and engages him to locate his kidnapped daughter.

7. In the Chase novel, Fenner takes Miss Blandish to a high-rise hotel. When she's left by herself in room 860, she jumps to her death. Fenner and two police officers smash open the door, but too late. From the street below they hear people shouting and the sound of traffic grinding to a halt.

8. George Orwell, *Dickens, Dali and Others* (New York: Reynal & Hitchcock, 1946), 210, 211.

9. D. Streatfeild, *Persephone* (London: Routledge & Kegan Paul, 1959), 23, 25.

10. John M. Reilly, ed., *Twentieth Century Crime and Mystery Writers* (New York: St. Martin's, 1980), 293.

Deathtrap (1978)

Ira Levin (United States, 1929–2007)

Ira Levin's first novel, written at the age of twenty-two, was the psychological thriller *A Kiss Before Dying* (1953), which won the Mystery Writers of America's Edgar Award as best first novel. It was turned into a movie twice (1956, 1991) and has become a suspense classic. Levin's later novels were equally impressive: *Rosemary's Baby*, a horror yarn of modern day Satanism (1967; filmed 1968); the science fiction *This Perfect Day* (1970) and *The Stepford Wives* (1972; filmed 1975, 2004); *The Boys from Brazil*, depicting the hunt for former Nazi Dr. Josef Mengele (1976; filmed 1978); *Sliver*, a murder mystery unfolding in a luxurious Manhattan apartment building (1991; filmed 1993); and *Son of Rosemary*, a sequel to *Rosemary's Baby* (1997).

At twenty-five, Levin adapted Mac Hyman's novel *No Time for Sergeants*, the misadventures of a hillbilly drafted into the United States Air Force, into a TV script, and two years later into his first play, a Broadway comedy that opened on October 20, 1955, ran for 796 performances, and was named best play of its season. Subsequently, Levin penned several thrillers that fared poorly on the New York stage: *Interlock* (1958), *Drat! the Cat!* (1965), and *Dr. Cook's Garden* (1968). *Veronica's Room* (1975) had a moderate run.

In 1978 *Deathtrap* took the town by storm. Not since Anthony Shaffer's *Sleuth* (1970) was there a twisty thriller on Broadway that so intrigued and bamboozled critics and audiences.

The action takes place in Sidney Bruhl's colonial house in Westport, Connecticut. Sliding doors up-stage open onto a foyer in which the audience sees the front door, entrances to the living room and kitchen, and the stairway to the second floor. French doors open out to a shrubbery-covered patio. Down-left is a fieldstone fireplace. The room's furnishings are tastefully chosen antiques: a few chairs, several bookcases, a buffet with liquor decanters, and—centrally located—Sidney's cluttered desk, full of papers, reference books, an electric typewriter, and a telephone. Framed theatrical posters and a collection of guns, handcuffs, maces, swords, and battle-axes are displayed on the walls.

Scene 1 unfolds during an afternoon on a sunny day in October. At rise, Sidney Bruhl ("about fifty, an impressive and well-tended man wearing a cardigan sweater over a turtleneck shirt") is seated thoughtfully at his desk. His wife Myra ("in her forties, slim and self-effacing, in a sweater and skirt") enters quietly with an ice bucket, which she places on the buffet. Sidney relates to her that he has just finished reading the script of a murder play called *Deathtrap*, which came in the morning mail from a former student, Clifford Anderson, for his evaluation. Sidney can't remember Clifford for sure—perhaps he was the "enormously obese" student with "a glandular condition—four hundred pounds."

Thrillers are Sidney's specialty, but his last four plays have failed. He is envious of his student for having written a play that can't miss, will run for years, and no doubt be sold to the movies. "It will be right up there with *Sleuth* and *Dial "M" for Murder*," says Sidney and adds jocularly that he's tempted "to beat the wretch over the head with the mace there, bury him in a four-hundred-pound hole somewhere and send this off under my own name to David Merrick or Hal Prince."

Sidney phones Anderson at his home in nearby Milford. He informs his former student that he's working on a new play himself, about a Dutch clairvoyant named Helga ten Dorp, who happens to live next door in Westport, but he'll drop what he is doing if Anderson will come by this evening to discuss revisions of *Deathtrap*, bringing the original script with him so they can use it in consultation. Anderson agrees to come.

Sidney has aroused his wife's curiosity—would he really commit murder to steal a hit play? Sidney laughs: "I only kill when the moon is full." He toys with an ornate dagger and reassures Myra that "committing murder on paper siphons off the hostile impulses."

As the lights come up in scene 2, Sidney has unlocked the front door from the outside and is leading Clifford Anderson into the foyer. Anderson is in his mid-twenties and free of obvious defects—a handsome young man in jeans and boots, wearing a heavy sweater. He carries a bulging manila envelope. Myra, who has been fretting in the study, hurries to greet them.

Clifford moves about, studies the posters, recognizes the mace that was used in *Murderer's Child*, the dagger from *The Murder Game*, and the axe that chopped heads in *For the Kill*. As they get comfortable, Clifford relates that he became enthralled with thrillers after seeing his first play, Sidney Bruhl's *Gunpoint*. Sidney confides that he became hooked when attending *Angel Street*. Clifford unfastens his envelope and submits the original manuscript of *Deathtrap* to Sidney. There are no carbon copies, he says. Myra is seated in a corner chair, needlework in her lap, sipping a glass of wine. She soon comes up with the suggestion that the two men collaborate on *Deathtrap*—"Do for Mr. Anderson—what George S. Kaufman did for you."

Clifford says that he'll think about the offer but would still like to get a second opinion. He fits the two copies of his manuscript into the envelope. Sidney declares that he's working on another play, based on the life of famed magician Harry Houdini. Myra becomes concerned when Sidney tosses a pair of antique handcuffs to Clifford and asks him to lock the handcuffs onto his wrists for a demonstration. Myra winces when Clifford, impressed, handcuffs himself. Sidney instructs him to turn his wrists and pull. Clifford follows the direction but remains handcuffed. He makes several more attempts—in vain. Sidney pretends to look for a key by rummaging about the desktop and opening drawers. He then crosses to the wall and touches various weapons. He plucks a garrote and suddenly whips it around Clifford's throat, pulling at its two handles. Myra screams, "Oh—God! My God!" but Sidney, grimly determined, strains at the garrote handles.

Myra turns away, moaning, as blood trickles down Clifford's wire-bound throat. Pop-eyed, the young man falls forward by the fireplace. Sidney kneels, unlocks and removes the handcuffs, wipes them with a handkerchief, and replaces them on the wall. He crouches again and unwinds the garrote from Clifford's throat, wipes the garrote, and returns it to its place. He then walks to the desk, opens the manuscripts, tears out the first page of each, throws the torn pages into the fireplace and sets them afire.

Sidney then turns the ends of the hearthrug over Clifford's body, tells the anguished Myra to help him, and they both lift the rug-wrapped Clifford. Together, they heft him up between them and carry him toward the French doors as the lights fade to darkness.

When the lights fade up on scene 3, Myra is sitting with an empty brandy glass in her hand, lost in thought. Sidney enters through the French doors, wipes his shoes, brushes dirt from his trouser legs, closes the doors, and pulls the draperies over them. "In a month or so, if we haven't been arrested, I want you to leave," says a tearful Myra. The doorbell chimes. Composing himself, Sidney opens the door. It is Helga ten Dorp, their neighbor—"a stocky strong-jawed Teutonic woman in her early fifties." She introduces herself as a "psychic" and seems to be in the throes of considerable distress. She apologizes for disturbing them so late at night and explains that she felt "pain" emanating from the Bruhl home.

Helga is taken aback by the sight of the weapons. Sidney explains, "They're antiques, and souvenirs from plays." Helga walks around and mutters, "Is danger here. Much danger." She touches Myra's cheek, says,

"Be careful" and goes out the front door. Sidney takes Myra in his arms and kisses her on the lips. He suggests that they turn in, switches off the desk lamp, and crosses to bolt the French doors when Clifford, covered with dirt, comes through the draperies and seizes his hand. Myra cowers, paralyzed with terror. Clifford forces Sidney to the desk and down onto it. He beats and smashes Sidney's head, each blow audible, until Sidney lies still. Clifford turns and advances on Myra, who gasps, clutches her chest, and hangs frozen over a chair arm for a moment. Then her eyes glaze and she slips down slowly to the floor. Clifford crouches, checks her partly concealed body, holding her wrist, touching her throat. He stands up and says, "She's dead. I'm positive."

Sidney begins to stir and gets up from the desk. Rubbing himself and straightening his jacket, he comes and stands by Clifford. They look down at Myra. Clifford takes out a handkerchief and wipes dirt from his face and fake blood from his neck. "I've been telling people for days that Myra was under the weather," says Sidney. "Not that any supporting evidence is needed, really." He picks up the *Deathtrap* manuscripts, throws them in the fireplace, and strikes a match. He then gives car keys to Clifford to get his things and dials a phone. With suitable throb, he leaves a message for the family doctor: "It's urgent. My wife's had a heart attack."

Clifford returns with two garment bags, a large plaid suitcase, and a tennis racket. The phone rings. Sidney picks it up, holds it for a moment while he gets into the right frame of mind, and with the grief of a bereaved husband tells the doctor, "I gave her mouth-to-mouth resuscitation for ten or fifteen minutes but—it's no use." The curtain falls.

In act 2, scene 1, the draperies are open to bright morning sunlight. Clifford is typing rapidly on an old Smith-Corona while Sidney is lolling in his chair over a blank sheet of paper. Porter Milgrim, a middle-aged attorney, arrives on the scene and Sidney introduces him to his secretary, Clifford Anderson. Milgrim takes several documents from his briefcase and informs Sidney of the disappointing figure of $22,000 left him in Myra's will. Upon the lawyer's departure, a quarrel erupts between Sidney and Clifford when the former discovers that his young lover is working on a play, *Deathtrap*, "A Thriller in Two Acts," in which the circumstances of Myra's death are recaptured. Clifford convinces Sidney to collaborate with him on the play: "Let people talk; we'll blush all the way to the bank."

On a stormy night punctuated by thunder and lightning, Helga ten Dorp rings the doorbell and asks for candles. She corners Sidney, warns him of the "young man in boots" and urges Sidney to send Clifford away immediately. Upon her departure, Sidney goes to the fireplace and takes a pistol from over the mantel, carefully resetting the safety catch. The storm grows in intensity as Sidney faces Clifford and pulls the trigger.

Clifford smirks and tells Sidney that he had anticipated the turn of events and exchanged the bullets with blanks. Clifford snatches a revolver from the wall and orders Sidney to cuff himself through the arm of a chair. He tucks his gun in his belt, reaches into Sidney's jacket, takes bills from a wallet, and heads up the stairs to pack. Sidney shucks off the cuffs, rises, takes a small armed crossbow from the wall, and ratcheting it, hurries to the foyer. He aims the bow upstairs, says, "Cliff, those were Houdini's," and fires an arrow. Clifford falls, part of him coming into view.

Sidney picks up the gun Clifford used and puts it in its place. He also returns the crossbow and the handcuffs, putting them where they belong. He drags Clifford's body down the stairs and into the study, and places an axe next to it. He then goes to the telephone and dials Operator. He asks for the police department and utters, "My name is Bruhl. I live out on Rabbit Hill Road. I just killed my secretary. He was coming at me with an axe. . . . I shot him with a medieval crossbow. . . . His name was Cli—" A hand clutches Sidney's throat and pulls him backward. Clifford comes up from behind and stabs Sidney repeatedly with the crossbow bolt. He finally stops stabbing, hauls himself erect, glassy eyed, the bolt in hand, his chest bloody, and crumples to the floor. Sidney, his hands to his own bloody chest, gasps, twitches, and dies. Loud thunder, vivid lightning, and blackout.

In a short, perhaps unnecessary last scene, the psychic ten Dorp goes through a trance and conjures the happenings that led to the double death of Sidney Bruhl and Clifford Anderson. Ten Dorp and lawyer Milgrim decide to utilize the event in a co-written new thriller, *Deathtrap*; they'll share the proceeds equally.

* * *

Deathtrap premiered at Broadway's Music Box Theatre on February 26, 1978, featuring a sterling cast: John Wood (Sidney Bruhl), Marian Seldes (Myra Bruhl), and Victor Garber (Clifford Anderson). Robert Moore directed and William Ritman designed the scenery. The critics were decidedly divided. Clive Barnes found *Deathtrap* "a most agreeable thriller—handsomely funny, totally undemanding, often, thrill-gaspingly surprising."[1] Howard Kissel lauded "an absolutely ingenious comedy-thriller . . . an extraordinary polished piece of craftsmanship."[2] John Beaufort opined that "Mr. Levin has a fiendishly clever way of mixing chills with laughter, clues and climaxes . . . the author spins out his well-made plot with infectious relish."[3]

On the other hand, Richard Eder complained that "after the initial scene or two, Mr. Levin has simply written the surprises. They grow less and less surprising, and their startlement ebbs. Too many intellectual pratfalls too close together and we lie there and refuse to get up."

Eder also objected to the "unpleasant vivid quality to the murders or the feigned murders. The garroting, bludgeoning, stabbing, shooting, and crossbow killing are staged too fleshily for what can only, by its nature, be a play of wit."[4] Douglas Watt scoffed at "a trashy Ira Levin thriller" that the playwright "didn't really know how to finish. A better ending might have found the author handcuffed to his plot."[5] Edwin Wilson pointed out that *Deathtrap* "has more twists and turns than a slalom run on a ski slope" but believed that "the chief flaw in the play is a lack of human feeling among the characters. . . . In *Deathtrap* there is so much emphasis on reversals that there is little time to get to know the characters well enough to care about them."[6]

The entire pool of reviewers expressed admiration for John Wood in the role of Sidney Bruhl, showering him with such plaudits as "John Wood is delicious," "It's really a delight watching him do anything," and "This is fantastic virtuoso acting." Bob Lape said, "John Wood, whose Broadway appearances are nothing short of electrifying, is a total delight."[7]

Despite the mixed reception by the press, *Deathtrap* had a whopping run of 1793 performances. The Barter Theatre of Abingdon, Virginia presented the play on August 5, 1981 for twenty-three performances; the Studio Arena Theatre in Buffalo, New York mounted *Deathtrap* later that year, on December 4, 1981, for thirty-two showings. London's Noel Coward Theatre revived the play in September 2010, directed by Matthew Warchus, featuring Simon Russell Beale (Sidney Bruhl), Jonathan Groff (Clifford Anderson), Claire Skinner (Myra Bruhl), and Estelle Parsons (Helga ten Dorp). Davidson-Valentini Theatre of Hollywood, California produced *Deathtrap* in April 2012, directed by Ken Sawyer, for a one-month run.

Scripted by Jay Press Allen and directed by Sidney Lumet,[8] *Deathtrap* was transferred to the screen in 1982, featuring Michael Caine (Sidney Bruhl), Christopher Reeve (Clifford Anderson), Dyan Cannon (Myra Bruhl), Irene Worth (Helga ten Dorp), and Henry Jones (Porter Milgrim).

* * *

Born in New York City in 1929, Ira Levin was educated at Drake University in Des Moines, Iowa and at New York University, earning his degree in philosophy and English in 1950. That same year, he began to write for television, contributing scripts to NBC's *Clock* and *Lights Out* series, and later to ABC's *U.S. Steel Hour*. He served with the U.S. Army Signal Corps from 1953 to 1955, penning training films, and then settled down to a writing career.

In addition to the blockbuster *No Time for Sergeants*, Levin penned another comedy for Broadway, *Critic's Choice* (1960), in which Henry Fonda starred as a theatre critic, Parker Ballantine, whose wife writes an awful play and he must decide whether to review it. *Critic's Choice* ran at the Ethel Barrymore Theatre for 189 performances and was made into a film in 1963 with Bob Hope and Lucille Ball.

Levin had several suspense-themed plays produced in New York, but none achieved the success of *Deathtrap*. *Interlock*, billed as "a psychological melodrama," is the story of a wily, wealthy New York widow confined to a wheelchair following a mysterious boat accident that killed her husband. The widow, Jeanette Price, has engaged a German refugee, Hilde Hahn, to be her companion but is now attempting to steal Hilde's fiancé, Paul Schildger, by guile and trickery, eventually blaming Hilde for misplacing a diamond bracelet and using the incident as an excuse for firing her. The girl pleads with Paul to leave with her. Instead, Paul succumbs to the temptation of permanent luxury and remains behind.

Interlock opened at the ANTA Theatre on February 6, 1958, garnering positive reviews for the actors—Celeste Holm (Mrs. Price), Maximilian Schell (Paul Schildger), Rosemary Harris (Hilde Hahn)—but negative ones for the play. "A near-miss," wrote Walter Kerr.[9] "Easy to forget," sighed Robert Coleman.[10] "The evening has been ruined by a devil's brew of dullness, obviousness, foolishness and sheer clumsiness," sniffed Richard Watts Jr.[11] *Interlock* ran for only four performances.

Taking place in an Army post in a New England State, *General Seeger* begins with preparations for a celebration dedicated to a young first lieutenant, William J. Seeger Junior, who was killed while saving two recruits from an exploding hand grenade. The lieutenant's father, General William J. Seeger, is proud of his heroic son. The general made sure that the memorial would be a full-scale pomp-and-ceremony event. However, the lieutenant's widow, Helena, arrives on the scene and reveals that her late husband was not a hero but had killed himself to escape the army. She blames his demise on his domineering father, the general, who perpetually dictated every step for his son. Under Helena's relentless resolve to expose the truth, the general wilts, probes the circumstances of his son's death, and calls off the dedication. His decision, which goes against the will of his superiors, means the destruction of a lifetime career, but with it, a spiritual redemption.

General Seeger premiered at the Lyceum Theatre on February 28, 1962, staged by George C. Scott who also played the title role, and lasted but three performances.

Levin wrote the book and lyrics of *Drat! The Cat!* (Milton Schafer composed the music)—a musical spoof unfolding in late-nineteenth-century Manhattan, centering on a female cat burglar with a yen for precious stones and the bumbling rookie police officer who falls in love with her. The duo croon their admiration for "the marvelously keen new detective" and the doctor "who's his foil" in a number dedicated to Sherlock Holmes and Dr. Watson. High points include an elaborate ballet danced on the waterfront, depicting the theft of a jewel-encrusted Japanese idol; a costume ball that turns into bedlam upon the disappearance of a forty-three-carat diamond worn by a society dowager; and a scene taking place in a basement where the rookie finds himself chained to a post, is threatened by the masked Cat, but insists on fulfilling his sworn duty.

Directed and choreographed by Joe Layton and designed by David Hays, *Drat! The Cat!* opened at the Martin Beck Theatre on October 10, 1965, starring Elliott Gould as police detective Bob Purely and Lesley Ann Warren as socialite Alice Van Guilder, alias The Cat. The critical reception was mixed. John McClain declared that he "had a good time,"[12] Walter Kerr lauded Joe Layton "who has handled the choreographic side of his duties with considerable relish,"[13] and John Chapman called David Hays's scenery "the funniest part of the show. . . . It revolves, it sinks, it pops up and it flitters around town from a masquerade ball to a pier to a spooky forest near Yonkers."[14]

The naysayers included Norman Nadel, who complained of a "sometimes faltering slapstick script"[15] and Richard Watts Jr., who found the endeavor "resolutely un-funny" and summed up his review, "All in all, I can't say that I found *Drat* humorous, likeable or enlivening."[16]

The critics were unanimous in praising Lesley Ann Warren, calling her "charming," "entrancing," "a real comer with a magnificent figure," and "an athletic and well-formed maiden of talent." One enamored reviewer, John Chapman, said, "I just wish I could catch up with Lesley Ann Warren, but my wife probably wouldn't turn me loose."[17] Howard Taubman dedicated the lion's share of his review to the actress, rhapsodizing "a pretty, lissome girl with eyes brighter than any polished buttons. . . . The Cat is a kitten. In her skintight black costume, with its front panel of pink, its trim of black fur and long, black tail, this girl is as mischievously sinuous a feline as you're likely to encounter anywhere on Broadway."[18] Decorative and multi-talented, Warren was not enough of a lure; she mewed through *Drat! The Cat!* for only eight performances.

The protagonist of *Dr. Cook's Garden* is young doctor Jim Tennyson who, upon the completion of his internship, returns to the Vermont village of Greenfield Center—described as "the healthiest, happiest town in the world"—and discovers the secret of the local veteran physician: Dr. Leonard Cook has poisoned thirty people he deemed undesirable in order to maintain the purity of his community. In a tense climax, Dr. Cook attempts to poison Tennyson with sodium cyanide but in the nick of time succumbs to a fatal heart attack.

Directed by the playwright and designed by David Hays, *Dr. Cook's Garden* premiered at the Belasco Theatre on September 25, 1967, featuring Keir Dullea as Dr. Tennyson and Burl Ives as Dr. Cook. The play was savaged by the entire cadre of morning-after critics. John Chapman opined that Ira Levin "seems to have aimed for suspense and goose-pimples, but the first audience found these in short supply."[19] Clive Barnes termed the play "ridiculous,"[20] while Richard Watts Jr. growled at "a disappointing attempt at medical melodrama.[21]" *Dr. Cook's Garden* closed doors after eight performances.

Veronica's Room is a twisty horror play in which twenty-year-old Susan Kerner, a student at Boston University, is lured to a gloomy mansion in a Boston suburb by a shady middle-aged couple, coaxed to impersonate a dead girl, and finds herself entangled in a game of life or death. "It was a melodrama with a difference," wrote Otis L. Guernsey Jr. in *The Best Plays of 1973–1974*, "in that our foolhardy heroine does *not* escape the clutches of the villains, and it turns out that their deeds are motivated by a variety of dark perversions. . . . The old couple, it turns out, are an incestuous brother and sister who have produced a necrophiliac offspring upon whom they dote, in an atmosphere so noxious that murder seems almost a cleansing act. . . . *Veronica's Room* was a raw, red helping of evil served up for the pure flavor of it."[22]

Veronica's Room opened at the Music Box Theatre on October 25, 1973, directed by Ellis Rabb and designed by Douglas W. Schmidt. Arthur Kennedy and Eileen Heckart played the heavies, with Regina Baff as their victim. "The play is meaty, suspenseful, and brilliantly acted," cheered critic Geoffrey Holder.[23] "Engrossing . . . well executed," agreed Leonard Harris.[24] But other reviewers were unhappy: "A murky old thriller-mystery-horror piece," sniffed Kevin Sanders.[25] "*Veronica's Room* poses a puzzle in the first act and tries to resolve it with three or four new puzzles in the second act. Result: frustration. . . . This is a jigsaw puzzle with too many pieces," frowned T. E. Kalem.[26] "It is laughably mechanical and as embarrassing as a sunken-eyed, foul-breathed English professor confiding his sado-masochistic dreams in the college cafeteria," scowled Jack Kroll.[27]

Veronica's Room ran for seventy-five showings. The play was revived at off-Broadway's Provincetown Playhouse on March 8, 1981, directed by Arthur Savage, running for ninety-seven performances. In England, Adrian Reynolds staged *Veronica's Room* at the Haymarket Theatre in Basingstoke, opening on January 6, 1994, winning kudos from the critic of the *Guardian* as "a creepy production" that "has a good atmospheric set and strong performances,"[28] and the reviewer of the *Financial Times* who wrote, "It is clever, knotty, scary and well worth seeing."[29] An unorthodox choice, *Veronica's Room* was produced by Israel's Habimah National Theatre at its experimental basement auditorium in 1997, translated into Hebrew, and directed by Avi Malka. The play ran an hour and fifteen minutes without intermission, and was characterized by an overuse of musical background to emphasize changes in mood, exemplifying a consistent fallacy in the Israeli theatre of that time.

In the comedy *Break a Leg*, the producer, playwright, and cast of a European theatre concoct schemes to get rid of a cynical, devastating, and hated drama reviewer. Should they find the means to blackmail him, a cause to humiliate him, or a reason to exile him? Or should they simply push him off the roof of a tall building?

Directed by Charles Nelson Reilly and designed by Peter Larkin, *Break a Leg* opened at the Palace Theatre on April 29, 1979 and closed that evening. The casting of Jack Weston as the producer, René Auberjonois as the critic and Julie Harris as an unemployed actress did not save a production lambasted by real-life New York critics, who called it "backstage claptrap," deemed it "beyond repair," and found it "about as funny as a broken leg."

Reminiscent of Paddy Chayefsky's *The Tenth Man*, Levin's *Cantorial* deals with a Jewish mystical theme. The plot revolves around young Yuppie lovers who move into a former synagogue on the Lower East Side of Manhattan and are soon haunted by the eerie voice of a long-dead cantor, raised in prayerful song. At first they try to exorcise the ghost but gradually it dominates their lives and moves them to investigate their roots.

Cantorial was first presented in New York City at the Jewish Repertory Theatre on October 27, 1988, staged by Charles Maryann. On February 14, 1989 the production moved to off-Broadway's Lamb's Theatre for a run of more than 120 performances. The Forum Theatre Group of Metuchen, New Jersey presented *Cantorial* on October 27, 1991 for six showings.

Based on an unproduced play by Levin, in 2003 CBS-TV presented *Footsteps*, in which Candice Bergen appeared as Daisy Lowendahl, a best-selling novelist who is struggling to recover from a nervous breakdown and decides to confront her fears by spending a night alone in her isolated beach house. "The film's real joy is Bergen," wrote the *New York Times*. "Convincingly switching from weepy victim to a resourceful heroine, she makes Daisy a woman for whom you can root, rather than just a pawn on a thriller chessboard. Those are footsteps to follow."[30]

Ira Levin died in Manhattan from a heart attack on November 12, 2007, at the age of seventy-eight.

Acting Edition: Dramatists Play Service.

Awards and Honors: *Deathtrap* was a top ten selection in *The Best Plays of 1977–1978*. It received a Tony Award nomination for Best Play in 1978 and won the 1980 Mystery Writers of America's Edgar Award as Best Play. Ira Levin's novel, *A Kiss before Dying*, won the 1954 Mystery Writers of America's Edgar for Best First Novel. His novel *This Perfect Day* garnered the 1992 Prometheus Hall of Fame Award. In 1997, Levin received the Bram Stoker Award for lifetime achievement from the Horror Writers Association.

NOTES

1. *New York Post,* February 27, 1978.
2. *Women's Wear Daily,* February 27, 1978.
3. *Christian Science Monitor,* March 1, 1978.
4. *New York Times,* February 27, 1978.
5. *Daily News,* February 27, 1978.
6. *Wall Street Journal,* March 2, 1978.
7. *WABC-TV7,* February 26, 1978.
8. Sidney Lumet was born in 1924 in Philadelphia, Pennsylvania to parents who were veterans of the Yiddish stage. He made his professional debut at the Yiddish Art Theatre at age five. As a child, he appeared in Broadway productions, notably in Sidney Kingsley's *Dead End* and Kurt Weill's *The Eternal Road,* both produced in 1935. During World War II he was stationed in India and Burma. After the war, he became involved with the Actor's Studio and formed his own off-Broadway theatre. In 1951 he began writing and directing for television, contributing episodes to *Crime Photographer, Danger,* and *You Are There.* Early directorial assignments included *Don Quixote* for *CBS Television Workshop* (1952) and *The Philadelphia Story, The Show-Off,* and *Stage Door* for *The Best of Broadway* (1954–1955). He went on to direct episodes for *The Elgin Hour, Frontier, The United States Steel Hour, The Alcoa Hour, Studio One,* and *Hallmark Hall of Fame.* For *Omnibus* he directed *School for Wives;* for *Kraft Theatre, All the King's Men;* for *The Dupont Show of the Month, The Count of Monte Cristo;* for *Sunday Showcase, The Sacco-Vanzetti Story;* for *Play of the Week, The Dybbuk, Rashomon,* and *The Iceman Cometh.* In 1957, Lumet directed his first feature film, the jury-room drama *12 Angry Men,* launching a long, prolific, and highly regarded motion picture career. Among his notable movies are *The Fugitive Kind* (1960), based on the Tennessee Williams play *Orpheus Descending; A View from the Bridge* (1961), from the play by Arthur Miller; *Long Day's Journey into Night* (1962), from the Eugene O'Neill drama; *The Pawnbroker* (1964); *The Hill* (1965); *The Group* (1966); *Network* (1976); *The Sea Gull* (1968), inspired by Anton Chekhov's play; *The Verdict* (1982); and *Daniel* (1983), an adaptation of E. L. Doctorow's novel *The Book of Daniel.* Many of Lumet's films were riddled with crime, intrigue, and suspense elements, including *Fail-Safe* (1964), *The Deadly Affair* (1967), *The Anderson Tapes* (1971), *Child's Play* (1972), *Serpico* (1973), *The Offence* (1973), *Murder on the Orient Express* (1974), *Equus* (1977), *Dog Day Afternoon* (1975), *Prince of the City* (1981), *The Morning After* (1986), *Running on Empty* (1988), *Family Business* (1989), *Q & A* (1990), *A Stranger among Us* (1992), *Guilty as Sin* (1993), *Night Falls on Manhattan* (1996), *Gloria* (1999), *Find Me Guilty* (2006), and *Before the Devil Knows You're Dead* (2007).
9. *New York Herald Tribune,* February 7, 1958.
10. *Daily Mirror,* February 7, 1958.
11. *New York Post,* February 7, 1958.
12. *New York Journal-American,* October 11, 1965.
13. *New York Herald Tribune,* October 11, 1965.
14. *Daily News,* October 11, 1965.
15. *New York World-Telegram,* October 11, 1965.
16. *New York Post,* October 11, 1965.

17. *Daily News*, October 11, 1965.

18. *New York Times*, October 11, 1965.

19. *Daily News*, September 26, 1967.

20. *New York Times*, September 26, 1967.

21. *New York Post*, September 26, 1967.

22. Otis L. Guernsey Jr., ed., *The Best Plays of 1973–1974* (New York: Dodd, Mead, 1974), 17.

23. *NBC-TV4*, October 27, 1973.

24. *WCBS-TV2*, October 25, 1973.

25. *WABC-TV7*, October 25, 1973.

26. *Time*, November 12, 1973.

27. *Newsweek*, November 5, 1973.

28. *Guardian*, January 8, 1994.

29. *Financial Times*, January 8, 1994.

30. *New York Times*, October 10, 2003.

Buried Child (1978)

Sam Shepard (United States, 1943–)

Buried Child, Sam Shepard's Pulitzer Prize–winning drama, "combines the formulas of the prodigal son and a murder mystery to create a meta-realistic style that almost seamlessly melds the surreal and real," writes Laura J. Graham in *Shepard in an Hour*.[1]

The brew of realistic action and symbolic implications unfolds in a dilapidated central Illinois farmhouse, inhabited by a bizarre, dysfunctional family. The interior includes an old wooden staircase, frayed carpets, a rickety green sofa, and a large, old-fashioned television set. Around the house are dark elm trees.

It is raining outside when the curtain rises on Dodge, a once successful farmer who is now a grizzled, old, sickly alcoholic. He sits on the flea-ridden couch, facing the TV, slides his hand under the cushion, pulls out a bottle of whiskey, takes a long swig, and puts the bottle back in its hiding place. He then pulls a pack of cigarettes from his sweater, lights one, and goes through a violent, spasmodic coughing attack. From upstairs comes the nagging, acid voice of Dodge's wife, Halie, as she dresses for an assignation with the preacher, Father Dewis.

Tilden, their oldest son, who sports a butch haircut and proves to be a burnt-out simpleton, enters with ears of corn in his arms. He dumps the corn on Dodge's lap, and the old man pushes all the corn off onto the floor. Tilden starts picking up the corn one ear at a time, throwing the husks into the center of the room and dropping the ears into a pail. "Corn functions as a major symbol: Native American and Aztec myth frequently associate corn with primal generative power and renewal and rebirth," writes Graham.[2]

Halie, about sixty-five with pure white hair, descends the stairs dressed completely in black, pulling on elbow-length black gloves. She goes into a tirade about her favorite dead son, Ansel, who could have become "a genuine hero" and "a great basketball player." She rebukes Dodge for "sitting here day and night, festering away! Decomposing!" and warns him that her son Bradley will take over the household. Dodge retorts "He's not my flesh and blood! My flesh and blood's buried in the back yard!" This obscure statement refers to the play's title and is a signpost of a secretive, horrible event that is sure to surface later.

Dodge coughs violently and clutches his chest. He swallows some pills. Tilden helps him to lie down on the sofa, covers him with a blanket, and switches off the television. Dodge falls asleep. Tilden reaches carefully under the cushion and pulls out the bottle of booze. He takes a long swig and sticks the bottle in his hip pocket. He then looks around at the husks on the floor and spreads them over the entire length of Dodge's body, symbolically indicating that the family's patriarch has been disempowered by his wife and children.

Tilden exits quietly. The figure of Bradley appears on the porch. He holds a wet newspaper over his head as protection from the rain. He struggles with the doorknob and pushes himself through the screen door. Bradley is a big man. His left leg is wooden, having been amputated above the knee after a chainsaw accident. He is about five years younger than Tilden.

Bradley looks at Dodge's sleeping face and shakes his head in disgust. He pulls out a pair of electric hair clippers from his pocket. He jabs his false leg and goes down on one knee. He violently knocks away some of the cornhusks and begins to cut Dodge's hair, metaphorically castrating him, as the lights dim slowly to black.

Act 2 unfolds at night. The rain is still coming down and Dodge is still asleep on the sofa. His hair is cut extremely short and in places his scalp is cut and bleeding. All the cornhusks have been cleared away. Shelly—nineteen, black-haired, very beautiful—and Vince—Tilden's son, about twenty-two—enter the porch. Vince carries a black saxophone case. As they walk into the room, we learn that Vince hasn't seen his family for more than six years. Dodge jerks up to a sitting position and glares at them. Shelly explains that she's Vince's girlfriend, and says that they're on their way to New Mexico. Dodge does not seem to recognize his grandson. He searches for his bottle under the pillow, knocks over the nightstand, and starts to rip the stuffing out of the sofa. Shelly wants to leave, but Vince stops her.

Tilden walks in from the courtyard, just as he did before; this time his arms are full of carrots. He sees the newcomers and stands still. Vince calls at him, "Dad," but Tilden drops the carrots into Shelly's arms and strides off. Dodge whines, "They'll steal your bottle! They'll cut your hair! They'll murder your children!" Tilden returns with a pail, milking stool, and knife. He sets the stool center stage and looks at Shelly. She takes the knife from him, sits, and begins to scrape the carrots.

Dodge keeps complaining about his missing bottle and Vince says that he'll get one for him at the town's liquor store. Shelly is concerned about staying in the house without him, but Vince assures her, "I'll come right back."

Dodge lights a cigarette, coughs, and stares at the TV. Shelly continues to scrape the carrots and Tilden moves closer to her. He whispers in her ear, "We had a baby. . . . Little baby. . . . Dodge killed it. . . . Dodge drowned it. . . . Nobody could find it. Just disappeared. Cops looked for it. Neighbors. Nobody could find it."

Dodge cautions Tilden not to tell the stranger anything, but Tilden pursues his narrative by telling Shelly that rumors were flying: "Kidnap. Murder. Accident," but finally "everybody just gave up." Shelly attempts to rise but Tilden firmly pushes her back, whispering that Dodge is the only one who knows where the child is buried. "Wouldn't even tell why he did it," says Tilden. "One night he just did it."

Shelly is trembling. The sound of Bradley's leg squeaking is heard off left. Bradley appears behind the screen door, takes off his raincoat and shakes it out. He stares at Shelly, and Tilden explains that she and Vince are driving to New Mexico. Bradley limps over to Shelly while Tilden suddenly bolts and runs off. Bradley stares at Shelly and asks her to open her lips wide. He forces his fingers into Shelly's mouth, symbolically raping her, as the lights black out.

Act 3 takes place in the morning. The carrots, pail, and stool have been cleared away. Bradley is sound asleep on the sofa under Dodge's blanket. His wooden leg is leaning against the couch. The shoe is still on it. Dodge is sitting on the floor, propped up against the television. Shelly's rabbit fur coat covers his chest and shoulders. Shelly enters from the kitchen and crosses toward Dodge, balancing a steaming cup of broth on a saucer. Halie appears on the porch, accompanied by Father Dewis, a distinguished-looking Protestant priest dressed in a traditional black suit and white clerical collar. Both Halie and Dewis are slightly drunk and giddy. Their body language intimates that they are lovers who apparently spent the night together. The adulterous Father Dewis symbolizes the deterioration of ethics in America even by the so-called guardians of society's morals.

Halie and Father Dewis enter the room laughing but stop in their tracks when they see Shelly. Halie looks at Dodge asleep on the floor and at Bradley stretched on the sofa. With a shriek of embarrassment, she covers the wooden leg with Dodge's coat. She then pulls out a silver flask from the priest's vest pocket and takes a sip. "I came here with your grandson for a little visit," says Shelly, "a little innocent friendly visit." Halie ignores Shelly, who suddenly rises, grabs Bradley's wooden leg, clutches it to her chest, and furiously emotes, "I really believed when I walked through that door that the people who lived here would turn out to be the same people in my imagination. But I don't recognize any of you. Not one." She moves around, staring at each of them. "I know you've got a secret," she says, and threatens to call the police.

Dodge complains that Shelly behaves "like a detective or something," then changes demeanor and agrees to tell Shelly everything. Halie threatens Dodge that if he "tells this thing," he'll be "just as good as dead" to her. Bradley cries, "We made a pact! . . . You can't break that now!" But Dodge, gaining momentary power over his wife and sons, relentlessly reveals to Shelly that all was well with the family and the farm until Halie got pregnant again "Outa' the middle of nowhere. . . . In fact, we hadn't been sleepin' in the same bed for about six years." It turned out that the father of the baby boy was Tilden, so Halie became both mother and grandmother. "We couldn't let a thing like that continue," says Dodge. He drowned the baby—"Just like the runt of a litter"—and buried him in the courtyard. The act of incest and the resultant murder are indicative of a breakdown in the morality of the typical American family.

Suddenly Vince comes crashing onto the porch floor and lands on his stomach in a drunken stupor. He mumbles that upon leaving the house he attempted to drive away, but discovered that he is inescapably attached to his roots. Vince hauls himself slowly to his feet. He has a paper shopping bag full of empty booze bottles. He takes them out one at a time and smashes them at the opposite end of the porch. Shelly sets down the wooden leg and picks up Vince's saxophone case and overcoat. She asks Vince to go and get the car—they're going to leave. Vince pulls out a big folding hunting knife and pulls open the blade. He jabs the blade into the screen porch door and starts cutting a hole big enough to climb through. Father Dewis takes Halie by the arm and escorts her up the stairs.

Bradley crawls toward his wooden leg. Vince climbs into the room through the ripped screen, moves the leg, and keeps pushing it with his foot so that it's out of Bradley's reach. Dodge whispers to Vince, "Go ahead, take over the house," and proclaims his last will and testament: The house and its furnishings go to his grandson, Vincent; the tools, including the chain saw and drill press, go to his eldest son, Tilden.

Shelly urges Vince to leave with her immediately, but he mutters, "I just inherited a house. . . . I've gotta carry on the line. I'll see to it that things keep rolling." Shelly sets down the saxophone case and overcoat, says, "Bye Vince," and exits off the porch. Dewis comes down the stairs and hurriedly leaves. Vince crosses to Dodge and realizes that his grandfather is dead. He lies down on the sofa, arms folded behind his head, staring at the ceiling, not unlike Dodge at the beginning of the play.

Halie's voice is heard from above, expressing pleasant surprise at seeing through the window corn, carrots, potatoes, and peas, all blossoming so early in the year—"It's like a paradise out there, Dodge . . . a miracle . . . maybe it was the rain." Richard Gilman, in his introduction to *Sam Shepard: Seven Plays*, theorizes: "The mysterious field behind the house that everyone knows to be arid nevertheless produces vegetables in abundance. The fantastic field is a metaphor for fecundity, of course, and at the same time works as a hope for future life against the bitter, hidden truth which emerges at the end in the form of the murdered, 'buried' child."[3]

Tilden appears from the courtyard, dripping with mud. In his hands he carries the corpse of a small child. As Halie's voice continues to be heard, Tilden slowly makes his way up the stairs, carrying the dead boy to his mother's room. The lights keep fading as Tilden disappears above, then go to black.

* * *

Buried Child is the middle work in Sam Shepard's trilogy painting the American family as odd and dysfunctional and dealing with the corruption of traditional American values. *Curse of the Starving Class*, 1978, preceded it; *True West*, 1980, followed. *Buried Child* premiered at the Magic Theatre, San Francisco, on June 27, 1978. It was directed by Robert Woodruff with the following cast: Joseph Gistirak (Dodge), Catherine Willis (Halie), Dennis Ludlow (Tilden), William M. Carr (Bradley), Betsy Scott (Shelly), Barry Lane (Vince), and Rj Frank (Father Dewis).

On October 19, 1978, Woodruff staged *Buried Child* in New York at Theatre for the New City with a different cast: Richard Hamilton (Dodge), Jacqueline Brooks (Halie), Tom Noonan (Tilden), Jay O. Sanders (Bradley), Mary McDonnell (Shelly), Christopher McCann (Vince), and Bill Wiley (Father Dewis). The play moved to the Theatre de Lys (now the Lucille Lortel Theatre), where in 1979 it became the first off-off-Broadway play to win the Pulitzer Prize.

In 1995, Gary Sinise directed a somewhat revised version of *Buried Child* at the Steppenwolf Theatre in Chicago. The *Chicago Tribune's* Richard Christian wrote that "the script was transformed and revivified by the electric-shock treatment of director Gary Sinise into a roaring, stomping, wheezing, unfailingly fascinating gallery of American grotesques. . . . The language, the characters, the predominant themes are all there, but juiced up by Sinise's patented brand of stage energy into a bizarre American folk tale that is at once hilarious and horrifying."[4] Ben Brantley of the *New York Times* believed that "*Buried Child* emerges as a bona fide classic: a work that conveys the mystical, cannibalistic pull of family ties even as they unravel."[5]

However, *Variety's* Lewis Lazar was less content. While finding *Buried Child* "crackling with energy" and "grimly funny," the reviewer sniffed at a production that "never fully penetrates the 'stench of sin,' as Shepard puts it, inside the decrepit central Illinois farmhouse where the play's dysfunctional family lives. It's mostly a surface show of acting prowess with too much of a coarse comic edge. . . . Sixteen years after its premiere, *Buried Child* seems less startling than it once did. Shepard settles much of the time for superficially celebrating the kinky bizarreness of his Gothic characters instead of fully developing them or weaving a larger theme from the dark humor."[6]

The Steppenwolf production came to New York's Brooks Atkinson Theatre on April 30, 1996, marking Shepard's Broadway debut. In a gamut of opinions, critic Ben Brantley lauded a "dazzlingly acted production" and a play that "actually appears to have grown more resonant, funnier and far more accessible in the 17 years since it won the Pulitzer Prize,"[7] while Donald Lyons complained that "*Buried Child* drowns its naturalism in a rain of symbolic, mythic, universalizing gimmickry."[8] Linda Winer appreciated "a gleefully brazen production,"[9] but Nancy Franklin sniffed: "At three hours, the play is a long haul."[10]

Buried Child ran for seventy-two performances and was nominated for five Tony Awards, but did not win any.

* * *

Samuel Shepard Rogers VII was born at the army outpost of Fort Sheridan, Illinois, in 1943, during World War II. His father, Samuel Rogers VI, was a member of the Army Air Corps and a bomber pilot, a military service that had a profound influence on young Shepard. In 1955, the family settled in the middle-class California suburb of South Pasadena, and later that year moved to a ramshackle livestock ranch in Duarte, California. The Rogers family proved to be dysfunctional, with a hard-drinking father insisting on military-style discipline. Violent arguments took place between father and son, mostly over money. The specter of his father later became a major factor in Shepard's writings.

After graduating from Duarte High in 1961, Shepard spent a year at Mount Saint Antonio Junior College, majoring in agricultural science. He played the drums for a semiprofessional band, acted in several college plays, and auditioned to join the touring Bishop's Company Repertory Players. When accepted, he used the opportunity to escape home, toured the country, and in 1963, at the age of nineteen, left the troupe to remain in New York. He changed his name to Sam Shepard—to create an identity that would separate him from his family.

Shepard worked at various jobs in Manhattan, including waiting tables at the then-popular nightclub The Village Gate, where he saw some of the best comedians of the era—Woody Allen, Dick Cavett, Richard Pryor—and was exposed to legendary jazz artists. He also met Ralph Cook, founder of off-off-Broadway's Theatre Genesis. In the early 1960s, the off-Broadway movement began to come into its own, with such milestone productions as the enormously popular revival of Bertolt Brecht and Kurt Weill's *The Threepenny Opera*; The Living Theatre's drug drama *The Connection* and the prison drama *The Brig*; Jean Genet's brothel fable *The Balcony* and the anti-racist *The Blacks*; the intimate, long-running musical *The Fantasticks*; the sparkling and entirely hilarious American premiere of Anton Chekhov's *A Country Scandal* (*Platonov*); and Brendan Behan's bittersweet *The Hostage*.

Off-off-Broadway companies, dedicated to experimental, non-commercial works, were emerging. The small theatres were hungry for new plays and, rebelling against the prevailing realism of such playwrights as Eugene O'Neill, Tennessee Williams, and Lillian Hellman, encouraged avant-garde theatrical styles. One-acts by Becket, Ionesco, Pinter, and Albee made a strong impression.

"I was very lucky to have arrived in New York at that time," said Shepard later, "because the whole off-off-Broadway theatre was just starting—like Ellen Stewart with her little café, and Joe Cino, and the Judson Poets' Theatre and all these places. . . . On the Lower East Side there was a special sort of culture developing. . . . It was a very exciting time."[11] In 1964, off-off-Broadway's Theatre Genesis produced a double bill by Shepard, *Cowboys* and *The Rock Garden*. *Cowboys*, staged on a floor covered with sand and gravel, describes two friends rousting around Manhattan. *The Rock Garden* is composed of three monologues delivered by members of the same family who are detached from one another: a sick mother, lying in bed, talks about baking a special sort of cookie; a father talks about his obsession with collecting rocks from different sojourns to the desert; their son talks about orgasm and ends up literally coming all over the place. The last monologue was included in 1969's phenomenally successful revue performed entirely in the nude, *Oh, Calcutta!*[12]

Shepard continued to pen one-act plays, most of which were tinged with autobiographical touches, notably the estrangement between father and son. The plays were staged by such innovative directors as Jacques Levy, Wynn Handman, and Tom O'Horgan. Joseph Chaikin, founder of Open Theatre, had a significant influence on Shepard's work and the two have worked together on various projects. "Hallucination, frenzied music, and the battle between old age and youth, these are the hallmarks of Shepard's generally short plays that brought him a growing reputation and a limited off-off-Broadway audience," wrote theatre scholar Robert Brustein.[13]

Shepard's first three-act play was *Operation Sidewinder*, composed of twelve satirical scenes divided by rock music interludes. The plot hinges around an Air Force computer fought over by a power-mad military, Black revolutionaries, and Indian tribes. Amid controversy, the play opened at Lincoln Center's Vivian Beaumont Theatre on March 12, 1970 and ran for fifty-two performances.

In addition to *Buried Child*, the better known among Shepard's forty-some plays are arguably *The Tooth of Crime*, *True West*, *Fool for Love*, and *A Lie of the Mind*. *The Tooth of Crime*, first performed at the Open Space, London, on July 17, 1972, under the direction of Charles Marowitz, illustrates on a bare stage a confrontation between a veteran rock "king" and his young challenger. *True West*, premiering at San Francisco's Magic Theatre on July 10, 1980, directed by Robert Woodruff, unfolds in a Southern California suburb and relates the clash between two brothers, a drifter and a successful screenwriter. The protagonists of *Fool for Love*, Eddie and May, are former lovers who meet in a cheap motel room in an attempt to reconcile. Along the way, they discover that they share the same father, an alcoholic who led a double life. Shepard himself directed the play for Magic Theatre for an opening on February 8, 1983. It came to New York later that year and was filmed in 1985. Set in the American West, the story of *A Lie of the Mind* alternates between two families connected by the marriage of Jake and Beth. They all struggle for meaning after Jake batters Beth so severely that she is hospitalized with brain damage. Shepard directed the play at the off-Broadway's Promenade Theatre, where it opened on December 5, 1985.

While establishing himself as one of the distinguished playwrights of modern American drama, Sam Shepard also carved a respectable career as a television and motion picture actor. Among his sixty films, notable are *Frances* (1982), in which he portrayed, under the fictional name of Harry York, the first husband of actress Frances Farmer; *The Right Stuff* (1983), wherein he played pilot Chuck Yeager; *Dash and Lilly* (1999), enacting the role of mystery writer Dashiell Hammett; *Hamlet* (2000), playing the ghost of the prince's murdered father; *Black Hawk Down* (2001), appearing as William F. Garrison, the commander of Task Force Ranger; *The Assassination of Jesse James by the Coward Robert Ford* (2007), as Frank James; and *Blackthorn* (2011), in the role of Butch Cassidy. "The character is played by Sam Shepard," wrote the *Los Angeles Times*, "who wears the dust, the boots, the bravado and the rest as if they were designed for him alone."[14]

Acting Edition: Dramatists Play Service.

Awards and Honors: *Buried Child* won the Pulitzer Prize for Drama in 1979 and the play's revival was nominated for a Tony Award in 1996. Sam Shepard's *True West* was nominated for a 1983 Pulitzer Prize, a Drama Desk Award, and a 2000 Tony Award. *Fool for Love* was nominated for a 1984 Pulitzer. *A Lie of the Mind* won the 1986 Drama Desk Award for Outstanding New Play. Shepard won ten Obies (awards given by the *Village Voice* for distinguished achievements off and off-off-Broadway). He was an Academy Award nominee for Best Supporting Actor for 1983's *The Right Stuff*, and wrote the screenplay of *Paris, Texas*, voted Best Film at Cannes in 1984. In October 2011, Shepard was the first recipient of the newly established Ellen Stewart Award, created in honor of the founder of off-Broadway's La MaMa Experimental Theatre Club in New York City.

NOTES

1. Laura J. Graham, *Shepard in an Hour* (Hanover, N.H.: Hour Books, 2010), 19.
2. Graham, *Shepard in an Hour*, 20.
3. *Sam Shepard: Seven Plays* (New York, Bantam, 1981), xxiv.
4. *Chicago Tribune*, October 2, 1995.
5. *New York Times*, October 9, 1995.
6. *Variety*, October 16, 1995.
7. *New York Times*, May 1, 1996.
8. *Wall Street Journal*, May 1, 1996.
9. *Newsday*, May 1, 1996.
10. *New Yorker*, May 20, 1996.
11. Ellen Oumano, *Sam Shepard* (New York: St. Martin's, 1986), 29.
12. The notorious revue *Oh, Calcutta!* was conceived by Kenneth Tynan and performed in the nude; it had contributions by Sam Shepard, Samuel Beckett, Jules Feiffer, John Lennon, and others. It opened at New York's Eden Theatre on June 17, 1969, and transferred to the Belasco Theatre on February 25, 1971, for 1314 performances. *Oh, Calcutta!* was revived at the Edison Theatre on September 24, 1976, for a whopping run of 5959 showings.
13. Robert Brustein, Introduction to *Shepard in an Hour*, by Laura J. Graham (Hanover, N.H.: Hour Books, 2010), vii.
14. *Los Angeles Times*, October 7, 2011.

The Penultimate Problem
of Sherlock Holmes (1978)

John Nassivera (United States, 1950–)

John Nassivera's *The Penultimate Problem of Sherlock Holmes* was first pre-sented by the Dorset Theatre Festival in Dorset, Vermont, on August 17, 1978 under the direction of Jill Charles. When the spectators took their seats, a Paganini violin concerto was being piped into the auditorium. Before the rise of the curtain, Paganini faded into the pensive squawking of Sherlock Holmes's Stradivarius.

At 221B Baker Street, early on the evening of April 13, 1891, Holmes is standing by the window, absently running the bow across the strings to the chagrin of Dr. Watson.

Mrs. Hudson ushers in Inspector Lestrade of Scotland Yard and Mrs. Leonora Piper from Boston. Mrs. Piper is an internationally acclaimed medium, visiting London as a guest of the British Society for Psychical Research. Holmes was asked to verify her authenticity. The world's fore-most consulting detective believes that Leonora Piper is a quack practic-ing "parlor games."

Holmes locks the door and dims the gas lamp. Mrs. Piper begins a sé-ance by slipping to the floor and speaking in a far-off voice. It is the voice of Ellen Watson, the doctor's late wife, assuring him, "I am very happy . . . you must be too."

Another echo is heard: "Does the name Auguste Dupin mean any-thing to you?" Holmes says that he knows of the French detective who some fifty years earlier solved "the so-called *Murders in the Rue Morgue*." Through the alcove drapes, Monsieur Dupin appears, carrying an ebony cane and speaking with a heavy French accent. He introduces himself, "Mesdames, messieurs, enchanté. I am Auguste Dupin, detective extraor-dinaire," and tells Holmes that, alas, he will soon die in the mountains, far from his home on Baker Street. "It is a *fait accompli*. I have reached these conclusions through the application of my Calculus of Probabilities."

Dupin asks Watson to check his heartbeat with a stethoscope. "There seems to be no pulse at all," exclaims Watson. Dupin confides that he has had no pulse since 1845, "the year of the completion of my last and most famous case, known among yourselves as the case of the Purloined Letter." Dupin magically brings forth a flower, which he offers to Mrs. Hudson, then steps off stage through the audience aisle and calls from the rear of the house, "Mr. Holmes, beware of Conan Doyle." Watson is astounded: "My God, Holmes, he walked through that wall!"

Mrs. Piper moans, and Irene Adler emerges through the curtains— "a tall woman, striking for her combination of cold, calculating mystique and her personal beauty." She is *the woman*—the one and only who softened Holmes's heart. Irene warns the Great Detective that "someone is exerting pressure" on his mortal enemy, Professor James Moriarty, to confront him in "a fight to the death." Adler slinks away and Holmes sighs: "She died some months ago, Watson . . . she was the daintiest thing under a bonnet on this planet."

The following morning, Holmes and Watson wonder if Mrs. Piper's machinations were achieved through the power of suggestion under hypnosis. Suddenly, a glass windowpane is shattered and a rock rolls to the floor. As Watson bends to pick it up, an arrow flies over his head and lands in the window alcove. There is a piece of paper around it: "Tomorrow evening at 9:00, Professor Moriarty will call. The game is up, Mr. Holmes, the curtain falls. Sincerely yours, Arthur Conan Doyle."

Professor Moriarty proves to be ascetic looking—"His shoulders rounded from much study. His face protrudes forward and slowly oscillates from side to side in a curiously reptilian manner." With a slight stutter he warns Holmes that it would grieve him "to take any extreme measure . . . you stand in the way not of an individual, but of a mighty organization. You must stand clear, Mr. Holmes, or be trodden underfoot."

"It's been a grand duel," says Holmes. The two antagonists exchange a look of appreciation and raise a toast.

HOLMES: To the Napoleon of Crime.
MORIARTY: To the world's greatest detective.

The next night, as the tower clock rings three times, a tall gentleman enters the Baker Street premises and confronts Holmes: "Your episode with Mrs. Piper has not pleased me, Mr. Holmes. I did not enjoy your performance. You have begun to displease me intensely, therefore, you shall simply come to an end. . . . On May 4, 1891, Mr. Holmes, I shall kill you at Reichenbach Falls. I shall kill you off and have done with you once and for all. . . . The game is up. Mr. Holmes, I am Arthur Conan Doyle."

In the last scene of the play, unfolding three years later, Holmes and Doyle meet again, but this time the detective has the upper hand. "Did you really think that you killed me at Reichenbach Falls?" he chuckles, and recounts that when Moriarty rushed at him on the edge of the precipice, he slipped through the professor's grip with a quick movement of baritsu, the Japanese style of wrestling, and watched as his mortal enemy clawed the air, kicked madly for a few seconds, then fell and struck a rock.

Moriarty enters through the curtains. Both he and Holmes lock the doors and surround Doyle. "What is it you want?" asks the author uneasily.

"It's elementary, Mr. Doyle," says Holmes. "We demand our lives."

Moriarty adds, "You cannot stop us, Doctor. No one can stop us. We shall live. We are immortal now."

Enter Watson, Dupin, Adler, Lestrade, and Mrs. Hudson. Doyle, confused and menaced, zigzags among the characters, but cannot escape and falls to his knees. A shower of loose pages descends from above, surrounding him.

* * *

Two years after its world premiere in Dorset, Vermont, *The Penultimate Problem of Sherlock Holmes* made it to New York City, presented by the Hudson Guild Theatre on May 17, 1980. David Kerry Heefner directed a cast headed by Keith Baxter (Holmes), Curt Dawson (Watson), and Edward Zang (Moriarty).

A Program Note informed the non-Sherlockians in the audience that "on May 4, 1891, Sherlock Holmes and Prof. James Moriarty, after a chase across the continent, met in hand-to-hand combat at Reichenbach Falls, Switzerland. Both men apparently fell to their death. An account of the case was titled *The Final Problem* and appeared in *The Strand* magazine. . . . It was not until April 5, 1894, that Holmes reappeared in London. . . . A description of Holmes' return is to be found in *The Adventure of the Empty House*."

Most press reviews were negative. Mel Gussow sighed, "Unfortunately, the game is up before it is afoot. . . . The final problem is not in the performance, but in the flaccid writing."[1] Marilyn Stasio yawned, "You'll probably be as bored silly as I was . . . the production has a disastrously whimsical tone that comes close to self mockery."[2] Christopher Sharp found the play "an overly literary speculation" and most of the performances "lackluster."[3] Terry Curtis Fox wrote, "The result is not even stale champagne but flat club soda."[4]

Positive appraisals came from Steven Hart, who found that the play "pleasantly blends dialogue, suitable to the master sleuth, and a plot of myriad convolutions"[5] and John Beaufort, who believed that "This adventurous New York premiere is the ultimate Hudson Guild Theatre production of the 1979/80 season."[6] Keith Baxter as Holmes and Edward Zang as Moriarty notched several complimentary endorsements.

The Penultimate Problem of Sherlock Holmes was presented by the Off-stage Company of San Antonio, Texas, in 1984, and by the Pacific Spindrift Players, Pacifica, California, in 1988.

* * *

Playwright John Nassivera was born in Glens Falls, New York, in 1950. A graduate of Boston University, Columbia University, and McGill University where he received his PhD in Comparative Literature, Nassivera has been teaching courses in English, drama, playwriting, and speech communication at Green Mountain College, Poultney, Vermont, since 1997. Prior to his tenure at GMC, Nassivera lived in Manhattan, where he was literary manager for New Dramatists and coproducer of a number of shows. His own plays include *The Orchard*, an adaptation of Anton Chekhov's *The Cherry Orchard*, and *Four of a Kind*, depicting a quartet of women at Barnard College.

In addition to *The Penultimate Problem of Sherlock Holmes*, Nassivera offered another criminous play, *Making a Killing*, at the Dorset Theatre Festival, a company he founded in 1967 and where he serves as producing director to this day. *Making a Killing* opened on August 2, 1984, under the direction of Anthony McKay. The play spotlights an audacious public relations scheme concocted to enhance interest in a new Broadway show by "arranging" the fake suicide of the playwright. On a split stage divided between a cottage in Vermont and an office in Manhattan, the playwright, his agent, the producer, and the star of *Once and Ever After* circle around each other in a game that gradually becomes more and more sinister.

Acting Edition: Samuel French, Inc.

NOTES

1. *New York Times*, May 19, 1980.
2. *New York Post*, May 21, 1980.
3. *Women's Wear Daily*, May 21, 1980.
4. *The Village Voice*, May 26, 1980.
5. *The Villager*, May 22, 1980.
6. *Christian Science Monitor*, May 23, 1980.

The Little Sister (1978)

Stuart Gordon (United States, 1947–) and Carolyn Purdy-Gordon (United States, 1947–)

Raymond Chandler's Knight of the Mean Streets, private investigator Philip Marlowe, has fiercely protected the interests of his clients in eight novels, eight movies, several radio and television series—and one play. *The Little Sister* (1949) was converted to the stage by Stuart Gordon and Carolyn Purdy-Gordon in a style faithful to the original novel; the story is told in a succession of vignettes unfolding from Marlowe's point of view. The detective never leaves the stage, sharing his thoughts and feelings with the audience through narratives and semi-poetic images.

Dispensing with some sub-plots and secondary characters, the adapters streamlined a very complex tale. Much of the action takes place in Marlowe's drab Hollywood office. As the play begins, the detective stalks a bluebottle fly and manages to swat it when the doorbell rings. Orfamay Quest, a petite, neat, prissy-looking girl, enters. She has just arrived from Manhattan, Kansas, in search of her brother, Orrin, who seems to have vanished. She cannot afford Marlowe's fee of "forty bucks a day and expenses," but offers a twenty dollar bill. Orfamay inquires whether Marlowe drinks—"I don't think I'd care to employ a detective that uses liquor in any form and I don't approve of tobacco."

Marlowe asks, "Would it be all right if I peeled an orange?"

Orfamay pulls out a snapshot of her missing brother and older sister, Leila. Marlowe reaches out and takes off Orfamay's glasses. Orfamay steps back and stumbles. Marlowe grabs her and she pushes against his chest. "I suppose you do this to all your clients," Orfamay whispers. She reaches an arm around his neck and pulls. They kiss. She nestles in Marlowe's arms and lets out a long sigh. "In Manhattan, Kansas, you could be arrested for this," she coos.

The paltry sum of twenty dollars plunges Marlowe into a trail of blackmail, treachery, cover-ups, and murder. In a seedy Bay City hotel he meets George Hicks, a muscular small-time hood who ends up with an ice pick through his neck. In the lining of Hicks's toupee, Marlowe finds a photographic negative of movie actress Mavis Weld with ex-gangster Sonny Steelgrave.

In his quest to find Orrin, the detective meets the glamorous, ambitious Mavis, her friend Dolores Gonzales, a hot-blooded Latin American starlet, and Dolores's lover, Vincent Lagardie, a dope-peddling doctor who has a habit of pricking the ball of his thumb and licking it. Both Mavis and Dolores are enamored with Steelgrave, but that does not preclude their making overtures to Marlowe. Strapping on a Luger pistol fails to help Marlowe when Mavis hits the shamus over the head with a .32 automatic or when Dr. Lagardie offers him a drugged cigarette.

Orrin Quest, too, turns up dead from an ice pick puncture. Police Lieutenant Christy French and Officer Fred Beifus enter the picture, hound Marlowe, arrest and third-degree him, with Beifus slapping his face with a heavy pigskin glove. But Marlowe withholds any and all information, remaining, as always, faithful to his client.

Steelgrave becomes the third victim in *The Little Sister*. Mavis Weld, who turns out to be Orrin and Orfamay's sister Leila, tells Marlowe that she shot Steelgrave in revenge because he killed her brother. It seems that Orrin had attempted to blackmail his actress sister by threatening to publish a compromising photo of Leila and Steelgrave.

Interrogated again by the police, Marlowe stays mum. Lieutenant French, while pulling off his belt and wrapping it around his right hand, assures Marlowe that he won't be Mr. Nice Guy any more. Coppers, barks French, spend their lives turning over dirty underwear and sniffing rotten teeth, go up dark stairways to get a gun punk with a skinful of hop and sometimes they don't get all the way up. And now, sniffs the lieutenant, as if all that was not enough to make them entirely happy, they've also got detective Marlowe, hiding information and dodging around corners, suppressing evidence and framing set-ups.

Marlowe responds that a private eye wants to play ball with the police. Sometimes, says Marlowe, he just gets in a jam without meaning to and has to play his hand the way it's dealt.

Back in his office, Marlowe, despondent, berates himself for "starting out cheap and ending cheaper still." He reaches for a bottle of whiskey when Orfamay arrives to announce that she's going home. Marlowe snatches her bag and fishes out $2000 in new bills.

Marlowe drops the bills back into the bag. He tells Orfamay that he concluded that her brother Orrin blackmailed his sister and then when a small-time crook like Hicks got wise to his racket, he snuck up on Hicks and knocked him off with an ice pick in the back of the neck. It probably didn't even keep Orrin awake that night.

Marlowe accuses Orfamay of setting up her brother so they could kill him, betraying him for blood money. He hopes she'll be happy with it.

Marlowe tears the incriminating photo into shreds, strikes a match, and drops it into an ashtray along with the negative. He then goes to meet Dolores Gonzales and draws from her a confession that it was not Mavis but she who shot Steelgrave. She had to kill him, she says. He was the one man she really loved and she would not share him.

In order to condense the proceedings and avoid a shift in locale, Dr. Lagardie is spotlighted eavesdropping before rushing toward Gonzales—"You've lied to me again! You still love him!" He then stabs her with a silver letter opener. (The original novel pictures the demise quietly, with Marlowe finding Gonzales's body in her apartment, on the couch, held in the arms of her ashen, catatonic lover-killer. "I guess somebody lost a dream," says an ambulance intern as he bends over and closes the dead woman's eyes.)

* * *

The Little Sister premiered at the Organic Theatre, Chicago, during the 1978–1979 season. The two adapters undertook the additional tasks of director (Stuart Gordon) and performer (Carolyn Purdy-Gordon in the triple roles of Orfamay Quest, Mavis Weld, and Dolores Gonzales). Mike Genovese portrayed Marlowe. The dramatization is listed in *Drury's Guide to Best Plays* by James M. Salem (Metuchen, N.J.: Scarecrow Press, 1987).

Chandler's novel of *The Little Sister* was transformed to the screen as *Marlowe* in 1969. Unlike the brooding film versions of Raymond Chandler's *Farewell, My Lovely* (as *Murder, My Sweet*, 1944), *The Big Sleep* (1946), *Lady in the Lake* (1946), and *The High Window* (as *The Brasher Doubloon*, 1947), *Marlowe* is a sunny, bright endeavor peppered with comic touches. James Garner departed from the hardboiled demeanor of Dick Powell, Humphrey Bogart, Robert Montgomery, and George Montgomery with a frothy, bemused interpretation.

In *Raymond Chandler in Hollywood*, Al Clark calls Garner's Marlowe "a sleuth with a suntan," asserting that "Marlowe would have a suntan only if he had been tied to a stake in the middle of the Mojave desert pre-applied with factor 15. . . . Marlowe, now charging a hundred dollars a day plus expenses, should have a slightly forbidding air about him that discourages people from taking liberties. Garner looks as if he would invite them to kick sand in his face. He is insufficiently crumpled and excessively well-groomed, too intrinsically lightweight as a presence and as a personality to play the role with any conviction."[1]

Clark reports that Garner and director Paul Bogart insisted on stripping the tough screenplay by Stirling Silliphant of any semblance of violence.

"It creates a difficult problem when you're dealing with a Philip Marlowe story," complained Silliphant. "You have to find bodies, get beaten up, shoot people, and hack your way around Los Angeles. . . . A lot of the vigor, anger, and cynicism had been eroded."[2]

It should be noted, however, that Stephen Pendo, in *Raymond Chandler on Screen*, believes that "the Marlowe character fitted Garner's screen image, an image that developed largely out of his role in the late 1950's television series, *Maverick*. . . . Physically, he more closely matches Chandler's detective than any other actor who has played the detective. . . . *Marlowe* accurately captures the mood of *The Little Sister* and remains faithful to the novel in terms of Marlowe's character. The film is, in fact, the most underrated 'Marlowe' picture."[3]

The cast of *Marlowe* included Gayle Hunnicut (Mavis), Rita Moreno (Dolores), Sharon Farrell (Orfamay), Carroll O'Connor (French), Kenneth Tobey (Beifus), Jackie Coogan (Hicks), and Paul Stevens (Lagardie). Bruce Lee took over as the novel's henchman, playing Winslow Wong, foot-kicking and demolishing Marlowe's office in the most memorable scene of the picture. Pocket Books published a movie-tie-in paperback titled *Marlowe* in 1969. Simon & Schuster's Fireside line published an illustrated edition of *The Little Sister* by Michael Lark, with cover art by Steranko, in 1997.

* * *

Born in Chicago in 1888, Raymond Thornton Chandler moved to England with his mother as a small boy. He received his education at Dulwich College, London, further studying in France and Germany, before eventually returning to the United States. His various occupations on both sides of the Atlantic included teaching, accounting, bookkeeping, ranching, soldiering, freelance reporting, managing a sporting goods firm, and working as an administrator at various oil companies. He began writing for pulp magazines in 1933, contributing twenty novelettes to *Black Mask* and other mystery monthlies, gradually developing the character of his hero sleuth until, settling on the name Philip Marlowe, chiseling him as a modern knight "in search of a hidden truth," immune to the corruptive forces around him.

In his 1944 manifesto, *The Simple Art of Murder*, Chandler proclaims: "Down these mean streets a man must go who is not himself mean, who is neither tarnished nor afraid. . . . He must be a complete man and a common man, and yet an unusual man. . . . He is a relatively poor man, or he would not be a detective at all. He is a common man or he could not go among common people. He has a sense of character, or he would not know his job. . . . He is a lonely man and his pride is that you will treat him as a proud man or be very sorry you ever saw him. He talks as the man of his age talks, that is, with rude wit, a lively sense of the grotesque, a disgust for sham, and a contempt for pettiness."[4]

In addition to *The Little Sister*, Philip Marlowe solves the cases of *The Big Sleep* (1939), *Farewell, My Lovely* (1940), *The High Window* (1942), *The Lady in the Lake* (1943), *The Long Goodbye* (1953), and *Playback* (1958). Robert B. Parker completed *Poodle Springs* (1962, unfinished) in 1989. Parker also penned, in 1991, *Perchance to Dream*, a sequel to *The Big Sleep*. Marlowe will make another comeback in a novel written by John Banville, to be published in 2013.

Marlowe appears in the short story collections *The Simple Art of Murder* (1950) and *The Smell of Fear* (1965). Chandler's novelettes were compiled in eleven volumes, notably the much-sought paperback originals published by Avon: *Five Murderers* (1944), *Five Sinister Characters* (1945), and *Finger Man and Other Stories* (1946). *Raymond Chandler's Philip Marlowe: A Centennial Celebration* (1988), edited by Byron Preiss, collects twenty-three Marlowe tales by prominent contemporary mystery writers and Chandler's *The Pencil*, the only short story originally written about Marlowe.[5] Joan Kahn edited *The Midnight Raymond Chandler*, an omnibus, in 1971. Library of America published Chandler's *Novels and Other Writings, 1943–1954* and *Stories and Novels, 1933–1942*—both in 1995.

Chandler's scripts for the cinema, sometimes with others, include the classic film noir *Double Indemnity* (1944), based on the James M. Cain novel and directed by Billy Wilder; *And Now Tomorrow* (1944); *The Unseen* (1945); *The Blue Dahlia* (1946); and *Strangers on a Train* (1951), from Patricia Highsmith's novel, directed by Alfred Hitchcock. Universal Pictures purchased a story for the screen titled *Backfire*, written by Chandler in 1947 as a proposal for an original screenplay. However, by the time Chandler completed the script early in 1948, Hollywood was going through a post–World War II recession and the project was cancelled. Santa Teresa Press published the initial seven-page treatment of *Backfire*, with a preface by Robert B. Parker, in a limited edition in 1984. The final draft was rediscovered and published as *Raymond Chandler's Unknown Thriller* by Mysterious Press in a slipcased first edition of 250 copies in 1985.

Considered the poet laureate of detective fiction, Chandler's novels have been touted as American classics transcending the genre. Most scholars maintain that his early works are his best. However, T. R. Steiner, in *St. James Guide to Crime & Mystery Writers*, lauds "the invention and tight plotting" of *The Little Sister*, adding: "Whatever Chandler's ultimate status in American letters, for the modern detective story his blend of realism, romance, verbal wit, and satire bordering on tragedy has proven to be the archetype."[6]

There is widespread Chandleresque literature, notably *Raymond Chandler Speaking*, edited by Dorothy Gardiner and Kathrine Sorley Walker (1962); *Down These Mean Streets a Man Must Go* by Philip Durham (1963);

Raymond Chandler: A Checklist (1968), *Chandler before Marlowe* (1973), and *Raymond Chandler: A Descriptive Bibliography* (1979), all three edited by Matthew J. Bruccoli; *The Notebooks of Raymond Chandler* (1976) and *Selected Letters* (1981) both edited by Frank MacShane; *The World of Raymond Chandler*, edited by Miriam Gross (1977); *Letters: Raymond Chandler and James M. Fox*, edited by James Pepper (1978); *Chandlertown* by Edward Thorpe (1983); *Hardboiled Burlesque: Raymond Chandler's Comic Style* by Keith Newlin (1984); *Something More Than Night* by Peter Wolfe (1985); *The Critical Response to Raymond Chandler*, edited by J. K. Van Dover (1995); biographies of Chandler by Frank MacShane (1976), Jerry Speir (1981), and William Marling (1986).

A Raymond Chandler manuscript collection is housed in the Department of Special Collections, University of California Research Library, Los Angeles. Chandler had served as president of the Mystery Writers of America in 1959, the last year of his life.

* * *

Born in Chicago in 1947, Stuart Gordon graduated from the city's Lane Technical High School, attended the University of Wisconsin at Madison as an anthropology major, enrolled in drama classes, and then established his own Screw Theatre. In 1969 Gordon dropped out of the university and moved his acting troupe to Chicago where he formed the Organic Theatre Company in 1970. The group traveled to New York, Los Angeles, and Europe, and launched David Mamet's career with the world premiere of his play *Sexual Perversity in Chicago*. Gordon's wife, Carolyn Purdy-Gordon (born in Michigan in 1947), was a leading actress at Organic. In the fall of 1968 the couple was arrested on obscenity charges for a production of *Peter Pan* in which Peter became the leader of hippies, Captain Hook became Mayor Daley, and the pirates became the Chicago police—all going on an acid trip in a Neverland populated by naked females. The charges were dropped in November 1968.

Other plays directed by Gordon at the Organic Theatre Company include his own *Warp!* (1971), a science-fiction adventure, which was moved to Broadway for a short run in January–February 1973 featuring John Heard, and was adapted into a graphic novel in 1980; Ray Bradbury's *The Wonderful Ice Cream Suit* (1974); stage versions of Mark Twain's *Huckleberry Finn 1* and *Huckleberry Finn 2* (both in 1975); *Bleacher Bums* (1977), an improvisation-based comedy that ran for seven years in Los Angeles; and *E/R* (1982), a hospital comedy that inspired a 1984–1985 television series starring Elliott Gould.

In 1985 Gordon left for the west coast and joined Empire Pictures to direct the company's first big hit, *Re-Animator*, an up-to-date version of H. P. Lovecraft's 1922 short story, "Herbert West—Reanimator." Jeffrey Combs played a young medical student who develops a serum to bring the dead back to life. Gordon continued to make his directorial mark in cinema's horror genre with *From Beyond* (1986), in which a scientist searches for the sixth sense; *Dolls* (1987), the tale of an elderly couple who create murderous dolls in an isolated mansion; *The Pit and the Pendulum* (1991), inspired by Edgar Allan Poe's story and filled with graphic scenes of torture; *Fortress* (1992), wherein much of the action unfolds in a futuristic maximum security prison run by a sadistic warden; *The Wonderful Ice Cream Suit* (1998), based on a short story and a play by Ray Bradbury, about five Los Angeles Latinos who buy one classy white suit which, they believe, will help them realize their dreams. *Dagon* (2001) is adapted from H. P. Lovecraft's 1932 novella "The Shadow Over Innsmouth" (rather than his 1919 short story "Dagon"), with an updated plot that moves the idol worshippers from the fictional town of Innsmouth, Massachusetts to a fictional town in Spain. *Edmond* (2005), scripted by David Mamet, features William H. Macy in the role of a middle-aged executive who heeds a tarot reading and embarks on an all-night odyssey through the city's underbelly. In *Stuck* (2008), a collision with an oncoming car leaves a man, played by Stephen Rea, enmeshed in the windshield where he is left to die in the garage of a nasty driver. Carolyn Purdy-Gordon appeared in supporting roles in many of her husband's films.

Gordon penned and directed suspenseful episodes for *Honey, I Shrunk the Kids: The TV Show* (1998), *Masters of Horror* (2005, 2007), and *Fear Itself* (2008).

In 2009 Gordon came back to the legitimate stage, directing his actor-friend Jeffrey Combs in a one-man play, *Nevermore . . . An Evening with Edgar Allan Poe*. The show premiered successfully in Los Angeles and went on national tour.

Acting Edition: The Dramatic Publishing Company.

Awards and Honors: Raymond Chandler garnered Mystery Writers of America Edgars for Best Motion Picture—*Murder, My Sweet* (1946), and Best Novel—*The Long Goodbye* (1955). Stuart Gordon was nominated for the Joseph Jefferson Award for Director of a Play in 1974, 1976, 1977, and 1982. He won the award in 1975 for his direction of *Huckleberry Finn 1* at the Organic Theatre Company in Chicago. Carolyn Purdy-Gordon was nominated in 1976 for the same award as Actress in a Principal Role in *Switch Bitch*, also at the Organic.

NOTES

1. Al Clark, *Raymond Chandler in Hollywood* (Los Angeles: Silman-James, 1996), 163.

2. Clark, *Raymond Chandler in Hollywood*, 163.

3. Stephen Pendo, *Raymond Chandler on Screen* (Metuchen, N.J.: Scarecrow, 1976), 126, 130.

4. Chris Steinbrunner and Otto Penzler, eds., *Encyclopedia of Mystery and Detection* (New York: McGraw-Hill, 1976), 78.

5. On March 24, 2012, the Ruskin Group Theatre of Los Angeles presented an adaptation by Ed Horowitz of Raymond Chandler's short story "The Pencil" at the Santa Monica Public Library. The staged reading was directed by Edward Edwards, who also appeared as author Chandler pounding on his typewriter and narrating the continuity. Paul Schackman played Phillip Marlowe.

6. Jay P. Pederson, ed., *St. James Guide to Crime & Mystery Writers* (Detroit: St. James Press, 1996), 170.

Sweeney Todd, the Demon Barber of Fleet Street (1979)

Book by Hugh Wheeler (United States, England-born, 1912–1987), music and lyrics by Stephen Sondheim (United States, 1930–)

Although some scholars claim that Sweeney Todd and Margery Lovett are characters based on a real-life murderous barber and his partner in crime,[1] the assumption is strongly disputed by other historians. It seems more likely that the duo are fictional creations who first appeared in an 1846 "penny dreadful" (Victorian-era pulp fiction) serial titled *The String of Pearls*, published anonymously and attributed to either Thomas Peckett Prest or James Malcolm Rymer, authors who created a number of gruesome villains. The eighteen weekly installments of the barber's homicidal exploits, published in *The People's Periodical* (no. 7–24, from November 21, 1846 to March 20, 1847), were immensely popular, and even before the last chapter saw light, *The String of Pearls*, dramatized by George Dibdin Pitt (1799–1855) was produced on February 22, 1847, subtitled "The Fiend of Fleet Street."

The play opened at the Britannia Theatre, Hoxton, London, a venue dedicated to explicit horror entertainment similar to Paris's Grand Guignol, with Mark Howard as Sweeney Todd. Dozens of imitations followed, produced in and around London throughout the remainder of the nineteenth century. Notable is *Sweeney Todd, the Barber of Fleet Street: or the String of Pearls* by Frederick Hazleton (c.1825–1890) which premiered at The Old Bower Saloon, Stangate Street, Lambeth, London, in 1865.

Sweeney Todd continued to have a stage life in the twentieth century. The Dibdin Pitt version was produced at New York's Frazee Theatre in 1924, featuring Robert Vivian in the lead, running for sixty-seven performances. The *New York Times* wrote that "It turned out to be a flavorous old melodrama, which, as is the way with these old pieces, has turned comic in the spots where it was not seriously meant."[2] Four years later, *Sweeney Todd* by Matt Wilkinson, starring Matt Wilkinson, played at London's Regent Theatre for twelve showings.

The English actor Tod Slaughter first appeared as Sweeney Todd in Frederick Hazleton's adaptation at London's Kingsway Theatre in 1932 and continued to make a career of portraying the character.[3] Rod Godfrey enacted *The Demon Barber*, a version by Donald Cotton, at the Lyric, Hammersmith in 1959. That same year, the Royal Ballet Company produced a one-act ballet adaptation, with music by Malcolm Arnold and choreography by John Cranko, at the Shakespeare Memorial Theatre, Stratford. Donald Britton danced the role of Todd. Based on George Dibdin Pitt's original, a musical, *Sweeney Todd the Barber*, with book, music, and lyrics by Brian J. Burton, premiered at the Crescent Theatre, Birmingham, England, on June 16, 1962, with Frank Jones in the title role, and a treatment "serious rather than comic," by Austin Rosser was first presented at the Dundee Repertory Theatre, Scotland, on September 23, 1969, featuring Paul Humpoletz.

In 1973, a dramatization by British playwright Christopher G. Bond played at the Theatre Royal, Stratford East, London. Stephen Sondheim saw this production, in which for the first time the title character (played by well-known British television actor Brian Murphy) is painted with sympathy. Sondheim negotiated for the rights to convert the play into a musical, wrote the music and lyrics, and recruited Hugh Wheeler to pen the book. Called "a musical thriller," *Sweeney Todd, the Demon Barber of Fleet Street* opened at New York's Uris Theatre on March 1, 1979. It expresses the tale almost wholly musically, with very little spoken dialogue. Twenty-six songs are identified in the program.

The action unfolds in Victorian London's Fleet Street and its environs. A prologue sung by the entire company, "The Ballad of Sweeney Todd," invites the audience to attend the tale of a barber who "shaved the faces of gentlemen who never thereafter were heard of again."

The lights fade up on an alley near the London docks. A small boat appears in the background. Sweeney Todd and Anthony Hope disembark. Anthony is a young, cheerful country-born sailor with a duffle bag slung over his shoulder. Todd is a heavy-set, saturnine man in his forties, morose and brooding. A ragged beggar woman offers her favors, but they repel her. She scuttles away, turns to give Todd a piercing look, and wanders off.

Todd lapses into a reminiscence of a "foolish" London barber and his "beautiful, virtuous" wife and tells Anthony, via a song called "The Barber and His Wife" how another man, "a pious vulture of the law," entered the picture and destroyed their happiness. Anthony departs. Todd stops outside a meat-pie shop. Inside, the proprietor, Mrs. Nellie Lovett (renamed from Margery in the original story), "a vigorous, slatternly woman in her forties," is flicking flies off the trays of pies with a dirty rag. Todd enters. At first Mrs. Lovett takes Todd for a potential customer but soon she admits in song that "these are probably the worst pies in London."

Todd expresses interest in the room above Mrs. Lovett's shop. She relates that a barber—Benjamin Barker, his name was—and his young wife, Lucy, once lived there. Judge Turpin and his right-hand man, the Beadle Bamford, lusted for Lucy, so they arranged to have the barber deported to a penal colony in Australia, leaving Lucy alone with her year-old daughter, Johanna.

As Mrs. Lovett sings "Poor Thing," her narration is acted out. We see a masked ball in progress at Judge Turpin's house. The Beadle leads a scared Lucy, offers her champagne, hurls her to the floor and holds her there as the judge, naked, mounts her. The masked dancers pirouette around as the judge rapes the terrified woman.

The flashback vanishes. Todd reveals that he is Benjamin Barker. Mrs. Lovett tells him that his wife poisoned herself with arsenic. Judge Turpin subsequently adopted Johanna and brought her up "like his own." Todd bemoans the fact that after fifteen years in a "living hell," he lost the dream of coming back home "to a loving wife and child." He vows revenge. Mrs. Lovett sympathizes with him. She fetches some gleaming, silver-handled razors that once belonged to Barker and tells him that she kept them in case "the poor silly blighter'll be back again someday."

The lights come up on the façade of Judge Turpin's mansion. At the upper level appears an exquisitely beautiful girl with a long mane of shining blonde hair—Johanna. Anthony passes by, sees her, and stands transfixed, immediately smitten. Their eyes meet. He purchases a cage with a bird from a sleepy salesperson and motions to Johanna to come down to get it. She hesitates, nods, and shyly slips out of the door. Anthony moves toward her, holding out the cage. Their fingers touch. They stand so absorbed with each other that they do not notice the approach of Judge Turpin, followed by the Beadle. The judge shouts, "Johanna! Johanna!" and the girl scurries into the house. The judge warns Anthony that if he sees his face on this street again, the young man will "rue the day" he was born. The Beadle takes the cage from him and wrings the neck of the bird. "Next time it will be your neck," threatens the Beadle. Wandering away, Anthony sings "I'll steal you, Johanna, I'll steal you."

Lights fade and come up on St. Dunstan's marketplace where Signor Adolfo Pirelli, a hair-cutter and tooth-puller, has parked his caravan. Pirelli's adolescent, simple-minded assistant, Tobias Ragg, is selling hair tonic to a crowd that includes Todd, Mrs. Lovett, and Beadle Bamford. Todd mocks Pirelli's elixir as worthless, "an arrant fraud," and challenges the mountebank to a shaving competition. The Beadle serves as umpire as Pirelli and Todd strop their razors, lather the faces of two men, and shave them. The Beadle examines the job, finds Todd's customer "smooth as a baby's arse" and pronounces him the winner. Pirelli pushes Tobias to a chair, forces open his lips, thrusts the extractor into the mouth, causing his assistant to moan and scream. Conversely, Todd extracts a tooth with a tiny tug and a single deft motion. The Beadle declares him "the two-time winner." Mrs. Lovett announces to the crowd that "Sweeney Todd's Tonsorial Parlor" is located above her meat pie shop on Fleet Street.

Consumed with passion, Judge Turpin tells his ward Johanna that he intends to marry her at once. The Beadle recommends an expert barber who will spruce the judge up to make him more attractive to a young woman. Meanwhile, Anthony returns and attracts Johanna's attention. She throws him a key. In her room, between kisses, the two lovers hatch a plan to elope. Anthony goes to Todd's barbershop and asks permission to bring Johanna there while he hires a coach to take the two of them to Plymouth.

Anthony hurries out as Pirelli and Tobias start up the stairs without ringing the bell. Pirelli tells Mrs. Lovett that he has "a little business" with Mr. Todd; would the signora take care of his assistant? Mrs. Lovett leads Tobias down the stairs to her shop, puts out a stool for the fellow to sit on and hands him a piece of pie. He starts to eat greedily. Upstairs Pirelli drops his Italian accent and, reverting to an Irish brogue, says, "Call me Danny, Daniel O'Higgins." He tells Todd that he remembers him as Benjamin Barker; he won't tell this to his friend Beadle Bamford if the barber will hand him half his profits every week, "share and share alike."

Todd gazes at Pirelli-O'Higgins for a long moment, then jumps at him, grabs the blackmailer by the throat and, after a protracted struggle, slashes his throat with a razor. When Tobias goes up to fetch his master, Todd tells him that Pirelli has left.

Todd hides Pirelli's body in a chest. He confesses his deed and its motive to Mrs. Lovett and she sympathizes. She picks up Pirelli's purse, takes out the money, and puts it down her bosom. Downstairs Judge Turpin clangs the bell and Mrs. Lovett scuttles out. The judge settles in the barber's chair and allows himself to be lathered for a shave. Todd savors the situation, flourishes the razor, preparing to dispose of the enemy who has walked into his trap. The judge makes conversation, tells Todd of his plan to marry Johanna and they both sing an ode to "Pretty Women." Just as Todd raises his arm in an arc and is about to slice the judge's throat, Anthony bursts in with an announcement, "She'll marry me Sunday, we leave tonight." The judge leaps up angrily, spilling the basin, knocking the razor from the barber's hand, and strides out and down the stairs.

Todd, bitterly disappointed, orders Anthony to leave. Mrs. Lovett goes up. There's the problem of disposing of Pirelli's corpse. The enterprising Lovett has a suggestion: It's a shame for anything to go to waste these days with supplies scarce, business slow, and debts piling up. What with the price of meat, maybe she and Mr. Todd could be of mutual assistance. Todd grasps her intent and accepts her suggestion with enthusiasm. They sing "A Little Priest," questioning the different flesh tastes of men of cloth, politicians, soldiers, and artists, concluding that they won't "discriminate great from small" and will serve them all. The act ends with the two of them brandishing "weapons"—he a butcher's cleaver, she a wooden rolling pin.

The curtain of act 2 rises on a prosperous outdoor garden next to the pie shop. Tobias, in a waiter's apron, serves a crowd of contented customers, shoos the beggar woman away, and draws business with the song "God, That's Good!" Mrs. Lovett, in a fancy gown, collects money, gives orders, and addresses patrons individually.

Upstairs, Todd is opening a huge crate that has just arrived, revealing an elaborate barber chair that tilts forward at the pull of a lever to slide its occupant down through a trap door to Mrs. Lovett's invisible cellar below. He tests the chair with a stack of books. It works admirably.

A customer arrives. Todd ushers him into the chair, lathers his face, and slashes his throat. He pulls the lever and the customer disappears down the chute. A second customer enters and his fate is similar to that of the first. Night falls. A wisp of smoke rises from the bake-house chimney. In the alley nearby the beggar woman coughs and spits, and in a rage croons, "Smoke! Smoke! Sign of the devil." She shuffles off while Anthony is searching the streets of London for Johanna, whom the judge has removed from her home and hidden away.

At last Anthony discovers Johanna's whereabouts: The judge has committed her to Jonas Fogg's Asylum. When Anthony passes by, he hears weird and frightening sounds, the cries and gibberish of the inmates. Echoing through is Johanna's voice, singing about her lost wedding. Anthony beats wildly on the door. The Beadle swaggers up, tells him that the girl is "as mad as the seven seas" and whistles for the police. Anthony runs away to Mrs. Lovett's pie shop, enters while she nuzzles up to Todd on the love seat, and tells them what happened to Johanna. Todd suggests that he penetrate the madhouse in disguise as a wigmaker ready to pay top price for hair that is "corn-yellow" like Johanna's. This way, Anthony can find the girl and rescue her, at pistol point if necessary.

Todd writes a note to Judge Turpin, notifying him that Johanna has taken refuge with him, hoping that this will entice the judge to come back to the barbershop in search of his ward. Todd hurries to Judge Turpin's house, knocks on the door, and hands him the letter.

In the evening, after the shop is closed, Tobias declares his allegiance to his new employer, Mrs. Lovett. "Nothing's gonna harm you," he sings, "Not while I'm around." Mrs. Lovett gives Tobias a bonbon from her purse. Tobias recognizes the purse as having belonged to his former master, signor Pirelli. Concerned, Mrs. Lovett tells Tobias that Mr. Todd bought the purse in a pawnshop and gave it to her for her birthday. She entices Tobias to help her bake the pies, instructs him how to operate the meat grinder, and leaves, slamming the door behind her. Tobias happily turns the handle of the grinder, not realizing that she has locked him in.

Mrs. Lovett goes upstairs to find Todd. At that moment the Beadle comes with official business; there have been complaints "about the stink from your chimney." Todd enters, having delivered his note to the judge. Mrs. Lovett persuades the Beadle to patronize the barbershop before inspecting the bake-house.

For Tobias, one shock follows another as, taking a bite of one of the pies, he finds some hair and a fingernail; then the Beadle's corpse comes tumbling down the chute. Terrified, Tobias tries to flee. Finding the door locked, he notices an open trapdoor and escapes into the cellar.

At Fogg's Asylum Anthony inspects the female inmates and finds Johanna. When Fogg attempts to prevent their escape, Anthony draws a pistol but can't bring himself to shoot. Johanna takes the weapon, holds it with both hands, and pulls the trigger. Fogg falls. She and Anthony run out. Compelled by Fogg's death, the lunatics tear down the wall and pour out onto the street. Amid police whistles, they lustily sing "City on Fire!"

Todd and Mrs. Lovett try to wheedle Tobias out of hiding, but they cannot find him. Lights come up on the tonsorial parlor. Anthony and Johanna enter. She is disguised in sailor garb. They kiss and he rushes off to hire a coach to take them out of London. Johanna paces nervously, then sits in the barber chair, her hand moving to inspect the lever. The beggar woman can be seen below approaching the pie shop, calling for the Beadle. Johanna jumps from the chair, looks wildly around, sees the chest, and clambers in, closing the lid just as the beggar woman comes shuffling in. She whimpers, clutches an imaginary baby, rocks it, and mumbles a lullaby. Todd appears, razor in hand. He orders the beggar woman to go but time is running out—down below Judge Turpin is ringing the bell, arriving in response to Todd's note. Frantically, Todd slits the beggar woman's throat, puts her in the chair, and launches her down the chute.

The judge enters and asks for his ward. Todd assures him that Johanna is totally repentant and coaxes the judge to take a shave to make him look his best for the meeting with the girl. The two of them reprise "Pretty Women," following which Todd reveals himself to the judge as Benjamin Barker, then viciously cuts his throat and releases him down the chute.

Johanna emerges from the trunk. Dressed in a sailor's uniform, Todd mistakes her for an intruder and slashes at her, but she manages to escape and runs out.

Todd goes down and finds Mrs. Lovett tending to the corpses of the judge and the beggar woman. When she opens the oven doors, the light from the fire illuminates the beggar woman's face. Todd drops his razor in horror upon recognizing his wife Lucy, whom he thought was dead. Todd is furious at Mrs. Lovett's deception; she explains that by telling him that his wife took poison, she hoped to spare Todd the bitter truth about Lucy's degradation, lying because she loves him.

Concealing his anger, Todd puts his arm around Mrs. Lovett affectionately and waltzes her toward the oven. He flings her into the furnace and slams the doors shut. She screams and black smoke belches forth.

Todd sinks to the floor, cradles his beloved wife in his arms, and reprises "The Barber and His Wife." Tobias emerges from the cellar, his hair now completely white from the horror of his experience, his mind reeling with shock and fear. He notices the beggar woman and bends down to examine the body. Todd pushes him violently aside. Tobias staggers back, sees Todd's fallen razor, picks it up, pulls Todd's head back, and fatally slashes his throat. Todd lies dead across the body of his wife.

Anthony, Johanna, and several constables burst into the bake-house. Seeing the carnage, they all stop. Tobias begins to turn the handle of the meat grinder, faces front and leads the company in "The Ballad of Sweeney Todd." The assorted victims—beggar woman, Judge Turpin, Todd, Mrs. Lovett, Pirelli, and the Beadle—join the song, belting "Attend the tale of Sweeney Todd! He served a dark and a hungry god!"

The company exits. Todd and Mrs. Lovett are the last to leave. They look at each other and begin to exit in opposite directions. Todd glares at the audience malevolently for a moment, then slams the iron door of the oven. Blackout.

* * *

Directed by Harold Prince and designed by Eugene Lee, *Sweeney Todd, the Demon Barber of Fleet Street* opened at Broadway's Uris Theatre on March 1, 1979, featuring Len Cariou (Sweeney Todd), Angela Lansbury (Mrs. Lovett), Victor Garber (Anthony Hope), Sarah Rice (Johanna), and Edmund Lyndeck (Judge Turpin). It was called by critics "a staggering spectacle" (Douglas Watt),[4] "sensationally entertaining" (Clive Barnes),[5] "total theater, a brilliant conception and a shattering experience" (Howard Kissel),[6] and "Broadway at its best" (Jack Kroll).[7] Edwin Wilson wrote, "Mr. Sondheim's score—in its range, in its depth, in its rightness—is probably his best so far."[8] Richard Eder applauded the direction by Harold Prince as "always powerful."[9] John Beaufort believed that "the two principal roles are acted and sung [by Len Cariou and Angela Lansbury] with amazing bravura."[10] Joel Siegel proclaimed, "*Sweeney Todd* is more than a great musical. Like *West Side Story* 20 years ago; like *Oklahoma* 30 years ago, *Sweeney Todd* has cut a new boundary."[11]

Sweeney Todd ran for 557 performances. During the run, George Hearn replaced Cariou and Dorothy Loudon replaced Lansbury. Denis Quilley played the title role in a 1980 London production, George Hearn in a 1980–1981 tour of the United States, Timothy Nolen in 1984 productions presented by the Houston Grand Opera and by the New York City Opera. Leon Greene undertook the part in a 1985 London revival, Bob Gunton in a 1989 Broadway revival, Alun Armstrong in a 1993 award-studded London revival. Timothy Nolen portrayed Todd again at the Goodspeed Opera House, East Haddam, Connecticut, in 1996, Kelsey Grammer in a concert presentation at the Ahmanson Theatre, Los Angeles, in 1999, George Hearn again in a 2000 concert version produced by the New York Philharmonic at Avery Fisher Hall, and that same year Bryn Terfel slit throats at the Lyric Opera of Chicago. Brian Stokes Mitchell played the homicidal barber in a 2002 Kennedy Center, Washington, D.C. revival, and Paul Hegarty in a 2004 West End production, directed by John Doyle, notable for having no orchestra and a ten-person cast playing the score themselves on musical instruments that they carry on stage. That version came to New York in 2005 with Michael Cerveris as a guitar-playing Todd, and went on a 2007–2008 Canadian and U.S. national tour with David Hess in the role. Irish tenor David Shannon starred as Todd in a highly successful Dublin production in 2007, Jeff McCarthy in a 2010 staging by the Barrington Stage Company in Pittsfield, Massachusetts, Franco Pomponi in a 2011 Paris production, and Michael Ball in a 2011 reincarnation that played at The Chichester Festival and came to the West End the following year.

The musical was presented on television by RKO/Nederlander and the Entertainment Channel on September 12, 1982, directed by Terry Hughes, featuring George Hearn and Angela Lansbury, and was transferred to the screen in 2007, scripted by John Logan, directed by Tim Burton, starring Johnny Depp and Helena Bonham Carter.[12]

* * *

Christopher Godfrey Bond (London-born, 1945), whose 1973 version of *Sweeney Todd* formed the basis of the Hugh Wheeler-Stephen Sondheim musical, is a seasoned actor, director, and playwright. He lived and worked in Liverpool for fifteen years, eventually becoming artistic director of both the Everyman and Playhouse Theatres. He subsequently became artistic director of the Half Moon Theatre in London's East End from 1984 to 1989. He has worked extensively as a director in Scandinavia, Israel, and the United States and has written more than thirty plays, including *Downright Hooligan, Tarzan's Last Stand, Judge Jeffreys, Under New Management,* and new versions of Stoker's *Dracula,* Wycherley's *The Country Wife,* Gay's *The Beggar's Opera,* and Verdi's *Macbeth.*

Hugh Callingham Wheeler was born in Hampstead, London in 1912, the son of a civil servant. He was educated at Clayesmore School in Dorset and the University of London, where in 1933 he received a BA degree in English with honors. He migrated to the United States the following year and became a naturalized citizen in 1942. During World War II he served in the U.S. Army Medical Corps.

Wheeler had his ups and downs on Broadway. Generally, his dramas and comedies did not fare well: *Big Fish, Little Fish* (ANTA Theatre, March 15, 1961—101 performances), is about a small-press editor surrounded by hangers-on. *Look: We've Come Through* (Hudson Theatre, October 25, 1961—five performances), depicts the developing relationship between a girl-with-a-past and a young man with a homosexual history. *Rich Little Rich Girl*, based on a play by Miguel Mihura and Alvaro de Laiglesia (a pre-Broadway tryout, for two weeks, at the Walnut Street Theatre, Philadelphia, October 26, 1964), is a comedy of murder involving a South American dictator. *We Have Always Lived in the Castle*, dramatized from a Gothic novel by Shirley Jackson (Ethel Barrymore Theatre, October 19 1966—nine performances), is a moody drama tinged with subtle horrors. *Truckload* (Lyceum Theatre, September 6, 1975—closed after a week of previews) tells of hitchhiking across the country.

Wheeler did, however, contribute the libretto for some very successful musicals, winning Tony, Drama Critics Circle, and Drama Desk Awards: *A Little Night Music* (Shubert Theatre, February 25, 1973—600 performances), based on the 1955 Ingmar Bergman film, *Smiles of a Summer Night*, about a weekend of romance and sex at a country estate; *Irene* (Minskoff Theatre, March 13, 1973—604 performances), an adaptation of a 1919 musical focusing on the behind-the-scenes romance between a fashion designer and his female associate; *Candide* (Chelsea Theatre Center of Brooklyn, December 11, 1973—forty-eight performances; transferred to the Broadway Theatre, March 10, 1974—740 performances), a revised book of the 1956 musical based on Voltaire; and *Pacific Overtures* (Winter Garden, January 11, 1976—193 performances), additional material to the book by John Weidman regarding Admiral Perry's arrival in 1853 in isolated Japan. Wheeler's last contribution to Broadway was the book for the musical *Meet Me in St. Louis*, based on the 1944 film of the same title, about a family living in St. Louis, Missouri on the eve of the 1904 World's Fair (George Gershwin Theatre, November 2, 1989—252 performances).

For the cinema, Wheeler co-wrote the screenplays for *Five Miles to Midnight* (1962), *Something for Everyone* (1969), *Cabaret* (1972), *Travels with My Aunt* (1973), and *Nijinsky* (1980).

Prior to his stage and screen career, from 1936 to 1957, Wheeler jointly penned, with Richard Wilson Webb and other collaborators—under the pseudonyms Patrick Quentin, Q. Patrick, and Jonathan Stagge—thirty-three highly regarded detective novels, a true-crime paperback original (*The Girl on the Gallows*, 1954), and a collection of criminous tales, *The Ordeal of Mrs. Snow and Other Stories*. Several of his novels have been transformed into films—*Homicide for Three* (1948, from *Puzzle for Puppets*), *Black Widow* (1954, from *Fatal Woman*), *Female Fiends* (1958, from *Puzzle for Fiends*), *The Man in the Net* (1959, from a novel of the same name), and *Ladies Man* (1960, from *Shadow of Guilt*). "All of the Q. Patrick/Patrick Quentin/Jonathan Stagge novels," wrote R. E. Briney in *Twentieth Century Crime and Mystery Writers*, "are characterized by intricate plots, cleverly planted clues, and endings which legitimately surprise the reader."[13]

Born in New York City in 1930, Stephen Sondheim was educated at Williams College, where he won the Hutchinson Prize for musical composition. He began his professional career writing scripts for TV's *Topper* series. For his first Broadway credit, Sondheim composed the theme song of N. Richard Nash's 1956 drama, *Girls of Summer*. His ascent on Broadway began with his lyrics for *West Side Story*, *Gypsy*, and *Do I Hear a Waltz?* He continued to provide music and lyrics for many Broadway hits, becoming one of the giants of the modern American musical.

Among Sondheim's early successes was *A Funny Thing Happened on the Way to the Forum* (1962). In the 1970s he peaked with *Company* (1970), *Follies* (1971), *A Little Night Music* (1973), *Pacific Overtures* (1976), and *Sweeney Todd, the Demon Barber of Fleet Street* (1979). Along the way he provided additional lyrics for a revival of *Candide* (1973), wrote the music and lyrics for Aristophanes's *The Frogs* (1974), provided the lyrics for the musical cabaret *By Bernstein* (1975), and spawned a show dedicated to his body of work: *Side by Side by Sondheim* (1977).

The indefatigable composer-lyricist continued to score mightily during the 1980s: *Sunday in the Park with George* (1984), *Into the Woods* (1987), and *Jerome Robbins' Broadway* (1989), which included Sondheim's "You Gotta Have a Gimmick" from *Gypsy* and "Comedy Tonight" from *A Funny Thing Happened on the Way to the Forum*. Less spectacular were *Merrily We Roll Along* (1981) and *A Little Like Magic* (1986), a puppet show that included "Send In the Clowns." Sondheim also contributed to various revues: *Marry Me a Little* (1980), *You're Gonna Love Tomorrow* (1983), *Barbara Cook: A Concert for the Theatre* (1987), *Liliane Montevecchi on the Boulevard* (1988), *Together Again for the First Time* (1989), and *Putting It Together* (1993).

In 1991, Sondheim composed *Assassins*, an experimental musical that probes the minds of men who attempted to assassinate U.S. presidents. Three years later he collaborated with James Lapine on *Passion*, the tale about a triangular love affair in 1863 Milan.

Several of Sondheim's major shows were revived in London and New York during the 1980s, 1990s, and the first decade of the twenty-first century. In 1996, he teamed with playwright George Furth on a whodunit, *Getting Away with Murder*, which was savaged by the critics and ran at Broadway's Broadhurst Theatre for only seventeen performances.

In 1953, Sondheim wrote ten episodes for the television comedy series *Topper*. For the silver screen, he coauthored with Anthony Perkins the mystery *The Last of Sheila* (1973); wrote the score for *Stavisky* (1974), based on the life of financier and embezzler Alexandre Stavisky, who died mysteriously in 1934; composed the music for the epic *Reds* (1981); and contributed five songs to *Dick Tracy* (1990).

Acting Edition: Applause, Theatre Book Publishers.

Awards and Honors: A top ten selection in *The Best Plays of 1978– 1979*. Winner of the New York Drama Circle Award for Outstanding Musical and recipient of eight Tony Awards—for Best Musical, Best Book of a Musical (Hugh Wheeler), Best Music and Lyrics (Stephen Sondheim), Best Actor in a Musical (Len Cariou), Best Actress in a Musical (Angela Lansbury), Best Direction of a Musical (Harold Prince), Best Scenic Design (Eugene Lee), and Best Costume Design (Franne Lee). The British 1980 production garnered the Laurence Olivier Award and the London Standard Drama Award for Best New Musical and Best Actor (Denis Quilley). A 1993 London revival won the Olivier Award for Best Musical Revival and Best Actor in a Musical (Alun Armstrong). A 2005 Broadway revival garnered Drama Desk Awards for Outstanding Revival of a Musical and Outstanding Director of a Musical (John Doyle). The 2007 movie version received two Golden Globe Awards, one for Best Picture, Comedy or Musical and one for Best Actor, Comedy or Musical (Johnny Depp). The film was also nominated for three Academy Awards, winning for Art Direction.

In 1963, Hugh Wheeler was given a Special Edgar Allan Poe Award by the Mystery Writers of America for *The Ordeal of Mrs. Snow and Other Stories*, a collection also included in [Ellery] *Queen's Quorum*. Wheeler won the Tony Award and the Drama Desk Award for Best Book of a Musical in 1973 (*A Little Night Music*), 1974 (*Candide*), and 1979 (*Sweeney Todd*). He was nominated posthumously for a Tony for the book of *Meet Me in St. Louis* (1990).

Stephen Sondheim received seven Tony Awards, more than any other composer, winning Best Score for *Company* (1971), *Follies* (1972), *A Little Night Music* (1973), *Sweeney Todd* (1979), *Into the Woods* (1988), and *Passion* (1994), and a special Tony for Lifetime Achievement in the Theatre (2008). Sondheim won the Pulitzer Prize for *Sunday in the Park with George* (1985) and an Oscar for Original Song, "Sooner or Later," in *Dick Tracy* (1991). With coauthor Anthony Perkins, Sondheim received the Mystery Writers of America 1974 Edgar Award for Best Motion Picture Screenplay for *The Last of Sheila*.

Sondheim served as president of the Dramatists Guild, the professional association of playwrights, composers, lyricists, and librettists, from 1973 to 1981. In 1982 he was elected into The Theatre Hall of Fame and a year later was inducted into the American Academy of Arts and Letters. He was an honoree at the 1993 Kennedy Center Celebration of the Performing Arts. In 1996 President Clinton presented him the National Medal of the Arts. In 2010, the 1,055-seat venue on Manhattan's West 43rd Street that had been named after actor-producer Henry Miller was renamed to honor Stephen Sondheim. In 2011 Sondheim received New York City's highest prize for achievement in the arts, The Handel Medallion.

NOTES

1. Popular culture historian Peter Haining argues in his book *Sweeney Todd* (1993) that the title character was a real-life figure committing his crimes around 1800, and Professor Robert L. Mack, in *The Wonderful and Surprising History of Sweeney Todd* (2007) presents what he theorizes are the tale's factual origins.

2. *New York Times*, July 19, 1924.

3. Tod Slaughter (1885–1956) was an English actor best known for playing melodramatic villains on stage and screen. Born as Norman Carter Slaughter in Newcastle, he launched his stage career at the age of twenty, initially playing leading man roles and young heroes like Sherlock Holmes and D'Artagnan in *The Three Musketeers*. During World War I he served in the Royal Flying Corps. After the war, he managed several theatres and established a company that concentrated on Victorian blood-and-thunder melodramas. In 1931 he won acclaim playing Long John Silver in *Treasure Island* and body snatcher William Hare in *The Crimes of Burke and Hare*. Soon thereafter he garnered kudos in the title role of *Sweeney Todd, the Demon Barber of Fleet Street*, and, like Lon Chaney, Boris Karloff, and Bela Lugosi, his subsequent career became geared to macabre fare. During World War II he appeared on stage performing *Jack the Ripper*, *Landru*, and *Dr. Jekyll and Mr. Hyde*. In 1935, Slaughter made his first motion picture, *Maria Marten or Murder in the Red Barn*, in the role of a cold-blooded murderer, and the following year reprised on screen another of his stage triumphs, *Sweeney Todd, the Demon Barber of Fleet Street*. Adding to his gallery of flamboyant villains was *The Crimes of Stephen Hawke* (1936), in which Slaughter portrays a kind moneylender by day who, masquerading as the "Spine Breaker," is a ruthless murderer by night. In *The Ticket-of-Leave Man* (1937), Slaughter appears as an arch criminal concocting a bank robbery, while in *Sexton Blake and the Hooded Terror* (1938) he is "The Snake," the elusive leader of a band of masked criminals. *Crimes at the Dark House* (1939), loosely based on Wilkie Collins's *The Woman in White*, has Slaughter as the cunning Sir Henry Glyde, who disposes of his wealthy wife and replaces her with a lookalike. In *The Face at the Window* (1939), Slaughter leads a double life as a Parisian aristocrat and as the notorious killer nicknamed "The Wolf." He returned to the character of Sweeney Todd in *Bothered by a Beard* (1945) and to the role of a grave robber in *The Greed of William Hart* (1948).

4. *Daily News*, March 2, 1979.

5. *New York Post*, March 2, 1979.

6. *Women's Wear Daily*, March 2, 1979.

7. *Newsweek*, March 12, 1979.

8. *Wall Street Journal*, March 6, 1979.

9. *New York Times*, March 2, 1979.

10. *Christian Science Monitor*, March 7, 1979.

11. *WABC-TV7*, March 1, 1979.

12. Earlier films about the demon barber of Fleet Street were made in 1926 (starring G. A. Baugham), 1928 (starring Moore Marriott), 1936 (starring Tod Slaughter), and 1970 (titled *Bloodthirsty Butchers*, with John Miranda). On radio, the Sweeney Todd's saga was broadcast in Australia (1925), inspired an episode in *The New Adventures of Sherlock Holmes* (1946) and was featured on the Canadian Broadcasting Corporation's *CBC Stage Series* (1947). On television, Todd used his shiny razor in an episode of the ITV series *Mystery and Imagination* (1970), in the CBC-TV series *The Purple Playhouse* (1973), in a television movie commissioned by British Sky Broadcasting, starring Ben Kingsley (1998), and in a BBC television drama featuring Ray Winstone (2006).

13. John M. Reilly, ed., *Twentieth Century Crime and Mystery Writers* (New York: St. Martin's, 1980), 1236.

Murder at the Howard Johnson's (1979)

Ron Clark (United States, Canada-born, 1933–) and Sam Bobrick (United States, 1932–)

The action of the comedy-thriller *Murder at the Howard Johnson's* takes place in three different rooms of a hotel, "somewhere in America." The curtain rises on room 514 a week before Christmas. It is a typical blue-and-orange Howard Johnson hotel suite, furnished with a nondescript bed, two small bed tables, two armchairs, a dresser, and a television on a stand.

Arlene Miller, an attractive woman in her forties, is seated on the bed, motionless, obviously troubled. Doctor Mitchell Lovell, a contemporary of Arlene's, enters from the bathroom, goes downstage, and brushes his hair in front of an imaginary mirror. We soon learn that Mitchell is a dentist, and that Arlene, his lover, is the wife of patient Paul Miller. Arlene expresses slight concern over a husband "who loves me so much. . . . He gave me everything. A house, furniture, clothing, silverware. . . . I have five watches." She is certain that Paul will never agree to a divorce. Mitchell confesses that he purposely treated Paul with the wrong sized bridge in order to cause him "terrific pain." He embraces Arlene passionately and they begin to go over a plan they have hatched:

MITCHELL: One. I open the door.
ARLENE: Two. I say, "Come in, Paul."
MITCHELL: Three. I hit him over the head with a lamp.
ARLENE: Four. I give him a karate chop in the neck.
MITCHELL: Five. I hit him over the head with a chair.
ARLENE: Six. I shove a handkerchief in his mouth so he won't scream.
MITCHELL: Seven. I give him an injection and he sinks to his knees.
ARLENE: Eight. We drag him into the bathroom.
MITCHELL: And nine, we dump him into the bathtub face down and hold his head under water for as long as it takes.

It is six o'clock. Paul Miller, a used-car salesman who has been lured to the hotel on the pretext of a business deal, is surprised to find his wife and dentist there. He is taken aback when they confront him with a declaration of their love. Mitchell suggests that Paul must have suspected something: his wife went to see the dentist two or three times a week, sometimes even on Sunday, and didn't return home until midnight. Paul says that he trusted Arlene and asks her what went wrong. Arlene begins: "You're shallow, you're dull, you're gloomy, you never smile." Paul's entire wardrobe is grey, complains Arlene, while Mitchell's closet is filled with color and life—there are reds and greens and yellows. "There's adventure in Mitchell's closet," announces Arlene. "Excitement, a lust for life."

Arlene goes to the door and places the "Do Not Disturb" sign outside. She then locks the door and tells Paul, "We're going to kill you." Mitchell pulls out a white dentist jacket from his bag and proceeds to put it on. Paul chuckles at the "two amateurs" who, he is certain, "don't have the guts" to take his life. Smiling, he allows them to tie his hands and feet to a chair.

Arlene puts on a floozy wig and, imitating a sexy hooker, explains to Paul that she registered at the desk as Kitty Latour; when they find his body, they'll connect it to this girl. "It's a perfect crime," says Mitchell. "You came here to meet this hooker, you had sex in the bathtub, you hit your head and you drowned."

Mitchell takes a hypodermic needle from his bag and ejects some of the liquid into the air. He tells Paul, who reacts with growing concern, that after giving him a shot in both arms and legs, they'll bounce him into the bathtub.

Mitchell and Arlene drag Paul into the bathroom. Following a loud splash, they return quietly, go about gathering their things, put on their coats, turn off the lights, and shut the door behind them. The faint sound of Christmas music is heard from outside. Paul suddenly emerges staggering out of the bathroom, still attached to the chair. He has the shower curtain wrapped around him and is soaking wet. The Christmas music swells as the lights fade out.

Scene 2 unfolds six months later, on the 4th of July, in room 907 of the same hotel. Paul enters with a bucket of Kentucky Fried Chicken and offers it to Arlene. But his wife says frantically, "I'm a rotten person," and declares that she intends to take a bottle of sleeping pills, sit on the window sill and stab herself. Paul takes the vial of pills from Arlene and promises to change, even stop drinking.

While they munch on chicken, Arlene cries that dentist Mitchell Lovell has ruined her life and Paul mutters, "People like him should be destroyed. I'll kill him! I'll kill him!" Arlene takes a pistol out of her handbag and hands it to Paul. She explains that she purchased the weapon at Sears—"It's their own brand"—and assures Paul that after getting rid of

Mitchell "it'll be wonderful; just you and me." She suggests that Paul hide in the closet, that she'll coax Mitchell to bed, and the minute they start making love, Paul will jump out of the closet and shoot him.

Mitchell enters with a bottle of wine. He removes his pants and gets into bed. Arlene joins him. The closet door opens and Paul comes out, gun in hand. He tiptoes to the front of the bed and stands there pointing the gun at Mitchell, who is startled. "Shoot him, Paul," cries Arlene. She breaks away from Mitchell and jumps off the bed. Mitchell runs behind Arlene and uses her as a shield. She kicks Mitchell in the leg, runs to Paul's side, and keeps goading him to shoot, but he hesitates. He suggests that a better way to get rid of Mitchell is to push him out the window to make it seem like suicide. Under the threat of the gun, Mitchell climbs onto the window, sits on the sill, pushes himself off, and disappears. Arlene screams. Unexpectedly Mitchell pops up outside the window—there's a ledge.

Six months later, on New Year's Eve, Paul and Mitchell meet in room 1015. As they converse, we realize that Arlene has left with a twenty-five-year-old millionaire, Malcolm Dewey. Calling her a whore, a bitch, and a slut, they create a hangman's scaffold on a small wooden platform with a protruding arm on top from which hangs a rope. Mitchell mumbles unhappily that hanging Arlene is an expensive endeavor—the room, the wood, the nails, and the rope cost more than $100.

They spread around items belonging to Malcolm Dewey—a cape, a top hat, galoshes, and a scarf smeared with Arlene's lipstick. They have no doubt that the "evidence" will send Dewey up the river for life.

There is the sound of a key in the door. Arlene enters calling "Malcolm" and is surprised to encounter Paul and Mitchell. She tells them that Dewey has expanded her vision to a higher plateau; they have no sex, but with Malcolm she escaped her mundane way of life. Paul and Mitchell place a phone call to Malcolm Dewey. Mitchell utilizes a Spanish accent, introduces himself as Mr. Zapata, a rich businessman from Mexico, and invites Dewey over to discuss expanding his operation south of the border.

They place the rope around Arlene's neck and tighten it. The rope snaps. Arlene immediately runs to the door but the doorknob is stuck. Paul chases Arlene but stops midway, clutching his chest in pain. Concerned, Arlene and Mitchell help Paul to the bed and place some pillows behind him. Arlene rushes to the bathroom and returns with a glass of water. "I'm a loser," whispers Paul. "It's as simple as that. That's all I've ever been."

Arlene blames herself for being the guilty party "of this whole mess," but the men decide that "no one is as guilty as Malcolm Dewey." They begin to form a plan for his demise when there is a knock on the door. Malcolm's voice is heard: "Mr. Zapata!" A slow curtain begins to descend.

MITCHELL: I'll fill the bathtub.
PAUL: I'll fix the rope.
MITCHELL: I'll hit him with a lamp.
PAUL: I'll push him out the window.

The curtain is down.

* * *

Staged by Marshall W. Mason, *Murder at the Howard Johnson's* premiered at the John Golden Theatre in New York City on May 17, 1979. The three actors—Tony Roberts (Mitchell Lovell), Bob Dishy (Paul Miller), and Joyce Van Patten (Arlene Miller)—were applauded by the critics, but the play was snubbed. "Bob Clark and Sam Bobrick, the writers, are adept enough at turning out funny one-liners," wrote Douglas Watt, "but the jokes can't support the comic situation they've built, even slight as it is, for the duration of the evening."[1] Richard Eder opined that "the authors have created comic sketches, not comic characters and have given the performers nothing to renew themselves with. As the plot winds along it becomes less of a vehicle and more of a road, and a tiring one at that."[2] Clive Barnes was facetious: "The tension is not that unbearable. . . . Maybe the authors should have tried their luck with Ramada."[3]

The one more-or-less positive assessment came from Joel Siegel: "As a play I'd have to give this a C minus, but as a comedy it rates a good healthy B plus."[4]

Murder at the Howard Johnson's closed its doors after only four performances. But its catchy title, modest set, small cast, and the novelty of a homicidal comic situation viewed from three angles garnered a following. Community theatres and summer stock companies have presented the play constantly. *Murder's* most recent showing took place in Eastpointe, Michigan, where the Broadway Onstage Live Theatre presented it from September 11 through October 10, 2010.

* * *

Born in Canada in 1933, Ron Clark is an American playwright and screenwriter. He began his professional career in the 1960s, contributing to various television shows, including *The Danny Kaye Show* (1963), *The Jimmy Dean Show* (1963), and *The Smothers Brothers Comedy Hour* (1967–1968). During the 1970s he began writing plays with collaborator Sam Bobrick; their first play was *Norman, Is That You?* It premiered at the Lyceum Theatre in New York City on February 9, 1970, directed by George Abbott, and featuring Lou Jacoby and Maureen Stapleton as middle-aged, conservative parents who are aghast at discovering that their son is gay.

Clark and Bobrick's second Broadway venture was *No Hard Feelings* (1973), a comedy about a middle-aged electrical-fixtures tycoon who falls apart when his wife leaves him for a young lover. *Wally's Café* (1981) is a three-character play depicting a New Jersey couple who open a family-run diner near Las Vegas and their first customer is a young woman from Quincy, Illinois who yearns to go to Hollywood for fame and fortune.

All of the Clark-Bobrick Broadway plays had brief runs. Clark did better when writing and supervising the one-man, stand-up comedy show *Jackie Mason's The World According to Me!* that ran in New York twice, in 1986 and 1988. Clark remained active in writing for television and film up through the early 1990s. His television credits include, among others, *The Paul Lynde Show* (1972–1973), *Hot L. Baltimore* (1975), *E/R* (1985), *Silver Spoons* (1985–1987), *The Dick Van Dyke Show* (1988), *Moonlighting* (1989), *The Man in the Family* (1991), and *Baby Talk* (1991–1992). His screenplays include an adaptation of his play *Norman, Is That You?* (1976), the Mel Brooks comedies *Silent Movie* (1976), *High Anxiety* (1977), and *Life Stinks* (1991), as well as *Revenge of the Pink Panther* (1978), Peter Sellers's final escapade as bumbling Inspector Clouseau.

Sam Bobrick was born in Chicago, Illinois in 1932. His parents wanted him to be an accountant, and he joined the Air Force, where he worked in accounting for four years. After the service he enrolled at the University of Illinois, switched from law to journalism, and with a BS degree wound up in New York City. His initial positions were in the mailroom at ABC and as an office boy on *The Ray Bolger Show*. He began his life as a writer in the 1950s, penning gags for Robert Q. Lewis's radio show and dialogue for television game shows. Eventually, he landed on *Captain Kangaroo*, writing two or three shows a week, and on *The Andy Griffith Show*, for which his first script won a Writers Guild Award.

Bobrick immersed himself in a three-prong career—writing for television (*Gomer Pyle U.S.M.C.*, *Get Smart*, *Bewitched*, *Good Morning, Miss Bliss*, *Saved by the Bell*) composing songs (one of which was recorded by Elvis Presley; others were included in three MAD magazine albums), and penning plays. He met Ron Clark when both were hired to write for *The Kraft Music Hall* program. Bobrick moved to Los Angeles in 1962 and has since written thirty plays, most of them comedies. "There is nothing more satisfying to me than sitting in the audience and hearing people laugh," he told interviewer Tom Tugend. "I want people to leave the theatre feeling good. Life is tough enough. Why send an audience home suicidal? It only cuts into future ticket sales."[5]

Crime-tinged plays by Bobrick include 1983's *Hamlet II (Better Than the Original)*, a zany parody of Shakespeare's masterpiece with a much happier ending, and *Are You Sure?* (a murder mystery—or is it?—that unfolds in someone's mind—or does it?); in a case of shifting realities, it is unclear whether David wants to kill Caroline, Charley wants to kill David, or Caroline wants to kill everyone. In *Death in England* (1992), Inspector Edward Mirabelle of Scotland Yard is called to solve the bizarre case of several deaths in a London household. *The Steinway Case* (2003) is the story of two jurors on a murder trial who get involved romantically only to discover that they disagree about the verdict. *Flemming*, first produced in Germany in 2008, is a spoof of film noir thrillers from the 1940s and 1950s. Henry Flemming, bored by his privileged but mundane life, sells his lucrative brokerage firm and becomes a private detective. To the horror of his wife Karen, their living room soon begins to fill up with dead bodies. *The Psychic* (2010) is Adam Webster, a down-on-his-luck writer who in desperation to pay the rent, has put a sign in his apartment window, "Psychic Readings $25." The characters who show up get entangled in a hilarious homicide. *A Little Bit Wicked* begins with the blissful third marriage of a wealthy old man to a much a younger woman. Soon her somewhat sinister brother arrives for a short visit and shows no sign of leaving. Dark motives surface and a murder is committed.

For the movies, Bobrick provided the story of *The Last Remake of Beau Geste* (1977), a Foreign Legion parody, and scripted *Jimmy the Kid* (1983), based on a Donald Westlake novel, about the kidnapping of a wealthy youngster by a gang of incompetent bunglers.

Acting Edition: Samuel French, Inc.

Awards and Honors: Ron Clark was a member of the writing team nominated for an Emmy for Outstanding Writing Achievement in Music and Variety, *The Smothers Brothers Comedy Hour* (1968). Clark also shared a nomination for a Writers Guild Award for Best Comedy Written Directly for the Screen, *Silent Movie* (1977). Sam Bobrick won Writers Guild Awards for *The Andy Griffith Show*, *Get Smart*, and *The Kraft Music Hall*. He received an Emmy nomination for *The Smothers Brothers Comedy Hour*, and a Theatre L.A. Ovation nomination for *Lenny's Back*, a one-man show about Lenny Bruce. Bobrick is also the recipient of an Angie (International Mystery Festival Award, named for Angela Lansbury) for *Flemming*. Bobrick's *The Psychic* won the 2011 Mystery Writers of America Edgar for Best Play.

NOTES

1. *Daily News*, May 18, 1979.
2. *New York Times*, May 18, 1979.
3. *New York Post*, May 18, 1979.
4. *WABC-TV7*, May 20, 1979.
5. *Jewish Journal*, December 8, 2010.

Agnes of God (1980)

John Pielmeier (United States, 1949–)

Martha Livingston, a court-appointed psychiatrist, is assigned to determine the sanity of a young nun, Agnes, accused of strangling her own newborn baby with its umbilical cord and discarding the body in the convent's wastebasket. Who fathered the child and who actually killed it are among the key investigative queries of *Agnes of God*.

On the stark, bare stage, a clash develops between the cynical chain-smoking psychiatrist—an atheist, ex-Catholic—and the formidable, miracle-prone Mother Superior, Miriam Ruth, who insists that Agnes knows nothing about sex and birth and "hasn't been troubled, except by God." Livingston accuses Ruth of killing the baby herself, to avoid a scandal. The Mother Superior claims that while she did assist in the birth, she was panicked by "so much blood," and left to get help. At that point, she says, both mother and baby were alive.

Through hypnotic interrogation, Livingston elicits from Agnes details of a tortured childhood warped by a sadistic mother, an abusive upbringing that has affected her ability to think rationally. The simple-minded, haunted nun confesses to the killing, saying it was done to "save" the baby girl and "give her back to God." The siring of the infant remains an enigma—could it have been God's, or that of a visiting priest, or a local field hand? All three women—Agnes, Livingston, and Miriam Ruth—are forced to face some harsh realities in their own lives, and to examine their common faith.

* * *

Agnes of God was baptized as a stage reading at the O'Neill Theatre Center in Waterford, Connecticut on July 26, 1979, under the direction of Robert Allan Ackerman. Doctor Martha Livingston was portrayed by Jo Henderson, Mother Miriam Ruth by Jacqueline Brooks, Sister Agnes by Dianne Wiest. The first fully mounted production of *Agnes of God* opened on March 9, 1980 at the Actors Theatre of Louisville, Kentucky, directed by Walton Jones, with Adale O'Brien, Anne Pitoniak, and Mia Dillon. It was then presented at Center Stage, Baltimore, Maryland; Stage West, Springfield, Massachusetts; Old Globe Theatre, San Diego, California; Geva Theatre, Rochester, New York; and Players State Theatre, Coconut Grove, Florida.

The drama's Broadway debut took place at the Music Box Theatre on March 30, 1982, staged by Michael Lindsay-Hogg, featuring Elizabeth Ashley, Geraldine Page, and Amanda Plummer. The New York critics hailed the three stars but condemned the play: "While *Agnes of God* aspired to be both a chilling thriller and a stirring reaffirmation of the power of faith, it fails on both counts," wrote Frank Rich.[1] "Cleverly executed blood and guts evening in the theatre with aspirations beyond dramatic butchery. However, with so much theological musing, there is less in this than meets the sky," sighed Clive Barnes.[2] "A good deal of mumbo-jumbo obscuring the central issues, which has to do with faith and miracles," sniffed Douglas Watt.[3] "Uninteresting, unfascinating play . . . overwrought and underwrought," scowled Dennis Cunningham.[4] "For all its pretensions to serious analysis of psychological vs. ecclesiastic dogmas, *Agnes of God* amounts to little more than old-fashioned sensational melodrama," objected John Beaufort.[5] "If *Agnes of God* just fails as an example of the playwright's craft it shines as a demonstration of three actresses' seductive art," opined Richard Corliss.[6]

However, Ron Cohen of *Women's Wear Daily* found *Agnes of God* "a theatrical event" and complimented playwright Pielmeier: "His writing is taut, his scenes bristle with conflict and his dialogue has occasional eloquence as well as clarity."[7]

A sort of miracle occurred when *Agnes of God* overcame the mostly negative reception, running heftily for 599 performances and selling to the movies. The 1985 motion picture version, scripted by Pielmeier and directed by Norman Jewison, starred Jane Fonda, Anne Bancroft, and Meg Tilly in the three tour-de-force roles. The play was also released as an audiobook, performed by Barbara Bain and Emily Bergl, Los Angeles Theatre Works, in 2001.

* * *

Born in Altoona, Pennsylvania, in 1949, John Pielmeier earned a BA degree from the Catholic University of America in 1970 and an MFA degree from the Pennsylvania State University in 1978. He began his career as an actor, affiliated with the repertory companies of the Actors Theatre of Louisville, Kentucky; the Guthrie Theatre, Minneapolis, Minnesota; Milwaukee Rep; Alaska Rep; Baltimore's Center Stage; and the Eugene O'Neill National Playwrights' Conference, Waterford, Connecticut.

During the 1980s, Pielmeier penned two other Broadway ventures. The drama *The Boys of Winter* (Biltmore Theatre, December 1, 1985—nine performances) cast Matt Dillon and Wesley Snipes as members of a Marine Unit on a dangerous mission during the Vietnam War. The thriller *Sleight of Hand* (Cort Theatre, May 3, 1987—nine performances) depicts a small-time magician named Paul (played by Harry Groener) with a penchant for practical jokes. Paul's girlfriend, Sharon (Priscilla Shanks), is a dancer rehearsing an Edgar Allan Poe musical, "Poe on Toe." On Christmas Eve, a visitor arrives in Paul's Manhattan's loft, exhibiting a gun and a badge, and introducing himself as Dancer, a police detective (Jeffrey DeMunn). "Now the plot muddles," wrote critic Clive Barnes, "and there are enough twists to make a corkscrew go straight. . . . Despite the absence of disguise—sometimes regarded as essential to the genre—I thought this was one of the best thrillers since *Sleuth* and last season's unlucky *Corpse*."[8]

Barnes's colleagues were less kind. "*Hand* is, on the surface, an old-fashioned thriller with good performances and wonderfully sinister sets and lighting . . . but its effectiveness lies chiefly in the hand being quicker than the brain," smirked Don Nelson.[9] Frank Rich believed that the playwright aimed for "a witty, shriek-inducing entertainment in the tradition of *Deathtrap, Sleuth* and *Wait Until Dark*," but ended up with "a remotely credible, let alone coherent, plot."[10] Jack Curry was blunt: "*Sleight of Hand* is slight entertainment. . . . No doubt within a very short time the entire production will stage a disappearing act of its own."[11]

Three one-act plays of suspense by Pielmeier are included in *Haunted Lives*, produced in Edinburgh, Scotland, in 1984. The first playlet, *A Witch's Brew*, takes place in a darkened basement of a remote farmhouse, where Daed, his sister Jule, and her boyfriend Tucker nervously explore the macabre secrets of the shallow graves scattered about. The main characters of *A Ghost Story* are two hikers who find shelter from a winter blizzard in an isolated Maine cabin. They while away the time by telling each other supernatural yarns. What begins as fanciful storytelling suddenly turns into blood-curdling reality. In *A Gothic Tale*, a man named Isaac is kept prisoner in the tower of an island mansion by a woman, Eliza, who warns her captive that unless he confesses his love for her, he will die. Just before Isaac expires from starvation, a large cupboard is opened to reveal the ghoulish remains of other men who have preceded him.

Pielmeier's additional plays include *Courage*, a one-man show looking into the intimate life of J. M. Barrie, presented at the Actors Theatre of Louisville, 1983; *Impassioned Embraces*, a collection of short plays and monologues, at the Repertory Theatre of St. Louis, 1989; *Willi*, a one-man show inspired by the speeches of mountaineer Willi Unsoeld, at Seattle's Contemporary Theatre, 1991; and the book for *Young Rube*, a musical based on the early years of cartoonist/inventor Rube Goldberg, at the Repertory Theatre of St. Louis, 1993.

Pielmeier returned to the suspense genre with *Voices in the Dark*, initially commissioned and produced by Seattle's Contemporary Theatre in October 1994, eventually making it to Broadway's Longacre Theatre on August 12, 1999. Judith Ivey starred as Lil, a radio talk show host who is menaced by a mysterious caller. Critic Ben Brantley said that *Voices in the Dark* "has managed to throw in elements from just about every shivery woman-in-jeopardy plot of the last six or seven decades. It has evoked, to its detriment, everything from old-fashioned telephone-centered shockers like *Sorry, Wrong Number* and *Midnight Lace* to carnage-in-the-woods movies like *Friday the 13th*. . . . Even the smart and resourceful Ms. Ivey can't overcome the humiliation of having to make like Jamie Lee Curtis in her scream queen period, brandishing a butcher knife while sobbing in terror."[12]

Fergus McGillicuddy, on the other hand, opined that John Pielmeier "has crafted an intelligent, masterfully plotted, and superbly engrossing tale of obsession, psychological tension, and consequences."[13]

Voices in the Dark ran for sixty-eight performances and garnered a Mystery Writers of America Edgar Award for Best Mystery Play.

For television, Pielmeier has written and produced more than twenty films, including *The Shell Seekers* (1989), *Through the Eyes of a Killer* (1992), *Original Sins* (1995), *Forbidden Territory: Stanley's Search for Livingston* (1997), *Happy Face Murders* (1999), *Flowers for Algernon* (2000), *Hitler: The Rise of Evil* (2003), *The Capture of the Green River Killer* (miniseries, 2008), adaptations of two Patricia Cornwell mysteries, *At Risk* and *The Front* (2010), and an eight-hour miniseries based on Ken Follett's best-selling novel *The Pillars of the Earth* (2010).

Pielmeier's latest venture is a stage adaptation of William Peter Blatty's 1971 novel, *The Exorcist*, about a ten-year-old girl possessed by the devil and the Roman Catholic priest who tries to save her. The Geffen Playhouse of Los Angeles hosted the July 3, 2012, world-premiere opening under the direction of John Doyle.

Acting Edition: Samuel French, Inc.

Awards and Honors: *Agnes of God* was a top ten selection in *The Best Plays of 1981–1982*—"certainly one of the highlights of the season."[14] Tony Award, 1982: Amanda Plummer, Best Featured Actress in the title role. Drama Desk Award, 1982: Amanda Plummer, Outstanding Featured Actress in a Play. For his 1985 screenplay of *Agnes of God*, John Pielmeier earned a Writers Guild of America Award nomination for Best Screenplay Based on Material from Another Medium. Pielmeier's *Voices in the Dark* won the 1999 Edgar Award for Best Play. In 2003, Pielmeier was inducted into the Blair County, Pennsylvania Arts Hall of Fame. His musical *Slow Dance with a Hot Pickup* garnered four 2007 New Hampshire Theatre Awards, including Best New Play and Best Production of a Musical. For his 1983 television movie, *Choices of the Heart,* about slain American missionaries in El Salvador, Pielmeier received a Christopher Award, the Humanities Award, a Writers Guild of America nomination for Best Teleplay, and an Honorary Doctorate of Letters from St. Edward's University in Austin, Texas.

NOTES

1. *New York Times,* March 31, 1982.
2. *New York Post,* March 31, 1982.
3. *Daily News,* March 31, 1982.
4. *WCBS-TV2,* March 30, 1982.
5. *Christian Science Monitor,* April 19, 1982.
6. *Time,* April 12, 1982.
7. *Women's Wear Daily,* March 31, 1982.
8. *New York Post,* May 4, 1987.
9. *Daily News,* May 4, 1987.
10. *New York Times,* May 4, 1987.
11. *USA Today,* May 4, 1987.
12. *New York Times,* August 13, 1999.
13. www.talkinbroadway.com/world/voices.htm, August 12, 1999.
14. Otis L. Guernsey Jr., ed., *The Best Plays of 1981–1982* (New York: Dodd, Mead, 1982).

Nuts (1980)

Tom Topor (United States,
Austria-born, 1938–)

Newspaperman Tom Topor utilized psychiatric cases at New York's Bellevue Hospital as a springboard for *Nuts*, a courtroom drama about inmate Claudia Faith Draper, who is intent on proving herself mentally fit to stand trial for slaughter-in-the-first-degree rather than being institutionalized indefinitely. Claudia, a high-priced hooker, believes that eventually she will be able to prove herself innocent of killing a violent client.

The court action takes place on the seventh floor of Bellevue. Frank Macmillan, representing the district attorney's office of New York County, claims that two examining psychiatrists found the defendant to be unfit to stand trial. Dr. Herbert Rosenthal, the unit chief of the hospital's prison ward, testifies that following a series of examinations the patient was diagnosed as a paranoid schizophrenic, severely out of touch with reality, dangerous to herself and others.

Claudia's bewildered mother, Rose, states on the witness stand that after she divorced Claudia's father and married Arthur Kirk, her daughter's behavior changed: she started to keep to herself, treated Kirk as if he had the plague, and acted as if she didn't trust anyone. During cross-examination of the self-assured Arthur Kirk by Claudia's court-appointed lawyer, Aaron Levinsky, it becomes evident that the stepfather abused his stepdaughter: "I washed her, and I dried her, and I sprinkled her, and I dried her, and I sprinkled her all over with talcum . . . young skin, soft, you touched it, you felt you were touching something magic."

Pugnacious and sardonic, Claudia Draper takes the stand in the third act of *Nuts*, relating her story of a tortured childhood, an unhappy marriage, an abortion, irregular income as a massage therapist, and enrollment at New York University's Law School paid for by offering "favors" to men. She gets a hundred dollars for "a straight lay," says Claudia, a hundred for "a hand job," a hundred for "head" and a hundred and fifty for "rimming." Claudia insists that she knew what she was doing "every goddam minute" and is responsible for her behavior. "I won't be nuts for you," she declares. Judge Murdoch concurs: "I will remand the defendant to the custody of the Commissioner of Corrections to await trial on the felony charge of manslaughter in the first degree."

Ultimately, Claudia makes peace with her parents; in the 1987 motion picture version, however, Claudia solely reunites with her mother, a more persuasive conclusion. Coscripted by Topor and directed by Martin Ritt, the all-star cast included Barbra Streisand in, arguably, her best screen performance as Claudia, Richard Dreyfuss as defense attorney Levinsky, Robert Webber as the prosecutor, Maureen Stapleton as mother Rose, Karl Malden as stepfather Kirk, Eli Wallach as a hostile psychiatrist, and James Whitmore as Judge Murdoch.

A Recorder's announcement notifies us that "on June 15th, 1979, Claudia Faith Draper was tried in the State Supreme Court, New York County, on a charge of manslaughter in the first degree" and acquitted.

* * *

Off-off-Broadway's Theatre at St. Clements presented a workshop draft of *Nuts* in June 1974. On February 23, 1980, WPA Theatre offered a revised version under Steve Zuckerman's direction, a production that was cosponsored by Universal Pictures and moved to Broadway's Biltmore Theatre on April 28, 1980. The critics hailed Anne Twoney as Claudia (the actress won a Theatre World Award for her "outstanding" performance), but were sharply divided regarding the merits of the play. "A slashing courtroom drama. . . . *Nuts* is a play that bares its teeth right from the start and plunges forward through three terse acts," wrote Douglas Watt,[1] while Frank Rich called the play "a courtroom melodrama without suspense, a moral debate without passion, a soap opera with more laughs than tears . . . a mess."[2] Clive Barnes hailed *Nuts* as "quite simply terrific, old time, belt them in the aisles, the guts and if necessary the kidneys, theatre,"[3] but Christopher Sharp believed that "while the play may not be nutty it is very foolish."[4] Joel Siegel announced that "Tom Topor knows his way around a courtroom. . . . He's just opened one of Broadway's best plays of 1980";[5] simultaneously, Dennis Cunningham complained that *Nuts* "is rather long on the craft of putting a play together, is woefully short on creating characters. . . . *Nuts* certainly has its heart in the right place, but not, however, its head."[6] The play ran for ninety-six performances.

Nuts gathered steam during the first decade of the twenty-first century with productions at the Altarena Playhouse in Alameda, California (2004); the Raven Playhouse in North Hollywood, California (2008); and the Lee Center for the Performing Arts in Alexandria, Virginia (2010).

* * *

Tom Topor, born in Vienna, Austria, in 1938, was brought to London in 1939 and came to New York ten years later. He earned his BA degree at Brooklyn College in 1961. He began his writing career as a reporter for the Paterson, New Jersey, *Morning Call*, the *New York Times*, the *New York Daily News*, and mostly the *New York Post*, for which he covered police stations, courtrooms, and hospitals. He simultaneously pursued his interest in theatre as actor, director, stunt man, and playwright.

In 1969, Topor followed his calling as a playwright with several one-act plays staged off-off-Broadway. *Answers* depicts a suspect interrogated at the headquarters of Homicide South in Manhattan for a crime about which he claims to know nothing (WPA Theatre, June 8, 1972). *But Not For Me* is about the odd things that people do, or don't do, for love (Theatre at Noon, May 10, 1976). *Romance: Here to Stay* focuses on a husband and wife who prove to be hopelessly inept bank robbers (Theatre of the Riverside Church, December 1, 1978).

For television, Topor scripted and directed *Judgment* (1990), based on the real-life story of a Louisiana priest accused of molesting young parishioners; penned *Perfect Murder, Perfect Town* (2000), a miniseries inspired by the murder of six-year-old JonBenét Ramsey; collaborated with Norman Mailer on *American Tragedy* (2000), a teleplay focused on attorney Johnnie Cochran's defense of O. J. Simpson; served as creative consultant on *The Glimpse of Hell* (2001), in which a Navy officer, in charge of a gun turret on the battle ship USS *Iowa*, becomes the scapegoat of higher-ups' ineptitude when an explosion destroys the turret and kills forty-seven sailors; and teamed with other writers on adapting Nelson DeMille's novel, *Word of Honor* (2003), wherein the Army recalls an ex-lieutenant to stand trial for a massacre committed by his platoon in a Hue hospital.

For the silver screen, Topor wrote *The Accused* (1988), in which rape victim Sarah Tobias (played by Jodie Foster), enraged at the light sentence her attackers received, prods a female prosecutor, Kathryn Murphy (Kelly McGillis), to charge those who encouraged the men who gang-raped her in a sleazy roadhouse. Foster won a Best Actress Academy Award, a Golden Globe Award, and a National Board of Review Award for her portrayal.

Acting Edition: Samuel French, Inc.

Awards and Honors: A top ten selection in *The Best Plays of 1979–1980* ("*Nuts* was for two of its acts, the most gripping courtroom session in years and a survivor of its weaker third.")[7] Tom Topor won the Writers Guild of America Award for his script of the 1990 made-for-television film, *Judgment*.

NOTES

1. *Daily News*, April 29, 1980.
2. *New York Times*, April 29, 1980.
3. *New York Post*, April 29, 1980.
4. *Women's Wear Daily*, April 30, 1980.
5. *WABC-TV7*, April 28, 1980.
6. *WABC-TV12*, April 28, 1980.
7. Otis L. Guernsey Jr., ed., *The Best Plays of 1979–1980* (New York: Dodd, Mead, 1980), 15.

Extremities (1980)

William Mastrosimone (United States, 1947–)

Sexual assault rears its ugly head in William Mastrosimone's taut, violent *Extremities*. What begins as a lazy day in the old New Jersey farmhouse Marjorie shares with two female roommates turns nightmarish when a stranger, Raul, shows up at the door when she's alone. Under the pretext of looking for a friend, he enters the house, rips out the phone wire, latches onto Marjorie's hair, pulls her down, mounts her, and forces a pillow over her face. "You gonna be nice?" he taunts. "Tell me you love me. . . . Touch me. All over. Nice. Touch my hair. My mouth. My neck. . . . And touch me down there. . . . And tell me you wanna make love." As Raul proceeds to rape her, Marjorie manages to grab an aerosol can and spray insecticide in his face. He screams, holding his eyes. Marjorie attempts to run for the door, but Raul grabs her legs. Struggling to escape, she yanks an extension cord from the socket, loops it around her tormentor's neck, and pulls.

Raul finds himself blindfolded and bound in a tangle of cords, clotheslines, belts, and other household implements. He threatens: "You call the cops? You don't got a fuckin' case! They gotta Miranda me! And let me go! And then one day I come back. . . . Get you in some parking lot and carve up that teasin' face." Enraged, Marjorie dumps a kettle full of hot water on him. Then she drags Raul to the fireplace, pokes him with a poker, douses him with ammonia, and brandishes a match. "I started a graveyard near the woods for the animals that get killed up on the highway," she says. "This time I dig deeper. . . . I want to hear you scream under the dirt, like me under the pillow." Queried, Raul discloses that while patching up potholes for the County "you come ridin' down the highway on your bike in your little white shorts. . . . You was beautiful. . . . I said 'How ya doin?' You didn't say nothing, looked at me like I was a dead dog. You pissed me off so I came back here to fuck you."

Marjorie's roommates, Terry and Patricia, return home from work. Horrified, they want to call the police, but Marjorie objects: "Police. Charges. Arraignment. Lawyers. Money. Time. Judge. Jury. Proof. His word against mine . . . that animal goes free . . . then what do I do? Come home and lock myself up. Chainlock, boltlock, deadlock. And wait for him. Hear him in every crack of wood, every noise in the wall, every twig tapping on the window." Cunningly, Raul manipulates Terry and Patricia to gain sympathy, but Marjorie keeps saber rattling an array of menacing tools—a noose, a spade, a claw hammer, tweezers, a hunting knife. Finally, Raul breaks down, admits to serial rapes, and whimpers for help. Marjorie sends her friends to get the police.

* * *

William Mastrosimone writes in an afterword of the Acting Edition of *Extremities* that the idea for the play came from a real-life rape case in which the culprit escaped punishment while the victim "quit her job, lost her pension, and bought a one-way ticket to the opposite coast."[1] The playwright relates that for two years producers rejected his controversial drama. "The first production was in a community college by amateurs. The town council made a motion to ban the play. . . . The next production was in a hole in the wall in Philadelphia. The reviews ran the spectrum from loathing to worship (which has always been the trend)."[2]

In July 1980, *Extremities* was presented by Rutgers Theatre Company, directed by John Bettenbender, who repeated the assignment for the Fifth Annual Festival of New American Plays at the Actors Theatre of Louisville, bringing with him Ellen Barber and Danton Stone to duplicate the roles of Marjorie and Raul. Critic Mel Gussow dispatched: "The play provoked an almost visceral response from the audience—from enthusiasm to hostility. I found a sordid little melodrama . . . contrived and untruthful to its central situation."[3]

Extremities represented the United States in the Baltimore International Festival, June 1981, with Gordana Rashovich as Marjorie. Susan Sarandon took over the role, with James Russo cast as Raul and Ellen Barkin as Terry, when *Extremities* opened at New York's Westside Arts Center, Cheryl Crawford Theatre, on December 22, 1982, under the direction of Robert Allan Ackerman. Reviewer Frank Rich asserted that the play "does exert a fascination that may keep those with strong stomachs riveted . . . but *Extremities* ultimately blurs the issues rather than illuminate them."[4] Clive Barnes found *Extremities* "a feeble play, feebly given, that never lives up to the modest pretensions of its theme."[5] John Beaufort declared that "*Extremities* never rises above the level of headline sensationalism."[6] However, Douglas Watt concluded that the play provides "a good, nasty, jolting evening of playgoing"[7] and T. E. Kalem testified that *"Extremities holds the playgoer transfixed."*[8]

Extremities raised its high-voltage curtain for 325 performances. Karen Allen and Farrah Fawcett substituted in the role of Marjorie during the long run. Helen Mirren portrayed Marjorie at London's Duchess Theatre, where the play opened on November 26, 1984, advertised as "unsuitable for children." That production also received both positive and negative reviews. Milton Shulman applauded "a powerful and disturbing thriller" and opined that "if the events themselves are melodramatic and far-fetched, nevertheless the moral dilemma is pertinent and stark."[9] Michael Billington found *Extremities* "a vigorous melodrama on a deeply serious theme: the dilemma faced by women who are victims of sexual violence. . . . Undeniably the play is lurid, violent and shocking; but then so is rape."[10] Steve Grant wrote, "It is a gripping, serious and well-constructed tale . . . Mirren is magnifico."[11] The naysayers included Lyn Carter, who sniffed, "This nasty gratuitously violent American play merely marginal-izes the issue, using rape as the springboard for that West End stalwart—the psychological thriller/melodrama. . . . Slick, sick and dangerously silly."[12] Michael Ratcliffe scowled, "It is a horrible dilemma and a horrible story, but almost entirely ludicrous in the hands of Mastrosimone, who has nothing new to say about violence and the banalities of everyday life or the contagious fever of revenge, while resolving the play's dilemma with a sticky smudge of compassion and a lazy trick."[13] John Barber moaned, "Painful to sit through, *Extremities* at the Duchess is a nasty and unhealthy piece of work. . . . It is yet another example of sanctimonious sensationalism: it combines sadism and sexual titillation, and presents both as if offering a worthy social message."[14] Francis King summed up his feelings with the statement, "Essentially, this is pornography."[15]

Extremities was produced in a Hebrew translation by the Library The-atre, Ramat-Gan, Israel, in 1993, eliciting a rave review from the critic of *Ha'aretz*, a leading Israeli newspaper, who found the play "important, sharp and pitiless, with wide implications about rape and its acceptance by society at large, providing the audience a gamut of emotions and lots to think about."[16]

Farrah Fawcett and James Russo were recruited to repeat their stage roles in a 1986 motion picture version, scripted by Mastrosimone and directed by Robert M. Young. The movie begins with an unnerving en-counter between Marjorie and a masked man in the parking lot of a local mall. The police seem indifferent. An early sequence introduces the rap-ist's wife and daughter as he peruses Marjorie's wallet at home. One week later, Raul shows up at Marjorie's isolated farmhouse—and the vicious confrontation begins.

* * *

William Mastrosimone was born in Trenton, New Jersey in 1947. He attended The Pennington School and received an MFA in playwriting from Mason Gross School of the Arts, part of Rutgers University, where his first play, *Devil Take the Hindmost*, was produced in 1977, winning the David Library of the American Revolution Award. Mastrosimone made his professional debut with the highly praised *The Woolgatherer*, the story of a rough, hard-drinking truck driver, Cliff, who drifts into the life of a shy, daydreaming five-and-dime salesgirl named Rose. Despite their differences, Cliff and Rose end up falling in love. The play premiered at the Rutgers Theatre Company, New Brunswick, New Jersey in 1979, and subsequently was presented by off-Broadway's Circle Repertory Company (1980), Center Stage, Baltimore (1981), and Chicago's Goodman Theatre (1982). Also in 1982, a production of *The Woolgatherer* in Los Angeles received the L.A. Drama Critics Award for Best Play.

In the early 1980s, the Actors Theatre of Louisville, Kentucky premiered Mastrosimone's *A Tantalizing*, about a lonely professional woman who brings a once-elegant tramp to her home (1982), and *The Undoing*, depicting another relationship, this one between a guilt-ridden woman searching for redemption and the stranger who comes to work for her in a poultry slaughterhouse (1984).

The Seattle Repertory Theatre presented several Mastrosimone plays during the 1980s: *Shivaree*, wherein a hemophiliac, sheltered youth finds love with a belly dancer, in 1983 (in 1996, the play was shown in New York by the Hudson Guild Theatre); *Cat's Paw*, in which a terrorist who killed twenty-seven people plays a cat-and-mouse game with a reporter in an attempt to justify his action (1986); and *The Understanding*, about a retired stonemason who refuses to leave his home to make way for a new highway (1987). *The Understanding* was transported to off-off-Broadway's South Street Theatre in 1989 and, named *A Stone Carver*, produced by off-Broadway's Soho Rep in 2006.

Other plays by the prolific Mastrosimone include *Nanawatai!* (an Afghan word that means "sanctuary"), picturing the capture and execution of a Soviet tank crew in Afghanistan—for which he did research in that country disguised as a freedom fighter. The play premiered in Bergen, Norway in 1984, and was subsequently produced by the Los Angeles Theatre Center in 1985. A homeless teenage thief is the protagonist of *Tamer of Horses*, a drama mounted by the Crossroads Theatre Company, New Brunswick, New Jersey in 1985. *Sunshine* is a character study of a glass booth porn queen and was presented by off-Broadway's Circle Rep in 1989.

Mastrosimone analyzes teen violence in *Like Totally Weird*, in which Hollywood youngsters, inspired by brutal action movies, go on a rampage.

Bang Bang You're Dead, based on a real-life event, focuses on a high school student who murders his parents and five classmates. *Like Totally Weird* premiered at the Actors Theatre of Louisville in 1998; *Bang Bang You're Dead* was first presented in 1999 at Thurston High School in Springfield, Oregon, where a school shooting had occurred a year earlier.

The heroine of *The Afghan Women* is an Afghan-American physician who returns to Afghanistan to found an orphanage and takes a stand against a warlord who wants to use children as hostages until he gets to the border of Pakistan. The drama premiered at the Mill Hill Playhouse in Trenton, New Jersey in 2003. In *Dirty Business*, a party girl is caught between the mafia and the newly elected president of the United States. The play debuted at the New Works Festival, Florida Stage, in West Palm Beach, Florida in 2008.

For the cinema, Mastrosimone scripted *The Beast of War*, aka *The Beast* (1988, based on *Nanawatai!*); *With Honors* (1994), in which a Harvard student accidently drops his thesis paper down a grate and finds himself blackmailed by the homeless man who found it; and *Bang Bang You're Dead* (2002), from his drama about high school violence.

Mastrosimone's contributions to television include the 250-minute biography *Sinatra* (1992); *The Burning Season* (1994), based on the true story of a Brazilian rubber tapper who was murdered in the mid-1980s when leading a protest against industrialists planning to burn the rainforest for a new road and ranch land; *Benedict Arnold: A Question of Honor* (2003), the story of the Revolutionary War's notorious traitor; and half a dozen episodes of *Into the West* (2005), a miniseries about settlers and Native Americans.

In his introduction to *William Mastrosimone: Collected Plays*, M. E. Comtois opines that the playwright's works "Challenge us, sometimes to make us recoil in shock or at least become unsettled. . . . Fresh insights enrich us and we are reminded of that endless human diversity—indeed human potential—that we so often never recognize on our own."[17]

Acting Edition: Samuel French, Inc.

Awards and Honors: A top ten selection in the *Best Plays of 1982–1983*: "The standard-bearer for domestic playwriting . . . raised provocative questions with the melodrama."[18] Outer Critics Circle Awards, 1982–1983—Best off-Broadway play and John Gassner Playwriting Award. Los Angeles Drama Critics Award for Best Play of 1982—*The Woolgatherers*. NAACP Award for Best Play of 1987—*Tamer of Horses*. 1988 Roxanne T. Mueller Award for Best Film at the Cleveland International Film Festival—*The Beast*, based on *Nanawatai!* New Jersey Governor's Walt Whitman Award for Writing, 1989. Honorary Doctorate of Humane Letters, Rider College, 1989. Golden Globe Award for Best Mini-Series on television—*Sinatra*—in 1992. Humanities Prize for *The Burning Season*, 1995. A Daytime Emmy Award for *Bang Bang You're Dead* (2002). Western Heritage Award (2006) for *Into the West*.

NOTES

1. William Mastrosimone, *Extremities* (New York: Samuel French, 1985), 66.
2. Mastrosimone, *Extremities*, 68.
3. *New York Times*, March 29, 1981.
4. *New York Times*, December 23, 1982.
5. *New York Post*, December 23, 1982.
6. *Christian Science Monitor*, January 5, 1983.
7. *Daily News*, December 23, 1982.
8. *Time*, January 3, 1983.
9. *Daily Mail*, November 27, 1984.
10. *Guardian*, November 27, 1984.
11. *Time Out*, November 29, 1984.
12. *City Limits*, November 30, 1984.
13. *Observer*, December 2, 1984.
14. *Daily Telegraph*, November 27, 1984.
15. *Sunday Telegraph*, December 2, 1984.
16. *Ha'aretz*, Tel-Aviv, Israel, July 6, 1993.
17. M. E. Comtois, *William Mastrosimone: Collected Plays* (Newbury, Vt.: Smith and Kraus), ix.
18. Otis L. Guernsey Jr., *The Best Plays of 1982–1983* (New York: Dodd, Mead, 1983), 26.

Tricks of the Trade (1980)

Sidney Michaels (United States, 1927–2011)

Playwright Sidney Michaels was nominated for Tony Awards in three successive seasons in the 1960s. *Tchin-Tchin*, a comedy borrowed from the French about a haughty Englishwoman (played by Margaret Leighton) and an earthy Italian construction worker (Anthony Quinn), opened at Broadway's Plymouth Theatre on October 25, 1962 and ran for 222 performances. It was nominated for a Tony for best play in 1963, losing to Edward Albee's *Who's Afraid of Virginia Woolf?*

Michaels's *Dylan*, a biographical portrayal of the poet Dylan Thomas, with Alec Guinness in the title role, opened at the Plymouth on January 18, 1964, ran for 273 performances and was nominated for a best play Tony, losing to John Osborne's *Luther*. Later that year, Michaels wrote the book and lyrics for the musical *Ben Franklin in Paris*, a fictionalized account of the American statesman in the French capital. It opened at the Lunt-Fontanne Theatre on October 27, 1964, ran for 215 showings, and earned Michaels his third Tony nomination, only to lose to Joseph Stein, author of *Fiddler on the Roof*.

A subsequent project, a collaboration with composer Richard Rodgers on a musical, *The Beautiful Woman*, about Egyptian queen Nefertiti, was abandoned. Another team effort, with composer Mitch Leigh, *Halloween*, tried out on the road with Jose Ferrer and Barbara Cook but never made it to Broadway. *Goodtime Charley*, a 1975 musical about Joan of Arc, featuring Ann Reinking and Joel Grey, came to Broadway's Palace Theatre on March 3, 1975, but gasped after 104 performances.

In 1980, Michaels detoured to the suspense genre with *Tricks of the Trade*, which he dubbed "A Romantic Mystery." A cold war spy story, the action unfolds in a posh psychiatry office on Central Park South in Manhattan. There are two main characters in the play—Dr. August Browning, an unorthodox analyst who may or may not have a license to practice, and is not averse to solving crossword puzzles during $75-an-hour sessions; and Diana Woods, a young, attractive new patient who may or may not need psychological help and vehemently objects to having her picture taken. Off stage, communicating via intercom, is secretary Judy. Lurking in the shadows are two goons, Howard and Paul, characters eliminated in the published edition of the play.

Over the course of nearly a year, a battle of wits develops between August and Diana. In an attempt to add bits of color, the encounters occur during Halloween, Thanksgiving, Christmas, and Valentine's Day. At some point, left alone in the office, Diana opens the doctor's desk and finds, deep in a drawer, a gun. She also discovers a safe hidden behind a bookcase.

August cross-examines Diana about the shooting murder of "a friend" in Czechoslovakia. She claims to be engaged to an art dealer but he, too, is found dead, seemingly of suicide. Eventually both August and Diana admit to being double agents, and confess their love for each other.

In a climactic scene, Diana enters stealthily, manipulates the combination of the hidden safe, and takes out a microfilm. The lights are suddenly switched on. August stands by the door, gun in hand. He declares that he has no doubt that she's Nadia, a feared KGB agent, with an anagram to Diana. She hands him the microfilm. He attaches a silencer to the gun but, soon thereafter, surprises Diana by laying the weapon aside and burning the microfilm in an ashtray. They hug passionately and agree to flee to Rio de Janeiro. Diana bemoans the loss of the microfilm, which could have been sold for a million dollars. August suggests that she write down names and addresses of Russian spies who are implanted in the West; he'll sell the list in West Berlin, and the money will ensure their cozy life in Brazil. Diana consents, sits at the desk, and writes.

August buzzes the intercom. In a minor surprise, he tells Diana that there wasn't anything on the burnt microfilm; it was blank. Now that he has her list of Russian operators, two gents from the CIA are waiting for her in the outer office.

Diana exits. Doors slam shut. August sits, lights a cigarette, and stares emptily at the audience, as the lights slowly fade away to darkness.

* * *

Directed by Gilbert Cates, *Tricks of the Trade* opened at Broadway's Brooks Atkinson Theatre on November 6, 1980. George C. Scott portrayed Dr. August Browning. Scott's real-life wife, Trish Van Devere, played Diana Woods. The reception of the morning-after critics was devastating.

"*Tricks of the Trade* is a dog of a thriller," wrote Douglas Watt, who continued to call the play "feeble," "confused," "silly," "indigestible stew," and "a murky pell-mell exercise."[1] Frank Rich complained, "The entire story is unbelievable, right down to the smallest details."[2] Douglas Cunningham bemoaned "a rickety vehicle" and called the playwright "the real villain of the evening."[3] Clive Barnes scoffed, "Despite a final slew of obvious surprises all I could care about was the number of signs around the theatre all tantalizingly named EXIT."[4]

Tricks of the Trade closed its doors after one performance.[5]

* * *

Sidney Ramon Michaels was born in New York City in 1927. His parents divorced when he was young and he moved with his father, Max Michaels, to Brookline, Massachusetts. Sidney made his first contact with show business through his father, a producer of burlesque shows and a theatre manager in Boston. After high school, Sidney served in the Coast Guard and then studied drama at Tufts University, graduating in 1950.

In addition to penning plays and musicals, Sidney Michaels wrote for television and the movies. His screenplays include *Key Witness* (1960), about a Los Angeles man, played by Jeffrey Hunter, who witnesses a gang murder. The mob members terrorize him and his family to keep him from testifying against them. *The Night They Raided Minsky's* (1968), starring Jason Robards, is a comedy about the birth of striptease. *Cry of the Innocent* (1980) is the story of a former Green Beret, now an insurance executive, enacted by Rod Taylor, who seeks revenge against the people who caused a plane crash in Ireland that wiped out his family.

Michaels contributed episodes for television's *Johnny Staccato* (1959–1960), which featured John Cassavetes as a private detective; *The Deputy* (1959–1961), a western starring Henry Fonda as Marshal Simon Fry; and *Bob Hope Presents the Chrysler Theatre* (1963–1967), an anthology of dramas, comedies, thrillers, westerns, and musicals, all introduced by comedian Bob Hope. Michaels shared writing credits on the 1967 television adaptation of the Rodgers & Hammerstein musical *Carousel*, starring Robert Goulet as Billy Bigelow, the ill-fated carousel barker.

Michaels died of Alzheimer's disease on April 22, 2011 in Westport, Connecticut. He was 83.

Acting Edition: Samuel French, Inc.

Awards and Honors: Sidney Michaels was nominated for Best Play Tony Awards in three consecutive years in the 1960s—for *Tchin-Tchin*, *Dylan*, and *Ben Franklin in Paris*.

NOTES

1. *Daily News*, November 7, 1980.
2. *New York Times*, November 7, 1980.
3. *WCBS-TV2*, November 6, 1980.
4. *New York Post*, November 7, 1980.
5. Three years later, in 1983, Arthur Bicknell's *Moose Murders* shared a similar fate: It received unanimous negative reviews and closed after one performance.

Zooman and the Sign (1980)

Charles Fuller (United States, 1939–)

Brandishing a switchblade knife, Zooman, a black Philadelphia teenager, addresses the audience in the opening monologue of *Zooman and the Sign*, admitting that he fatally slashed a foreigner who was at the wrong place at the wrong time. Drawing a gun, he reports that he unwittingly killed a little girl who was hit by a stray bullet.

Reuben and Rachel Tate, parents of the twelve-year-old girl who was killed, mourn the senseless loss. Their grief erupts into fury when they learn that although the neighbors were on their porches at the time of the shooting and must have witnessed it, no one has come forward to help the police with their investigation. People are reluctant to become involved. Bitterly, Reuben, a former professional boxer and current bus driver, posts a sign over his porch: "The killers of our daughter, Jinny, are free on the streets because our neighbors will not identify them."

The sign annoys the community, and they blame the Tates for smearing the reputation of the middle-class neighborhood and reducing real-estate values. Reuben gets into a fistfight at a local bar and is thrown through the window. Stones are hurled at the Tate home and threats to burn the house down pour in. The harassment of the Tates is reminiscent of the Stockmanns in Henrik Ibsen's *Enemy of the People*.

Rachel wants the sign removed, for the sake of peace, but Reuben insists that it stays up until somebody comes forward.

Eventually the police arrest Zooman's accomplice, a kid named Stockholm, who confesses to the shooting. While the law is looking for Zooman, in the dark of night he attempts to rip the sign off the Tate home. Uncle Emmett Tate, frightened and half-asleep, shoots him. Another meaningless killing.

* * *

Zooman and the Sign is an uncompromising, gritty play in which the author condemns the African-American community for apathy, urging

145

them not to rely on outside help, but to save themselves from a suffocating, deadly environment. "His play is an indictment of Black Americans who capitulate to tyrannical punks within their midst," wrote Frank Rich upon the presentation of *Zooman and the Sign* by the Negro Ensemble Company at off-Broadway's Theatre Four on December 7, 1980.[1]

Artfully, the playwright manages to build sympathy for the young killer, Zooman, who questions his unsavory way of life when he, too, is prematurely cut off. "He is turning into a creature capable of imagining, understanding, the plights of others. . . . [T]he author has made us feel nearly as much for the slayer as for the slain," opined Walter Kerr in a follow-up piece. "If the play is not entirely realized, it is rich in contradiction, in a challenging overlap of right and wrong, in stage figures who are plausible people rather than handy tags."[2]

Directed by Douglas Turner Ward and featuring Giancarlo Esposito in the title role, *Zooman and the Sign* ran for thirty-three performances, then returned on June 20, 1981, for forty-four more. On November 22, 1994, the play was revived at Second Stage Theatre under the direction of Seret Scott, with Larry Gillard Jr., provoking Ben Brantley to comment, "*Zooman* remains a bracing and unfortunately relevant piece of theatre."[3] Clive Barnes lamented, "*Zooman and the Sign* is far more timely and topical now than it was more than a decade ago."[4] But other critics felt that *Zooman* had lost its punch. Howard Kissel commented, "Though the play is full of insights, it tries to make too many points too facilely."[5] James Hannaham claimed, "It seems out of context and watered down at Second Stage."[6] George Evans called it a "Minor, schematic play."[7] *Zooman and the Sign* ran through January 15, 1995.

Off-Broadway's Signature Theatre Company mounted *Zooman and the Sign* at Peter Norton Space on March 24, 2009, directed by Stephen McKinley-Henderson, with Amari Cheatom as Zooman. It ran for a month.

Fuller wrote the screenplay *Zooman* for a made-for-TV movie in 1995. Khalil Kain enacted the title role, with Louis Gossett Jr. as Reuben Tate, Cynthia Martells as Rachel Tate, and Charles S. Dutton as Emmett Tate.

*　*　*

Charles Henry Fuller was born in Philadelphia, Pennsylvania in 1939. His father was a printer and young Charles developed a fondness for reading and writing while helping him proofread galleys. He attended a Roman Catholic high school and enrolled at Villanova University (1956–1958). In 1959 he joined the Army, serving in Japan and South Korea. He left the army in 1962 and later studied at La Salle University (1965–1967). In 1967 he cofounded the Afro-American Arts Theatre in Philadelphia, codirecting it until 1971, when he moved to New York City.

Prior to *Zooman*, Charles Fuller penned *The Village: A Party* (1968), a play portraying a community of racially mixed couples. The drama was produced at the McCarter Theatre in Princeton, New Jersey, in 1968. Re-titled *The Perfect Party*, it traveled to off-Broadway's Tambellini's Gate Theatre in 1969 for twenty-one performances. Fuller's *Candidate*, the story of a black politician running for mayor of a northern city, was performed at the Henry Street Settlement in 1974. *In the Deepest Part of Sleep*, a play about a black youth who overcomes the turmoil caused by his emotionally disturbed mother, played at off-Broadway's St. Mark's Theatre in June 1974 for thirty-two showings. In 1976, the Negro Ensemble Company presented *The Brownsville Raid* at the Theatre de Lys, for 112 performances. The play is Fuller's dramatization of an actual 1906 incident in which an entire black army regiment, stationed in Texas, was falsely accused of instigating a violent public disturbance and dishonorably discharged. Fuller also wrote the libretto for *Sparrow in Flight* (1978), a musical biography of Ethel Waters.

In 1981, Fuller's *A Soldier's Play,* combining mystery and sociology through a murder investigation at an Army base in Louisiana, won the Pulitzer Prize. The Negro Ensemble Company staged the play at off-Broadway's Theatre Four for 468 performances. In 1988, Fuller collaborated with several other playwrights on the book of the musical *Urban Blight*, produced by the Manhattan Theatre Club and featuring Laurence Fishburne, which ran for forty-eight showings. *We,* a series of Civil War plays by Fuller that included *Sally, Prince, Jonquil,* and *Burner's Frolic*, were produced by the Negro Ensemble Company at Theatre Four during 1989–1990.

Fuller wrote *The Sky Is Gray* (1980) for PBS, a teleplay about a young black boy who comes of age in 1940s Louisiana, grappling with poverty and racism. For CBS, Fuller penned *A Gathering of Old Men* (1987), a drama unfolding in a Louisiana sugarcane plantation after a white farmer is shot and racial tensions boil. *The Wall* (1998), an episode for "The Badge," focuses on three items left at the Vietnam Veterans Memorial Wall—a pencil holder, a sheriff's badge, and an electric guitar—each connecting the living to the dead. *Love Songs* (1999) consists of three connected segments about simple folk who try to find love and peace in their lives.

Fuller is a member of the Dramatists Guild; Writers Guild East; and P.E.N. board of directors, American Division.

Acting Edition: Samuel French, Inc.

Awards and Honors: A top ten selection in the *Best Plays of 1980–1981*— "off Broadway's standout."[8] Two 1980–1981 Obie Awards: Playwriting, Charles Fuller; Performance, Giancarlo Esposito. Charles Fuller received a Creative Artist Public Service Award, 1974; Rockefeller Foundation Fellow, 1975; Endowment for the Arts Fellow, 1976; Guggenheim Fellow,

1977–1978; the Pulitzer Prize for Drama for *A Soldier's Play*, 1982; Academy Award nominations for best picture and screenplay for *A Soldier's Story*, 1984; honorary degrees from La Salle University, 1982; Villanova University, 1983; Chestnut Hill College, 1985.

NOTES

1. *New York Times*, December 8, 1980.
2. *New York Times*, December 21, 1980.
3. *New York Times*, December 12, 1994.
4. *New York Post*, December 12, 1994.
5. *Daily News*, December 12, 1994.
6. *Village Voice*, December 27, 1994.
7. *Variety*, January 1, 1995.
8. Otis L. Guernsey Jr., ed., *The Best Plays of 1980–1981* (New York: Dodd, Mead, 1981), 27.

Dracula (1980)

John Mattera (United States, 1953–)

Bram (Abraham) Stoker (1847–1912) was an Irish civil servant before moving to London as business manager for the great actor Sir Henry Irving. Legend has it that in the fiftieth year of his life, following a hefty dinner, Stoker had a nightmare about a vampire rising from his tomb, and thus the story of Dracula was born.[1] But there is little doubt that Stoker was well versed about the literary vampires who preceded his *Dracula*— Lord Ruthven in John Polidori's *The Vampyre* (1819), Sir Francis in *Varney the Vampyre, or The Feast of Blood* (1847) by James Malcolm Rymer, and the lesbian vampires in Sheridan Le Fanu's *Carmilla* (1872).

Stoker selected the name of his vampire from historical sources dating back to the fifteenth century about a ferocious, bloodthirsty Romanian prince, Vlad III (1431–1476), called Dracul—"The Devil." The novel *Dracula*, published in 1897, still stands as one of the most brooding and horrifying works in the English language. It has spawned many theatrical adaptations over the years.

In 1980, John Mattera dramatized Bram Stoker's novel faithfully, keeping the title *Dracula* but adding a few twists of his own. The first act transpires in an antique bedroom at Dracula's castle in Varna, Transylvania, and we see firsthand how Jonathan Harker, a visiting lawyer from England, is seduced by three pale brides of the Count. In the second act, the action shifts to the elegantly furnished home of Henry and Martha Westenra, the proud parents of Lucy, Harker's fiancée. The house is located not far from London and is adjacent to a mental asylum run by a friend, Dr. Peter Seward, and an old, ruined estate, Carfax, recently purchased by a titled foreigner. The Westenras have not heard from Harker for a while and are concerned. Adding to their anxiety is a change that has come over Lucy. Despite the young woman's engagement to Jonathan, she seems sullen and depressed.

Dr. Seward and Professor Van Helsing are enlisted for advice and help, but they cannot save Lucy's friend, Mina Murray, who falls prey to the vampire's fangs and graphically perishes on stage (in most other adaptations of *Dracula*, Mina succumbs behind the scenes).

R. M. Renfield, an asylum inmate, is very active in the Mattera version. Renfield explains to Van Helsing that he munches on flies and spiders "to absorb their life, of course. . . . It's the way of nature. The spider eats the fly; the bird eats the spider; the cat eats the bird; the dog eats the cat; and, and, if, if I eat them all, if I drink their blood, I will live forever." Renfield attempts to protect his Master by claiming that Dracula is a vegetarian who eats only "Health foods; granola, soy beans, carrot juice." But at the end Renfield joins the vampire hunters in their exploration of Carfax, sneaks up behind the Count and plunges a stake through his back. "How ironic," gasps Dracula, "That after centuries of conquest, I am felled by an imbecile."

In a sardonic final scene we learn that Dr. Seward couldn't cope with what happened and is now an inmate himself, while Renfield is a free man. Solicitor Harker returns home to Lucy. "Oh, Jonathan," she exclaims as she rushes to embrace him. As the lights dim, we see Jonathan's face over Lucy's shoulders. His teeth are sharp and extended.

* * *

John Mattera is a member of the Dramatist's Guild and Horror Writers of America. *Dracula* is his most successful adaptation with continuous productions in the United States and Canada. His other known work is a 1983 dramatization of *Time after Time*, based on the time-travel book by Karl Alexander in which Jack the Ripper has used H. G. Wells's time machine to disappear into the future and Wells decides it's his responsibility to bring him back to England and to justice. The action begins in 1890s London and jumps to the fume-filled streets of modern San Francisco.

Mattera is also the author of several one-act plays. In *An Open and Shut Case* (1981), young, handsome Harold Benton is married to rich, elderly, disabled Elizabeth. Harold convinces Elizabeth to hire a nurse, cook, housekeeper, and gardener as part of his plan to murder her. But Harold's scheme goes awry in an unexpected way. *Frankenstein* (1981), adapted by Mattera with Stephen Barrows, changes the premise of the original Mary Shelley novel by the last-minute revelation that it was not the Monster who killed Victor Frankenstein's young brother and fiancée, but a madly jealous Henry Clerval, Victor's best friend. *Abra-Cadaver* (1982) is a twisty murder mystery. As the play starts, Jack and his girlfriend Christine plot to kill Marie, Jack's wife. We later learn that Christine has informed Marie of the plot and they are working together to do in the unsuspecting Jack.

However, Jack is hatching another scheme—and so is Marie! And there's still one more twist in store before the final curtain.

In 1998, Mattera penned *The Mirror of Dori Gray*, loosely based on the novel *The Picture of Dorian Gray* by Oscar Wilde, changing the gender of the lead characters. Here Dori Gray's flaws are reflected not in a portrait hidden away in a dusty attic, as in the original story, but rather in a mirror that she carries in her purse. Dori is seen at first as a naïve adolescent but as time marches on, she is consumed by vanity, ambition, and greed. Mattera's other works include numerous short stories. Simultaneously he has worked with emotionally disturbed adolescents and is currently a principal with the state of Connecticut. His job is to ensure that orphans receive an appropriate education.

* * *

Born in Dublin, Ireland, Bram (Abraham) Stoker was a sickly child who grew up to become a sinewy, six-foot-two athlete. Stoker planned to follow in his father's footsteps as a civil servant, but at Trinity College the young man changed course after falling under the spell of Romantic poets Byron, Keats, and Shelly. He excelled in the debate society, and joined the dramatic club. He also began reviewing theatrical productions in Dublin's *Evening Mail*—without pay.

A glowing account by Stoker of Henry Irving's *Hamlet* brought the two together and in 1878 Stoker was engaged as the business manager of Irving's theatre in London, the Lyceum, a position he held for twenty-seven years, until the famed actor's death in 1905. Among the productions Stoker serviced were Shakespeare's *Hamlet*, *The Merchant of Venice*, *Romeo and Juliet*, *Macbeth*, *Cymbeline*, and *Richard III*, as well as Boucicault's *The Corsican Brothers* (from Dumas), W. G. Wills's adaptation of Goethe's *Faust*, Conan Doyle's *Waterloo*, Cervantes's *Don Quixote*, Tennyson's *Becket*, Sardou's *Dante*, and *The Bells*, a conversion by Leopold Lewis from the French, in which Irving portrayed his signature role—an Alsatian village burgomaster, Mathias, who years ago bludgeoned to death a Jewish merchant for his gold and has ever since been haunted by the sound of the bells on his victim's sleigh.

Well liked and respected, Stoker developed cordial and friendly relationships with luminaries of literature and the arts, on both sides of the Atlantic, including Oscar Wilde (with whom he remained friendly despite "stealing" and marrying Wilde's sweetheart, Florence Balcombe), Alfred Tennyson, Arthur Conan Doyle, George Bernard Shaw, Henry James, Franz Liszt, James Whistler, Walt Whitman, and Mark Twain.

Though heavily taxed with the myriad details of running a theatre company, controlling its budget and preparing its tours, Stoker made time to write eighteen books. His nonfiction output is composed of *Duties of Clerks of Petty Sessions in Ireland* (1879), *A Glimpse of America* (1886), *Personal Reminiscences of Henry Irving* (1906), *Snowbound, the Record of a Theatrical Touring Party* (1908), and *Famous Impostors* (1910), in which he theorizes that Queen Elizabeth I had died as a baby and court officials secretly substituted her with an infant boy. *Under the Sunset* (1881) is a volume of fairy tales. "Not gruesome like the Grimm Brothers' or fanciful like Hans Christian Anderson," asserts Barbara Belford in the biography *Bram Stoker*. "The tales are almost biblical, permeated with allegories of good and evil and an atmosphere of dreamlike unease."[2]

Stoker's first novel was *The Snake's Pass* (1891), a yarn of contraband and buried treasure. *The Shoulder of Shasta* (1895) recounts a mismatched summer romance between a delicate San Francisco girl and a grizzly mountain man while *Miss Betty* (1898) connects an heiress with a dashing highwayman. *The Mystery of the Sea* (1902) is centered on letters written in cipher and the *Jewel of Seven Stars* (1903) on an ancient Egyptian curse (filmed as *Blood from the Mummy's Tomb*, 1972, and *The Awakening*, 1980). Filled with demonic women are *The Lady of the Shroud* (1909) and *The Lair of the White Worm* (1911, filmed in 1989). A discarded chapter from *Dracula* was published posthumously as the title short story in the collection *Dracula's Guest* (1914, filmed in 1936 as *Dracula's Daughter*).

Acting Edition: The Dramatic Publishing Company.

NOTES

1. Reportedly, Mary Shelley and Robert Louis Stevenson also dreamed, respectively, of *Frankenstein* and *Dr. Jekyll and Mr. Hyde* before committing their masterpieces to paper.

2. Barbara Belford, *Bram Stoker* (New York: Knopf, 1996), 139.

The Picture of Dorian Gray (1980)

Jack Sharkey (United States, 1931–1992)

In 1889, during dinner at a London restaurant, the American publisher Joseph M. Stoddart challenged Arthur Conan Doyle and Oscar Wilde to come up with an unusual yarn for his *Lippincott's Monthly Magazine*. Doyle offered Stoddart his second Sherlock Holmes novel, *The Sign of Four*, and Wilde created *The Picture of Dorian Gray*.

The Picture of Dorian Gray, Wilde's longest prose narrative, appeared as the lead story in the June 20, 1890 issue of *Lippincott's*. Wilde revised the novel, adding several chapters, for a book publication by Ward, Lock and Company in April 1891.[1]

The Picture of Dorian Gray has since been adapted to the stage, screen, and television many times. In 1980, the prolific playwright Jack Sharkey and composer/lyricist Dave Reiser collaborated on "a musical drama" based on the novel. They dedicated their work to Oscar Wilde, "poet, novelist, dramatist, lecturer, raconteur—and frightening philosopher." In a foreword to the published manuscript, Sharkey and Reiser state that they

> read the book thoroughly, noticed several scenes that would play eminently well onstage, and several moments that could be rendered in song quite easily—but we also noticed something else, something that began pervading our minds with its downright creepy possibilities: Oscar Wilde had not only written a novel—he had written what amounted to a *mystery story*—a mystery story *without* a solution! Or—and this is when we started getting goosebumps—*was* there a solution—an implied solution—all clues given—just waiting for the reader to ferret them out and realize the enthralling truth?![2]

Poking and sniffing between the lines of Wilde's novel, the two collaborators came up with answers to such tantalizing queries as why does the Alan Campbell character agree to help Dorian dispose of the body of a man he murdered? Why does Dorian abruptly decide to go to an opium den? What is Gwendolyn Langdon's secret? Who was the beautiful Hetty

Duval whom the fickle Dorian loved above all other women? And why does Dorian determine, in the last scene of the book, to destroy the portrait he has posed for?

Set in and about London in the mid-1800s, the Sharkey-Reiser musical begins at the studio of Basil Hallward, where the renowned artist is putting the finishing touches on the portrait of the aristocrat Dorian Gray, who seems bored with the endeavor. The cynical, foppish Lord Henry Wotton arrives for a visit and is intrigued by Dorian, "a young man whose male vitality is just barely able to prevent our seeing him as beautiful." Hallward, facing the portrait, sings "The Best I've Ever Done." He turns the canvas on the easel toward the audience, and we see Dorian as "a truly magnificent picture of youth, against a brilliant background of flowers and blossom-laden boughs and brilliant blue sky."

Hallward presents the portrait to Dorian with a comment, "This picture will always show you at the height of your youth," to which the young man responds, "How I wish it could be otherwise, that the picture could change and grow old, and I could remain this way forever."

Dorian begins to lead a life of debauchery and vice. He gets entangled with several ill-fated romances, wooing and discarding a naive young actress, Sybil Vane, who commits suicide, and a high-society beauty, Gwendolyn Langdon, who ends up as a tart in an opium den. As time passes, Dorian remains young and good-looking while his portrait gradually changes, first with a cruel smirk, and later as a misshapen, monstrous creature. An unseen chorus sings,

> His sins grew more than scarlet, they were blacker than the Pit!
> And still he searched afar for darker deeds he might commit!

Basil Hallward pays a visit to Dorian and admonishes him for his growing notoriety. Dorian takes Basil to the attic and pulls aside the cloth that covers the portrait. Basil staggers back with a cry of horror: "This is the face of a satyr—the eyes of the devil!" Says Dorian: "It is the face of my soul."

Basil sings "Prayer," pleading with Dorian to "kneel in devout supplication . . . put an end to all your sinful ways . . . and ask God to be your guide." Dorian picks up a small, sharp fruit knife lying on a dusty trunk and stabs Basil again and again. Basil topples, and as the lights fade out— the hands in the picture are now dripping with blood.

By threatening Alan Campbell, a medical student who has been in love with Gwendolyn Langdon, that he will inform Gwen's mother, Lady Margaret, that her daughter has become a waterfront prostitute, Dorian solicits Alan's help in getting rid of most of Basil's body with acid, and burying the rest of the cadaver in a hole dug in his garden. "It might do wonders for your daffodils," chuckles Dorian.

Alan reveals to Dorian that Gwen has borne his child. Dorian, shocked, rushes to an opium den to face his former lover. Gwen and several hags croon, "In praise of addiction," at the end of which she hurls the dregs of her drink into Dorian's face. James Vane, Sybil Vane's brother, now older, grayer but still a powerful sailor, appears on the scene, accuses Dorian of causing his sister's suicide and draws a gleaming knife, but Dorian points at his youthful appearance and convinces James that he couldn't be "the man you seek for a crime committed before my own time."

James lets Dorian go. Gwen laughs raucously and relates to James that "Dorian Gray hasn't aged in a generation; something protects him, he never gets caught." James sings hoarsely, "I will track him down, I will seek him, I will hack him down where he stands" and follows Dorian to his country estate. But during a hunting escapade, as the hunters follow a small scurrying animal, they mistakenly shoot James, who was hiding behind a shrub.

For the first time, Dorian feels pangs of remorse. He sobs and tells his latest sweetheart, Hetty Duval, "the most radiantly beautiful blond woman on the face of the earth," that he is vile. Hetty says that she would like to become his wife and confides that she is the adopted daughter of the Duvals; she is actually "the bastard child of an unfortunate woman," Gwendolyn Langdon. Dorian realizes to his horror that Hetty is his daughter. He rushes to the attic and uncovers the portrait, now revealing young Dorian in the full bloom of youth and beauty. Dorian snatches the knife with which he killed Basil Hallward, and intends to stab the portrait when he hears approaching footsteps. He hides behind a curtain. Hetty enters. Dorian emerges, looking like the monster from the canvas in all his repellent horror.[3] Hetty shrieks in terror and recoils. The monster moves toward her, hands outstretched. She backs away and topples backward through the upper window, hurtling headlong to her death.

The Monster cries, "Oh, no," grabs a hand-mirror, glances at his face, crumples and falls lifeless on the floor near the portrait. The lights dim swiftly, with a spotlight lingering briefly on the painting, seen with all its pristine beauty, as the curtain descends.

* * *

The dark, supernatural elements of *The Picture of Dorian Gray* have attracted filmmakers since the early days of the cinema. Silent pictures based on the novel were made in 1910, 1913, 1915, 1916, 1917, and 1918. Most notable is MGM's 1945 version, scripted and directed by Albert Lewin, starring Hurd Hatfield as Dorian Gray, George Sanders as Lord Henry Wotton, and Angela Lansbury as Sybil Vane. *Dorian*, aka *Pact with the Devil* (2001), is a modernization derived from the Wilde story, depicting a New York model (played by Ethan Erickson) selling his soul to his manager-devil (Malcolm McDowell). Played by Stuart Townsend, Dorian Gray is one of the Victorian hero/villains gathered in the 2003 adventure movie *The League of Extraordinary Gentlemen*.

London audiences saw a stage adaptation of the novel, by G. Constant Lounsbery, at the Vaudeville Theatre, on August 28, 1913, directed by and starring Lou Tellegen, running for thirty-six performances. Disappointed New Yorkers went to the Broadway productions of *The Picture of Dorian Gray* in May 1928, adapted by David Thorne (Biltmore Theatre, sixteen performances); in July 1936, adapted by Jeron Criswell (Comedy Theatre, sixteen performances); and in August 1936, adapted by Cecil Clarke (Comedy Theatre, thirty-two performances), all panned by the critics. A similar fate befell the off-Broadway offerings at the Bleecker Street Playhouse, in August 1956, of an adaptation by Justin Foster presented arena-style and called by the *New York Times* "superficial and amorphous,"[4] and at the Showboat Theatre, in August 1963, of a version adapted and directed by Andy Milligan. According to the *Times*, "nothing that Wilde might have done in this extravagant search for experience could have been as horrifying as what the company associated with *The Picture of Dorian Gray* did to his memory last night."[5]

"A working script for the stage from the novel by Oscar Wilde," concocted by Jim Dine, was published by London's P. Petersburg in 1968. That same year, a one-man show of *Dorian*, penned and performed by John Stuart Anderson at London's New Arts Theatre, was lambasted by playwright David Hare, who asserted that "Anderson isn't capable of feeling each character anew when he's just whipped away from the last."[6] Anderson revamped his adaptation into an ensemble play, to be performed by a cadre of eight actors.

In 1972, John Osborne, the angry young man of Britain's theatre, concocted his own version of *The Picture of Dorian Gray*, which was performed three years later at London's Greenwich Theatre to lukewarm reviews. Musicalizations of *The Picture of Dorian Gray* were created by the Hungarian Matyas Varkonyi (1990); Americans Lowell Liebermann (1996), Allan Reiser and Don Price (1996), and Richard Gleaves (1997); and finally by the Canadian team of Ted Dykstra and Steven Mayoff (2002).

One of the more successful dramatizations of *The Picture of Dorian Gray* was presented by off-Broadway's Irish Repertory Theatre in 2001. Realizing that the tale is too well known to hold any shock value, adapter-director Joe O'Bryne decided, as reported by the *New York Times*, to "rediscover Wilde's wit and language. The Lord Henry character gets most of the Wilde-icisms, many of them still ringing with relevance."[7]

The Wilde story inspired a dance-drama conceived by Robert Hill for the American Ballet Theatre, premiering at Manhattan's City Center in 2003, and a rock opera written and produced by Barry Gordon, showcased at off-Broadway's Barrow Group Theatre in 2005. A Czech musical induced by the novel debuted in Prague a year later.

In addition, 2008 was rife with Dorian Gray appearances: an Australian dramatization by playwrights Greg Eldridge and Liam Suckling; a dance adaptation of the story by choreographer Matthew Bourne that made its debut at the Edinburgh International Festival; a Grand Guignol style production by Canadian Ian Case, staged for Halloween at Craigdarroch Castle in Victoria, British Columbia; and a version with book, music, and lyrics by Randy Bowser, premiering at Pentacle Theatre in Salem, Oregon. In 2009, *The Picture of Dorian Gray* was adapted by Linnie Reedman, with music by Joe Evans, for a run at London's Leicester Square Theatre. It played to full houses.

* * *

Jack Michael Sharkey and David Reiser belong in the group of prolific American playwrights whose works are constantly performed by little theatres across the land but seldom in New York City. Others are Tim Kelly, Wilbur Braun, Wall Spence, James Reach, Don Nigro, Fred Carmichael, Jules Tasca, and F. Andrew Leslie.

In addition to *The Picture of Dorian Gray*, Sharkey and Reiser teamed on the musicals *Betsy* (1975), about Betsy Ross and how she came to sew America's first flag; *Woman Overboard!* (1975), a madcap romantic comedy taking place on a Caribbean cruise; *What a Spot!* (1976), a parody of Robinson Crusoe, unfolding on a desert island inhabited by an amorous gorilla named Lolita; *Ichabod* (1977), a song-and-dance adaptation of the story by Washington Irving about the village schoolmaster and the Headless Horseman; *Not the Count of Monte Cristo?* (1977), a play-within-a-play wherein three ragtag actors attempt to stage a musical version of the Dumas classic; and *Operetta!* (1978), part nostalgic tribute and part hilarious send-up of the quaint musical form of yesteryear.

Sharkey and Reiser had a banner year in 1982 with *And on the Sixth Day*, a rollicking romp highlighted by verbal battles between God and Satan; *My Husband the Wife*, a wacky comedy that focuses on domestic squabbles; and *Saloonkeeper's Daughter*, an unblushing musical melodrama featuring a flamboyant villain, a damsel in distress, and a stalwart but brainless hero.

It's Not the End of the World, Is It? (1983), depicts a family and neighbors who go to the safety of a backyard atomic bomb shelter when an erroneous alarm is sounded. In *Jekyll Hydes Again* (1984), Junior Jekyll, fresh out of medical school, rediscovers the formula that changed his father into Mr. Hyde. Junior tastes the potion and turns into a monster. However, this musical version ends happily. The publisher, Samuel French, promises that "the show is ebullient, the dialogue is priceless and the songs range from frightening to charming to hilarious." *Zingo!* (1985) is a fast-moving farce about two unsavory corporations competing over the formula for a top-secret flavor.

In *Love with a Twist* (1986), Sharkey and Reiser dramatize several O. Henry stories, including "The Gift of the Magi" and "The Last Leaf." *Coping* (1987) pokes fun at such dilemmas as how to deal with a fickle spouse, a fiancé whose hobby is stealing cars, and a daughter who brings home a boyfriend with purple hair and earrings. *The Pinchpenny Phantom of the Opera* (1988) retells the Gaston Leroux story, utilizing a tacky single set and a chorus of two with one guest soprano. The soprano's life is threatened by strangulation, electrocution, poison fleas, and a falling chandelier; the theatre director wants one of the chorus girls to star in the show.

On his own, Sharkey penned the mystery comedies *The Creature Creeps* (1977), mixing mayhem and silliness high in the Carpathian Mountains of Transylvania; *The Murder Room* (1977), a zany spoof of crime thrillers with secret chambers, sliding panels, and trap lids galore; and *Par for a Corpse* (1980), in which guests in a Catskills resort are murdered one by one. The curtain of *While the Lights Were Out* (1988) rises on a blonde in black lace holding a bloody dagger while standing over a dead man.

* * *

Chicago born Jack Sharkey began writing when he was ten years old. He graduated from college with a BA in Creative Writing, taught school for several years, then enlisted in the Army. Based in New Mexico, he wrote, produced, and directed shows for the Enlisted Men's Club. From 1957 to 1958, Sharkey worked as a copywriter for Sears, Roebuck and Company, then went to New York and began a freelance writing career. At first he penned science fiction stories, published in *Galaxy*, *Amazing*, *Fantastic*, *Worlds Beyond*, and *Alfred Hitchcock's Mystery Magazine*, as well as detective novels, notably *Murder, Maestro, Please* (1960) and *Death for Auld Lang Syne* (1962). Beginning in 1965 he dedicated himself exclusively to playwriting. He has published eighty-two comedies, musicals, and thrillers under his own name and four pseudonyms—Rick Abbot (*Dracula: The Musical*, 1982), Monk Ferris (*Let's Murder Marsha*, 1984), Mike Johnson (*The Perfect Murder*, 1989), Mark Chandler (*Doctor Death*, 1991). Sharkey passed away in 1992 after a bout with cancer.

David Reiser, the music department chair of a large Chicago suburban high school, has written scores and lyrics for nearly fifty musicals since 1970. In addition to his work with Jack Sharkey, Reiser collaborated with others on *Robin Hood* (1971), capturing the escapades of the Sherwood Forest rogue and his merry men; *Ballet Russes* (1990), the story of the legendary Russian ballet company during the years prior to World War I; *Alas! Alack! Zorro's Back!* (1995), an updated adventure about the masked, swashbuckling hero; and *I Want My Mummy!* (1995), in which Baroness Frankenstein opens her castle to monsters of the world who cannot adjust to modern society. The guests include the Mummy, a Werewolf, a Vampire, The Invisible Man, the mad Igor, a Medusa, and a descendent of Dr. Jekyll.

Aladdin and the Magic Lamp (1996), retells the classic rags-to-riches tale of a poor tailor's son who discovers a magic lamp containing a genie. *Mrs. Scrooge* (1997) is a musical adaptation of Charles Dickens's classic "A Christmas Carol" but the genders are reversed, and all the lead characters are female. *The Real Story of Little Red Riding Hood* (1998) dramatizes the immortal yarn from the wolf's point of view.

* * *

Oscar Fingal O'Flahertie Wills Wilde (1854–1900) was born to an Anglo-Irish family in Dublin, Ireland. He studied classics at Dublin's Trinity College, was an outstanding student, and received a scholarship to Magdalen College, Oxford, where he continued his education from 1874 to 1878. Decorative arts were his main interest. While at college, his long hair, flamboyant dress, and general demeanor were considered that of an "effeminate dandy."

After graduating from Oxford, Wilde returned to Dublin. He courted Florence Balcombe but she became engaged to Bram Stoker, author of *Dracula*. Wilde spent the next several years in Paris, went on a lecture tour in the United States, and settled in London, where he contributed articles and art reviews to the *Dramatic View* and *Pall Mall Gazette*. In 1885, he married Constance Lloyd, daughter of a wealthy Queen's Counsel, and they had two sons. In the early 1890s, Wilde's novel *The Picture of Dorian Gray*, two collections of fairy tales, and the volume *Lord Arthur Savile's Crime and Other Stories* established his literary reputation. On stage, he had a series of popular comedies.

However, Wilde's widely known homosexual encounters, notably with the young Lord Alfred Douglas, led in 1895 to three successive *cause célèbre* trials, at the conclusion of which he was convicted of "gross indecency" and sentenced to two years' hard labor. Upon his release, Wilde spent his last three years penniless in Paris. He died of cerebral meningitis on November 30, 1900. His tomb in Pére Lachais was designed by the sculptor Sir Jacob Epstein.

Accounts of the real-life trials of Oscar Wilde were published by H. Montgomery Hyde in 1975, by Jonathan Goodman in 1995, and by

Merlin Holland in 2003. Among others, biographies of Wilde include *The Life and Confessions of Oscar Wilde* (1914) by Frank Harris, *Oscar Wilde* (1987) by Richard Ellmann, and *The Stranger Wilde* (1994) by Gary Schmidgall. Peter Ackroyd penned *The Last Testament of Oscar Wilde* (1983), a fictional diary presumably written by Wilde when in exile in Paris after serving time in prison. In *The Wilde West* (1991), Walter Satterthwait conjectures Wilde's lecture tour in the United States as background for a tense mystery, in which the visiting author finds himself a suspect in the murder of prostitutes. The tour also inspired Louis Edwards's steamy adventure novel, *Oscar Wilde Discovers America* (2003).

In a twist, Wilde becomes a clever sleuth in Gyles Brandreth's lively detective stories *Oscar Wilde and the Candlelight Murders* (2007), *Oscar Wilde and the Ring of Death* (2008, aka *Oscar Wilde and a Death of No Importance*), *Oscar Wilde and the Dead Man's Smile* (2009), and *Oscar Wilde and the Nest of Vipers* (2010). While a student at Oxford, Brandreth wrote and produced the play *The Trials of Oscar Wilde* (1974). Other plays about Wilde include *Oscar Wilde* (1936) by Leslie and Sewell Stokes; *The Importance of Being Oscar* (1961), arranged and acted by Micheál MacLiammóir; *Dear Oscar* (1972), a musical with book and lyrics by Caryl Gabrielle Young; *Wildflowers* (1976) by Richard Howard; *Wilde West* (1988) by Charles Marowitz; *Stephen and Mr. Wilde* (1993) by Jim Bartley; *Gross Indecency* (1997) by Moises Kaufman; *The Judas Kiss* (1998) by David Hare; *Goodbye Oscar* (1999) by Romulus Linney; *Aspects of Oscar* (2001) by Barry Day; *A Man of No Importance* (2002) by Terrence McNally; and Brian Bedford's one-man show, *Ever Yours, Oscar* (2009), featuring Wilde's correspondence.

Two excellent motion pictures about Wilde's traumatic life in the straight-laced Victorian era were made in England in 1960: *Oscar Wilde*, with Robert Morley, and *The Trials of Oscar Wilde*, starring Peter Finch. A third biographical movie, *Wilde* (1998), featured Stephen Fry in the title role.

A naughty pastiche by Graham Greene, *The Return of A.J. Raffles* (1975), spotlights Oscar Wilde's lover, Lord Alfred Douglas, as he solicits the help of gentleman-burglar Raffles to penetrate the safe of his father—an act of revenge for stopping his allowance after the affair with Wilde became public.

An odd couple of the Victorian era, Sherlock Holmes and Oscar Wilde met on two occasions. In the play *The Incredible Murder of Cardinal Tosca* (1980), by Alden Nowlan and Walter Learning, good Dr. Watson learns from his roommate that his latest case revolved around a packet of compromising letters penned by Wilde. In Russell A. Brown's novel, *Sherlock Holmes and the Mysterious Friend of Oscar Wilde* (1988), Wilde, described as "a giant moth," arrives at 221B Baker Street to ask for the aid of the Great Detective in a case of blackmail in high society.

Acting Edition: Samuel French, Inc.

Awards and Honors: In 2000–2001, The New York Public Library for the Performing Arts marked the centennial of Oscar Wilde's death with a series of public programs that included lectures, readings of Wilde's works, and motion pictures based on his plays.

NOTES

1. In the summer of 2009, a Boston antiquarian, Peter L. Stern, offered a rare first edition of *The Picture of Dorian Gray*, in dust jacket and a custom quarter-morocco slipcase, for $100,000.

2. Jack Sharkey and Dave Reiser, *The Picture of Dorian Gray* (New York: Samuel French, 1982), 9.

3. The playwrights suggest that "the monster" be another actor, in either grotesque makeup or a hideous head-covering rubber mask, who changes places with Dorian when he hides behind the curtain.

4. *New York Times*, August 18, 1956.

5. *New York Times*, August 29, 1963.

6. *Plays and Players*, September 1968.

7. *New York Times*, March 23, 2001.

The Green Archer (1980)

Tim Kelly (United States, 1931–1998)

In the early 1980s, the prolific American playwright Tim Kelly adapted to the stage two novels by the equally prolific English writer Edgar Wallace—1923's *The Green Archer* and 1926's *The Black Abbot*. Both dramatizations take us back to the era of unapologetic melodrama; each transpires in the 1920s in a medieval manor complete with sliding panels, secret passageways, and torture chambers. Ghostly apparitions roam shadowy corridors. The lights flicker on and off at opportune moments while the wind howls outside.

The Green Archer's Garre Castle, a fortress of stone and mortar, is located in Berkshire, England, and belongs to Abel Bellamy, a former Chicago gangster. The sanctuary is a combination sitting room, library, and office. Down-right are stairs that lead to an unseen tower room. Up-right, heavy doors open into a hallway. Up-center is a recessed library lined with bookshelves filled with handsomely bound volumes. Stage-left is another set of doors leading into Bellamy's bedroom. At stage-right there is a fireplace. The furniture includes a sofa, armchair, and table with a tablecloth that reaches the floor. On top of a desk is a telephone, files, writing materials, and a letter opener.

The master of the house, Abel Bellamy, enters wearing a dressing gown. He is described as "a commanding figure. Beyond middle years, he's anything but handsome. He enjoys taunting people, controlling them, bending them to his will. He can be, by turns, sadistic, amusing and oddly hospitable."

Bellamy begins the day by rebuking his housekeeper, Mrs. Coldstern—"a woman dressed in severe black"—and squeezing the hand of his male secretary, Julius Savini—"a trim man, on the swarthy side, neatly dressed." Savini pulls away, nursing his knuckles, and Bellamy smirks, "I have the strength of a young ox."

It soon becomes clear that Bellamy engaged Savini because of the secretary's shady past; he has a hold on him. Calling Savini "slick," "a liar," and "a crook," Bellamy warns him that "people who displease me have the habit of—dropping out of sight. Here today, gone tomorrow. Poof."

They hear voices from the hallway as Lily, a pretty, eighteen-year-old maid, tries to stop an aggressive newcomer. The doors fling open with considerable force and Charles Creager enters. Like Bellamy, he's a domineering fellow with a powerful voice and gruff manner. Bellamy orders Savini to leave the room and confronts Creager. We learn that Creager is a former prison guard who has been blackmailing Bellamy for a monthly "pension," keeping mum about Bellamy's checkered past. Creager requests one large lump sum, "and I'm off your back for good." A heated discussion ensues, provoking Creager to dip into his pocket and take out a revolver. Bellamy doesn't flinch. Mrs. Coldstern enters and announces that the American journalist has arrived for his appointment. Spike Holland enters—"young, glib, ambitious." With a meaningful look at Bellamy, Creager invites the reporter to come to his house—Rose Cottage, Field Road, New Barnet—for "something that'll make a sensation."

Creager exits. Spike asks Bellamy if the Green Archer is a ghost or a stunt. Savini brings in a small tray with a medicine bottle, spoon, and glass of water. Bellamy requests that Savini taste the medicine first, before sipping it. He then opens the door abruptly and Mrs. Coldstern tumbles in. It's plain that she has been listening at the keyhole. Bellamy laughs, "One of these days you'll fall flat on your inquisitive face and break your nose." He asks the housekeeper to relate to the reporter the history of the Green Archer. "The Green Archer of Garre Castle was at one time the most famous ghost in London," says Mrs. Coldstern. "The original Archer was hanged by one of the owners of Garre Castle in 1487. He was hanged for stealing deer." Mrs. Coldstern points to a ceiling oak beam: "That's where they swung him." Since then, declares the housekeeper, the Green Archer has haunted Garre Castle, seeking revenge.

Spike jots down some notes and says with satisfaction, "The *Globe* hasn't had a decent ghost story for months." Bellamy invites Spike to stay for a few days, and the reporter is delighted. Later, when the others leave the room, Bellamy pulls a key chain from around his neck. He looks toward the bookshelves for a moment, changes his mind, drops the chain back under his shirt, and exits up the tower steps. After a moment, Creager enters stealthily from a passageway hidden behind a tapestry. He pulls out his revolver, makes sure it is loaded, and quickly follows Bellamy.

Silence. Suddenly, from the steps above, Creager's voice is heard: "Who are you? Get back! Get away from me!" A shot rings, then another.

Creager stumbles into sight. He tries to make it to the sofa but falls to the floor with a dying gasp. Embedded in his chest is an arrow. A hooded figure dressed in green emerges from the shadowy steps, holding a bow. On the phantom's back we can make out a quiver and arrows, as the curtain descends.

The second scene begins with Lily, the maid, and Spike, the journalist, discussing the strange case of Creager, whose corpse was found by the potting shed; there are rumors that he was "a regular gangster in America." Lily, whose function is mainly to provide comic relief, opines that "if Mister Creager had an arrow in his chest, he stuck it there himself. Suicide, that's my guess."

Enter John Wood, an English social worker based in Belgium, described as "a handsome chap with a pleasant personality." Wood tells Bellamy that he represents an orphanage in search of a new location and expresses interest in Garre Castle.

Left by himself, Bellamy locks the doors, takes out the key chain, and crosses to the bookshelves. He pulls out a large red volume halfway, which opens a section of the wall to reveal a passageway leading to a dungeon. A flickering lantern inside casts frightening patterns on the wall. From the recesses of the dungeon comes the pitiful sound of a woman weeping. Bellamy moves out of sight, down, down, down, into the catacombs of Garre Castle.

The lights come up on scene 3, illuminating Bellamy behind his desk, his shirt open, checking his heartbeat with a stethoscope. He swallows two pills and washes them down with water. Mrs. Coldstern ushers in "the man from the agency" and, after a few tart questions, Bellamy hires the conservatively dressed Phillips for the position of butler.

Two more Americans join the cadre of characters—the widow Mrs. Howett, "a gracious woman, somewhat on the sophisticated side," and her adopted daughter, Valerie, "lovely enough to grace the cover of a fashion magazine." The Howetts have rented Bellamy's adjacent cottage and are delighted to make his acquaintance. Bellamy, unexpectedly gracious, offers to guide Mrs. Howett around the mansion. Valerie and Savini remain alone and we realize that she's paid the secretary for letters that he's swiped from Bellamy's private files and delivered to her—letters about a woman named Elaine Held, Valerie's long-lost mother.

Later that day, Bellamy sends Mrs. Coldstern through the bookcase's secret opening, turns on the radio for soft music, and sets the table for "a little dinner party." The housekeeper returns, followed by Elaine Held— "A few years younger than Bellamy, her hair falls loosely around her shoulders and her complexion is pale due to her captivity in the castle dungeons." Bellamy asks Elaine to sit and enjoy green salad and fried potatoes. He then springs the news that "Valerie's here. Your daughter."

Elaine gasps. Bellamy fills her plate and says, "If you had married me instead of my brother we'd be sitting here as man and wife, not prisoner and keeper." Elaine mumbles that eight years of imprisonment should be enough to squelch Bellamy's appetite for revenge, but he insists, "I'm only sorry my brother didn't know I was behind his ruin." He admonishes Elaine for refusing to marry him after Michael's suicide and for calling him "a brute," "a devil," "an animal." His only comfort, says Bellamy, is punishing her over and over again. He's had Valerie's room wired for sound and Elaine will be able to hear her daughter's voice and movements—but will never be able to meet her.

Mrs. Coldstern, affected by Elaine's plight, exclaims, "I'll get the police!" and rushes to the telephone. Bellamy pounces, wraps the phone cord around the housekeeper's throat, and keeps tightening it. She makes a gurgling sound and drops to the floor behind the desk, dragging the telephone with her. With difficulty, she manages to rise and grasp the letter opener. Bellamy grabs her wrist, forces the housekeeper to her knees, and plunges the knife into her belly. She clutches at it to no avail—and expires. Elaine trembles fearfully while Bellamy chuckles, "I suppose this means another call to the people at Happy Domestic Help."

In act 2 it is revealed that some of the manor's staff and guests are not who they seemed to be. Phillips, the "perfect butler," is in reality a private investigator, Jim Featherstone, hired by Mrs. Howett and Valerie to track the whereabouts of Elaine Held. Julius Savini's wife, Fay, arrives on the scene and we realize that the secretary has uncovered Bellamy's safe below the table, under a floor plank. The Savinis plan to steal the large sum of money stored inside.

The Green Archer turns out to be John Wood, who under the guise of a social worker, concealed his true identity—Michael Bellamy Jr., Abel Bellamy's nephew. As the masked Green Archer he roamed the nooks of Garre Castle in search of his mother, Elaine Held. The impersonation gave him the opportunity to watch his uncle, whom he had never met, and be close to Valerie, the stepsister he's never known.

The shock of confronting the nephew he thought dead proved the final blow to Abel Bellamy's precarious health. He clutches his chest tightly and falls, dying. Elaine Held is released from the dungeon and ecstatically embraces her son Michael and stepdaughter Valerie. Spike Holland observes the family reunion and announces that he's "going to have one fantastic story for the *London Globe*."

* * *

The Green Archer, published in 1923, is widely considered one of Edgar Wallace's top novels. The book was chosen for inclusion in *The Encyclopedia of Murder and Mystery* by Bruce F. Murphy: "*The Green Archer* combines ghosts, gangsters, and murder. . . . A mysterious green archer appears on the grounds of the castle, sometimes acting as a Robin Hood and saving damsels in distress."[1]

The Green Archer was filmed as a silent serial in 1925 and as a talkie serial in 1940. The 1925 film, released by Pathé, was directed by Spencer G. Bennet and had ten chapters, the first one titled "The Ghost of Bellamy Castle" and the last one "The Smoke Clears Away." Columbia's 1940 serial, directed by James W. Horne, was divided into fifteen chapters, beginning with "Prison Bars Beckon" and concluding with "The Green Archer Exposed." In both movies, Abel Bellamy uses Garre Castle as a base for his underworld ring.

Tim Kelly's dramatization of *The Green Archer* was copyrighted in 1980. Two years later, Kelly adapted to the stage another popular Edgar Wallace novel, 1926's *The Black Abbot*, under the title *The Mystery of the Black Abbot*. Like *The Green Archer*, here too the dastardly proceedings unfold in an English ancestral home, Fossaway Manor, the centuries-old residence of the Alford family.

The current lord is Harry Alford, eighteenth Earl of Chelford. His domain covers farmlands and abbey ruins. "The sitting room breathes an atmosphere of mystery and shadows," says the playwright. Down-right is a fireplace; above it hangs the portrait of a handsome, aristocratic woman, the family's deceased matriarch. Also attached to the wall is an ancient dagger. Up-right is a majestic grandfather clock and up-center are French windows that open onto a lawn. Up-left is a large chest, "deep enough to conceal a body." Next to it stands a volume-filled bookcase. Down-left is an old library table stacked with manuscripts and maps. The furnishings were once expensive but are now worn and faded.

The play begins with a bizarre prologue. Outside, a storm howls. The light is dim. Silhouetted at the windows is the outline of a robed figure, a monk. The face is hooded but two points of red light indicate the specter's eyes peering into the room. The wind continues to rage as the eyes stare at the audience. Finally the lights fade out; the "eyes" continue to glow for a moment before the stage is plunged into complete darkness.

The lights come up on Mary Wenner, secretary to Lord Alford. Mary, "efficient and alert," is at the library table, checking manuscripts, when the butler, Thomas Luck, enters and announces that a parcel of books has arrived from London for his lordship. Thomas reacts to a clap of thunder by peering out of the window and commenting that this is the sort of night that "*he*" fancies." Mary rebukes Thomas for believing in the Black Abbot, who, she says, is nothing but a ghost story. "It's wicked for people to say Fossaway Manor is haunted," she pouts.

Richard Alford, Harry's half-brother—"a handsome young man, forceful and direct"—enters and sends Thomas to get the luggage of Miss

Cordelia Lynwood, who has just driven up for the weekend. Lynwood—
"an attractive woman dressed conservatively"—is an estate appraiser.
Harry Alford—"an academic type"—comes down to meet her, and Lynwood asks about the Chelford treasure; legend has it that gold bars taken
from a Spanish galleon were stored somewhere on the property during
the reign of Good Queen Bess. "Our respected forefathers have searched
for it for hundreds of years," says Richard.

Lynwood expresses an interest in "the resident ghost," the Black Abbot.
Harry pooh-poohs the story as "a myth." He reports that about eight hundred years ago the Black Abbot of Fossaway was assassinated on order of
an Alford ancestor. Since then, from time to time, says Harry, his "ghost"
has supposedly wandered about.

Alice, a young maid in uniform, enters with a small parcel. Harry
rips away its cover and, excited, holds a book. He lights a candle at the
library table and asks to be left alone. Mary gives Harry a pill container
and he remains by himself, reading aloud. An apparition garbed in a
monk's robe comes into view at the French windows. Suddenly, the
specter begins to howl—a hideous, spiraling wail. Petrified, Harry turns
and sees the "thing." The Black Abbot remains in the background as the
curtain descends.

Scene 2 begins with the arrival of Leslie Gwyn, Harry's fiancée—
"young, beautiful, lively"—and her brother, Arthur—"a hearty type,
full of gusto and a love of life." Arthur relates to Lynwood that he
played Cupid when introducing his sister to Harry. "Harry is a perfect
match for my sister," adds Arthur jocularly. "A young heiress is prey
for fortune hunters."

Later in the day, Arthur meets with Fabrian Gilder, a law clerk, and
we learn that Arthur has recently lost heavily betting on the horses. To
avoid embarrassment and a lawsuit, he must get money fast. Arthur escorts Gilder to the front door and Miss Lynwood enters. The portrait of
Harry's mother draws her attention and she moves to the mantelpiece.
She does not notice a gloved hand parting the nearby drapes indicating
that someone is watching her. Harry enters from the hallway, remarks
that everyone thinks that he's a hypochondriac, and pops a pill. Lynwood
smiles and exits.

The hooded Black Abbot slinks in from behind the drapes, pounces on
Harry, holds him in an armlock, and with a red, chloroformed handkerchief covers his nostrils. Harry drops to the floor. The maid Alice walks
in, reacts, screams, and runs away. The Black Abbot leaps to the mantelpiece and grabs the antique dagger. The dagger is lifted high and, then—it
plunges. The Black Abbot raises the dagger and again thrusts it down.

The following morning, Leslie and Richard converse nervously while
staring at the blank space on the wall where the sword previously hung.

Harry has disappeared, and both his fiancée and his brother are not sure if he's alive. The local constables are searching for him. A police sergeant from Scotland Yard, "Monkey" Puttler, arrives on the scene, walking "with something of a simian stoop." He has a tendency to jut out his lower lip when lost in thought.

A suspicion of foul play points at lawyer Fabrian Gilder, who came to the manor yesterday and, upon departing, instead of returning to London, spent the night at the village inn. Sergeant Puttler also learns that a next-door neighbor, Mrs. Leonard, has been quarreling with Harry about the estate's borders. The Sergeant interrogates Alice and she relates how she had witnessed a deadly encounter between the missing lord and a ghost.

> PUTTLER: The ghost—was it a man or a woman?
> ALICE: How should I know? A ghost is a ghost.

The Sergeant goes to inspect the premises. Secretary Mary Wenner quietly meets lawyer Gilder and we realize that they have joined forces to unearth the castle's hidden treasure. Mary confides to Gilder that she has studied the plans of Fossaway Manor and knows where it is. As the two of them remain locked in their hush-hush conversation, the Black Abbot passes behind the French windows with dagger in hand. The conspirators hear a groan and slowly butler Thomas comes into view from a passageway located behind the fireplace. Thomas's eyes are wide open and his breathing labored. He holds out a hand covered with blood, imploring help. He groans for the last time and drops, dying from a stab wound. Sergeant Puttler rushes in and kneels by the body. Mary stutters, "First Harry, and, now, Thomas. Who's next?"

Act 2 begins on a light note as the neighbor, Mrs. Leonard—"a forceful, opinionated, no-nonsense woman"—pokes fun at the Scotland Yard investigator: "Monkeys have long arms. You represent the long arm of the law. I suppose that's how you got that absurd nickname."

The Sergeant tells Richard and Leslie that the real name of butler Thomas was Sleisser and that he did time at Dartmoor Prison for theft. No doubt he planned to rob Fossaway Manor. Suddenly the sound of a rifle crack comes from the grounds, firing into the room. A china figurine on the mantelpiece smashes. Richard pulls Leslie to the floor. The Sergeant takes out a revolver from inside his jacket, cautiously moves to the French windows, and exits. Richard and Leslie follow.

Mary and Gilder come out from the library. Mary motions to the lawyer to check that no one is hovering outside the room and pulls a hardly noticeable wall lever; the fireplace moves enough to allow a person to slip into a narrow passageway. Mary goes through, followed by Gilder. Richard enters the room in time to see the lawyer disappear. The fireplace is pulled back into position from inside. Richard crosses to the corner chest, opens its lid, and removes a costume—the Black Abbot outfit! He puts on the robe and covers his face with the hood as the lights fade.

In the next scene, Sergeant Puttler continues his investigation. He holds a hunting rifle and cross-examines Mrs. Leonard. The feisty neighbor insists that she fired at a bevy of quail. She has no doubt that ballistics will prove that the bullet fired into the room did not come from her sporting shotgun. The Sergeant shifts his attention to Cordelia Lynwood, who reveals that she's not an appraiser but a psychiatrist. Richard admits that he hired Lynwood to check the sanity of his brother Harry and sign commitment papers. "Harry had moods," says Richard. "He often went into the village and got into mischief. There was only one way I could keep him inside the house—by posing as the Black Abbot. The Black Abbot terrified him."

The end of the fireplace moves a little. Mary Wenner and Fabrian Gilder enter cautiously carrying a long metal box. When they realize that the Sergeant, Richard, and Leslie are in the room watching them, they keep their composure. Gilder announces that the box contains the hidden treasure; Miss Wenner has discovered it and no doubt she's due for a handsome reward.

Richard bangs open the lock of the box and lifts the top. Instead of a bar of gold, he takes out a sheet of music. "Ancient music," says Richard. "The monks must have stored their music scrolls behind a false wall."

Suddenly the lights flicker. Alice screams off stage. Richard, Puttler, and Gilder hurry out. The grandfather clock strikes with an eerie tone— nine, ten, eleven, twelve, thirteen! Mary moves nervously to the clock and pulls aside its panel to reveal the body of Cordelia Lynwood, the psychiatrist. Her dead eyes stare; her blouse is blood-stained. Mary rushes out for help. Slowly, the lid of the chest rises and from its interior appears—the Black Abbot! He gets out of the chest and pulls back the hood. The features are distorted because of a nylon stocking over the head. The apparition pulls off the stocking. It's Harry Alford! No explanation is given as to how Harry survived the vicious stabbings inflicted upon him at the end of scene 2.

Harry convinces Leslie that they're both in danger, takes her hand and pulls her to the French windows. They exit onto the lawn. Mary re-enters the room ahead of Richard, Arthur, and Puttler, and points at Lynwood's corpse. The Sergeant is puzzled. "Seems we got another Black Abbot running about the place," he muses.

The wind continues to howl during the last scene. The fireplace is pushed. The robed figure of Harry appears, with Leslie behind him. She's wary, exhausted, and fearful; she doesn't know who to believe, Richard or Harry. Harry draws a dagger from his robe and orders Leslie to sit on a chair. He crosses to the chest, opens it, and takes out rope. "You betrayed me, you have no love for me," he says. In one swift movement he flings the rope over the back of the chair and around Leslie's torso. "Don't struggle, don't scream," he warns, and as he continues to talk his dementia becomes more pronounced. No, he didn't kill Thomas and Miss Lynwood; the Black Abbot killed them. Harry raises the dagger high when a shot rings from behind the fireplace. The bullet hits Harry in the back. He groans, falls, and dies. The fireplace moves and Sergeant Puttler appears first, followed by Richard, who dashes to Leslie and unties her. Alice peeks out carefully and announces, "I'm giving my two weeks' notice."

The Mystery of the Black Abbot was first presented at The Drama Center, Los Angeles, directed by Darrell Sandeen. The two Black Abbots were portrayed by Jimmy Williams (Harry Alford) and Joseph Taggart (Richard Alford). In the published acting edition of the play, the author suggests that "there are any number of ways to approach the script. . . . Directors can go with a straight 'drawing room' approach climaxing with 'thrill after thrill.' Or, with restraint, the spoof or parody approach will prove effective. It can also be done as a stylized piece reflecting the sort of play that, in years past, was enormously popular with audiences. Whatever the approach, the end result should be the same—an evening of escapist entertainment, designed to give the viewer a good scare and a laugh."[2]

* * *

Richard Horatio Edgar Wallace (1875–1932), the illegitimate son of parents who were trouping in provincial theatres, ended his formal education at a boarding school when he was twelve years old. He held a series of menial jobs in a rubber factory, a shoe shop, a printing firm, and on a fishing trawler. At eighteen, Edgar joined the Royal West Kent Regiment, eventually transferring to the Medical Staff Corps in South Africa. He served as a war correspondent for Reuters during the Boer War and wrote battle poems, later collected in *The Mission that Failed* (1898) and *Writ in Barracks* (1900).

Upon returning to London, Edgar became a reporter for the *Daily Mail*, a racing editor, and a drama critic. Unable to find a publisher, he manufactured *The Four Just Men* on his own, coupled with a publicity stunt of offering a 500-pound reward to any reader who could guess how the locked-room murder of the British Foreign Secretary was committed. The challenge resulted in a great financial loss, for there were several correct solutions. However, the popularity of *The Four Just Men* began the Edgar Wallace era in print and on stage.

It is said that during the late 1920s and early 1930s, one out of every four books published in England was by Edgar Wallace. A prolific writer of thrillers, credited with some 175 novels and hundreds of short stories, Wallace was the first to make a specialty of detective drama.

An early effort, *The African Millionaire*, initially performed in 1904 in Cape Town, South Africa, was a typical melodrama of the time, complete with high-flown dialogue, asides to the audience, broad humor, and black-and-white characters—a larger-than-life hero, a hissable villain, a damsel in distress, a long-lost son, and a dangerous Russian adventuress. The proceedings included blackmail, two murders, a native rebellion against white rule, hand-to-hand combat in a dark mineshaft, and the final victory of true love.

Wallace continued his apprenticeship in the theatre by penning several one-act plays, of which *The Forest of Happy Dreams* stands out. It was adapted from a tale in *Sanders of the River* (1911), the first of twelve short-story collections logging the adventures of a British commissioner. In 1921, Wallace wrote and produced a sentimental drama called *M'Lady*, spotlighting the tribulations of a plumber's wife, Mrs. Carraway, whose criminal husband is serving a life sentence in Broadmoor for the murder of a police officer. Mrs. Carraway attempts to raise her daughter in high society but her husband unexpectedly turns up, threatening to topple their way of life. Fortunately, he dies of heart failure, after a devoted shop assistant destroys his bottle of medicine. Some twenty years later, Lillian Hellman would utilize the same murder device in *The Little Foxes*.

M'Lady opened at London's Playhouse Theatre on July 18, 1921, was panned by critics, and closed after twenty-three performances. Wallace novelized the play under the title *The Lady of Ascot* in 1930.

Wallace's first theatrical success was soon to come. With distinguished actor-manager Gerald du Maurier serving as his mentor, Edgar wrote, revised, and tightened a stage adaptation of his 1925 novel, *The Gaunt Stranger*, naming it *The Ringer*. The saga of a notorious vigilante who assassinates dastardly evildoers clever enough to escape the arm of the law was presented at Wyndham's Theatre, London, on May 1, 1926 and became the rage of town.

The floodgates opened. During the next six years, Wallace penned more than half a dozen plays with various degrees of success. *The Terror* (1927), dramatized from his 1926 novel *The Black Abbot*, included such familiar melodrama ingredients as the old mysterious house built over dark dungeons, a hidden treasure in the vault, the master criminal disguised as the mildest character, the Scotland Yard detective masquerading as a drunken ne'er-do-well, the hooded figure appearing on moonlit nights and leaving a trail of corpses in its wake. *The Yellow Mask* (1928), book by Wallace, music by Vernon Duke, followed a robbery of the crown jewels from the Tower of London by an accented foreigner and his getaway on his yacht with a kidnapped girl. The hero, her lover, comes to the rescue aboard a plane. *The Man Who Changed His Name* (1928) is the story of Nita Clive, a striking woman of twenty-five, who learns that her husband, a wealthy businessman, may be a notorious Canadian fugitive who murdered his wife, her mother, and her paramour. Among the dramatis personae of *The Squeaker* (1928) are two unknowns: who among them is the leader of a dangerous crime organization, and who is the Scotland Yard inspector hunting him? The action of *The Flying Squad* (1928) takes place in a shadowy den on the bank of the Thames, which serves as the headquarters of a lucrative cocaine smuggling enterprise, complete with electrical warning signals and a hidden trap door, under which runs a sweeping, deadly current. *The Lad* (1928) tells of a comic criminal who invades a country house in search of loot and is mistaken by the staff as a private detective. *Persons Unknown* (1929) is a restrained melodrama that focuses on an ace reporter's pursuit of a mysterious blackmailer who stabbed a "person unknown" in the street. *The Calendar* (1929), "A Racing Play in Three Acts," was inspired by Wallace's own familiarity with the milieu of this noble sport. The protagonist is a racehorse owner who finds himself in dire financial straits with a muddy reputation.

Following a trip to the United States, during which he visited Chicago's Al Capone headquarters and the garage that had been the scene of the St. Valentine's Day Massacre, Wallace returned home and during four feverish days dictated the entire manuscript of *On the Spot* (1930), generally considered his best play. Charles Laughton was cast as Tony Perelli, the Capone figure, with Emlyn Williams portraying his laconic henchman and Gillian Lind enacting his Chinese mistress.

After the success of *On the Spot* came a few failures. *The Mouthpiece* (1930) was marred by a flimsy story line about an heiress unaware of the pending fortune soon to be bestowed upon her, and a gang of opportunists planning to marry her to one of their own. Fascinated with Sing Sing prison, which Wallace toured during his American visit, and struck by its death chamber and electric chair, he concocted *Smoky Cell* (1930), a grim yarn punctuated by a soundtrack rattling with the staccato of automatic weapons and screams of police sirens. It depicts a clash between a police captain and a dangerous inmate. The proceedings of *The Old Man* (1931) occur within the "Coat of Arms" tavern. Throughout, a bearded old man appears in the background, lurking in the shadows, stealthily climbing stairways, peeking through keyholes. It is rumored that the enigmatic character has escaped from a nearby asylum for the criminally insane. Before the play ends, the Old Man is a silent witness to a clandestine rendezvous, to the setting of a room on fire, and to an extortion scheme.

In *The Case of the Frightened Lady* (1931), Wallace returned to the pure mystery thriller. The elegant Lord Lebanon arrives in Scotland Yard's headquarters to complain about his domineering mother and a pair of gun-slinging henchmen whom she had hired to keep an eye on him. After two strangulations—of Lebanon's chauffeur and physician—we learn in a surprising turnabout that instead of the imperious mother, the lord himself, mad as a hatter, is the villain of the piece. The action of *The Green Pack* (1932) transpires in Angola, then Portuguese West Africa. Three hired gold prospectors who for eighteen months "have gone where the foot of white man has never trod," before unearthing a rich mine, are double-crossed by their English employer. When the man is found shot to death with his own revolver next to him, a tense third act poses the tantalizing question: Which of the three friends killed their nemesis?[3]

Tireless, Wallace also produced plays in the West End, importing from America *Brothers* (1929), by Herbert Ashton Jr., a drama of the New York underworld, and wrote a number of screenplays, including 1931's *The Hound of the Baskervilles*.

In Hollywood, with Merian C. Cooper, Edgar Wallace conceived the idea of a horror picture about prehistoric monsters and submitted a 110-page first draft, but his contribution was cut short when he caught a cold and died of double pneumonia on February 10, 1932, before the filming of *King Kong*.

Chris Steinbrunner and Otto Penzler, editors of *The Encyclopedia of Mystery and Detection*, opined that Edgar Wallace is "probably the most popular 'thriller' writer of all time. . . . Wallace's books still sell more than a million copies a year, and motion pictures and television programs based on his stories are everywhere." Steinbrunner and Penzler believe that Wallace's furious pace led to writing that is "slapdash and cliché-ridden, characterization [that] is two-dimensional, and situations [that] are frequently trite, relying on intuition, coincidence, and much pointless, confusing movement to convey a sense of action. The heroes and villains are clearly labeled, and stock characters—humorous servants, baffled policemen, breathless heroines—could be interchanged from one book to another."[4]

On the other hand, Phyllis Hartnoll, editor of *The Oxford Companion to the Theatre*, finds that "In all his works [Wallace] showed unusual precision of detail, narrative skill, and inside knowledge of police methods and criminal psychology, the fruits of his apprenticeship as a crime reporter."[5]

Wallace's large output consists mainly of criminous novels, short stories, plays, and film scenarios, but he also wrote non-genre tales, science fiction, historical surveys, social criticism, poetry, an autobiography (*People*, 1926, also published as *Edgar Wallace by Himself*, 1932), and a personal log (*My Hollywood Diary*, 1932).

Penelope Wallace, the author's daughter, devoted to keeping her father's legend alive, considered *On the Spot*, *The Case of the Frightened Lady*, and *The Ringer* to be Wallace's best works, an evaluation *The Cambridge Companion to the Theatre* agreed with. In a letter dated November 24, 1989, Penelope Wallace wrote that when *On the Spot* was performed in Chicago, "gangsters in the audience sent up a note congratulating the author on writing it like it was! One theory I heard was that my father had not really died of pneumonia but had been 'bumped off' for lifting the lid on gangsterdom!"[6]

In 1969, Penelope Wallace organized an Edgar Wallace Club, which evolved into the Edgar Wallace Society, headquartered in Oxford, England. The club, now defunct, drew members from around the globe and issued a quarterly fanzine, *The Crimson Circle*, commemorating the achievements of the "King of Thrillers."

* * *

Tim Kelly (1931–1998) was born in Saugus, Massachusetts, a small New England town near Boston. At the age of twelve, he got a $50 check for a story he wrote about a dog that went to war, published in the *Victorian*. As an adolescent, Kelly was attracted to the low-key horror films produced by Val Lewton (*Cat People, I Walked with a Zombie, The Body Snatcher*), and to the imaginative works of Edgar Rice Burroughs and L. Frank Baum. Impressed by the plays of Arthur Miller and Tennessee Williams, he began to write for the stage. Kelly attended Emerson College in Boston and earned an MFA in playwriting at the Yale School of Drama.

Kelly's first play, *Widow's Walk*, "A Mystery Thriller in Three Acts," was published in 1963. Since then, with more than 300 plays to his credit, Kelly has become the unsung hero of America's hinterland theatres. While his works are rarely produced in New York, they are constantly performed across the United States by small theatres and amateur societies. The plays, published under several pseudonyms, cover a wide range of genres: whodunit, true crime, horror, science fiction, adventure, western, melodrama, youth plays, and children's plays. Kelly's heroes include Sherlock Holmes, Robin Hood, and Hawkshaw the Detective, while the villains are Dracula, Frankenstein, The Wolfman, the Zombie, The Invisible Man, Sweeney Todd, Jack the Ripper, and Dr. Jekyll and Mr. Hyde. Kelly adapted to the stage works by Victor Hugo, Alexandre Dumas, Sheridan Le Fanu, Charles Dickens, Wilkie Collins, Robert Louis Stevenson, H. G. Wells, Oscar Wilde, Mark Twain, Edgar Allan Poe, and Edgar Wallace—interweaving horrific elements with sly humor.

Kelly recreated the world's foremost consulting detective in the one-act *The Last of Sherlock Holmes* (1970), *Sherlock Holmes Meets the Phantom* (1975), and *Beast of the Baskervilles* (1984); the full-length *The Hound of the Baskervilles* (1976), *Sherlock Holmes* (1977), and *The Adventure of the Speckled Band* (1981); and the musical *Sherlock Holmes and the Giant Rat of Sumatra* (1987). Named after the famous sleuth, Shirley Holmes, a young coed, is the heroine of Kelly's *If Sherlock Holmes Were a Woman* (1969). Kelly's *The*

Adventure of the Clouded Crystal (1982) deals with a stormy relationship between Sir Arthur Conan Doyle and magician Harry Houdini.

For younger audiences, Kelly spotlighted Alice in Wonderland, Cinderella, Tom Sawyer, the Three Musketeers, the Wizard of Oz, and Zorro.

Kelly died on December 7, 1998 after suffering a brain hemorrhage in his Hollywood, California home. He was cremated, per his request.

Acting Edition: Both *The Green Archer* and *The Mystery of the Black Abbot* were published by Baker's Plays.

Awards and Honors: Edgar Wallace's short story collection, *The Mind of Mr. J. G. Reeder* (1925) is included in Howard Haycraft and Ellery Queen's *Definitive Library of Detective-Crime-Mystery Fiction*; in *Queens Quorum, a History of the Detective-Crime Short Story as Revealed by the 106 Most Important Books Published in This Field Since 1845*; and in H. R. F. Keating's *Crime & Mystery: The 100 Best Books*. Boston's Emerson College has twice honored Tim Kelly for his "Contributions to the Field of Playwriting." In 1991 Kelly beat more than 300 entries to win the Elmira College Original Playwriting Contest with his blood-and-thunder drama *Crimes at the Old Brewery*. The play, depicting the squalor of Manhattan's Five Points during the 1850s, premiered, under Amnon Kabatchnik's direction, at the college's Emerson Theatre on March 7, 1991. Helen Hayes attended.

NOTES

1. Bruce F. Murphy, *The Encyclopedia of Murder and Mystery* (New York: St. Martin's, 1999), 217.

2. Tim Kelly, *The Mystery of the Black Abbot* (Boston: Baker's Plays, 1982), 79.

3. Edgar Wallace's more important plays—*The Ringer, The Squeaker, The Flying Squad, On the Spot,* and *The Case of the Frightened Lady*—are scrutinized in Amnon Kabatchnik's *Blood on the Stage, 1925–1950,* published by Scarecrow Press in 2010.

4. Chris Steinbrunner and Otto Penzler, eds., *Encyclopedia of Mystery and Detection* (New York: McGraw-Hill, 1976), 407.

5. Phyllis Hartnoll, ed., *The Oxford Companion to the Theatre* (London: Oxford University Press, 1951), 832.

6. Penelope Wallace and Amnon Kabatchnik, author of this chronology, corresponded for many years until her death in 1997.

Frankenstein (1981)

Victor Gialanella (United States, 1949–)

On the night of June 19, 1816, four friends were trapped by a storm at a lodge in the Swiss Alps. Trying to pass the time, they decided to concoct ghost stories. Lord Byron hosted this impromptu party, and his guests included Byron's physician, Dr. John Polidori, the poet Percy Bysshe Shelley, and Shelley's lover, young Mary Wollstonecraft Godwin, daughter of the author William Godwin.[1]

That night two important works were born. Polidori would embellish his ghost story and come up with the novella *The Vampyre*, introducing the enigmatic, suave undead Lord Ruthven; and Mary would build on her story and write the gothic novel *Frankenstein; or, The Modern Prometheus*. Shelley edited Mary's manuscript and *Frankenstein* was first published, in three hardcover volumes, on January 1, 1818.

Five years later, Richard Brinsley Peake adapted the novel to the stage under the title *Presumption; or, The Fate of Frankenstein*. James Wallack enacted Dr. Frankenstein, and Thomas Potter Cooke, a renowned stage villain, portrayed the monster.[2] The play scored a huge success. Within three years, fourteen other dramatizations of *Frankenstein* were mounted on English and French stages, of which the important ones are *The Monster and the Magician* by John Kerr and *The Man and the Monster* by Henry M. Milner, both produced in London in 1826. These were the torchbearers of more than one hundred plays utilizing the Frankenstein theme.[3]

In the twentieth century, the first play to present a Frankenstein motif was *The Last Laugh* (1915) by the American playwrights Charles W. Goddard (1879–1951) and Paul Dickey (1885–1933). *The Last Laugh* lampoons the Frankenstein saga by having its wild action swirl around a wooden crate containing a body wrapped in bandages—the centerpiece in the private laboratory of a doctor intent on creating human life.[4]

In 1927 came Peggy Webling's *Frankenstein: An Adventure in the Macabre*. Actor-manager Hamilton Deane, basking in the success of his dramatization of Bram Stoker's *Dracula*, added Webling's *Frankenstein* to his company's repertoire, and *Dracula* and *Frankenstein* ran alternatively in the English provinces, with Deane himself portraying the two monsters.

Deane brought *Frankenstein* to London's Little Theatre on February 10, 1930. Though the reviews were caustic and *Frankenstein* closed doors after seventy-two performances, producer Horace Liveright planned to export the play to New York in 1931 and engaged John L. Balderston to doctor it. But Liveright was wiped out by the stock market crash, could not mount a stage production, and sold his option to Universal Studios. The Webling-Balderston play served as the basis for Universal's two classic horror films—*Frankenstein* (1931) and *Bride of Frankenstein* (1935), both directed by James Whale, both starring Boris Karloff as the monster and Colin Clive as his creator.

Many other dramatizations of Mary Shelley's story were written and produced throughout the twentieth century. Gladys Hastings-Walton's version was seen in Glasgow in 1936. Donald F. Glut reports that the adaptation remained faithful to the original novel, and adds, "Miss Hastings-Walton tried to show the very real horror of man's being replaced by the machines that he created."[5]

During the early 1940s, the drama department at Fairmont High School in Manion, Indiana, presented a spoof, *Goon with the Wind*, in which a young student who would later rise to fame—James Dean—portrayed the Frankenstein monster.

The stage is divided into three parts in David Campton's 1959 *Frankenstein: The Gift of Fire*—Victor Frankenstein's laboratory, his friend Henri Clerval's house, and a blank, neutral space. "This arrangement," states a production note, "made it possible for the scenes to flow into each other almost cinematically."[6] In the first scene we learn that Victor has often secluded himself in a hidden laboratory. He tells Henri, "In centuries to come my name will be whispered with awe."

During a thunderstorm, a gigantic creature with "patchwork features" emerges from a covered sheet. Henri pleads with Victor to kill the giant. Victor attempts to prove that the creature possesses human emotions by giving it a doll. The creature cradles the doll in his arms, then, with one jerk, detaches the head from the body. Convinced that the creature must be destroyed, Victor offers him a poisoned flask, but relents, knocks the flask from the creature's hand, and urges, "Leave this place. Hide. Go to the mountains."

The plot now takes a turn and becomes a murder mystery. Master William, Victor's young brother, is discovered dead in his bed amid splattered blood. The maid Justine, who was found in the child's room, is accused of his murder. The argument against her is that the snow beneath the window was unmarked. Despite Victor's protestations that Justine has not committed the crime, she is found guilty. Before Henri Clerval can corroborate Victor's testimony, he is found dead on the town's old roadside, his spine broken.

At the climax, the monster enters Clerval's house through a window and confronts Elizabeth, Victor's fiancée. In a departure from the original novel and from all other stage adaptations, as the creature advances menacingly towards Elizabeth, she shoots him point blank with a pistol. The creature staggers and falls. Victor pleads with Elizabeth to forgive him. He has learned his lesson. Everything will be different—next time.

* * *

In the mid-1950s, the avant-garde Living Theatre Company, founded by Julian Beck and Judith Malina and known for its offbeat productions of *The Connection* and *The Brig*, began to rehearse their interpretation of *Frankenstein* while on a European tour. It was a sharp departure from the original novel. Pierre Biner, in his book *The Living Theatre*, writes that for Beck and Malina, "the play's philosophical foundation is embedded in the idea that the world must be changed, that a new man must evolve, and all human suffering must be eliminated. The motives of Dr. Frankenstein are to be found in that idea."[7]

Running six hours (an abridged version ran three and one-half hours), the play evolved from a skeletal script developed by actors' improvisations during rehearsals. The curtain rose on the tossing of a girl into a coffin. "From that point," relates Donald F. Glut, "the stage erupted into a series of murders and executions in numerous brutal ways, with the long-haired members of the cast screaming and howling and running through the audience. Dr. Frankenstein (played by Beck) entered the scenes and began to dismember the various corpses so that the dead could be given new life. While Dr. Frankenstein labored on his monster, Jewish cabbalists imitate him by building a female Golem. Sigmund Freud assisted in the creation of the Frankenstein monster. Blood was pumped into the corpse creation of Frankenstein."[8]

* * *

Written by Sheldon Altman and Bob Pickett, *I'm Sorry, the Bridge Is Out, You'll Have to Spend the Night*, is a musical spoof on horror movies of the 1930s and 1940s. The show opened at Hollywood's Coronet Theatre on April 28, 1970. The zany plot centers on Dr. Frankenstein's quest to obtain a suitable brain for his monster. A storm brings down the bridge and forces John David Walgood and his pretty fiancée Mary Ellen Harriman to take refuge in the castle. The couple, innocent and naïve, are oblivious to danger when surrounded by the Mummy, the Wolfman, Igor, and other creatures that go bump in the night.

More stage adaptations of Shelley's novel followed. *Frankenstein's Monster* by Sally Netzel was presented at the Dallas Theatre Center in the summer of 1972. Wolfgang Deichsel's *Frankenstein* played in Paris during the 1972–1973 season. In 1974, the prolific Tim Kelly penned a two-act *Frankenstein* (aka *The Rage of Frankenstein*) that unfolds entirely in a chateau on the shores of Lake Geneva, Switzerland. Five years later, *The Frankenstein Affair* by Ken Eulo was produced at off-Broadway's Courtyard Playhouse, rotating the action between Mary Shelley's bedroom and Dr. Frankenstein's laboratory in an attempt to illustrate a parallel between the author's tribulations in her marriage with those of the monster.

* * *

On January 4, 1981, the monster made it to Broadway. *Frankenstein* by Victor Gialanella premiered at the Palace Theatre under the direction of Tom Moore, featuring David Dukes (Victor Frankenstein), Keith Jochim (The Creature), Dianne Wiest (Elizabeth Lavenza), and John Carradine (blind hermit DeLacey).

The action of the play takes place in and around the Frankenstein Estate, Geneva, Switzerland in the mid-1800s. The first scene unfolds in a graveyard shrouded by fog. Two villagers, Hans Metz and Peter Schmidt, are barely seen as they pull a body from an open grave. A pick and a shovel are lying on the ground next to it. Victor Frankenstein enters carrying a lantern and instructs the men to leave the body "in the usual place . . . the money will be waiting." Schmidt confides that the corpse is that of a hanged man.

They hear the sound of an approaching carriage. Victor hurriedly leaves. The carriage appears in the background, its door opens, and Henry Clerval emerges, a proper, articulate gentleman in his late twenties. Henry asks for directions to the Chateau Frankenstein; he has been a friend of Herr Frankenstein since their university days at Inglestadt. Henry is advised to drive two kilometers to a fork in the road and take a right. He mounts the carriage and the two grave robbers begin to wrap the body as the lights fade.

In the elegant sitting room of the Chateau, Victor is standing by the fireplace and the lovely Elizabeth Lavenza is seated in an armchair reading the story of Rumpelstiltskin to William, Victor's eight-year-old brother, who lies on the floor in front of her with his dog, Fritz. Justine Moritz, a young maidservant, sits embroidering in a side chair. Soon Justine leads William and his dog off to bed, at which time Victor and Elizabeth draw together slowly and kiss. They are interrupted by the entrance of Lionel Mueller, the local magistrate, his wife Frau Mueller, and Victor's father, Alphonse Frankenstein. Alphonse declares, "We have a surprise for you," and Henry Clerval enters, presenting himself with a mock flourish. Victor embraces Henry.

There is a distant rumble of thunder—the beginning of a storm that continues to build throughout the evening. Alphonse announces that Victor and Elizabeth are engaged to be married and everyone bustles about in a flurry of congratulations. Lightning flashes as Metz and Schmidt appear behind the French doors. Victor joins them and escorts them out. Elizabeth tells Henry that she invited him because Victor "is not the man we used to know." Her fiancé has transformed the tower rooms into a laboratory, ordered machinery and equipment, and hired villagers to construct an enormous dynamo in the stream beneath the tower to produce electricity; he has not confided the nature of his work.

Later that evening Victor reveals to Henry that he's "capable of reanimating life" and asks his friend to join him in "the creation of life—in a man." Henry is shocked and Victor, heated, says that by his capability to control life and death, disease will forever be removed from the human race.

Victor ushers Henry to the laboratory, a wide room filled with an assortment of electrical and chemical apparatus. Cables and wires run everywhere in a maze of interconnections. On a large operating table in the center rests the recently delivered body. The thunderstorm continues to build as Henry secures a large strap across the dead man's chest and Victor throws switches. Machinery throbs and pulses. The table begins a slow ascent toward the ceiling, accompanied by a deafening crack of thunder and a huge flash of lightning. The table descends and the machinery winds to a halt. Victor checks the pulse of the figure and declares, "It's alive!"

Victor and Henry celebrate the monumental achievement but soon realize that they have no control over the creature, who crashes out the window and disappears.

The following scene, borrowed from the movie *The Bride of Frankenstein*, pictures the creature's arrival in the isolated cottage of a blind hermit, DeLacey, who teaches the strange newcomer how to speak. While the creature is out getting wood, the grave robbers, Metz and Schmidt, enter and begin to put items into their bags. DeLacey attempts to stop them and calls for help. Metz tightens a scarf around the blind man's neck and strangles him—the first of a number of brutal, violent acts described graphically throughout the play.

The creature enters carrying a bundle of wood, looks at the body, and starts toward Metz, who pulls a knife and jams it into the creature's stomach. He doubles over, almost falls, then pulls out the knife, crosses to Metz and drives the tines of a pitchfork into him. Metz falls with a scream. The creature kneels by DeLacey, rocks him gently, and cries out a word he has recently learned, "Friend!"

Act 2 recounts the travails of the creature as he returns to the Frankenstein Chateau, plays with Little William, and inadvertently smothers the boy and kills his dog. A confrontation in the laboratory results with the creature pushing Henry against the high-voltage electrical machine; Henry shakes violently and crumples to the floor, dead. A year later, on Elizabeth's wedding day, the creature does not realize his own strength when he strangles her in the bedroom. Victor shoots the creature who, mortally wounded, manages to lift Victor, place the struggling scientist across his shoulders and bend him backwards until Victor's back breaks with an audible crack. The creature shrugs off the body onto the ground, says, "Farewell, Frankenstein," crosses to the bank of electrical switches, and pulls them one by one. The machinery begins to spark and smoke. Flames lick up and the lab begins to crumble until it falls upon itself, the creature, and his creator.

In the published acting edition of *Frankenstein*, playwright Victor Gialanella suggests that the destruction of the laboratory "can be accomplished by the use of flashpots, smoke, flickering colored lights and the appropriate accompanying sound. At the very end, almost simultaneously with the curtain, a few chunks of painted Styrofoam thrown from the wings or dropped from the flies add greatly to the illusion."[9]

Upon the opening of *Frankenstein* at New York's Palace Theatre on January 4, 1981, the reviews were unanimously negative. Frank Rich wrote, "This playwright has merged the most memorable scenes from James Whale's 1931 Hollywood version with random scraps from the 1816 Shelley novel only to end up with a talky-stilted mishmash."[10] Clive Barnes asserted that "the special effects proved to be neither special nor effective enough to save the show."[11] Douglas Watt sniffed, "The one truly monstrous thing about this effort by a fledging playwright, Victor Gialanella, that came to the Palace last night is the clumsy writing."[12] John Beaufort frowned, "The actors work zealously. . . . But for all their efforts and for all the special effects, the Gialanella treatment seldom rises above the level of spectacular hokum."[13] Christopher Sharp concluded that "Victor Gialanella's new play at the Palace is not scary, not funny, not dramatic, not melodramatic, not even entertaining."[14]

The television critics, too, were disappointed. "At the end of *Frankenstein* the entire set falls apart in spectacular fashion," said Dennis Cunningham. "But, much earlier on, the play falls apart—in no particular fashion."[15] Joel Siegel lamented, "Victor Gialanella managed, somehow, to turn the classic tale of gothic terror into a mumble-jumbled Victorian melodrama."[16]

Frankenstein played for only one performance; it opened and closed on January 4, 1981, losing the entire investment of two million dollars.

* * *

Due to his fertile imagination, Victor Gialanella is a long way from his early days working in his father's Newark, New Jersey butcher shop. Growing up, he always wanted to be a writer. He penned and produced plays in high school. He majored in theatre at Catholic University, but left after his sophomore year to join regional and touring companies.

Gialanella rose from the ashes of 1981's *Frankenstein* to become a prolific television soap opera writer for *Guiding Light* (1983–1987), *Days of Our Lives* (1995–2008), and *One Life to Live* (2006–2007). He has been leading a quiet, mundane life with his wife, Cindy, their two daughters, and assorted cats in their Peters Township home in Pennsylvania while concocting complicated plots of bigamy, infidelities, and divorces. "The networks think we're hacks," Gialanella said. "We're the bastard children. It's done on the fly and from the hip. Prime time has a week to shoot an hour. Soaps shoot an hour a day and we crank it every day, 52 weeks a year."[17]

Acting Edition: Dramatists Play Service.

Awards and Honors: Victor Gialanella won a Daytime Emmy Award for Best Writing (*Guiding Light*, 1986) and a Writers Guild of America Award for Best Writing (*Days of Our Lives*, 1999).

NOTES

1. William Godwin (1756–1863) wrote *Things As They Are; or, The Adventures of Caleb Williams* (1794), the very first novel about detecting a murder.

2. According to scholar Donald F. Glut, T. P. Cooke played the Frankenstein monster 365 times, and, like Boris Karloff over a century later, became identified with the role. Donald F. Glut, *The Frankenstein Legend* (Metuchen, N.J.: Scarecrow Press, 1973), 29.

3. *Hideous Progenies* by Steven Earl Forry recounts the plots and production data of *Frankenstein* dramatizations from the nineteenth century to the present (Philadelphia: University of Pennsylvania Press, 1990).

4. In addition to *The Last Laugh,* Charles W. Goddard and Paul Dickey collaborated on *The Ghost Breaker* (1913), a farcical thriller that ran for seventy-two performances on Broadway and spawned three movie adaptations in 1922, 1940, and 1953; *The Misleading Lady* (1913), depicting the abduction of a budding actress by a hard-boiled adventurer; and *The Broken Wing* (1920), relating the antics of a wealthy American rancher and a smiling but dangerous Mexican bandit. Suspense plays written by Dickey are described in Amnon Kabatchnik's *Blood on the Stage, 1900–1925* (Lanham, Md.: Scarecrow Press, 2008), 189–92. Charles William Goddard penned the original story of *The Perils of Pauline* (1914), a torch-blazing serial that had Pearl White menaced by the dastardly Koerner—and his cohorts, bloodthirsty, if stereotyped, Indians, Orientals, Gypsies, and pirates—through twenty cliff-hanging episodes, on land, in the air, and underwater.

5. Glut, *The Frankenstein Legend*, 45.

6. David Campton, *Frankenstein* (London: J. Garnet Miller, 1973), 6.

7. Pierre Biner, *The Living Theatre* (New York: Horizon Press, 1972), 111.

8. Glut, *The Frankenstein Legend*, 49.

9. Victor Gialanella, *Frankenstein* (New York: Dramatists Play Service, 1982), 64.

10. *New York Times*, January 5, 1981.

11. *New York Post*, January 5, 1981.

12. *Daily News*, January 5, 1981.

13. *Christian Science Monitor*, January 6, 1981.

14. *Women's Wear Daily*, January 6, 1981.

15. *WCBS-TV2*, January 4, 1981.

16. *WABC-TV7*, January 4, 1981.

17. http://boards.soapoperanetwork.com/topic/21135.

A Talent for Murder (1981)

Jerome Chodorov (United States, 1911–2004) and Norman Panama (United States, 1914–2003)

During the 1970s, the whodunit became an endangered species. Only half a dozen thrillers—*Sleuth* (1970) contained twists galore, *Child's Play* (1970) presented an aura of supernatural menace, *Night Watch* (1972) had a wallop of a surprise ending, *The Runner Stumbles* (1976) re-created a real-life murder case, *The Crucifer of Blood* (1978) took us back to the gaslight era of Sherlock Holmes, and *Deathtrap* (1978) thoroughly bamboozled us—sweetened an otherwise starched decade.

This scarcity triggered high expectations for *A Talent for Murder*, which arrived at the Biltmore Theatre on October 1, 1981, pumped up by the reputation of its writing team—Jerome Chodorov and Norman Panama, and its leading actors—Claudette Colbert and Jean-Pierre Aumont. Sadly, the "mystery comedy" turned out to be less than suspenseful and sparsely humorous. A producer's note in the playbill stated, "In the tradition of the 'whodunit,' and in fairness to future audiences, we request that you not reveal the plot details of *A Talent for Murder*." Alas, there are few "plot details" in the play mystifying enough to warrant such secrecy.

A Talent for Murder is the story of Anne Royce McClain (played by Colbert), America's foremost suspense novelist, "second only to the immortal Agatha," who has sixty-eight best-sellers to her name and, naturally, a plush estate, "Twelve Oaks," in the foothills of the Berkshires. Anne, in her seventies, is ailing and reliant on a wheelchair, though she sometimes gets out of it for no discernable reason, except, perhaps, to model a succession of chic dresses designed by Bill Blass.

The house is full of strange contraptions, including a sealed garage from which oxygen can be drained, utilized to test the murder methods exhibited in Anne's books. Aiding Anne with her experiments, and serving as butler-cook-bartender-chauffeur, is Rashi, an East Indian paroled convict. Also in the household are Anne's personal physician, Dr. Paul Merchand (Aumont), an urbane, chess-playing Frenchman in his mid-sixties, and her granddaughter Pamela, a twenty-five-year-old victim of a plane crash who is brain-damaged.

The play begins on a happy note as a telegram arrives to notify Anne that she has been awarded an Edgar Prize by the Mystery Writers of America for *The Case of the Purple Shoes*. But this is Anne's birthday and to her chagrin some unsavory relatives are arriving to celebrate—Lawrence McClain, Anne's ineffectual son, editor of a failing poetry magazine; his wife Sheila, beautiful, ambitious and greedy; and Mark Harrison, Pamela's husband, an aggressive car dealer with a penchant for nymphets.

The family, coined by Anne "a nest of vipers," is anxious to lay hands on her fortune, most especially a $15.7 million art collection peppered with paintings by Matisse, Braque, Modigliani, and Picasso. Led by the ruthless Sheila, they intend to put Anne away in an eldercare institution. "I'm talking about an exclusive senior citizen's home in Palm Beach," confides Sheila sweetly. Anne learns of the plan through sophisticated bugging devices scattered about her home.

In the evening, when the family members leave the house for a Tanglewood concert, Anne addresses Sheila: "You drive with me." She wheels to her desk and slips a cassette into the tape recorder. Sheila's voice is heard, cajoling the others to commit Anne to an institution.

Anne flicks off the machine. She reaches for a brooch, removes it, and explains that it is a mini-microphone like the one she used in *The Deadly Voice*—"Five hundred and sixty-four thousand hard cover; a million, four-eighty paperback." She offers Sheila $100,000 settlement if she divorces Larry and gets her "miserable bones" out of the family. "You're a firebug and a loonie," says Sheila. "There'll be no trouble putting you away. And that's just what I'm going to do."

The next morning, Sheila is found dead of suffocation in the locked garage, but it was not Anne who had locked the door. Without much ado, over a nightcap, Anne discloses to Doctor Marchand that she knows he committed the murder by riding Pamela's bike from the theatre to the house, setting the trap, and bicycling back. The clue? Purists will consider it unfair, for the audience has no chance to observe it: "When you returned at the end of the intermission, I noticed your right cuff was turned up, a strange oversight for a man of your sartorial elegance," says Anne. "So I dropped in at your cottage, and I found the trousers with a smear of grease from Pam's bicycle . . . I know you did it for Pam and me and as murders go, it was terribly sweet." They begin to play chess, and the curtain falls.

* * *

"Miss Colbert, who continues to reverse the normal process of time, and Mr. Aumont are both ineffably charming," wrote critic Clive Barnes, while concluding sadly: "*A Talent for Murder* needs every bit of luster it can muster. A *Sleuth* or *Deathtrap* it isn't."[1] The other reviewers were even less accommodating: "A woefully creaky thriller," hooted Douglas Watt.[2] "Messrs. Chodorov and Panama have created such a flimsy charade that one ceases to care very much whodunit or why," frowned John Beaufort.[3] "None of the characters is at all intriguing. The only reason for so creaky a vehicle arriving is a chance to exhibit two aging movie stars," sneered Howard Kissel.[4] Frank Rich echoed his colleagues' sentiments: "But, really! While no one expects Miss Colbert, now or ever, to play *Medea*—or even *The Little Foxes*—surely she can find a stage vehicle, however light, that gives her more drive than a wheelchair."[5] Dennis Cunningham was blunt: "All sorts of gimmicky embroidery are sewn onto that basic premise. But it all remains gimmicky embroidery, and never for a moment do the proceedings become compelling."[6]

Ordinarily, such a trouncing would engender an immediate closing notice, but the two "aging movie stars" evidently had enough drawing power for seventy-two performances. In 1984, BBC-TV cast Angela Lansbury and Sir Laurence Olivier in a follow-up production.

* * *

Born in New York City in 1911, Jerome Chodorov worked as a runner on Wall Street and as a reporter for the *New York World* before setting off for California. There he began his screenwriting career with *The Case of the Lucky Legs* (1935), a Perry Mason case that he adapted from an Erle Stanley Gardner novel, and there he met Joseph Fields (1895–1966) who became his long-time writing partner. They collaborated on the screenplays of half a dozen movies, including *The Gentleman from Louisiana* (1936), a yarn about horse-race fixing; the thriller *Reported Missing* (1937); *Rich Man, Poor Girl* (1938) with Lana Turner; the Bob Hope comedy *Louisiana Purchase* (1941); and the Western adventure *Man from Texas* (1948). Chodorov's suspense films include *Conspiracy* (1939), in which an American freighter's radio officer gets entangled in a foreign espionage caper, and *Murder in the Big House* (1942), wherein a crusading reporter gets himself thrown in prison in order to reveal the connection between the murder of a Death Row inmate and the town's crooked politicians. *Lucky Luciano* (1973) is the real-life story of a ruthless underworld boss who is jailed, pardoned, and sent back to Sicily, where he again becomes a Mafia kingpin.

In the early 1950s, Chodorov was named a communist during the House Un-American Committee hearings and was blacklisted in Hollywood for most of the decade. He continued to script several films uncredited and went to London to work with renowned film producer Alexander Korda.

Chodorov and Fields's main contribution to the Broadway stage was in the area of light comedy: they coauthored the hits *My Sister Eileen* (1940), *Junior Miss* (1941), *The Anniversary Waltz* (1954), and the milestone musical *Wonderful Town* (1953). On his own, Chodorov wrote the book for the long-running musical *I Had a Ball* (1964) and the short-lived *Three Bags Full* (1966) as well as the librettos for *Dumas and Son* (1967) and a revised version of *Pal Joey* (1978).

Chodorov and Fields teamed on the farce *The Ponder Heart* (1956), adapted from Eudora Welty's novella, in which a lovable country bumpkin is on trial for the murder of his wife, who actually died of fright during a severe thunderstorm. Chodorov's sentiment for suspense was also expressed in his Broadway direction of Alec Coppel's *The Gazebo* (1958), a mystery-comedy about a suburban television writer who is being blackmailed and decides that murder is the only way out. He shoots the bad guy and plants his body in a gazebo's fresh concrete foundation. Complications ensue.[7]

Increasingly hard of hearing and with his sight failing, Chodorov stopped writing by the early 1990s. In 2003 he attended the opening night of a Broadway revival of *Wonderful Town*. The show was still running when he died the following year in Nyack, New York at the age of 93.[8]

Norman Panama was born in Chicago in 1914. Teamed with Melvin Frank (1913–1988) since their student days at the University of Chicago, the pair wrote radio shows for Bob Hope and Milton Berle in the late 1930s, and later penned such Hope screen vehicles as *My Favorite Blonde* (1942), *Monsieur Beaucaire* (1946), *That Certain Feeling* (1956), *The Facts of Life* (1960), and several *Road* movies. For Eddie Cantor, they scripted *Thank Your Lucky Stars* (1943), and for Danny Kaye, *Knock on Wood* (1954), *White Christmas* (1954), and *The Court Jester* (1956). Based on the popular cartoon strip, Panama and Frank created *Li'l Abner* for Broadway in 1956, and three years later filmed it in VistaVision. On a more serious note, the duo wrote and directed the motion picture *Above and Beyond* (1952), in which Robert Taylor enacted the role of Paul Tibbets, the U.S. pilot who dropped the atomic bomb on Hiroshima.

Panama continued to make his mark as a prolific screenwriter, director, and producer through the 1980s. He died in 2003 in Los Angeles from complications of Parkinson's disease.

Acting Edition: Samuel French, Inc.

Awards and Honors: *A Talent for Murder* won the 1982 Mystery Writers of America's Edgar Award for Best Play. Jerome Chodorov's *Wonderful Town* garnered a Tony Award for Best Musical in 1953. With his co-writer Melvin Frank, Norman Panama was nominated for a Best Screenplay Oscar three times, for *Road to Utopia* (1945), *Knock on Wood* (1954), and *The Facts of Life* (1960).

NOTES

1. *New York Post*, October 2, 1981.
2. *Daily News*, October 2, 1981.
3. *Christian Science Monitor*, October 7, 1981.
4. *Women's Wear Daily*, October 2, 1981.
5. *New York Times*, October 2, 1981.
6. *CBS-TV*, October 1, 1981.
7. A synopsis of the plots, production data, and critics' evaluation of both *The Ponder Heart* and *The Gazebo* can be found in *Blood on the Stage, 1950–1975* by Amnon Kabatchnik (Lanham, Md.: Scarecrow Press, 2011).
8. Jerome Chodorov's older brother, Edward Chodorov (1904–1988), was also a playwright, author of the nerve-wracking *Kind Lady* (1935).

A Soldier's Play (1981)

Charles Fuller (United States, 1939–)

Charles Fuller's *Zooman and the Sign* (1980) was centered on the random killing of a twelve-year-old girl by a young African American thug. *A Soldier's Play* also begins with a murder—the shooting of a black army sergeant by an unknown assailant in Ft. Neal, Louisiana during World War II. In both plays, Fuller challenges African Americans to find their identity within white society.

Structurally, *A Soldier's Play* develops along the traditional formula of the whodunit. Tech Sergeant Vernon C. Waters, staggering drunk on his way to the barracks, is shot twice by a shadowy figure holding a .45-caliber pistol. It is generally presumed that the Ku Klux Klan committed the murder, but Richard Davenport, a black captain attached to the military Police Corps Unit, is sent to investigate the matter. Amid clashes with the dubious white captain in charge of the 221st Company—"This case is not for you! By the time you overcome the obstacles to your race this case would be dead!"—Davenport grills the black enlisted men who were under Waters's command. In quick, kaleidoscopic flashbacks, unfolding on various raked levels connected by stairs or ramps, Waters is exposed as a much-hated taskmaster, continuously spewing abuse at the "lazy, shiftless Negroes" under his charge. He stripped Staff Sergeant James Wilkie of his stripes, triggered a fistfight with Private First Class Melvin Peterson, and had "a crazy hate" for the popular Private C. J. Memphis.

Davenport discounts the involvement of the Klan because the victim was found with his stripes and insignia intact. The white officers—Lieutenant Byrd and Captain Wilcox—scuffled with Waters outside the "colored" NCO club, but insisted that "He was alive when we left!" A ballistic check of their guns cleared the officers. Finally, Davenport concludes that Waters was not the victim of white racists but was killed by Pfc. Peterson. It is then revealed that "the entire outfit, officers and enlisted men, were wiped out in the Ruhr Valley during a German advance."

Beneath the veneer of this murder mystery, there is an unflinching, palpable exploration of tensions among blacks, and, as aptly stated by critic Frank Rich, "a relentless investigation into the complex, sometimes cryptic pathology of hate." Rich pointed out that "for all his venom and cruelty," Waters "was also a prideful man who refused to toady to whites and who often wanted the best for his fellow Blacks."[1]

* * *

A Soldier's Play was produced by the Negro Ensemble Company at off-Broadway's Theatre Four on November 10, 1981. Douglas Turner Ward directed a cast headed by Charles Brown as Davenport, Adolph Caesar as Waters, and two actors who would soon make it to the big time: Denzel Washington as Peterson and Samuel L. Jackson as fellow recruit Private Louis Henson. Walter Kerr declared playwright Fuller to be "one of the contemporary American theatre's most forceful and original voices. . . . You should make Mr. Fuller's acquaintance. Now."[2]

A Soldier's Play ran for 468 performances. In 1984, scripted by Fuller, it was effectively transformed to the screen as *A Soldier's Story*—with a number of original cast members, including Caesar and Washington reprising their roles, under the direction of Norman Jewison. Off-Broadway's Second Stage Theatre revived the play October 17–November 27, 2005, staged by Jo Bonney. "Mr. Fuller uses clean-lined conventions to elicit disconcertingly blurred shades of racism, resentment and self-hatred among Black men waiting to fight in a white man's army," wrote critic Ben Brantley.[3] "Fuller's script can be programmatic, with its flashback structure and whodunit setup, and it concludes with some back-patting speechifying. But he compensates with scenes of rich social, temporal and psychological texture," opined Robert Simonson.[4] "A murder investigation that serves to explore the complex shades of racism, the 1981 Pulitzer Prize-winning play perhaps remains too entrenched in whodunit mechanics to bring a full charge to its deeper issues," deemed David Rooney. "But Second Stage's taut revival enlists a strong ensemble to tell an engrossing story of deeply rooted injustice." [5]

Acting Edition: Samuel French, Inc.

Awards and Honors: Pulitzer Prize, 1982; New York Drama Critics Circle Award—Best American Play, 1981–1982; Outer Critics Circle Award—Best off-Broadway Play, 1981–1982. A top ten selection in *The Best Plays of 1981–1982*—"first-rate theatre in a production perfectly suited to its off-Broadway environment."[6] Scripted by Charles Fuller, *A Soldier's Story* won the 1985 Mystery Writers of America's Edgar Award for Best Motion Picture.

NOTES

1. *New York Times*, November 27, 1981.
2. *New York Times*, December 6, 1981.
3. *New York Times*, October 18, 2005.
4. *Time Out New York*, October 20, 2005.
5. *Variety*, October 18, 2005.
6. Otis L. Guernsey Jr., ed., *The Best Plays of 1981–1982* (New York: Dodd, Mead, 1983), 24.

Cards on the Table (1981)

Leslie Darbon (England)

Leslie Darbon, who transformed Agatha Christie's *A Murder Is Announced* to the stage, was also responsible for adapting *Cards on the Table*, Christie's 1936 novel. While Darbon's earlier effort was too cumbersome, *Cards on the Table* progresses smoothly and relentlessly toward its denouement.

In the Christie tradition, Darbon removed Poirot from the stage adaptation. He also extracted another sleuth from *Cards on the Table*, Colonel Race of the British Secret Service. It is up to Superintendent Battle of Scotland Yard and Mrs. Ariadne Oliver, renowned author of mystery novels (and arguably Agatha Christie's alter ego), to solve the fatal stabbing of London socialite Shaitana during a bridge game.[1]

As the curtain rises, four people are playing cards in the luxurious drawing room of Mr. Shaitana's house: Dr. David Roberts, a charming, gregarious man with impeccable taste; Mrs. Lorimer, a graceful, intelligent woman of sixty-three; Major Bruce Despard, aged thirty-five, a dashing adventurer with an eye for the ladies; and Anne Meredith, a shy, timid person of twenty-five.

Mr. Shaitana, the host, described as "the original, oily Levantine you wouldn't trust to sell you a second-hand car," chats in the corner with writer Ariadne Oliver, "a big, rather magnificent-looking lady with wild uncontrollable hair." Mrs. Oliver confides that she almost killed famous Finnish detective Sven Hjerson in her latest book. To tell the truth, she hates writing, but "it's better than working for a living."

Shaitana shocks Mrs. Oliver when he whispers that all four of his four guests have committed murder and have so far gotten away with their crimes.

A few hours later, Shaitana is found dead in the big armchair by the fireplace. On the floor next to the body lies a long, thin, evil-looking stiletto.

Superintendent Battle takes charge. It turns out that each of the bridge players had been blackmailed by the host, threatened with exposure of their past misdeeds. Who among them is the killer?

Mrs. Oliver conjectures that perhaps all four conspired to commit the murder, but Inspector Battle downplays the notion: "They didn't know each other," he states.[2]

By assessing the character of the players through rubber scorecards, the investigators conclude that it was Dr. Roberts who slipped over to Shaitana while sitting out a dummy hand and boldly stabbed him.[3]

* * *

Cards on the Table, directed by Peter Dews, premiered at London's Vaudeville Theatre on December 9, 1981, with Gordon Jackson as Superintendent Battle and Margaret Courtenay as Mrs. Oliver. The reception by the critics went from sarcastic to vitriolic. Michael Billington believed that the real victim of a foul and dastardly murder was a play called *Cards on the Table*. "What I want to find out is who killed it?" Billington demanded from director Dews an explanation of his whereabouts during the month prior to the opening, and concluded that the real culprit was Leslie Darbon, the adapter, sentencing him to solitary confinement "until you write a better play than this."[4]

Benedict Nightingale did not mince words: "It is vile, abominable, a stinker among stinkers."[5]

But Agatha Christie and Leslie Darbon had the last laugh. *Cards on the Table* ran for nine months, closing on September 4, 1982, and joined the Christie canon of worldwide revival by little theatres and summer stock.

Acting Edition: Samuel French, Inc.

NOTES

1. While in the novel *Cards on the Table* Superintendent Battle plays second fiddle to Hercule Poirot, he appears on his own in *The Secret of Chimneys* (1925); *The Seven Dials Mystery* (1929); *Murder Is Easy*, aka *Easy to Kill* (1939); and *Towards Zero* (1944). Ariadne Oliver joined Poirot in *Mrs. McGinty's Dead* (1952); *Dead Man's Folly* (1956); *Third Girl* (1966); *Hallowe'en Party* (1969); and *Elephants Can Remember* (1972). Mrs. Oliver is the sole sleuth of *The Pale Horse* (1961).

2. In an earlier novel, *Murder on the Orient Express*, aka *Murder in the Calais Coach* (1934), Christie utilized the audacious solution of a collective culprit.

3. Across the Atlantic, in New York City, amateur detective Philo Vance identified the cold-blooded murderer of *The Canary Murder Case* (1927) by observing a poker game.

4. *Guardian*, London, December 10, 1981.

5. *New Statesman*, London, December 10, 1981.

The Hound of the Baskervilles (1982)

Anthony Hinds (England, 1922–)

In 1959, the British Hammer Company made a movie of *The Hound of the Baskervilles* featuring Peter Cushing (Sherlock Holmes), Andre Morell (Dr. Watson), and Christopher Lee (Sir Henry Baskerville). Years later, one of the film's producers, Anthony Hinds, penned a stage adaptation of *The Hound,* calling it "an entertainment based on the classic story by Sir Conan Doyle." Hinds divided the action into three acts unfolding in two settings—the study in Baker Street and the hallway of Baskerville Hall.

The play follows the proceedings of the Doyle novel, but Hinds inserted a number of innovations:

Each scene opens with "menacing" or "mysterious" music, sometimes accompanied by "an ear splitting clap of thunder." Holmes energizes his mental faculties by playing chess. For reasons best known to the playwright alone, country physician James Mortimer is called Basil Mortimer, housekeeper Eliza Barrymore becomes Alice Barrymore, and the Devonshire neighbor, Mr. Frankland, changes into Lady Franklyn. When Mortimer narrates to Holmes the story of "profane and godless" Sir Hugo who "came to lust after the daughter of yeoman holding lands near to the Baskerville estate," a door at the rear of the auditorium crashes open and the figure of a young girl in peasant costume comes running down the aisle. Sobbing, she reaches the stage, but stops fearfully at the sight of Sir Hugo standing there, leering. The girl utters a terrified scream, turns, and runs back the way she came. Sir Hugo hurries after her, calls for his horse at the rear of the theatre, and the spectators hear the clatter of horses' hooves thundering away.

The auditorium is used liberally for entrances and exits by the actors and for imaginary walls, notably the one decorated with (invisible) family portraits.

A mustached hansom cabbie is summoned to the Baker Street flat and is interrogated by Holmes regarding the bearded man who followed

Sir Henry through the streets of London (other stage adaptations of *The Hound* have omitted this auxiliary character).

Selden, the escaped convict who in most stage renditions is an off-stage figure, makes a clandestine entrance by night and takes away parcels of clothing left for him by the Barrymores. Soon Selden's body comes hurtling through the window, dropping at Watson's feet. The convict scratches at the carpet as if trying to pull himself up, but convulses and dies.

Beryl Stapleton, perpetually browbeaten by her brother Jack, finds the gumption to suddenly, startlingly kiss Sir Henry "full on the mouth."

Paying homage to the tradition of classical whodunits, Holmes marshals a gathering of all "concerned with this terrible affair" for a climactic denouement.

Holmes deduces that the culprit, Jack Stapleton, is a professional actor—"Now what sort of a man is it who can disguise himself so convincingly. . . . Performing here, in Devon, at the Theatre Royal in Exeter—he learned that he had a relative nearby, a very rich relative. He also learned of the legend. He rented a cottage nearby under a false name, bought a wolfhound, trained it."

Stapleton grabs a gun from Watson and leaps down the auditorium. Watson starts after him. Stapleton fires. Watson is saved by his watch—it's a wreck, but it stopped the bullet. Stapleton runs out through the rear of the theatre. The sound of a baying hound is heard, first from a distance, then louder and louder. A terrible scream reverberates and Stapleton staggers in, stumbles up an aisle, gasping, whimpering. He gets to the edge of the stage, tries to reach out for Beryl, spins around—revealing a red gash where his throat was torn out—and falls to the ground.

Anthony Hinds's *Hound* was performed by the Steeple Aston Players, Oxfordshire, England, in March 1982. The play was published by New Playwrights' Network in 1991.

* * *

Englishman Anthony Hinds, born in 1922 and educated at St. Paul's School, is the son of the founder of Hammer Films, William Hinds. Anthony became immersed in the cinema in 1946 and eventually contributed mightily, as writer and producer, to the success of his father's company. Under the pseudonym John Elder, he scripted *The Curse of the Werewolf* (1961), *The Phantom of the Opera* (1962), *The Kiss of the Vampire* (1963), *The Evil of Frankenstein* (1964), *Dracula: A Prince of Darkness* (1966), and *The Mummy's Shroud* (1967) and continued to pen horror fare during the 1970s.

As a producer, Hinds worked on many low-budget thrillers before hitting it big with *The Quatermass Experiment,* aka *The Creeping Unknown*

(1955), based on the BBC-TV serial by Nigel Kneale. Hinds served as producer of Hammer's *The Hound of the Baskervilles* (1959), the first Sherlock Holmes movie filmed in color. Among his motion picture follow-ups: *The Stranglers of Bombay* (1960), *The Curse of the Werewolf* (1961), *Paranoiac* (1963), *The Damned* (1963), *Fanatic* (1965), and *The Lost Continent* (1968).

For British television, Hinds produced the series *Journey to the Unknown* (1968–1971), and wrote (as John Elder) *The Masks of Death* (1984), with Peter Cushing reprising his role of Sherlock Holmes and John Mills portraying Dr. Watson—both involved in the kidnapping of a German prince before World War I.

Acting Edition: New Playwrights' Network.

Whodunnit (1982)

Anthony Shaffer (England, 1926–2001)

Anthony Shaffer, who demonstrated his love-hate feelings for the genre of suspense fiction in *Sleuth* (1970) and *Murderer* (1975), again bit the format that fed him in a broad comic spoof titled *Whodunnit*.

An earlier version of the play, *The Case of the Oily Levantine* (1979), had a brief run in London. After extensive rewrites, the author described the work in a *New York Times* interview with Newgate Callendar as, "a comedy of manners, an evocation of Agatha Christie and her British society milieu. It's a slight piece, really more a comedy than a thriller. I simply say to the audience that we're going to play a game. All the facts will be given, mistakes will be made, all kinds of false clues planted. But we will play it as fair as we can."[1]

The game unfolds during the 1930s in the Library of the Orcas Champflower Manor, a grand eighteenth-century room with dark wood paneling, bookcases stretched to the ceiling, an ornamental display of antique swords, and sinister hidden nooks. Archibald Perkins, a tipsy, ancient, gray-haired butler, ushers in, one by one, six strangers who have arrived for a leisurely weekend in the country. All are archetypes of the classic detective story: An Old Sea Dog, A Dotty Aristocrat, A Sweet Young Thing, A Black Sheep, An Eccentric Archeologist, and An Oily Levantine who is blackmailing the lot. The host, A Respectable Family Lawyer, also finds himself at the mercy of the dastardly Levantine, Andreas Capodistriou.

During a howling storm, while Capodistriou kneels down and bends his head in prayer, the gaggle of guests sneak in; each snatches a sword and hides behind the bookcases. There is a crack of thunder and lightening. Suddenly a sword flashes and Capodistriou's head is struck off his body. It bounces downstage spurting blood as the act 1 curtain falls.

In act 2, the plot twists in surprising fashion. We realize that the action heretofore has been a charade by a troupe of actors recruited by the victim, Capodistriou, a much-hated talent agent. Inspector Bowden, an unconventional Scotland Yard detective, and his sergeant, a stolid police officer, grill each of the guests, with a finger pointed from one to the other. Exasperated, the inspector says, "I know it's a trifle old hat, but I'm going to reconstruct the crime." During the reconstruction, with the guests taking their previous positions and again lifting their respective swords, a second murder occurs. This time Silas Bazely, the host, staggers from his cranny with a knife in his back.

Inspector Bowden concludes that the murderer is left-handed and soon arrests "The Butler," Perkins, "the only actor here who has a career sufficiently valuable to justify murdering a man who would continue to take twenty-five percent of it." The inspector proudly announces, "In spite of the cliché, this will in fact be just about the first time in a major criminal enterprise that irrefutably, incontestably, indisputably, and incontrovertibly the butler did it!"

Playwright Shaffer has spruced up the proceedings with a taped Voice of the Murderer delivered via an amplification system sped up to conceal the gender and identity of the speaker, tantalizing the audience to solve the case prior to the denouement. Some hidden clues are sprinkled throughout. Good-natured, satirical darts are aimed at the prolific Edgar Wallace, G. K. Chesterton's Father Brown, John Dickson Carr's Dr. Fell, and Hercule Poirot's "Grey Cells," as well as toward other sacred cows of the Golden Age. However, none of the gimmicks and innuendos can mask a certain dullness. A lazy continuity and patched plot twists are especially disappointing when compared to the rich texture, elegant wit, and ghoulish ingenuity of Shaffer's *Sleuth* and *Murderer*.

* * *

Whodunnit opened at Broadway's Biltmore Theatre on December 30, 1982 and was lambasted by bloodthirsty critics. "The Christie magic has not rubbed off and the humor is as heavy as a flatfooted bloodhound barking up the wrong tree," growled Clive Barnes.[2] "I'm afraid *Whodunnit* just won't do it . . . the game's less afoot than underfoot," groaned Douglas Watt.[3] "*Whodunnit* is neither flesh nor fowl nor good red herring," complained Jack Kroll.[4] "*Whodunnit* has all the pieces: dual identities, double bluffs, a first-act curtain murder, a second-act twist. As a mystery it's a technical triumph. As theatre it's a crime. Whodunthat? The playwright," rasped Joel Siegel.[5] Most of the reviewers felt that director Michael Kahn did "nothing to bail the writing out," staging the play "as if it were a joke rather than a comedy, and the result is a dulling of the plot's edges." But by and large the aisle men complimented Andrew Jackness for having "designed the ultimate country house library for a murder," and Patricia Zipprodt for costumes that were "ingeniously tacky." The performances of George Hearn—"splendid as the blackmailing Levantine," and Fred

Gwynne as "a bumbling sleuth who looks like the hound of the Basker-ville in tweed," were also lauded.

Despite its negative critical reception, *Whodunnit* ran for 157 perfor-mances. Perhaps audiences flocked to solve the mystery of the double "n" in the play's title.

* * *

Anthony Joshua Shaffer was born to a Jewish family in Liverpool, England, in 1926. His twin brother was renowned playwright Peter Shaffer. In the 1940s, Anthony worked in coalmines in Kent and York-shire. In 1950, he graduated with a law degree from Trinity College, Cambridge University, and began practicing as a barrister the following year. Concluding that the money was inadequate, Shaffer switched to copywriting ads and in the early 1950s penned three thrillers in collabo-ration with his brother: *The Woman in the Wardrobe* (1951) and *How Doth the Little Crocodile?* (1952), under the joint pseudonym Peter Anthony, and *Withered Murder* (1955), bylined with their full names—all featur-ing a private detective named Mr. Verity, "an immense man just tall enough to carry his breadth majestically." By the end of the 1960s Shaf-fer changed course again, this time to playwriting.

Shaffer's first produced play, 1963's *The Savage Parade*, unfolds in a wine cellar in Tel Aviv, where a former high-ranking Nazi, hunted down in South America and brought to Israel in 1962, is interrogated by Haga-nah "judges" to determine whether he is "guilty in the first degree, or was an accomplice, in the death of six million Jews, gassed, burned, beaten, starved, shot, frozen, entombed, or otherwise put to death." In this initial effort, Shaffer established his knack for surprising plot maneuvers.

Shaffer's flagship play is 1970's *Sleuth*. It depicted a deadly cat-and-mouse game between a cynical playwright and his wife's lover in a style that both reveres and mocks parlor-room murder mysteries. His other stage ventures continued to display prankish and fiendish manipulations of the audience, constantly shifting, twisting, and shunning the obvious. *Murderer* (1975) is a send-off triggered by famous real-life assassinations. The play begins with a sequence during which painter Norman Bar-tholomew dismembers the corpse of his model, tossing arms, legs, and torso into a stove. Director Clifford Williams and designer Carl Toms of *Sleuth* contributed their sleight-of-hand expertise. *Widow's Weeds*, first produced in Australia in 1977 and ten years later in England, is a comic thriller about a lower-middle-class housewife in suburban London who has been selected to appear in a television commercial. Complications ensue. *The Case of the Oily Levantine* (1979), which became *Whodunnit* in its 1982 New York incarnation, came next. Shaffer's last play, *The Thing in the Wheelchair*, revolves around a paralyzed old woman tortured by her sadistic female caretaker. It was mounted posthumously in 2001 in Australia but there have been no other productions yet.

Shaffer is the author of several television dramas, notably an adaptation of Wilkie Collins's 1868 classic, *The Moonstone* (BBC, 1992). He has also written a number of screenplays, including *Forbush and Penguins* (1972), an adventure shot in the Antarctic; the harrowing *The Wicker Man* (1973), novelized by Shaffer and Robin Hardy in 1978; Alfred Hitchcock's thriller *Frenzy* (1974); *Absolution* (1979), a boys' school melodrama starring Richard Burton, novelized by Shaffer in 1981; and three Agatha Christie conversions—*Death on the Nile* (1978), *Evil under the Sun* (1982), and *Appointment with Death* (1988)—all featuring Peter Ustinov as Belgian detective Hercule Poirot.

Shaffer died of a heart attack in London in 2001. In an article in the magazine *Mystery Scene*, Joseph Goodrich reports that "a protracted battle over his estate began in 2004 when his mistress claimed she was entitled to a portion of Shaffer's estate. Her claim was dismissed but other complications ensued. More than ten years after Shaffer's death, legal matters show no sign of resolution." On a happier note, Goodrich proclaims that "the best of Shaffer's work continues to delight, engross and mystify the viewer. A firm believer in that old-fashioned virtue, entertainment, he worked hard to make it all look easy."[6]

Acting Edition: Samuel French, Inc.

Awards and Honors: Anthony Shaffer's *Sleuth* was a top ten selection in *The Best Plays of 1970–1971*. The play won the Antoinette Perry (Tony) Award, 1970–1971—Best Play; Mystery Writers of America Edgar Allan Poe Awards—Best Play, 1971, and Best Motion Picture Screenplay, 1973.

NOTES

1. *New York Times*, December 26, 1982.
2. *New York Post*, December 31, 1982.
3. *Daily News*, December 31, 1982.
4. *Newsweek*, January 17, 1983.
5. *WABC-TV7*, December 30, 1982.
6. Joseph Goodrich, "Anthony Shaffer: Grand Artificer of Mystery," *Mystery Scene* 124 (Spring 2012).

Moose Murders (1983)

Arthur Bicknell (United States, 1951–)

A satire on the mystery genre, *Moose Murders* joined 1980's *Tricks of the Trade* in the dubious distinction of garnering unanimous negative reactions from New York reviewers and dropping the curtain after its one and only performance—the play opened, and closed, at the Eugene O'Neill Theatre on February 22, 1983. "*Moose Murders* shouldn't happen to a moose," wrote Douglas Watt. "We are told early in the game that Wild Moose Lodge has an evil reputation. Talk about under-statement."[1]

"Playwright Arthur Bicknell and director John Roach would do well to learn something all children are told—that being funny involves much more than being silly," admonished Christopher Sharp.[2]

"This ensemble stumbles about mumbling dialogue that, as far as one can tell, is only improved by its inaudibility," jested Frank Rich.[3] "The good news is most of these characters will be dead before the night is out," announced Joel Siegel,[4] "and, quite probably, countless others in the audience," added Dennis Cunningham.[5] Clive Barnes called *Moose Murders* a "murderously uncomic murder comedy,"[6] but for unknown reasons voted it as his second choice for Best Play on the fourth ballot polled by the New York Drama Circle.

Wild Moose Lodge is located in the heart of the Adirondack Mountains, its walls decorated with stuffed game, most notably three moose heads. The caretaker, Joe Buffalo Dance, is a mock American Indian who speaks with an Irish brogue. "The Singing Keenes" are the in-house entertainers: Snooks, an off-key crooner, and husband Howie, her blind accompanist. They are soon joined by the Holloway family, the lodge's new owners: Hedda, a WASP matriarch; her husband Sidney, a somnambulist quadriplegic confined to a wheelchair; their drug-crazed, Oedipus-complexed, twenty-year-old son Stinky; Gay, their twelve-year old daughter, a tap-dancing Shirley Temple clone; Lauraine, another sibling, in her thirties, plain and simple-minded; and Nelson Fay, Lauraine's manipulative husband. With the dysfunctional family comes Nurse Dagmar, an exotic Nazi, who perpetually barks orders but screams fearfully at the slightest provocation.

Scheming to inherit the "legendary Holloway fortune," Lauraine and Nelson intend to bump off the rest of the family. "Sweet Momma, I'll see her dead," squeals Lauraine. "And brother precious. . . . And little Gay . . . Daddy too . . . right on down the line!" Thunder booms, the electricity goes off. When light is restored, it is Lauraine who is found lying on the floor strangled.

We soon learn that Nelson is actually in cahoots with Nurse Dagmar to eliminate them all. However, the veritable unholy alliance turns out to be between the Nurse and Sidney, who is only pretending to be an invalid. No, no—in still another twist, Hedda and Nelson are revealed to be passionate lovers and the real culprits who have undertaken to massacre husband, wife, and siblings. Hedda serves her daughter Gay a poison-laced vodka martini before cackling joyfully, "I've got the whole Holloway fortune to myself and the son-in-law I've always wanted."

Notwithstanding *Moose Murders*' reputation as a legendary flop, many community groups and dinner theatres have produced it. In 2007, the "mystery farce" was mounted by Repertory Philippines, an English-language theatre company in Makati City, Philippines. A year later, on February 22, 2008, the twenty-fifth anniversary of the play's Broadway opening-and-closing, *Moose Murders* received a stage reading, by amateur thespians, at the Rochester, New York Contemporary Art Center, with the hope that it will find new life "as a work of art."[7] The experience with the Rochester troupe galvanized Bicknell to write a new play expressly for this company. On February 19, 2010, Bicknell's *What Is Art?* premiered at Rochester's MuCCC Theatre. The plot is centered on the creation and marketing of a piece of public art in a small Texas town in the 1970s. Bicknell was present to talk about his life as a notorious playwright.

Arthur Bicknell now lives in Springfield, Massachusetts, and is the chief publicist for Merriam-Webster. In addition to *Moose Murders*, his other published play is the historical drama *Masterpieces*, an imaginative reconstruction of the lives of Branwell Brontë and his sisters Charlotte, Emily, and Anne.

Acting Edition: Samuel French, Inc.

NOTES

1. *Daily News*, February 23, 1983.
2. *Women's Wear Daily*, February 23, 1983.
3. *New York Times*, February 23, 1983.
4. *WABC-TV7*, February 22, 1983.
5. *WCBS-TV2*, February 22, 1983.
6. *New York Post*, February 23, 1983.
7. *New York Times*, April 21, 2008.

Postmortem (1983)

Ken Ludwig (United States)

The action of Ken Ludwig's whodunit *Postmortem* unfolds in a unique setting—the William Gillette castle in Hadlyme, Connecticut.

William Hooker Gillette (1853–1937), the son of a United States senator, was a distinguished actor-director-playwright. As a young boy, Gillette constructed a miniature puppet theatre and initiated a journal, signposts of things to come. To the chagrin of his parents, Gillette, a product of Yale, Harvard, and the Massachusetts Fine Arts Institute, embarked upon a theatrical career, joining stock companies. It is said that a neighbor, Mark Twain, was instrumental in getting Gillette his first professional appearance at the Globe Theatre in Boston in 1875.

Gillette's Broadway debut occurred in Twain's *Gilded Age* (1877)—a one-line role as the foreman of a jury. He later won accolades for his performances in J. M. Barrie's *The Admirable Crichton* (1903), Henri Bernstein's *Samson* (1908), Victorien Sardou's *Diplomacy* (1914), Clare Kummer's *A Successful Calamity* (1917), J. M. Barrie's *Dear Brutus* (1918), and as star of many of his own plays.

Gillette's first effort as a playwright, *The Professor* (1881), a bittersweet drama about two scientists who compete for the affection of their lovely assistant, was greeted by hostile critics, but audiences flocked to its 151 performances. Gillette's subsequent plays, *Esmeralda* (1881), rotating around a lovable farm girl, and *Digby's Secretary* (1884), concerning a timid parson, were also snubbed by the press albeit achieving popular success, playing, respectively, 350 and 200 performances.

Gillette gained recognition and esteem with his two Civil War spy melodramas, *Held by the Enemy* (1886) and *Secret Service* (1895). He was among the first exponents of a natural rather than over-dramatic style of acting and the producing of realistic stage settings in full detail. Gillette's major success was the penning of the four-act *Sherlock Holmes*, based on several stories by Arthur Conan Doyle, and starring in the title role.

Sherlock Holmes opened on Broadway in 1899, was received enthusiastically by critics and audiences, ran for 256 performances, and spawned a London production and a succession of English and U.S. touring companies. Holmes became Gillette's signature role as he continued to portray the world's foremost consulting detective for many years, amassing 1,300 performances. It was Gillette who popularized Holmes's deerstalker cap and meerschaum pipe.

Largely on the profits from *Sherlock Holmes*, Gillette built a castle on 115 acres of land in southern Connecticut. It was patterned after a medieval fortress, took five years to build, and was completed in 1919. Gillette frequently brought the cast of his latest New York revival to the castle for a weekend of leisure and good food. Following Gillette's death in 1937, "Gillette Castle," as it came to be known, was opened to visitors and tourists by the state of Connecticut. And it is here where the dastardly deeds of *Postmortem* unroll.

The living room of "Gillette Castle" is described as "expansive and eccentric" with an imposing frame of rough fieldstone walls and a nineteen-foot ceiling supported by massive oak frames. Upstage center are two French doors leading to a flagstone terrace. Double doors at stage right lead to a reception hall and the front door of the house. A staircase leads to a balcony and the bedrooms. A chandelier hangs from the ceiling, its lights controlled by switches in the form of carved oak handles near all the doors.

The furnishings contain a wingback chair, a sofa covered in chintz, a drop-leaf table, and a sturdy desk. Also noticeable are an electric gramophone and a wall portrait of a beautiful woman in her mid-thirties. Scattered around the room are great mementos of Sherlock Holmes, including the Persian slipper filled with shag tobacco, the deerstalker cap, and the meerschaum pipe. On the desk, the Stradivarius is propped against several scrapbooks. A large dagger with a jeweled handle hangs on one of the walls.

Scene 1 takes place on a Saturday night in April 1922, about 11:30 p.m. When the curtain rises, we hear the sound of a car screeching to a halt. The front doorbell buzzes and the butler Macready, stooped and whiskered, pushing retirement, enters and plods through the room. He disappears briefly to open the front door and soon a noisy young couple bounds into the room. Bobby Carlyle, a handsome fellow with a boyish face, wears a stylish motoring coat and cap, complete with rakish goggles. May Dison, a pretty girl in her mid-twenties, at the moment slightly disheveled, seems troubled and nervous. Bobby tosses his cap and gloves carelessly on a chair and joyfully tells Macready that they have beaten William Gillette in a car race from a Manhattan theatre and arrived first. May relates that Gillette received a standing ovation from an enthusiastic audience and Bobby laughingly adds that the actor left the theatre wearing the deerstalker hat and the cape from act 1. "The man actually believes that he's Sherlock Holmes," chuckles Bobby.

Bobby and May ask about Bates, Gillette's old-time butler, and Macready explains that Bates has fallen ill—pneumonia—and was taken to a hospital. Macready was engaged as a temporary replacement.

Mary looks up at the wall painting and Bobby tells her that the woman, Maude Redding, who was Gillette's fiancée, killed herself. Bobby vividly remembers the "worst damn night" of his life when at three a.m. he woke up at the sound of a shot, ran down, and out on the terrace found Gillette kneeling beside the body of Maude. "She looked beautiful, except for one perfect little hole in her forehead," says Bobby.

Looking for a cigarette, Bobby opens May's purse. He gingerly pulls out a revolver. May explains that she keeps the gun for protection, feeling unsafe in the big city of New York.

Enter Leo and Marion Barrett. Marion, Gillette's sister, in her forties, plays the adventuress Madge Larrabee in *Sherlock Holmes*. Leo, her husband, a few years older, portrays arch-villain Professor Moriarty. The conversation turns to Maude, who shot herself exactly a year ago. Macready enters unnoticed and collects the coats. Leo watches Macready suspiciously, then approaches the butler and accuses him of lying about Bates's illness. A quarrel ensues, at the end of which Leo grabs the dagger from the wall and Macready, frightened, fishes a gun from his pocket. "Get back! Get back!" shouts Macready and fires the weapon into the ceiling as a warning. All freeze.

Macready pulls off a wig and tells Leo, in his Sherlock Holmes voice, "You bastard, I could have had them going all night!" He removes his whiskers, peels the spirit gum from his face, takes off the Macready coat, and dons a suit jacket that has been draped over the desk chair since the scene began. "Bates is on vacation, living it up in Atlantic City," says Gillette.

Lilly Warner, Gillette's and Marion's aunt, appears on the balcony. She's in her late sixties or early seventies, wearing a hostess gown. Lilly comes down the staircase relating that even as a child, Gillette "liked to play dress up. When he was six years old, he put on one of my best hats and started prancing around, telling everyone that he was Ellen Terry."

Gillette announces that he has invited for the weekend one more guest, Louise Parradine, one of Maude's good friends who was staying in the castle the night Maude died. "She got hysterical," recalls Bobby. "They had to inject her." Leo remembers that Louise, who at the time played the role of a French maid on Broadway, left the show after that night.

Louise Parradine appears in the doorway. In her mid to late thirties, Louise is tall and striking. Gillette greets her and kisses her hand. Louise apologizes for being late but Gillette shrugs it off, saying, "It's a pity that the taxi had a flat tire." Louise is perplexed, "How did you know that?" Gillette explains his deduction by pointing to a stub that fell on the floor when Louise took off her gloves. Meticulously dressed, she surely did not leave her apartment with yellow mud caked on her left shoe. If it was engine trouble, she would have stayed in the car. "But you couldn't expect the poor fellow to jack it up while she sat inside," concludes Gillette.

Louise tells her astonished listeners that she has become a medium. She realized her new calling when one night, after her breakdown, when still in the hospital, she heard a voice, looked up, and there was Maude. "We're going to have a séance," declares Gillette.

Scene 2 begins with a flash of lightning and a crack of thunder. While a storm is raging outside, Louise instructs Gillette, Lilly, Bobby, May, Marion, and Leo to sit at the table and switches off the lights. Only a single lamp remains on, throwing long, weird shadows along the walls. Louise takes a seat between Gillette and Leo, closes her eyes, and soon begins to gasp and moan. Suddenly she calls, "May . . . May Redding. . . . Are you there?" The table thumps. A different voice emerges from Louise's lips, a feminine voice, heavy and sad: "May . . . May Redding. . . . I love you. . . . I miss you. . . . You know the truth. . . . It was murder. . . . *Murder!*"

Slowly, on the back wall, facing May, the image of a woman's head begins to form, larger than life. They all stare at the image as it begins to fade. May sinks to the floor, sobbing hysterically. Gillette runs to the hall wall and switches on the lights. Everyone huddles around May, helping her up. May blurts that Maude was her sister and it is likely that she was murdered.

Soon the guests depart for their rooms. Gillette and Louise remain. Gillette presses a button on the underside of the table. The image of Maude appears on the wall. He lets his finger up and the image fades. "Well done," says Gillette. "You even sounded like Maude." Shaken, Louise asks Gillette to hold her and she kisses him fiercely. May suddenly hurries onto the balcony, about to say something—but she sees them and stops. She stares at them, frozen in shock, as the lights fade.

Later that night, Gillette, wearing a patterned silk dressing gown—much the same outfit that Holmes wears when at leisure in Baker Street—affirms to his aunt Lilly his belief that Maude was murdered. He remains noncommittal when Lilly begs him to "stay out of it." An hour later, Gillette goes through a tense confrontation with May, who accuses him of murdering Maude. Her sister left her a letter in which she stated that her fiancé's love has turned to jealousy and hatred, and her life was in danger. Gillette retorts by telling May that on that fateful night a year ago, her sister was "frightened of something" and in a panic wanted to leave at once. She wouldn't tell Gillette what it was. He left for his bedroom to change when he heard the shot. He knew she was murdered the moment he found her. But the police "couldn't have cared less." As far as they were concerned, it was cut and dried: she owned a gun; it was in her hand, no signs of a struggle.

A gunshot explodes, shattering a window. Gillette orders May to get down and leaps straight at her, pinning her to the floor—as two more gunshots explode, shattering two more windows. "You're bleeding," exclaims May. He crawls across the room for his gun, jumps to the door, and fires several shots in quick succession. He then stumbles and falls to his knees. Lilly comes down the steps and May shouts for her to call a doctor. Lilly rushes to the telephone and asks the operator to send an ambulance—in a hurry.

Act 2 takes place in the following evening. Bobby theorizes to May that "everybody" had a motive to kill Maude: Leo, tired of playing second banana on the stage, wreaks his revenge; Marion, jealous of Maude's looks and talent; Lilly, terrified of losing her darling boy; Gillette himself, if Maude didn't want him after all. "And you," says Bobby to May, pointing out that she concealed the fact they were sisters and obviously inherits whatever estate Maude had.

Gillette strides in, dressed formally for a party, his left arm in a sling. Louise descends the staircase, dressed in a seductive gown, and expresses her anticipation of soon meeting the great Sarah Bernhardt: "I shall look in her eyes and see Medea, Camille, Hamlet." May goes to change while Leo and Bobby exit to the billiard room. Gillette pounds at Louise: "What happened?" Louise reports that the man she was to keep an eye on sat around all day, reading, and made one telephone call about four o'clock. Gillette informs her that the police found the man's gun in the courtyard bushes. "He must have thrown it there, after the shooting," says Gillette. Louise warns the actor-detective that he could be mistaken, but Gillette stands his ground and quotes Conan Doyle: "Exclude the impossible, and whatever remains, however improbable, must be the truth."

Lilly and Marion come down the stairs, both dressed for the party. Gillette, however, apologizes for changing his mind and staying home; his arm is "killing" him and he'd better take it easy. After the partygoers leave, Gillette takes off the sling and tosses it away. He opens the desk's top drawer and takes out his gun. He snaps the barrel open and turns the cylinder to confirm that it's loaded.

The lights fade and come on for the last scene, taking place later that night, about ten o'clock. The stage is dark. A match is struck—Gillette lighting his pipe. He sits on the floor, reclined against the sofa. After several seconds, he hears a noise, springs silently to his feet, and moves quickly to the down right corner of the room, gun in hand. May enters, carrying her purse, and turns on the lamp next to the sofa. She's momentarily startled when Gillette addresses her, "What the hell are you doing here?" then says that she was worried about him and walked back by herself. Gillette insists that she return to the Bernhardt party; she can take his car. "You're waiting for the killer," realizes May and proclaims that she's determined to stay. "I love you so much," she adds. Gillette reminds May that she's twenty-six years old while he's fifty-one, but the girl responds, "It doesn't matter."

After an awkward pause Gillette leaves for the kitchen to fix them some food. Left by herself, May, embarrassed, tries to regain her composure. She suddenly hears a noise from the terrace and crosses to the French doors. She pushes both doors open and a dark figure leaps at her, wrapping his hand around her mouth. "It's me, Bobby," he whispers.

Bobby hurriedly tells May that it occurred to him that she's an intended victim and that Gillette is her sister's killer. She should leave with him immediately; they'll drive to New York. But May refuses. Gillette's voice is heard asking May to get the door. Bobby darts behind a curtain and May opens the door. Gillette enters with a large tray loaded with sandwiches, plates, and cutlery. He puts the tray on the coffee table and sends May to get iced tea he'd made. Bobby comes out of hiding and smashes Gillette's head with a bottle. The actor staggers, then falls to the floor, unconscious. With enormous effort, Bobby manages to drag Gillette through a door and out of sight.

May returns from the kitchen. With growing panic, she looks for Gillette. The doorbell rings. Louise appears on the terrace. May rushes to her with relief. She points at Bobby and accuses him of attempting to kill Gillette. Bobby says that May has gotten it all wrong, that it was Gillette who killed Maude. Suddenly, violently, Louise strikes Bobby on the back of his head with the butt of a revolver. He slumps forward and topples to the floor, onto his back. May looks at Louise incredulously, then the truth dawns on her: "You."

Louise advances toward May and demands to know where Gillette is. The actor appears in the doorway with a gun in his hand. Louise grabs May by the hair, places her revolver to May's temple, and orders Gillette to drop his gun. He hesitates, then tosses his gun onto the sofa. "It's me you want," says Gillette quietly, "which is why you agreed to come here this weekend, agreed to a séance. Now, why don't you let her go?" Addressing May, Gillette explains that her sister and Louise were lovers; Maude fell in love with him, and Louise couldn't bear it. She begged Maude to stay with her, eventually threatened her, finally shot her through the head.

Louise shoves May aside and fires at Gillette. May screams and Gillette takes a step toward Louise. She fires two more shots but he doesn't move. Louise realizes that the revolver is loaded with blanks. She drops the weapon to the floor, darts to the wall and grabs the dagger. "I'll kill you," she shouts maniacally. Suddenly a shot rings out, then four more in quick succession. Louise is thrown back against the wall, drops the dagger, and collapses to the floor. May is kneeling by the sofa with Gillette's gun in both hands.

It takes a while for May to snap out of a state of shock. Gillette sends her to her room. When she begins to climb the stairs he suggests that after tomorrow's performance they get some dinner, nothing fancy.

* * *

Postmortem was first presented at the American Stage Festival, Milford, New Hampshire, in July 1983. Larry Carpenter directed and Patrick Horgan portrayed William Gillette. The fictional name of an actor, "Ross Patterson," appeared in the program for the character of butler Macready.

The play was subsequently produced at the Cleveland Playhouse on January 18, 1985, staged by Dennis Zacek, featuring Thomas S. Oleniacz as Gillette and "Harold Merton" as Macready. The Little Theatre of Ottawa, Canada, mounted *Postmortem* on October 21 to November 9, 2002, directed by Peter Cochrane. On this occasion, the program notations avoided coyness and billed Michael Kennedy for enacting both Macready and Gillette.

Other regional theatres that presented *Postmortem* include Bergen County Players, Oradell, New Jersey; Long Beach Playhouse Studio Theatre, Long Beach, California; Paris Performers Theatre, Paris, Ontario, Canada; and California Actor's Theatre, Longmont, Colorado.

* * *

Born in York, Pennsylvania, Kenneth D. Ludwig was educated at the York Suburban Senior High School, graduating in 1968; York Haverford College, studying music theory and composition, earning his BA, magna cum laude, in 1972; his LIM from Trinity College, Cambridge, England; and his JD from Harvard in 1976. He also studied music at Harvard with Leonard Bernstein.

For many years, Ludwig has been leading a double life: practicing law with the Washington, D.C. firm of Steptoe and Johnson while becoming an internationally acclaimed playwright.

Ludwig's first play of note was *Sullivan and Gilbert*, taking place behind the scenes at the Savoy Theatre in London, where the famed Victorian-era composer and dramatist have been feuding for months but their admiration for each other eventually wins the day. *Sullivan and Gilbert* premiered at National Arts Center of Canada in 1983, followed by a run at the Kennedy Center, Washington, D.C.

Ludwig's first Broadway play, *Lend Me a Tenor*, is a comedy rotating around the presentation of the opera *Otello* as a fundraiser for the Cleveland Opera Company. The madcap happenings include a chain reaction of mistaken identity, plot twists galore, double entendres, and split-time entrances and exits through many doors. *Lend Me a Tenor* was presented originally at a summer theatre, American Stage Festival, Milford, New Hampshire, produced by Andrew Lloyd Webber. A London production opened on March 6, 1986 at the Globe Theatre, where it ran for ten months. Directed by Jerry Zaks, the comedy came to Broadway's Royale Theatre on March 2, 1989, received nine Tony Award nominations, and ran for 476 performances. *Lend Me a Tenor* has been translated into at least twenty languages and produced in over thirty countries. Staged by Stanley Tucci, a Broadway revival opened at the Music Box Theatre on April 4, 2010, and closed after six months. A musical adaptation was presented in May 2006 as a staged reading at the Utah Shakespearean Festival in Cedar City, Utah; followed by rewrites, it opened as a full-scale production in London's West End in June 2011.

Inspired by the 1930 musical *Girl Crazy*, Ludwig adapted the Guy Bolton-John McGowan book but kept the George Gershwin music and Ira Gershwin's lyrics in *Crazy for You*, the story of Bobby Child, the rich son of a New York banking family, who yearns to become a Broadway hoofer. Failing an audition, Bobby escapes to a Nevada coal-mining town where he saves a bankrupt theatre, stages a spectacular show, and falls in love with a spunky local girl. *Crazy for You* opened at the Shubert Theatre on February 19, 1992, won the Tony Award for Best Musical, and ran for 1,622 performances. A subsequent London production opened at the Prince Edward Theatre on March 3, 1993 and ran for nearly three years. *Crazy for You* was revived in London's West End in 2011.

Ludwig's *Moon Over Buffalo* is also a show business comedy, focusing on a second-rate traveling theatre performing *Cyrano de Bergerac* and *Private Lives* in Buffalo, New York. The leading actors of the company are George and Charlotte Hay, who find themselves on a collision course about personal and professional matters. George's infidelity and Charlotte's dreams of becoming a movie star are part of the conflict. A telephone call from Frank Capra adds a sense of panic; the famed movie director is flying into town to catch their matinee: he may want them to replace Ronald Colman and Greer Garson in *The Twilight of the Scarlet Pimpernel*.

Directed by Tom Moore and starring Carol Burnett and Philip Bosco as the Hays, *Moon Over Buffalo* opened at New York's Martin Beck Theatre on October 1, 1995, ran for 309 performances, and came to London's Old Vic in October 2001 starring Joan Collins and Frank Langella.

Ludwig's sole failure on Broadway was *The Adventures of Tom Sawyer*, a musical adaptation of stories about Mark Twain's famous character. Directed by Scott Ellis, the show opened at the Minskoff Theatre on April 26, 2001 and lasted only twenty-one performances.

Twentieth Century, Ludwig's adaptation of the 1932 Ben Hecht-Charles MacArthur comedy, premiered at Signature Theatre in Arlington, Virginia before moving to off-Broadway's Roundabout Theatre in 2004, starring Alec Baldwin as an egomaniacal theatre producer and Anne Heche as a temperamental actress.

Out of town plays by Ludwig include *Shakespeare in Hollywood*, a comedy poking fun at the movie industry of the 1930s. The plot hinges on the making of *A Midsummer Night's Dream* at the Warner Brothers lot. The characters include gossip columnist Louella Parsons, director Max Reinhardt, and actors James Cagney, Dick Powell, Joe E. Brown, Groucho Marx, and Johnny Weissmuller/Tarzan. *Shakespeare in Hollywood* premiered at Arena Stage, Washington, D.C. on September 5, 2004.

The farce *Leading Ladies* centers on down-on-their-luck Shakespearean actors who con their way to a multi-million-dollar inheritance. It was first presented by the Alley Theatre, Houston, Texas on October 15, 2004 under the direction of the author. Since then *Leading Ladies* has played at the Divadlo Na Fidlovačce, Prague, Czechoslovakia; Kanata Theatre, Ottawa, Ontario, Canada; and The Gateway Theatre, Richmond, British Columbia.

Be My Baby is the story of an irascible Scotsman and an uptight Englishwoman unexpectedly thrown together. Starring Hal Holbrook and Dixie Carter, the play opened the 2005–2006 season at the Alley Theatre in Houston, Texas. Ludwig's stage adaptation of Alexandre Dumas's swashbuckling *The Three Musketeers* premiered on December 6, 2006 at the Bristol Old Vic for an eight-week run during the Christmas season, while his dramatization of Robert Louis Stevenson's adventurous *Treasure Island* was first presented at the Alley Theatre, Houston, Texas, on May 23, 2007. In the fall of 2008, *Treasure Island* migrated to Theatre Royal, Haymarket in London.

The comedy *The Fox on the Stairway*, unfolding in the taproom of a country club, mixes golf, alcohol, and romance. It debuted at the Signature Theatre, Arlington, Virginia on October 10, 2010, with subsequent productions mounted by the George Street Playhouse, New Brunswick, New Jersey, and Gulfshore Playhouse, Naples, Florida.

Acting Edition: Samuel French, Inc.

Awards and Honors: Ken Ludwig's *Sullivan and Gilbert* won the Ottawa Critics' Circle Award for Best Play of 1983. *Lend Me a Tenor* was a top ten selection in *The Best Plays of 1988–1989* as well as a nominee for a Laurence Olivier Award as Comedy of the Year in 1986, a Best Play Tony Award in 1989, and Best Revival Tony in 2010. *Crazy for You* was a top ten selection in *The Best Plays of 1991–1992* and won the 1992 Tony Award for Best Musical. *The Game's Afoot*, produced by the Cleveland Playhouse, Cleveland, Ohio, in November 2011, won the 2012 Mystery Writers of America's Edgar Allan Poe Award for Best Play.

Pack of Lies (1983)

Hugh Whitemore (England, 1936–)

In 1961, Helen and Peter Kroger were found guilty of spying for Russia by a London court and sentenced to twenty years' imprisonment. In 1969 they were exchanged for a Briton jailed in Moscow.

Shortly after the Krogers' release, Cedric Messina, the producer of BBC's *Play of the Month,* learned from a young journalist, Gay Search, that the Russian spies were her neighbors and that her family had played a key role in their capture. Messina, excited by the story, telephoned playwright Hugh Whitemore, who subsequently met with Miss Search and penned *Act of Betrayal,* a docudrama that was transmitted in January 1971.

"The subject and its implications stayed in mind," wrote Whitemore in his foreword to the acting edition of *Pack of Lies.* "In addition to the themes of loyalty and deception, I became increasingly occupied with the role of the ordinary citizen in our society. Is it ever possible for the average, relatively powerless, man or woman to make anything more than a token stand against officialdom? Is it not potentially risky to allow the state greater moral license than the individual? . . . With those thoughts in mind, I decided to rework the basic story of *Act of Betrayal* in a larger, less restricted, more fictionalized form. *Pack of Lies* is the result."[1]

The play takes place in Ruislip, a suburb of London, during the autumn and winter of 1960–1961. The action unfolds in the sitting room and adjacent kitchen of a small semidetached house, "typical of the thousands of suburban homes that were built between the wars." The curtain rises on a quiet domestic scene: Barbara Jackson is preparing breakfast and her husband Bob is reading the morning paper. Their teenage daughter, Julie, wearing a school uniform, dashes down the stairs, sits at the table and complains: "People don't have tea with breakfast anymore. It's so old-fashioned—and boring."

The doorbell rings. Enter Helen and Peter Kroger, the friendly neighbors from across the street. Helen, tall and large-boned, is a bubbly forty-something, while Peter, in his fifties, is quiet and earnest. They brought a present for Barbara's birthday—an artist's easel. Barbara is grateful but good-naturedly points out that her birthday is a week away. We soon learn that the Jacksons and the Krogers have become the best of friends since Peter and Helen arrived from Canada and settled in Ruislip five years earlier.

The Jacksons' cozy, routine way of life changes one day when a call from Scotland Yard's Superintendent Smith informs them that a gentleman named Mr. Stewart will pay them a visit regarding a "very important" matter.

Mr. Stewart arrives wearing a trilby hat, a raincoat, and a dark blue suit. After an awkward pause, Stewart relates that he knows about Bob's position in the aircraft industry—on classified material—at Aircraft Research. Julie asks Stewart if he's a police officer. "Not really, no," grins the visitor. "In actual fact, I'm a civil servant—and that as we all know, can cover a multitude of sins."

Steward paces slowly across the room as he gradually explains the purpose of his visit. The authorities have become very interested in "one particular chap" and are anxious to find out what he does, where he goes, "and so on." The man has been followed. He comes to this area most weekends. Stewart exhibits a photograph, but Bob, Barbara, and Julie declare that they've never seen him.

Stewart asks about the Krogers. "They're our best friends, really," says Barbara. "He's a bookseller." Bob adds: "Book dealer. Antiquarian books, you know, first editions."

Stewart confides that his outfit, MI5, has decided to station observers in various parts of the district to find out where the suspect goes. The observer, a young lady named Thelma, has to be concealed. They need a room for a couple of days—Saturday and Sunday. It is all very confidential. No, there's no danger of any physical violence, he assures them.

Thelma arrives the following evening. She is in her late twenties, a sturdily built ex-Army woman. She wears a sweater and slacks. After an uneventful Saturday, Barbara joins Thelma for a chat on Sunday afternoon. They suddenly look out the window. The Krogers' front door opens and a man comes out. Barbara recognizes the man in the photograph, the man Mr. Stewart is looking for. Thelma goes to make a call. Stewart arrives and theorizes that the man must have arrived in Ruislip yesterday and presumably spent the night with the Krogers. His car, a white Studebaker Farina, license number ULA 61, was parked on the next street.

Bob and Barbara press Stewart to explain what the pursued man has done. Stewart reveals that he has entered the country illegally with a false passport under the assumed name of Gordon Lonsdale. "We think he may be working—covertly—for a foreign government," says Stewart.

Bob and Barbara insist that their friends the Krogers could not be involved with the stranger's actions; they have known Peter and Helen for five years! Helen is always telling stories about her life on a farm in Canada, how she could climb trees better than any of the boys. While Helen is still a sort of a tomboy, Peter is quiet, bookish, intellectual. He used to have a bookshop in the Strand, London, but now it's a mail-order business; he sends out lists and catalogues from home. As she relates the data about the Krogers, Barbara bows her head and fights back tears.

Stewart asks the Jacksons' permission to "trespass" upon their hospitality for a few more days. He understands how painful and unpleasant it is, but "unfortunately—it has to be done."

Though *Pack of Lies* is an espionage yarn, the play contains little cloak-and-dagger action. The most suspenseful scene has Barbara, alone, cutting vegetables, when Helen and Peter arrive unexpectedly carrying baskets. "We're making an early start on the Christmas shopping," says Peter. Helen asks, "Who's the mystery man, huh?" Yesterday afternoon she saw a guy walking across the street and it looked like he was coming from here, she winks playfully. Barbara tries to control her nervousness when explaining that the man is an old acquaintance. Impulsively, Barbara asks the Krogers to come for a small party on Saturday evening, but Helen demurs, "Saturday's always difficult for us. . . . Peter likes to do his accounts at the weekend." Helen and Peter exit. Barbara remains motionless as the curtain descends.

In act 2 the surveillance continues. Sally, a pleasant, rather plain thirtyish woman has taken over for Thelma, watching through the second-floor window to see what is going on at 45 Cranley Drive across the street. The front doorbell rings. Tense, Barbara opens the door to Helen, who mock-accuses Barbara for avoiding her and, glancing at empty mugs on the table, laughingly queries if she has a lover hidden away upstairs. Barbara plunges the mugs into the sink. Helen expresses concern about Barbara's health—"You look kinda pale"—and offers to go upstairs to get some pills. Barbara, irritated, exclaims, "Helen! Please don't fuss!" Helen, startled, soon leaves.

Barbara tells Stewart that she can no longer tolerate the situation. "Every time I see Helen, every time she comes around—it makes me feel quite ill," she says. Bob asks if Gordon Lonsdale is "a spy of some sort." Stewart confides that it's almost certain that Lonsdale is a high-ranking officer in the KGB—Russian intelligence—who has been compiling information about British submarines and underwater detection techniques.

Barbara, Bob, Julie, and their guests Helen and Peter are gathered around a decorated Christmas tree when the hall phone rings. Julie goes to pick it up, returns and tells her father, "It's Mr. Stewart." Bob glances sharply at Barbara and hurries to the phone. Helen mumbles, "Stewart . . . Stewart

. . . I've heard that name before . . . Stewart Granger . . . James Stewart."
Bob comes back into the sitting room and tells Barbara, "Merry Christmas.
That's all. He just said, 'Merry Christmas.' Nice of him."

Stewart appears on a Saturday to inform the Jacksons that their ordeal
is almost over. He explains that their neighbors' home serves as Lonsdale's transmitting station. He brings them information that they dispatch
to KGB headquarters, either hidden in books that Peter Kroger posts
to fictitious clients in various parts of Europe or by radio. The Krogers
are American—not Canadian. Barbara struggles to prevent herself from
weeping: "I trusted Helen. I thought she was brash and noisy and sometimes a bit silly—but I trusted her. I loved her." She tells Stewart that she
wishes he'd never come to her home. Bob tries to stop her, but Barbara
continues, "Helen may have lied to us—but you've gone one better. You
made us do the lying. . . . Helen's lying and we're lying—we're all playing
the same rotten game."

The front doorbell rings. Barbara looks out the window. It's Helen.
Stewart suggests that they let her in, goes to the kitchen, and exits
through a back door. Bob ushers Helen in. She tells them that she and
Peter have decided it's time to move on and are planning to go to Australia, where Peter has friends. "Just think of it," squeals Helen, "all that
sun, all those sexy young Aussies just waiting for Helen Kroger to put
in an appearance."

Distant church bells chime during the Jacksons' final meeting with
Stewart. He tells them that Lonsdale was picked up outside the Old Vic,
following which Superintendent Smith and his men invaded the house
across the street and arrested the Krogers "on suspicion of offences
against the Official Secrets Act." Helen Kroger was stopped when she
tried to throw a six-page letter, written in Russian, into the boiler. A radio
transmitter was found hidden under the kitchen floor. The Krogers are
now being interrogated at the Bow Street Police Station.

Both Barbara and Julie weep. Bob steps forward and addresses the
audience, relating that the Krogers were sentenced to twenty years' imprisonment. It was discovered that Helen was a colonel in the KGB. Julie
went to visit her in Holloway Prison, and Helen told her, "I'll never forgive your mother—never." After eight years, announces Bob, the Krogers
were released in exchange for an Englishman who had been jailed by the
Russians. They flew to Poland to start a new life. A few weeks after that,
on a Sunday afternoon, Barbara went into the kitchen, sat down in a chair,
and died of a heart attack.

* * *

Pack of Lies was first presented at the Theatre Royal, Brighton, England,
on October 11, 1983 and subsequently at the Lyric Theatre, London, on

October 26. The play was directed by Clifford Williams and designed by Ralph Koltai. The cast included Judi Dench (Barbara Jackson), Barbara Leigh-Hunt (Helen Kroger), and Richard Vernon (Stewart). Dench won the Laurence Olivier Award as Best Actress for her performance. The play ran for nearly a year.

Director Williams and designer Koltai repeated their assignments when *Pack of Lies* came to New York's Royale Theatre on February 11, 1985. The leading roles were played by Rosemary Harris (Barbara Jackson), Dana Ivey (Helen Kroger), and Patrick McGoohan (Stewart).

The reviews were mixed. Douglas Watt called *Pack of Lies* a "tidy little play . . . an ironic study of a loss of friendship, leaving behind a sadly bewildered woman. On its own quiet terms, it succeeds."[2] Clive Barnes recommended "Hugh Whitemore's absolutely engrossing play. . . . It is amazing how well *Pack of Lies* holds the interest, even though you know the outcome, there is no mystery, and scarcely any suspense."[3] John Beaufort admired "a first-rate Anglo-American production of a superior British drama."[4] Joel Siegel believed that "watching *Pack of Lies* is like reading a terrific thriller, or seeing an undiscovered early Hitchcock."[5]

Conversely, Howard Kissel sniffed at "the sheer dullness of *Pack of Lies*. . . . Even in 1962, a play like Whitemore's would have seemed a rather weak cup of tea."[6] Frank Rich wrote, "The playwright, who has the aspirations but not the skills of a Graham Greene or John le Carré, may be too high-minded for his own good. *Pack of Lies* comes across as a terribly polite English attempt at a Lillian Hellman melodrama; it's too flimsy and low-keyed to support its weighty polemical message."[7]

Pack of Lies ran for 120 performances. Both Harris and McGoohan were nominated for Tony Awards, and she won a Drama Desk Award for Outstanding Actress in a Play. In 1987, Whitemore (under the name of Ralph Gallop) adapted *Pack of Lies* for the American television program *Hallmark Hall of Fame*. It starred Ellen Burstyn (Barbara Jackson) and Alan Bates (Stewart) and received three Emmy nominations: for Outstanding Drama/Comedy Special, Outstanding Lead Actress in a Miniseries, and Outstanding Writing in a Miniseries or Special.

In 2009, *Pack of Lies* toured the United Kingdom. A year later, the play was performed by Saughtonhall Drama Group and won the Edinburgh Fringe Evening News EDNA "Best Drama" Award.

* * *

Hugh Whitemore was born in Tunbridge Wells, England, in 1936. He studied for the stage at London's Royal Academy of Dramatic Art, where he is now a member of the Council. He began his writing career in British television with both original teleplays and adaptations of classic works by Somerset Maugham (*The Three Fat Women of Antibes*, 1969; *The Closed*

Shop, 1970), Charles Dickens (*David Copperfield*, 1974–1975), and Daphne du Maurier (*Rebecca*, 1979, and *My Cousin Rachel*, 1985). For *Midsomer Murders*, a British television detective series, Whitemore contributed the episode *Blue Herrings* (2000), in which Detective Chief Inspector Tom Barnaby investigates a cycle of suspicious deaths at a nursing home.

For American television, Whitemore scripted *Concealed Enemies* (1984), about the Alger Hiss case; *The Final Days* (1989), adapted from the book by Bob Woodward and Carl Bernstein, depicting the Watergate case and the fall of Richard Nixon (played by Lane Smith); *The Gathering Storm* (2002), which focused on the troubled marriage of Winston Churchill (Albert Finney) and his wife Clementine (Vanessa Redgrave) prior to World War II; and *My House in Umbria* (2003), based on a novella by William Trevor, spotlighting an eccentric British romance novelist (Maggie Smith) who lives in Umbria in central Italy. While traveling, the train she is on is bombed by terrorists; a local police officer investigates the explosion. *Into the Storm* (2009) continues the storyline of *The Gathering Storm*—Winston Churchill (now portrayed by Brendan Gleeson) during World War II.

Whitemore's motion picture credits include *Decline and Fall of a Bird Watcher* (1969), adapted from a novel by Evelyn Waugh, depicting strange happenings in a boys' school; *Man at the Top* (1973), in which the protagonist (played by Kenneth Haigh) gets immersed in shady business endeavors; *All Creatures Great and Small* (1974), a drama describing rural English life as seen through the eyes of a budding author; *The Return of the Soldier*, based on Rebecca West's novel about a shell-shocked soldier who returns home from World War I with a loss of memory; *84 Charing Cross Road* (1987), the story of a longtime correspondence and growing friendship between a New York woman (portrayed by Anne Bancroft) and a British bookseller (Anthony Hopkins); and *Utz* (1992), a drama about an elderly, dying man and his lifelong obsession with collecting porcelain figurines.

In addition to *Pack of Lies*, Whitemore focused on real-life figures in his plays *Stevie* (1977), centered on English poet and novelist Stevie Smith; and *Breaking the Code* (1986; adapted for television, 1996), about British mathematician Alan Turing, who was a key player in the breaking of the German Enigma code during World War II (for which he was decorated). He also shattered the English code of sexual discretion as an open homosexual (for which he was arrested on a charge of gross indecency); *The Best of Friends* (1988; filmed for TV, 1991), covering the ideas exchanged and the lively friendship spanned from 1924 through 1962 among playwright George Bernard Shaw, the Abbess of Stanbrook Abbey in Worcestershire, Dame Laurentia McLachlan, and the curator of Fitzwilliam Museum in Cambridge, Sir Sidney Cockerell; *My Darling Clemmie* (2008), a return to Whitemore's favorite topic—Winston and Clementine Churchill; and *The Last Cigarette* (2009), based on the diaries of the playwright Simon Gray, who had died of cancer a year earlier. The play shows Gray facing his fate with unflinching courage.

In *It's Ralph* (1991), a frustrated couple spends a weekend in a country cottage that, like their marriage, is in need of repair. *A Letter of Resignation* (1997) pictures political immorality: The War Minister has an affair with a call girl; the call girl with a Russian spy who had been set up by MI5. *Disposing of the Body* (1999) is the story of a clandestine, passionate affair between a man and a woman married to others that ends with a violent act. In 2003, Whitemore adapted Luigi Pirandello's *As You Desire Me*, a drama exploring the mysteries of memory and identity. Whitemore's plays have been translated into many languages and produced throughout the world.

Acting Edition: Samuel French, Inc.

Awards and Honors: Hugh Whitemore received a special Communications Award from the American Mathematical Society (for 1986's *Breaking the Code*), the Scripter Award in Hollywood (for 1987's *84 Charing Cross Road*), and the Script Prize at the Monte Carlo Festival (for 1997's miniseries, *A Dance to the Music in Time*). Whitemore twice won a Writers' Guild of Great Britain Award for his teleplays, and garnered an Emmy Award for his television films *Concealed Enemies* (1984) and *The Gathering Storm* (2002). *My House in Umbria* (2003) was nominated for nine Emmy Awards, including Outstanding Writing for a Miniseries, and for a Golden Globe Award for Best Miniseries or Motion Picture Made for Television. Whitemore is a Fellow of the Royal Society of Literature.

NOTES

1. Hugh Whitemore, *Pack of Lies* (New York: Samuel French, 1985), 7.
2. *Daily News*, February 12, 1985.
3. *New York Post*, February 12, 1985.
4. *Christian Science Monitor*, February 19, 1985.
5. *WABC-TV7*, February 11, 1985.
6. *Women's Wear Daily*, February 12, 1985.
7. *New York Times*, February 12, 1985.

Corpse! (1983)

Gerald Moon (England, 1943–)

Gerald Moon, an actor-playwright, pinched an idea from *The Red House Mystery*, purloined a piece from *The Prisoner of Zenda*, borrowed a scene from *Dial M for Murder*, finagled the theme of *The Prince and the Pauper*, adopted the spirit of *Sleuth*, and added a few new wrinkles for his self-coined "Comedy Thriller"—*Corpse!*

The preposterous shenanigans of *Corpse!* occur on December 11, 1936, when King Edward VIII abdicated the throne of England, and unravel within two flats inhabited by identical twin brothers. Evelyn Farrant, a fey, unemployed actor, lives in a dilapidated SoHo basement on groceries that he shoplifts from Fortnum and Mason. Rupert Farrant is a suave society gent who enjoys a luxurious dwelling in Regent's Park. Rupert had inherited the family riches from their unsavory father, abuser of the twins' mother. Evelyn, with a Norman Bates fixation, vows revenge. His plan is to engage the unscrupulous Major Walter Powell to kill Rupert so that he may assume his identity. "I need an executioner," he tells the major, an expert sniper known in the army as "One Shot Wally." Overwhelmed by Evelyn's soliloquies from *Hamlet* and an offer of 10,000 pounds, Powell undertakes the assignment.

The Major calls on Rupert and coaxes him to visit his "expiring" brother. "The news that Evelyn is dying is the best Christmas present I'm likely to receive," says Rupert cheerfully. Soon Major Powell finds himself ensnared in a cat-and-mouse game with the twins—shooting each of them at least twice, suspecting there might be triplets, being struck unconscious by a poisonous sword, dueling with one of the brothers, who impales him through the heart against a bar mirror. Secondary dramatic personae who partake in the wheels-within-wheels proceedings are Mrs. McGee, Evelyn's amorous middle-aged landlady who does not understand his sexual escapades—"I've never known a man with so many nephews"—

and Constable Hawkins, who is more concerned with Rupert's car being left with its lights on than with the bloody cadavers scattered around.

* * *

Corpse! premiered at the American Stage Festival Theatre, Milford, New Hampshire, in 1983. Keith Baxter, who previously played several distinct characters in *Sleuth* (1970), appeared as the vile twin brothers in the London production (which opened at the Apollo Theatre on July 26, 1984 for a six-month run) and in New York (Helen Hayes Theatre, January 5, 1986—121 performances). The dexterous Mr. Baxter won high praise for his dead ringer impersonations as well as his swift, nimble, almost simultaneous appearances and getaways stage right and left. Milo O'Shea enacted the jack-in-the-box Major Powell in both London and New York (called Ambrose in England, Walter in America). John Tillinger and Alan Tagg served, respectively, as director and designer for the duo productions, utilizing four trick escapes with split-second sleight of hand.

The New York critics were divided in their verdicts: "It is a most adroit example of that dear old theatrical form, the crime farce," cheered Clive Barnes,[1] but Douglas Watt scoffed, "If the combination of ham and corpse brings to mind turkey, I'm afraid that just can't be helped."[2] Howard Kissel stated, "It is an evening of light-hearted entertainment,"[3] while Frank Rich called the play "a forgettable Boulevard entertainment."[4] John Beaufort found *Corpse!* "less scary than *Sleuth* or *Deathtrap*. But it is more comic than either";[5] however, Edward Wilson wrote "the action and the jokes soon become predictable."[6]

Corpse! has subsequently been presented in Sweden, Denmark, Japan, South Africa, Austria, Poland, Bulgaria, Italy, and Spain. A six-month tour in Australia culminated with a smash-hit opening in Sydney, where it ran for ten months. America and the United Kingdom hosted successful road tours. Playwright Moon took over the lead role when *Corpse!* went into the West End for the second time at the Strand Theatre in 1988. Moon also directed and portrayed the twin roles in UK productions at The Redgrave Theatre, Farnham; The Repertory Theatre, Dundee; and The Byre Theatre, St. Andrews. In 1987, the play was performed, in English, at the English Theatre of Hamburg, Germany, and was revived there in 1995 and again during the 2006–2007 season.

* * *

Gerald Moon began his theatrical career as an actor on British television. He played Gangster #1 in *The Casting Session*, a 1968 entry in the series *Half Hour Story*; a Gardener's Boy in *Twelfth Night*, a 1969 offering by *ITV Saturday Night Theatre*; the recurring role of Robert Bean in the

1969 series *Thicker Than Water*; George Formby Sr. in 1972's *The Reluctant Juggler*, an episode of 1972's *The Edwardians*; a sea captain in the 1976 TV-movie *Ubu roi*; and feature roles in the series *A Horseman Riding By* (1978) and *Shoestring* (1979).

In addition to *Corpse!* Moon penned the whodunit *Deadly Maneuvers*, set against the glittering backdrop of the coronation of Queen Elizabeth II. A Machiavellian plot corkscrews in unexpected directions as members of the wealthy Beaumont family compete for power. Among the questions raised are who's the killer? who's been killed? and has anyone been killed at all? *Deadly Maneuvers* premiered at the Haymarket Theatre in Basingstoke, England, on January 20, 2000.

Land of Lies, written by Moon in collaboration with Hugh Janes, is a drama based on the life of Magda Quandt, a cultured divorcee who joined the National Socialist Party after hearing Joseph Goebbels speak at a rally in 1929. They seduced each other and got married. Soon Magda became entwined in her husband's web of deceit, and her privileged life, as mother figure of the German nation, ended in Hitler's bunker where she took the lives of her children before committing suicide. *Land of Lies* opened at the Cockpit Theatre, London, on September 29, 2003.

Acting Edition: Samuel French, Inc.

NOTES

1. *New York Post*, January 6, 1986.
2. *Daily News*, January 6, 1986.
3. *Women's Wear Daily*, January 6, 1986.
4. *New York Times*, January 6, 1986.
5. *Christian Science Monitor*, January 13, 1986.
6. *Wall Street Journal*, January 22, 1986.

Execution of Justice (1984)

Emily Mann (United States, 1952–)

On November 27, 1978, Dan White, a former member of San Francisco's Board of Supervisors, shot and killed Mayor George Moscone and gay City Supervisor Harvey Milk. White was charged with two counts of murder, but was instead convicted on two counts of voluntary manslaughter and sentenced to seven years and eight months in prison. Less than five years later, he was paroled. White subsequently committed suicide, gassing himself in his own garage.

In writing her docudrama *Execution of Justice*, Emily Mann drew on the trial transcript, published news reports, and interviews related to the notorious case. She also incorporated into the proceedings projected images of San Francisco scenes and audio dialogue from the Oscar-winning film *The Times of Harvey Milk* (1984).

The play unfolds in quick episodes. Act 1 is titled "Murder." The curtain rises on a bare stage. Images of Milk and Moscone are projected on a white screen overhead, accompanied by hot, fast music. A video depicts Dianne Feinstein, the President of the San Francisco Board of Supervisors, as she tearfully announces that Mayor Moscone and Supervisor Milk have been killed. A shaft of light illuminates Dan White praying on his knees next to a church window. His wife, Mary Ann, runs in breathlessly and crumples when he says, "I shot the Mayor and Harvey."

The lights change. A police officer articulates the atmosphere in which the killings occurred, illustrating his point by confronting a nun in drag, Sister Boom Boom, who is heavily made up and sashays on spiked heels. The cop complains of a city "stinkin' with degenerates," populated with "shaved-head men with tight pants, chains everywhere, French-kissing on the street. . . . It's disgusting. . . . Dan White showed you could fight City Hall."

The trial of the People of the State of California versus Daniel James White commences. Prosecutor Thomas F. Norman and Defense Attorney

Douglas Schmidt are selecting the jury. Joanna Lu, a television reporter, declares on camera that "by all accounts, there are no blacks, no gays, and no Asians" on the jury, and that "most of the jurors are working and middle-class Catholics. . . . Dan White will certainly be judged by a jury of his peers."

The defendant has entered a plea of not guilty to each of the charges. Prosecutor Norman addresses the audience and it soon becomes clear that the auditorium spectators are called upon to serve as jurors. Norman presents defendant White—a war veteran, a decorated firefighter, a respected ex-policeman—as a conscientious member of the Board of Supervisors who had resigned because of personal financial pressures. Then, when he wanted to withdraw his resignation and return to that post, Major Moscone and Supervisor Milk objected. On November 27, White went to City Hall carrying his police .38, entered by a window to avoid the metal detector at the front door, and walked into the mayor's office. Upon learning that he wasn't going to be reappointed, he shot Moscone four times, went to Milk's office and, reloading, put five or six bullets into Milk. He then called his wife and arranged to meet her at the cathedral. He went from there to the police station to give himself up.

Defense Attorney Schmidt points out that throughout his adulthood, Daniel White had suffered from a mental disease—"depression, sometimes called manic depression or unipolar depression." Financial stress and his underlying mental illness culminated in his resignation on November 10, 1978. When he asked for his job back, he was given the runaround and finally learned from a television interviewer that his request had been denied. The mayor ignored more than a thousand petitions on his behalf. Furthermore, White believed that Harvey Milk had been acting to prevent his reappointment. Schmidt emphasizes that White came from a vastly different lifestyle than Milk "who was a homosexual leader and politician." Dan White, says Schmidt, deeply believed in the traditional American values of family and home.

Schmidt asserts that it was "not particularly unusual" for White to take his .38 caliber revolver with him when he went to City Hall. Dan White was an ex-policeman; for him to carry a gun was "common practice." Besides, he added, White's life was threatened continuously by the White Panther party and other radical groups.

Prosecutor Norman calls to the stand several witnesses who were at City Hall on the fateful day; they identify Dan White as the person who entered the building through a window and went into the mayor's office; gunfire was heard. White later came out, proceeded down the hall, and entered Harvey Milk's office; five or six shots rang out and White left the building.

The action detours to the office of homicide Inspector Frank Falzon. White, sobbing, says that he's been under "an awful lot of pressure lately"—financial pressure, family pressure. He found out that Supervisor Milk was working against him. He is not sure why he took his gun with him that morning. When the mayor told him that he was not going to be reappointed, "he was all smiles. . . . Then I, I just shot him, that was it, it was over." White relates that he then went to Harvey Milk's office. "He started kinda smirking. . . . I just got all flushed, and, and hot, and I shot him." He left and called his wife to meet him at St. Mary's cathedral. There he told her what occurred. She was horrified but said she loved him and would stick by him. She came with him to the Northern Police Station.

Act 2 is titled "In Defense of Murder." The trial continues with Defense Attorney Schmidt examining Inspector Falzon and other witnesses who have known White for years. They testify about White's distinguished career as a firefighter, police officer, and city supervisor. Joseph Freitas Jr., a former district attorney, believes that the friction between White and his victims was a political fight over who controlled the city, not a hate crime against a gay person.

The defense then brings in several psychiatrists to testify as to the defendant's state of mind. The first, Dr. Jones, concluded that White was "enraged and anxious and frustrated in addition to his underlying depression." Dr. Blinder asserts that White became increasingly frustrated by what he perceived to be corrupt behavior at City Hall. Gradually, White began to abandon his usual program of exercise and good nutrition and started gorging himself on junk foods; he couldn't sleep, was dazed, confused, had crying spells, stopped shaving, became increasingly ill, and wanted to be left alone.

When the mayor put his arm around him, continues Dr. Blinder, seemingly concerned about White's future, the defendant felt "as if I were in a dream." He started to leave, then inexplicably turned around and like a reflex drew his revolver. "He had no idea how many shots he fired," says Dr. Blinder. "The similar event occurred in Supervisor Milk's office." Dr. Blinder approaches the jury: "In susceptible individuals, large quantities of what we call junk food, high sugar content food with lots of preservatives, can precipitate antisocial and even violent behavior."

The most emotional moment in court occurs during the testimony of Dan White's wife, Mary Ann, who speaks about their courtship, their life together, and the fateful morning of November 27. As Mary Ann stumbles off the stand, her husband, softly sobbing, shields his eyes.

The background screen depicts a candlelight march dedicated to the memory of Harvey Milk, and a funeral attended by mourners, headed by Mayor Moscone's wife.

Attorney Schmidt sums up for the defense, contending that even though Dan White is guilty, the degree of his responsibility and his state of mind are at issue. "Heat of passion fogs judgment," declares Schmidt, "makes one act irrationally. . . . It was a man broken, shattered. . . . Something happened to him and he snapped." Schmidt asks the members of the jury to come up with the verdict of "voluntary manslaughter, nothing more, nothing less," and points out that White, his child, and his family will have to live with the deed for the rest of their lives.

Prosecutor Norman states that the evidence laid before the jury *screams* for a ruling of murder in the first degree. Dan White brought a gun to City Hall with extra cartridges; he went around the corner and climbed through a window; he appeared, according to witnesses, to be calm as he approached the Mayor's office; he shot the Mayor twice in the body, then shot him in the head twice more; he reloaded his gun, went across the hall and "put three bullets into Harvey Milk's body, two more delivered to the back of his head." Norman insists that these were deliberate, premeditated, and cold-blooded *executions*.

The jury returns a guilty verdict of voluntary manslaughter.

A television reporter relates on camera that Dan White was sentenced to seven years and eight months in jail, the maximum sentence for two counts of voluntary manslaughter. The lenient verdict led to rioting by homosexuals and their sympathizers. On the screen are projected images of a riot—angry faces, police cars burning, City Hall being stormed, a line of police officers in riot gear. Then another image appears on the screen: Execution of Justice. A gavel echoes, and the curtain descends.[1]

* * *

Emily Mann began writing *Execution of Justice* on a commission from San Francisco's Eureka Theatre in 1982. The play was first produced on March 8, 1984 by the Actors Theatre of Louisville, Kentucky, eliciting a positive nod from reviewer Holly Hill who called it an "epic drama."[2] *Execution of Justice* was subsequently produced by Baltimore's Center Stage; Theatre Cornell in Ithaca, New York; Seattle's The Empty Stage; Arena Stage in Washington, D.C.; the Abbey Theatre in Houston, Texas; Berkeley Rep; San Jose Rep; and the Guthrie Theatre of Minneapolis, Minnesota.

Mann directed and Ming Cho Lee designed *Execution of Justice* when it opened at New York's Virginia Theatre on March 13, 1986. The lead actors were John Spencer (Dan White), Mary McDonnell (Mary Ann White), Peter Friedman (Douglas Schmidt), and Gerry Bamman (Thomas F. Norman). Stanley Tucci, Wesley Snipes, Donal Donnelly, and Earl Hyman appeared in several small roles.

The play received mostly negative reviews. Douglas Watt called it "an interminable play" that "executed the audience . . . it induces practically unrelieved tedium. . . . In Mann's and the designer's hands the stage is so filled with gimmickry that the result is distracting and often incoherent."[3] Clive Barnes opined that "the proceedings lack suspense" and did not ignite "outrage . . . and this kind of play, about justice's miscarriage, either fires one with a sense of outrage or, in the final count, fails."[4] Conversely, Ron Cohen believed that *Execution of Justice* "succeeds in striking fashion. . . . It's a big, horrific play, but Mann, as both playwright and director, moves with sureness and balance through much of it. . . . The 22-member company turn in a uniformly strong performance. . . . *Execution of Justice* would validate any Broadway season with an insightful seriousness of purpose."[5]

The play ran for twelve performances.[6]

Early in 2011, a bill was introduced for approval by the California Legislature to mandate schools to teach gay history. Harvey Milk, one of the first openly gay elected officials in the United States, may take a prominent place in the state's history books.

* * *

Emily Betsy Mann was born in Boston, Massachusetts on April 12, 1952. Her father was a professor of American history, first at MIT, then at Smith College, and finally at the University of Chicago. Her mother was a remedial reading specialist. Playwright, director, and actress, Mann staged productions at such top resident companies as the Tyrone Guthrie Theatre in Minneapolis; the Cincinnati Playhouse; the Brooklyn Academy of Music; the American Place Theatre in New York; the Actors Theatre of Louisville; the Hartford Stage Company; and the Mark Taper Forum in Los Angeles.

In 1990, Mann was appointed Artistic Director of the McCarter Theatre in Princeton, New Jersey, where she staged more than thirty productions, including the world premieres of Christopher Durang's *Miss Witherspoon*, Theresa Rebeck's *The Bells*, Steven Dietz's *Last of the Boys*, and Nilo Cruz's *Anna in the Tropics*, a 2003 Pulitzer Prize winner. Notable plays helmed by Mann at the McCarter were *The Glass Menagerie* and *Cat on a Hot Tin Roof*, both by Tennessee Williams, *The Matchmaker* by Thornton Wilder, *All Over* by Edward Albee, and *The Tempest* and *Romeo and Juliet* by William Shakespeare.

As a playwright, Mann carved a reputation by penning documentary dramas she called "theatre of testimony," beginning with *Annulla Allen: Autobiography of a Survivor* (1977), based on interviews she conducted with a Polish Jewess who escaped a Nazi concentration camp by pretending to be Aryan. *Still Life* (1980) is a distillation of interviews with three characters from Minnesota who speak directly to the audience—Mark, an ex-marine and Vietnam veteran; Cheryl, his wife, mother of his children; and Nadine, his friend, a divorced artist. "It is about violence in America," writes Emily Mann. "The Vietnam War is the backdrop to the violence at home. . . . I have been obsessed with violence in our country since the 1960s."[7] *Having Our Say: The Delany Sisters' First 100 Years* (1995) tells the saga of two black centenarian sisters, while *Greensboro: A Requiem*

(1996) covers the murder of young communists by the Ku Klux Klan. *Mrs. Packard* (2007) dramatizes how in 1861 the Reverend Theophilus Packard had his wife committed to a psychiatric hospital because of a disagreement as to how to raise their children.

The indefatigable Mann also adapted and directed August Strindberg's *Miss Julie* (1993), Federico Garcia Lorca's *The House of Bernarda Alba* (1997), Isaac Bashevis Singer's *Meshugah* (1998), and Anton Chekhov's *The Three Sisters* (1992), *The Cherry Orchard* (2000), *Uncle Vanya* (2003), and *The Seagull* (2008).

Mann is a member of the Dramatists Guild and serves on its Council.

Acting Edition: Samuel French, Inc.

Awards and Honors: *Execution of Justice* won the HBO New Plays USA Award, the Helen Hayes Award, and the Bay Area Critics Award. The play was nominated for a 1986 Drama Desk Award for Outstanding New Play and is a top ten selection in *The Best Plays of 1985–1986*. Emily Mann's *Still Life*, which opened off-Broadway under her direction in 1981, won six Obie Awards, including Distinguished Playwriting and Distinguished Directing. Mann's 1995 Broadway production of *Having Our Say* was nominated for a Tony Award for Best Play and Best Direction; the play won a Joseph Jefferson Award as well as an NAACP Award. Mann's numerous awards include a Guggenheim, NEA Playwrights Fellowship, CAPS Award, McKnight Fellowship, a Dramatists Guild of America Hull-Warriner Award, and the Rosamond Gilder Award for Outstanding Creative Achievement in the Theatre. In 2002, Mann received an Honorary Doctorate of Arts from Princeton University.

NOTES

1. Dan White was paroled after five years in 1984. The following year he was found dead of carbon monoxide poisoning in the garage of his wife's home in San Francisco, California.

2. Otis L. Guernsey Jr., ed., *The Best Plays of 1983–1984* (New York: Dodd, Mead, 1984), 60.

3. *Daily News*, March 14, 1986.

4. *New York Post*, March 14, 1986.

5. *Women's Wear Daily*, March 14, 1986.

6. *Milk* (2008), a biographical motion picture about the life of Harvey Milk, written by Dustin Lance Black and directed by Gus Van Sant, starred Sean Penn in the title role and Josh Brolin as Dan White. The film earned high praise and garnered eight Academy Award nominations, including Best Picture. It won for Best Acting in a Leading Role (Penn) and Best Original Screenplay (Black).

7. Emily Mann, *Testimonies: Four Plays* (New York: Theatre Communications Group, 1997), 34.

Over My Dead Body (1984)

Michael Sutton and Anthony Fingleton

You don't have to be a Golden Age devotee to be charmed by the parody *Over My Dead Body*, but it helps. The tongue-in-cheek action takes place in the Reading Room of The Murder League, London, a literary society composed of crime authors, complete with well-filled bookcases, a suit of armor, a grandfather clock, a weapons display case, a cast-iron figure of a raven on the mantel, and a number of framed portraits: Poe, Doyle, Chesterton, Sayers, Christie—the greats of detective fiction.

The heroes are a trio of elderly writers down on their luck, characters borrowed from Robert L. Fish's Murder League Trilogy *The Murder League* (1968), *Rub-a-Dub-Dub* (1971), and *A Gross Carriage of Justice* (1979). Trevor Doyle, Dora Winslow, and Bert Cruikshank, proud authors of such classics as *The Fatal Touch* (where a blind woman is killed by a poison absorbed through the skin from the coating on her Braille cards), and creators of series protagonists Eustace St. Claire, the renowned Luxembourgian sleuth; Sir Hugh Enfield, who once outpolled Sir Winston Churchill as the Most Admired Man in Great Britain; and Gustav Carr, the one-legged crime-solving midget. These founding members of the Murder League bemoan the passing of an era in which people were "committing murder with elegance, with style: the bloodstained rose, the nursery rhyme scrawled on the hallway mirror, the snake slithering down the bell pipe."

Adding salt to their wounds is an arrogant young newcomer, Simon Vale, who writes under the influence of the American "hard-boiled dicks." Vale's sex-and-splatter *Blood On My Hands* is at the top of the best-seller list. "I really don't care *who* killed Roger Ackroyd or *what* Mrs. McGillicuddy saw," smirks the handsome, well-dressed Vale. "And as far as I'm concerned, it's perfectly all right if Trent's case is his last. . . . When are you going to realize that the world isn't as innocent as it was forty years ago? Maybe then people could accept the murders of vicars in rooms locked from the inside, but they can't now." Leo Sharp, Vale's crass

American agent who is visiting the author, also insists that the modern writer must have "the killer instinct."

Our old-timers are downcast. "Dora, can it be true, are we so out of touch with reality?" asks Trevor. "Maybe we are," answers Dora sadly. "Perhaps Simon is right and people can no longer accept someone being murdered with the venom of a Tasmanian tarantula." Then and there they decide to commit a murder as it might have occurred in one of their books—a locked room affair with a touch of the baroque. "Think of it, Dora," says Trevor feverishly, "After we've done it, there'll be a virtual renaissance of red herrings." They determine to kill "someone who deserves to die"—the Baker Street Bludgeoner, a contemporary Jack the Ripper who had recently "splattered the brains of five young women all over the pavement." The newspapers announced that the police "are most anxious to question a man seen leaving the scene of the crime wearing a dark overcoat and a scarf of the Stewart tartan." The description matches Leo Sharp's attire, so Trevor, Dora, and Bert believe that they have unearthed the culprit. The threesome plan to assassinate Sharp using an elaborate scheme—sure to delight John Dickson Carr fans—that will leave the body behind a locked and barricaded door, shot, stabbed, and strangled, hanging by his neck from a chandelier. Chloroform, a sword-stick, a bayoneted rifle, a fishing line, a long rope, and a gorilla suit help create a perfect, bizarre murder. No wonder Chief Inspector Smith and Detective Sergeant Trask are bamboozled.

The plot takes a twist when forensics ascertains that Leo Sharp's death was not caused by shooting, stabbing, or strangulation, but by poison. It turns out that Dora, Trevor, and Bert, despite their meticulous efforts, did not kill Sharp after all. Their nemesis, Simon Vale, angered by a professional disagreement, murdered his agent by grinding Xanax pills into a powder and mixing them with an alcoholic beverage (copycatting the modus operandi in Bert's *Murder on the Menu*). Furthermore, Vale is unmasked as the Bludgeoner, annihilating the poor women to gain insight into a murderer's psyche. "It's common knowledge I draw my works from life," he explains to the astounded trio as he holds them at gunpoint. "That's why they are so popular." In the nick of time, the antique mantel clock chimes and its mace hits Simon's head with a loud crack. Simon slumps heavily to the ground. Dora, Trevor, and Bert now begin to compose *The Case of the Second Clock* wherein Gustave Carr, Eustace St. Claire, and Sir Hugh Endfield join forces to defeat the notorious Baker Street Bludgeoner.

Over My Dead Body premiered at the Hartman Theatre, Stamford, Connecticut, on November 2, 1984. Edwin Sherin directed, with Fritz Weaver, Tammy Grimes, and Thomas Toner portraying, respectively, Trevor, Dora, and Bert. The lampoon played at the Savoy Theatre in London on

February 20, 1989, directed by Brian Murray, featuring Donald Sinden, June Whitfield, and Frank Middlemass.

* * *

Born in Cleveland, Ohio, in 1912, Robert Lloyd Fish was educated at Case School of Applied Science (now Case-Western Reserve University), graduating with a BS in 1933. He served three years in the National Guard, Ohio 37th Division. Married and the father of two daughters, Fish worked for many years as a consulting engineer on vinyl plastics in Brazil, Argentina, England, Korea, Taiwan, Columbia, Mexico, and Venezuela before settling in Trumbull, Connecticut. He was forty-seven years old when, in 1960, he submitted the parody "The Adventure of the Ascot Tie" to *Ellery Queen's Mystery Magazine*.

Fish became a prolific and successful writer, continuing to demonstrate his farceur mastery through Sherlockian pastiches in which an inept sleuth called "Schlock Homes," assisted by "Dr. Watney," operates from 221B Bagel Street. The outrageous tales were collated in *The Incredible Schlock Homes* (1966) and *The Memoirs of Schlock Homes* (1974). Highly regarded for his skill and versatility, Fish also penned caper stories about smuggler extraordinaire Kek Huuygens (*The Hochmann Miniature*, 1967; *Whirlygig*, 1970; *The Tricks of the Trade*, 1972; *The Wager*, 1974; *Kek Huuygens, Smuggler*, 1976), and exotic mysteries featuring Brazilian police captain Jose da Silva (*The Fugitive*, 1962; *Isle of the Snakes*, 1963; *The Shrunken Head*, 1963; *Brazilian Sleigh Ride*, 1965; *The Diamond Bubble*, 1965; *Always Kill A Stranger*, 1967; *The Bridge That Went Nowhere*, 1968; *The Xavier Affair*, 1969; *The Green Hell Treasure*, 1971; *Trouble in Paradise*, 1975).

Under the pseudonym of Robert L. Pike, Fish wrote police procedurals about the astute Lieutenant Clancy of Manhattan's 52nd precinct (*Mute Witness*, 1963, the basis for the film *Bullitt*; *The Quarry*, 1964; *Police Blotter*, 1965); and, on the other side of the continent, about the resourceful Lieutenant Jim Reardon of the San Francisco Police Department (*Reardon*, 1970; *The Gremlin's Grampa*, 1972; *Bank Job*, 1974; *Deadline 2 A.M.*, 1976). Among the author's other achievements are *The Assassination Bureau, Ltd.*, 1963, completion of a Jack London espionage manuscript, filmed in England in 1969; *Tales of O'Brien*, 1965, novelization of a TV play; *Pursuit*, 1978, a yarn of international intrigue; and the editing of *With Malice Toward All*, 1968, and *Every Crime in the Book*, 1976.

"Although Robert L. Fish did not begin his writing career until he was in his late forties, he made up for his late start by the quality and versatility of his talents," writes Mary Ann Grochowski in *Twentieth-Century Crime and Mystery Writers*. "Ranging from Sherlockian parodies to fascinatingly realistic police procedural novels, Fish's short stories and novels are witty and well-plotted, alternating between expertly crafted humor and breath-taking suspense."[1]

Acting Edition: Dramatists Play Service.

Awards and Honors: Robert L. Fish won the Mystery Writers of America Edgar Allan Poe Award, Best First Novel, 1963, for *The Fugitive*; Mystery Writers of America Edgar Allan Poe Award, Best Short Story, 1972, for "Moonlight Gardener" (published in *Argosy*). He was elected President of the Mystery Writers of America in 1978. After his death in 1981, MWA created the Robert L. Fish Award, given annually to the best short story emerging from the organization's writer training program.

NOTE

1. John M. Reilly, ed., *Twentieth-Century Crime and Mystery Writers* (New York: St. Martin's, 1980), 564.

Fatal Attraction (1984)

Bernard Slade (Canada, 1930–)

In the 1970s, Canadian Bernard Slade contributed to the Broadway scene several bittersweet plays, notably the two-character *Same Time, Next Year*, arguably the most successful romantic comedy ever to grace the stage. *Same Time, Next Year*, about Doris and George, a couple who are married to others but meet annually in a country inn for sex and conversation, opened at the Brooks Atkinson Theatre on March 14, 1975 under the direction of Gene Saks, with Ellen Burstyn and Charles Grodin, and ran for 1453 performances. The play won the Drama Desk Award as Outstanding New Play and was nominated for a Best Play Tony. It was a hit at London's Prince of Wales Theatre in 1976 and was presented in more than forty languages worldwide. Scripted by Slade, *Same Time, Next Year* was made into a movie in 1978, starring Ellen Burstyn and Alan Alda, endowing the author with an Academy Award nomination.

Slade's next Broadway offering, *Tribute*, the story of a father, Scottie Templeton, who is dying of cancer and wants to mend his relationship with his estranged son, premiered at the Brooks Atkinson Theatre on June 1, 1978, staged by Arthur Storch and featuring Jack Lemmon. *Tribute* ran for 212 performances and garnered Tony and Drama Desk nominations for Lemmon. The actor reprised the role of Templeton in a 1980 motion picture, also scripted by Slade.

Slade's *Romantic Comedy* depicts a playwright, Jason Carmichael, who stifles his feelings for his writing partner, Phoebe Craddock, over many years. Directed by Joseph Hardy, the play opened at the Ethel Barrymore Theatre on November 8, 1979 and ran for 396 showings. Anthony Perkins and Mia Farrow portrayed the pair but in the 1983 movie version, adapted by Slade, the roles went to Dudley Moore and Mary Steenburgen.

Unlike its predecessors, Slade's fourth Broadway outing, *Special Occasions* (Music Box Theatre, February 17, 1982), about a divorced couple (played by Suzanne Pleshette and Richard Mulligan) who find a new piquancy in their relationship, was met with savage reviews and closed after one performance. The play was filmed twice: in Spain, as *Grandes Ocasiones* (1998), and in France as *Les Grandes Occasions* (2006).

In the 1980s, Slade detoured into the suspense genre with two fiendishly clever thrillers—*Fatal Attraction* and *An Act of Imagination*, aka *Sweet William*.

The entire action of *Fatal Attraction* (which has nothing to do with the popular 1987 film of the same title) takes place over a period of three October days in the living room of a remote Nantucket beach house. The room is furnished with comfortable country antiques and includes a chintz sofa, chairs, a table used for eating, and a stereo. There are overflowing bookshelves and casually piled classical record albums.

When the curtain rises, the stereo is playing a recording of "Gymnopédies II" by Satie. Blair Griffin enters down a flight of stairs carrying several unframed canvases, which she leans against another pile of paintings. Blair, a well-known movie actress, is "thirty-five years old but looks much younger with the slim body of a teenager. Everything she does has a graceful, feminine delicacy, and she exudes an aura of vulnerable fragility."

Blair hears the motor of a car, picks up a pair of binoculars, crosses out onto the deck, and watches the car approaching along the coast road. She goes into the kitchen and re-enters with a cheeseboard containing some large slabs of cheese, bread, and fruit. She plunges a kitchen knife into the cheese where it remains in the upright position providing a subtle but ominous note.

The front door opens. Enter Morgan Richards, "a handsome man in his mid-forties." The two regard each other for a moment and the tension between them becomes palpable. Morgan, Blair's estranged husband, tells her that their kids are fine and that he came from Boston in a rented station wagon to pick up his canvases; an exhibition of his paintings will open in Washington the next week. Morgan warns Blair that Tony Lombardi, a paparazzo who has been shadowing them for years, followed him by car and is parked nearby.

Morgan goes upstairs for his canvases. Blair moves to a bookcase, removes several volumes, and pushes a concealed button. A five-by-three-foot square of floor down-left slides open, revealing a Jacuzzi. Blair puts her hand in to test the water. She then presses another button and the Jacuzzi's top slides back, concealing it by a strip of wooden floor.

Blair exits to the kitchen, takes a coffeepot from the stove. Tony Lombardi walks in through the front door. "He is a seedy thirty-four with an intense, kinetic energy." Lombardi carries a canvas bag that presumably contains his cameras and film. He looks around, notices the cheeseboard, takes the knife, tests the sharpness of the blade, and slides it down inside his boot. Blair enters with a coffee tray.

Tony expresses his nervousness about, at long last, meeting Blair face-to-face with "no camera between us." He confesses that for fifteen years he has photographed Blair and Morgan during various events—"Both your weddings, funerals. Even when you had your kids—I was there." No, their posing for pictures won't do—"It's the hunt. The tracking—the chase—the moving target—and—click—the kill."

Morgan, carrying a large portrait of Blair, comes downstairs. Tony greets him, "Hi, I'm Tony Lombardi. We've never met formally," and, unexpectedly, plunges the knife through Blair's face on the canvas, and into Morgan's stomach. Morgan's face assumes a surprised expression as Tony withdraws the knife. Blood starts seeping through the slit created on the canvas. Morgan slowly crumples on the floor. Tony moves to a corner, kneels, and retches. Blair, her eyes enormous, screams and screams as the lights black out.

Scene 2 commences two hours later. The body of Morgan has been removed. Two small silver candlesticks are also missing. Police Sergeant Doris Aylesworth, "a pleasant looking, appealing woman in her mid-thirties," is sitting at the table writing in a notepad. Lieutenant Gus Braden enters, "wearing rumpled, old fishing clothes . . . flawed, idiosyncratic, a physical wreck of a man probably in his early fifties with an attractive, likable, lived-in face." He tells Doris that he was "out in the boat" when summoned. On the dock, he was greeted by his assistants who were spastically hopping up and down. "Haven't had so much excitement in this embalmed little community," says Gus," since that whale washed ashore and the Mayor's dachshund tried to hump it." While Gus ambles around, leisurely examining the room, Doris reports that the victim was stabbed in the stomach and the body is now at the morgue. The culprit is known: The ex-wife ran out, got in a station wagon—her husband had rented it in Boston—drove to the phone on Highway 3, called the police station, and asked for Gus Braden. The lieutenant is astonished; he only met Blair Griffin once and that was four years ago, on the Phil Donahue talk show, when he was hawking his mystery novel *Scenario for Murder*. Based on Blair's information, the description of Tony Lombardi is out and, says Doris, "it's only a matter of time before we pick him up."

Gus examines the bookshelves. Doris has already noticed that his book is there. "Looks like she owns every mystery and crime book ever written," says Gus.

Blair appears on the landing and comes down the stairs. Her manner is warm, pleasant, controlled. She asks Gus and Doris if they would "care for a drink or a cup of coffee." Doris exits to the kitchen to make coffee.

Blair tells Gus that Lombardi was always a nuisance but, over the years, she had become used to him. About six months ago he started to be really intrusive—tried to get a shot of her children at school and interrupted a complicated take on a movie set. So she decided to take Lombardi to court for harassment—invasion of privacy. On the morning that the case was going to come to trial, Lombardi accosted her in the corridor of the courthouse, pleaded with her to drop the charges; feeling sorry for him, she dropped the suit.

Gus assures Blair that Lombardi will be apprehended. There are only three ways off the island—by plane, by ferry, or by charter boat—and they're all under watch.

Blair confides to Gus that her emotional connection to Morgan ended months ago and that they were in the process of getting a divorce; it was to become final next week. That's why she asked Morgan to come to her home—to pick up his paintings. Gus relates that he too has gone through a painful divorce.

"Can you think of any reason Lombardi would want to kill your husband?" asks Gus. She cannot. Suddenly they hear a gentle rapping against the front door. The newcomer turns out to be Maggie Stratton, Blair's agent, "an extremely beautiful woman probably in her mid-forties." Maggie tells them that she was on her way here from Los Angeles with a script. At the Boston airport she saw a television news flash about the Nantucket murder and is very concerned. The phone rings. Blair answers it, listens for a moment, and hangs up. It was the undertaker, she says, asking for some of Morgan's clothes. Blair goes upstairs.

"You don't look like a police detective," says Maggie. Gus asks, "What's a detective supposed to look like?" "Humphrey Bogart," she smiles. They converse. Maggie opines that Blair is very calculating—"she's like a human computer." Off screen, says Maggie, Blair is the best actress in the world—"she's the consummate con artist." But Maggie does not believe that Blair had anything to do with Morgan's death—she has absolutely nothing to gain.

Gus calls and arranges a room for Maggie at the Harbor House. She leaves. Blair descends the stairs, dressed in a robe. She confides to Gus that Maggie had an affair with her husband—"That's the reason our marriage broke up." Gus departs. Blair turns out the lamps. The room is now illuminated by burning logs. She moves to the stereo, selects a tape, and we hear Bartok's "Concerto for Orchestra." She then bolts the door and crosses to the Jacuzzi controls. The Jacuzzi top slides open and a soaking wet Tony Lombardi, holding the kitchen knife, leaps out. The music from the stereo rises to a loud, discordant pitch as Tony advances towards Blair. When he reaches her, he bends to put the knife on the coffee table and roughly embraces her. They sink to the floor, obscured from view by the coffee table. As the sex act takes place, Blair's hand comes up and grasps the knife. It is plunged down with great force. After a moment, Blair scrambles to her feet, pulls the robe around her, and goes to the phone. Tony, knife in the back, pulls himself to his feet. He slowly staggers towards Blair; his mouth utters the word "why?" and he sprawls to the floor at her feet. She stares down at him for a moment, turns away, and begins to dial as the curtain falls.

Act 2, scene 1, transpires an hour and a half later. The stage is empty and dark except for glowing embers in the fireplace. The front door is pushed open and Maggie Stratton enters with a flashlight. The beam of the flashlight plays over the room and we now see that the Jacuzzi top is closed. Maggie picks up a poker and is about to poke embers when she hears the sound of an approaching car. With poker still in hand, she moves to the stairs and quickly ascends. Gus enters, takes in the room, goes to the Jacuzzi, pushes a button, and the top slides open. Gus kneels, puts his arm into the water and pulls Lombardi's wet canvas bag out by the straps. He opens the bag and brings out two cameras, some lenses, and Morgan's wallet, watch, and ring.

Doris appears in the doorway. She tells Gus that Blair is waiting outside in the police car. "Considering in one day she's watched her husband being stabbed to death," says Doris, "and then was raped and killed another man—she's fair." Doris adds wryly that Blair Griffin is big news again—reporters are pouring into town.

Blair enters wearing a rain slicker over her robe. Looking pale and slightly disoriented, she exits upstairs to change. Gus and Doris theorize that Blair hired Lombardi to kill her husband, hid Lombardi in the Jacuzzi, then got rid of him. Gus sends Doris to check on all outgoing calls from the house over the last ten days. Blair comes down. Over coffee, Gus finds himself confiding to Blair that he was married with two kids and divorced after twenty years. He was working in the narcotics division out of Boston and was assigned to the porno movie ring case that inspired his best-selling book. Several magazines published biographical profiles that made him seem "like a combination of Sam Spade and Albert Schweitzer." He was both attracted and repelled by being famous, became impossible at home, and left his wife for "a twenty-two-year-old tootsie." A sense of intimacy develops between Gus and Blair. She murmurs, "Something happened between us . . . something really nice."

A phone call from Doris reminds Gus that his daughter, a music major at Georgetown University, is giving her first solo recital the next day. Gus promises to be back after Morgan's funeral and turns to leave. Blair kisses him on the lips and, with overtones of something in the air, he exits.

Maggie Stratton, poker in hand, silently appears at the top of the stairs. She comes down and deposits the poker by the fireplace. The two women look at one another for a moment, then embrace and kiss passionately. Maggie sits on the sofa. Blair stretches out and puts her head in Maggie's lap. Maggie strokes her hair and expresses concern about the police investigation—somebody has been sniffing around asking questions in the L.A. office. Blair assures Maggie that Lieutenant Gus Braden has "bought everything." Maggie is still skeptical: "Suppose he hasn't?" Blair shrugs, "Oh, then we'll just have to kill him."

Act 2, scene 2 takes place in the late afternoon of the next day. Gus confronts Blair, laying out a motive for the killing of Morgan. Following their divorce, he had planned to get married again and request custody of their children. Blair's claim that Morgan had an affair with Maggie Stratton was a "big lie," says Gus, a decoy to stop the police from looking for the other woman in Morgan's life. Gus is certain that Blair got Lombardi to murder her husband. It was all planned in advance—the Jacuzzi, the rape, the killing, making it look like a break-in robbery—everything.

Blair confesses that Gus hit upon the truth and adds that Morgan had found out about her intimate relationship with Maggie. "He threatened to make it public if I didn't give him the children," says Blair. "And I'd rather die than lose them. . . . The real truth is that, without them, I couldn't survive, because—without them, I am nothing."

Gus does not understand why Blair had so easily and completely admitted to instigating Morgan's murder. Blair grins and says that she has "a nice, warm, ace in the hole": She knows that Gus has fallen in love with her. "We're a perfect match," she declares. "We're very much alike. We're two of a kind. We live by instinct, not convention." She assures Gus that they can have a *wonderful* life together. She has no doubt that her children would adore him. "Most of all," she concludes, "we'd have each other."

There's only one stumbling block, says Blair, Maggie Stratton. She'll take care of it. All she needs is a drug, a pill that will knock Maggie out for ten, fifteen minutes. She'll put it in a glass of red wine. Maggie will pass out. Blair will open the Jacuzzi, place Maggie in, close the top, turn on the water—she drowns. She'll then put Maggie in her car—"she doesn't weigh much"—drive it two hundred yards to Randall's Point and let it roll over the edge into the sea. It will be adjudged an accident—the victim was drinking and didn't know the road.

Gus looks at the Jacuzzi, then crosses to the window to look at Randall's Point. "There's one more thing," says Blair. "I'd really like you to make love to me." He turns, moves back to Blair, and kisses her. The lights fade.

Act 2, scene 3 unfolds at 9:00 p.m. the next evening. It is raining outside. A small table by the curtained window has been set for two. There is a bottle of red wine and two glasses but only one is full. The Jacuzzi top is open. Blair is mopping up some water from the floor. Gus enters, wearing a wet raincoat, a gun, and holster. Blair tells him that "it's all over"—Maggie's car is now at the bottom of the cliff. She didn't need to use the pills. After five brandies Maggie decided she wanted to take a Jacuzzi. "It made everything ridiculously simple," continues Blair. "We're home free, Gus."

Maggie silently appears from behind a curtain with a poker in her hand. She clubs Gus from behind. He slumps down. The two women drag him to the Jacuzzi. His body disappears with a splash. Blair presses the button and the Jacuzzi top closes. She then turns the tap on. After a moment, Blair surprisingly says that she's sorry to see the police lieutenant go—"he was smart, funny, decent, with just enough larceny to make him human." Maggie watches with incredulous eyes as tears roll down Blair's cheeks.

There is a clap of thunder and a flash of lightning outside. The women decide it's time to press the button and open the Jacuzzi. They are transfixed as Gus, soaking wet, rises slowly out of the Jacuzzi. Blair grabs Gus's pistol, points it right at him, and fires. There is a loud explosion but Gus moves forward and takes the weapon from her. "Blanks," he says. Doris, gun in hand, and carrying a large towel, enters. Gus tells Blair and Maggie that in case they're wondering, Doris turned the water off at the main.

Doris escorts Maggie out to the police car. Blair asks Gus why he didn't go along with her plan to abscond together. He shrugs: "I wanted to be rich and famous again. This case is going to make a hell of a book." Undeterred, Blair suggests that if he teams with her on the book—"a collaboration between the detective and the murderer"—it is a *guaranteed* best seller. She even has a title—"Fatal Attraction."

Gus looks at her with a mixture of amazement and admiration. She moves to him, embraces him, kisses him. Behind his back she is holding a knife she has picked from the table. The knife waves slightly. Is she going to use it?

She breaks the embrace and hands him the knife. "Pick up the phone, Gus," she urges. "Phone your publisher." She flashes her beautiful, vulnerable smile at him and exits. Gus gazes at the phone, starts out, but stops. He turns back, and is staring at the tantalizing phone as the curtain falls.

* * *

Fatal Attraction premiered at the St. Lawrence Center Theatre in Toronto, Canada on November 8, 1984. The production was directed by Tom Troupe. The cast included Dawn Wells (Blair Griffin), Ken Howard (Lieutenant Gus Braden), Robin Ward (Morgan Richards), Tony Noll (Tony Lombardi), Bette Ford (Maggie Stratton), and Jayne Eastwood (Sergeant Doris Aylesworth).

The thriller reached London's Theatre Royal Haymarket on November 26, 1985, staged by David Gilmore, featuring Susannah York (Blair Griffin) and Denis Quilley (Gus Braden).

Fatal Attraction was produced by California's Costa Mesa Civic Playhouse in 1990. Critic Mark Chalon Smith of the *Los Angeles Times* believed that "the plot has more than its share of incongruities" and sneezed at one of the play's climaxes: "My favorite was when the missing photographer emerges, a la Dracula from his crypt, out of the spa in the living room. These sorts of 'rising from the dead' moments of terror are so overused, they evoke giggles instead of shivers."[1]

Two years later, *Fatal Attraction* was presented by the Bayway Arts Center in East Islip, New York. The *New York Times'* Leah D. Frank appreciated the play's setup: "Genuine clues and red herrings are mixed together in a stew consisting of a love-starved police lieutenant, a brittle Hollywood agent, a perky and cynical policewoman, a famous artist, a freelance celebrity photographer, and, of course, the movie star." However, concluded the reviewer, "What is remarkable about this production is that it has all the proper production elements but none of that indefinable theatrical magic that makes a play worth sitting through."[2]

Fatal Attraction garnered renewed interest, on both sides of the Atlantic, during the first decade of the twenty-first century. In 2002, the thriller was mounted by the Richmond Hill Barn Theatre, Geneseo, Illinois. Reviewer Jill Pearson of the *River Cities' Reader* lauded a tale of "love, deceit, cunning, and sex appeal."[3] Conversely, Ruby Nancy of *Quad City Times* wrote, "the play is pointless and so ostentatiously overwrought it wouldn't even work as melodrama."[4]

In November 2003, *Fatal Attraction* was presented by the Western Players, Swindon, Wiltshire, England; in July 2006, by Theatre Palisades, Pacific Palisades, California; in March 2011, by the Archway Theatre Company, Horley, Surrey, England; in June 2011, by Pasadena City College, Pasadena, California; and in September 2011, by the Bingley Little Theatre, Bingley, England, advertised as "a crackling tale with many twists and turns right up to, and including, the very last scene."

The published acting edition of *Fatal Attraction* includes a production note that offers several ways of constructing the all-important Jacuzzi, and the suggestion that "Dry ice can be used to disguise the fact that there is no water in the Jacuzzi."[5]

* * *

Bernard Slade followed *Fatal Attraction* with *An Act of the Imagination*, another twisty mystery, first produced under the title *Sweet William* on September 15, 1987 at the Yvonne Arnaud Theatre in Guildford, Surrey, England. The time: Late afternoon of a sunny day in 1964. The setting: The living room–study of a house in Hampstead on the outskirts of London. The room is furnished with a pleasing mixture of English and French country antiques. The beamed ceilings and use of muted fabrics give it a lived-in, appealing ambience.

At rise we hear the serene, soothing "The Girl With the Flaxen Hair" by Debussy. Arthur Putnam—"mid to late fifties, a gentle daydreamer"— is sitting at his desk smoking a pipe, writing on a pad. His wife, Julia Putnam—"late forties, very beautiful, warm, graceful"—is reclining in a chair, reading the last pages of a novel, *Signs of Life*, still in manuscript form. She tells Arthur that she finds his story "poignant, evocative, sexy, passionate, terribly sad and thoroughly satisfying." Her only concern is, will a romantic novel jar Arthur's multitude of readers who are ac- customed to his gritty mysteries, published under the pseudonym T. L. Quentin. Arthur agrees—he'll use another pen name.

Enter Simon Putnam, Arthur's son from an earlier marriage—"a very attractive, charming, young man in his mid-twenties." A strained sense between father and son becomes evident when Simon asks for financial support to open an American-style diner in "a perfect location." Arthur pooh-poohs the idea.

A neighbor, Detective Sergeant Fred Burchitt—"a spry, friendly Londoner in his mid-fifties"—arrives to invite the Putnams to the open- ing night of *Gaslight*, the well-known psychological thriller by Patrick Hamilton being mounted by a local troupe. The director, his daughter, recruited him to play the detective of the piece. Julia begs off, as she'll be away doing research for her next radio broadcast. Arthur explains that he's been invited on that date to give a talk at the Mystery Writers Society at the Garrick.

Arthur surprises the visitor by exhibiting a loaded revolver and tells him that "there's a possibility someone's trying to kill me." Two peculiar incidents have happened to him lately. A few days ago, when waiting for a train in the Leicester Square tube station, someone shoved him in the back. He stumbled forward but fortunately didn't fall onto the rails but against the front of the first car. Yesterday, the steering in his Bentley suddenly malfunctioned. He was again lucky because he was traveling at about ten miles per hour.

Sergeant Burchitt considers whether Arthur is in danger as a result of his involvement in MI5, the intelligence unit of the War Office. Burchitt leaves. Arthur tells Julia that he intends to attend the sergeant's show; he just wanted to take the pressure off, for in the past, when old Fred knew Arthur was there, he completely went to pieces, forgot his lines, stumbled around "and generally made a complete ass of himself."

In view of the vivid sensuality expressed in *Signs of Life*, Julia confronts Arthur with the query, "Have you been having a love affair?" He answers

"No," simply and sincerely. "So why is your book so damned believable?" she pursues. "It was an act of the imagination," he insists.

Brenda Simmons—"vaguely bohemian appearance, underlying neurotic sexuality"—arrives on the scene. She corners Julia with an announcement that she has been having an affair with her husband for the last eight months. She has just found out that the famous mystery writer T. L. Quentin is none other than Arthur Putnam. Her dad has read *Exhibition for a Dead Painter* and she recognized Arthur's picture on the cover. For 5,000 pounds she'll go away and keep quiet. At that moment Arthur enters. Brenda crosses to him and attempts to hug him, but he pushes her away. He insists that the woman is lying and, losing control, grabs Brenda and starts to violently shake her like a rag doll. Brenda manages to get away from him and, with tears in her eyes, goes to the door, threatens Arthur that she'll do something "you'll never forget," and exits. Arthur, his face ashen, sinks into a chair and says quietly, "I swear—before God— I've never seen that woman in my life."

At 10:30 the next morning, Sergeant Burchitt arrives to tell Arthur that Brenda Simmons has left a suicide note in her rented room and the police have every reason to believe that she is dead. On her way out, the girl met briefly with her landlady, Mrs. Prockter, and told her she was off to meet someone on Hampstead Heath. In one of the rain shelters on the Heath the police found signs of a struggle: blood on the floor, some strands of hair, a bloodstained shoe. The body has not been found yet, but there's a search party out right now. Also in the shelter, a button was found, and it matches the missing button on Arthur's jacket. Furthermore, Arthur's car, his Bentley, was seen in Brenda's neighborhood that evening. Before the sergeant came in, the Bentley was searched. Brenda's other shoe was found in the glove compartment.

Arthur insists that he has not seen the woman, that he attended *Gaslight* from the back of the auditorium, but he is led out by the sergeant. In a startling revelation, Julia and her stepson Simon, now by themselves, kiss passionately and review their successful entrapment of Arthur. As they discuss the case, their motives become clear: Simon complains that he was tired of groveling for handouts; Julia bemoans living for twenty years with a man who "even when he was present—was absent."

The last scene unfolds in the early evening, some weeks later. A storm is brewing outside. Simon is leafing through newspapers. Julia enters with a tray containing sandwiches and coffee. The doorbell rings. The newcomer—"classically beautiful"—introduces herself as Brooke Carmichael, the wife of a diplomat. She has just returned from Chile and learned that Arthur Putnam is on trial for murder. She knows he is innocent, because she's the woman with whom Arthur had the affair. During the two hours that Arthur was supposed to have murdered the girl, he was with her. They met at Heathrow Airport and spent time in the first class lounge before she boarded her flight. Because of the delicate circumstances, dear, honorable Arthur kept quiet about it. No wonder she fell in love with him. It was not just a sordid, sexual fling.

Realizing that the situation is hopeless, Julia sighs and her shoulders slump in resignation. Simon, however, is not ready to give up. He solicits from Brooke the information that no one else knows of the airport meeting, moves to the end table, and slides a gun into his side pocket. There's a clap of thunder when Simon fires the gun, the bullet splattering Brooke's brains on the wall behind (a production note in the printed version of the play states that there's a simple way of achieving this effect).

Julia, her eyes open, starts to scream. Simon quickly moves to put his hand over her mouth. "It's done, it's all over," he says. "It was the only way." He hurriedly rattles that he'll drive the body to the coast, take it out in his boat, weigh the body down, and dump it in the ocean. He urges Julia, "This is no time to be squeamish," and she helps him get a tarpaulin from the window seat. As they intend to drop the tarp beside the corpse, to their horror they realize that it has vanished!

Slowly Brooke emerges above the sofa. Sergeant Burchitt and Arthur enter. The sergeant explains wryly to the dumbfounded Simon and Julia that Brooke Carmichael is actually Phoebe, a police officer, and adds, "I'm arresting you on the charge of attempted murder." He flips a panel around the wall so that the bloody matter disappears, and chuckles, "Special effects. I rigged it myself earlier in the day when Arthur told me about the attachment between you and his son." Arthur then confides that he has known about the clandestine relationship for about a year, almost as soon as it started, but was hoping for a change of heart.

Burchitt and Phoebe escort Julia and Simon out to the police car. Left alone, Arthur crosses to the stereo and presses a button, and we hear the strains of "The Girl with the Flaxen Hair." He sits at the desk in the position in which we first discovered him, takes up his pen, and begins to write. Another pool of light gradually comes up on Julia, dressed as she was in the beginning of the play, reclining in the chair downstage-left, reading a manuscript. In an ending reminiscent of George M. Cohan's classic *Seven Keys to Baldpate* (1913), we realize that the whole preceding adventure was Arthur's Act of the Imagination.

Directed by Val May, *An Act of the Imagination* was first produced, under the title *Sweet William*, on September 15, 1987, at the Yvonne Arnaud Theatre, Guildford, Surrey, England. The lead actors included Michael Craig (Arthur Putnam), Myree Dawn Porter (Julia Putnam), Paul Herzberg (Simon Putnam), and David Baron (Detective Sergeant Fred Burchitt). In the United States, the play was performed for several weeks at the Rector Little Theatre, Union College, Barbourville, Kentucky, in 2005.

* * *

Bernard Slade was born to British parents in St. Catherines, Ontario, Canada, in 1930. He was educated in England, returned to Canada at eighteen, and embarked on a ten-year career as an actor. He began performing in summer stock, first at International Players, Kingston, later with the company he founded with his wife Jill Foster, in Vineland, Ontario—The Barn Theatre.

In 1964, Slade and his family moved to Los Angeles, where he has written extensively for film and television. He began as a writer and story editor on the situation comedy *Bewitched* (ABC, 1964–1972) and went on to create seven popular series on three networks: *Love on a Rooftop* (ABC, 1966–1967), *The Flying Nun* (ABC, 1967–1970), *Mr. Deeds Goes to Town* (ABC, 1969–1970), *The Partridge Family* (ABC, 1970–1974), *Getting Together* (ABC, 1971–1972), *Bridget Loves Bernie* (CBS, 1972–1973), and *The Girl with Something Extra* (NBC, 1973–1974).

Slade is a member of the Dramatists Guild of America. His anecdotal memoir, *Shared Laughter*, was published by Key Porter Books in 2000.

Acting Edition: *Fatal Attraction* and *An Act of the Imagination*—Samuel French, Inc.

Awards and Honors: In 1975, Bernard Slade received a Drama Desk Award and was nominated for a Tony as author of Best Play, *Same Time, Next Year*. In 1979, he was nominated for an Oscar for adapting the play to the screen.

NOTES

1. *Los Angeles Times*, June 7, 1990.
2. *New York Times*, February 16, 1992.
3. *River Cities' Reader*, August 14, 2002.
4. *Quad City Times*, August 15, 2002.
5. A variation on *Fatal Attraction*'s Jacuzzi deathtrap can be found in two earlier thrillers. *The Flying Squad* (1928) by Edgar Wallace unfolds in a shadowy den on the bank of the Thames. It serves as headquarters of a lucrative cocaine-smuggling enterprise, complete with electrical warning signals and a hidden trapdoor, under which runs a sweeping, deadly current. In Rufus King's *Invitation to a Murder* (1934), a deadly trapdoor looms in the great hall of a centuries-old mansion on the coast of southern California. By the touch of a secret lever an unsuspecting person is plunged through the floor to swift-running waters deep below the house. The mistress of the estate, Lorinda Channing, is adept at gripping and twisting the fatal knob, thus disposing of bothersome antagonists. Both *The Flying Squad* and *Invitation to a Murder* are entries in *Blood on the Stage, 1925–1950* by Amnon Kabatchnik (Lanham, Md.: Scarecrow Press, 2010).

The Mystery of Irma Vep (1984)

Charles Ludlam (United States, 1943–1987)

In 1915, French director Louis Feuillade directed the celebrated silent serial *Les Vampires*, in which the actress Musidora played an exotic dancer
who assumes command of a secret society that terrifies Paris with a series
of murderous activities. An investigative reporter, Philippe Guérande
(portrayed by Édouard Mathé), attempts to expose the gang's operations
and bring the criminals to justice.[1]

Seven decades later, in 1984, Charles Ludlam, founder of off-Broadway's notorious Ridiculous Theatrical Company, penned the burlesque-
spoof *The Mystery of Irma Vep*, combining elements from Feuillade's film
with splices from *Rebecca*, *The Mummy*, and *The Wolf Man*, recycles from
Shakespeare and Ibsen, and snatches from Victorian melodrama.

The Mystery of Irma Vep, arguably Ludlam's masterpiece, has a cast of
two, each playing four different characters. A quick-change device is at
the core of the play's magical effect. "The idea of creating the illusion of
an actor exiting out one door and immediately entering through another
across the stage dressed as a different character was the hook around
which Ludlam built the show," wrote Rick Roemer in *Charles Ludlam and
the Ridiculous Theatrical Company*.[2]

The curtain opens on the study of "Mandacrest," the Hillcrest estate near
Hampstead Heath, England. There are a desk and chair, two deep arm-
chairs, and a fireplace with a mantel over which hangs a portrait of Lady
Irma in her prime. African masks, an Egyptian mummy case, and a painted
Japanese screen are signs that the Hillcrests have travelled the world.

At rise, lightning flashes and thunder rumbles. Nicodemus Underwood, a stableboy, enters from the garden through French doors, carrying a basket. His left leg is deformed and the sole of his shoe is built up
with wood. The housekeeper, Jane Twisden, begins to arrange flowers
in a bowl. As the two servants chat we learn that Nicodemus had his leg
mangled by a wolf when saving his master, Lord Edgar Hillcrest. Still

devoted to her former mistress Irma, Jane finds it difficult to accept the new lady of the house, Enid. Sneers Jane, "She's so, so—common. She'll never live up to the high standards set by Lady Irma."

Thunder claps and Jane shrieks. Protectively, Nicodemus tries to put his arm around her but Jane eludes his embrace. "Don't you get any ideas about me," she sternly says. "You are beneath me and beneath me you're going to stay." Nicodemus retorts, "Someday you might want to get beneath me," and chases Jane around the room, requesting a kiss.

They hear footsteps above. Jane rebukes Nicodemus for waking up their new mistress, who "sleeps all day and is up all night." Nicodemus theorizes that Lady Enid had acquired the habit when performing on the stage. Jane is shocked: "The stage! Ugh! How disgusting!"

Nicodemus exits. Jane lights the fire as Lady Enid comes down the stairs. She looks about the room, stops by the portrait over the mantel, and stares at it for a long time. Jane, cold but cordial, soon departs to prepare dinner.

Lord Edgar enters, dragging the carcass of a wolf, supposedly the one that has been killing lambs and howling all night. Lady Enid rushes to Edgar and plants a kiss on his lips. The Lord retreats, points at the painting, and says, "Not in front of—" Lady Enid begs her husband to forget the past and make a fresh start. She insists that he blow out the memorial candle burning near the picture and goes to change for dinner. Lord Edgar summons Nicodemus and orders him to burn "every hide and hair" of the dead wolf. The Lord would also like the mantel picture taken down and burnt with the wolf.

Jane returns, approaches the carcass wearily, and exclaims, "It's no rejoicing there'll be this night, Nicodemus Underwood. He's killed the wrong wolf."

Later that evening the storm has passed. Jane is stoking the last embers of fire and Lady Enid comes downstairs in her dressing gown. Jane launches into the history of the Hillcrest family. The sound of howling reminds Jane that Miss Irma used to keep a wolf, Victor, as a pet. Bigger than a dog, relates Jane, Victor's happiest hours were spent stretched out at Miss Irma's feet, his huge purple tongue lolling out of his mouth. Lord Edgar locked him out when it came time for her to deliver her child. A tragedy occurred when one winter day Victor and the boy, also named Victor, went out to the heath to play in the fallen snow; the wolf came back without the boy. At dusk they found the child in the mill run, dead. His throat had been torn apart. Lord Edgar wanted Victor destroyed but Lady Irma fought against it. When the Master came to shoot the wolf, Lady Irma turned him loose upon the heath. Jane climaxes her tale with a bombshell: The boy was killed by a wolf that left human tracks in the snow—probably a werewolf, a human that takes the form of a wolf at night.

Jane retires to bed and Lady Enid stays up to read Lord Edgar's treatise on ancient Egyptian mythology. Suddenly a pane of the French door shatters. A bony hand reaches in through the curtains and opens a latch. A gaunt figure slowly enters the room. The clock strikes one. The intruder emits a hissing sound, leaps, and catches Enid by her long hair and drags her toward the mantel. Enid grabs roses from the vase and presses their thorns into the intruder's eyes. He groans and releases her. She stabs him with scissors from Jane's sewing basket. The creature clasps his hand over Enid's mouth and drags her through an upstage door, amid her high-pitched screams for help. Shriek follows strangled shriek as the intruder seizes her neck in his fang-like teeth. Lord Edgar and Jane run downstairs. They find the door leading to the cellar locked. They use a crowbar and force the door open.

Nicodemus enters through the French door carrying the limp body of Lady Enid. Her long hair hangs down, covering her face. There are several drops of blood on her nightgown. Nicodemus exits stage right with the body. He soon re-enters and tells Lord Edgar that he saw something strange moving in the heath. A horrible face appears at the window. Laughing shrilly, the thing bangs against the windowpanes. Nicodemus musters his courage and goes outside to face the creature. Sounds of a struggle are heard. A wooden leg, one that had formerly belonged to Nicodemus, is thrown inside. Nicodemus crawls in, whispers in horror that the creature appeared first as a dog, then as a wolf, and finally as a woman. It tore off his leg and started chewing on it; if it hadn't been wood, it would have eaten it.

Lord Edgar retrieves a gun from the wall, shouts, "It's Victor! Victor came back to haunt me!" and runs out. Running steps, shots, and howling are heard. Jane rushes in and takes another gun down from the wall. Nicodemus struggles for the gun and it goes off unexpectedly, causing the picture of Irma Vep to ooze blood.

The next day Lord Edgar is hovering near Lady Enid, who sits in a chair by the fire. She is numbed and quasi-catatonic. Lord Edgar begins to believe in lycanthropy, mummy legends, and vampirism. He tells Nicodemus that he plans to embark on a journey for Cairo where he'll organize an expedition to Giza and explore Numidian ruins. Meanwhile, due to her delicate mental condition, he'll arrange for Lady Enid to rest in a private sanitarium.

The second act unfolds in various places in Egypt. Lord Edgar has hired the services of Alcazar, a shady guide, who leads him to the Valley of the Kings. Lord Edgar goes down by rope to the tomb of Princess Pev Amri, slowly opens the sarcophagus, and finds a mummified woman. They unwrap the mummy's hand, which holds a scroll. It reads, "She who sleeps but will one day wake," and unrolls to describe the invocation that will return the princess to life once more. Alcazar exits backward making a salaam. Lord Edgar lights a charcoal brazier, intoning, "Katara katara katara rana! Ecbatara Ecbatra Soumouft!"

Pev Amri flutters her eyelashes and opens her eyes. She mumbles in ancient gibberish. Overcome by "lips silent for three thousand years now beg to be kissed," Lord Edgar bends down and kisses the princess. She slaps him.

Lord Edgar runs out to get Alcazar while the mummy returns to her sarcophagus. Alcazar follows Lord Edgar in, obviously dubious. He slowly opens the case. Inside stands the mummy as before, only this time with the wrappings partially removed, revealing a hideously decomposed face. Lord Edgar decides to take the ancient Egyptian to England. He and Alcazar carry out the sarcophagus as the lights fade.

Act 3 takes us back to Mandacrest. It is autumn. Jane is dusting the mummy case. She tells Nicodemus that Lady Enid has returned from the sanitarium and is in her bedroom—"she sleeps all day and she's up at night." A bell tinkles. Jane goes upstairs to her mistress and Nicodemus is left alone in sight of a full moon. "No! No! No!" he screams and turns to the audience. His face has become that of a wolf. He runs about the room on his tiptoes with his knees bent. He sniffs, scratches, howls, and flees through the French doors.

The sound of a wolf howling in the distance echoes when Lady Enid comes downstairs. She and Jane sit by the piano, playing duets and drinking toddies. Lady Enid confides that she and Lord Edgar are drifting apart. "It's a terrible thing to marry an Egyptologist," she says, "and find out that he's hung up on his mummy." Jane talks Lady Enid into wearing one of the lovely dresses in the closet to surprise Lord Edgar, knowing full well that if Edgar were to see Enid in one of Irma's old dresses, he would explode. Jane exits to lay out the dress.

Lord Edgar enters and tells his wife that he went to the village to purchase silver bullets. A young dairy maid was found badly mauled. It seems that the werewolf has struck again.

Later that night, Lady Enid, wearing a different frock, discovers a pretty ornament on the fireplace. When she touches it, it triggers a sliding panel, revealing a cage with a shrouded woman. She claims to be Irma Vep, the first Lady Hillcrest, held prisoner because she alone knows where a secret treasure of jewels is hidden. Footsteps are heard and Lady Enid quickly closes the panel.

Lord Edgar is aghast at Lady Enid for wearing one of Irma's dresses. He yelps that this was the dress that Irma wore the night she died. He tears the dress and Lady Enid bursts into tears, complaining that he doesn't love her. He responds that he cannot show his love for lingering fear of his first wife. Lady Enid cries: "The woman has an unearthly power over you, Edgar."

They argue and Lord Edgar leaves in a huff. Lady Enid pulls the figurine, again revealing the shrouded woman. She opens the cage. Irma flies out, shrieking madly. She seizes Enid by the throat, turns her back to the audience, and leans over her. Enid sinks to her knees. Says Irma: "Oh triple fool! Did you not know that Irma Vep is "vampire" anagrammatized!" Lady Enid reaches up and rips off Irma's face, which is a rubber mask, exposing Jane, the real vampire, who admits to killing Lady Irma and the boy Victor. Wielding a meat cleaver, Jane attacks Enid, who backs over to the mummy's case and deftly moves aside as Jane stumbles into it.

Enid slams the door and holds it shut. Jane begins to pound on the door and manages to open it. Enid is saved by Nicodemus who, as a werewolf, bursts through the French doors, grabs Jane, and drags her out the way he came, howling. He immediately returns with only Jane's dress. Lord Edgar dashes in and fires a volley of shots. "Thank you," whispers Nicodemus, and dies.

In the final scene, Lord Edgar and Lady Enid are seated comfortably in their drawing room, musing upon the recent events. Lord Edgar announces that he intends to publish his invaluable discovery of the ancient, hideously shriveled mummy. Lady Enid, unable to bear it any longer, asks her husband to forgive her and sheepishly admits that she was "the mummy" in the tomb and that Alcazar is her father, actually Professor Lionel Cuncliff of Cambridge University, a leading Egyptologist. The sarcophagus was from an Egyptian restaurant in London closed for a number of years. A theatre designer was engaged to make it look like a tomb. She did it to win Lord Edgar over from the spell of his first wife, hoping that it would make her husband believe that their love was destined.

Lord Edgar lovingly forgives Lady Enid. Holding hands, they stand in the doorway, with their backs to us, looking up at the sky as the lights fade to darkness.

* * *

"Ludlam once remarked that he had worked backwards in *Irma Vep*," wrote Rick Roemer in *Charles Ludlam and the Ridiculous Theatrical Company*,

> starting with the theatrical devices and then developing the story. . . . In order for two actors successfully to play four characters apiece with quick changes, Ludlam had to map out the end and work backward toward the beginning, carefully planning each exit and entrance to avoid an actor colliding with himself on stage. According to Ludlam: "A playwright can usually bring on any character at any time he wants, but I couldn't because it involved a change—an exit which had to be justified and covered—and

then you had to think of where the various characters had gone and where you had left them and how you could get them back on. It's really a kind of Rubik's Cube effect. Every time you try to change one element, all the other elements go out of whack. It's that precise."[3]

The Mystery of Irma Vep was first produced by the Ridiculous Theatrical Company at off-off-Broadway's One Sheridan Square Theatre in September 1984, running for 331 performances. It featured Charles Ludlam as Lady Enid Hillcrest and stableboy-werewolf Nicodemus Underwood, and Everett Quinton as Lord Edgar Hillcrest and housekeeper-vampire Jane Twisden (among other characters).

Critic Mel Gussow of the *New York Times* complimented the "perfervid imagination of Mr. Ludlam as author, director and star," expressed admiration for "the two actors quick-change costumes, characters and genders," and applauded "a penny dreadful" that turned into "a double tour de force."[4] *The American Weekly*'s David Kaufman agreed: "Ludlam and his single cohort—Everett Quinton—portray seven different characters in such rapid succession, that there were times I could swear I saw more than two people on stage. Even Houdini would be impressed, if not astonished."[5] Center Stage of Baltimore, Maryland produced *The Mystery of Irma Vep* on May 1, 1991, with Wil Love and Derek D. Smith, eliciting a mixed evaluation by *Baltimore Sun* reviewer J. Wynn Rousek, who found it "a corny, campy, melodramatic horror story . . . frequently tasteless, always unsubtle, generally hilarious production."[6]

Eight years later, on November 11, 2009, Baltimore's Everyman Theatre presented *Irma Vep* with the duo Clinton Brandhagen and Bruce R. Nelson. *Baltimore Sun*'s Mary Carole McCauley reported that "Three dressers and a stagehand conduct a carefully choreographed dance that allows two actors to make up to 50 full costume changes during each performance, complete with Victorian-era petticoats, wigs, false teeth and top hats—often in two seconds or less."[7]

Irma Vep was produced by Theatre Three in Port Jefferson, New York, on January 23, 1993, featuring Scott Hofer and Bill van Horn. *New York Times*' Leah D. Frank found the show "wickedly funny. . . . Murder, mayhem, skullduggery and a few other vices invade the plot like a swarm of Gothic killer bees."[8]

The play was revived at off-Broadway's Westside Theatre from September 1998 through July 1999 with Everett Quinton (now enacting Lady Enid and Nicodemus) and Stephen DeRosa (Lord Edgar and Jane). *Curtain Up* reviewer Elyse Sommer found the "lush new production" tinged with "a master's silliness brought to the level of great comedic timing by two perfectly matched comic talents."[9]

The gothic spoof was mounted by the Park Square Theatre, Saint Paul, Minnesota, from July 26 to August 24, 2003; at Howmet Playhouse in Whitehall, Michigan, from August 1 through 4, 2007; by the Balagula Theatre, Lexington, Kentucky, from October 5 through 16, 2008; at the Old Globe Theatre of San Diego, California in its summer 2009 season; at the Hayworth Theatre, Los Angeles, in March 2009; at Theatre in the Park, Raleigh, North Carolina, on October 23, 2009, for three successive performances at 7 p.m., 9:30 p.m., and midnight; and at the Court Theatre, Chicago, Illinois in November 2009, with Eric Hellman and Chris Sullivan in the multiple roles. The *Chicago Critic* wrote: "*The Mystery of Irma Vep* is a hilarious adventure mystery and door-slamming farce that is part horror movie, part melodrama, part Grand-Guignol, and part drag show pastiche."[10] The play was also seen at Space 916 in Hollywood, California in the fall of 2009 and 2010, featuring Michael Lorre and Kevin Remington, and at the distinguished Flinton Summer Theatre in Flinton on Sea, England, as part of its 2010 season celebrating seventy years of repertory theatre.

Often mounted in the United States, in 2003 *The Mystery of Irma Vep* became the longest-running play ever produced in Brazil. It set a Guinness world record for the longest run of a play with the same cast—Marco Nanini and Ney Latorraca. Nanini and Latorraca reprised their roles in the 2006 Brazilian motion picture *Irma Vap—O Retorno* (*Irma Vep—She's Back!*).

* * *

Born in Floral Park, New York, and raised on Long Island, Charles Ludlam was encouraged by his parents to explore his vivid imagination. As a child, he presented backyard vignettes with other neighborhood kids. In his senior year at Harborfields High School, where he was known as a rebel and outcast, he established, with a group of friends, a "Students Repertory Theatre," performing dramas by August Strindberg and Eugene O'Neill in a loft studio on Northport's Main Street. He subsequently appeared in plays produced by amateur companies and worked backstage in summer stock. He pursued his interest in theatre by traveling to New York City and seeing commercial and experimental plays. Off-Broadway's avant-garde The Living Theatre proved to be of significant influence on young Ludlam, and he later said that Julian Beck, its artistic director, "is sort of my idol." In 1964, upon receiving a degree in dramatic literature from Hofstra University, he came to New York with the zeal of creating new theatrical forms.

In 1966, Ludlam joined off-off-Broadway's avant-garde Playhouse of the Ridiculous. During rehearsals of his farce *Conquest of the Universe*, he clashed severely with director John Vaccaro and was fired from his own play. Ludlam left with seven other key members of the group and in 1967 founded the Ridiculous Theatrical Company, launching a most illustrious career as playwright, director, designer, and actor, and helping make off-off-Broadway a significant part of the New York theatre. His initial plays were inchoate exercises, but beginning with *Big Hotel* (1967), he wrote more structured works, mostly pastiches of Greek mythology, Shakespeare, and Victorian melodramas. Ludlam usually directed and appeared in his plays, often with his lifetime companion Everett Quinton. During the late 1970s and early 1980s, the company secured a permanent home at One Sheridan Square in the heart of Manhattan's Greenwich Village. Ludlam also taught or staged productions at New York University, Connecticut College for Women, Yale University, and Carnegie Mellon University.

Though centered on broad comedy, many of Ludlam's twenty-nine plays are tinged with criminous elements and suspenseful moments. Checking into *Big Hotel* (1967) are Mata Hari, Norma Desmond, Svengali, and a suicidal Russian ballerina. Santa Claus checks in, too, and is murdered. The dastardly deeds of *Bluebeard* (1970) take place in an alchemical laboratory located on an island off the coast of Maine and are based on H. G. Wells's horror novel, *The Island of Dr. Moreau*. *Hot Ice* (1972) is the saga of an underground war between the Cryogenic Society (an organization that believes in freezing the dead in the hope of later resuscitation) and the Euthanasia Police (who are devoted to the ideal of the "good death"). The play is cast in the mold of a gangster epic. *Medea* (1984) reiterates the basic plot of the ancient murderous mother with high camp vision. Set in a pet shop in Lower Manhattan, *The Artificial Jungle* (1986) borrows ingredients from James M. Cain's *The Postman Always Rings Twice* and *Double Indemnity* as well as from Emile Zola's *Thérèse Raquin*. The owner lives in the back with his mother and bored wife. They hire a drifter to work in the shop and soon the newcomer plots with the wife to feed her husband to the piranhas.

Among the plays that Ludlam adapted from another source, adding his own pastiche wrinkles, are *Corn* (1972), a backwoods version of *Romeo and Juliet*, set in an Appalachian town; *Camille* (1973), from *La Dame Aux Camelias* by Alexandre Dumas fils; *Stage Blood* (1974), tinkering with *Hamlet*; *Jack and the Beanstalk* (1976), a retelling of the children's classic; *Der Ring Gott Farblonjet* (1977), a parody of Wagner's Ring Cycle; *The Enchanted Pig* (1979), a camp combination of King Lear, The Three Sisters, Cinderella, and The Frog Prince; *A Christmas Carol* (1979), from Charles Dickens's classic story; *Le Bourgeois Avant-Garde* (1983), from Molière's *Le Bourgeois Gentilhomme*; and *Salammbo* (1985), from Flaubert's similarly titled novel.

The Grand Tarot (1969) borrows ideas from Antonin Artaud's theatre of cruelty and is based on the figures of Tarot cards. *Eunuchs of the Forbidden City* (1971) sardonically captures the corrupt history of Tsu Hsi, the last empress of China. *Galas* (1983) is a tribute to Maria Callas.

In March 1987 Ludlam was diagnosed with pneumocystis pneumonia and died two months later, at the age of forty-four, in Manhattan's St. Vincent's Hospital, extinguishing prematurely a shining light of downtown theatre. A front-page obituary in the *New York Times* proclaimed Ludlam "one of the most innovative and prolific artists in the theatre avant-garde."[11] Everett Quinton, Ludlam's partner, tried to no avail to keep the Ridiculous Theatrical Company going; after a two-year financial struggle, he decided to throw in the towel.

Acting Edition: Samuel French, Inc.; *The Mystery of Irma Vep* is also included in *The Complete Plays of Charles Ludlam* (Harper & Row, 1989).

Awards and Honors: *The Mystery of Irma Vep* was the recipient of a Drama Desk Award and an Obie Award for Ensemble Performance, both in 1985, as well as a 1999 Lucille Lortel Award for Outstanding Revival. Charles Ludlam won a 1973 Obie Award for Distinguished Performances in *Corn* and *Camille*, and a 1987 Obie for Sustained Achievement. He also won the 1986 Rosamund Gilder Award for distinguished achievement in the theatre. Ludlam garnered fellowships from the Guggenheim, Rockefeller, and Ford Foundations, and grants from the National Endowment for the Arts and the New York State Council on the Arts. In December 1987, New York City named a short block fronting his theatre in Sheridan Square "Charles Ludlam Lane." The New York Public Library for the Performing Arts hosted an exhibition dedicated to the plays of Charles Ludlam on January 11–March 5, 2005. Later that year, Michael Baron wrote and directed a nostalgic tribute to Ludlam, *The Whore of Sheridan Square*, which performed for several weeks at off-off-Broadway's La Mama Experimental Theatre Club. On August 19–22, 2010, Ludlam was remembered by the screening in New York of "Charles Ludlam on Film," a collection of short, silent, unfinished, and rarely seen films that he directed and acted.

NOTES

1. Louis Feuillade (1873–1925) was born in Lunel, France, to a family of modest wine merchants. At a young age, he developed a keen interest in poetry and drama. Feuillade went to Paris in 1898 and after several years of struggle and poverty, he started to sell screenplays to Gaumont, soon getting a chance to direct them himself. In 1907, Feuillade was appointed artistic director of the company. By 1925, the year of his death, he had made more than 600 silent films (many ten

minutes long) in a wide variety of genres—comedies, bourgeois dramas, biblical epics, exotic adventures, and complex mysteries. Feuillade is most remembered for his masterful, crime-tinged silent serials *Fantômas* (1913–1914), *Les Vampires* (1915), *Judex* (1916), and *Barrabas* (1919). He is credited with launching many of the thriller techniques used by Fritz Lang, Robert Siodmak, Alfred Hitchcock, and others. *Irma Vep*, a 1996 movie made by French director Olivier Assayas, starring Hong Kong actress Maggie Cheung, is the story of a film company's disastrous attempt to remake Louis Feuillade's *Les Vampires*.

2. Rick Roemer, *Charles Ludlam and the Ridiculous Theatrical Company* (Jefferson, N.C.: McFarland, 1998), 136.

3. Roemer, *Charles Ludlam*, 138.

4. *New York Times*, October 4, 1984.

5. *American Weekly*, October 17, 1984.

6. *Baltimore Sun*, May 2, 1991.

7. *Baltimore Sun*, November 15, 2009.

8. *New York Times*, January 24, 1993.

9. http://www.curtainup.com/irmavep.html.

10. http://www.chicagocritic.com/mystery-of-irma-vep.

11. Quoted in David Kaufman's *Ridiculous! The Theatrical Life and Times of Charles Ludlam* (New York: Applause, 2002), ix.

Cliffhanger (1985)

James Yaffe (United States, 1927–)

James Yaffe's sole contribution to Broadway was *The Deadly Game* (1960), his adaptation of a radio play by Swiss playwright Friedrich Dürrenmatt. In a secluded Alpine retreat, three retired men of law—a judge, a prosecutor, and a defense attorney—relive their glory days by playing legal charades with stranded strangers. In the background hovers the ominous gaunt figure of a fourth elderly gentleman, who has served the municipality as its official hangman.

The Deadly Game received mixed reviews, ran for thirty-nine performances, had a somewhat longer span in London during the 1966–1967 season, and, slightly revised, was presented off-Broadway in 1966 for 105 showings. The play was televised in India (1971), Italy (1972), and the United States (1982).

Yaffe's 1985 *Cliffhanger*, "A Thriller in Two Acts," has not reached New York but made its rounds in the hinterland. Unlike *The Deadly Game*, the play is light in texture. The curtain rises on the house of Henry Lowenthal, a sixtyish philosophy professor. It is late May, the end of the semester. The professor sits in an easy chair in the living room, reading a book while his middle-aged wife, Polly, is in the pantry, preparing a pot of coffee and humming a jaunty tune. Henry is expecting his appointment to an endowed chair so that he and his wife can enjoy their golden years with honor and dignity.

The warm, cozy atmosphere changes with the arrival of Henry's successor, Edith Wilshire, who brusquely announces that she will not recommend him for the position. Edith's manner is so calculated and cruel, that the usually gentle professor seizes a bust of Socrates and strikes his tormentor a heavy blow. Edith gasps, blood spurts from her mouth, then she sinks to the floor, a dead weight.

Recapturing his equanimity, Henry intends to call the police, but Polly stops him. They begin to hatch a foolproof way to dispose of the body. Complications arise in the form of a rather odd student, Melvin McMullen, who happened to witness the professor's violent action from the window. Melvin is willing to keep mum if the professor agrees to elevate his failing grade and let him pass the course. Henry sends him packing. The curtain of the first scene comes down when the professor and his wife, both in a trance, pick up the body and begin to carry it outside. They intend to load Edith into her car and drive to "some cliff or precipice or something."

A police lieutenant, Dave DeVito, arrives on the scene. He is in his thirties, described as "tall, husky, but with an earnest manner and a hint of sensibility." DeVito explains to the Lowenthals that even though Professor Wilshire obviously died by accident, when an experienced climber falls off a mountain, it's possible that she committed suicide. Henry states that "it really isn't conceivable. . . . She was so attached to life." The lieutenant mentions that the Phi Beta Kappa key that Professor Wilshire always carried on a chain is missing and cannot be found.

When DeVito leaves, Henry and Polly scurry around in panic, searching for the key. They are on their knees when Melvin McMullen wanders in through the front door. He watches them with mild curiosity, and finally speaks up: "Is this what you're looking for?" He takes the chain and the Phi Beta Kappa key from his pocket, dangles it in front of the shocked Lowenthals, and, with a smirk, again proposes an exchange: his silence against Henry's promise that he won't flunk him in Ethics.

Henry loses his cool and picks up the Socrates bust. Melville rushes out, and a moment later his motorbike can be heard racing away. The Lowenthals believe that all is lost, when Lieutenant DeVito arrives with an astounding bit of information: the student Melvin McMullen showed up at the police station. He looked shifty and overexcited, so they took his prints—and they were the same as the set found on a wineglass inside Professor Wilshire's cabin. They frisked Melvin and found in his pocket the Phi Beta Kappa key. Obviously, the murderer had torn it off while struggling with her. DeVito laughs and relates that Melvin told him a cock-and-bull story about Henry, blaming the professor for the murder.

DeVito admits with a red face that Melvin "kinda stole my gun," escaped from the police station, and disappeared on his motorbike. Henry attempts to tell DeVito the truth but the lieutenant brushes him off and leaves.

Henry puts on a record—"I've Got You Under My Skin"—and he and Polly start dancing a fox-trot, vintage 1940s. As they move about, there is a stirring in the pantry. The sheets part and Melvin rises to a sitting position. He is a horrendous sight—face caked with blood, clothing torn, eyes wild. Holding a gun, he cautiously crosses to the living room. "I'm going to kill you, Professor," he says. "Both of you!"

Henry attempts to calm Melvin by promising to go to the police and confess. But the student continues to babble, inadvertently revealing that he had killed Professor Wilshire when she refused to authorize a change in his grade. He pushed Wilshire over a cliff. When she was earlier thrown over the edge by the Lowenthals, the chairwoman fell only three feet down into a little hollow. She came climbing up, fuming. "It was the wrong time to ask about my grade, I guess," states Melvin. She laughed at him and Melvin picked up a rock and hit her. When he pushed Wilshire down, he made sure she fell all the way.

Henry rebukes Polly for her mistake in checking Wilshire's pulse and is happily dumbfounded by the fact that he did not murder the chairwoman. Melvin retreats toward the hallway and complains that people always believe him to be a weakling. He exclaims, "I'll show you who's a weakling" and once more points the gun. At this moment DeVito appears behind him, picks up the bust of Socrates, and brings it down on Melvin's head. The student falls to the ground.

Soon DeVito hauls a groaning Melvin to his feet and hustles him to the hallway. Henry stops him, still feeling that he should tell the police lieutenant the whole story. But Polly puts her hand on Henry's arm and pleads, "Once in your life, you *will* be practical, won't you?" Henry throws up his hands, a gesture of surrender, and bids DeVito goodbye.

Polly now begins to convince Henry to forget about retirement and become Chairman of the Philosophy Department, now that both Edith and Melvin won't bother him any more.

First produced at the Alliance Theatre in Atlanta, Georgia, *Cliffhanger* was presented at the Lamb's Theatre, in New York City, on February 7, 1985, directed by David McKenna. Henry and Polly Lowenthal were portrayed by Henderson Forsythe and Lenka Peterson. Vintage Theatre presented the play as part of its Summer of Suspense '96 series, at the Corning, New York Glass Center. Amnon Kabatchnik directed. *Cliffhanger*'s box-office receipts exceeded those of such classics as *Ten Little Indians* and *Dial "M" for Murder*. Pennsylvania's Bristol Riverside Theatre mounted *Cliffhanger* in August 2004, while Broadway Onstage Live Theatre of Eastpointe, Michigan produced the play in January 2005.

* * *

James Yaffe was born in 1927 in Chicago to a middle-class Jewish family. He attended Yale University from 1944 to 1948, graduating summa cum laude. In 1948 he began to contribute episodes to television's *Studio One*. During the 1950s and 1960s he wrote for *The United States Steel Hour*, *The Elgin Hour*, *The Defenders*, *The Nurses*, and *The Alfred Hitchcock Hour*.

Beginning with 1953's *The Good-for-Nothing*, Yaffe published several novels, often capturing the milieu of his upbringing. That same year he started penning crime stories for *Ellery Queen Mystery Magazine*. In 1958, Yaffe based his novel *Nothing But the Night* on the Nathan Leopold-Richard Loeb murder case of 1924.

Following *The Deadly Game* and prior to *Cliffhanger*, Yaffe came up with *Ivory Tower* (1969), coauthored with Jerome Weidman, a courtroom drama that played in various resident theatres. The protagonist, Simon Otway, a famous American writer who lived in Paris during World War II, is accused of treason for calling on the invading Allied forces, in several radio broadcasts, to lay down their arms and stop the bloodshed. By the end of a prosecutor's grueling cross-examination, Otway begins to crack and eventually, in tears, admits that his broadcasts caused American soldiers to die.

One hopes that the deadly events of *Cliffhanger* are not autobiographical, but it should be noted that since 1981 James Yaffe has been an English professor and writer-in-residence at Colorado College in Colorado Springs. Yaffe's series character, Mom, introduced in the *Ellery Queen Mystery Magazine* and catapulted to hardcover in *A Nice Murder for Mom* (1988), followed her son Dave from the Bronx out to Mesa Grande, Colorado, where the quick-witted Jewish mother solves crimes over Sunday brunches and homemade chicken soup. The focal point of *A Nice Murder for Mom* is the simmering rivalry between two college professors that reaches a deadly conclusion. A subsequent novel, *Mom Doth Murder Sleep* (1991), reveals that the hallowed community theatre is nothing but a cesspool of intrigue, mayhem, and bloodshed. The seventy-five-year-old sleuth gets entangled with the murder of an actor in a production of *Macbeth*. There are several more novels in the series, published by St. Martin's Press. The complete "Mom" short stories are collected in *My Mother, the Detective*, published in 1997 by Crippen and Landru.

Acting Edition: Dramatists Play Service.

Awards and Honors: James Yaffe's *The Deadly Game* was a top-ten selection in *The Best Plays of 1959–1960*.

The Mystery of Edwin Drood (1985)

Book, Music, and Lyrics by Rupert Holmes
(England/United States, 1947–)

Charles Dickens, the great English author, inserted elements of crime in many of his books. *Oliver Twist* (1837–1839) introduces a gallery of underworld characters dominated by Fagin and Bill Sikes. The plot of *Barnaby Rudge* (1841) revolves around two murders and mistaken identities. *Martin Chuzzlewit* (1843–1844) is populated with corrupt, greedy, and scheming hucksters on both sides of the Atlantic. *Bleak House* (1852–1853) features Inspector Bucket, the first signature detective-hero in English literature, investigating a tale of murder in which an innocent suspect has been arrested on circumstantial evidence. *Hunted Down* (1859) is a story about murder-for-insurance-money. London police officers play prominent roles in *Great Expectations* (1861) and *Our Mutual Friend* (1864–1865).

Dickens's bona fide detective novel, perhaps written to compete with the success of *The Moonstone* (1868) by his friend Wilkie Collins, was *The Mystery of Edwin Drood* (1870). The novel was to consist of twelve monthly installments in *All the Year Round* but the story remained unfinished at Dickens's death. Regrettably, he left no notes indicating how the plot would proceed or what the conclusion was to be. Dickens's secret died with him.

The main character of *The Mystery of Edwin Drood* is John Jasper, a young choirmaster at Cloisterham Cathedral, the guardian of his orphan nephew, Edwin Drood, who is a few years Jasper's junior. In spite of his position of trust, Jasper is an opium addict. Drood, an apprentice engineer, is engaged to Rosa Bud, a beauty attending a finishing school in Cloisterham. The late fathers of Edwin and Rosa had been close friends and each had requested in his will that their children marry one another. As the years passed, however, Edwin and Rosa realized that they were not in love and had no desire to tie the knot.

Rosa realizes that Jasper is in love with her. Afraid of his infatuation, Rosa does not dare to tell anyone about it, but, ill at ease in his presence, she ceases to study music with him.

Two youths from Ceylon—now called Sri Lanka—arrive on the scene, an English brother and sister orphaned in the far-off island. The girl, Helena Landless, joins Rosa's class at finishing school. Neville Landless begins study under one of the officials at the Cathedral, Reverend Crisparkle. Crisparkle introduces the newcomers to his friends Jasper and Drood. Neville Landless and Rosa Bud fall for one another. Jasper, distraught, takes note of a quarrel that developed between Neville, who has a volatile temper, and Edwin.

At one of his clandestine visits to an opium den, Jasper meets Durdles, a cemetery caretaker. Durdles guides Jasper on a dead-of-night tour of old crypts beneath the Cathedral. Jasper steals a key to an underground tomb from Durdles's pocket.

During the next Christmas season, Reverend Crisparkle attempts to patch up the animosity between Landless and Drood. After mutual apologies and a congenial evening together, the two young men take a walk. On Christmas morning, Drood is reported missing by his uncle. Drood's body is not found, but his watch and pin are discovered on the riverbank. Landless is accused of foul play.

Rosa and Helena are convinced of Landless's innocence and win Crisparkle over to their side. The Reverend vouches for Landless and helps him leave Cloisterham for a refuge in London. Jasper vows to unearth evidence to incriminate the murderer. He meets Rosa and as they walk in the school garden, he confesses his love for her. Jasper warns Rosa that he has sufficient evidence to send Neville Landless to the gallows and will use his knowledge unless Rosa agrees to marry him.

Rosa leaves school and goes to London, where she seeks the protection of her old guardian, the lawyer Hiram Grewgious. Grewgious arranges to have Rosa remain in safe lodgings in London.

One day, a white-haired stranger arrives in Cloisterham. He introduces himself as Dick Datchery and takes rooms across from Jasper's home. He constantly sits behind an open door. Whenever he hears a remark about John Jasper, he makes a chalk mark on the inside of the door. His curiosity evidently piques when he observes a haggard old woman confront Jasper, reminding him that she was the proprietor of an opium den that he had visited and describes an act of violence he committed in a drug-addicted state. Datchery adds another chalk mark to those behind the door.

Here the novel ends, for Dickens died suddenly from a stroke, leaving the narrative incomplete. Many puzzlements remain unsolved: Is Edwin Drood dead? Did John Jasper, a Jekyll and Hyde persona, kill him? Is Dick Datchery a disguised detective? Through the years, many tantalized authors and scholars have attempted to complete the story and have concocted various solutions. Almost all are in agreement that John Jasper either murdered or attempted to murder Edwin Drood. Did Drood survive a murderous assault by his uncle?

Allen I. Borowitz elaborates in *The Armchair Detective* on "the psychological significance of Jasper's crime. For Edmund Wilson, Jasper represents, like [Dostoyevsky's] Raskolnikov, the duality of man and his innate simultaneous capacity for good and evil. Jasper lives in the respectable milieu of Victorian society and at the same time is what today we might call a 'drop-out'; he is a dope addict and a brutal murderer."[1] A 1935 motion picture version, scripted by John L. Balderston and Gladys Unger, depicts Jasper (played by Claude Rains) as the murderer of his nephew Drood (David Manners), with Neville Landless (Douglass Montgomery) impersonating old Datchery to unravel the mystery. In the end, Jasper, cornered, escapes to the belfry of the Cathedral, where he jumps to his death.

Other scholars believe that Drood did not die but returned to Cloisterham disguised as Datchery, carefully monitoring his uncle's movements and awaiting an opportunity to avenge the attempted killing. Dissenting theories regarding Datchery's identity focus on Neville or Helena Landless, Rosa Bud, and Hiram Grewgious. A far-fetched speculation depicts the Opium Woman as Jasper's mother. On one assumption all the literary investigators agree: *Edwin Drood*, if completed, would have been a great, perhaps the greatest, detective novel.

* * *

The Mystery of Edwin Drood was adapted to the stage by Walter Thompson (Surrey Theatre, London, November 4, 1871) and by J. W. Comyns Carr (His Majesty's Theatre, London, January 4, 1908). Almost eight decades later, Rupert Holmes, a composer and arranger of pop albums, wrote the book, music, and lyrics of his first full-scale musical, basing it on the Dickens novel. "Though the show is set in 1880, I didn't want to write Gilbert and Sullivan-styled music," Holmes told interviewer Stephen Holden of the *New York Times*. "It is a composite of influences, from the Episcopalian hymnal, English vaudeville music, Gilbert and Sullivan, and traditional Broadway."[2] Produced by the New York Shakespeare Festival, *The Mystery of Edwin Drood* debuted at Central Park's Delacorte Theatre on August 21, 1985.

The curtain rises on Mr. William Cartwright, the Chairman of the Music Hall Royale Company, who welcomes the audience to the premiere presentation of *The Mystery of Edwin Drood*. It is 1873. Members of the troupe, scattered in the auditorium, join the chairman in singing "There You Are," introducing the show as "a musicale with dramatic interludes." The chairman explains that since Mr. Dickens didn't live to finish the story, the audience will be asked to vote upon key questions regarding the outcome of the plot. The chairman further advises "those among you who arrived alone" that they may find the ingénues willing to provide companionship during the show and beyond; however, "all goods are to be returned tomorrow morning, none the worse for wear."

The chairman raps his gavel and the play begins. The lights fade up to reveal the home of John Jasper. A church organ plays a somber recessional hymn as Jasper enters in cassock, robe, and scarf. The chairman introduces him as "choirmaster, composer, organist, and vocal instructor," played by "your very own Mr. Clive Paget." Paget/Jasper, obviously the principal thespian of Theatre Royale, acknowledges the ensuing applause with a rakish smile, then instantly steps into character and croons, as Jasper, "A Man Could Go Quite Mad," complaining of boredom that "grinds my brain down to the grain."

The chairman introduces Mr. Cedric Moncrieffe as the Reverend Septimus Crisparkle. In character, the reverend enters Jasper's home, comments that the choirmaster looks "a little worn," and departs as Edwin Drood arrives. Drood is portrayed by Miss Alice Nutting, wearing moustache, cap, and trousers "to charming effect."

Uncle and nephew raise a cup of wine to Rosa Bud, betrothed to Drood. Drood emotes moodily that their late parents had arranged their marriage "at birth." The young man observes that Jasper looks "frightfully ill." His uncle forces a smile and mumbles that he has been forced of late to seek treatment in London for "a condition," which later turns out to be his opium addiction. Drood is concerned. They clasp hands and croon "Two Kinsmen," expressing mutual devotion.

The conservatory of the Nun's House, a seminary for young women in Cloisterham—a charming room with a piano near French windows, beyond which are trellises and the hint of foliage—is revealed. Several young girls giggle and twitter around the room. They scatter when Jasper enters with a music manuscript in hand. Jasper wishes Rosa "the happiest of birthdays." As a birthday present, he has written a love ballad for her, "Moonfall." Rosa is reluctant to sing it but yields to Jasper's insistence. Her emotional tension is evident.

Reverend Crisparkle enters with Neville Landless and his twin sister, Helena, and introduces them as orphaned visitors from Ceylon. Now their brutish stepfather has also died and they have come to start a new life in Cloisterham. Neville has been entrusted to his care and Helena will be living at Nun's House. "It was well my stepfather died when he did, or I might have killed him," confesses Neville, who is ultimately revealed as hot-tempered, a meaningful bit of information. He confides that "Helena tried on more than one occasion to flee their stepfather's cruel and miserly hand, even disguising herself as a boy," a statement that may later be interpreted as a clue. Neville is dazzled by Rosa and learns that she is engaged to Edwin Drood. Helena and Rosa establish a rapport.

Chairman Cartwright introduces "the Clown Prince of the Music Hall Royale," Nick Cricker, who is to play Durdles, the caretaker of the Cathedral's tombs, and Cricker's son, "following in his old dad's footsteps," who is portraying Deputy, the caretaker's boy-assistant. The stage manager of the company, James Throttle, enters and whispers a hurried word in the chairman's ear. After an awkward pause, Cartwright tells the audience that the actor cast in the role of Thomas Sapsea, the town's mayor, will not be appearing tonight due to an incident in an adjacent bar. He himself, Chairman William Cartwright, will undertake the role. Sapsea's wife has passed away and Durdles displays a ring of keys, unlocks the door leading to the catacombs beneath the Cathedral, and ushers the mayor in. "The crypt is a national treasure," announces Durdles to the audience, and adds pointedly, "Just a while ago, Mr. Jasper asked if I'd take him down into the crypts to see it."

Eerie music starts softly as the action shifts to an opium den, operated by Princess Puffer (played by Miss Angela Prysock), in the East End of London. Puffer sips gin and fills clay pipes for her nearly comatose clients. She bemoans the fact that "crime don't pay" and "there ain't much profit in the wages of sin." In bed 11, John Jasper bolts up from beneath the blanket and calls for laudanum so that he will be able to continue with his hallucination of Rosa Bud. "I must be rid of him," he whispers in a daze, and his dream is manifested with the ballet "Jasper's Vision." Two opium smokers begin a languid struggle to the death and Jasper watches with fascination as a murder transpires.

Reverend Crisparkle is chatting amiably with Rosa and Drood as they stroll down Cloisterham's High Street. They meet the Landless twins. Drood talks of his grand plan to travel with Rosa to Egypt where he'll take over his family's engineering company and build a road from Cairo to Alexandria with stones taken from the pyramids. The idea of such desecration of ancient monuments angers Neville and a verbal rift ensues. Jasper and Sapsea enter and listen. Jasper remarks that he fears "the hot-blooded Eastern temperament of Neville. . . . There is something of the tiger in his blood." Jasper theorizes on the duality of human nature; he senses that "beneath Neville's tainted English accent and adopted English manners, there is a heathen Landless, a tribesman Landless, a half-blooded, half-bred half-caste who would kill as easily as he would comb his sleek hair!" Sapsea is skeptical but Jasper sings "Both Sides of the Coin," at the end of which the mayor promises to keep a careful eye upon the duplicitous Neville Landers.

With a musical shiver, the scene changes to a chamber within the crypts. Labyrinthine corridors are implied. To the left is the prominently labeled tomb of Mrs. Thomas Sapsea. Jasper emerges from the mausoleum, a lantern in his hand. We see Durdles lying semi-comatose near the foot of a stone stairwell. Jasper holds up Durdles' keys and removes one of them. He is suddenly startled to hear a sound from above and watches in terror as Deputy twists his way down the staircase looking for his master. Stepping from the shadows, Jasper seizes Deputy violently. The boy, held by the throat, goes limp just as Durdles stirs. Jasper changes his raging disposition to benign concern and bends over Deputy, presumably to aid him. "You are ripe for the asylum, Mr. Jasper," cries Deputy before rushing up the stairs.

Durdles comes out of his wine-induced daze, notices his key ring on the floor, and realizes that the key to the tomb of Mayor Sapsea's wife is missing. Jasper expresses his puzzlement, and the two men mount the stairs.

On Christmas Eve, Edwin and Rosa stroll near the ruins of Cloisterham. They finally articulate their real feelings with the song "Perfect Strangers" and vow to remain close, like brother and sister. Rosa gives Edwin a clasp of her mother's, symbolizing their enduring friendship. Edwin believes that the breaking-off of their engagement will come as "a terrible blow" to his uncle Jasper. Rosa asks that they keep their change of plans from him for a while.

With Christmas music in the background, a thunderstorm is approaching and dinner is being served at Jasper's home. The guests include Reverend Crisparkle, Neville and Helena, Drood and Rosa. Soon Neville and Drood begin to clash and their animosity toward one another is evident in the song "No Good Can Come From Bad." Drood pulls the carving knife savagely from the bird; Neville does likewise with the carving fork. They almost cross swords but eventually the two are persuaded to shake hands and, as Jasper pours more wine, become inebriated.

The wind howls. Drood decides to saunter down to the River Weir to observe the storm. Neville offers to join him while Reverend Crisparkle will escort the ladies home. Jasper lends Drood his caped coat. The sky erupts as the guests depart.

The next day, Christmas, the storm has subsided. The chairman announces that Edwin Drood has disappeared. There has been no sign of him since he went walking with Neville the previous evening. Rosa, concerned, prays for Drood's safety. Reverend Crisparkle sends his assistant Bazzard to see if there is any news. There isn't.

Jasper and Mayor Sapsea huddle on a street corner. They are certain that murder has been committed and Jasper points out that Neville Landless was seen fleeing the district. A search ensues. Dogs are heard barking in the background, and villagers cry, "There he is!" and "Stop! Stop!" Deputy rushes in and exclaims, "We've hunted down Neville Landless." Bazzard enters and exhibits a coat he's discovered under a rock by the river. Jasper identifies it as his coat, the one he gave Drood the night before. The coat has been badly torn and is bloodstained. Jasper tells Bazzard that from now on he'll be devoting himself to "fasten the crime of murder upon the murderer."

Jasper exits. Philip Bax (Bazzard) and William Cartwright (Sapsea) step out of their *Edwin Drood* roles briefly. They wonder why Charles Dickens wrote in the small role of Bazzard unless he intended something significant for Crisparkle's assistant later in the plot. Kindly, the chairman allows Bax/ Bazzard to sing a song he has written, "Never the Luck." The thespian seizes the moment, hoping to "waltz" his way into the audience's heart. Several sympathetic actors step quietly from the wings to observe.

On applause, Neville Landless is pushed on stage by townspeople, who kick him and hurl abuse. Reverend Crisparkle separates Landless from his assailants. Rosa watches fearfully. Jasper, wearing a black armband, argues that the temperamental stranger was the last person to spend time with the missing Drood. Neville states that he does not recall the events by the river for he was under the influence of the potent wine poured last night by Jasper. Mayor Sapsea inquires about bloodstains found on Neville's shirtfront. Neville explains that the stains occurred when he was forcefully dragged by the men to this encounter. Horace, the district's constable, places Neville under arrest for murder. Helena defends her brother by pointing out that no body has been found. All agree that this is legally true; Neville is released.

Jasper corners Rosa. She flinches but summons up the resolve to tell him that she will no longer take musical instruction from him. Jasper smiles, twists her arm, and confesses that he loves her "madly." Rosa is gripped in fascinated terror. They reprise "The Name of Love" and "Moonfall" as a blood-red moon emerges from the clouds. The Cathedral bell chimes midnight and the curtain falls.

Six months have passed, and there has been no sign of Edwin Drood. Act 2's curtain rises on the mail train pulling into Cloisterham Station. John Jasper, dressed in mourning, gets off the train, back from another "treatment" in London. The chairman announces that "two Enquiring Sleuths are about to appear on the scene"—Princess Puffer, the old hag we met at the opium den, and Dick Datchery, "a ragged bundle of a man with a long platinum hair and beard." Puffer and Datchery step from the train and head downstage simultaneously, oblivious to each other. They sing "Setting Up the Score," relating that they came to Cloisterham "on the scent" to solve the mystery of Edwin Drood's disappearance.

On High Street, Reverend Crisparkle encounters Mayor Sapsea and tells him that his assistant Bazzard is away on business. It is unclear at this point whether that bit of information is a clue or a red herring. Datchery asks for lodging near the Cathedral and the mayor mentions an available room in the upstairs of Jasper's house. Datchery exits, limping pronouncedly. All, including Puffer, feel that there is something suspicious about Datchery but the mayor warns against jumping to premature conclusions. Sapsea, Durdles, and Deputy croon "Off to the Races," in which they agree that "quick conclusions often lead the best of us astray."

Rosa and Helena enter. At the sight of Rosa, Princess Puffer is stunned and gasps for breath. Apparently she now has "one of the bits of information" for which she came to Cloisterham. Determined to get the rest, she sings "Don't Quit While You're Ahead." The entire company joins for a reprise but their voices and the music abruptly cease. The orchestra members frantically thumb through their music looking for the next page of the score. The actors step out of character and anxiously peer in the direction of the chairman as if to ask what's going on. The audience may get the uncomfortable feeling that something has gone wrong, that the play has collapsed. The chairman steps forward and says with great sadness, "Ladies and gentlemen, it was at this point in our story that Mr. Charles Dickens laid down his pen forever. And so, my dear friends, this is all we shall ever know for sure about the Mystery of Edwin Drood. Tonight, however, at least within the confines of this humble theatre, we shall together solve, resolve and conclude (gavel once) The Mystery (gavel twice) of Edwin Drood (final gavel)."

The chairman explains that most literary experts agree that Dick Datchery is actually someone "we have already met," a character from act 1 who is roaming Cloisterham disguised as Datchery so as to better investigate the disappearance of Drood. The role of Datchery, continues the chairman, has been portrayed by that mistress of male impersonation, Miss Alice Nutting, who has also appeared as Edwin Drood. With a flourish, Datchery twirls off his/her coat, beard, and wig to reveal, in abbreviated costume and tights, a fetching Alice. But, warns the chairman, this does not mean that Edwin Drood is Dick Datchery, nor does it mean that Drood is necessarily alive.

> CHAIRMAN: Which brings us to our first key question: Is Edwin Drood dead—or alive? Mr. Charles Dickens experimented with many different titles for our story, for example:
> NUTTING/DROOD: The Loss of Edwin Drood
> CONOVER/HELENA: The Flight of Edwin Drood
> GRINSTEAD/NEVILLE: The Disappearance of Edwin Drood
> CHAIRMAN: But nowhere the Death or Murder of Edwin Drood.

Then the chairman asks the cast to vote about the fate of Edwin Drood and they unanimously agree that Drood is dead—except for Alice Nutting, who maintains that Drood is alive, blames her colleagues for petty jealousy, and stalks out in a huff.

The next question is "Who is Datchery?" Helena in disguise, a trick she used when fleeing her cruel stepfather as a child? Neville, trying to clear his name? Reverend Crisparkle, responsible for Neville, aiming to clear his ward's name? Bazzard, the reverend's assistant, who may, or not, have gone away on business? Rosa—did she take it upon herself to investigate the disappearance of her fiancé? The chairman asserts that Datchery is definitely not John Jasper, Durdles, Deputy, Mayor Sapsea, or Princess Puffer, for they all shared—in Mr. Dickens's novel and in our play—scenes with him.

The chairman calls for a vote by audience applause to determine Datchery's identity. The character chosen leaves the stage to change costume into Datchery's disguise.

The last question is "Who is the murderer?" John Jasper, the obvious villain of the piece? Did Rosa Bud mean to kill Jasper in revenge for his lustful advances, but killed Drood by mistake, as he was wearing Jasper's coat? Did temperamental Neville Landers murder Drood in lieu of their continuous rift and thereby eliminate a rival for Rosa Bud? Aware of her brother's uncontrollable temper, did Helena Landless kill Drood so that Neville would not be tempted to do so? Did Reverend Crisparkle believe Jasper to be the incarnation of Satan and killed Drood accidently because he was wearing Jasper's coat? Did Princess Puffer make the same mistake while intending to kill Jasper in order to protect Rosa from his advances? And, perhaps most far-fetched, did Bazzard murder Drood in an effort to boost his role in the show?

While the chairman and the suspects reprise "Setting Up the Score," the lights come up in the auditorium, members of the cast circulate among the viewers and tally hand-raised votes. At last the chairman declares, "Ladies and Gentlemen, we have determined the murderer in our midst!"

It is dawn as the curtain rises on the streets of Cloisterham. Princess Puffer is asleep in a corner of the Cathedral. Rosa Bud, dressed for a journey, is hurrying along. The princess stops Rosa and relates that she knew her when she was an infant; she was Rosa's nanny. Since those days, the princess sings, she has been on "The Garden Path To Hell"—betrayed by a man, taking to drink, losing her looks, becoming a drug addict. There immediately follows "Puffer's Confession," in which the old woman tells how a while back, one of her clients ordered laudanum wine and cried out "Rosa Bud."

Puffer accuses Jasper of being the murderer. The choirmaster is dragged from his house by Constable Horace and other villagers. With maniacal joy he sings "Jasper's Confession," admitting that he strangled his nephew when drunk.

Durdles, the gravedigger, who has been loitering about, bursts forward and bellows, "You're a bad one, Jasper, but you're not a murderer!"

Durdles explains that on that stormy night he saw Jasper carry Edwin Drood to the Cathedral and down to the crypt, depositing the body in the tomb of Mrs. Sapsea. But, says Durdles, the young man was still alive. Another person crept in and throttled Edwin Drood. There was a flash of lightning—and he saw who it was!

Durdles savors the moment as he regards the candidates—Bazzard, Reverend Crisparkle, Helena Landless, Neville Landless, Princess Puffer, and Rosa Bud. The audience is questioned again. Five different versions of the song "Murderer's Confession" are available, one of them to be sung according to the identity of the culprit. If Bazzard is the murderer, he expresses his joy in at last being the object of everyone's attention. "I saw the chance to be a legend in my time," he sings. If Crisparkle is the murderer, we see a gradual change transform him into a fanatic, capable of getting rid of the "Satan" Jasper, but mistakenly killing his nephew, who was wearing Jasper's coat. Also confessing to the same mistake are Helena, Princess Puffer, and Rosa, who collapses center-stage, pounding the ground as she moans, "I killed my good, true Ned." If the murderer is Neville; the man from Ceylon went after his rival for the affections of Rosa.

The chairman stresses the need for a happy ending. He asks the audience to resolve one final question: Which two in our story shall be our lovers tonight and live happily ever after? The chairman names "the lovely Miss Rosa Bud," "Temptress Helena Landless," and "the highly experienced Princess Puffer." The men include Mayor Thomas Sapsea, the Reverend Crisparkle, Neville Landless, John Jasper, Durdles, and Bazzard. The audience votes again, by applause, and a brief scene commences to go with each possible pairing.

After the happy couple reprises "Perfect Strangers," the chairman wonders what Edwin Drood might say if he could speak from beyond the grave. There is ominous rumbling beneath the ground. Suddenly, the crypt of Mrs. Sapsea rises from below as it pushes stone and dusty earth aside. From its doorway emerges a cheery Edwin Drood!

Drood declares, "I'm alive! Halloo all!" and sings "The Writing on the Wall," ready to reveal what really happened on the night of his disappearance. He found himself awake in "dark beyond belief," fought for every breath down in the crypt, and managed to escape. He didn't return to Cloisterham until he could discern who attempted to kill him.

The band plays "Don't Quit While You're Ahead" as the cast takes their individual and company bows.

* * *

The Mystery of Edwin Drood was presented by the New York Shakespeare Festival at Central Park's Delacorte Theatre on August 4, 1985, with a press opening on August 21. The musical was directed by Wilford Leach and choreographed by Graciela Daniele. The cast included George Rose (Chairman William Cartwright/Mayor Thomas Sapsea), Howard McGillin (Clive Paget/John Jasper), Betty Buckley (Alice Nutting/Edwin Drood), Patti Cohenour (Deirdre Peregrine/Rosa Bud), Jane Schneider (Janet Conover/Helena Landless), and John Herrera (Victor Grimstead/Neville Landless).

The critics issued split verdicts. Frank Rich described the musical as "jolly and rollicking," attributing its "ingenuity" to Rupert Holmes, "the author of the show's book, music and lyrics."[3] Howard Kissel stated, "With great skill and smoothness, Holmes turns both words and music into a more serious direction, achieving remarkable depth and beauty."[4] Patricia O'Haire enjoyed "the play-ending lottery where the audiences hisses, boos, applauds and votes on who they feel should be the villain of the piece."[5] John Beaufort lauded "the incomparable George Rose as the actor-manager and master of ceremonies" and the "excellent cast of singing actors."[6]

Conversely, Sylviane Gold believed that "Mr. Holmes's music, lyrics and book all take themselves much too seriously. . . . The work is at odds with itself: the music-hall approach undercuts the musical's essential seriousness, while the dramatic duets and trios and sextets weigh down the lighter music-hall elements."[7] Linda Winer complained that "Dickens' storytelling genius has vanished in Holmes's adaptation. Instead of trusting the characters and the mystery to build their own suspense, *Drood* undercuts its momentum with cutesy tangents. . . . Things don't perk up until the audience choose the murderer, who confesses in song. Long before that, however, it's hard to care who did what to whom."[8]

There were also mixed evaluations regarding the contributions by director Wilford Leach ("might have been more inspired in his staging") and choreographer Graciela Daniele ("choreography is downright dreary").

The Mystery of Edwin Drood ran for twenty-four performances and, slightly revised, transferred to Broadway's Imperial Theatre on December 2, 1985. Critics Frank Rich, Howard Kissel, and John Beaufort again sang the praises of the "rich score by adapter-composer Rupert Holmes," the "boisterous, good-humored music hall quality," and George Rose's "grandly comic performance." The reviewers concluded that *Edwin Drood* is "as pleasurable an evening as Broadway has seen in years." The show ran for 608 performances. Cast replacements included Loretta Swit and Karen Morrow in the part of Princess Puffer, Donna Murphy and Paige O'Hara in the title role.

Drood opened in London in May 1987. George Rose (later Clive Revill) and Jean Stapleton went on a U.S. National Tour in 1988.

"*Drood* has to be seen in three ways," writes biographer Claire Tomalin in *Charles Dickens: A Life*. "First, as the unfinished mystery which has received

extraordinary attention just because it is a puzzle left by Dickens and offers itself for endless ingenious speculation by those who enjoy thinking
up solutions. Secondly, as half a novel that cannot be regarded as a major
work, and that has divided opinion sharply even among Dickens's warm-
est admirers. . . . And thirdly, as the achievement of a man who is dying
and refusing to die, who would not allow illness and failing powers to keep
him from exerting his imagination, or to prevent him from writing: and as
such it is an astonishing and heroic enterprise."[9]

* * *

His birth name David Goldstein, Rupert Holmes was born in 1947 in
Cheshire, England, to a British mother and an American father, a U.S.
Army officer and bandleader. The family moved to Nanuet, New York,
in 1950, and the boy grew up with music as his major interest. In 1965 he
enrolled in the Manhattan School of Music to study composition. He left
school three years later and became a pop performer-writer-producer. He
played the piano for both The Cuff Links and The Buoys, with whom he
had his first international hit, "Timothy," in 1971. He wrote jingles and
pop tunes for Wayne Newton, Dolly Parton, Barry Manilow, the Plat-
ters, and the Drifters. In 1974, he released his first album, the cult classic
"Widescreen," a collection of cinematically inspired pop songs. Since then
Holmes has enjoyed much success in the popular song market, including
gold albums sung by Barbra Streisand. "Brass Knuckles" was the first
pop song ever reviewed in *Ellery Queen's Mystery Magazine*. "Escape," included in his album *Partners in Crime*, was the last #1 record of the 1970s
and the first #1 record of the 1980s.

Holmes followed *Drood* with two fiendishly clever comedy-thrillers:
Accomplice, a play-within-a-play in which hardly anything is what
it seems (Richard Rodgers Theatre, April 26, 1990—fifty-two performances) and *Solitary Confinement*, bamboozling the viewers from the
moment they open the playbill and read the biographical sketches of
non-existing actors to the final curtain when it is revealed that one
dexterous thespian (Stacy Keach) played a reclusive, eccentric tycoon
and all of the six suspects in a breach of the seemingly secure Jannings
Industries building (Nederlander Theatre, November 8, 1992—twenty-
five performances). Also for Broadway, Holmes penned the hit *Say
Goodnight, Gracie*, inspired by the life and times of comedian George
Burns (Helen Hayes Theatre, October 10, 2002—364 performances). After the death of both librettist Peter Stone and lyricist Fred Ebb, Holmes
joined the creative team of *Curtains*, a parody of murder mystery plots
in which the hated leading lady of "Robbin' Hood of the Old West" is
murdered during the opening night curtain call (Al Hirschfield Theatre,
March 22, 2007—511 performances).

Plays by Holmes that have not made it to Broadway include *The Hamburger Hamlet*, a futuristic, ecological Armageddon comedy about students of a California high school who yearn to reclaim their lost culture and try to piece together fragments of a play called "The Hamlet" by Mister William Shakespeare. Written for young actors, the play was first mounted by the Drama Department of Cleveland University in 1990. With book, music, and lyrics by Holmes, *The Picture of Dorian Gray*, adapted from the novel by Oscar Wilde, previewed in England in 2001. A musicalization of *Marty*, based on the screenplay by Paddy Chayefsky, was first produced at the Huntington Theatre, Boston in 2002 while *The First Wives' Club—The Musical*, based on the film *The First Wives Club*, played at the Old Globe Theatre in San Diego in 2009. Holmes next penned the book for the musical *Robin and the 7 Hoods*, inspired by the film of the same name, presented at the Old Globe in 2010. A stage adaptation of John Grisham's courtroom drama, *A Time to Kill*, premiered at the Arena Stage, Washington, D.C., running in May and June 2011. Criminous elements play a major role in *Goosebumps* (1988), based on the books by R. L. Stine, and *Thumbs* (2001), in which two enterprising women match wits with a devious killer. Future endeavors by Holmes include a revision of Agatha Christie's trial play *Witness for the Prosecution* and, rumor has it, a stage adaptation of Dashiell Hammett's hardboiled novel *The Maltese Falcon*.

For television, Holmes created the 1996 Emmy Award-winning series *Remember WENN* (1996), writing the theme song and all fifty-six episodes. His melodies were incorporated into the soundtrack of many TV shows, including *The Partridge Family*, *The Simpsons*, *ER*, *Six Feet Under*, and *Bewitched*, as well as feature films such as *A Star Is Born*, *Jaws: The Revenge*, *Shrek*, and *Mars Attacks!*

In 2003 Holmes published his first novel, *Where the Truth Lies*, the tale of a vivacious, free-spirited investigative journalist who is bent on unearthing celebrity secrets and gets involved in a long-ago murder. The novel *Swing* (2005) fuses suspense and music in a narrative of intrigue set in 1940, during the big band era. A jazz saxophonist falls for a Berkeley student and finds himself entangled in a sinister coil of spiraling secrets. *The McMasters Guide to Homicide* (2009) describes the inner workings of the McMasters Academy, the world's leading institution devoted to the study of murder.

Theatre critic William F. Hirschman interviewed Rupert Holmes for *Mystery Scene* magazine: "He recognizes a kinship between the skills to puzzle out the plot of a mystery and the equally intricate structuring of a script or a melody or a lyric. 'Lyric writing is like writing a crossword puzzle that has to rhyme,' says Holmes. 'You know the ultimate destination of your lyric and you have to figure out how to get there. . . . I know what the plot hinges on, I know most of the twists. As I get to know my characters, and they become real to me, they usually lead me on a merry chase. They tend to invent stuff and sometimes I'm breathtakingly surprised by what they've done . . . don't think about whether what you're going to write will be clever or fit your message. If you know your characters, what would they really do?' It's a technique that has served him well."[10]

Acting Edition: Tams-Witmark Music Library. The libretto was also published by Nelson Doubleday, Inc.

Awards and Honors: *The Mystery of Edwin Drood* was nominated for eleven 1986 Tony Awards, winning for Best Musical. Rupert Holmes garnered the Tony for Best Book and Best Original Score. The New York Drama Desk presented identical honors to *Drood* and Holmes. The musical won a 1986 Special Edgar Award from the Mystery Writers of America and was a top ten selection in *The Best Plays of 1985–1986*. In 1991, Holmes's *Accomplice* received a Best Play Edgar Award. Two years later, *Say Goodnight, Gracie* was nominated for a Best Play Tony Award. In 2007, *Curtains* was nominated for a Best Musical Tony and Holmes was nominated for Best Book of a Musical; he won the Drama Desk Award for Outstanding Book of a Musical.

NOTES

1. *Armchair Detective* 10, no. 1 (January 1977): 82.
2. *New York Times*, August 2, 1985.
3. *New York Times*, August 23, 1985.
4. *Women's Wear Daily*, August 23, 1985.
5. *Daily News*, August 23, 1985.
6. *Christian Science Monitor*, August 28, 1985.
7. *Wall Street Journal*, August 23, 1985.
8. *USA Today*, August 23, 1985.
9. Claire Tomalin, *Charles Dickens: A Life* (New York: Penguin, 2011), 389.
10. *Mystery Scene* 113 (Winter 2010).

The Mask of Moriarty (1985)
Hugh Leonard (Ireland, 1926–2009)

In an introduction to his published play *The Mask of Moriarty*, Hugh Leonard relates that "a title, *The Face of Moriarty*, shot into my mind, and within a day or two *Face* had become *Mask* to make it alliterative, and also because I probably knew subconsciously that a theme of the play would have to do with identity. Usually, I know hardly anything about a play when I sit down to write it . . . with *Moriarty*, I had my subject ready-made—an adventure-cum-detective story—and two characters known more widely than any figures of history, so I was further along than usual."[1]

The Mask of Moriarty opens on a sketchy setting: the balustrade of Waterloo Bridge. A fog is rolling in from the river. A police constable, Herbert Travesty, ambles along, meets a misshapen man walking with an ape-like crouch, and greets him, "Oh, it's you, sir. Beg pardon, Doctor Jekyll, didn't recognize you in the fog. Good night, sir." The man does a double take, growls, and shuffles off. The pastiche style of the proceedings is set.

The American Gwendolyn Mellors and her English maid, Alice Binns, sashay along. They meet Travesty, introduce themselves, and tell him that they "are expecting a gentleman." The constable warns the ladies that "after dark this is a place of wickedness." Gwen offers him and her maid Smith Brothers lozenges. Travesty strolls away chewing. Big Ben strikes the quarter hour and Bunny St. John Manders—blond and handsome—enters.

We learn that Bunny is Gwen's newly discovered half-brother. He is on his way to meet a dastardly blackmailer in an attempt to "save a friend's good name." Bunny declares that he will not hesitate to send the "vile cur" to the bottom of the Thames. Gwen pleads with him to go to the police, but Bunny, determined, stalks off. Gwen, overcome, sways as if about to faint, takes a small revolver from her handbag, and sends Alice after Bunny: "Give it to him . . . take it or he is a dead man." Alice, frightened, exits running.

Constable Travesty rushes in and asks Gwen whether she heard a cry for help. Alice reappears walking slowly toward them, one hand holding the revolver, the other against her abdomen. She goes into Gwen's arms, whispers, "Murder. . . . The Men . . . the two men . . . they have killed—" and falls dead. Travesty bends over Alice and looks up—"I'm afraid she's dead . . . stabbed through the 'eart."

Bunny enters. "You must have passed her assailants in the fog," says Travesty as he removes his cape and covers the body. Bunny insists that there was no one on the bridge and queries, "Who would have wished to kill a harmless servant girl?"

The scene shifts to 221B Baker Street. Sherlock Holmes, meerschaum pipe in his mouth, stops playing the violin, welcomes a visitor, John Watson, and astounds him by deducing that the good doctor and his wife had a falling out "of such severity as to necessitate your removal from home to your club." Proof is provided by unpolished boots, which Mrs. Watson would never permit, and a minute grey stain on the elbow of Watson's overcoat, which matches the color of a freshly repainted railing at the doctor's club. Watson complains that the wife has become jealous without cause—"Oh, Holmes, if only women were people."

Gwen Mellors and Bunny St. John Manders are ushered in and disclose the circumstances of "a murder that could not possibly have happened, and yet an inoffensive girl lies dead." Bunny believes that his arrest is imminent though he is not guilty. He mentions that he was associated with the hero who fell three years ago in the Transvaal, A. J. Raffles, but Holmes says, "Hmm . . . never heard of him."[2] When Bunny tells of the constable who had participated in the Waterloo Bridge events, Holmes scoffs at the British policeman "who sees nothing, hears nothing and writes down everything."

Burly, bowler-hatted Inspector Lestrade enters and declares, "Mr. Harry St. John Manders, I arrest you for the murder of—" but Holmes stops him and asks for forty-eight hours to prove Bunny's innocence. Lestrade consents.

The plot thickens when Professor James Moriarty, Holmes's nemesis, engages a shady plastic surgeon to alter his face so that it resembles the Great Detective. Disguised as Holmes, Moriarty assassinates the Waterloo Bridge constable, Herbert Travesty, and enters 221B Baker Street. Watson, Gwen, Bunny, and Lestrade listen with admiration as Moriarty/Holmes analyzes the case of the slain maid: "To the murderer, Alice Binns was nothing, a means to an end . . . her life was thrown away so that you, Bunny, would be accused of her murder, found guilty and put to death."

Moriarty/Holmes shakes Gwen warmly by the hand and congratulates her for being "the most self-possessed taker of human life I have ever met. . . . Here is your murderer, Lestrade."

Moriarty/Holmes proceeds to prove that Gwendolyn Mellors is not Gwendolyn Mellors but an impostor who came from America with a cold-blooded plan to dispose of the man who thought she was his sister and gain the family's fortune. The maid Alice was not stabbed but poisoned by a Smith Brothers lozenge containing strychnine. "Alice Binns came to you, to warn you. . . . She said 'The two men!' What she meant was the box containing lozenges, with the likeness of those two most excellent Smith Brothers on the lid. She thought to save you from being poisoned. She came into your arms—into the knife."

Moriarty/Holmes accepts the compliments of a beaming Watson, and asks Gwen how she disposed of the murder weapon. She moves to him and whispers in his ear. Suddenly, he gasps, notices blood dripping from his hand, and realizes that "Gwen" has killed him. Moriarty staggers blindly across the room, goes into the bathroom area, and there is a long cry. Watson, shocked, exclaims, "My God! He has fallen into a pit of some kind and plunged two floors downward into Mrs. Hudson's bedroom."

LESTRADE: What a 'orrible fate.

Just as they are mourning the demise of the Great Detective, Holmes enters, approaches Gwen, and through a vent in her dress pulls out a lethal-looking strip of pointed steel—"Your murder weapon, Lestrade. . . . Take her away."

* * *

The Mask of Moriarty was first performed at the Gate Theatre, Dublin, Ireland, on October 4, 1985, and ran through November 30, with Tom Baker (who played Doctor Who in the British television series) starring as Holmes, supported by Slan Stanford (Watson), Brian Munn (Moriarty), and Ingrid Craigie (Gwen). *Variety* believed that the first act of the play "bubbles over with humor" and "things become funnier" as the play progresses.[3]

Critic Desmond Rushe dispatched to the *New York Times* a summation by various Irish newspapers in which there was recognition of the playwright's "fabulous comic talent" but a sense that "the spoof exceeded its limits and was too long."[4]

The English premiere of *The Mask of Moriarty* took place at the Haymarket Theatre, Leicester, on June 16, 1987. The London reviewers were divided. Robin Turner praised Hugh Leonard for "such a deft lightness of touch that you are charmed into accepting anything."[5] Eric Shorter called

Moriarty a "breathtakingly ingenious spoof"[6] and John Peter chirped, "it is an amusing, garrulous piece of hocus pocus."[7]

Martin Hoyle objected to "the play's slovenly construction" and pouted, "many of the jokes are achingly predictable."[8]

In the United States, *Moriarty* was presented at The Blackfriers Theatre, Rochester, New York, 1988–1989, directed by John Haldoupis, featuring Kevin S. Sweeney as Holmes and Paul C. Pope as Watson, and at the Williamstown Theatre Festival, Williamstown, Massachusetts, 1994, under the direction of John Tillinger, marqueeing Paxton Whitehead (Holmes), David Schramm (Watson), and Jane Krakowski (Gwen). Whitehead repeated the assignment three years later at the Old Globe Theatre, San Diego; at the Paper Mill Playhouse, Millburn, New Jersey, 1988; and at the Rich Forum, Stamford, Connecticut, 1998.[9] In 1999, *Moriarty* was produced by the University of Washington in Seattle and by Hartnell College, Salinas, California.

* * *

Hugh Leonard (a pseudonym for John Keyes Byrne) was born in Dublin in 1926 to an unmarried woman named Annie Byrne. His mother immediately gave him up for adoption. It is reported that he eventually located her but was unable to bring himself to meet her. He was raised as Jack Keyes by his adoptive parents, Nicholas and Margaret Keyes.

Leonard was educated at the Harold Boys' School and the Presentation College at Glasthule in County Dublin. From 1945 until 1960 he worked in the Irish civil service. After attending an Abbey Theatre production of Sean O'Casey's *The Plough and the Stars*, Leonard was affected powerfully and began to write plays of his own. When the Abbey undertook to present his dramas *The Big Birthday* (1956), *A Leap in the Dark* (1957), and *Madigan's Lock* (1958), Leonard left his day job and became a full-time writer. Since then he has penned more than thirty plays, three of which were produced in New York: *The Au Pair Man* (nominated for a Best Play Tony Award in 1974), *Da* (world premiere at the Olney Theatre, Washington, D.C., 1973; winner of Tony Award as Best Play on Broadway, 1978), and *A Life* (nominated for a Tony in 1981).

In addition to *The Mask of Moriarty*, Leonard wrote several plays tinged with criminous elements: *The Poker Session* (1963), in which a family poker game becomes tense when it is revealed that one of the players has just been released from a mental institution; *Nothing Personal* (1975), wherein a home party starts jovially but becomes increasingly sinister as one of the guests realizes that he has been kidnapped and is facing execution; and *Kill* (1982), unfolding in Kill House—seventy-five miles from Dublin—where the tenants go through bribery, blackmail, and crimes of the flesh. In 1995, Leonard adapted to the stage *Great*

Expectations, Charles Dickens's Victorian tale of young Pip's ascent through the English social classes.

Leonard wrote seven screenplays, including the script for *Da* (1989). Among his more than 120 original television episodes are contributions to several suspense series: *Blackmail* (1965), *Public Eye* (1965), *Simenon* (1966), *The Informer* (1966), *Out of the Unknown* (1966–1967), *Late Night Horror* (1968), *Detective* (1969), *Father Brown* (1974), and *The Inspector Alleyn Mysteries* (1993). For the *Sherlock Holmes* series, Leonard adapted *A Study in Scarlet* and *The Hound of the Baskervilles* (both in 1968).

Leonard participated in the television serializations of Charles Dickens's *Great Expectations* (1967), *Nicholas Nickleby* (1968), *Dombey and Son* (1969), and *Hunted Down* (1985). Leonard also had a hand in the miniseries of Emily Brontë's *Wuthering Heights* (1967), Fyodor Dostoyevsky's *The Possessed* (1969), and Wilkie Collins's *The Moonstone* (1972).

Extremely prolific, Leonard also penned novels, essays, children's books, radio plays, and two volumes of autobiography, *Home Before Night* (1979) and *Out After Dark* (1989). For more than thirty years he wrote a weekly column in the Irish *Sunday Independent* newspaper, in which he often came up with prickly theatre critiques, debunking, among others, the playwright Brendan Behan. The trouble with Ireland, he said, was that it was "a country full of genius, but with absolutely no talent."

Acting Edition: Brophy Books, Dublin and London.

Awards and Honors: In 2009, the Dun Laoghaire-Rathdown County Council Arts Office established The Hugh Leonard Award "to celebrate the significant contribution he made to Irish theatre, TV and film."

NOTES

1. Hugh Leonard, *The Mask of Moriarty* (Dublin: Brophy Books, 1987), 6.
2. Not content with borrowing Sherlock Holmes from the canon of Arthur Conan Doyle, playwright Hugh Leonard invades the writings of E(rnest) W(illiam) Hornung, Doyle's brother-in-law and creator of gentleman-burglar A. J. Raffles and his sidekick Bunny St. John Manders.
3. *Variety*, October 16, 1985.
4. *New York Times*, October 8, 1985.
5. *Guardian*, June 18, 1987.
6. *Daily Telegraph*, June 20, 1987.
7. *The Times*, London, June 21, 1987.
8. *Financial Times*, June 18, 1987.
9. Paxton Whitehead previously portrayed Sherlock Holmes in the Broadway production of Paul Giovanni's *The Crucifer of Blood* (Helen Hayes Theatre, September 28, 1978—236 performances).

Les Misérables (1985)

Screenplay by Alain Boublil (France, Tunisia-born, 1941–) and Claude-Michel Schönberg (France, 1944–), Music by Schönberg, Lyrics by Herbert Kretzmer (England, South Africa–born, 1925–)

Les Misérables, Victor Hugo's 1862 masterpiece, is a multilevel novel unfolding in France during 1815 to 1835. It is not only a dramatic narration packed with pounding incidents but also a social study of poverty and slum life. Incorporated in *Les Misérables* were memories of Hugo's own childhood glimpses of Paris, and early experiences that left their mark.

The core of the plot revolves around the convict Jean Valjean, sentenced to a term of five years for stealing a loaf of bread to feed his starving sister and her family. Despite Valjean's unusual physical strength, his multiple attempts to escape are foiled and his sentence is increased. The 1985 musical version of *Les Misérables* condenses the sprawling action of the original novel, dispenses with several subplots, and eliminates secondary characters. But the main incidents remain, conveyed entirely by song and dance.

The curtain rises on a chain gang laboring under a scorching sun and lamentably singing about being forgotten ("Work Song"). After nineteen years of imprisonment, Jean Valjean, prisoner 24601, is released on parole. He is reminded by police inspector Javert, a severe, fanatical lawman, that he'll have to display a yellow ticket-of-leave, the insignia of an ex-convict, for the rest of his life ("On Parole").

True enough, Valjean realizes that his papers are like "the mark of Cain"; he cannot get a job and no innkeeper will give him food or lodging. Finally, the kind Bishop of Digne offers him shelter. The next morning, two constables escort Valjean back. It seems that he has stolen some artifacts. The bishop pretends that they were a gift and adds two silver candlesticks, suggesting that Valjean left them behind. The constables exit and the bishop tells the former convict that he "must use this precious silver to become an honest man." Valjean is shaken, admonishes himself for becoming "a thief in the night," and in "Soliloquy" promises his benefactor to change his ways—"another story must begin."

Eight years later, Valjean, having assumed a new identity as Monsieur Madeleine, is a wealthy factory owner and the mayor of Montreuil-sur-Mer. One of his workers is the beautiful Fantine, who is sending money to her illegitimate child, Cosette, now living with an innkeeper and his wife. Fantine rejects the lewd advances of the foreman and is dismissed. She recalls better days in the song "I Dreamed a Dream," when she was "young and unafraid." Desperate for money, Fantine sells her locket and her golden hair, and wanders to the red-light district, where she is urged by an old crone to join her establishment ("Lovely Ladies"). When a rough sailor abuses her, Fantine fights back and a brawl ensues. Javert, now stationed in Montreuil, arrives on the scene and Fantine pleads with him to spare her from going to jail. Valjean, the mayor, orders Javert to let Fantine go and, noticing her fragile state, takes her to a hospital.

In a nearby alley, a runaway cart pins down an elderly peasant. Javert watches as the mayor lifts the heavy cart and saves the man's life. The inspector knows only one man of such prodigious strength, a former convict named Jean Valjean.

Valjean visits Fantine in the hospital. Feverish and dying of consumption, Fantine elicits from Valjean a promise that he'll look after her daughter Cosette. He vows that "the child will want for nothing" ("Fantine's Death"). When Javert arrives to arrest him, Valjean asks for three days before submitting himself, but Javert refuses ("The Confrontation"). They fight; Valjean knocks Javert unconscious and escapes.

The action moves to a tavern in Montfermeil run by a roguish innkeeper, Thénardier, and his shrewish wife. The Thénardiers have been abusing eight-year-old Cosette, who works for them, while pampering their own daughter, Éponine. Cosette dreams of a better life ("Castle on a Cloud") before Madame Thénardier sends her to fetch water from the well in the dark. While the innkeepers and their customers drink and sing, Valjean finds Cosette wandering in the woods, "trembling in the shadows." He pays the Thénardiers 1,500 francs to let him take her away ("The Waltz of Treachery").

Ten years later, Valjean and Cosette live happily together in a modest house on the outskirts of Paris. Marius Pontmercy, a young lawyer estranged from his aristocratic family because of his liberal views, notices Cosette and her guardian on one of their evening walks, and is struck by the girl's beauty. Not realizing that the tomboyish Éponine is in love with him, Marius asks her to discover where Cosette lives ("Éponine's Errand"). Éponine leads Marius to Cosette and then prevents her father's gang from robbing Valjean's home ("The Attack on *Rue Plumet*"). Marius and Cosette hit it off.

Revolutionary Parisian students meet in a coffee shop to prepare for a takeover of the streets ("The ABC Café—Red and Black"). Marius joins them at the barricades. All anxiously ponder what "tomorrow" will bring ("One Day More") as the curtain falls.

At the barricades, the students expose Javert as a government spy and prepare to lynch him. Valjean intercedes and lets the inspector go. Javert warns Valjean that he'll strike no deals and will still pursue him. "Once a thief, forever a thief," says Javert before leaving.

A rousing musical number unfolds at the barricades. The superior forces of the army crush the rebel students. Éponine is one of the first to be shot. She dies in Marius's arms, gasping, "I'm at rest/A breath away from where you are." Almost all on the barricades are killed. Having learned that Cosette loves Marius, Valjean carries away the wounded young man down a manhole into the Paris sewers. During hours of wandering underground, they pass by Thénardier, who is looting dead bodies of their rings and gold teeth ("Dog Eats Dog").

When at last Valjean and Marius reach the sewer's exit, they are confronted by Javert, who has been waiting for them. Valjean pleads with Javert to give him one hour to bring Marius to the home of his grandfather, and Javert reluctantly agrees. Alone on a bridge over the Seine, Javert sings of his torment: as a man of law he finds himself indebted to a thief and is reluctant to return to prison the man who had saved his life ("Soliloquy—Javert's Suicide"). He throws himself into the swollen river.

Time has passed. When Marius recovers, he and Cosette plan to get married ("Wedding Chorale"). In a departure from the original story, Valjean convinces Marius to keep his checkered past from Cosette. A wedding procession and a dancing celebration ensue.

In the final scene, Valjean prepares for his death and the spirit of Fantine arrives to take him to heaven. Marius and Cosette visit Valjean's lodging, and find him on his deathbed. Valjean peacefully croons, "Now you are here again beside me, now I can die in peace for now my life is blessed." The souls of Fantine and Éponine guide him to paradise while the young men who died on the barricades join in a finale that promises a better tomorrow. The musical omits Valjean's bequeath to Cosette of the bishop's silver candlesticks and his burial in a grave with no name on the stone.

* * *

In 1973, French composer Alain Boublil attended the premiere of *Jesus Christ Superstar* in New York. He was overwhelmed by the Andrew Lloyd Webber–Tim Rice rock musical and after the performance walked the streets of Manhattan thinking of a suitable theme for a rock opera of wide scope and emotional intensity to compare to *Jesus Christ Superstar*. "Inspiration came at dawn," relates Edward Behr in *The Complete Book of Les Misérables.* "Why not deal with the single most important event in French history—the French Revolution?"[1]

Back in Paris, Boublil elicited composer Claude-Michel Schönberg to join him on *La Révolution Française,* a show that ran for a season in Paris, yielding a bestselling record. The next step that led to the evolution of *Les Misérables* occurred in London. Boublil saw a revival of *Oliver!* produced by a young man called Cameron Mackintosh. While watching the Charles Dickens characters in the musical, Boublil began seeing in his mind's eye the characters of Victor Hugo's *Les Misérables*—Valjean, Javert, Cosette, Marius, and Éponine. He broached the idea to Schönberg, who immediately said, "Let's do it."

It took two years for Boublil and Schönberg to come up, in 1980, with a two-hour demonstration tape. Later that year, in September 1980, a stage version directed by Robert Hossein was mounted at the Palais des Sports in Paris, running for 100 performances. During that time Cameron Mackintosh became an established, highly successful producer with *Cats* and *Little Shop of Horrors* (*Phantom of the Opera* was still in the distant future). Upon hearing the recorded *Les Misérables,* Mackintosh undertook to produce it in London, struck a deal with Broadway's James Nederlander for a New York production, and hired Trevor Nunn, the artistic director of the Royal Stage Company who has staged a memorable eight-and-a-half-hour show of Dickens's *Nicholas Nickleby.*

After a period of crises and behind-the-scene struggles, rehearsals for *Les Mis'* commenced in July 1985. Clashes continued to erupt when producer Mackintosh insisted that the show could not be longer than three hours. The first preview lasted for almost four hours and cuts were made prior to an October 8, 1985 opening at London's Barbican Arts Center. "After a long, emotional standing ovation, all those associated with *Les Misérables* believed they had a hit on their hands," reports Edward Behr. "But the first batch of critics' comments, with only a few exceptions, ran the gamut from faint praise to scathing contempt."[2]

However, public opinion differed from that of the critics, and within three days the show was playing to full houses. On December 4, 1985, *Les Mis'* was transferred to the Palace Theatre. With some revisions, it moved again, on April 3, 2004, to the more intimate Queen's Theatre where it celebrated its 10,000th performance on January 5, 2010 and where it is still playing.

In December 1986 *Les Misérables* crossed the Atlantic and played for eight weeks at the Kennedy Center in Washington, D.C. The musical came to New York's Broadway Theatre on March 12, 1987, amassing an advance sale of more than $11 million—the most in U.S. theatre history at the time. Recruited from the London production were Colm Wilkinson (Jean Valjean) and Frances Ruffelle (Éponine). Terrence Mann played Javert.

The morning-after critics were split in their verdicts. Frank Rich declared, "The ensuing fusion of drama, music, character, design and movement is what links this English adaptation of a French show to the highest tradition of modern Broadway musical production."[3] Clive Barnes found the show "simply smashing"[4] while Jack Curry exclaimed, "It is a phenomenon."[5] John Beaufort applauded Colm Wilkinson's "magnificent performance as Valjean" and Terrence Mann's "fierce portrayal of Javert."[6] Jack Kroll hailed "the dazzling work of set designer John Napier and lighting designer David Hersey."[7] William A. Henry III admired the staging conceived by director Trevor Nunn and his associate John Caird, "using one huge revolving turntable inside another—on which sets come and go and characters move from one scene into the next—to achieve a fluid, cinematic style."[8]

Conversely, Howard Kissel gleaned in *Les Misérables* "a Monarch Notes version of the Victor Hugo novel. It gives you sketches of the plot, characters and themes, but no suggestion of the depth of the original."[9] Lida accused the show's writers, Alain Boublil and Claude-Michel Schönberg, of having "filled their stage with every imaginable musical theatre cliché" and lamented "tepid, watered-down stuff."[10] Edwin Wilson found "the character treatment simplistic and the plot overloaded. In the final 30 minutes there are at least four points at which the play should have ended."[11]

The yea-sayers won. *Les Misérables* ran for 6,680 performances in sixteen years. When it closed on May 18, 2003, it was the second-longest-running Broadway musical after *Cats*. In 2006, it fell to third place when *The Phantom of the Opera* took the lead.

Following the double successes of London and New York, *Les Mis'* productions were mounted across the United States (notably in Boston, Salt Lake City, St. Louis, Los Angeles, Philadelphia, Pittsburgh, and by a bus-and-truck tour) and throughout the world, translated into twenty-one languages (notably in Seoul during the 1988 Olympic Games, Sidney, Vienna, Oslo, Budapest, and Tel Aviv). A Broadway revival opened on November 9, 2006 and ran for 463 showings. The musical came to the Ahmanson Theatre in Los Angeles for a June 14–July 31, 2011 run, setting a box-office record, playing to 97 percent capacity in the 2,074-seat house.

On October 8, 1995 *Les Misérables* celebrated its tenth anniversary with a concert production at London's Royal Albert Hall. The cast was assembled from various international productions, singing in their native languages. The Twenty-Fifth Anniversary Concert of *Les Misérables* was held at the 02 Arena, London, on October 3, 2010 with the return of all the original cast members of 1985 performing the final reprise of "One Day More."

* * *

Victor Hugo's *Les Misérables* was filmed many times in various countries. The first known motion picture version was made in 1909; Maurice Costello played Jean Valjean and William V. Ranous portrayed Javert in three short silent parts produced by the Vitagraph Company in the United States. France produced a silent version in 1913, adapted and directed by Albert Capellani. Four years later, Frank Lloyd wrote the scenario and directed a 100-minute American feature that starred William Farnum (Jean Valjean) and Hardee Kirkland (Javert). A 359-minute French version was made in 1925 under the direction of Henri Fescourt.

An early sound short, titled *The Bishop's Candlesticks*, depicting the "bishop" sequence in *Les Misérables*, was produced by Paramount Pictures in 1929, featuring Walter Huston as Jean Valjean and Charles S. Abbe as the bishop. In 1931, Japan came up with a talkie feature adapted by Masashi Kobayashi and directed by Tomu Uchida. A major French talkie of *Les Misérables*, running for 281 minutes, was made in France in 1934, starring Harry Baur (Jean Valjean), Charles Vanel (Inspector Javert), and Jean Servais (Marius Pontmercy). America's answer came a year later with an all-star cast that included Fredric March (Valjean), Charles Laughton (Javert), Cedric Hardwicke (Bishop Bienvenu), Florence Eldridge (Fantine), Rochelle Hudson (Cosette), and John Bill (Marius).

Additional movie versions of the Hugo novel were made in the Soviet Union (1937), Egypt (1944), Mexico (1944), Italy (1948, with Valentina Cortese playing both Fantine and Cosette), Japan (1950, starring Sessue Hayakawa as Valjean), and the United States (1952, directed by Lewis Milestone and featuring an impressive cast that included Michael Rennie, Robert Newton, Sylvia Sidney, Debra Paget, Cameron Mitchell, and Edmund Gwenn). Jean Gabin and Bernard Blier portrayed Valjean and Javert in a 1958 French adaptation, and still more film versions were produced in Brazil (1958) and South Korea (1961). Jean-Paul Belmondo enacted Valjean in a new 1995 French version and Liam Neeson was attracted to the role in 1998, supported by Geoffrey Rush (Javert), Uma Thurman (Fantine), and Claire Danes (Cosette)—an American production filmed in Prague.

Les Misérables was adapted to television in the United States (1949), England (1952), France (1964, a miniseries of ten episodes), England again (1967, a miniseries of ten episodes), Spain (1971), France again (1972), Mexico (1974), England again (1978, with Richard Jordan as Valjean, Anthony Perkins as Javert), France again (1982, a miniseries starring Lino Ventura as Valjean), East Germany (1987), and France again (2000, featuring Gérard Depardieu).

In March 2011 Cameron Mackintosh signed Tom Hooper to direct a British film version of the musical by Alain Boublil, Claude-Michel Schönberg, and Herbert Kretzmer. The screenplay is by William Nicholson. The cast includes Hugh Jackman (Valjean), Russell Crowe (Javert), Anne Hathaway (Fantine), Amanda Seyfried (Cosette), Eddie Redmayne (Marius), Sacha Baron Cohen (Thénardier), and Helena Bonham Carter (Madame Thénardier). The movie will be distributed by Universal Pictures. Principal photography of the film commenced in March 2012 in various locations, including London and Paris.

* * *

Librettist Alain Boublil was born in Tunisia in 1941. He is best known for his collaborations with composer Claude-Michel Schönberg (born in Vannes, France in 1944) on musicals produced in Paris, London, and New York. In addition to *Les Misérables*, these include *La Révolution Française* (1973), the first-ever French rock musical; *Miss Saigon* (1989), based on Giacomo Puccini's *Madame Butterfly*, the tale of a doomed romance involving an Asian woman abandoned by her American lover, which played in both London and New York for ten consecutive years; *Martin Guerre* (1996), a mistaken-identity plot drawn from a real-life historical event; *The Pirate Queen* (2006), a musical about the sixteenth-century adventuress Grace O'Mally; and *Marguerite* (2008), set in World War II occupied Paris and inspired by the novel *The Lady of the Camellias* by Alexandre Dumas fils.

Born in South Africa in 1925, Herbert Kretzmer relocated in London in the mid-1950s and pursued twin careers as journalist and lyric writer. A prolific writer on the *Sunday Dispatch* and the *Daily Express*, Kretzmer interviewed John Steinbeck, Truman Capote, Tennessee Williams, Henry Miller, Louis Armstrong, Duke Ellington, and Cary Grant. In 1962, he became senior drama critic of the *Daily Express*, a post he held for eighteen years, covering about 3,000 first nights. Kretzmer wrote lyrics for BBC's satire *That Was the Week That Was*, the French singer Charles Aznavour, and Anthony Newley's musical film *Can Hieronymus Merkin Ever Forget Mercy Humppe and Find True Happiness?* In addition to *Les Misérables*, Kretzmer wrote the lyrics for the West End musicals *Our Man Crichton*, based on J. M. Barrie's satirical play *The Admirable Crichton*, and *The Four Musketeers*, a spoof on the Alexandre Dumas adventure novel.

Awards and Honors: A top ten selection in *The Best Plays of 1986–1987*. Tony Awards in 1987 for Best Musical, Best Book of a Musical (Alain Boublil and Claude-Michel Schönberg), Best Original Score (Claude-Michel Schönberg and Herbert Kretzmer), Best Direction of a Musical (Trevor Nunn and John Caird), Best Scenic Design (John Napier), and Best Lighting Design (David Hersey). In 1987, Drama Desk Awards for

Outstanding Musical, Outstanding Music (Claude-Michel Schönberg), and Outstanding Set Design (John Napier). Boublil and Schönberg's *Miss Saigon* was nominated for ten 1991 Tony Awards, including Best Musical and Best Original Score. Their *Martin Guerre* won the 1997 Laurence Olivier Award for Best New Musical; *Marguerite* was short-listed in the Best Musical category in the Evening Standard Drama Awards, 2008. In 1988, Herbert Kretzmer was elected a Chevalier de L'Ordre des Arts et des Lettres. In 1996, he received an Honorary Doctor of Letters at Richmond College, London, and in 2011, an Honorary Doctorate from Rhodes University in South Africa.

NOTES

1. Edward Behr, *The Complete Book of Les Misérables* (New York: Arcade Publishing, 1989), 47.

2. Behr, *The Complete Book of Les Misérables*, 140.

3. *New York Times*, March 13, 1987.

4. *New York Post*, March 13, 1987.

5. *USA Today*, March 13, 1987.

6. *Christian Science Monitor*, March 13, 1987.

7. *Newsweek*, March 23, 1987.

8. *Time*, March 23, 1987.

9. *Daily News*, March 13, 1987.

10. *Women's Wear Daily*, March 13, 1987.

11. *Wall Street Journal*, March 16, 1987.

Never the Sinner (1985)
John Logan (United States, 1961–)

On May 21, 1924, nineteen-year-old Nathan Leopold and eighteen-year-old Richard Loeb, students at the University of Chicago, kidnapped a friend, Bobbie Franks, killed him, then attempted to extract a ransom from Franks's parents. Obsessed with Nietzsche's "superman" theory, Leopold and Loeb believed that they had committed the perfect crime. But they hadn't: Leopold dropped his designer glasses at the scene of the crime and the police quickly traced them. The investigators also found the typewriter on which they had typed the ransom note. Leopold and Loeb were tried, defended by renowned attorney Clarence Darrow, found guilty, and sentenced to life imprisonment. Loeb was killed in a prison brawl in 1936. Leopold was paroled in 1958; he died in Puerto Rico in 1971.

In an introduction to the published play *Never the Sinner*, playwright John Logan recounts that in 1977, when he was attending high school in Millburn, New Jersey, he had an after-school job shelving books at the local public library. The blood-red binding of *Compulsion* by Meyer Levin caught his eye, and upon reading the book he couldn't shake the story from his mind: "Why did they do it? Why would two young men with every advantage in the world decide to murder an innocent fourteen-year-old boy? What were the demons lurking behind Loeb's flashing good looks? Behind Leopold's saturnine intellect? Those questions stayed with me—and stimulated my continued work on the play—for the past twenty years."[1]

While a senior in the theatre department at Northwestern University, Logan took a playwriting course "on a lark." In class, he began to write a play about Leopold and Loeb. As the fates would have it, the Northwestern Library Special Collection was home to the Elmer Gertz Collection; Gertz was Leopold's parole attorney and amassed a large volume of information on the case. "So," writes Logan, "the gates were unlocked, and the pages spilled forth."[2] He buried himself in a stream of intimate letters between Leopold, Loeb, and Darrow, in full trial transcripts, and in psychiatric reports, police statements, and newspaper accounts.

The first version of *Never the Sinner* was produced at Northwestern in 1983 at the end of Logan's senior year. On opening night the play ran for three hours and had almost twenty characters, including Clarence Darrow's wife and Mrs. Franks. A revised, condensed version that had seven actors was produced at the Stormfield Theatre, Chicago, in 1985, running just over two hours. In 1990, *Never the Sinner* was presented at the Playhouse Theatre in London, staged by Geoff Bullen. "With the tenacious support of Terry McCabe, who directed the first professional Chicago production . . . the committed work of actors like Donna Powers Branson in Chicago and Dennis O'Hare and Ben Daniels in London," relates Logan, "I tried to shape the spine of the play so that it charted more elegantly the intricate ebbs and flows of the relationship between Leopold and Loeb."[3]

In 1994, *Never the Sinner* was offered at the Space Theatre in Adelaide, Australia, staged by Rob Crosner. Three years later, in the summer of 1997, the play was presented by the Signature Theatre in Arlington, Virginia. The Signature production came to New York under the sponsorship of the National Jewish Theatre on December 1, 1997. Critic D. J. R. Bruckner of the *New York Times* called *Never the Sinner* "a remarkable play . . . based on years of research, including some sealed family archives."[4] The production subsequently reopened at off-Broadway's John Houseman Theatre on January 24, 1998. Ethan McSweeny directed and Lou Stanari designed the highly regarded show. The cast was headed by Jason Patrick Bowcutt (Nathan Leopold), Michael Solomon (Richard Loeb), and Robert Hogan (Clarence Darrow). In shaping the play to its final form, Logan admittedly "cannibalized" the ideas of talented producers, directors, designers, and actors.

The action of *Never the Sinner* unfolds in short vignettes that rotate, back and forth, from court proceedings to flashbacks leading to the murder of Bobby Franks. Three court reporters function as a chorus to relate the progression of the case and the nation's hypnotic involvement in the "trial of the century." It soon becomes clear that the audience will serve as the jury.

Leopold, "dark and brooding" and Loeb, "bright and airy" are led in handcuffs to their place in the courtroom. "The People of the State of Illinois versus Nathan Leopold Jr. and Richard Loeb for the crime of murder," announces the bailiff, and Judge John R. Caverly takes his seat. Reporter 1 exclaims that "Clarence Darrow, Attorney for the Defense, entered the courtroom loaded down with weathered law books." Reporter 2 declares, "State's Attorney Robert Crowe stalked in—a slick symphony of sinewy ambition."

As the court proceedings begin, glimpses of the past reveal Leopold and Loeb's fascination with Nietzsche's theory of the *Übermensch*—the *Superman*—who "is aloof to the petty concerns of mankind" and "is exempt from the laws that bind the common run of humanity." Loeb, who calls Leopold "Babe," leads him in a waltz and spins him around the stage while suggesting that the two of them "live up to their exalted potential and stun the world."

In court, State's Attorney Crowe describes how the accused, two young men with "expensively cut suits" and "slicked back hair," cruised the streets of Kenwood in search of their victim. "Consider their smiles as they seduced little Bobby Franks into the car," barks Crowe. "As they pulled shut the door and mercilessly beat him to death. As they pushed him into that sewer." Crowe wishes "to tear those superior smirks from their faces" and asks for "the extreme penalty, for death."

A flashback describes Loeb and Leopold hatching a plan to stop a passerby in Lincoln Park, pretend to have guns in their coat pockets, and rob the man's wallet. Loeb is obviously the leader; Leopold is at first reluctant, but after Loeb's sneer, "You're pathetic. Some Superman," Leopold agrees to go along.

They elevate their scheme from robbery to kidnapping and murder. Callously, they consider killing one of their fathers but discard the idea. Who among their student friends is a natural, ideal target? Finally, Leopold says, "Leave it to fate! Why don't we just cruise the Harvard School area and take whomever fits us." Loeb likes the idea, grabs Leopold's face and kisses him passionately, almost violently, and races off.

In court, psychologist Dr. White testifies, to hushed, mesmerized spectators, about a pact made between the accused men: "Leopold would take part in crimes primarily to accommodate Loeb, and Loeb would take part in sexual acts primarily to accommodate Leopold."

The reporters announce: "Body of boy found in swamp!" "Kidnapped rich boy found dead!" "Bobby Franks found dead in marshes!" "All city hunts for killers! Police call crime the strangest and most baffling in Chicago history!" "Al Capone Declares: Organized crime not responsible for Franks' murder!"

In a flashback sequence, Loeb and Leopold peruse a newspaper story about a pair of spectacles found near Bobby Franks' body. Loeb angrily admonishes Leopold for carelessly dropping his "fucking glasses" at the scene of the crime.

The unique hinges of the spectacles lead police to Leopold. Confronted with this evidence, Leopold and Loeb confess their crime. A flashback pictures Loeb and Leopold cruising in a "car"—three plain wooden chairs are used to suggest the vehicle. Leopold is driving. They stop to observe a neighborhood baseball game. Bobby Franks emerges from the playground and walks toward his home. He's alone. Leopold and Loeb pull up beside Franks and offer him a lift. Inside the car, without any warning, Loeb and Leopold smash the boy twice over the head with a chisel. Loeb lets out a savage scream as he batters Franks and drags his body to the back seat. Leopold recoils from the splattered blood and whispers, "My God! My God!" Loeb explodes into giggles, expresses joy at committing the deed "within a block" of Franks' home, and gushes, "Everything turned out beautifully; it was a work of art."

Clarence Darrow meets Loeb and Leopold in the jail's anteroom and asks them to confide the story of Franks' murder—and the lights fade out.

Act 2 continues to mingle past incidents and present court proceedings. A grim scene pictures the two protagonists pushing the body of Bobby Franks into a culvert on the marshes. Loeb wipes mud and blood from his clothes while Leopold stands still, looking down at the dead boy. "The acid didn't work," says Leopold anxiously, but Loeb assures him that it doesn't matter, that no one will find the corpse "in this god forsaken spot." They plan to send a ransom note to Franks' parents.

In court, Darrow throws a bombshell by changing his clients' plea to "Guilty on all counts." He informs Judge Caverly that he will present testimony regarding the mental state of the accused that will explain—not justify—their actions. "The darkest recesses of the human mind are in question here," announces Darrow. "We must take that fact into account to arrive at a just verdict of punishment." Reporters 1, 2, and 3 note the change of plea with exclamation marks. However, Reporter 2 states that "foxy Mr. Darrow might be outfoxed yet, as Judge Caverly is popularly known as a 'Hanging Judge.'"

Prosecutor Crowe, who demands the death penalty, and Defense Attorney Darrow go through a series of clashes. "They're boys, Bob. Boys. And they're scared," says Darrow. Crowe retorts: "You want to throw away the law? If we do that, what will we have left?" The verbal duel climaxes with Darrow calling Crowe "a cold bastard," and the prosecutor sallying, "and you are a blind old man." Darrow softens his tone: "I could look at them like you do, Bob. I could damn these boys for what they did. . . . I can see the sin in all the world. And I may well hate that sin, but never the sinner."

In their separate jail cells, Leopold and Loeb are interviewed by reporters. "That killing was an experiment," says Leopold. "It is just as easy to justify such a death as to justify an entomologist in killing a beetle on a pin!" And Loeb remarks coolly, "I know I should be sorry I killed that young boy and all, but I just don't feel it." The reporters remain speechless.

In the jail yard, Leopold and Loeb sit watching a baseball game. "If they hang us—would they do that together? At same time?" asks Loeb. Leopold nods, "Probably. They have two gallows here, side by side." Loeb mutters, "Then I hope they hang us."

In court, Dr. White testifies that despite the defendants' intelligence, their emotional development has been arrested "somewhere under the age of ten."

In his summation, Crowe demands the death penalty as proportional to the turpitude of the crime: "Hang these heartless 'supermen'! Hang them!" Darrow, however, claims that the boys were not in their right minds when they committed the crime, *"because they were made that way. Because somewhere, somehow, in the infinite processes that go into the making of a boy or a man something . . . slipped."*

In the jail anteroom, Leopold and Loeb await the verdict. They look at each other.

LEOPOLD: Dick, why did we kill Bobby Franks?
LOEB: I don't know.
LEOPOLD: I don't know either. . . . We're not Supermen, are we?
LOEB: No. I guess not.

Reporter 1 announces: "September 10th—Dickie and Babe escape the noose. Judge's Verdict: Life Plus Ninety-Nine Years."

* * *

D. J. R. Bruckner of the *New York Times* found John Logan's play "remarkable. . . . Other plays, and movies and books about the case have tended to foreground the sex; Mr. Logan treats it as fairly normal and concentrates on the personalities of the men and on the moral environment they lived in, with a result that the world is uglier and the killers somehow colder and more sinister than ever. . . . Michael Solomon's Loeb is brutal and sentimental at once; manipulative, impulsive, devious. . . . Jason Patrick Bowcutt has a trickier assignment in Leopold, who has to move from thrill to horror to wonder so fast and often that you question his sanity."[5]

Playwright Logan has a different take on the two murderers: "In the end, I feel great pity for Leopold and Loeb. . . . To say that Leopold and Loeb were 'monsters' is too easy. To say that they were 'evil' is too facile. . . . Leopold and Loeb were human beings. Just like the rest of us. They were tormented. They were brutal. They lacked any true moral, ethical compass. They could not find their way in our sunlit world, so they embraced the darkness. In that darkness they had each other. The real provocation of Leopold and Loeb is that we all could, given some unkind twists of fate and character, be them."[6]

* * *

In addition to *Never the Sinner*, other plays inspired by the Loeb-Leopold case include *Rope* (1929) by Patrick Hamilton; *Leopold and Loeb* (1997) by George Singer; *Thrill Me* (2003), a musical with book, lyrics, and music by Stephen Dolginoff; and *Dickie and Babe* (2008) by Daniel Henning.

Englishman Patrick Hamilton (1904–1962) is remembered today mostly for his 1938 play *Gaslight* aka *Angel Street* and his 1941 Jack the Ripper novel *Hangover Square*—both filmed effectively in memorable motion pictures. *Rope* was Hamilton's first play. The action unfolds continuously on the first floor of a house in Mayfair, a fashionable neighborhood in London. Wyndham Brandon and Charles Granillo, Oxford students and lovers, share the apartment. When the curtain rises, the living room is completely darkened save for the pallid gleam of lamplight from the street below. Silhouetted are the figures of Brandon and Granillo, bending over a chest, working intensely, when suddenly the lid of the chest falls with a bang. The two young men sink exhausted into armchairs and light cigarettes. Against the two pinpoints of light they begin to converse. We learn that they have just strangled, by rope, young Ronald Kentley, a fellow undergraduate, deposited his body in the chest, and are expecting Ronald's father, his aunt, and several friends to come around for supper. For an extra thrill, the guests will be seated around the chest. "This is the complete story," says Brandon, "The complete story of a perfect crime."

They switch on a lamp. Brandon is tall and blond, Granillo, slim and dark. Brandon goes to switch on the light in the hall and returns fuming, his eyes blazing, holding a slip of blue paper in his hand. He castigates Granillo for neglecting to find a Coliseum ticket that dropped from their victim's pocket. The ticket later becomes the clue that leads to the downfall and capture of the two murderers.

Directed by Reginald Denham, an authority on stage suspense,[7] *Rope* played at West End's Ambassador Theatre in 1929, featuring Brian Aherne and Anthony Ireland as Brandon and Granillo, ran for 131 performances, and later that year came to New York's Masque Theatre, under the title *Rope's End*, for 100 showings. The *New York Times* found it "a novel diversion of pure morbidity."[8] Alfred Hitchcock brought *Rope* to the screen in 1948, featuring John Dall and Farley Granger as the youthful killers uncovered by their former professor, enacted by James Stewart.[9]

George Singer's *Leopold and Loeb* is an episodic, less-than-profound play produced by Artists Theatre Company at off-Broadway's 28th Street Theatre under Renee Philippi's direction, with Brian Weiss as Leopold and Marc Palmieri as Loeb. Reviewer D. J. R. Bruckner recounted that playwright Singer "focuses on the killers' convoluted and mostly unspoken sexual passions . . . but the dialogue so rigorously prevents both characters from revealing any self-awareness, that viewers are likely to conclude that evil really is banal."[10]

The action of Stephen Dolginoff's musical *Thrill Me* is book-ended between a prologue and an epilogue that take place in a Chicago pardon conference room. The year is 1958 and it is the fifth hearing for prisoner Nathan Leopold. As Leopold responds to queries by voice-over committee members, flashbacks picture his submissive relationship—psychologically and physically—with Richard Loeb, a charismatic Nietzsche disciple. Step by step Loeb draws Leopold into a crime spree motivated by a sense of superiority, capped by the fatal stabbing of a young boy in a remote, wooded area. Leopold dropping a pair of prescription glasses at the crime scene botches their perfect crime. At the conclusion there is a twist: It is Stephen Dolginoff's theory that Leopold left the incriminating glasses behind purposely, counting on the pair's verdict of life imprisonment and thus having the fickle Loeb forever to himself.

Thrill Me has only two characters, Leopold and Loeb, so we are told, not shown, by word and song, such events as the execution of the murder, the police investigation, and the trial. The erotic relationship between the two protagonists is heightened with long kisses at the end of several scenes.

Thrill Me was first produced by a non-Equity troupe under the direction of Martin Charnin of *Annie* fame. The ninety-minute musical, containing sixteen songs, was presented for six performances at New York's 2003 Midtown International Theatre Festival. Christopher Totten played Nathan Leopold and Matthew Morris enacted Richard Loeb. In 2005, *Thrill Me* was revived for a limited run by off-Broadway's York Theatre Company, staged by Michael Rupert, featuring Matt Baur (Leopold) and Doug Kreeger (Loeb). Reviewer Frank Scheck of the *New York Post* opined that the Leopold-Loeb case "seems to resist musicalization. . . . While, thankfully, the tragic subject matter isn't trivialized, it results in a ponderous, tedious evening, the most endearing aspect of which is its brevity."[11]

Thrill Me came to Hollywood, California in 2008, a production mounted by the Havok Theatre Company at the Hudson Backstage. Critic Steven Mikulan complimented director Nick DeGruccio for knowing "the difference between thrill and shock," and keeping the evening "from lapsing into Grand Guignol."[12] Kathleen Foley found Stewart W. Calhoun and Alex Schemmer, who played Leopold and Loeb, respectively, "so convincingly boyish that they resonate not as mere monsters, but as kids trapped in an escalating game of triple dare . . . they deliver wrenching performances that force us to care, almost in spite of ourselves."[13]

In March 2008, Daniel Henning directed his own play, *Dickie and Babe*, for the Blank Theatre Company of Hollywood, California, a production running simultaneously, two blocks away, from *Thrill Me*. According to David No of the *Los Angeles Times*, Henning "has set an ambitious if strangely academic goal for himself—to tell the Leopold and Loeb story as objectively as possible, minimizing conjecture and dramatic embellishments."[14] Not unlike John Logan before him, for three years Henning immersed himself in court transcripts, medical reports, letters, and other documents, and pulled out verbatim dialogue from historical records. He even visited the Chicago neighborhood where the killers lived and retraced their path.

Books about the Leopold-Loeb case include *The Amazing Crime and Trial of Leopold and Loeb* (1924) by Maureen McKernan; *Life Plus 99 Years* (1958) by Nathan Freudenthal Leopold; *A Handful of Clients* (1965) by Elmer Gertz; *The Crime of the Century* (1975) by Hal Higdon (reprinted in 1999 under the title *Leopold and Loeb: the Crime of the Century*).

A low-budget but highly stylized motion picture, *Swoon* (1992), depicts the execution of the crime, the investigation, the trial, and the final fate of the two killers. *Swoon* was scripted and directed by Tom Kalin and starred Daniel Schlachet (Loeb) and Craig Chester (Leopold).

* * *

John Logan was born in San Diego, California, in 1961. The youngest of three children, he grew up in California and New Jersey before moving to Chicago to attend Northwestern University, where he graduated in 1983. Following *Never the Sinner*, Logan wrote *Hauptmann* (1986), about the German immigrant Bruno Richard Hauptmann, who was convicted of kidnapping and murdering the Lindbergh baby; *Riverview* (1991), a musical melodrama set at Chicago's famed amusement park; and *Red*, the story of artist Mark Rothko that opened at London's Donnar Warehouse in December 2009, ran for two months, and transferred to Broadway for a limited run, winning the 2010 Tony Award for Best Play.

In 1996, Logan penned a made-for-TV movie about storm chasers, *Tornado!* Three years later, he concocted another television contribution, *RKO 281*, examining the struggle of young Orson Welles in making the greatest American film of all time, *Citizen Kane*. At the end of the twentieth century, Logan began writing and producing feature movies in a gamut of genres. *Bats* (1999) is a horror flick about hordes of mutated killer bats attacking a southwestern community. *Any Given Sunday* (1999) covers the world of pro football. *Gladiator* (2000) is a spectacle of ancient Rome. *The Time Machine* is an adaptation of the H. G. Wells classic and *Star Trek: Nemesis* is an impressive entry in the series—both science-fiction films made in 2002. *Sinbad: Legend of the Seven Seas* (2003) was called by Leonard Maltin an "entertaining animated blend of adventure, fantasy, comedy and romance as bad-boy Sinbad takes on a noble mission to save his boyhood friend—the prince."[15] *The Last Samurai* (2003) depicts a clash of cultures as an American cavalry officer arrives in 1876 Japan to train the emperor's soldiers, while *The Aviator* (2004) is a screen biography of billionaire Howard Hughes, who sets out to conquer Hollywood. *Sweeney Todd: The Demon Barber of Fleet Street* (2007) is a stylized, brooding adaptation of the Stephen Sondheim–Hugh Wheeler musical about a vengeful barber in nineteenth-century London. *Coriolanus*

(2011), inspired by Shakespeare's tragedy, follows the blood-splattered path of a centurion exiled from Rome and returning as the head of an army to take his revenge on the city. *Rango* (2011) is a computer-animated family film about a pet chameleon who wanders into an old western town, presents himself as a tough drifter, becomes sheriff, and encounters gunslinging outlaws, bank robbers, and a crooked mayor.

Acting Edition: Samuel French, Inc.; Overlook Press.

Awards and Honors: John Logan won the 1999 Writers Guild of America Award for Best TV Adapted Writing for *RKO 281*. He was nominated for a 2000 Academy Award and a BAFTA Award for Best Original Screenplay, *Gladiator*. In 2004, he was nominated for an Academy Award, a BAFTA Award, and a Writers Guild of America Award for Best Original Screenplay, *The Aviator*. In 2010, Logan won a Tony Award for Best Play for *Red*. Two years later, he garnered an Annie Award from the International Animated Film Society for Writing in a Feature Production for *Rango* (*Rango* also won Academy, BAFTA, and Annie Awards for Best Animated Feature Film).

NOTES

1. John Logan, *Never the Sinner* (Woodstock, N.Y.: Overlook, 1988), 12.
2. Logan, *Never the Sinner*, 13.
3. Logan, *Never the Sinner*, 15.
4. *New York Times*, December 2, 1997.
5. *New York Times*, December 2, 1997.
6. Logan, *Never the Sinner*, 16.
7. Among the thirty plays that Reginald Denham directed on Broadway were the criminous *Suspense* (1930), *Ladies in Retirement* (1940), *Suspect* (1940), *Guest in the House* (1942), *The Two Mrs. Carrolls* (1945), *Portrait in Black* (1947), *Dial "M" for Murder* (1952), *Sherlock Holmes* (1953), *Bad Seed* (1954), and *Hostile Witness* (1966).
8. *New York Times*, September 20, 1929.
9. Patrick Hamilton was contracted to pen the screenplay of *Rope*, Alfred Hitchcock's first picture filmed in color. The director's conceit was to shoot it without cuts, unraveling continuously in the apartment where the murder is committed. The task was too strenuous for Hamilton, who was replaced, successively, by Hume Cronyn and Arthur Laurents. A synopsis of Patrick Hamilton's *Rope* and *Gaslight*, the plays' production data, and critics' evaluation can be found in Amnon Kabatchnik, *Blood on the Stage, 1925–1950* (Lanham, Md: Scarecrow Press, 2010).
10. *New York Times*, June 4, 1997.
11. *New York Post*, June 9, 2005.
12. *LA Weekly*, February 1–7, 2008.
13. *Los Angeles Times*, February 1, 2008.
14. *Los Angeles Times*, January 27, 2008.
15. *Leonard Maltin's 2011 Movie Guide* (New York: Plume, 2010), 1252.

The Phantom of the Opera (1986)

Book by Richard Stilgoe (England, 1943–) and Andrew Lloyd Webber (England, 1948–), Music by Andrew Lloyd Webber, Lyrics by Charles Hart (England, 1961–)

The horrifying events that took place in the catacombs of the Paris Opera House, where Erik, a mysterious, masked, half-crazed musician reigned supreme, first came to light in a 1910 novel by Gaston Leroux, a French writer of detective and action melodramas.

Gaston Leroux (1868–1927), described as a "red-bearded" man with a "large, exuberant personality," started his literary career as a newspaper reporter, first writing drama reviews, then covering courtroom events, and later doing exclusive interviews with celebrities. He eventually became a roving correspondent across Europe, Asia, and Africa.

Influenced by Edgar Allan Poe and Arthur Conan Doyle, Leroux also began to write detective stories. His first international success was the 1907 classic whodunit *Le Mystére de la Chambre Jaune* (*The Mystery of the Yellow Room*), in which a murder is committed behind impenetrable sealed doors. Although he may have borrowed the surprising solution of this locked-room puzzle from Israel Zangwill's *The Big Bow Mystery* (1892), critics consider the Leroux book one of the first important titles in the history of the genre. Leroux dramatized *The Mystery of the Yellow Room*—adding elements from 1908's *The Perfume of the Lady in Black*—as a five-act thriller.[1]

However, it is *The Phantom of the Opera* that has preserved Leroux's reputation, undoubtedly kept alive by its many film adaptations. Lon Chaney, Claude Rains, and Herbert Lom portrayed the shadowy character of Erik, lurking in subterranean passages, instigating a series of murderous deeds to further the career of a beautiful young singer, Christine Daaé.[2]

A phenomenally successful musical adaptation of *The Phantom of the Opera* was created in 1988 by Richard Stilgoe (book), Andrew Lloyd Webber (music), and Charles Hart (lyrics). A prologue unfolds on the somewhat run-down stage of the Paris Opera, where an auctioneer is disposing of props from old productions. When the auctioneer finds a disassembled chandelier, he reminds the souvenir-hunters that it once played a part in "the strange affair of the Phantom of the Opera, a mystery never fully explained."

As the auctioneer lights the chandelier to show it off, there is a great flash, the overture commences, and the chandelier rises to its former place above the audience while the auditorium is restored to its former gilded glory of 1881.

Act 1 opens on a dress rehearsal of *Hannibal*, with a ballet sequence created around a huge mechanical elephant. The opera's retiring owner, Lefêvre, introduces the new managers—Richard Fermin and Giles André—to the company, including the leading singers (Carlotta Giudicelli and Ubaldo Piangi), the director (Reyer), the leading dancer (Meg Giry) and her mother, the ballet mistress (Mme. Giry). Lefêvre asks Carlotta to sing "Think of Me" in honor of the occasion. During Carlotta's song, a backdrop falls from the flies and crashes to the stage, narrowly missing her. Joseph Buquet, the chief scene-shifter, enters and suggests that a ghost—"the Phantom of the Opera"—may have caused the accident.

Mme. Giry informs Fermin and André that she discovered a message from the Phantom in her dressing room, ordering the new managers to continue to leave Box 5 empty for his use; she further demands that they continue to pay him the customary 20,000 francs a month.

Unwilling to perform under these "dangerous circumstances," Carlotta and Piangi decide to leave. Meg Giry suggests that dancer Christine Daaé, who has been taking voice lessons from an enigmatic teacher, could sing the role.

The opening night performance receives applause and bravos, especially from Raoul, the Vicomte de Chagny, in one of the boxes. After taking her bows, Christine walks toward her dressing room, followed by Meg. Suddenly a disembodied voice is heard calling "Christine, bravi, bravi, bravissimi." Christine enlightens Meg with the song "Angel of Music" that an "unseen genius" has been guiding her vocal development.

Outside the dressing room, the new managers are congratulating themselves on the success of the understudy. Raoul, carrying a champagne bottle, knocks on the door. Christine admits him, and they discover that they were childhood friends. They reminisce about those early days in the song "Little Lotte." Raoul insists that Christine have supper with him and goes to fetch his hat. In his absence, Christine hears the Phantom's voice instructing her to look in the mirror. An apparition wearing a half-mask becomes visible on the other side of the glass. The Phantom's hand reaches through the mirror and draws Christine to him. When Raoul re-enters the dressing room, it is empty.

The Phantom leads Christine to a trap door in the stage and they descend deeper and deeper through a zigzagging walkway. Far down, they climb into a gondola that slowly glides across the misty waters of an underground lake, a surreal image borrowed from the 1925 silent movie. As they cross the lake toward the Phantom's lair, they sing "The Phantom of the Opera," which glorifies the Phantom's power to dwell inside Christine's mind.

When they arrive at their destination, the boat turns into a bed and occupies the center of the stage. The place is lit by giant candelabras. A huge pipe organ is prominent on one side, and a large mirror, covered by a dustsheet, on the other.

The Phantom seats himself near the organ and croons "The Music of the Night," telling Christine that from the moment he heard her sing, he wanted to bring her to this site to purge her thoughts "of the life she knew before" and savor the "sweet intoxication" of the music he'll compose for her. Christine, curious about her benefactor, moves behind him, reaches out and tears the mask from his face. It is horribly disfigured and she screams. The Phantom springs up and turns on her furiously but he softens in the song "Stranger Than You Dream It," pleading with Christine to turn her fear into affection. Christine hands him back the mask, and the Phantom prepares to take her back to the real world of the opera.

Backstage, scene-changer Buquet demonstrates to the ballet dancers the use of the Punjab lasso in the song "Magical Lasso." The trap opens and the shadow of the Phantom, bringing Christine back, scares the girls away. In their office, the two managers, Fermin and André, read to each other missives they've received, signed "Opera Ghost": he applauds Christine's performance, sniffs at the "lamentable messy" dances, and complains that his fees haven't been paid.

Piangi enters with Carlotta, who has also received a mysterious note warning her of dire consequences if she undertakes the leading role of the countess in the forthcoming production of *Il Muto*. The managers assure Carlotta that they won't take orders from a ghost. In the song "Prima Donna" they plead with her to play the part. The Phantom's voice echoes: "So, it is to be war between us!"

During the performance of *Il Muto*, Raoul defiantly seats himself in Box 5. The Phantom appears high up on the catwalk and rocks the immense chandelier above the auditorium. Suddenly Carlotta loses her voice, emitting strange toad-like sounds. Piangi leads the diva, sobbing, offstage. The managers announce the substitution of Christine in the role.

As the performance commences, the garroted body of Buquet falls to the stage floor, creating pandemonium. Christine cries out for help and Raoul rushes to her side. She asks him to take her to the roof of the Opera House, where she believes they'll be safe. With the twinkling lights of Paris in the background, Raoul tries to convince her that the ghostly Phantom doesn't really exist (in "Why Have You Brought Me Here") but Christine insists that she has seen the Phantom with her own eyes (in "Raoul, I've Been There"). They kiss and hurry off, planning to run away together after the show. The Phantom emerges from behind a statue of Apollo and expresses his feelings about Christine's betrayal: "You will curse the day / You did not do / All that the Phantom / Asked of you."

On stage, the performers (with Christine wearing Carlotta's costume) are taking their bows. The Phantom appears high up, laughing maniacally, once more rocking the chandelier. Released from its hook, the massive chandelier slips down and, with a blinding flash, swings madly over the orchestra pit and crashes at Christine's feet. The curtain closes.

Act 2 takes place six months later. The opera is celebrating the New Year with a gala costume party. The large gathering of opera personnel sing "Masquerade" about the identities hidden behind the variety of colorful disguises. After six months of peace, all toast the new chandelier. Raoul and Christine join the throng—they're engaged, but Christine insists on keeping their engagement a secret, with her ring suspended by a gold chain around her neck.

A tall, sinister, scarlet-garbed figure with a skeletal head, purporting to be Red Death, enters and becomes the center of attention. It is the Phantom, who asks, in the song "Why So Silent?" why the celebrants have suddenly fallen still. He takes from under his robe a bound manuscript, announces its title, "Don Juan Triumphant," and throws it to manager André. He then crosses to Christine and pulls the chain holding her engagement ring. There's a flash of light and the panicky guests run off.

Backstage, Raoul implores Mme. Giry to tell him what she knows about the Phantom. Mme. Giry reveals that many years ago a traveling circus passed through the city. Its main attraction, locked in a cage, was a physically disfigured scholar and composer. He escaped and was never recaptured. It was said that he had died, but Mme. Giry doesn't believe it, "For in this darkness / I have seen him again."

Under Reyer's supervision, Carlotta and Piangi rehearse the Phantom's opera. There is much confusion until the piano starts to play the score by itself, causing them all to fall silent and then sing part of "Don Juan Triumphant." On opening night, the orchestra is tuning up and the managers are conferring with the police, setting a trap for the Phantom; it includes a marksman, hidden in the pit with a clear view of Box 5.

The final scene of the opera has Don Juan (Piangi) preparing for his latest conquest, Aminta (Christine). Don Juan goes behind a curtain to disguise himself as his servant for the assignation. When he emerges to greet the arriving Aminta, it is the Phantom, not Piangi, who takes the stage as Don Juan. "The Point of No Return" is the song they sing to each other. Christine becomes aware that it is the Phantom who is singing with her. When Don Juan offers her a ring, she pulls off his mask, exposing the Phantom's horrifying skull to the audience. The police close in. The Phantom sweeps his cloak around Christine, and they vanish. The curtain is pulled aside upstage, revealing the body of Piangi, who has been garroted. In the midst of the ensuing confusion, Mme. Giry offers to show Raoul where Christine and the Phantom have gone. She leads him off.

In the labyrinth underground, the Phantom navigates the gondola forward. Offstage, the mob is heard in pursuit, singing "Track Down This Murderer." Raoul and Mme. Giry are seen making their way down the slope to the edge of the water, where Raoul plunges in. In the Phantom's lair, a wax doll of Christine is sprawled on a large throne. As they enter, Erik takes the bridal veil from the dummy and places it on Christine's head. Raoul emerges from the lake and begs the Phantom to show some compassion and free the woman he loves. The Phantom places the Punjab lasso around Raoul's neck and offers Christine a choice between his love and Raoul's death. To Raoul's horror, Christine places a long kiss full on the Phantom's misshapen lips. When they separate, the Phantom, stunned and trembling, slowly moves toward the organ, takes a lit candle, crosses to Raoul, and burns the thread on which the lasso was held.

The pursuing mob is heard approaching. The Phantom, in a major turnabout, motions Raoul and Christine toward the boat and urges them, "Leave me alone—forget all you've seen." He declares "I love you," as Christine departs. The gondola pulls away. The Phantom sits on the throne, gathering his cloak around him. Soon the mob reaches the lair. Meg walks to the throne and courageously pulls the cloak away—revealing empty air. The Phantom has vanished, leaving behind his white mask.

* * *

Produced by Cameron Mackintosh and directed by Harold Prince, *The Phantom of the Opera* premiered at Her Majesty's Theatre, London, on October 9, 1986. The entire cadre of critics praised the physical production elements but some expressed disappointment about the merit of the book, lyrics, and score. Among the content aisle men were Jack Tinker, who applauded "Andrew Lloyd Webber's triumphant re-working of this vintage spine-tingling melodrama,"[3] and Richard Barkley, who found the show "a gorgeous operatic extravaganza that is a thrill to the blood and a sensual feast to the eye."[4] Michael Billington was entranced by the "shrewd idea of going back to Gaston Leroux's original 1911 novel."[5] "So we get a story that mixes horror and romance in equal proportions. . . . It is a Beauty and the Beast myth about a disfigured hero who can only express his love for a soprano by becoming her musical inspiration. . . . It is refreshing to find a musical that pins its faith in people, narrative and traditional illusion."[6] David Nathan wrote, "The show is held together by Hal Prince's superb direction which never fails to direct attention to the heart of a scene."[7] Michael Coveney admired designer Maria Bjornson's "luxuriant but deftly manageable swags, curtains and, for the opening Act Two masked ball, a recreation of the Opera's grand staircase."[8] Michael Crawford, in the title role, was called by John Barber "superb—tense, controlled, tigerish . . . Sarah Brightman [Andrew Lloyd Webber's spouse, in the part of Christine] makes a remarkable West End debut with her pure, wide-compass voice and rhythmic sense of melody."[9]

The naysayers included Nigel Williamson, who gleaned in the musical "a real load of old hokum";[10] Ros Asquith, who lamented the absence of "tragedy, tenderness and terror" and scoffed at "a great deal of clever opera pastiche and some frankly third rate special effects";[11] and Joan Smith, who sighed at "a one-song show; once the evocative number is out of the way, Lloyd Webber and his lyricist, Charles Hart, meander aimlessly, tunelessly and forgettably."[12]

A megahit in the West End, *The Phantom of the Opera* crossed the Atlantic and came to Broadway's Majestic Theatre on January 26, 1988, amid a great deal of hoopla, empowered by a then-huge $8 million budget and an advance sale of $18 million. Three actors from the London production arrived with it: Michael Crawford (Erik, the Phantom), Sarah Brightman (Christine Daaé), and Steve Barton (Raoul de Chagny). The show garnered several rave reviews, a few mild endorsements, and a smattering of negative reactions.

"Phantastic!" proclaimed Clive Barnes, who went on to offer kudos to director Harold Prince ("has proved a wizard"), designer Maria Bjornson ("elegant visual imagination"), and actor Michael Crawford ("awe-inspiring creation of the Phantom").[13] "Britain's Andrew Lloyd Webber has triumphed again," wrote John Beaufort, "this time with a musical extravaganza that may be his most accomplished as well as his most popular to date."[14] Allan Wallach gushed, "The triumph of *The Phantom of the Opera* lies in the amalgam of virtually all its elements into as gloriously theatrical a show as we've had in recent memory."[15]

Conversely, Howard Kissel found that "the characters are not fleshed out, the lyrics are forgettable and the melodramatic plot is not as evocative as it might be."[16] Frank Rich frowned at "a characteristic Lloyd Webber project—long on pop professionalism and melody, impoverished of artistic personality and passion. . . . With the exception of 'Music of the Night,' Mr. Lloyd Webber has again written a score so generic that most of the songs could be reordered and redistributed among the characters (indeed, among other Lloyd Webber musicals) without altering the show's story or meaning."[17] David Lida stated harshly, "I don't recall a single lyric, nor a note of Andrew Lloyd Webber's music, which is a dull mishmash of serious opera, opera parody and rock 'n' roll riffs. It is weighted down by ponderous and repetitive love ballads."[18] Joel Siegel sneered, "Though the lyrics are mediocre at best, the spoken dialogue manages to be even less than that, and Sarah Brightman, the composer's wife, couldn't act scared on the IRT at four o'clock in the morning."[19]

William A. Henry III attempted to explain the extraordinary anticipation that *Phantom* has aroused: "The show apparently taps into yearnings for a transporting sensory and mystical experience: in a word, for magic. On that primal level, despite considerable and at times embarrassing shortcomings, *Phantom* powerfully delivers. The story may be muddled, the characters sketchy, some performances shallow and the music often slushily derivative. So what. For those who seek an equivalent to a ride through the Haunted Mansion at Walt Disney World—seemingly a vast proportion of today's Broadway audience—*Phantom* is a brilliantly manipulated journey, scary yet ultimately unthreatening."[20]

Despite the mixed reviews, *The Phantom of the Opera* has had a phenomenal run. In 2004, when the show turned sixteen, critic Clive Barnes marked the occasion with a *New York Post* article, headlined "Lush Phantom Still Haunting," in which he announced that the show still "seems band-box fresh," has remained "taut and ship-shape," and is "one of the all-time best Broadway musicals."[21] On January 9, 2006, *Phantom* played its 7,486th performance and became Broadway's longest-running show ever, surpassing *A Chorus Line* (thirteen years) and *Cats* (eighteen years). In October 2011, *Phantom* celebrated its twenty-fifth anniversary. On Saturday, February 11, 2012, the musical made show business history with the 10,000th Broadway performance of an $8 million production that became an $845 million hit. *Phantom* has played in 27 countries and 145 cities, from Budapest to Melbourne and Cape Town, grossing $5.6 billion worldwide as of April 2012.

The Phantom of the Opera has also had several successful touring companies across the United States. In 2006, *Phantom* was cut to roughly ninety minutes and radically restaged (by Harold Prince) for a $35 million Las Vegas production, a whopping budget that far surpassed even the priciest of Broadway musicals of the time. Andrew Lloyd Webber co-produced a 2004 motion picture based on the musical, and largely financed its $70 million budget. Directed by Joel Schumacher and starring Gerald Butler and Emmy Rossum as Erik and Christine, the film was greeted by hostile reviewers. Lou Lumenick of the *New York Post* suggested that Schumacher "has not so much directed the movie version as embalmed it. . . . Butler is the least frightening Phantom in screen history. . . . The falling chandelier, the signature moment of *Phantom*, has been moved from the end of the first act to climax the movie—by which point non-devotees may need to be roused from their sleep by their companions."[22] A. O. Scott of the *New York Times* opined that "this screen version, for all its wailing emotionalism and elaborate production design, lacks both authentic romance and the thrill of memorable spectacle. . . . Full though it is of bellowings and screechings about love, art and the spirit of music, *The Phantom of the Opera* is remarkably lacking in tenderness or grace."[23]

Andrew Lloyd Webber began working on a sequel to the *Phantom of the Opera* in 1990. Collaborating with author Frederick Forsyth, he set the proceedings in New York City at the turn of the twentieth century. The project soon fell apart and Forsyth went on to utilize some of their ideas in his 1999 novel *The Phantom of Manhattan*. Lloyd Webber returned to the sequel in 2006, teaming with a number of writers and directors. He was finally satisfied by a treatment penned by Ben Elton. In 2008, Lloyd Webber first announced that the sequel would likely be called *Phantom: Once Upon Another Time*. However, the title was later changed to *Love Never Dies*.

Lloyd Webber originally intended for *Love Never Dies* to open in London, New York, and Shanghai simultaneously in the autumn of 2009. The plan was altered and delayed several times. By October 2009, the Shanghai idea had been dropped in favor of an Australian production. Eventually, Lloyd Webber announced that the show would begin previews in London on February 20, 2010, followed by a Broadway production later that year. Directed by the American Jack O'Brien, *Love Never Dies* officially opened on March 9, 2010 and was savaged by most critics. Lloyd Webber closed the show for a few days of changes to no avail; the London production ended its disappointing run after nearly eighteen months with the loss of a $12 million investment. The Broadway opening has been postponed indefinitely. An Australian production debuted on May 21, 2011 at Melbourne's Regent Theatre, directed and choreographed by a local creative team. Lloyd Webber hopes to bring that endeavor to New York in the future. Meanwhile, a DVD of the Australian show was released in the United States on the twenty-fifth anniversary of *The Phantom of the Opera*.

* * *

Andrew Lloyd Webber was born in South Kensington, London in 1948 to a musical family. His father was organist and composer William Lloyd Webber; his mother, Jean Hermione Webber, was a noted piano teacher; his younger brother Julian became an internationally famous concert cellist. At an early age, Andrew and Julian presented mini-musicals in a toy theatre to an audience of their parents and guests. Trips to the West End in the company of his aunt Violet whetted Andrew's appetite for musical theatre. He attended Westminster School, where he participated in shows by writing songs, directing, and performing, and went on to Magdalen College, Oxford, and the Royal College of Music.

Webber's early work includes a suite for the theatre, which he wrote at age nine, and an unproduced musical, *The Likes of Us*, with lyrics by Tim Rice, about the establishment of homes for destitute children in nineteenth-century England.

The Webber-Rice collaboration paid dividends on an international scale with three musicals of which the first, *Joseph and the Amazing Technicolor Dreamcoat*, was inspired by the Old Testament story, in the Book of Genesis, of Joseph and his brothers (Colet Court, a preparatory school in London, 1968; Edinburgh International Festival, 1972; West End's Albery Theatre, 1973; Brooklyn, New York's Academy of Music, 1976 and 1977; off-Broadway's Entermedia Theatre, 1981; Broadway revivals 1982 and 1993; West End revivals 1991, 2003, 2007; a U.S national tour, 2005; a U.K. tour, 2010).

Webber-Rice's *Jesus Christ Superstar* tells the story of the last seven days in the life of Jesus of Nazareth (a recorded album, 1970; Broadway's Mark Hellinger Theatre, 1971, 711 performances; a show directed by Tom O'Hargan, famous for *Hair*, that was restaged for Universal Amphitheater, Universal City, California and filmed in Israel; Paris and West End, 1972; Broadway revivals 1977, 1995, 2000, 2012).

Evita covers the career of Argentina's First Lady Eva Perón (West End, 1978, 2900 performances, Olivier Award for Best New Musical; Broadway, 1979, 1567 performances, Tony-winning production, book, and score; film, 1996; West End revival, 2006; Broadway revival, 2012).

Lloyd Webber put music to T. S. Eliot's whimsical poems and added lyrics by Trevor Nunn in *Cats* (London, 1981; New York, 1982, 7485 performances, Tony winner for Best Musical, Best Book of a Musical, Best Original Score). *Starlight Express* is a rock musical centered on a child who dreams that his toy train comes to life. The entire cast performs wearing roller skates (London, 1984, 7461 performances; New York, 1987, 761 showings). *Cats* and *Starlight Express* were still running when *The Phantom of the Opera* came to Broadway in 1988.

Aspects of Love spotlights the romantic entanglements of an actress with several men and a woman (West End, 1989; Broadway, 1990). *Sunset Boulevard*, based on a 1950 Billy Wilder film of the same title, revolves around Norma Desmond, a faded star of the silent era, living in a decaying Los Angeles mansion (London and Los Angeles, 1993; New York, 1994; Canada and Germany, 1995; Australia and U.S. tour, 1996; UK tour, 2001; West End revival and the Netherlands, 2008; Sweden, 2009; Japan, 2012). *Whistle Down the Wind*, inspired by a 1961 movie that in turn was based on a novel by Mary Hayley Bell, tells the story of a group of children who mistake an escaped convict hiding in a barn for Jesus Christ (world premiere, directed by Harold Prince, at the National Theatre, Washington, D.C., 1996; West End, 1998; UK tour, 2001; West End revival, 2006; U.S. tour, 2007–2008;

U.K. tour, 2010). *By Jeeves*, based on the P. G. Wodehouse stories, tells how the enterprising valet Jeeves unravels the romantic complications of his master, Bertie Wooster (original version, West End, 1975; rewritten version, West End, 1996; Goodspeed Opera House, 1996; Broadway, 2001).

The Woman in White, a musical adaptation of Wilkie Collins's 1859 novel, presents one of the most famous literary villains of Victorian literature, Count Fosco, as he hatches a nefarious plan to usurp the estate of heiress Laura Fairlie (London, 2004; New York, 2005).

Other compositions by Lloyd Webber include the scores for the British motion picture thrillers *Gumshoe* (1971) and *The Odessa File* (1974); a one-act musical, *Cricket*, set against the backdrop of Cricket Club matches, commissioned for Queen Elizabeth's sixtieth birthday, first performed at Windsor Castle on June 18, 1986; and additional songs for a stage musical of *The Wizard of Oz*, an adaptation of the 1939 film and L. Frank Baum's 1900 novel. It premiered at London's Palladium on March 1, 2011 to pre-opening sales of 10 million pounds. Michael Crawford, the "Phantom of the Opera," portrays the Wizard.

In 2000, Lloyd Webber purchased ten London theatres, making him a dominant force in the world's largest theatrical district. He has arguably been the most popular stage composer of the late twentieth century and, with more than a billion dollars in the bank, certainly the wealthiest. John Snelson, a British music and theatre historian, writes in his biography *Andrew Lloyd Webber* that

> Before Andrew Lloyd Webber, one must turn to the historic Broadway invasion of Arthur Sullivan's music and W. S. Gilbert's words and stories in the late 1870s and early 1880s (*H.M. Pinafore, The Pirates of Penzance, The Mikado*) to find a British theater composer who so consistently conquered American popular culture. From the New York arrival of *Jesus Christ Superstar* in 1971 to the present, the sun has yet to set on the Lloyd Webber era either on Broadway or in London's West End. *Evita, Joseph and the Amazing Technicolor Dreamcoat, Starlight Express*, and *Sunset Boulevard* all enjoyed considerable popular acclaim from the late 1970s to the mid-1990s, and in 1997, one Lloyd Webber show, *Cats*, surpassed the record of *A Chorus Line* for longest-running Broadway show. Lloyd Webber's megahit eventually lost its ninth life in New York and London after eighteen years (1982–2000) and twenty-one years (1981–2002), respectively. Meanwhile, *The Phantom of the Opera* (London, 1986; New York, 1988) continues its spectacular run on both sides of the pond.[24]

Born in Camberley, Surrey, England in 1943, Richard Henry Simpson Stilgoe was brought up in Liverpool, where he sang in the church choir and was lead singer of a group called Tony Snow and the Blizzards. He was educated at Monkton Combe School in Somerset and at Clare College,

Cambridge, and became a member of the Cambridge University Footlights. Stilgoe made his name on the BBC television program *Nationwide*, followed by a consumer affairs program called *That's Life!* for which he wrote comic songs satirizing various minor domestic misfortunes. He became famous for his ability to write a song from almost any source material at prodigious speed, a knack he utilized in a one-man show that has played all over the world. Well known for his wordplay, Stilgoe appeared continuously on quiz shows. His collaboration with Lloyd Webber began with the lyrics for the opening number of *Cats*, continued with the book and additional lyrics for *The Phantom of the Opera*, and the lyrics for *Starlight Express*.

Lyricist Charles Hart was born in London in 1961 to a family with a theatrical background: his father was an antiquarian book dealer who had once been an actor; his mother was the daughter of Glen Byam Shaw, one-time director of the Royal Shakespeare Company. Hart was educated at Desborough School, Maidenhead, Robinson College, Cambridge, and the Guildhall School of Music and Drama in London. He began writing lyrics as a child and was motivated to turn professional in the 1970s when his grandmother, actress Angela Baddeley, starred in a London production of Stephen Sondheim's *A Little Night Music*. Hart attracted the attention of Andrew Lloyd Webber and producer Cameron Mackintosh, who were judges of the Vivian Ellis Awards for musical theatre writers, with an entry based on *Moll Flanders*. They hired him as a lyricist for *The Phantom of the Opera* a year later. Since then Hart has gained an enviable reputation with miscellaneous songs written for BBC Radio, BBC TV, and Granada TV.

Awards and Honors: A top ten selection in *The Best Plays of 1987–1988* and winner of a 1988 Tony Award as Best Musical. Andrew Lloyd Webber was the recipient of Drama Desk Awards for Most Promising Composer— *Jesus Christ Superstar* (1972) and Outstanding Music—*Evita* (1980), *Cats* (1983), and *The Phantom of the Opera* (1988). Lloyd Webber garnered Tony Awards for Best Original Score—*Evita* (1980), *Cats* (1983), and *Sunset Boulevard* (1995); for the latter he also won for Best Book of a Musical. Lloyd Webber and lyricist Tim Rice received an Academy Award in 1997 for Best Original Song, "You Must Love Me," from the film version of *Evita*. Lloyd Webber was knighted in 1992, and nominated a life peer in 1997.

NOTES

1. The plot, production elements, and critical reception of the play version of Gaston Leroux's *The Mystery of the Yellow Room* are provided in Amnon Kabatchnik's *Blood on the Stage, 1900–1925* (Lanham, Md.: Scarecrow Press, 2008), 166–72.

2. The 1925 silent film version of *The Phantom of the Opera* is considered a classic. Carl Laemmle, Universal's president, allocated a production budget of one

million dollars, then an incredible expenditure for a movie. A good portion of it went to the construction of a convincing facsimile of the Paris Opera House, still the largest in the world (it covers a site of nearly three acres, stands seventeen stories high—seven of them below street level—with huge basements for storage of scenery and costumes). *The Phantom of the Opera* serves as the finest showcase for Lon Chaney's unique pantomimic art. He was born in 1883 to deaf-mute parents, and thus learned to express himself, from an early age, through his forceful face and well-coordinated body. He began to work as an actor in 1913 and appeared in some 100 films before attracting attention in a William S. Hart Western of 1918. He was often cast in roles that required complete change of appearance. He was facially scarred by a tiger's claws in *Where East Meets West*, crippled in *The Miracle Man*, legless in *The Penalty*, armless in *The Unknown* (in this one he learned how to hold cigarettes with his toe). Among Chaney's varied portrayals were an ape-man in *The Blind Bargain*, a mad doctor in *The Monster*, and a circus harlequin in *He Who Gets Slapped*. In *The Unholy Three*, he was not only Echo, the sideshow ventriloquist, but also the kindly old grandmother, the criminal genius whose perverse personality surfaces after hours. In *London after Midnight* he played a double role—a ghoulish, crouching, bat-winged creature and a gentle, bespectacled Scotland Yard inspector. Among Chaney's celebrated roles was Quasimodo in *The Hunchback of Notre Dame*. This superstar of the silent era, who was nicknamed "The Man of a Thousand Faces," realized that it took more than putty and false hair to create a believable character. His monstrosities, however warped in body and spirit, were still human. Amidst the potboiling action of *The Phantom of the Opera*, the disfigured, obsessed Erik elicits our understanding and sympathy.

3. *Daily Mail*, October 10, 1986.

4. *Sunday Express*, October 12, 1986.

5. The London and New York theatre critics mistakenly said that Gaston Leroux's original novel was written in 1911. *Le Fantome de L'Opera* was published in Paris in 1910. London's Mills & Boon and New York's Bobbs-Merrill published the novel's English translation in 1911. A rarity, the American first edition, with a chipped dust jacket, was offered by Between the Covers, a New Jersey antiquarian, for $55,000.

6. *Guardian*, October 11, 1986.

7. *Jewish Chronicle*, October 17, 1986.

8. *Financial Times*, October 10, 1986.

9. *Daily Telegraph*, October 11, 1986.

10. *Tribune*, October 24, 1986.

11. *City Limits*, October 16, 1986.

12. *Sunday Today*, October 12, 1986.

13. *New York Post*, January 27, 1988.

14. *Christian Science Monitor*, January 27, 1988.

15. *New York Newsday*, January 27, 1988.

16. *Daily News*, January 27, 1988.

17. *New York Times*, January 27, 1988.

18. *Women's Wear Daily*, January 27, 1988.

19. *WABC-TV7*, January 26, 1988.

20. *Time*, February 8, 1988.

21. *New York Post*, February 4, 2004.

22. *New York Post*, December 22, 2004.

23. *New York Times*, December 22, 2004. A non-musical follow-up motion picture version, produced in 1989, strayed from the original Gaston Leroux novel by shifting the action to modern New York City. A young Broadway singer, Christine Day, comes across a piece of music written nearly 100 years before by an unknown musician named Erik Destler. Once Christine sings his music, she is transported back to 1881 London, where she is coached by a mysterious, protective "Phantom" and becomes the star of the London Opera House. Robert Englund of *A Nightmare on Elm Street* fame portrays Christine's Svengali.

24. John Snelson, *Andrew Lloyd Webber* (New Haven: Yale University Press, 2004), ix.

The Musical Comedy Murders of 1940 (1987)

John Bishop (United States, 1929–2006)

A snowed-in Westchester mansion, replete with sliding doors, revolving bookcases, and secret passages, serves as the scene of the crime in a murder mystery parody that laces together *The Cat and the Canary*, *The Mousetrap*, and Hollywood espionage movies of World War II. "When the play opens it is midnight naturally," notes the playbill of *The Musical Comedy Murders of 1940*.

A backers' audition for an upcoming musical is rudely interrupted by the reemergence of the elusive Stage-Door Slasher, a black-hooded figure who has killed three chorus girls during a previous show, *Manhattan Holiday*, and is now bent on resuming his bloody spree. The figure stealthily appears from behind a drape, stabs to death the household maid, Helsa Wenzel, and hides the body in a walk-in closet.

The audition was called by a wealthy, eccentric Broadway "angel," Elsa von Grossenkneuten, who has assembled the troupe of actors to unmask the murderer. There is an undercurrent of lesbianism in Elsa's character; one of the Slasher's victims was Elsa's "very close friend." Loitering around the mansion is an Irish police sergeant, Michael Kelly, hired by Elsa to conduct the investigation incognito.

Cut off from civilization by a heavy storm, the members of the company become stalking prey for the mysterious Slasher. Among them are tenor Patrick O'Reilly, "a rather large, rather sinister man with a saber scar across his left cheek," and dancer Nikki Crandall, "a beautiful young woman in her twenties who occasionally wears glasses." The director is Ken De La Maize, "a handsome man in his mid-forties whose clothes and tan are Hollywood, and whose all-star movies haven't been released yet." Roger Hopewell is the composer who steals from either Jerome Kern or Sigmund Romberg and "must have that martini." Bernice Roth, the librettist, "dresses like a gypsy dancer; her arms are piled with bracelets which rattle every time she moves." The producer, Marjorie Baverstock, is "anywhere from thirty-five to sixty years of age." None of them turns out to be what he or she or seems to be.

The plot thickens when a Nazi submarine "is believed to have landed men on the shore off Long Island," and Marjorie is subsequently found with a sword pinning her to a chair. Dogs howl from afar, lights go out at opportune moments, bodies keep popping out of revolving closets, and identical triplets make for a carousel of mistaken identities. Unfazed by the mayhem swirling around her, Bernice keeps concocting lyrics for the upcoming production. "I'm creating," she calmly announces.

Poking fun at the genre, Sergeant Kelly sets the scene for the traditional reconstruction of "the moment before the crime," during which time the sinister bookcase slides open and an arm grabs the poor officer around the throat, pulling him back into the opening. Period heroes Ellery Queen, Philo Vance, Orphan Annie, Jack Armstrong, and Don Winslow of the Navy provide inspiration throughout the loopy happenings. The deciphering of a coded notebook leads to a frenetic climax wherein O'Reilly declares he is not Irish but Italian—"Lt. Tony Garibaldi, N.Y.P.D., working under cover on the case of da Stage Door Slasher." But in a follow-up twist, he is discovered to be a Gestapo agent-saboteur by Nikki, who is actually Ensign Nicole Crandall, U.S. Naval Intelligence.

Another disclosure occurs when the maid Helsa removes her wig to reveal that she is a man—a female impersonator who does "Lotte Lenya, Josephine Baker, and a great Dietrich." "Helsa" killed his twin sister— "We were never close. And I needed her identity." In a final wrinkle, Ken, the director, is found to be the Slasher. His motive? "My father left my mother for a ballet dancer." Ken's last unreleased movie, *Berlin Calling*, starred Paul Lukas, Helmut Dantine, Conrad Veidt, George Coulouris, Oscar Homolka, and Merle Oberon.

* * *

Directed by playwright John Bishop, *The Musical Comedy Murders of 1940* was first presented by off-Broadway's Circle Repertory Company on February 4, 1985, for four showings, as a work-in-progress. Circle mounted a full-scale production on January 7, 1987 for eighty-eight performances. The critics' reaction was mixed. Mel Gussow found the "backstage comedy-thriller" lacking "both satiric specificity and biting wit. The humor is inconsistent and the plot is top-heavy with trivia."[1] Allan Wallach maintained that "The spy story seems like a confusing afterthought, and the whodunit remains a mystery."[2] However, Clive Barnes raved: "Funny! Very funny! . . . Here is a most agreeable evening of no redeeming social value, but with engaging and adroit silliness that brings a smile to the mind."[3] Howard Kissel declared "Good news for the boondocks!

There's no need to revive *Ten Little Indians* next season. You can do *The Musical Comedy Murders of 1940* instead."[4]

The melodrama was transferred to Broadway's Longacre Theatre on April 6, 1987. Edwin Wilson called it "a spirited spoof of both murder mysteries and old-fashioned musicals."[5] Joel Segal stated, "No big stars but big, big laughs."[6] Jack Curry guaranteed that "*The Musical Comedy Murders of 1940* will knock you dead."[7]—and so it did for 136 screwball performances.

* * *

John Bishop had one previous play produced on Broadway—*The Trip Back Down*, a highly praised drama about an over-the-hill race car driver who comes to terms with himself. The play began as a workshop project at off-off-Broadway's T. Shreiber Studio on October 1, 1975, and was eventually promoted to uptown's Longacre Theatre on January 4, 1977 for seventy performances. Due to the warm reception granted to *The Trip Back Down*, Bishop was invited to join the reputable Circle Repertory as a playwright in residence.

In addition to *The Musical Comedy Murders of 1940*, Bishop hatched criminous plots in three other plays nurtured by Circle Rep, albeit on a more serious note: *The Harvesting* (1984) is a whodunit unfolding in a seemingly idyllic middle-America town during Independence Day, with a detective digging into a family's past and unearthing closet skeletons to solve a double murder. *Borderlines* (1988) is composed of two one-acts depicting, respectively, a witness being grilled about murders and a police stakeout. *Empty Hearts* (1992) is the story of a husband on trial for killing his wife.

Circle Rep also presented a number of non-crime plays by Bishop: *Cabin 12* (1978); *Winter Signs* (1979); *The Great Grandson of Jedediah Kohler* (1981); and *How Women Break Bad News* (1982). Simultaneously, Bishop directed and acted in a string of Circle productions.

Off-off-Broadway contributions by Bishop include *The Skirmishes* (one-act plays) at New York Stageworks (1982), and material for *Urban Blight*, a musical revue shown at Manhattan Theatre Club (1988). He also wrote the book for a musicalization of Sinclair Lewis's *Elmer Gantry*, produced at Ford Theatre in Washington, D.C. in 1988 and again in 1995, and by La Jolla Playhouse in San Diego, California in 1991.

Circle Rep dissolved in 1997 and Bishop moved west. Later that year he founded Circle West in Los Angeles. Among the plays that the company produced was Bishop's *Legacies*, a police-detective drama. While in L.A., Bishop was hired to do rewrites on the suspense motion pictures *Sliver* (1993), *Clear and Present Danger* (1994), *Beverly Hills Cop III* (1994), and *Primal Fear* (1996). He also scripted the movie *The Package* (1989), a political thriller depicting an attempt to assassinate the Secretary General of the Soviet Union when he was visiting Chicago. Gene Hackman, Dennis Franz, and Joanna Cassidy portray the heroes who confront power-hungry military despots played by John Heard and Tommy Lee Jones.

John Dickson Bishop was born on May 3, 1929, in Mansfield, Ohio, the son of a foreman for Westinghouse. He majored in theatre at Carnegie Mellon University in Pittsburgh and began his career as an actor at the Cleveland Playhouse. He also served in the Marines. Bishop died of cancer on December 20, 2006 in a clinic in Bad Heyburn, Germany, far from his Encino, California home. He was 77.

Acting Edition: Dramatists Play Service.

NOTES

1. *New York Times,* January 8, 1987.
2. *New York Newsday,* January 8, 1987.
3. *New York Post,* January 8, 1987.
4. *Daily News,* January 8, 1987.
5. *Wall Street Journal,* April 22, 1987.
6. *WABC-TV7,* April 6, 1987.
7. *USA Today,* April 7, 1987.

Perfect Crime (1987)

Warren Manzi (United States, 1955–)

As of early 2012, the longest-running mystery play in London has been Agatha Christie's *The Mousetrap*, which opened in the West End in 1952 and is still drawing throngs. The longest-running thriller in New York has been Warren Manzi's *Perfect Crime*, which opened off-Broadway in 1987 and is still raising its curtain, albeit to half-empty houses.

While *The Mousetrap* is an intriguing whodunit boasting a wallop of a surprise ending, the puzzling element of *Perfect Crime* is its longevity. The play underwent major changes while switching locations five or six times. In the published acting edition, Warren Manzi relates that "way back, the script was too long, and too many people were confused." The playwright acknowledges "the belief, and the guts to endure the longest set of previews in the history of the American Theatre" by actors, designers, technicians, theatre managers, and administrators who have contributed greatly to the process of *Perfect Crime* as it has developed through its off-Broadway run.[1] But although the play has been trimmed from a three-and-a-half-hour running time to about half that, it still remains too cumbersome and incoherent in many of its plot maneuvers. The long run of *Perfect Crime* may arguably be attributed to an endorsement by a second-string *New York Times* reviewer and blind faith by persistent producers who have maintained low overhead.

The action of *Perfect Crime* takes place in and around the sitting room of the Brent home in Windsor Locks, Connecticut, "an out-of-the-way, wealthy community." Margaret Thorne Brent is a psychiatrist. She uses the sitting room and an adjacent office for consultations. The furniture is comfortable and there are full bookcases, a stereo system, a television set, and a brick fireplace. Stairs lead to a landing; doors open to the kitchen and the basement. There are no windows, but during the day sunlight streams in through a skylight.

The curtain rises on a stormy Sunday night. A clock chimes ten. A reading lamp behind an armchair throws a dim light. A man enters from the front door. He is wearing a tuxedo and is bone dry. He moves swiftly to a desk, opens a drawer, takes out a .45 automatic, and examines the weapon.

Suddenly the stereo goes on, operated by a timer. At the same time, the phone rings. The man snatches the receiver, not noticing that the kitchen door is slowly opening; a hand appears. Someone is listening as the man is addressing "Margaret" on the line, telling her that he could have overcome anything if she had really loved him. The man hangs up and sits in the armchair, reading a magazine and munching on cake. A red-haired girl in a green dress appears on the landing. We can't see her face. The man stands up and points the gun at her. The girl produces a revolver and fires. The man collapses to the floor, drops the gun, and begins to crawl toward the office. The girl keeps firing as the man disappears into the office. The girl follows, shutting the door behind her. The hand clutching the kitchen door disappears. We later find out that the clandestine listener was the household cook, Mrs. Johaneston.

Scene 2 unfolds the following night. The TV is on, visible to the audience, with a gaggle of girls singing a jingle. There is drilling in the office. The phone rings. Dr. Margaret Thorne Brent enters from the office, wearing a smock covered with paint and carrying an electric drill. She crosses to the telephone and tells the pharmacist on the other end that she always keeps extra insulin in the house for her diabetic husband. Another call comes in and Margaret clicks the phone back and forth, informing the Granville Employment Agency that her cook didn't show that morning and tells American Express that she needs a platinum card.

While conversing on the phone, Margaret also pays attention to the television screen, where an interviewer, David Breuer, introduces Dr. Margaret Brent, a psychiatrist and author of the recently published whodunit *Killing the King*. The TV interview and Margaret's telephone discourse continue simultaneously. Breuer solicits from Margaret the information that her husband, Harrison Brent, is also a psychiatrist, now retired; he's been sick with diabetes. In her book, she says, a woman kills her husband; the clues are "psychological ones."

There is a knock on the door and Margaret switches off the TV. She notices the .45 on a chair and puts it on the mantel on her way to the door. Inspector James Ascher is standing in the doorway. Margaret picks up the drill, tells Ascher that she's "just finishing this bookcase thing" and exits into the office. Drilling is heard as the inspector scrutinizes a painting on the chimney, high above the fireplace opening—an arid desert, a scorching sun, a man on his knees, another man with no face standing over him. In the bottom left-hand corner there's a skull, in the top right-hand corner, a dog.

The drilling stops and Margaret returns. She explains that her husband, Harrison Brent, painted that picture right on the bricks eight months ago when they moved to America from London. Ascher listens politely and Margaret tells him that he is "much nicer" than the other police officer, Detective Giarrusso, who's been here all day asking for her husband. Margaret says that Harrison went walking, for his health, through the woods. Ascher changes topics and asks whether Margaret owns a red wig. "No, not my style," answers Margaret. Ascher now reveals that he's following up on a report that her husband was shot five times by a red-haired woman of average height wearing a green dress. The housekeeper, Mrs. Johaneston, witnessed it all.

Ascher reads Margaret her Miranda rights, "You have the right to remain silent," when she swipes the .45 off the mantel, aims it at the inspector, and demands to know the details of Mrs. Johaneston's statement. A man appears on the upstairs landing, drying his hair with a towel, the same man who appeared in scene 1. Margaret introduces him as her husband, W. Harrison Brent, "late of London, before that Harvard, now retired, caused by diabetes." Margaret hands Harrison the .45: "Here's your toy," and addresses Ascher wryly, "Is that the man Mrs. Johaneston saw last night? The one who was shot five times?" The inspector stalks out in a huff.

In scene 3 Margaret is in session with a patient, Lionel Mcauley. She allows Lionel to turn the tables and bombard her with a succession of queries. She patiently tells him that her husband, a diabetic, painted the strange wall picture and that even though her favorite fantasy is "murdering my husband," she won't kill him because the money would go back to his family. At some point Lionel grabs Margaret by the throat, releases her, and reveals that he followed her last night to Brenner's Pharmacy and saw a man in the car with her. They drove to Elm Street and the man, carrying a brown bag, went into an apartment building.

Margaret sends Lionel upstairs to fetch a gun from the night table and a brown hatbox from the walk-in closet. Lionel returns and opens the box to reveal a red wig. He aims the gun at Margaret and shoots six times. It soon becomes clear that the gun was loaded with blanks. Margaret instructs Lionel to sit down, relax, and sleep.

Scene 4 begins with Ascher showing Harrison Brent his police badge and Harrison proving to be a disciple of Sherlock Holmes with a series of deductions, pinpointing the inspector's expensive collar, shirt, and tie but ten-dollar pants and five-dollar shoes: "So, you crave expensive things but can only afford half the ensemble." Harrison concludes that Ascher wants to use Margaret for his Big Case and is searching for a Vital Clue.

Margaret enters in a running outfit, out of breath. She asks Ascher if he has a heavy caseload, and the inspector tells her that there's only been one murder in this town in the last five years: a naked red-headed girl of about eighteen fished out of Scotty's Pond. She was beaten to death and her murderer threw her body into the pond. They couldn't identify the girl and she's still listed as Jane Doe.

The phone rings. It's Detective Giarrusso on the line. Ascher hangs up and informs Margaret and Harrison that their cook, Mrs. Johaneston, was found dead in her apartment on Elm Street. Someone beat her bout the head with a blunt instrument.

Ascher leaves. Harrison expresses concern: the detective won't give up. Margaret assures him that her hypnotism of Lionel Mcauley is working and the police will believe that he's the killer. There's nothing to worry about.

Act 2 unfolds two nights later. Mozart's String Quartet in C Major is heard on the stereo. Lionel asks Margaret why she keeps hypnotizing him and telling him repeatedly about a young girl, Carlotta Donovan. There's a knock on the door. Margaret pushes Lionel out the kitchen door, asks him to leave by the footpath, and promises to meet him the next day. She then moves to the front door and throws it open. Ascher enters and questions Margaret about Mrs. Johaneston, who was murdered Monday night with a baseball bat. Margaret admits that she hated the cook, who was "a sneak" and "the town gossip." Through a heated cross-examination, Ascher and Margaret get close to each other and, unexpectedly, he takes her in his arms and they kiss. Margaret crosses to the liquor cabinet and prepares two drinks. Ascher takes a hardcover book out of his pocket: Killing the King by Margaret Thorne Brent. "I finished your book," he says. There's a passage in the chapter "Murder" that he particularly liked: "You must commit the crime so no one can tell a crime has been committed. That was what the perfect crime was."

Margaret describes how last Sunday she acted out a theory described in her book, wearing a green dress and a red wig, gun in hand. The cook Johaneston must have seen it. Ascher asserts that whoever killed Mrs. Johaneston also killed Jane Doe. The plot thickens when, following Ascher's exit, Margaret tells Harrison that she plans to have Lionel Mcauley kill the inspector on Sunday night.

In scene 6, Lionel is discovered wearing a red dress, a wig, and high heels. While he teaches Margaret to dance the cha-cha, he babbles that he knows why she has taken him under her wing; it's because she's aware that he ruthlessly got rid of his wife's lovers, pushing one down an elevator shaft, blowing up the other guy's car. Margaret hands Lionel the .45. He understands that she is setting him up to be accused of being the baseball bat killer. He doesn't mind; he doesn't have the courage to kill himself.

Saturday night. A thunderstorm. The clock chimes. Lionel appears on the landing. He's wearing a green dress and red wig, brandishing a gun. He descends. A man leaps out of the office, grabs Lionel's gun-hand, and drags him into the office. A cracking sound is heard repeatedly and Lionel screams. We hear a baseball bat dropping to the floor. The man emerges from the office, stained with blood. He wipes himself with a handkerchief, exits to the kitchen, and returns carrying a suitcase. He goes to the phone, dials, and makes a flight reservation from Kennedy Airport to Heathrow, England under the name of Phillip Reynolds.

A man's voice is heard on the tape recorder, the real Harrison Brent explaining to his wife that Carlotta Donovan simply admired his paintings. Reynolds listens for a moment, then heads for the front door and exits. Margaret comes down the stairs in evening dress. The doorbell rings. It is Ascher. The inspector puts his gun on the coffee table and informs Margaret that his men dragged Scotty's Pond again and found a lady's makeup kit stamped with the initials C. D. In a secret compartment, under the lipstick, the police discovered a crucifix engraved with the initials W. H.—no doubt for W. Harrison, Margaret's husband. Ascher theorizes that for some unknown reason Carlotta Donovan had fatally shot Harrison and Margaret avenged his death by killing Carlotta, disfiguring her with a baseball bat so that she wouldn't be recognized, and throwing her body in the pond.

Unknown to Ascher, Margaret then called a former beau, Phillip Reynolds, in London, told him that she loved him, that she always loved him, and Phillip agreed to impersonate Harrison. Every Sunday night she and Phillip have been replaying what happened, in search of the one clue left by Carlotta in a taped message. Last Sunday night, when enacting the scene, Mrs. Johaneston saw Phillip eating a piece of cake, which the diabetic Harrison would never do. A chatterbox by nature, she would've told everyone, and had to go.

As if the head of the viewer has not been swimming enough, Ascher adds another wrinkle to the plot when deducing that the enigmatic, disorganized painting over the fireplace indicates that the bricks have been switched; Margaret must have taken them out and buried Harrison's body in the fireplace.

Police sirens are approaching. Margaret puts the barrel of Ascher's gun to her temple. Her hands shaking, she pulls the trigger. Ascher wipes off the burn and tells her that he loaded the gun with blanks. He helps her to a chair and throws open the front door. Red and blue flashing lights envelop the room.

* * *

Directed by Jeffrey Hyatt, *Perfect Crime* opened at off-Broadway's Courtyard Playhouse on April 17, 1987. The cast included Perry Pirkkanen (Inspector James Ascher), G. Gordon Cronce (W. Harrison Brent),

Marc Lutsky (Lionel Mcauley), and W. MacGregor King (David Breuer, who appears on a videotape). Catherine Russell, who portrayed the lead role of Margaret Thorne Brent, has stayed with the production since the premiere, moving with it to several off-Broadway venues: the Second Stage; the McGinn-Gazale Theatre; Intar Theatre; the Harold Clurman Theatre; Theatre Four; Duffy Theatre, a renovated burlesque house in Times Square; and finally, the Snapple Theatre Center at the corner of 50th Street and Broadway, where it is still running. Russell has never taken a sick day or a vacation day. She has missed only four performances, to attend her siblings' weddings, and currently holds the world record for the most performances as a character in a play.

Reviewer D. J. R. Bruckner of the *New York Times* wrote: "Warren Manzi has the makings of a crackling thriller in *Perfect Crime*, playing at the Courtyard Theatre. Its tension holds tight even while it ridicules conventions of the genre."[2]

In its third year, when playing at the Harold Clurman Theatre on 42nd Street's Theatre Row, the production's advertising flyers blazoned quotes from the *Village Voice* ("Mr. Manzi has a way with unexpected violence!") and *WNEW* ("A good old-fashioned murder mystery!").

In its fifth year, when playing at Theatre Four, the *Daily News* earmarked the show's 2,025th performance and its becoming "the longest-running straight play in off-Broadway history."[3] In its twelfth year, when performing at the Duffy Theatre, *Perfect Crime*'s posters featured blurbs by the *New Yorker* ("A cunning little whodunit!"), *Fox Live News* ("One of the biggest hits off-Broadway!"), and the *Newhouse Newspapers* ("May well outdistance *The Mousetrap*!"). In its eighteenth year playing at the Snapple Theatre Center, Jason Zinoman of the *New York Times* called *Perfect Crime* "one of the great curiosities of the New York theatre. . . . Fans of cheap genre novels and twisty murder mysteries may have fun puzzling out the labyrinthine plot."[4]

In 2011, *Perfect Crime* celebrated twenty-four years and almost 10,000 performances in New York.

* * *

Warren Manzi was born in Lawrence, Massachusetts in 1955. When very young, he was influenced by his mother, who was an aficionado of detective fiction, and found himself immersed in the works of Arthur Conan Doyle, Agatha Christie, Raymond Chandler, and Erle Stanley Gardner. In high school he became interested in drama, wallowing in Chekhov, Ibsen, Strindberg, and Moliere. Future heroes were Pirandello, Tennessee Williams, and Englishmen Pinter, Osborne, and Stoppard.

A 1980 graduate of the Yale School of Drama, that same year, at age twenty-five, Manzi appeared on Broadway as Mozart in *Amadeus*. Simultaneously, an early version of the play *Perfect Crime* drew the interest of

veteran producer Morton Gottlieb, and Manzi became the youngest author ever to have a play optioned for Broadway. The project never mate-
rialized and Manzi moved to Hollywood to write screenplays and appear
in movies. He had a supporting role in *Nuts* (1987), a screen adaptation of
Tom Topor's courtroom drama about a call-girl accused of murder, a role
undertaken by Barbra Streisand. Upon his return to New York, Manzi became the artistic director of the Actors Collective, a not-for-profit theatre
company, where *Perfect Crime* began its run.

At the Actors Collective, Manzi staged, among other productions, An-
ton Chekhov's *The Three Sisters* and Kurt Vonnegut Jr.'s *Between Time and
Timbuktu*. For the Garrett Players of Lawrence, Massachusetts he directed
Harold Pinter's *The Birthday Party*, Samuel Becket's *Waiting for Godot*, Joe
Orton's *Loot*, and the musicals *Annie*, *Fiddler on the Roof*, and *A Funny
Thing Happened on the Way to the Forum*. Manzi also directed dramas and
musicals for the New England Theatre Conference.

In an interview conducted by blogger Adam Szymkowicz in 2001,
Manzi states, "I like plays that take you through a story and keep you on
the edge of your seat and on your toes."[5]

Acting Edition: Samuel French, Inc.

Award and Honors: Warren Manzi is the only person in the history
of the New England Theatre Conference annual festivals to win the Best
Director Award five times.

NOTES

1. Warren Manzi, *Perfect Crime* (New York: Samuel French, Inc., 1990),
unpaginated.

2. *New York Times*, July 1, 1987.

3. *Daily News*, September 4, 1992.

4. *New York Times*, October 3, 2005.

5. http://aszym.blogspot.com/2011/07.

Beyond Reasonable Doubt (1987)

Jeffrey Archer (England, 1940–)

When Lord Jeffrey Archer's courtroom drama *Beyond Reasonable Doubt* opened in London in late September 1987, the production followed the best-selling author's sensational libel suit. Lord Archer had taken the *Daily Star*, a tabloid, to court for a story alleging that he had spent the night with a prostitute. The jury delivered a verdict in Archer's favor to the tune of half a million pounds.

But to the surprise—and perhaps disappointment—of the first-night audience at London's Queens Theatre on September 22, 1987, *Beyond Reasonable Doubt* was not concerned with libel but with murder. Worse, the play's jury is persuaded to reach an incorrect verdict.

The first act of *Beyond Reasonable Doubt* takes place in the Central Criminal Court (The Old Bailey). The curtain rises on Mr. Justice Tredwell addressing the jury (i.e., the audience): "The case has already attracted much lurid publicity," says the judge. He instructs the viewers to concentrate on the evidence, and adds, "It is you and you alone who will decide if Sir David Metcalfe is guilty or not of murder."

The prosecutor, Anthony Blair-Booth, states that the indictment revolves around "the deliberate, non-accidental cold killing of Lady Millicent Metcalfe by the defendant, her husband." It gives him no pleasure, says Blair-Booth, to appear for the Crown against a man who was "an ornament of the Bar." However, continues the prosecutor, distressing as it is, the Crown will present a case that will prove, beyond reasonable doubt, that Sir David Metcalfe did willfully murder his wife in the early hours of March 24. Earlier that evening the two of them had quarreled; later, Sir David grasped the opportunity to "deliberately and knowingly" administer a lethal overdose of the drug Cyclotoxelix to Lady Metcalfe.

Blair-Booth calls to the stand Detective Chief Inspector Richard Travers, who testifies that the Metcalfes' housekeeper, Eileen Rogers, came to the Wimbledon police station and stated that she had witnessed Sir David

319

poison his wife. He had put a Cyclotoxelix pill in her tea though he must have known that Lady Metcalfe had already taken the medication only a few hours earlier.

Sir David, who has elected to represent himself, cross-examines Inspector Travers.

> SIR DAVID: Inspector, if I had killed my wife in the manner indicated by the Crown, surely I could have destroyed the evidence quite simply by having her body cremated?
> INSPECTOR TRAVERS: Most criminals think they're cleverer than the law. That's usually how we catch them.

Blair-Booth calls housekeeper Rogers. She testifies that Sir David has a violent temper and "can always pick a quarrel over the slightest thing." On the fateful evening he came home drunk and hit Lady Metcalfe. Later, she saw him drop a red pill she takes only once a week into the Lady's tea. Upon cross-examination, Sir David produces three full pill bottles from the shelf on the dock. He asks Mrs. Rogers to identify the color of the pills in each bottle; she is wrong each time.

The next witness is the Metcalfes' family doctor, John Weeden, who ascertains that upon examining Lady Metcalfe's body in the early hours of March 24, he concluded that she had died of natural causes. In an answer to Blair-Booth's query, Dr. Weeden explains that any excess of the drug Cyclotoxelix could prove fatal. He had prescribed the drug to Lady Metcalfe for lymphosarcoma—cancer of the lymph glands. He adds that she was in considerable pain for the last fourteen months of her life.

Blair-Booth calls Lionel Hamilton, a solicitor, who testifies that Lady Metcalfe left a will bequeathing the bulk of the estate—just over one million pounds—to her husband.

That concludes the case for the prosecution. Sir David takes the stand and lets his junior counsel, Robert Pierson, question him. On the night in question he was awakened by a noise that seemed to come from downstairs, discovered that his wife was not at his side, ran down the steps, and found Millicent lying on the drawing-room floor. He picked her up and helped her to the sofa. She was badly shaken by the fall and asked for tea. He went to the kitchen immediately. When he returned with the tea, the pain had obviously become much worse. Millicent had two pill bottles in her hands and was fumbling with one of them, trying to open it. She handed the vials to him and asked him to put a pill in her tea. He did. He was concerned with his wife's condition and cannot remember the color of the pill. Millicent seemed to slip into a restful sleep. Later, he realized that she had started to grow cold and he could no longer hear her breathing. He called Dr. Weeden, who came within the hour and confirmed his worst fears. And, no, contrary to the housekeeper's testimony, he and his wife never quarreled. The only things they ever disagreed about were Dylan Thomas and cricket.

Blair-Booth cross-examines Sir David and elicits from him the information that preceding his wife's death, he had "a run of rather bad luck" and owed stockbrokers Gilbert and Goddard two hundred and eighty-one thousand pounds. Blair-Booth declares that Sir David found an easy way out—a chance to clear himself of embarrassing debts and an ailing wife. If it weren't for the courageous Mrs. Rogers, Sir David may have committed the perfect murder, he concludes.

The lights fade to a spot on the Judge, who addresses the audience-jury with the instruction, "If the evidence does not satisfy you beyond reasonable doubt you will bring a verdict of 'Not Guilty,' but on the other hand, if it does, your verdict, however unpalatable it may be—must be 'Guilty.'" The lights come up again and the Clerk of the Court faces front: "Mr. Foreman, do you find the prisoner, Sir David Metcalfe, guilty or not guilty of murder?" Everyone on stage stares fixedly at the audience as the curtain descends.

Act 2 is composed of a series of flashbacks showing what really happened. The lights fade up on the Metcalfe home in Wimbledon. Lady Metcalfe, in her late forties, and her housekeeper, Mrs. Rogers, are preparing a "pre-trial dinner party"—Sir David is set to defend Beverley Cutts, a woman who stabbed her lover seven times with a rusty pair of scissors. The guests are Lionel Hamilton, an old solicitor, and Robert Pierson, David's junior counsel. They reminisce about their earlier cases—the Halford murders; Humphries Ascott, "the arson killer"; Lang, "the hatchet murderer"; Charles McCulloch, "the body in the freezer"; and Alice Campbell, charged with "theft, adultery, perjury, blackmail and attempted murder."

The conversation shifts to their nemesis—Anthony Blair-Booth. Young Pierson learns that the prosecutor had proposed to Millicent before she consented to marry Sir David, so the rivalry between them is not only professional but also personal. The telephone rings. Sir David speaks to his broker and gets some bad news.

Later that evening, after the departure of their guests, Lady Metcalfe suffers a painful attack and collapses in a chair. She wearily tells her husband that there's no use fooling themselves—"we are talking of months at best." Mrs. Rogers enters, carrying a tray with a glass of water and a bottle of pills. "You must take your once-a-week pill tonight, my lady," she says. Lady Metcalfe swallows the pill and Sir David guides her to the stairs.

A week later, on the evening of March 23, Sir David enters the drawing room and sees his wife lying on the floor. He helps her to the sofa and she asks for tea. He exits to the kitchen and returns with a cup. She hands David a bottle of pills. Mrs. Rogers appears on the stairs and observes

David drop a pill into the tea, then sit next to his wife. Mrs. Rogers exits upstairs. David sobs, "Millie, please—don't go yet."

The last scene unfolds two weeks after the trial. Sir David is standing by the desk with his back to the audience. The doorbell rings and Lionel Hamilton enters. He rebukes Sir David for living "like a hermit" since the verdict. He notices a bottle of red pills on the table and Sir David explains that the police returned them. Hamilton attempts to cheer up his subdued friend and mentions an upcoming case, an "extraordinary" one, of a boy who killed his mother, having dabbled in black magic.

Sir David says that case is tempting but he cannot return to the Bar—because he *did* kill his wife. No, it was not an accident caused by exchanging pills. He deliberately mixed Millicent's tea with a red pill—that's what she wanted and he couldn't refuse her. He had the pleasure of beating Blair-Booth, but he knew it would be his last appearance in court. He asked Hamilton to come to his house because he thinks he should know the truth—the whole truth. Shortly before Hamilton arrived, says Sir David, he took a fatal dose of three Cyclotoxelix pills with a glass of wine.

Hamilton reaches slowly for the phone and dials 999 as the lights slowly fade and the curtain falls.[1]

* * *

Beyond Reasonable Doubt premiered at the Queens Theatre, London, on September 22, 1987, directed by Robert Gilmore and designed by Tim Goodchild. The main roles were portrayed by Frank Finlay (Sir David Metcalfe), Wendy Craig (Lady Metcalfe), Jeffrey Wickham (Anthony Blair-Booth), and Andrew Cruickshank (Mr. Justice Tredwell). Critic Kenneth Hurren of *Plays and Players* slammed the drama as "pretty awful," found the flashbacks "irrelevant padding," and lamented the "total lack of elements of plausibility."[2]

Despite the negative critical reception, *Beyond Reasonable Doubt* ran for more than 600 performances. The play's box-office bonanza may be attributed to the notoriety of the playwright's successful libel action against the *Daily Star*.

A second courtroom drama by Archer, *The Accused*, premiered at the Theatre Royal, Windsor, England on September 26, 2000 and had a nine-week regional tour before anchoring at the Haymarket Theatre, London, on December 5. Archer himself played the title role of Patrick Sherwood, a doctor charged with fatally poisoning his wife. Sherwood pleads "Not Guilty." At the end of the trial, the audience is assigned the role of jury, voting on Sherwood's guilt or innocence. The play was savaged by the critics. Benedict Nightingale of the *New York Times* opined that as soon as Archer's Doc Sherwood enters the witness box, the play "creaks monotonously along, like a wooden crate dragged down a corridor."[3] *The Accused* ran for eight weeks.

Art imitated life again, for simultaneously Archer was accused of perjury related to the 1987 case. The formal charges came hours before the opening night of *The Accused*. In July 2001 he was convicted of "perjury and perverting the course of justice." The jurors determined that he had asked two friends to provide a false alibi and compensated them for it during the *Daily Star* trial. A diary filled with bogus dates preserved by Archer's secretary served as the smoking gun. Archer was sentenced to four years and served half of his sentence. While incarcerated, he wrote the three-volume memoir *A Prison Diary*.

* * *

The son of a printer, Jeffrey Howard Archer was born in 1940 London and brought up in Somerset. He was educated at Wellington School and Brasenose College, Oxford, where he excelled in sports and was president of the Athletic Club. Archer ran the 100 yards in 9.6 seconds for Great Britain in 1966.

After leaving school, Archer trained for a while with the army and the police, then became a physical education teacher in several prep schools. He enrolled at Oxford and garnered an academic qualification in teaching. There have been claims that Archer provided false evidence of his academic qualifications to gain admission into Oxford. He was also plagued with rumors of financial wrongdoing during that period. However, that did not deter Mary Weeden, a chemistry student at St. Anne's College, Oxford, from marrying Archer in July 1966.

Soon thereafter, Archer entered politics and was elected to the Greater London Council, serving as a Conservative councilor from 1967 to 1970. At the age of 29, he was elected Member of Parliament (MP) for the Lincolnshire constituency of Louth. His ideology was to the left of the Conservative Party, and he rebelled against some of the party's policies, voting against restoring capital punishment, for example. In 1985 he was appointed deputy chairman of the Conservative Party by Margaret Thatcher but the following year he was forced to resign. This came on the heels of a scandal caused by an article in *The News of the World* that charged Archer with paying a "vice-girl."

Archer's books are peppered with heroic feats and crime elements. His first novel, *Not a Penny More, Not a Penny Less*, was published in both the United States and England in 1976 and was an instant success. The plot revolves around shady business deals and stock manipulation. His second novel, *Shall We Tell the President?* (1977), is a thriller depicting a plot to assassinate Edward Kennedy. His third, *Kane and Abel* (1979), tells the story of two men—one Polish, an illegitimate son of a Gypsy, the other a rich and privileged Bostonian. Their paths cross and they become bitter enemies, each determined to destroy the other. The book became an enormous best-seller, spawned two sequels, and was made into a television miniseries by CBS in 1985.

The following year, Granada TV screened a ten-part adaptation of Archer's *First Among Equals*, the saga of four ambitious MPs and their quest to become Prime Minister. *A Matter of Honour* (1986) is a tale about a letter that the receiver never opened, only to be passed to his son after his death. The opening of the letter changes the family's lives forever. *As the Crow Flies* (1991) begins in the east end of London at the turn of the twentieth century and follows the rags-to-riches career of Charles Trumper who, as a youth, ran a fruit cart. He eventually became the owner of some of the most successful businesses in England. *Honour Among Thieves* (1993) is a political thriller in which Saddam Hussein's emissaries steal the American Declaration of Independence and the CIA is on the hunt to recover the document. Israel's Mossad and New York's mafia get involved in the action. *The Fourth Estate* (1996) depicts the battle royale between media barons Rupert Murdoch and Robert Maxwell to control the British newspaper market.

In *The Eleventh Commandment* (1998), the chief of the CIA secretly orders the assassination of an international array of adversarial political figures. The proceedings move from the White House to the St. Petersburg hideaway of a Russian mafia boss. *Sons of Fortune* (2003) is the tale of Hartford, Connecticut twins who were separated at birth and grew up without knowing about each other. Eventually, both decide to run for governor of Connecticut. The truth surfaces when a car accident reveals that they share the same rare blood type.

Vincent Van Gogh's last painting, worth $70 million, is the MacGuffin of *False Impression* (2005), a twisty mystery novel that includes information about the September 11 attacks on New York and takes a breathtaking journey through several countries before the resolution. *The Gospel According to Judas* (2007), co-written with Frank Moloney, presents the events of the New Testament through the eyes of Judas Iscariot. *A Prisoner of Birth* (2008) is a contemporary retelling of Alexandre Dumas's *The Count of Monte Cristo*. Danny Cartwright, arrested for murder in a plot orchestrated by four friends, escapes from prison and unleashes his revenge upon the men who framed him. *Paths of Glory* (2009) is a controversial novel in which Archer supports the claim that George Mallory, an Englishman whose body was found in 1999 at 26,760 feet, was the first to conquer Mount Everest—before Sir Edmund Hilary.

Highly regarded short story collections in which Archer plays a cat-and-mouse game with the reader include *A Quiver Full of Arrows* (1980),

A Twist in the Tale (1989), *Twelve Red Herrings* (1994), *To Cut a Long Story Short* (2000), *Cat O'Nine Tales* (2006), *And Thereby Hangs a Tale* (2010).

Archer's books have been published in ninety-seven countries and translated into forty languages, with international sales passing 250 million copies.

Acting Edition: Samuel French, Ltd.

Awards and Honors: Jeffrey Archer was made a life peer in 1992; despite his criminal conviction at the Old Bailey, he retains the title of Lord.

NOTES

1. The verdict of "not guilty" awarded to a person charged with murder and later discovered to be guilty also occurred at the climaxes of *The Ware Case* (1915) by George Pleydell, *Witness for the Prosecution* (1953) by Agatha Christie, and *An Anatomy of a Murder* (1959) by Elihu Winer (based on the 1958 novel by Robert Traver).

2. *Plays and Players*, November 1987.

3. *New York Times*, January 7, 2001.

The Woman in Black (1987)

Stephen Mallatratt (England, 1947–2004)

Reminiscent of Bram Stoker's *Dracula*, in which a young lawyer, Jonathan Harker, travels to a remote village in Transylvania and plunges into a supernatural ordeal, *The Woman in Black*, adapted by Stephen Mallatratt from a novel by Susan Hill, centers on a young solicitor, Arthur Kipps, who is summoned to a small market town on the east coast of England and gets entangled in a ghostly affair.

The Woman in Black begins in a small Victorian theatre, on a stage devoid of scenery but cluttered with clothes, boxes, trunks, and furniture—including several chairs and a high stool. The auditorium lights remain on and working lights come up as the Actor, a middle-aged man, enters carrying a manuscript. The Actor comes downstage and tells the audience a Christmas Eve tale. He is soon interrupted from the back of the theatre by a gentleman named Arthur Kipps, who admonishes the actor for his monotonous interpretation and urges him, "Draw on your emotions, and our imaginations."

Kipps coaches the Actor to summon his energies. "We'll make an [Henry] Irving of you yet," says Kipps. But the Actor soon falters and slumps dejectedly into a chair. Kipps takes the manuscript and as the house lights go off, he prepares the audience for "a story, a true story, a story of haunting and evil, fear and confusion, terror and tragedy."

Kipps arranges the clutter of furniture into some order that can pass for a solicitor's office. He snaps his fingers and instantly the sound effects of a London street are heard: cars, horses, shouts from outdoor vendors. The Actor, now appearing as Tomes the Clerk, stands writing in a ledger. His desk might be a stool or a pile of boxes. Kipps enters briskly and tosses his briefcase on the desk. Tomes keeps sniffing as he sends Kipps to see Mr. Bentley. The Actor becomes Bentley and sits on the other side of the desk. Bentley instructs Kipps to go home, pack a bag, and take the afternoon train from King's Cross to the little market town of Crythin Gifford. There he'll wait for low tide and cross the causeway to Eel Marsh. His mission is to go to the house of the recently deceased widow, Alice Drablow, represent the firm at their client's funeral, and review her documents and private papers.

Kipps informs the viewers that he told his landlady that he would be away for a couple of nights and scribbles a note to his fiancée, Stella. Accompanied by the sound of a steam train, he arranges his compartment and sits reading a newspaper. After a while, the train slows down and draws to a halt. As the train moves on, Kipps changes his seat a few times and puts on a coat and hat against the cold.

The Actor is now Sam Daily, a local landowner who greets Kipps on the platform and directs him to the Gifford Arms Hotel. When Kipps mentions that he's on his way to Eel Marsh House, the desk clerk reacts strangely and abruptly turns away. "There seems to be a propensity for leaving conversations to hang in the air whenever Mrs. Drablow's name is mentioned," relates Kipps. "Doubtless in such a place as this, with its eerie marshes, sudden fogs, moaning winds and lonely houses, any poor old woman might be looked at askance."

A villager, Mr. Jerome, leads Kipps to a church. A priest's voice-over is heard followed by the echoing tread of the undertaker's men bearing a coffin down the aisle. In the center aisle stands the Woman in Black. Her clothes are dark and old-fashioned. She wears a black bonnet that partly obscures her face; from what can be seen, it appears she suffers from some terrible wasting disease. She is extremely pale, the thinnest layer of flesh is stretched tautly across her bones, and her eyes seem sunken. Upon seeing her, Kipps is momentarily shocked, then steadies himself. Mr. Jerome does not see her, nor is he aware that she's there.

The church changes into a graveyard. Jerome and Kipps stand over the edge of the stage, as if looking into the grave. The Woman in Black enters and hovers behind them. Kipps senses her presence but, again, Jerome does not see her. The Woman in Black moves away. Kipps asks Jerome about the "young woman with the wasted face." Jerome freezes and grabs Kipps's hand, evidently in extreme terror. He takes a deep breath and changes into a carriage driver, Mr. Keckwick, wearing an overcoat, cap, and high riding boots. He picks up a riding whip, arranges several chairs toward the audience, and sits facing front. We hear a pony drawing to a halt and Kipps climbs up behind Keckwick. They drive for a while, the silence broken by occasional harsh cries from birds.

Kipps dismounts, sends Keckwick and his carriage away, and walks through the marshes. He arrives in a small burial ground, where most of the gravestones are leaning or fallen, covered in lichens and mosses. The Woman in Black appears nearby, and slips away and out of sight. "I do not believe in ghosts," mumbles Kipps and begins to run until, breathlessly, he reaches Eel Marsh House and slams the door shut.

He switches on the lights and dumps bundles of documents on a makeshift table. From outside he can hear the sound of a pony and cart, followed by the shrill neighing of a horse in panic, a shout, and the terrified sobbing of a child. Kipps conjures the image of a pony and cart with a child sucked into the marshes' quicksand.

Kipps attempts to engage a local assistant to help review Mrs. Drablow's papers, but no one will agree to spend time at Eel Marsh House. Sam Daily does not like Kipps's staying alone there and lets the solicitor borrow his little dog, Spider, for company. Kipps begins sorting the papers into piles—those to be dealt with, those to discard. He notices a packet of letters dated about sixty years ago and signed for the most part "J," and occasionally "Jennet." The writer, a young woman and apparently a relative of Mrs. Drablow, was unmarried with a child. Her parents sent her away, and a son was born in Scotland. She refused to give up the child for adoption, saying repeatedly that they would never be parted. But eventually the young mother became desperate and allowed her infant son to be adopted by Morgan Thomas Drablow of Eel Marsh House, Crythin Gifford, and his wife, Alice.

Suddenly, from an inner room comes the sound of a rhythmic bump, bump, bump. A door slowly opens. Kipps shines his torch inside and sees a rocking chair in motion, moving backward and forward apparently of its own volition, echoing on the floorboards. Kipps looks around and notices that the room was a child's nursery, complete with a bed in the corner, a chest with old-style clothes for a small boy of six or seven, toys, and miniature musical instruments.

The wind begins to roar about the house, and from the darkness outside Kipps can hear a child's anguished cry. Spider runs out and away across the marshes. Kipps follows, calling for him and, horrified, sees the dog disappear beneath the whirling, sucking bog. Kipps lies down, reaches for the dog, and with an effort drags Spider onto firmer ground. Exhausted, Kipps lies in silence. He opens his eyes. The Woman in Black stands there, looking directly down at him. From the back of the auditorium, the audience hears the sound of a pony and a cart.

The Woman in Black exits and Samuel Daily enters. He helps Kipps get up and they hobble to Mrs. Drablow's house. Kipps picks up a small packet of letters and his overnight bag. Daily moves the skip to represent the cart once more and they drive off. Kipps reads aloud a death certificate: "Nathaniel Drablow, age six years; cause of death: drowning." He reads another: "Rose Judd, nursemaid; cause of death: drowning." And another: "Jennet Eliza Humfrye, spinster, age thirty-six; cause of death: heart failure." Samuel Daily explains that Jennet Humfrye was Mrs. Drablow's sister. Jennet gave up the child, the boy Nathaniel, to her sister, Alice Drablow, because she had no choice. At first Jennet stayed away, but the pain of parting from her son brought her back to Crythin. Initially, Alice would not let her see the boy, but Jennet threatened violence and her sister relented. Nathaniel became more and more attached to Jennet, and she planned to take him away. Before she could do so, the accident happened—the boy, the nursemaid, the cart and its driver, and the boy's little dog all drowned in the treacherous marshes and the hidden quicksand.

The bodies were recovered and from that day Jennet Humfrye began to go mad—mad with grief, anger, and a desire for revenge. She blamed her sister, who had let them go out that day, though it was no one's fault; the mist had come without warning. She also contracted a disease that caused her to waste away; the flesh shrank from her bones, her color was drained, she looked like a walking skeleton—a living specter. Jennet died eventually, and soon thereafter the hauntings began. Whenever she has been seen, in the graveyard, on the marsh, in the streets of town—a child has died in violent circumstances.

Kipps announces to the audience, "there is only the last thing left to tell." Upon his return home, he and Stella got married. A little over a year later, Stella gave birth to their child, a son, whom they called Joseph Arthur Samuel. Happy years ensued. One Sunday afternoon Kipps, Stella, and little Joseph went to a park outside London. There was festive air about the place and families strolled in the sunshine. One of the attractions offered a pony and cart on which rides could be taken, and Joseph gestured to it excitedly. Because there was room for only two, Stella took Joseph while Kipps remained to watch them merrily take the ride. Then, unexpectedly, Kipps saw the Woman in Black. Illuminated by a spotlight, she was staring at the ride. The soundtrack changes into the neighing of a startled horse, shouts from the driver, an exclamation of horror from a child, and finally a horrifying crash. The Woman in Black's spot fades out and she's gone.

Kipps relates that his son has been thrown against a tree and lay crumpled on the grass below, dead. Ten months later, Stella too died from her injuries. Kipps crosses and switches on the work lights. The Actor thanks him for sharing his emotional story and Kipps says that he hopes that the saga of the Woman in Black will now be laid to rest. He wonders where the Actor found the actress to play the role of a young woman with a wasted face. The Actor is puzzled: "A young woman? I did not see a young woman." Blackout.

* * *

The Woman in Black was first performed at the Stephen Joseph Theatre-in-the-Round in Scarborough, England, on December 11, 1987, with the following cast: Jon Strickland (The Actor), Dominic Letts (Arthur Kipps), and Lesley Meade (The Woman). The play was directed by Robin Herford and designed by Michael Holt. Director and designer repeated their tasks for a subsequent production presented at the Lyric, Hammersmith, London, on January 11, 1989, featuring Charles Kay (Actor), John Duttine (Kipps), and Nicola Sloane (Woman). The show transferred to the Strand Theatre in London's West End on February 15, 1989; to the Playhouse, London, on April 18, 1989; and to the Fortune Theatre, London, on June 7, 1989, where it has been running continuously with several cast changes. More than seven million people have seen it during the last twenty-two years. On June 29, 2012, *The Woman in Black* will reach its 9,000th performance.

The back cover of Samuel French's acting edition of *The Woman in Black* includes several laudatory blurbs: "Really gripping ghost stories on stage are all too few and far between, so all credit to Stephen Mallatratt"— *International Herald Tribune*. "A brilliantly effective spine-chiller without a trace of self-mocking absurdity"—*The Guardian*. "As immaculate an example of the Gothic horror story as you could wish for, building to its climax with the slow, purposeful precision of an Edwardian timepiece"—*City Limits*. The show is advertised by its producers as "The Most Terrifying Live Theatre Experience in The World."

The Woman in Black has been translated into a dozen languages and staged in more than forty countries around the world, with long runs in New Zealand, Japan, and Mexico. In the United States, the play was presented by Blood Curdling Productions in Chicago, Illinois (1998) and at the Whitefire Theatre in Sherman Oaks, California (2009).

In 1989, *The Woman in Black* was made into a television movie for Britain's ITV network, adapted by Nigel Kneale, best known as the creator of the *Quatermass* science fiction serials. The production starred Adrian Rawlins as Arthur Kidd (not Kipps), and Pauline Moran in the title role. In 1993, BBC Radio 5 broadcast an adaptation of the 1983 Susan Hill novel, featuring Robert Glenister as young Arthur Kipps and John Woodvine as old Arthur Kipps (who also narrated part of the story). In 2004, BBC Radio 4 broadcast a fifty-six-minute version, adapted by Mike Walker, with James D'Arcy as Arthur.

In autumn 2012, England's Hammer Films released a movie version adapted by Jane Goldman from the Susan Hill book, directed by James Watkins and starring Daniel Radcliffe of Harry Potter fame in the role of Arthur Kipps. Critic Manohla Dargis of the *New York Times* wrote,

A creaking, shrieking haunted-house amusement and a solid addition to the recently resurrected Hammer Films—the company where Christopher Lee and Peter Cushing once reigned—*The Woman in Black* makes the most of its old-fashioned virtues. . . . Schooled in the art of the quiet boo, director James Watkins fills the film with squeaking doors and floor-boards, pools of black, long silences and an assortment of moldering toys. Less gore is more here, and what a relief *The Woman in Black* isn't especially scary, but it keeps you on edge, and without the usual vivisectionist imagery.[1]

Sheri Linden of the *Los Angeles Times* found *The Woman in Black* "a good, old-fashioned ghost yarn of the Victorian Gothic persuasion."[2]

* * *

The son of a lower-class family, Stephen Mallatratt was born and bred in Mill Hill, north London. He attended Orange Hill School, caught the theatre bug in his teens, trained as an actor at the Central School of Speech and Drama, worked as a rep performer for the Ipswich Theatre, and was invited by famed playwright Alan Ayckbourn to join his company in Scarborough. Mallatratt originated roles in such Ayckbourn comic masterpieces as *Confusions*, *Absent Friends*, and *Bedroom Farce*, and penned for the company his first play, *An Englishman's Home*, a domestic drama about a snobbish, show-off husband whose wife leaves him.

Mallatratt later moved on to Bristol, where he took over the operations of the Little Theatre, casting a group of outstanding actors, including Daniel Day-Lewis and Pete Postlethwaite. Mallatratt returned to Scarborough in autumn 1985 and appeared in Ayckbourn's production of *The Brontës of Howarth* by Christopher Fry. When Ayckbourn took a sabbatical to join director Peter Hall as a National Theatre associate, Mallatratt stayed on as the stand-in resident author and wrote *The Woman in Black*.

Mallatratt appeared in the motion picture *Chariots of Fire* (1981) and in many television programs, including *All Creatures Great and Small* (1978), *Brideshead Revisited* (1981), and *The Adventures of Sherlock Holmes* (1984). He also wrote episodes for ITV's highly regarded series *Coronation Street* (1996–1999), *The Forsyte Saga* (2002), and *Island at War* (2004).

Mallatratt died of leukemia in 2004, aged 57, in Bristol, England. He is survived by three successive wives, actresses Vanessa Mallatratt and Eileen O'Brien and stage manager Emma London.

* * *

Susan Elizabeth Hill was born in Scarborough, North Yorkshire, England in 1942. She attended the local Convent School, where she became interested in theatre and literature. Hill enrolled in a girls' grammar school, Barr's Hill, where she studied English, French, History, and Latin, and proceeded to an English degree at King's College, London, graduating in 1963. Hill published her first novel, *The Enclosure*, in 1961, while still a student. It was panned for its sexual content.

Hill worked as a freelance journalist during 1963–1968, has been a monthly columnist for the *Daily Telegraph* since 1977, and has continued to publish a succession of novels. She became a Fellow of the Royal Society of Literature in 1972. In 1975, she married Shakespeare scholar Stanley Wells and moved to Stratford upon Avon. During 1986–1987, Hill was a presenter of BBC 4's "Bookshelf." In 1996, she established her own small publishing company, Long Barn Books.

Notable among Hill's books is *Mrs. De Winter*, a 1993 sequel to Daphne du Maurier's classic, *Rebecca*. In 2004, Hill launched a series of detective novels about the cases of Detective Chief Inspector Simon Serailler: *The Various Haunts of Men* (2004), *Pure in Heart* (2005), *The Risk of Darkness* (2006), *The Vows of Silence* (2008), *The Shadows in the Street* (2010), and *The Betrayal of Trust* (2011).

In the tradition of 1983's *The Woman in Black*, Hill penned the ghost stories *The Mist in the Mirror* (1992), *The Man in the Picture* (2007), and *The Small Hand* (2010). She has also written two volumes of memoirs, children's books, nonfiction, and radio plays, as well as edited several anthologies including *Ghost Stories* (1983 and 1990), *The Walker Book of Ghost Stories* (1990), and *The Penguin Book of Modern Women's Short Stories* (1991 and 1997). "A skilled editor of the work of others," states *British Council Literature*, "it is clear that Hill applies those editorial skills just as rigorously to her own prose. As a result, her writing reveals an enviable capacity for generating and maintaining suspense through the deployment of fast moving, agile plots. That one of her best loved novels, *The Woman in Black* (1983), is still running as an adaptation in London's West End (some 25 years after it was first published!), is an indication of the seductive power of her prose. . . . *The Woman in Black* is essentially a ghost story. Like a number of her books, it borrows imaginatively from the styles and conventions of the nineteenth century realist novel. . . . The text self-consciously signals its literary heritage through its title (a playful reversal of Wilkie Collins's Victorian ghost story, *The Woman in White*) and through its references and allusions to Dickens's *Great Expectations*. . . . *The Woman in Black* is by no means simply a faithful reproduction of the 'past masters' however. The compressed prose and the nuanced characterization, along with the clever use of silence and the unsaid suggest that this is also very much a modern novel about modern times."[3]

Acting Edition: Samuel French, Ltd.

Awards and Honors: Susan Hill won a Somerset Maugham Award for the Gothic novel *I'm the King of the Castle* (1970); the Mail on Sunday / John Llewellyn Rhys Prize for *The Albatross* (1971), a collection of short stories; and the Whitbread Novel Award for *The Bird of Night* (1972). *The Various Haunts of Men* (2004) was shortlisted for the Theakstons Old Peculier Crime Novel of the Year.

NOTES

1. *New York Times*, February 3, 2012.
2. *Los Angeles Times*, February 3, 2012.
3. http://literature.britishconcil.org/susan-hill.

To Kill a Mockingbird (1987)

Christopher Sergel (United States, 1918–1993)

Harper Lee's 1960 novel *To Kill a Mockingbird* won the Pulitzer Prize, has been translated into ten languages, sold well over thirty million copies in the United States and abroad, and continues to be widely taught in secondary schools. It was also made into a critically acclaimed motion picture—and was faithfully adapted to the stage by Christopher Sergel.

The play depicts the events that rocked imaginary-yet-real Maycomb, Alabama, in 1935, through the inquisitive eyes of Jean Louise Finch (nicknamed "Scout"), an alert, forthright six-year-old tomboy. Together with her older brother, Jeremy ("Jem") and their friend Charles Baker Harris ("Dill"), Scout tries to understand the web of racial undercurrents then prevailing in the South.

Motherless, Scout and Jem are being raised by their father, Atticus, a reserved, quietly impressive lawyer who does what he considers just. The children are disappointed that their father won't play touch football or show them how to shoot their air rifles. Calpurnia, a capable black housekeeper, helps discipline the siblings. Neighbors on the sleepy street include wise Maudie Atkinson, gossipy Stephanie Crawford, cranky Mrs. Dubose, and reclusive Arthur Radley ("Boo"), considered insane and dangerous.

Rumor has it that when Boo was in his teens, he took up with some bad fellows from Old Sarum. They were arrested on charges of disorderly conduct, disturbing the peace, and using abusive language in the presence of a female. Boo Radley was released to his father, who shut him up in the house; Boo has not been seen for fifteen years.

Atticus agrees to defend a young black man, Tom Robinson, accused of raping a nineteen-year-old white woman, Mayella Ewell, whose large family resides by the town dump. Her father, Bob Ewell, hopes that the pending trial will make him an important community man. Scout asks Atticus, "what's rape?" pouts that the kids at school snicker at his defending "niggers," and confides that most people think he is doing something wrong. Atticus explains that the one thing that does not abide by majority rule is a person's conscience.

The play pictures some of the novel's memorable moments: Atticus shooting a rabid birddog as the children learn that their father was "the deadest shot in Maycomb County"; the lynch mob surrounding the county jail, confronted by Atticus and swayed by the unexpected interference of little Scout; and the centerpiece of the drama, the trial. The audience is the jury. Scout, Jem, and Dill sneak into the balcony, sitting among the blacks to watch the court proceedings.

On the stand, Bob Ewell testifies that upon arriving home he found Tom Robinson raping his daughter. During cross examination Atticus has Ewell sign his name on an envelope, establishing him as left-handed. Young Dill understands: "Her *right* eye was blackened so it had to be someone left-handed."

Mayella, sworn in, insists that the "nigger yonder" took advantage of her and calls anyone who doesn't believe her "a yellow stinking coward."

Led by Atticus, Tom Robinson states that Mayella invited him into the house to fix an old door. Once inside, says Robinson, she jumped at him, hugged him, kissed his cheeks. He tried to leave but Mayella got in his way, blocking his path to the door. He tried to push her aside just as Mr. Ewell hollered through the window. He ran away.

In spite of Atticus's contention that circumstantial evidence indicated that someone who used his left hand beat Mayella Ewell savagely, and that Tom Robinson's left hand was crippled, the jury, as expected, finds the defendant guilty. When Atticus leaves the courthouse, the balcony spectators rise to their feet. Miss Maudie tells the disappointed kids that their father was the only man in the area who could keep the jury out so long in a case like this. He didn't get an acquittal, but he got something. "Maybe we're taking a little step, a little step along the way," says Miss Maudie.

Atticus plans an appeal, but word comes that Tom Robinson, despondent, made a feeble attempt to escape from the Enfield Prison Farm only to be gunned down by the guards. Gaining respect for their father and affected by the dramatic events that will influence the rest of their lives, Scout and Jem still have one more crucial experience in store: After a costume party for the town children in the school auditorium, they are viciously attacked by Bob Ewell as they walk back home.

Unexpectedly, Boo Radley comes to their rescue. There is a struggle in the dark, after which Boo carries the injured youngsters home. In the morning, Ewell is found dead. Sheriff Heck Tate declares that "Bob Ewell fell on his knife. He killed himself. Let the dead bury the dead."

As the stage lights dim, Scout wonders how Boo Radley, with all the bad stories about him, turned out to be *real* nice. Her father responds affectionately: "Most people are, Scout—when you finally see them."

* * *

To Kill a Mockingbird was transformed to the screen in 1962. Robert Mulligan directed a richly textured motion picture that earned Academy Awards for Horton Foote's screenplay and Gregory Peck's performance. The play was later adapted from the novel by Christopher Sergel, who was granted special permission to do so from Harper Lee. Producer-director Chris Hayes embellished Sergel's version when the drama toured regional theatres in the United Kingdom for nine months, before playing seven months at the Mermaid Theatre, London, in 1987. Four years later in the United States, director Robert Johanson of the Paper Mill Playhouse, Milburn, New Jersey, helped shape the final form of the play (with George Grizzard as Atticus).

A perennial favorite with provincial theatre audiences, *To Kill a Mockingbird* was presented during the 1990s by Denver Center Theatre, Denver, Colorado; ESIPA, Albany, New York; Wisdom Bridge Theatre, Chicago, Illinois; Actor's Theatre Series, Fullerton, California; Repertory Theatre of St. Louis, Missouri; Hippodrome Theatre Inc., Gainesville, Florida; Syracuse Stage, Syracuse, New York; Alabama Shakespeare Festival, Montgomery, Alabama; Fulton Opera House, Lancaster, Pennsylvania; Foothill Theatre, Nevada City, California; Great American History Theatre, St. Paul, Minnesota; Alliance Theatre, Atlanta, Georgia; Tennessee Repertory Theatre, Nashville, Tennessee; Montana Repertory, Missoula, Montana; and the Hanger Theatre, Ithaca, New York.

London saw two revivals of *To Kill a Mockingbird* in 1992. In 1997, it was filmed for the second time, directed by Scott Jacoby and Matt Moses, with Evan Nisenson portraying Atticus Finch. Matthew Modine starred as Atticus Finch in a 2009 production presented by Hartford Stage in Connecticut. The Lex Theatre of Hollywood, California offered the play during January–February 2011.

* * *

Except for two years spent on a schooner in the South Pacific and a year spent in the African bush, Christopher Sergel's entire life was devoted to playwriting and publishing. New York credits include dramatizations of Sherwood Anderson's *Winesburg, Ohio*, depicting life beneath the surface of a small town (Broadway's National Theatre, February 5, 1958—thirteen performances), and John G. Neihardt's *Black Elk Speaks*, an account of the conquest of the West from the perspective of a Sioux spiritual leader (off-Broadway's Entermedia Theatre, March 12, 1981—six performances).

Sergel also converted to the stage *The Mouse That Roared*, based on Leonard Wibberly's novel (Woodstock Academy, Woodstock, Connecticut—March 29, 1963), and *Pillow Talk*, from the screenplay by Stanley

Shapiro and Maurice Richlin (Concordia State Teachers College, Seward, Nebraska—February 14, 1963).

Other adaptations by Sergel include Kurt Vonnegut Jr.'s *Who Am I This Time?* and *Welcome to the Monkey House*; Hildegarde Dolson's *We Shook the Family Tree*; Sally Benson's *Meet Me in St. Louis*; Phil Stong's *State Fair*; Bel Kaufman's *Up the Down Staircase*; S. E. Hinton's *The Outsiders*; Christopher Morley's *Kitty Foyle*; James Hilton's *Lost Horizon*; and Frank Gilbreth and Ernestine Gilbreth Carey's *Cheaper by the Dozen*.

From television, Sergel borrowed Arthur Hailey's *Flight into Danger* and the series *Get Smart*, originally created by Mel Brooks and Buck Henry. The prolific playwright also adapted *Fame*, basing his stage treatment on the screenplay by Christopher Gore.

Sergel's output is available through the Dramatic Publishing Company, Chicago, founded by his great-uncle in 1885 and run by the Sergel family ever since. Sergel served as president of the company from 1970 until his death in 1993.

* * *

Nelle Harper Lee was born in 1926 in the small town of Monroeville, Alabama, the daughter of a lawyer. The youngest of four children, Lee befriended a schoolmate, Truman Streckfus Persons, who later became known as Truman Capote.

At five years old, Lee was affected deeply by a 1931 trial in the Alabama town of Scottsboro. Nine young black men were charged with the rape of two white women, and despite flawed testimony, the all-white jury found the men guilty and sentenced them to death. The convictions were repealed in subsequent trials and all but one of the accused were freed. The Scottsboro case inspired Lee's *To Kill a Mockingbird*.

Lee attended the all-female Huntington College in Montgomery (1944–1945) and studied law at the University of Alabama (1945–1949). She relinquished a position as a reservation clerk with Eastern Air Lines in New York City in order to devote herself to writing. In 1959, she worked as a research assistant for Truman Capote when he investigated the brutal murder of the Clutter family in Holcomb, Kansas, described starkly in his *In Cold Blood*.[1]

In 1960 J. B. Lippincott Company published *To Kill a Mockingbird*, Lee's first and only novel. To commemorate the novel's fiftieth anniversary in 2010, filmmaker Mary McDonagh Murphy produced the documentary *Hey, Boo*. A companion volume, *Scout, Atticus and Boo*, published by Harper, features Murphy's interviews with celebrities about the effect of Lee's book. Among the interviewees are Tom Brokaw, Andrew Young, and Oprah Winfrey. Lee herself refused to be interviewed for the book, and did not accept an offer by Winfrey to appear on her television show.

Lee has not spoken publicly about *To Kill a Mockingbird* for more than half a century. She lives quietly in her hometown of Monroeville, Alabama.

Acting Edition: The Dramatic Publishing Company.

Awards and Honors: Harper Lee—Pulitzer Prize for Fiction, 1961; Alabama Library Association Award, 1961; Brotherhood Award of National Conference of Christians and Jews, 1961; Best Sellers Paperback of the Year Award, 1962—all for *To Kill a Mockingbird*. In 1966, President Lyndon Johnson named Lee to the National Council of the Arts. She has received several honorary doctorates since then. In 1999, *To Kill a Mockingbird* was voted "Best Novel of the Century" by Library Journal. In 2005, Lee received the Los Angeles Public Library Literary Award. Two years later, President George W. Bush awarded her the Presidential Medal of Freedom, the highest civilian award in the United States. In the summer of 2010, in honor of the fiftieth anniversary of the publication of *To Kill a Mockingbird*, its publisher, HarperCollins, announced plans to issue four new editions of the novel, each with a different cover, and helped to organize parties, readings, scholarly discussions, and movie screenings.

NOTE

1. Harper Lee is a key character, portrayed by Catherine Keener, in the biographical movie, *Capote*, 2005. Lee was also played by Tracey Hoyt in the TV movie *Scandalous Me: The Jacqueline Susann Story* (1998), and by Sandra Bullock in the film *Infamous* (2006).

Hapgood (1988)

Tom Stoppard (England, Czechoslovakia-born, 1937–)

In 1968, Englishman Tom Stoppard wrote the farcical play-within-a-play *The Real Inspector Hound*, lampooning the genre of Agatha Christie-like parlor whodunits, which he believed to be formalistic and cliché-ridden. Twenty years later, in 1988, Stoppard threw satirical darts at the literature of espionage, as epitomized by Ian Fleming, Graham Greene, Len Deighton, John le Carré, and their ilk.

Hapgood unfolds during the Cold War. The action takes place over a period of four days among seven key locales. The curtain rises on the dressing area of a municipal swimming pool in East London. An impressively tailored American CIA man, a British secret agent in a swimsuit, and Russian spies sporting fur hats dodge in and out of various shower cubicles—all carrying identical briefcases of pale aqua. With a sense of the absurd, they swirl through a ballet of exchanged briefcases, entering and exiting the cubicles with split-second timing. Then out of a shower sashays Elizabeth Hapgood, the title character, carrying a pink umbrella over her head. Hapgood is a no-nonsense big wheel in the MI5 intelligence operation, called Mother by her underlings.

The introductory sequence establishes both the cloak-and-dagger contents and the comic style of the proceedings. A briefcase containing a disc with hush-hush nuclear particle data served as a device to flush the double agent who has been passing along top-secret scientific discoveries to Soviet authorities. Yet, as Hapgood and her associates watched the various briefcases change hands, they somehow missed the switch they were waiting for.

All indications are that the mole is one of a small circle of London espionage bureaucrats. Is it Joseph Kerner, the brilliant Russian atomic scientist who supposedly defected to England long ago? Ernest Ridley, the pugnacious cockney field agent? Ben Wates, a black American CIA operative? Paul Blair, the benign head of the department? Maggs,

Hapgood's twenty-something calm and professional secretary? Or is it, perhaps, Elizabeth Hapgood herself?

The briefcase, snatched by the Russians during the swimming-pool sequence, was sprayed inside with an aerosol can and bugged with a radio signal. The clues lead Hapgood and Blair to suspect Ernest Ridley as the traitor. Ridley's past reveals a number of botched operations: a caper in Athens in which a Russian target was missed and an American agent killed and, in Paris, a Bulgarian go-between was shot to death on his way to meet Ridley, who was caught in a traffic jam. Hapgood concludes that there are two Ridleys—twins.

The play abounds in twins and double images: twin Russian spies play a part in bamboozling British intelligence; at the zoo, Hapgood and Blair hold clandestine meetings in front of twin giraffes; in a photographer's studio we are introduced to Celia, who may be Hapgood's flamboyant, slutty twin sister or just a masquerading Elizabeth Hapgood. The scientist Kerner likens the world of espionage to particle physics, where an electron "can be here or there at the same moment . . . it defeats surveillance." That's what the twin theory is all about, he maintains.

The human side of Elizabeth Hapgood is revealed by the introduction of her young son, Joe, fathered out of wedlock by Joseph Kerner, with whom Hapgood is secretly in love. Hapgood takes time to attend Joe's rugby games at his school, St. Christopher's, and cheer him on to victory. At one such occasion, Kerner shows up and confesses that he has been passing along information to the Russians; they found out about Joe and threatened to harm the boy; he had no choice but submit the briefcase containing the crucial disc. Blair informs Hapgood and Kerner that the original disc was substituted with a fake one so the Russians never got the real data. Fearful, Hapgood sends secretary Maggs to check on her son at his school. The boy has left with a driver supposedly sent by his mother to pick him up. Seizing Joe must be the Russians' counter-move.

Ridley suggests that they turn over the disc in exchange for the kidnapped boy. Hapgood opens her safe and hands Blair a disc-box. Blair exits, followed by Kerner. Alone with Ridley, Hapgood confides that she gave her supervisor a dummy disc, and she has her own plan as to how to proceed from here. She orders Ridley to stay in touch with her on a radio. He leaves and Blair returns. Hapgood then calls the school and it becomes clear that Joe has not been abducted but is being used as a ruse to trap Ridley as the mole.

In a photographer's studio, Ridley meets Celia Newton, whom he believes to be Hapgood's twin sister. He tells Celia that he must obey her sister's instructions; they have an appointment in three hours. Celia tries to phone Hapgood, but Ridley pulls the phone cord from the wall. This infuriates Celia and she curses him soundly, but she is mollified by the sight of two batches of bank notes, 2,000 pounds in each, that will be hers when the job is completed. Ridley warns Celia that he'll deduct fifty pounds every time she uses foul language. "Fuck yourself," she replies, trying him. Ridley extracts a fifty-pound note and sets fire to it with his cigarette lighter. He then sends her off to bathe and change into the clothing he's brought.

Ridley and Celia enter Hapgood's empty office. While Ridley inserts a bugging device into a red desk telephone, Celia explains that her sister "was always the scholarship girl, and I was the delinquent." She lights a cigarette, and Ridley takes it away from her. Celia lapses into vulgarity, and Ridley burns another bill. The red phone rings. Ridley tells Celia that it is Joe's kidnappers calling, and orders her to answer with a request to talk to Joe. To give Celia's voice an edge of distress, he chops her hand across the knuckles. Celia whimpers into the phone, "I want to talk to Joe," and Ridley takes the instrument from her and gently replaces it. "You were fine," he says. "We can go now. Me first. Count twelve, and I'll see you outside." Ridley leaves. Secretary Maggs enters from a side door and we now learn for sure that Celia is a masquerading Hapgood.

In a cheap hotel room, Ridley is trying to reach Mother on his pocket radio, without success. He takes his gun out of his holster and checks it. Celia-Hapgood, lying on the bed, teases him, "I'm your dream girl, Ernie—Hapgood without the brains or taste." He grabs her, and there is no resistance.

A climactic scene returns to the swimming-pool area. It is night. Two identical Ridleys appear, carrying large flashlights. Ridley One enters Cubicle Two while Ridley Two waits. Hapgood enters from the lobby. Ridley instructs her, "Call the boy." Hapgood utters "Joe," and her son emerges upstage. Hapgood opens her bag, takes a disc-box from it, and slides it under the door of Cubicle Two. She goes to Joe, takes his hand, and leads him out through the lobby door, followed by Ridley. Ridley One comes out of Cubicle Two holding the disc that Hapgood had posted. Wates opens the door of Cubicle One with gun in hand. Blair strides in from upstage. Ridley tells Blair with a chuckle that he's aware that there never was any kidnapping, that it was all a scheme to entrap him. Hapgood quietly returns from the lobby. Ridley reaches for his gun when Hapgood shoots him.

Strobe lighting illuminates the stage as the décor changes from the cubicle area to the lobby outside. Ridley's body is carried on a stretcher while Ridley Two, in handcuffs, is being led away. Hapgood tells Blair that she'll never forgive him for actually bringing her son into the caper, which he'd promised to execute without the boy being present. Blair shrugs this off, convinced that she'll get over it.

BLAIR: One has to pick oneself up and carry on. We can't afford to lose. It's them or us, isn't it?

HAPGOOD: Oh, the KGB! The opposition! Paul, we're just keeping each other in business, we should send each other Christmas cards—oh, f-f-fuck it, Paul!

A coda takes place next to the rugby pitch. Hapgood stands on the touchline, watching the boys practice. Kerner, wearing an overcoat, approaches her. He has completed his arrangements for going back to Russia, he says, and has come to say goodbye. Joe runs over to his mother, and Hapgood introduces him to Kerner. Joe runs off to join his teammates, unaware that the stranger is his father.

Kerner begins to leave. Hapgood breaks down, "Oh, Joe." Off stage, the game starts with a referee's whistle. Hapgood collects herself, shifts her attention to the pitch, and soon cheers the St. Christopher squad. She turns around briefly and finds that Kerner is still there. When the curtain comes down it is ambiguous whether the scientist will return to Russia or remain in England with his lover and son.

* * *

Directed by Peter Wood and designed by Carl Toms, *Hapgood* opened at London's Aldwych Theatre on March 8, 1988. The cast included Felicity Kendal (Hapgood), Nigel Hawthorne (Blair), Roger Rees (Kerner), and Iain Glen (Ridley). The somewhat convoluted plot triggered a tepid reception from the press, with the *Times of London* inimitably declaring that the play's complexities "reduced le Carré to the narrative simplicity of Red Riding Hood," and the *Telegraph* admitting to "enjoying without understanding it."[1]

Critic Benedict Nightingale called *Hapgood* "a comic spy-thriller about the elusiveness of truth. If you want its flavor, imagine [John le Carré's novel] *Tinker, Tailor, Soldier, Spy* as it might have been written by Einstein in collaboration with Groucho Marx." Nightingale suggested that "it would have been no great compromise on Stoppard's part if he'd set up the surface aspects of the plot more clearly, and maybe even summed up its development from time to time. That way, both critics and audiences could better appreciate its riddles and ambiguities." Nightingale added: "Though *Hapgood* is never as hilarious as [Stoppard's] *Jumpers* at its best, not often as witty as *The Real Thing*, there's plenty of sly fun to help you through the choppier parts of your intellectual voyage."[2]

Hapgood crossed the Atlantic and was presented by the Center Theatre Group at UCLA's Doolittle Theatre, Hollywood, California, on April 12, 1989. Judy Davis took over the title role. The play came to New York's Lincoln Center Theatre on December 4, 1994, staged by Jack O'Brien, designed by Bob Crowley, featuring Stockard Channing (Hapgood), Josef Sommer (Blair), David Strathairn (Kerner), and David Lansbury (Ridley).

"The play gets a crystal-clear production at Lincoln Center," wrote reviewer Donald Lyons of the *Wall Street Journal*, lauding "Jack O'Brien's brisk, vivid direction," Bob Crowley's "fluid, mutable sets," and Stockard Channing's Hapgood—"counterfeiting a sexy twin, showing herself the best high comedienne in America."[3] Channing's performance was also hailed by *Variety* ("incomparable"),[4] *Daily News* ("marvelous"),[5] and *Newsweek* ("Her smart, sexy, tough, tender spy can do anything that James Bond can do").[6] However, Channing was downgraded by the *New York Post* ("seemed rather too stiff and matronly for the ebullient, eponymous master-spy Hapgood");[7] *Time* ("There's something a little frustratingly soft at her center");[8] and *New York Newsday* ("lacks both the arrogance to exploit Russian expatriates and the toughness to fend off unruly male colleagues").[9]

David Patrick Stearns of *USA Today* acclaimed *Hapgood* as "one of Tom Stoppard's most brilliant plays."[10] Conversely, David Richards of the *New York Times* believed that *Hapgood* "is likely to prove flummoxing. . . . It takes a nimble mind, an alert eye and graph paper to get to the bottom of this one."[11] Michael Feingold maintained in *The Village Voice* that "so much of *Hapgood*'s material has been better used in films, from *The Third Man* to *The Spy Who Came in From the Cold*."[12] *Hapgood* ran for 129 performances.

* * *

Born Tomas Straussler in Ziln, Czechoslovakia, Tom Stoppard's Jewish family fled their native land, moving to Singapore in 1939 when the Nazis invaded. Two years later, the Strausslers were forced to flee again, this time from the invading Japanese. Tom's father, Eugene, was captured and died in a prison camp. Tom's mother soon married a British Army Major, Kenneth Stoppard, and the family moved to England in 1946.

Stoppard attended boarding schools in Nottinghamshire and Yorkshire but left school early, "bored and alienated by everyone from Shakespeare to Dickens besides." He never went to a university. During the 1950s, he worked as a journalist for the *Western Daily Press* and the *Bristol Evening World*. His assignments included humorous pieces and theatre critiques. Mostly, he reviewed plays presented by the Bristol Old Vic Repertory. He claims that viewing a 1958 production of *Hamlet*, with Peter O'Toole in the title role, was a defining moment for him; that's when he decided to become a playwright.

Stoppard's first play, *Enter a Free Man*, about a dreaming, imaginative inventor who gradually succumbs to the mundane world around him, was aired in 1963 by British Independent Television and on March 28, 1968 it was eventually staged at London's St. Martin's Theatre, starring Michael Hordern. Stoppard's breakthrough came with *Rosencrantz and Guildenstern Are Dead*, a whimsical retelling of *Hamlet* from the point of view of its fringe characters. Said Stoppard: "Rosencrantz and Guildenstern are two people who have been written into a scheme of things and there's nothing they can do about it except follow through and meet the fate that has been ordained for them, which is to die violently."[13] Initially performed at the Edinburgh Fringe Festival by a group of Oxford undergraduates, the National Theatre Company presented the play at London's Old Vic in 1967. With this production, thirty-year-old Stoppard became the youngest playwright ever to have a play mounted by the prestigious group. *Rosencrantz and Guildenstern Are Dead* was also a hit in New York, where it received the Tony and Drama Critics' Circle awards for best play of 1967–1968. "Very funny, very brilliant, very chilling," wrote Clive Barnes in the *New York Times*.[14] Stoppard scripted and directed a movie version in 1990, featuring Gary Oldman and Tim Roth in the title roles.[15]

The laudatory reception of *Rosencrantz and Guildenstern Are Dead* catapulted Stoppard to the high echelons of British theatre. *The Real Inspector Hound* followed. During the late 1960s and early 1970s, Stoppard penned several one-act plays and radio and television episodes. Notable is the playlet *After Magritte* (1970), a dip into absurdism, revolving around an argument between spouses with a detective and a police officer drawn into the action.

Stoppard's next full-length play was *Jumpers*, a drama set in an alternate reality in which British astronauts have landed on the moon and "radical liberals" have taken over the British government. The play meshes farcical elements, lengthy speeches, and heavy philosophical references about the bizarre murder of an acrobat. *Jumpers* premiered at the Old Vic Theatre on February 2, 1972, with Michael Hordern and Diana Rigg in the lead roles. Under Peter Wood's direction, the play came to the Kennedy Center in Washington, D.C. on February 18, 1974, and moved to Broadway's Billy Rose Theatre on April 22, featuring Brian Bedford and Jill Clayburgh, running for forty-eight performances. The Royal National Theatre revived *Jumpers* in 2003, and the production migrated to Broadway the following year, receiving a Tony Award nomination for Best Revival.

Travesties unfolds primarily in Zürich, Switzerland during World War I. Author James Joyce, Dadaist founder Tristan Tzara, and communist revolutionary Vladimir Lenin are the main characters in a comedy that connects real-life characters with a presentation of Oscar Wilde's *The Importance of Being Earnest*. *Travesties* was first produced at the Aldwych Theatre in London on June 10, 1974, staged by Peter Wood, a director Stoppard would continue to work with in the coming decades. A subsequent production opened at New York's Ethel Barrymore Theatre on October 30, 1975, won the Tony Award as Best Play, and ran for 156 performances. The Royal Shakespeare Company revived *Travesties* in 1993.

Night and Day, a satire about the British news media, merges fiction and nonfiction as it unfolds in an imaginary African country called Kambawa. The press covers a tribal war in the country using linguistic manipulation and double meanings. The play premiered on November 8, 1978 at London's Phoenix Theatre, designed by Carl Toms and starring Diana Rigg. It ran for two years.

Somewhat autobiographical, *The Real Thing* spotlights a playwright in search of self, and questions the place of art in society. The play opened successfully at the Strand Theatre in London on November 16, 1982, and made it to New York's Plymouth Theatre on January 5, 1984, where it ran for 566 performances and won Tony Awards for Best Play, Best Actor (Jeremy Irons), and Best Actress (Glenn Close).

Arcadia unfolds with two parallel story lines, one beginning in 1809 and one in 1989, both set in Sidley Park, an English country home. In 1809, Thomasina Coverly, a precocious teenager who exhibits surprisingly advanced theories about mathematics, falls in love with her tutor, Septimus Hodge, a friend of Lord Byron, an unseen but pivotal character in the play. In the modern segment, Hannah Jarvis, an author, researches the identity of an elusive hermit who lived in Sidley Park in the early 1800s and concludes that it was Septimus Hodge. Directed by Trevor Nunn, *Arcadia* premiered at the Royal National Theatre in London on April 13, 1993 and won the Laurence Olivier and Evening Standard Awards for Best Play. *Arcadia* opened at New York's Vivian Beaumont Theatre in March 1995, again directed by Nunn but with a completely different cast, and ran for 173 showings. It was nominated for a Tony Award as Best Play. The Arena Stage in Washington, D.C. mounted a regional production of *Arcadia* in 1996–1997. David Leveaux staged a revival of the play at the Duke of York's Theatre in London, opening on May 27, 2009.

A memory play, *The Invention of Love*, portrays the life of homosexual poet A. E. Housman, surrounding him with many notable authors of his era, including Oscar Wilde, Frank Harris, and Jerome K. Jerome. Blending historical and fictional characters, the play was presented by the Royal National Theatre, London, on September 25, 1997, directed by Richard Eyre and starring John Wood. It ran for nearly a year in London and won the Evening Standard Award for Best Play. A Broadway run at the Lyceum Theatre commenced on March 29, 2001 and lasted 108 performances. Richard Easton portrayed the older Housman and Robert Sean Leonard the young. Both actors won Tony Awards for Best Actor and Best Featured Actor in a Play.

Stoppard's magnum opus is *The Coast of Utopia*, a mammoth drama divided into three parts—"Voyage," "Shipwreck," and "Salvage." The trilogy, with a total running time of nine hours, premiered at London's National Theatre on June 22, 2002, performing in repertory. Trevor Nunn directed. In 2006, Jack O'Brien staged the sequential plays at New York's Vivian Beaumont Theatre for a combined run of 124 performances. Set in pre-revolution Russia, the epic story features some seventy characters and covers a thirty-three-year period, 1833 to 1866. The main characters are author Ivan Turgenev, literary critic Bakunin Vissarion, and revolutionary thinker Alexander Herzen. *The Coast of Utopia* won 2007's Tony Award for Best Play.

Rock 'n' Roll focuses on the emergence of the democratic movement behind the Iron Curtain, with an emphasis on artistic dissent against the Communist Party. The action unfolds over several decades from 1968 to 1990, rotating between Prague, Czechoslovakia, and Cambridge, England, and culminates with a concert given by the Rolling Stones in Prague. *Rock 'n' Roll* was presented at London's Royal Court Theatre and ran from June 3 until July 15, 2006. The premiere of the play was attended by Václev Havel, the playwright and first president of the post-Communist Czech Republic, and Mick Jagger of the Rolling Stones.

Stoppard adapted for the British stage plays by Austrians Arthur Schnitzler (*Undiscovered Country; Dalliance*) and Johann Nestroy (*On the Razzle*); the Hungarian Ferenc Molnar (*Rough Crossing*); the Spanish Federico Garcia Lorca (*The House of Bernarda Alba*); the Italian Luigi Pirandello (*Henry IV*); and the Russian Anton Chekhov (*The Seagull*). In 1983, Stoppard wrote an English libretto of Prokofiev's opera *The Love of Three Oranges*. Ten years later, he penned an English narration for Lehar's operetta *The Merry Widow*.

The indefatigable Stoppard has also contributed extensively to film and television. He penned the screenplays of *The Human Factor* (1980), *Brazil* (1985), *Empire of the Sun* (1987), *The Russia House* (1990), *Billy Bathgate* (1991), *Shakespeare in Love* (1998), for which he won an Academy Award, *Enigma* (2001), *The Bourne Ultimatum* (2007), and *Anna Karenina*, based on the novel by Leo Tolstoy (2012). He teamed with Clive Exton on the half-hour teleplay *The Boundary*, aired live on the BBC series *The Eleventh Hour* July 19, 1975. *The Boundary* was later converted to a one-act play, published by Samuel French, London, in 1991. The teleplay reveals the secrets of a murder at a lexicographer's library with a touch of comic absurdity. The body of a woman is buried under disorderly piles of paper. It is Brenda, the wife of librarian Johnson and mistress of librarian Bunyans. Was she murdered by one of them? And why is a pane of glass in the French window broken? What is the connection between the white-flannelled cricketer outside and the hidden corpse inside?[16]

"As a playwright, Stoppard is both playful and thoughtful, both serious and absurd, and both faithful and irreverent," writes Mikhail Alexeeff in *Stoppard in an Hour*. "His legacy is one of innovation and impressive diversity. His inspiration often stems from established material, but his inventiveness sets him apart from his predecessors and contemporaries. In a popular culture that increasingly relies on remakes, retreads, and retooling, it is hard not to marvel at what Stoppard has consistently accomplished. Using a known story to draw an audience, Stoppard has made the tired fashionable, the arcane accessible, and the plodding fun."[17]

Acting Edition: Samuel French, Inc.

Awards and Honors: Tom Stoppard was appointed Commander of the Order of the British Empire (CBE) in 1978 and was knighted in 1997. This same year he was made an Officier de l'Ordre des Arts et des Lettres by the French government. He was recruited to the Board of the National Theatre in 1989. He won the Academy Award for *Shakespeare in Love* (1998), and Best Play Tony Awards for *Rosencrantz and Guildenstern Are Dead* (1968), *Travesties* (1975), *The Real Thing* (1984), and *The Coast of Utopia* (2007).

NOTES

1. Quoted in the *New York Times*, March 27, 1988.
2. *New York Times*, March 27, 1988.
3. *Wall Street Journal*, December 14, 1994.
4. *Variety*, December 5, 1994.
5. *Daily News*, December 5, 1994.
6. *Newsweek*, December 19, 1994.
7. *New York Post*, December 5, 1994.
8. *Time*, December 19, 1994.
9. *New York Newsday*, December 5, 1994.
10. *USA Today*, December 5, 1994.
11. *New York Times*, December 5, 1994.
12. *The Village Voice*, December 13, 1994.
13. *New York Times*, March 24, 1968.
14. *New York Times*, October 17, 1967.
15. A 2009 motion picture, *Rosencrantz and Guildenstern Are Undead*, written and directed by Jordan Galland, is a horror-comedy about an off-Broadway production of *Hamlet* financed by a pale entrepreneur who turns out to be a vampire. "Funny title, not so funny movie," wrote reviewer Gary Goldstein in the *Los Angeles Times* of July 16, 2010. "An ambitious satire of Shakespeare, vampires, small theatre, Tom Stoppard, serial womanizing, cops and more that starts off feeling clever and original but turns silly and diffused as its convoluted story spins out."
16. The English playwright Clive Exton (1930–2007) exhibited an affinity for matters of crime on stage (dramatizing Agatha Christie's *Murder Is Easy* in 1993), the silver screen (*10 Rillington Place*, 1970, based on the sensational John Christie-Timothy Evans murder case in 1940s England; *Crazy House*, 1973, called *Night of the Laughing Dead* in the United States, a horror spoof; *The Awakening*, 1980, an Egyptian tomb saga adapted from Bram Stoker's novel, *The Jewel of the Seven Stars*), and television (contributing to such shows as *Dick Baron—Special Agent*, *The Ruth Rendell Mysteries*, and *Poirot*, the enormously successful series starring David Suchet in what many believe is the definitive portrayal of the Belgian detective).
17. Mikhail Alexeeff, *Stoppard in an Hour* (Hanover, N.H.: Hour Books, 2010), 37.

M. Butterfly (1988)

David Henry Hwang (United States, 1957–)

On May 11, 1986, the *New York Times* announced that "a former French diplomat and a Chinese opera singer have been sentenced [in Paris] to six years in jail for spying for China after a two-day trial that traced a story of clandestine love and mistaken sexual identity. . . . Mr. [Bernard] Boursicot was accused of passing information to China after he fell in love with Mr. Shi [Pei Pu], whom he believed for twenty years to be a woman."[1]

American playwright David Henry Hwang utilized the account for his play *M. Butterfly*, changing names, adding characters, and creating fictional incidents.

From his sparsely furnished Parisian prison cell, in 1988, Rene Gallimard, sixty-five, breaks through the fourth wall and shares with the audience somewhat disordered, distorted recollections of an affair that began forty years earlier when he was on a diplomatic mission to China. In Peking he met Song Liling, an opera star, whom he calls "Butterfly, the Perfect Woman." Gallimard compares his experience to that of Benjamin Franklin Pinkerton, an American naval officer whose ship docks at the harbor of Nagasaki, Japan, the hero of Giacomo Puccini's opera *Madame Butterfly*. Pinkerton meets, marries, and has a child with a local geisha girl, Cio-Cio-San—"her friends call her Butterfly"—only to leave her behind and return to the United States. The distraught Cio-Cio-San commits suicide.

At the age of thirty-one, shy and introverted Gallimard married an older woman, Olga, whose father was the French ambassador to Australia. Gallimard was faithful to his wife for eight years until the day when, as a junior-level diplomat in Peking, he attended a private reception at the German ambassador's house, where Song Liling sang the death scene from *Madame Butterfly*. "Here was a Butterfly with little or no voice," relates Gallimard to the audience, "but she had the grace, the delicacy. . . . I wanted to take her in my arms—so delicate, even I could protect her, take her home, pamper her until she smiled."

Smitten with Song, Gallimard begins to attend the opera regularly. Song eventually invites Gallimard to her apartment, greets him wearing a sheer dressing gown, and mumbles, "I am your Butterfly." He kisses her roughly, starts to caress her, and opens her gown. "No, let me keep my clothes," she whispers, but promises to please him. He turns off the lamp.

Act 2 begins at Gallimard and Song's flat on the outskirts of Peking. Gallimard confides to the audience that over the years 1961 to 1963 they had settled into a domestic routine. Song would prepare a light snack and then, "ever so delicately," would please him with her hands and mouth. Gallimard is promoted to the rank of vice-consul, in charge of coordinating a revamped intelligence division. Song begins to express interest in her lover's work and asks about what is happening in Vietnam. Did the American president, John F. Kennedy, sign an order to bomb North Vietnam? When will the bombardment start? What cities are being targeted?

Song turns out to be a spy working for the Red Chinese government. She reports to her female supervisor, Comrade Chin, that the Americans will increase troops in Vietnam to 170,000 soldiers and 11,000 advisors. The United States will allow the Vietnamese generals to stage a coup and assassinate President Diem.

One evening, an inebriated Gallimard says that he wants to see Song naked. She demures but he insists. He crosses the room and grabs Song by the waist. He releases her, transfixed, when she utters, "I'm pregnant." Upon her next meeting with Comrade Chin, Song tells her that she needs a baby. When her lover told her to strip, she took a chance. If she can present him with an Asian baby with blond hair—he'll be hers for life!

Gallimard tells Song that he'll divorce his wife, marry her, and eventually they'll move to France. Song declines, for Gallimard is a diplomat with a skyrocketing career; what would happen if he divorced his wife to marry a communist Chinese actress?

In 1966 Gallimard is sent home to France. In Paris, he confesses to Olga that he has had a mistress for eight years and now wants a divorce. Olga says, "I hope everyone is mean to you for the rest of your life," and leaves.

Comrade Chin orders Song to travel to Paris, renew her contact with the diplomat, and continue compiling weekly reports of useful information. Song connects with Gallimard and they resume their relationship.

Act 3 unfolds fifteen years later. The lights come up on Song standing in front of a mirror, removing a wig and a kimono. It's revealed that Song is a man wearing a well-cut suit. The action shifts to a courthouse. On the witness stand, Song testifies that at his urging, Rene Gallimard got a job as a courier, handling sensitive documents. Rene had photographed them, and would then pass them to the Chinese embassy. When the judge asks whether Gallimard knew that he was a man, Song responds: "You know, Your Honor, I never asked."

Music from *Madame Butterfly*'s "Death Scene" blows over the house speakers when Song confronts Gallimard, removes his clothes, and asks the Frenchman to admit that he still adores him. But Gallimard coolly asks him to leave.

In his prison cell, in 1988, Gallimard bemoans, "Love warped my judgment, blinded my eyes." He wavers between reality and fantasy. Dancers appear and help him get into Song's kimono, whiten his face, redden his lips. They hand him a dagger and he sets himself in a harakiri position, the Japanese ritual of self-disembowelment. In an ironic reversal of the Puccini opera, it is not Song who commits suicide but Gallimard, who has finally realized that he has been the exploited Butterfly.

* * *

The original title of the play was *Monsieur Butterfly* but David Henry Hwang's wife persuaded him to emphasize the ambiguities of the situation. *M. Butterfly* opened at Broadway's Eugene O'Neill Theatre on March 20, 1988. John Dexter directed. John Lithgow portrayed Rene Gallimard and B. D. Wong enacted Song Liling. Critic Frank Rich found *M. Butterfly* "a visionary work that bridges the history and culture of two worlds. . . . One must be grateful that a play of this ambition has made it to Broadway." But the critic also had some misgivings, scoffing at repetitions, a preaching tone, and "overly explicit bouts of thesis mongering."[2] Clive Barnes raved: "It enriches, it fascinates, it offers thought to feed on."[3] Edwin Wilson saluted playwright Hwang for having "something to say and an original, audacious way of saying it . . . he ingeniously has woven together a real-life story and events from Puccini's opera *Madame Butterfly*."[4] David Henry admired Eiko Ishioka's "marvelous design" [of set and costumes], John Dexter's "excellent staging," and John Lithgow's "forceful performance as Rene Gallimard."[5]

Negative reactions were expressed by Jack Kroll, who maintained that "at every level the play defies belief,"[6] and Joel Siegel, who commented, "The story is so bizarre everyone's first reaction is: How could it happen? And in two and a half hours the playwright doesn't tell us."[7]

M. Butterfly won Tony Awards for Best Play, Best Director (John Dexter), and Best Featured Actor (B. D. Wong) as well as Drama Desk Awards in the same three categories. The play was further nominated for a Pulitzer Prize. It ran for 777 performances. David Dukes, Anthony Hopkins, Tony Randall, and John Rubinstein took over the part of Gallimard at various times. An audio recording of the play was produced by the Los Angeles Theatre Works with Lithgow and Wong reprising their roles.

Revivals of *M. Butterfly* were presented at Arena Stage, Washington, D.C. (2004); Philadelphia Theatre Company (2007); and Guthrie Theatre, Minneapolis (2010). The play also ran for a year in London's West End and has been produced in more than three dozen countries to date.

A Russian motion picture based on *M. Butterfly* was made in 1990, directed by Roman Viktyuk, with Kazakh tenor Erik Kurmangaliev in the title role. Three years later, Hwang scripted an American version that featured Jeremy Irons (Rene Gallimard) and John Lone (Song Liling). The movie was shot by director David Cronenberg in Budapest, Hungary.

* * *

David Henry Hwang was born in Los Angeles, California, in 1957. He was raised in San Gabriel, a suburb near Pasadena, by his father, a banker who grew up in Shanghai, and his mother, a piano teacher reared in the Philippines. Hwang graduated from Stanford University in 1979 with a BA degree in English and enrolled at the Yale School of Drama. He briefly studied with Sam Shepard and Maria Irene Fornés.

Hwang's early works focused on the role of Chinese Americans in the modern world. His first play, *FOB*, depicts the contrasts and conflicts between established Americans and new immigrants. The play premiered at the Stanford Asian American Theatre Project in 1979 under the direction of the author and was further developed at the National Playwrights Conference of the Eugene O'Neill Center. Its professional debut took place at off-Broadway's Joseph Papp Public Theatre on June 8, 1980. The following year, the Public Theatre presented Hwang's *Family Devotions*, a drama concerned with West-East clash within three generations of an Americanized Chinese family living in a Los Angeles suburb. The play was nominated for a Drama Desk Award.

Rich Relations is the story of a wealthy WASP family and the damage inflicted from parent to child, with many religious overtones. The play was first shown by off-Broadway's Second Stage Theatre on April 21, 1986.

Golden Child relates the struggles of a nineteenth-century Chinese family confronting westernization. The drama premiered at the Joseph Papp Public Theatre on November 19, 1986, directed by James Lapine. A revised version was tried out in California and Singapore, and opened at Broadway's Longacre Theatre on April 2, 1988. It was nominated for a Tony Award as Best Play.

Hwang's adaptation of Henrik Ibsen's *Peer Gynt*, a poetic, symbolic fantasy that deals with the degeneration of the human soul and the redeeming power of love, streamlined the complicated, episodic original and added many contemporary references. The work was commissioned by the Trinity Repertory Company in Providence, Rhode Island, where it debuted on February 3, 1998.

Tibet through the Red Box is an adaptation of the children's book by Peter Sis about a boy growing up in Prague in the 1950s. The play was commissioned by the Seattle Children's Theatre, where it opened on January 30, 2004.

The protagonist of *Yellow Face* is the author himself. Partly autobiographical, *Yellow Face* is a satire that raises questions of how politics and media function in society and what America really stands for. The play opened at the Joseph Papp Public Theatre on December 10, 2007. It won an Obie Award and placed Hwang as a finalist for the Pulitzer Prize. *Chinglish*, a comedy about the misadventures of an American businessman hoping to make his fortune in China, raised its curtain at Broadway's Longacre Theatre on October 27, 2011. Much of the dialogue is delivered in Mandarin, accompanied by supertitles in English, purposely mistranslated. Ben Brantley of the *New York Times* found the device of "merrily mutilated" language, "the principal source of this production's mirth." However, the critic remained dissatisfied: "While David Korins' nifty revolving set is meant, I think, to summon the whirligig dizziness of farce, *Chinglish* only rarely achieves the sort of momentum that sends audiences into the ether. Even when its characters are floating helplessly on the wings of unhinged words, this play feels too solidly grounded for its own good."[8] Despite the fact that *Chinglish* received generally favorable reviews and was named the number one new American play of 2011 by *Time* magazine, box office sales were modest and the comedy ended its run after 128 performances.

Short plays by Hwang include *The Dance and the Railroad*, which describes a strike in a coolie railroad labor camp in the mid-nineteenth century. Commissioned by the New Federal Theatre and presented at the Joseph Papp Public Theatre on July 16, 1981, the play was a finalist for the Pulitzer Prize for Drama. It was also produced on television by the ABC Arts channel, winning a CINE Golden Eagle Award. *The House of Sleeping Beauties* focuses on Japanese author Yasunari Kawabata, a 1968 Nobel Prize winner, and how he came to write a novella of the same name. The one-act was produced at the Joseph Papp Public Theatre on November 6, 1983, accompanied by Hwang's *The Sound of a Voice*, a ghost story inspired by Japanese folk tales and Noh theatre.

As the Crow Flies depicts the double life of an African American maid living in a Chinese home in Los Angeles. The playlet premiered at the Los Angeles Theatre Center on February 16, 1986, double-billed with Hwang's *The Sound of a Voice*. *Bondage* deals with issues of racial stereotypes by placing a fully disguised man and woman in a sadomasochistic parlor, playing out sexual games. The play premiered at the Actors Theatre of Louisville on March 1, 1992, featuring B. D. Wong and Hwang's wife, Kathryn Layng. Four years later, the Actors Theatre of Louisville presented Hwang's *Trying to Find Chinatown*, a playlet covering dilemmas of racial identity by pitting an Asian street musician against a Caucasian man who claims Asian American heritage. The violinist is not aware that the white man was adopted by Asian American parents. Also penned in 1996, a ten-minute piece by Hwang, *Bang Kok*, concerns two businessmen who share stories of prostitution in Thailand. In the climax, one of the men confesses to his friend that he has contracted AIDS. *Merchandising*, commissioned in 1999 by the Actors Theatre of Louisville's Humana Festival, tells of two filmmakers who lament the failure of their picture and the nature of marketing in Hollywood. *Jade Flowerpots and Bound Feet* is centered on a Caucasian woman who passes herself off as a minority to sell a book to a major publishing company. The play premiered on November 5, 2001 as part of a program of short plays dealing with Asian American identity, presented at the Joseph Papp Public Theatre. Six years later, the same off-Broadway theatre presented *The Great Helmsman*, a comedy about two women who are debating who will be chosen to spend the night with Chairman Mao Zedong. *A Very DNA Reunion*, dealing with the imprecise science of DNA technology, premiered as part of Chicago's Silk Road Theatre Project on March 8, 2010.

The untiring Hwang joined Linda Woolverton and Robert Falls in penning the libretto of *Aida*, a rock musical based on the Italian-language opera by Giuseppe Verdi. The musical, produced by Disney Theatrical, with a score by Elton John and lyrics by Tim Rice, premiered at Broadway's Palace Theatre on March 23, 2003. It was nominated for five Tony Awards and ran for 1852 performances, yielding an album with the original cast. In 2001, Hwang revised the book of Rodgers and Hammerstein's 1958 *Flower Drum Song*, about Wang Ta, the son of wealthy refugees from China residing in San Francisco's Chinatown, torn between his Chinese roots and assimilation into American culture. Following a tryout in Los Angeles, the musical came to Broadway in 2002, received mostly poor reviews, and closed after six months.

Hwang wrote the book, to music and lyrics by Phil Collins, of *Tarzan*, based on the 1912 Edgar Rice Burroughs story and the 1999 Disney animated film. After six weeks of previews, the musical officially opened at Broadway's Richard Rodgers Theatre on May 10, 2006. Despite mediocre reviews and poor ticket sales, *Tarzan* managed to keep its doors open for a run of 486 performances.

Hwang collaborated with Korean composer Unsuk Chin on an operatic rendition of Lewis Carroll's *Alice's Adventures in Wonderland* and *Through the Looking Glass*. *Alice in Wonderland* had its world premiere at the Bavarian State Opera on June 30, 2007 as part of the Munich Opera Festival. Teamed with Canadian composer Howard Shore, Hwang wrote the libretto of *The Fly*, an opera loosely based on David Cronenberg's 1986 film about a misguided, horrific scientific experiment. *The Fly* was commissioned by the Théâtre du Châtelet in Paris, where it opened on July 2, 2008.

For television, Hwang co-wrote with Frederic Kimball the special *Blind Alley* (1985), the story of two people, once linked by an interracial marriage, setting up their daughter's wedding. *The Monkey King* (2001), also known as *The Lost Empire*, is a four-hour television miniseries in which an American businessman encounters a beautiful, mystical Chinese lady who transports him to the ancient Chinese underworld.

The protagonist of the feature film *Golden Gate* (1994) is a 1950s G-Man (portrayed by Matt Dillon) who pursues a communist ring in San Francisco. The trail leads him to a young Chinese American woman (played by Joan Chen) whose father he helped to put in prison. *Possession* (2002), co-scripted by Hwang with Laura Jones and Neil LaBute, based on a novel by A. S. Byatt, is a puzzle-drama about two scholars, an impulsive American man (portrayed by Aaron Eckhart) and a cool British woman (Gwyneth Paltrow) who investigate an affair between two renowned fictional poets of the mid-1800s. LaBute directed.

M. Butterfly remains David Henry Hwang's most popular and critical success. He is acknowledged as the preeminent Asian American dramatist in the United States. He sits on the boards of the Dramatists Guild, Young Playwrights Inc., and the Museum of Chinese in the Americas. From 1994 to 2001, he served by appointment of President Bill Clinton on the President's Committee on the Arts and the Humanities.

Acting Edition: Dramatists Play Service.

Awards and Honors: In 1988, *M. Butterfly* received a Tony Award and a Drama Desk Award for Best Play. The play was nominated for a 1989 Pulitzer Prize for Drama. David Henry Hwang has received numerous grants, including fellowships from the Guggenheim and Rockefeller Foundations, and the New York State Council on the Arts. He has been honored with awards from the Asian American Legal Defense and Education Fund, the Association for Asian Pacific American Artists, the Organization of Chinese Americans, the Media Action Network for Asian Americans, the Center for Migration Studies, the Asian American Resource Workshop, and the China Institute. Hwang holds an honorary degree from Columbia College, Chicago. In 1998, the nation's oldest Asian American theatre company, East West Players of Los Angeles, christened its new main stage the David Henry Hwang Theatre. Hwang is the recipient of the 2012 Steinberg Award ($200,000) for playwriting, the most generous prize in theatre.

NOTES

1. Bernard Boursicot confessed to having passed at least 150 classified documents to Shi Pei Pu.

2. *New York Times,* March 21, 1988.

3. *New York Post,* March 21, 1988.

4. *Wall Street Journal,* March 22, 1988.

5. *Daily News,* April 10, 1988.

6. *Newsweek,* April 4, 1988.

7. *WABC-TV7.*

8. *New York Times,* October 28, 2011.

The Secret of Sherlock Holmes (1988)

Jeremy Paul (England, 1939–)

"When the American actor William Gillette wrote the first stage play about Holmes, he sent a telegram to Sir Arthur Conan Doyle asking: 'May I marry Holmes?'" relates author Jeremy Paul in the playbill of *The Secret of Sherlock Holmes*. "From England came the rabid reply, 'You may marry or murder or do what you like with him.' With this generous thought in mind (which was typical of Conan Doyle), I become the latest in the long line of 'loungers and idlers' who have meddled with the great man's works for profit and for pleasure. Many of the words you will hear are Conan Doyle's own, taken on and fashioned into an original mystery which I hope will intrigue Conan Doyle himself if he's looking in."

Paul, who during the 1980s penned many Sherlock Holmes episodes for Britain's Granada Television, recruited the series' stars, Jeremy Brett and Edward Hardwicke, to recreate the roles of Holmes and Watson in his two-character, ninety-minute stage play.

The action takes place in multiple settings including 221B Baker Street (complete with cluttered paraphernalia and chemical apparatus), Watson's modest study, a railway carriage, the Reichenbach Falls, and a neutral area from which the world's foremost consulting detective and his chronicler occasionally address the audience.

The play takes us down Memory Lane as Holmes and Watson reminisce about their first meeting when the good doctor came to inquire about lodging; Watson's growing awe at his roommate's extraordinary deductive prowess, vast knowledge of sensational literature and British law, and considerable skills as violin player, boxer, and swordsman; Holmes's contempt for Edgar Allan Poe's Auguste Dupin ("a very inferior fellow") and Emile Gaboriau's Monsieur Lecoq ("a miserable bungler"); the one woman who shook Holmes's equanimity, ravishing opera singer Irene Adler; Mycroft, Holmes's brother, who works for the British government and "has the greatest capacity for storing facts of any man living."

Following the case of *The Sign of Four*, Watson married heiress Mary Morstan and moved to other quarters. He confides to the audience that Holmes, who loathed "every form of society," remained on Baker Street "alternating between cocaine and ambition, the drowsiness of the drug and the fierce energy of his own keen nature."

After a visit with his friend, Holmes tells Watson about Professor Moriarty, "the Napoleon of Crime. The organizer of half that is evil and nearly all that is undetected in this great city."

With depressed affect, Watson tells us of his double loss: the sudden, tragic death of his wife, Mary, and the plunge of friend Sherlock, with a struggling Moriarty, into the abyss of Reichenbach Falls.

Then, three years later, an elderly, deformed bookseller who speaks in a croaking voice turns out to be Sherlock Holmes in disguise. Holmes recounts that Professor Moriarty rushed at him and they tottered upon the brink of the Falls. Holmes flipped his opponent with a baritsu maneuver and saw him fall a long way, striking a rock, bouncing off, and vanishing into the bottomless pit. In order to escape the wrath of Moriarty's henchmen, Holmes spent several years traveling incognito to Tibet, Persia, and the Sudan.

Watson surprises Holmes by stating that he always believed that the detective was alive because his brother Mycroft had instructed Mrs. Hudson "to keep these rooms just as they are."

In a pensive mood, Holmes tells his friend that he intends to retire to "a life of philosophy, agriculture—and bee-keeping. . . . One learns as much about human nature from the study of the bee, as from the study of people. . . . London has become a singularly uninteresting city since the death of the late, lamented Professor Moriarty."

Holmes begins to move around feverishly, and suddenly collapses. Delirious, he reveals a dark, Jekyll-and-Hyde, secret: "Watson, I propose to offer you . . . the hypothesis . . . that Professor Moriarty did not exist. That I invented him. . . . It was the summer of '87 that the idea first came to me. It may have sprung from one of my black fits. . . . I took the name from an old Mathematics Professor I had known at university, a dear, sweet man."[1]

Watson is incensed: "If you invented him for your amusement, it was at my expense! . . . If you did indeed create this monster, then what prompted you to destroy him?"

"I could not live with him," says Holmes quietly. "It was either him or me." However, the detective is certain that the Napoleon of Crime, like a many-headed hydra, will have successors—"As soon as one head is cut off, another grows in its place. It is essential to our well-being, Watson, that there will always, somewhere, be a Moriarty among us."

* * *

The Secret of Sherlock Holmes previewed at the Yvonne Arnaud Theatre in Guildford, and at the Richmond Theatre, Surrey, and opened at
Wyndham's Theatre, London, on September 22, 1988. The press generally praised Jeremy Brett and Edward Hardwicke: "First-rate playing";[2]
"the best Holmes and Watson, respectively, I have ever seen."[3] Director
Patrick Garland was complimented for "orchestrating the ebb and flow
. . . with a master touch."[4]

Conversely, Jeremy Paul's play was showered with negative verdicts:
"Worthy, but dull";[5] "woefully thin";[6] "another two-hander heavy on
prattle";[7] "a script of banality and lack of surprise";[8] and "the real mystery
of this curious 90-minute offering is why it should be occupying a West
End theatre."[9]

Despite the critical snub, *The Secret of Sherlock Holmes* ran at Wyndham's
for a year, closing on September 16, 1989. A successful eleven-week tour
in the English and Scottish provinces followed.

* * *

Born in 1939, Jeremy Paul was educated at King's School Canterbury
and St. Edmund Hall, Oxford. He sold his first television play, *Mr. More-
cambe*, while still a student. He has written, sometimes in collaboration,
several theatre works for the Orange Tree Theatre, Richmond, including
the musicals *The Lady or the Tiger* and *Scraps*.

Paul contributed to the television series *Upstairs, Downstairs*, *The Duchess of Duke Street*, *Danger UXB*, and *By the Sword Divided*. He has penned
more episodes for the Granada Television Holmes cycle than any other
writer, including *The Master Blackmailer* (based on *Charles Augustus Milverton*) and *The Last Vampyre* (based on *The Sussex Vampire*).

* * *

Jeremy Brett (1933–1995) is revered by Sherlockians as the most authentic and vibrant interpreter of the Great Detective. He was born Jeremy
Peter William Huggins in Berkswell, Warwickshire, England, educated at
Eton and the Central School of Speech and Drama, and in 1954 made his
professional stage debut in Manchester as a member of the Library Theatre. Roles he portrayed included Mercury in Giraudoux's *Amphytrion 38*,
Cassio in *Othello*, and Marc Antony in *Julius Caesar*.

Following a stint as Nicolai Rostov in the film version of Tolstoy's
War and Peace (1956), Brett joined London's Old Vic Theatre Company,
where he appeared as Patroclus in *Troilus and Cressida*, Malcolm in *Mac-
beth*, Duke of Aumerle in *Richard II*, and Paris in *Romeo and Juliet*. On the
West End, Brett sang in *Meet Me by Moonlight* (1957); starred in Frederick
Knott's thriller *Mr. Fox of Venice* (1959); and played the title role of *Ham-*

let (1961). At the National Theatre, Brett appeared in Shakespeare's *As You Like It, Love's Labour's Lost*, and *The Merchant of Venice*, and Ibsen's *Hedda Gabler*.

Across the Atlantic, on Broadway, Brett was elevated to the part of Troilus in *Troilus and Cressida* (1956), was featured in Rolf Hochhuth's *The Deputy* (1964), and had his name above the title in a revival of Frederick Lonsdale's *Aren't We All?* (1985).

In 1978, Brett broke house records in Los Angeles, San Francisco, and Chicago in the title role of *Dracula*. Two years later he made a complete turnaround, portraying a bumbling Dr. Watson, alongside Charlton Heston's Holmes, in a Los Angeles production of Paul Giovanni's *The Crucifer of Blood*.

Brett's motion pictures include *Svengali* (1955); *Girl in the Headlines*, aka *The Model Murder Case* (1963); *My Fair Lady* (1964); and *The Medusa Touch* (1978). His last films were *Mad Dogs and Englishmen* (1995) and *Moll Flanders* (1996).

On television, Brett made appearances on the *Hallmark Hall of Fame* (1960), *Armchair Theatre* (1964), *Mystery and Imagination* (1966), *The Baron* (1967), *Play of the Month* (1970), *Thriller* (1974), *The Supernatural* (1977), *The Incredible Hulk* (1978), *Hart to Hart* (1979), *Battlestar Galactica* (1980), and *Masterpiece Theatre* (1983). Among his more demanding TV roles were Dionysus in *The Bacchae* (1962); D'Artagnan in *The Three Musketeers* (1966); Captain Jack Absolute in *The Rivals* (1975); the title roles in *The Incantation of Casanova* (1967), *Lord Byron* (1970), and *Macbeth* (1981); Robert Browning in *The Barretts of Wimpole Street* (1982); and King Arthur in *Morte D'Arthur* (1982). Brett's tour de force characterizations were Basil Hallward, the victimized artist in *The Picture of Dorian Gray* (1976), and Maxim de Winter in the BBC's *Rebecca*, shown in the United States on *Mystery!* (1978).

In 1984, Brett was chosen to star in several Granada Television series: *The Adventures of Sherlock Holmes, The Return of Sherlock Holmes, The Casebook of Sherlock Holmes*, and *The Memoirs of Sherlock Holmes*—making the Great Detective his signature role.

In an interview with Judy Klemesrud of the *New York Times*, Brett declared that "playing the eccentric sleuth for such a long period took its toll. 'I used to be very gregarious,' he said. 'While playing Sherlock Holmes, I became a recluse. . . . He's a very complicated character, very uncomfortable to be around. I wouldn't cross the road to meet him. When you play him, you leave out love, you leave out affection. He's a walking brain who's very rude, and can't even say thank you.'"[10]

Afflicted with bipolar disorder and a failing heart, Brett passed away, in his sleep, on September 2, 1995.

R. Dixon Smith, whose credits include a biography of macabre author Carl Jacobi and a study of actor Ronald Coleman, writes: "As portrayed by Brett, Holmes is a fragile, brittle, reasoning machine. . . . On the other hand, Brett also exhibits great charm and expresses a wide range of moods through facial and physical mannerisms: the lean, ascetic face and piercing eyes; the indolent sweep of a hand; the use of both languid and staccato speech; the faraway, half-quizzical gaze of a man who lives within himself, as if he were searching for something he hasn't yet found; the enigmatic half-smile which plays upon his lips . . . the almost manic glee with which he pounces on a new lead."[11]

Michael Cox, the original producer of Granada Television's Sherlock Holmes series, called Brett "a perfectionist. The only person on the team with whom he lost his temper was himself; he was furious if he failed to live up to his own high standards. . . . Where Conan Doyle had created a character which seemed to belong to marvelous old black-and-white movies, Jeremy added his own style, panache and colour to the portrait."[12]

David Stuart Davies, a lifelong Sherlockian and freelance writer, opines that "Brett became not only *the* Sherlock Holmes of this generation but also, to many, the definitve impersonator of Arthur Conan Doyle's immortal sleuth. . . . He also touched—really touched—millions of people's lives. There was an unfathomable alchemy in the performance that was very special to so many . . . the mesmeric actor who became Conan Doyle's fabulous character on screen provided a buffer against those slings and arrows of the grey, mundane world."[13]

* * *

Born in London, Edward Hardwicke (1932–2011) was the son of distinguished actor Sir Cedric Hardwicke. Edward spent his early childhood in Hollywood, where he appeared, at the age of ten, uncredited, in MGM's *A Guy Named Joe*. Back in England, Edward trained at the Royal Academy of Dramatic Art and apprenticed at The Oxford Playhouse, The Nottingham Playhouse, and the Bristol Old Vic.

Hardwicke launched his London career by playing small parts in Old Vic Shakespearean plays during the 1950s. In 1962, Hardwicke appeared in Peter Ustinov's *Photo Finish*, and in 1964 he joined Laurence Olivier's National Theatre, getting major roles in Shakespeare's *Othello*, Ibsen's *The Master Builder*, Miller's *The Crucible*, and Stoppard's *Rosencrantz and Guildenstern are Dead*. In 2001, Hardwicke played the stubborn, proud Mr. Winslow in Terence Rattigan's *The Winslow Boy* at the Chichester Festival, Chichester, England.

Throughout the second half of the twentieth century, Hardwicke appeared in numerous motion pictures and on television. On the wide screen he was seen in *Men of Sherwood Forest* (1954), *Othello* (1965), *The Day of the Jackal* (1973), *Venom* (1982), *Shadowlands* (1993), *Richard III* (1995),

Photographing Fairies, in which he played Sir Arthur Conan Doyle (1997), *Elizabeth* (1998), *She* (2001), and *Oliver Twist* (2005).

On television, Hardwicke made notable guest appearances in *Invisible Man* (1959), *Journey to the Unknown* (1970), *Colditz* (1972–1974), *Thriller* (1974), *The Supernatural* (1977), *Lady Killers* (1980), *Oppenheimer* (1980), *The Chinese Detective* (1982), *Ruth Rendell Mysteries: Front Seat* (1997), and *Poirot* (2004). He also participated in the made-for-television movies *Oedipus the King* (1984), *The Biko Inquest* (1984), *Titus Andronicus* (1985), *The Alchemists* (1999), and *David Copperfield* (2000).

Hardwicke died of cancer on May 16, 2011, in Chichester, southern England, at the age of seventy-eight.

NOTES

1. The 1978 novel *The Last Sherlock Holmes Story* by Michael Dibdin presents a variation on the theme, albeit more ominous as Sherlock Holmes hunts for Jack the Ripper.

2. Francis King, *Sunday Telegraph,* September 25, 1988.

3. Clive Hirschhorn, *Sunday Express,* September 25, 1988.

4. Jack Tinker, *Daily Mail,* September 23, 1988.

5. Tim Clark, *Time Out,* September 28, 1988.

6. Michael Gillington, *Guardian,* September 24, 1988.

7. Jim Hiley, *Listener,* October 6, 1988.

8. Sheridan Morley, *Punch,* October 4, 1988.

9. Alasdair Buchan, *Today,* September 24, 1988.

10. *New York Times,* May 28, 1985.

11. R. Dixon Smith, *Jeremy Brett and David Burke* (Minneapolis: University of Minnesota Libraries, 1986), 22, 25.

12. Michael Cox, *A Study in Celluloid* (Cambridge, UK: Rupert Books, 1999), 21, 23.

13. David Stuart Davies, *Bending the Willow,* rev. ed. (Ashcroft, B.C.: Calabash Press, 2002), 9, 17.

Sherlock Holmes — The Musical, aka *The Revenge of Sherlock Holmes* (1988)

Leslie Bricusse (England, 1931–)

Leslie Bricusse, who created the book, lyrics, and score of *Sherlock Holmes — The Musical*, begins the proceedings with an 1897 prologue, which has the Great Detective and his arch-enemy Professor Moriarty meet face-to-face on a rocky cliff, "grapple ferociously on the precarious precipice," and finally fall into the chasm of Reichenbach Falls, apparently to their doom.

To the relief of Dr. Watson and the faithful Irregulars, Holmes returns to London alive and well. Upon her first glimpse of him, Mrs. Hudson reacts with horror and "faints dead away into his arms." Overcome with emotion, the landlady, Watson, and the Irregulars sing an ode to Holmes, calling him, "Without a doubt the greatest man on earth."

An attractive young artist, Bella Spellgrove, summons Holmes to The Royal Academy, where her painting, "Portraits of a Stranger," was jaggedly cut out. The missing portrait was of a "strangely solitary man . . . such piercing eyes, and a high, dome-like forehead."

Leslie Bricusse introduces a new wrinkle to the saga of Sherlock Holmes by the revelation that Bella is the daughter of Professor Moriarty, bent on avenging her father's death. Bella croons "Vendetta . . . Sherlock Holmes will die!" and is joined by her mother, Mrs. Moriarty, in entrapping the detective as the suspect in a murder committed in a locked room. Pompous Inspector Lestrade is delighted to find Holmes hovering over the body of a young girl with a blood stained swordstick in his hand.

A student of Houdini, Holmes manages to slip off his handcuffs. While the entire country is abuzz with the "daring escape of Sherlock Holmes," the Great Detective hunts for the female Moriartys. Watson senses that "Miss Spellgrove seems to have somewhat ruffled" Holmes's reasoning. Mrs. Moriarty, too, finds her daughter wavering in her quest for revenge. At some point, Bella says to Holmes, "I have been thinking. . . . If your powers were ever to be married to the mind of a Moriarty—just imagine what a great leap forward there might be in the process of evolution!"

It takes a few clever disguises by both Holmes and Bella for them to finally meet in a deserted waterfront warehouse for a showdown. Mrs. Moriarty aims a loaded pistol at Holmes's head but Bella stops her and the women plunge over the side of a bridge "in an eerily similar replay of Moriarty's own death."

Holmes receives by messenger a small bouquet of bright red-purple flowers and conjectures that Bella Moriarty is still alive. He vows to search for his new adversary, emoting, "And when I find her, this time I know—I shall never, never, ever let her go!"

Sherlock Holmes—The Musical was first presented at the Northcott Theatre, Exeter, England, on October 18, 1988. It was subsequently produced at the Cambridge Theatre, London, on April 24, 1989, under the direction of George Roman, featuring Ron Moody (Holmes), Derek Waring (Watson), and Liz Robertson (Bella). Retitled *The Revenge of Sherlock Holmes* and revised, the musical was mounted by Bristol Old Vic on March 11, 1993, staged by Bob Tomson, with Robert Powell (Holmes), Roy Barraclough (Watson), and Louise English (Bella).

* * *

Lyricist-composer Leslie Bricusse was born in London on January 29, 1931. His talent for songwriting became evident at Cambridge University where he was president of the Footlights Club and author of musical revues. Bricusse achieved his professional breakthrough in *Stop the World—I Want to Get Off,* a collaboration with Anthony Newley, a hit both in London (1960) and New York (1962); the major song was "What Kind of Fool am I?" *The Roar of the Grease Paint—the Smell of the Crowd* (1965) was another successful Bricusse-Newley musical. Bricusse continued creating Broadway lyrics with *Pickwick* (1965), *Victor/Victoria* (1995), and *Jekyll and Hyde* (1997). Among his many contributions to the screen are the title songs of James Bond's *Goldfinger* (1964) and *You Only Live Twice* (1967) as well as scores or lyrics for *Doctor Dolittle* (the song "Talk to the Animals" won an Academy Award, 1967), *Goodbye, Mr. Chips* (1969), *Scrooge* (1970), *Peter Pan* (1976), *Superman* (1978), *Victor/Victoria* (won an Oscar for Best Score, 1982), *Santa Claus* (1985), *Home Alone* (1990), *Hook* (1991), and *Bruce Almighty* (2003).

Acting Edition: Samuel French, Inc.

Awards and Honors: Leslie Bricusse was awarded an O.B.E. (Officer of the British Empire) in 2001.

The Adventure of the Sussex Vampire (1988)

Peter Buckley

Arthur Conan Doyle's trim, under-appreciated story *The Adventure of the Sussex Vampire* was published in the January 1924 issue of *Strand Magazine* and was included in 1927's collection *The Case Book of Sherlock Holmes*. It is the only affair in the Canon in which the Great Detective apparently confronts a supernatural creature.[1]

Holmes dismisses the notion of the undead, of walking corpses who can only be held in their grave by stakes driven through their hearts. "It's pure lunacy," he chuckles.

The topic presents itself when Robert Ferguson of the town of Cheeseman's, Lamberley, an old schoolmate of Watson's, arrives at 221B Baker Street with a curious, desperate plea. His beloved wife, a beautiful Peruvian, the stepmother of his fifteen-year-old son, Jacky, from a previous marriage, and the mother of their one-year-old baby, was seen by the nurse leaning over the infant, seemingly biting his neck. Horrified, the nurse told Ferguson what she saw. Of course, he would not believe her, because as far as he knew his wife was "ordinarily sweet and gentle."

While they were talking, recounts Ferguson, a sudden cry is heard. He and the nurse rushed to the nursery. He saw his wife rise from a kneeling position beside the cot and saw blood on both the child's exposed neck and on the sheet. His wife's lips were smeared with blood. Beyond all question—she had drunk the poor baby's blood. Since that day, says Ferguson, his wife has confined herself to her room and he has become "half demented."

In his 1988 stage adaptation of *The Sussex Vampire*, playwright Peter Buckley omits the Baker Street setting. Instead, the curtain rises on a manor at Cheeseman's, "a somewhat dark and foreboding place. . . . The interior of the sitting room mixes traditional Victorian furnishings with wall hangings depicting weapons, shields and artifacts from South American jungles."

A woman is bent over a bassinet, seeming to struggle with the baby within. The door opposite opens and a young lad, Jacky, pulls in Mrs. Mason, governess and nurse. "You see?" he shouts. "The baby! She's sucking the baby's blood!"

The woman, Mrs. Ferguson, turns around and glares at them. Jacky hobbles towards her[2]—"Look at her mouth! Blood! It's blood!" Mrs. Ferguson quickly covers her lips. The nurse screams. Blackout.

Under the glare of a spotlight, Dr. Watson addresses the audience to explain that a letter requesting his help came from Robert Ferguson. Watson enters the manor. Soon the sound of pounding on the outer door is heard. Dolores, a maid, confronts a filthy and half-crazed man who introduces himself gruffly as "a catcher of rats." He insults Dolores and accosts Watson. The good doctor is dumbfounded until the Rat Catcher changes demeanor and reveals himself to be Sherlock Holmes.[3]

Holmes questions the members of the household one by one: the anguished Robert Ferguson; his sickly teenage son, who nonetheless expresses joy in meeting the famous sleuth;[4] the grim nurse, Mrs. Mason, who declares, "this household is headed for tragedy"; the elderly stable hand, Michael Ashton, whose dog has developed "some sort of paralysis"; the Peruvian maid, Dolores, devoted to her mistress; and Mrs. Ferguson herself, "a woman of great beauty, but it is a beauty wracked by some power within."

Two incidents augment suspicion about Mrs. Ferguson. She chases Jacky in the hallway, swinging at him and beating him with all her might, and it takes both Holmes and Watson to restrain her. A while later, she sneaks into the nursery and is driven out by the vigilant nurse.

Holmes, ever rational, tells Watson that the idea of a vampire seems absurd; such things do not happen in criminal practice in England. When the detective notices an empty quiver among the scattered weapons, he deduces that the dog had been pricked by a poisonous arrow—"curare or some other devilish drug"—as a tryout for doing the same to the infant. Mrs. Ferguson recognized the symptoms. When seen rising from the child with blood on her lips, she was actually sucking his neck to draw the venom out, thereby saving the child's life. Realizing that her husband's son Jacky, jealous and angry at the attention given to the baby, is the culprit, she found herself in an untenable position and was forced, explains Holmes, "into her wretched silence."

Ferguson kneels by his wife and asks her forgiveness. Holmes suggests that a year at sea would be the best prescription for Master Jacky and whispers to Watson, "This, I fancy, is the time for our exit." The Fergusons embrace warmly as the lights fade out.

The Adventure of the Sussex Vampire was first produced by the Ferndale Repertory Theatre, Ferndale, California. The play was copyrighted in 1988.

* * *

The Sussex Vampire was an entry in the radio series *The Adventures of Sherlock Holmes*, aired on February 23, 1931. It was one of thirty-four programs presented by *WEAF-NBC*, New York, all written by Edith Meiser and featuring Richard Gordon (Holmes) and Leigh Lovell (Watson). Meiser's *The Sussex Vampire* was also an entry in the radio series *Sherlock Holmes*, aired on March 14, 1936, one of thirty-five programs presented by *WOR-MBS*, New York, featuring Richard Gordon (Holmes) and Harry West (Watson). Three years later it was part of the *Adventures of Sherlock Holmes*, aired on October 9, 1939, one of twenty-four programs originating from Hollywood, presented by *WLZ-NBC*, New York, starring Basil Rathbone (Holmes) and Nigel Bruce (Watson). *The Sussex Vampire* also featured in *Sherlock Holmes*, aired on December 21, 1947, one of thirty-nine programs originating from Hollywood, presented by *WOR-MBS*, New York, with a cast headed by John Stanley (Holmes) and Alfred Shirley (Watson). The story was again adapted for radio and aired by *BBC Light Programme*, London, on September 18, 1964 with Carleton Hobbs (Holmes) and Norman Shelley (Watson).

Despite its visual potential, *The Adventure of the Sussex Vampire* has rarely been seen on screen and television. *Sherlock Holmes en Caracas* (*Sherlock Holmes in Caracas*), a feature made in Venezuela in 1992, is a ninety-five-minute parody of *The Sussex Vampire*. In it Sherlock Holmes and Dr. Watson travel to Venezuela at the request of an old friend, now living in Maracaibo. He suspects that his young wife is jeopardizing the lives of his children. The denouement inverts the original story when Holmes concludes that the wife is, indeed, a vampire.

England's Granada Television produced a color version titled *The Last Vampyre*. Broadcast on January 27, 1993, it starred Jeremy Brett (Holmes) and Edward Hardwicke (Watson). Adapted by Jeremy Paul and directed by Tim Sullivan, the plot strays considerably from the original.

The Sussex Vampire was an entry in *Sherlock Holmes in the 22nd Century*, an animated series produced by America's *DIC Entertainment* and *Scottish Television Enterprises*, broadcast July 25, 1999 on UK's independent *ITV* network.

Acting Edition: Greatworks Play Service, Shell Beach, California.

NOTES

1. Several disciples of Conan Doyle brought together the Great Detective and the King of Vampires in pastiched novels: Fred Saberhagen in *The Holmes-Dracula File* (1975); Loren D. Estleman in *Sherlock Holmes vs. Dracula* (1978); T. A. Waters in *The Probability Pad* (1993); and Roger Zelazny in *A Night in the Lonesome October* (1993).

2. In the original story, young Jack walks with "a curious shambling gait," evidently "suffering from a weak spine." The play made Jack an invalid who drags his right foot and maneuvers with the aid of a metal-tipped walking stick.

3. Holmes's impersonation is not part of the Doyle story and its motivation here makes no sense—except to provide the character with theatrical bravado.

4. In the original tale, observes Watson, "the youth looked at us with a very penetrating and, it seemed to me, unfriendly gaze."

Stained Glass (1989)

William F. Buckley Jr.
(United States, 1925–2008)

During a pleasant lunch with several associates of the Doubleday publishing company, right-wing scholar and writer William Buckley was asked if he had recently read any action thrillers. Buckley said that he'd read Frederick Forsyth's *Day of the Jackal* the week before and thought it "tremendous." "Why don't you try writing a novel?" asked a Doubleday editor. Buckley pooh-poohed the notion but the next morning he found on his desk a proposed contract to write a novel for the publishing giant.

It so happens that Buckley had just seen the movie *Three Days of the Condor*, in which a CIA agent, played by Robert Redford, goes out for a hamburger and returns to the CIA's New York headquarters to find all nine of his colleagues shot dead. In due course, the agent discovers that the Mr. Big who ordered the killings is not a member of the Mafia or the KGB but a higher up in the government of the United States. He murdered the agents because they stumbled on a secretive CIA operation, the killings motivated by the necessity to safeguard against disclosing the plan. Buckley, himself a former CIA agent, also noted that famed espionage authors Graham Greene, John le Carré, and Len Deighton had equaled the morality of the CIA with that of the KGB. He decided to counter the cynical view of *Three Days of the Condor* and the three British authors by writing a book "in which it was never felt in doubt that the CIA, for all the complaints about its performance, is, when all is said and done, not persuasively likened to the KGB."[1]

The protagonist created by Buckley, Blackford Oakes, debuted in the novel *Saving the Queen* (1976). Oakes, born in 1925, appears on the scene at age twenty-two. He served in World War II as a fighter pilot and graduated from Yale University. At Yale, Oakes was on the swimming and lacrosse teams and was a member of the Zeta Psi fraternity. His main love interest is Sally Partridge, a Smith student, and a relationship between the two develops in later books.

An engineer by training, Oakes is recruited for the Central Intelligence Agency in his senior year, 1951. In Buckley's own words, Oakes is "distinctly American"—handsome, worldly, witty, confident, likable. A Cold Warrior, Oakes risks his life for the country he loves. A charmer, he also has a rebellious streak in the face of harsh authority.

Oakes's first assignment sends him to London to identify a high-level security leak close to the Queen of England. *Stained Glass* (1978) is the second of eleven books in the Blackford Oakes series. In it Oakes travels to West Germany, where he infiltrates the inner circle of a charismatic nobleman, Count Axel Wintergrin, who intends to run for the West German Chancellorship on a platform advocating the immediate reunification with East Germany. The Soviets react by threatening to invade Western Europe and trigger a third World War. A decision had been made in Washington to accede to the demands of the Kremlin and to prevent Wintergrin's election by all means necessary, even assassination.

Buckley's stage version of *Stained Glass* unfolds in a village in West Germany and in a sitting room outside Washington, D.C. High Up Stage Center hangs a large rose-colored stained-glass window. The light that shines through the glass goes through various stages of brilliance, depending on the time of day.

The set is divided into four playing areas, framed by fragmented Gothic arches. Stage right is a small living room in the Georgetown house of Secretary of State Dean Acheson. Stage Center is Bradford Oakes's small, cozy room in the Inn, nearby Anselm's Castle. Stage left is Count Wintergrin's formal living room; a part of St. Anselm's Castle, it abuts the Chapel. At the center is a large metal contraption with a seat in front of it, with turning knobs on either side. Directly below the stained-glass window is a desk. To its right and left are carpenters' horses and assorted masonry, the paraphernalia of a construction team. Whenever there is a change of scene, the lights illuminate the relevant area and organ music plays.

The first scene takes place in the Wintergrin living room. At rise, Countess Wintergrin is seated in a blue chair, brocading. She is described as "grey-haired, slim, dressed austerely but elegantly, age late sixties." At a desk, translating a document, is Erika Chadinoff, "young, striking, full-bodied." Count Wintergrin—"tall, rangy, brown-haired, 31 years old," and Blackford Oakes—"27, handsome, about six feet, faintly blond," enter from the chapel door. Wintergrin introduces Oakes to his mother as "the gentleman who, courtesy of the United States Government's Marshall Plan, is going to rebuild the chapel." The countess expresses surprise that such a young man will be in charge of renovating a famous twelfth-century chapel.

The countess babbles that the sanctuary was "all but destroyed" by American artillery seven years ago; she has no doubt that if her son wins the November elections and becomes prime minister, the Soviet Union will invade Germany "and the chapel would be destroyed all over again."

Wintergrin dismisses his mother's concern and introduces Oakes to Fräulein Erika Chadinoff, who joined his staff a week earlier as official translator and interpreter. The count tells Oakes that the chapel's glass must be reproduced in the same blue color as the original: "It cannot be different from what it was. I would as soon destroy the chapel."

The lights fade up on Dean Acheson's study. Allen Dulles, Director of Central Intelligence, confirms to Acheson that a CIA agent has been placed at St. Anselm. Rufus, an enigmatic big wheel at the CIA—"middle-sized, balding, heavy-set," reports that at this point the polls indicate that Adenauer is leading but Wintergrin's popularity seems to be growing. The three men exchange views about Stalin's threat not to "tolerate" the election of Wintergrin in Germany.

Signs of construction are visible everywhere. A desk is set up against one of the chapel's walls with blueprints slopped about. Only the bottom one-third of the great Rose Window is functioning as stained glass. No blue. The balance of the window is covered with black tarpaper. A light focuses on Wintergrin examining a blueprint with the aid of a magnifying glass. Oakes shifts the count's attention to a chromoscope and puts inch-square pieces of glass, framed in cardboard, into a slide tray. Wintergrin sits down, places his hands on either side of the instrument, and plays with the knobs. Slide 4-C-7 offers the closest tint of blue to the original but the count is not satisfied.

The action shifts to Oakes's study. Rufus arrives and listens unhappily as Oakes reports that Wintergrin "takes people in with this crazy unification business."

> RUFUS: Wintergrin simply can't be a prospective prime minister of West Germany.
> OAKES: I agree. But do you know, Rufus, sometimes I find myself thinking, *Jee-zus*, whose side are we on? The Germans who want to free the other half of the country? Or Stalin—who wants East Germany to continue as a satellite?

Rufus informs Oakes that Secretary Acheson was told that Stalin would mobilize one hundred and fifty divisions were the threat of Wintergrin not removed.

Erika and Oakes enter a room jesting, laughing. Their mood becomes grimmer when Erika tells the American that when translating that afternoon, she realized that Wintergrin is advising the Soviet Union that in the event of an invasion, "there are Germen scientists who will make available to the Government of West Germany the ultimate weapon"—an atomic bomb. Oakes suggests that they stop talking of world affairs, pours champagne, and switches on the radio for sentimental music. He puts his arm around her shoulders and kisses her on the nose. She reciprocates.

The lights fade out, then rise on the chapel. Wintergrin admits that his rating in the polls has dropped to 25 percent while Adenauer's has risen to 34. Oakes suppresses his elation. Two workmen come in—Andy Grossinger, tall and angular, and Alfred North Whitehead (A. W.), short and chubby. The count congratulates them on their excellent progress. Andy says modestly that it is his colleague, A. W., who is the true specialist in electrical schematics.

Roland Himmelfarb, chunky, mid-forties, an aide to Wintergrin, introduces the count at a televised news conference. In answer to a reporter, Wintergrin asserts that the Soviet Union is not satisfied to coerce the East Germans; it desires to influence the election in West Germany as well. Wellington adds that even though at the moment it is a "scientific impossibility" for Germany to have developed an atom bomb, "it does not follow that we cannot have *acquired* an atom bomb."

Rufus arrives for a meeting with Oakes. Oakes asks why it is necessary to kill Wintergrin; why not kidnap him for a few weeks or drug him with a concoction that will temporarily disable him, or jail him until the election is over? Rufus dismisses these ideas. Enter Grossinger and Whitehead. The two men report that the plan to have the count "meet with an accident" will not be easy to execute. A new security chief, Jürgen Wagner, has tightened the proceedings regarding entry to the chapel and its surrounding area. Wagner's apartment is on top and he has a view of the courtyard and the chapel. He has an alarm system and a direct line to the village police. A sniper could do the job, but Wintergrin's demise must look like an accident.

A. W. reveals that earlier in the day he discovered that the translator, Erika Chadinoff, has a tap on Oakes's telephone. Oakes's conversations feed into a recording machine in her room. There remains the question: Is Erika an informer for one of Wintergrin's political competitors or an agent of the Soviet Union?

In Washington, Acheson and Dulles discuss the revelation that Erika was hired by Wintergrin one week before Oakes got there, and Oakes's report that the German count has been receiving a lot of randomly motivated hate mail. The police arrested a young man at a rally with a loaded pistol in his pocket. Dulles jocularly reminds Acheson of Agatha Christie's *Murder on the Orient Express* in which the murdered man has thirteen knife wounds inflicted by thirteen passengers on the train. "That would be a hell of a coincidence," snickers Dulles, "if, a few days before the election, Count Wintergrin was simultaneously shot, stabbed, asphyxiated, poisoned, and drowned." In a more somber mood, Acheson states that if it turns out that the Americans have to dispose of the count, and if, "God help us," the operation is traced to the CIA, he will be "totally astonished, totally shocked by it."

Wintergrin, who has grown fond of Oakes, reveals to him that West Germany has acquired four atomic bombs and one of them is situated very near a concentration of Soviet military. Rufus meets Oakes in his study and tells him that a year earlier Erika had been studying at the Sorbonne, where she fell deeply in love and shared an apartment with a fellow student, Emile. He influenced her to join a communist cell at the university and study—alongside her school courses—espionage and counterespionage under a shadowy gentleman named Lazar. One day last April, Erika came home with the groceries and found Emile lying on their bed naked, dead, a bullet through his head. He was killed by the anti-Communist underground. Erika stayed loyal to Emile's ideas. Oakes admits to Rufus that he has been intimate with Erika but insists that he's never breached security.

Rufus informs Oakes that the newspaper *Die Welt* will report its poll in tomorrow's edition, giving Wintergrin 37 percent. If the ratings plummet to below 30, the operation will be called off. Meanwhile, the Russians offered the Americans "a sporting" proposition: pulling cards, to be drawn by their agents in the field, to decide who'll execute Count Wintergrin.

The bell rings. Rufus goes to the door and admits Colonel Boris Andreyevich Bolgin, Chief KGB agent for Western Europe, who is followed by Erika. Bolgin, described as "always somehow menacing, in gesture, in accent, in intonation," presides over the proceedings: a low card loses; which means the person drawing the lowest card "does the necessary business." Bolgin removes a checkered tablecloth and with a grand gesture invites Rufus to select a pack of cards, place it on the table, and spread the cards out, face down. Erika, with obvious nervousness, fingers a card, thinks better of it, gropes for another and turns it. It is the ten of clubs. Oakes reaches and slams down the five of clubs. "Pity, pity" chuckles Bolgin. "Pity pity pity pity pity pity."

The leisurely pace of the play now shifts and becomes more frenetic. Oakes hears a ring coming from the closet. He brings out a portable radio handset. He flicks on the audio switch and listens. Nothing. Oakes rushes to the chapel and tiptoes in. The security chief, Jurgen Wagner, is standing by a table with the contents of a huge box on top. Oakes walks in. "Detonators! Dynamite sticks! A radio!" yells Wagner. "All nicely hidden and padlocked in one big, disguised wooden case! You're under arrest, Mr. Oakes!" He reaches for his pistol. Oakes yanks a bottle of wine from Andy's open case and thrusts the neck end of it into Wagner's throat. Uttering a barely discernible groan, Wagner collapses. Oakes crosses, establishes that the security chief is dead, sprints to the radio lying on the table, and orders Andy Grossinger to come to the scene immediately. He then covers the body with a loose stretch of tarpaulin and begins to gather the objects scattered on the table. Andy walks in. In a fierce whisper, Oakes tells him what has happened and devises a plan to remove Wagner's corpse. It will fit into the supply box and will be taken out tomorrow morning in the pickup truck.

Count Wintergrin prepares to go off for a final campaign swing. His election as West Germany's Prime Minister is now all but assured. A. W. explains to Oakes the method of disposing of Wintergrin. When the count looks down the chromoscope to check the blue glass, Oakes is to depress a button in a cigarette-pack-sized transmitter. A module tucked into the chromoscope will be activated and .220 volts will flow from the hand touching the lever to the heart. The heart will stop—"no ands, ifs, or buts."

Oakes mumbles, "Axel Wintergrin could not be permitted to live in this world. And *I* am to be his executioner." He complains bitterly to Rufus that when joining the CIA he was never told that his duty would be to kill an ally in cold blood. In the chapel he confronts Erika and accuses her leader, Stalin, who has insisted that Wintergrin must die, of turning him into an executioner. "You do it," he says, and drops the transmitter into her purse.

Wintergrin enters with his aide Himmelfarb. Oakes tells him that at long last his mixture of colors has yielded the Anselin blue. Ecstatic, Wintergrin sits at the chromoscope and begins to adjust the knobs. Oakes trains his eyes on Erika. He spots her purse hanging on a wall hook. She is not going to do it!

A blast shakes the heavy chromoscope machine, followed by an explosion within it. Himmelfarb runs over, seizes the count by his shoulders and shouts, "Get a doctor!" Erika runs out, pausing only to snatch her purse. Later, in Oakes's room, A. W. tells him that he made two transmitters, to make sure that at least one would be "in reliable shape." He could tell by the way Oakes was standing with his hands out that he wasn't going to use the transmitter, so he pressed the button. No one knows that he did it, not even his coworker, Andy. "I don't plan to tell nobody. Ever," says A. W.

Oakes and his men continue to work on the renovation of the chapel. In the play's last scene, the Rose Window, totally restored, is brilliantly illuminated. Countess Wintergrin walks in, goes to the altar, kneels, and says a quick prayer. She then rises, congratulates Oakes, and hands him a letter "to be delivered to Mr. Blackford Oakes in the event of my death." She kept the nine-month-old letter until the completion of the work on the chapel. Oakes reads with deep emotion that Wintergrin knew for weeks that Oakes has been serving a certain force, but he was confident that whatever happened, Oakes would join him as a brother in the fight against tyranny. "Whatever your duty requires of you," the letter stated, "my confidence in your integrity will never . . . alter."

Oakes breaks down in a convulsive sob. Organ music begins to rise in volume as both Oakes and the countess kneel by the chapel's rail. The lights dim, except those on the stained-glass windows. They remain brilliant for a few seconds before the music and spots go off.

Stained Glass premiered at the Actors Theatre of Louisville, Kentucky, on March 1, 1989. The play was directed by Steven Schachter, with set design by Paul Owen. The cast included William Carden (Blackford Oakes), William McNulty (Count Axel Wintergrin), Barbara Gulan (Erika Chadinoff), Edward James Hyland (Rufus), Donald Symington (Dean Acheson), William Swan (Allen Dulles), John Dennis Johnston (Andy Grossinger), George Gerdes (Alfred North Whitehead), and Adale O'Brien (Countess Wintergrin).[2]

* * *

The sixth of ten siblings, William Frank Buckley Jr. was born into a wealthy Catholic family in 1925 in New York City. His father, William Frank Buckley Sr., was an oil baron with holdings in several countries. Buckley Jr. began his schooling with personal tutors at the family estate in Sharon, Connecticut, then was sent to Paris, where he attended first grade, and London, where he began to develop a love for music, sailing, hunting, skiing, and storytelling. Just before World War II, at age thirteen, he attended high school at the Catholic preparatory Beaumont College in England. Back in the United States, Buckley entered Millbrook School in Millbrook, New York, where he founded and edited the school's yearbook, *The Tamarack*, before graduating in 1943. He spent a year at the National Autonomous University of Mexico, was commissioned as a second lieutenant in the U.S. Army during World War II, and at the end of the war in 1945, he entered Yale University to study history, economics, and political science. He excelled as the captain of the debate team, served as chair of the *Yale Daily News*, and became a member of the secret, prestigious, and somewhat notorious Skull and Bones society. He graduated with honors in 1950. The following year he published his first book, *God and Man at Yale*, in which he argued that his alma mater had strayed from its Christian roots and its original educational mission.

Also in 1951, like some of his classmates in the Ivy League, Buckley was recruited into the Central Intelligence Agency (CIA). He served for nine months working as a political action specialist in the elite Special Activities Division under E. Howard Hunt. The two remained lifelong friends.[3]

In the early 1950s, Buckley worked as an editor for *The American Mercury*, but left after perceiving emerging anti-Semitic tendencies in the magazine. In 1955 he founded *National Review*, serving as editor in chief until 1990. During that time, *National Review* became the standard-bearer of American conservatism. In an attempt to define the boundaries of conservatism, Buckley and his editors excluded and denounced Ayn Rand, George Wallace, the John Birch Society, and anti-Semites. However, in 1957 Buckley argued that white supremacy in the South was a good idea as the black population lacked the educational, economic, or cultural development for racial equality. Buckley backtracked and in the mid-1960s renounced racism. He later grew to admire Martin Luther King Jr., and supported the creation of a Martin Luther King Jr. Day as a national holiday.

In 1965, Buckley ran for mayor of New York City as the candidate for the new Conservative Party. He did not expect to win; when asked what he would do if victorious, Buckley responded, "Demand a recount." He got 13.4 percent of the vote; fellow alumnus John Lindsay became mayor. Instead, Buckley garnered national exposure in his weekly PBS show *Firing Line*, hosting 1,504 episodes between 1966 and 1999. Beginning in 1962 and until 2008, he also wrote a twice-weekly syndicated column, "On the Right," which appeared in more than 300 newspapers. Along the way, Buckley had heated debates and feuds with Gore Vidal, Norman Mailer, and Carl Sagan. Even his antagonists praised Buckley's personal charm, sparkling wit, and a vocabulary that became the stuff of legend.

In 1973, Buckley served as a delegate to the United Nations. Three years later he penned his first spy novel, *Saving the Queen*, introducing CIA agent Blackford Oakes and Rufus, the enigmatic genius behind American intelligence operations.

Following his assignments in England (*Saving the Queen*) and Germany (*Stained Glass*), Oakes continued to travel, near and far, in nine more novels. In *Who's on First* (1980) he is sent to Hungary during the 1956 anti-Soviet uprising. Set in 1958, Oakes is shot down while flying a U-2 spy plane over the Soviet Union in *Marco Polo, If You Can* (1982). *The Story of Henri Todd* (1984) unfolds in 1961 Germany during the Berlin Wall crisis. *See You Later, Alligator* (1985) is set in Cuba in the early 1960s. Oakes meets Che Guevara in an attempt to ease tensions after the Bay of Pigs incident. Once again enmeshed in Cold War politics, in *High Jinx* (1986) Oakes goes inside the Soviet Union to monitor an internal power struggle within the Kremlin. Oakes revisits Cuba in *Mongoose R.I.P.* (1987) to determine the feasibility of overthrowing Fidel Castro, following the Cuban missile crisis of 1963. In *Tucker's Last Stand* (1990), Oakes is sent to Vietnam to assist in cutting off supply lines to the Viet Cong. In *A Very Private Plot* (1994), Oakes is called to testify before the U.S. Congress regarding a suspected domestic Soviet plot to assassinate Mikhail Gorbachev. *Last Call for Blackford Oakes* (2005) depicts a 1987 confrontation between Oakes and the infamous double agent Kim Philby (1912–1988) who was a high-ranking member of British intelligence and also a spy for the Soviet Union's KGB.

In *The Blackford Oakes Reader* (1999), Buckley explains where, when, why, and how he created the Blackford Oakes saga and provides a literary analysis of all the major characters in the series.

Buckley died at his home in Stamford, Connecticut in 2008. He was found lying on the floor of his study after a fatal heart attack. At the time of his death, he had been suffering from emphysema and diabetes. Notable members of the Republican establishment paying tribute to Buckley included President George W. Bush, former speaker of the House of Representatives Newt Gingrich, and former first lady Nancy Reagan.

Acting Edition: Samuel French, Inc.

Awards and Honors: In 1991, William F. Buckley Jr. received the Presidential Medal of Freedom from President George H. W. Bush. Buckley's PBS television program *Firing Line* won an Emmy Award in 1969. The paperback edition of the novel *Stained Glass* won the 1980 National Book Award as the best mystery story of the year. "I like to think it was not the narrative's suspense that overwhelmed the judges," wrote Buckley. "What the book did was to pose the central question of counterintelligence and espionage as conducted by a free society."[4]

NOTES

1. William F. Buckley Jr., *The Blackford Oakes Reader* (Kansas City: Andrews and McMeel, 1995), xv.

2. Adale O'Brien, who has been a bulwark of the Actors Theatre of Louisville, Kentucky, for many years, was first discovered in the role of damsel-in-distress Annabelle West in a long-running off-Broadway revival of John Willard's classic melodrama *The Cat and the Canary*, directed by Amnon Kabatchnik.

3. E.[verette] Howard Hunt was a controversial CIA agent and author of spy novels. Born in Hamburg, New York, in 1918, a graduate of Brown University in 1940 and a recipient of a Guggenheim Fellowship in 1946, Hunt was a scriptwriter and editor for the *March of Time* newsreel series and a correspondent for *Life* magazine before World War II. He served in the U.S. Naval Reserve, 1940–1942, and the U.S. Air Force, 1943–1946. From 1948 to 1970 he was involved with covert CIA activities in Washington and many world capitals including Paris, Vienna, Tokyo, and Montevideo. In 1971 he became a consultant at President Richard M. Nixon's White House, in charge of carrying out acts of political warfare. Two years later he was convicted of six counts of conspiracy in connection with the June 1972 break-in to the Democratic National Committee headquarters at the Watergate complex. He served thirty-three months in federal prison. His notoriety caused the reprinting of books that Hunt wrote years earlier under several pseudonyms—less-than-successful hard-boiled private eye and action-packed espionage yarns, many peppered with personal references. As Robert Dietrich, he wrote a dozen original paperbacks about Steve Bentley, a Washington accountant-troubleshooter. As David St. John, he created Peter Ward, a graduate of Brown

University whose Washington law practice was a cover for CIA activities. As Gordon Davis, he wrote about a Washington hotel detective. In 1974, Hunt published *Undercover: Memoirs of an American Secret Agent*, a full-scale, 338-page volume tracing the life of a bona fide spy from his childhood to the Watergate scandal. That same year, Hunt's life and fate were also covered in *Compulsive Spy: The Strange Career of E. Howard Hunt* by Tad Szulc. Following his release from prison, Hunt lived in Miami, Florida, until his death, caused by pneumonia, in January 2007, at the age of 88. William F. Buckley Jr. remembered Hunt as "a spy and a Cold Warrior, a companion and a confidant, a Watergate burglar and a broken man." (*New York Times*, March 4, 2007).

    4. Buckley, *The Blackford Oakes Reader*, xxv.

Travels with My Aunt (1989)

Giles Havergal (Scotland, 1938–)

Henry Pulling, a fifty-some retired bank manager whose only interest in life is cultivating dahlias, has suddenly been thrust into the picaresque world of his flamboyant aunt, Augusta Bertram. The meek, reclusive Henry is awed by the sprightly, red-headed, seventy-five-year-old who lives above the Crown and Anchor, a sleazy pub, with her valet-lover, "a very large middle-aged Negro" nicknamed Wordsworth.

"Age, Henry, may a little modify our emotions—it does not destroy them," says Aunt Augusta, who proceeds to shock her straight-laced nephew with her drinking bouts, lusty encounters, and zest for wild adventures.

Henry tastes his first whip of risk when Detective Sergeant Sparrow confiscates the urn containing his mother's ashes for drug analysis in a police laboratory. "It's quite possible that the man Wordsworth took out the ashes and substituted pot," says Sparrow. "You wouldn't want to see that urn every day and wonder, are those really the ashes of the dear departed or are they an illegal supply of marijuana?"

Aunt Augusta whisks Henry away on a series of nefarious escapades. She smuggles a case with ten-pound notes to Paris, a gold ingot hidden in a candle to Istanbul (where she outwits Colonel Hakim of the Turkish police), and an original Leonardo da Vinci, framed behind a photograph of Freetown Harbor, to Paraguay (where she sells it for $10,000 to O'Toole, a CIA agent who is tracking them).

Henry is amazed to find that all of Aunt Augusta's trials are designed to support the man she loves, Mr. Visconti (alias Izquierdo), hunted by Interpol as "a war criminal." Never mind that in the past the scoundrel absconded with her money; never mind that he is short, bald, and fat, with most of his teeth missing. When Mr. Visconti is in "a very low state," Aunt Augusta will do anything to help him.

The rollicking *Travels with My Aunt* shifts gears temporarily when the devoted Wordsworth, who follows Augusta to South America, is found stabbed to death. Did Visconti's henchmen commit the murder? At the end, Aunt Augusta marries Visconti and reveals that she is Henry's biological mother. The pensioned banker loses "the taste for dahlias," discovers that he enjoys the excitement of his new life, joins the import-export business that Visconti has established in Paraguay, and plans to marry the sixteen-year-old daughter of the local police chief.

* * *

Travels with My Aunt, adapted from Graham Greene's 1969 novel and directed by Giles Havergal (who also participated as one of the four male actors enacting twenty-five colorful, variegated characters, including a wolfhound), was first presented at the Citizens' Theatre in Glasgow on November 10, 1989. The play arrived in New York via London's West End (where it ran for sixteen months and won two 1993 Olivier Awards) and the Long Wharf Theatre, New Haven, Connecticut (October 14, 1994), settling at off-Broadway's Minetta Lane Theatre on April 12, 1995 for 199 performances.

In this production, Jim Dale played Aunt Augusta, while Brian Murray, Tom Becket, and Martin Rayner changed voice and nuance for all other personalities. The quartet shared, at various times, the role of Henry Pulling. Throughout, all were dressed in identical gray suits, with moustaches and eyeglasses, and wore no special makeup.

"It's a thoroughly engrossing evening that starts off looking like theatrical gimmickry but evolves into something far more involving as one is drawn inexorably into the tale," wrote reviewer Jeremy Gerard.[1] "Cheeky, offbeat and outrageously delightful," applauded Clive Barnes."[2] "Is kin to *Never on Sunday* and *Zorba,* in which timid retiring Anglo-Saxons learn that life should not be lived second-hand . . . a giddy, eccentric romp," chirped Howard Kissel.[3] "An exercise in high camp so inspired as to be quintessential theatre," raved John Simon.[4] "Mr. Havergal's play is a triumph of theatrical style over substance, totally eclipsing the slight, schematic and doggedly whimsical novel that is its source," opined Ben Brantley.[5]

Dissenting voices came from Jan Stuart: "The play's chief flaw . . . is that Aunt Agatha (Augusta) is never as compelling as Greene would have us believe,"[6] and Michael Feingold: "But in the long run the effect is dry and dispiriting."[7]

Travels with My Aunt was transformed to the screen in Panavision (MGM, 1972), directed by George Cukor, featuring Maggie Smith as Aunt Augusta, Alec McCowan as Henry Pulling, Louis Gossett Jr. as Wordsworth, and Robert Stephens as Visconti. Critic Leonard Maltin believes that the "deliberately paced film never really gets going, leaves viewer in midair like a final tossed coin."[8]

* * *

Born in Edinburgh, Scotland in 1938, Giles Havergal has had an impressive career as playwright, director, and actor. In addition to adapting to the stage Graham Greene's *Travels with My Aunt*, he also dramatized *Pamela, or, The Reform of a Rake* (1985) from a novel by Samuel Richardson; *The Gospels* (1991) from the Bible; *Summer Lightning* (1992) from a novel by P. G. Wodehouse; *David Copperfield* (2000) from Charles Dickens, which was performed at the Steppenwolf Theatre Company in Chicago; and *Brighton Rock* (2004), again from a Greene novel.

Havergal appeared on stage and in television, became the director of the theatre at Barrow-In-Furness in 1964, director of Watford Palace Theatre during 1965–1969 (where he staged, among others, the British premiere of Tennessee Williams's *Sweet Bird of Youth*), and in 1969 was nominated Director of the Citizens' Theatre in Glasgow. His numerous directing credits include Shakespeare's *Hamlet* and *The Taming of the Shrew*; Brecht's *The Caucasian Chalk Circle* and *Puntilla and Matti*; Shaw's *Pygmalion* and *Saint Joan*; Coward's *Private Lives* and *Blithe Spirit*; O'Casey's *Juno and the Paycock* and *The Plough and the Stars*; Miller's *The Crucible* and *Death of a Salesman*; and Orton's *Loot* and *Entertaining Mr. Sloan*.

Among the roles that Havergal played at the Citizens' Theatre were King Philip in Schiller's *Don Carlos*, Krapp in Ionesco's *Krapp's Last Tape*, and Ebenezer Scrooge in Dickens's *A Christmas Carol*.

* * *

Graham Greene was born in Berkhamsted, Hertfordshire, England in 1904. He was a sickly and sensitive child who instead of participating in sports chose to immerse himself in the reading of adventure stories by authors such as Rider Haggard, Joseph Conrad, and R. M. Ballantyne. Bullied by classmates for being the headmaster's son, Greene made several youthful suicide attempts. His parents sent him to a therapist in London at age fifteen. His analyst encouraged him to write. At Balliol College, Oxford he studied modern history and served as editor of *The Oxford Outlook*.

After graduating with a BA in 1925, Greene was employed by the *Nottingham Journal*, and moved on as a sub-editor to *The Times* in London. Influenced by his fiancée, Vivien Dayrell-Browning, Greene converted to Catholicism in 1926. A year later they got married, had two children, and in 1948 separated, but never divorced or remarried. In fact, religion plays an important role in many of Greene's works.

Much travelled, Greene was recruited into MI6, the British secret service agency, and was posted to Sierra Leone during World War II. Kim Philby, who would later be revealed as a Soviet double agent, was Greene's supervisor at MI6. Greene incorporated the places where he lived and the characters he met into the fabric of his novels.

Plays by Graham Greene are often occupied with questions of good vs. evil. There is the intellectual psychological thriller *The Potting Shed* (1957), tinged with autobiographical elements of the playwright's bleak outlook on Catholicism, his manic-depressive bouts, and suicidal tendencies.[9] In the metaphoric *Carving a Statue* (London, 1964; New York, 1968), the protagonist is a sculptor who has been working obsessively, for fifteen years, on a massive rendition of God the Father. Isolating himself from the real world, the sculptor despairs of ever molding God and turns his creative juices toward demon Lucifer instead. Lighter fare include *The Return of A. J. Raffles* (London, 1975), a rollicking resurrection of Greene's boyhood hero, E. W. Hornung's Amateur Cracksman. The farce *For Whom the Bell Chimes* (Leicester, 1980) revolves around the body of a murdered woman hidden in a bed enclaved behind the wall of a small studio.

Greene's masterpiece, *The Power and the Glory* (1940), a multi-layered novel about a hunted and haunted alcoholic priest, was dramatized by Dennis Cannan and Pierre Bost, and, starring Paul Scofield, "was given a powerful production by Peter Brook"[10] at London's Phoenix Theatre in 1956. Two years later, the adaptation was produced by New York's Phoenix Theatre, staged by Stuart Vaughan, running for seventy-one performances. "It is wonderful acting in a wonderful play that fills the Phoenix with power and glory," wrote Brooks Atkinson in the *New York Times*.[11]

Non-crime plays by Greene include *The Living Room* (London, 1953; New York, 1954); *The Complaisant Lover* (London, 1959; New York, 1961); and the one-act *Yes and No* (Leicester, 1980). In 2000, a recently discovered manuscript, *A House of Reputation*, was given its world premiere at Berkhamsted, England, Greene's birthplace. It is set in a brothel, reflecting the playwright's lifelong fondness for prostitutes and frequent visits to seedy houses of ill repute.

Together with director Carol Reed, Greene scripted the film noir masterpiece *The Third Man* in 1949, and novelized it the following year. Altogether, Greene wrote or co-wrote ten screenplays, including several based on his works: *Brighton Rock* (1947), *The Fallen Idol* (1948), *Our Man in Havana* (1960), and *The Comedians* (1967).[12]

Crime plays a dominant role in the bulk of Graham Greene's fiction, most notably in the novels he coined as "entertainments:" *Stamboul Train* (1932, U.S. title *Orient Express*), *A Gun for Sale* (1936, U.S. title *This Gun for Hire*), *Brighton Rock* (1938), *The Confidential Agent* (1939), and *The Ministry of Fear* (1943). All were impressively transferred to the screen. In 1943, *Brighton Rock* was dramatized by Frank Harvey and ran for 100 performances at West End's Garrick Theatre, featuring Richard Attenborough as Pinkie Brown, a psychotic teenaged gangster. In 2004, film composer John Barry and lyricist Don Black collaborated on a musical version of *Brighton Rock* that was lambasted by the critics and ran for less than a month at London's Almeida Theatre.

On July 15, 2009, the *New York Times* reported the discovery of an unfinished murder mystery novel by Greene, called *The Empty Chair*. Greene began writing the novel in 1926 and apparently abandoned it. He was twenty-two at the time, apprenticing with the *Times of London*. The manuscript, written in longhand, was discovered in 2008 in the Greene archive at the Ransom Center of the University of Texas. It is a country house whodunit with a protagonist who is "a sly, Columbo-like detective-inspector," said the *New York Times*.[13]

British TV presented adaptations of the short stories by Greene under the banner *Shades of Greene* in the fall of 1975.

The prolific author penned *The Little Steam Roller: A Story of Mystery and Detection* (1953) for the young readers' market, and, with Dorothy Glover, the catalogue *Victorian Detective Fiction* (1966). Among others, Greene edited *British Dramatists* (1942), *The Best of Saki* (1950), and, with his brother Hugh Greene, *The Spy Bedside Book* (1957). Various short pieces were collated in Greene's *The Lost Childhood and Other Essays* (1951) and *Collected Essays* (1969) while his numerous film criticisms were assembled in *Graham Greene on Film*, edited by John Russell Taylor (1972). Greene's autobiography *A Sort of Life* was published in 1971 and his memoir, *Ways of Escape*, in 1980. Other real-life accounts were delineated in *Revenge* (1963), *Getting to Know the General (1984)*, *Reflections* (1990), and *A World of My Own*, published posthumously in 1992.

Greene lived the last years of his life in Vevey, on Lake Geneva, Switzerland, where Charlie Chaplin lived as well, and the two became good friends. Greene died at age 86 of a blood disease in 1991 and was buried in Corsier-sur-Vevey cemetery.

Professor Norman Sherry's *The Life of Graham Greene, Volume I: 1904–1939*, won the 1990 Edgar Allan Poe Award from the Mystery Writers of America for best critical/biographical work. *Volume II: 1939–1955* (which details Greene's participation in British Intelligence during the Second World War) was released in 1995, *Volume III: 1955–1991* in 2004.

"The depth of Greene's work comes from the inexhaustible themes of guilt and redemption, of evil's influence on the innocent and vice versa," writes William L. DeAndrea.[14] George Woodcock concludes: "The criminal rather than the crime, the sinner rather than the sin, are Greene's ultimate concerns."[15]

Acting Edition: Dramatic Publishing; Oberon Books.

Awards and Honors: Outer Critics Circle Award, 1994–1995—cast of *Travels with My Aunt* for an outstanding ensemble performance; Lucille Lortel Award, 1995–1996—Best Actor in a play: Jim Dale; Graham Greene's *The Potting Shed* was a top ten selection in *The Best Plays of 1956–1957*: "*The Potting Shed* is the most truly dramatic of detective stories, a what-done-it, a shadowy trek backward from an effect to cause. . . . It has an emotional force born of its characters' harassed bafflement and needs."[16] Among other honors, Graham Greene was the recipient of the Hawthornden Prize (1941), Black Memorial Prize (1948), Chevalier of the Legion of Honor (1967), Shakespeare Prize, Hamburg (1968), Thomas More Medal (1973), Mystery Writers of America's Grand Master Edgar (1976), The Jerusalem Prize (1981), and the Order of Merit (1986). In 1956, Greene turned down an offer to be a Commander of the British Empire (CBE). In 2002, Giles Havergal received the CBE "in recognition of services to the theatre," and the Loving Cup from the Glasgow City Council.

NOTES

1. *Variety*, April 17, 1995.
2. *New York Post*, April 13, 1995.
3. *Daily News*, April 13, 1995.
4. *New York Magazine*, May 1, 1995.
5. *New York Times*, April 13, 1995.
6. *New York Newsday*, April 13, 1995.
7. *Village Voice*, April 25, 1995.
8. *Leonard Maltin's 1997 Movie and Video Guide* (New York: Signet, 1996), 1396.
9. A synopsis of *The Potting Shed*, the play's production elements, and its critical reception are provided in *Blood on the Stage, 1950–1975* by Amnon Kabatchnik (Lanham, Md.: Scarecrow Press, 2010).
10. *Theatre World Annual*, 1957.
11. *New York Times*, December 12, 1958.
12. An analysis of Graham Greene's motion pictures is provided in *Graham Greene: The Films of His Fiction* by Gene D. Phillips (New York: Teachers College Press, 1974).
13. *New York Times*, July 15, 2009.
14. William L. DeAndrea, *Encyclopedia Mysteriosa* (New York: Prentice Hall, 1994), 142.
15. John M. Reilly, ed., *Twentieth-Century Crime and Mystery Writers* (New York: St. Martin's, 1980), 701.
16. Louis Kronenberger, ed., *The Best Plays of 1956–1957* (New York: Dodd, Mead, 1957), 12.

A Few Good Men (1989)

Aaron Sorkin (United States, 1961–)

The military courtroom drama by a novice playwright, Aaron Sorkin, be-gan its artistic incubation at the University of Virginia in Charlottesville, then moved to the Kennedy Center in Washington, D.C., before playing Broadway for 497 performances. *A Few Good Men* reportedly brought twenty-eight-year-old Sorkin a six-figure deal with movie producer Da-vid (*Jaws*) Brown.

The action of *A Few Good Men* takes place in two diverse settings: Washington, D.C., and the U.S. Naval Base in Guantanamo Bay, Cuba. The time: summer 1986. Marine Lance Corporal Harold W. Dawson and Private First Class Louden Downey have been charged with conspiracy to commit murder, murder in the second degree, and conduct unbecoming a U.S. Marine. The victim, William Santiago, was an unpopular private in their platoon. Assigned to defend Dawson and Downey is Lieutenant Daniel A. Kaffee, a callow Harvard Law School graduate, who prefers playing baseball to pursuing the case.

Prodded by Lieutenant Commander Joanne Galloway ("Lieutenant, would you feel very insulted if I recommend to your supervisor that he assign different counsel?"), Kaffee discovers that Santiago had written to his senator for help, describing how he was dizzy and nauseated during a PT (physical training) run, had fallen behind when going down a rocky hill, and was deliberately pushed down the hill by his sergeant. He was put in remedial physical training and punished by filling sandbags every day after standing his post on the fence line. He is asking the senator to help in a transfer out of the RSC (rifle security company).

It seems that Santiago has penned eleven similar letters and put in for transfer six times. That triggered the ire of his commanders. Santiago, considered a traitor to the Marine Corps motto "Unit, Corps, God, Coun-try," was placed on "Code Red"—a form of hazing-like discipline that befalls enlisted men who don't measure up to standard. Dawson and

Downey stuffed a rag down Santiago's throat, accidentally suffocating him. The thrust of Kaffee's defense case is that the two Marines are fall guys willing to go to jail; higher-ups, condoning and instigating brutal treatment of men who don't fit the mold, are the real culprits.

In court, Kaffee gradually sheds his neophyte image when pitted against rigid, flag-waving Lieutenant Colonel Nathan Jessup, the formidable base commander, who barks at Kaffee: "We live in a world that has walls. And those walls have to be guarded by men with guns. Who's gonna do it? You? I have a greater responsibility than you can possibly fathom." Jessup looms larger than life in the courtroom but the reflection is shattered when Kaffee maintains that Jessup ordered the Code Red on Santiago and when it went awry, he signed a phony transfer order for Santiago. Kaffee submits Defense Exhibit A, the Tower Chief's log for Naval Air Station, NAVBASE, Guantanamo Bay, Cuba. It lists incoming and outgoing flights for Thursday, July 7 and Friday, July 8, and the lawyer points out that the logbook was forged to show that Santiago could not have left yet because on those dates no passenger-capable flights left the base.

Kaffee opens the logbook and crosses to Jessup. "Is that your signature?" he asks. Jessup nods, "That's my signature" and reluctantly admits that he ordered the Code Red against Santiago. The case against Dawson and Downey is dismissed while Jessup is placed under arrest. He makes a quick move toward Kaffee, but is grabbed by MPs who pull him back.

JESSUP: I'm gonna tear your eyes right outta your head and piss in your skull! You fucked with the wrong Marine! All you did here today was weaken the country. . . . You put people in danger. Sweet dreams, son.
KAFFEE: Don't call me son. I'm a lawyer. An officer of the United States Navy. And you're under arrest, you son of a bitch. [To the MPs] The witness is excused.

* * *

While not in the same league with Herman Wouk's *The Caine Mutiny Court Martial*, *A Few Good Men*, which opened at the Music Box Theatre on November 15, 1989, proved to be popular with critics and audiences. Clive Barnes declared it "A triumphant example of a now fashionably outmoded courtroom drama that sizzles with fun and entertainment."[1] Linda Winer agreed: "People who like courtroom dramas eat them like popcorn, and chances are, people like them are going to gobble *A Few Good Men* as if it were a gourmet brand."[2] Edwin Wilson stated: "Mr. Sorkin not only knows how to set up a scene, he has a sharp sense of humor, and he is greatly aided by director Don Scardino, who puts the cast members through their paces with a military precision that even the gung-ho colonel would have admired."[3] However, William A Henry III suggested that the play "suffers from bad timing" in view of "the flood tide of change in the Communist world that makes the military appear less vital."[4] Frank Rich found *A Few Good Men* "too predictable to satisfy as a courtroom entertainment, and its attempt to tie its plot to some larger moral issue, in the manner of Charles Fuller's *Soldier's Play* are lightweight."[5] Otis L. Guernsey Jr. and Jeffrey Sweet opined that "*A Few Good Men* puts on the airs of being a play about issues . . . but what it really is about is giving actors the opportunity to play their favorite scenes from old movies. A lot of those scenes are here—the wise-cracking female associate putting male chauvinists in their place, the wise-cracking side-kick tossing off one ironic quip after another when faced with a team of macho bullies. . . . Tom Hulce, Megan Gallagher and Mark Nelson batted Sorkin's snappy patter back and forth with great élan, and Stephen Lang snarled memorably as the principled villain."[6]

The motion picture adaptation that made young Sorkin a rich man was shot in 1992 by director Rob Reiner. Jack Nicholson is mesmerizing as Colonel Jessup; Kevin Bacon is eerily intense as Jack Ross, a fanatic captain; Tom Cruise and Demi Moore are solid as attorneys Kaffee and Galloway.

In 2005, Sorkin revised the play for a revival at London's Theatre Royal Haymarket, directed by David Esbjornson, with Rob Lowe as attorney Kaffee. Staged by Kenne Guillory, *A Few Good Men* was presented in March 2012 at the Sky Lounge, North Hollywood, California, squeezing the large cast into a small, black-box theatre.

* * *

Aaron Sorkin was born in Manhattan to affluent Jewish parents and was raised in the wealthy suburb of Scarsdale, New York. He attended Scarsdale High School where he became involved in the drama club. His interest in theatre was whetted when his parents took him to see such Broadway shows as *Who's Afraid of Virginia Woolf?* and *That Championship Season*.

In 1979 Sorkin enrolled at Syracuse University. He graduated in 1983 with a BA degree in musical theatre. He moved to New York City where he pursued an acting career while supporting himself driving a limousine, delivering singing telegrams, and handing out promotional fliers. It is said that one weekend, while house sitting at a friend's place, he found an electric typewriter, started typing, felt exhilarated, and from then on dedicated his life to writing. He sent his first play, *Removing All Doubt*, to his Syracuse theatre teacher, Arthur Storch, who was impressed and staged the play at the university. Sorkin's second play, the one-act *Hidden in This Picture*, a Hollywood satire, was presented at off-off-Broadway's West Bank Café in 1988, and he developed it into a full-length play called

Making Movies. *Making Movies* debuted in 1990 at off-Broadway's Promenade Theatre, directed by Don Scardino.

Sorkin got the idea for writing *A Few Good Men* from a phone conversation with his sister Deborah, who had graduated from Boston University's Law School and signed up with the U.S. Navy Judge Advocate General's Corps. She was on her way to Guantanamo Bay to defend a group of Marines who had come close to killing a fellow Marine in a hazing ordered by a superior officer. "I wrote [*A Few Good Men*] on cocktail napkins during the first act of Broadway shows where I was serving as a bartender," recalls Sorkin in an interview with broadcast journalist Charlie Rose on August 13, 2003.[7]

Following the success of the courtroom drama on Broadway, Sorkin wrote several drafts of the screenplay with veteran author William Goldman serving as his mentor. Goldman also submitted to Sorkin a story premise to be developed into the script that became *Malice*, a medical thriller released in 1993, featuring Alec Baldwin, Nicole Kidman, Bill Pullman, George C. Scott, and Anne Bancroft. Two years later, Goldman worked as a creative consultant on Sorkin's third screenplay, for *The American President*, in which the widowed President of the United States (played by Michael Douglas) is attracted to a lobbyist (Annette Bening) and decides to pursue her despite the advice of his political aides. During the 1990s, Sorkin served, uncredited, as a script doctor on *Schindler's List* (1993), *The Rock* (1996), and *Bulworth* (1998).

Sorkin went on to create *Sports Night* for ABC-TV, a comedy series about the behind-the-scenes happenings on a sports show. Although critically acclaimed, the 1998 show was cancelled after two seasons due to its low ratings. However, Sorkin's next television endeavor, *The West Wing*, depicting fictional life and politics in the White House, was honored with nine Emmy Awards for its season debut in 1999 and became a hit series on NBC.[8]

In 2001, Sorkin was arrested at Burbank Airport for possession of marijuana and crack cocaine. He was ordered by a judge to attend a drug diversion program. His drug addiction was widely publicized. Recovered, Sorkin created *Studio 60 on Sunset Strip*. Describing it as having "autobiographical elements," it was a 2006 show that began with high expectations but fizzled mid-season. A year later, Sorkin scripted the movie *Charlie Wilson' War*, about Texas congressman Charles Wilson, who funded the CIA's secret campaign against the former Soviet Union in Afghanistan.

After more than a decade away from the theatre, Sorkin adapted for the stage his screenplay *The Farnsworth Invention*, a drama centered on the bitter conflict that pitted Philo T. Farnsworth, a boy genius who invented television as a high school student in 1927, against David Sarnoff, head of the Radio Corporation of America. The play was presented by the La Jolla Playhouse in San Diego, California from February 20 through March 25, 2007. A subsequent presentation at the Music Box Theatre on Broadway had to surmount a stagehand strike and finally opened on December 3, 2007. It closed on March 2, 2008. Later that year Sorkin undertook to adapt for the movies the novel *The Accidental Billionaire* by Ben Mezrich, about the founding of Facebook. The film was released on October 1, 2010 under the title *The Social Network*, and Sorkin crossed the country to promote it through a series of screenings and interviews. Nicole Sperling of the *Los Angeles Times* spent two evenings with Sorkin and wrote: "The 49-year-old screenwriter behind such television shows and movies as *The West Wing*, *A Few Good Men* and this year's *The Social Network* is a complicated mix of humility and egoism—at once a self-depreciating goofball who struggles with insecurities and a confident titan of his field who recognizes that his name is itself a brand, one that melds fiction and reality into whip-smart dialogue delivered at breakneck speed."[9]

A triple threat, Sorkin created the TV series *The Newsroom* for HBO in 2012, is writing the script for a movie based on the life of Steve Jobs, and will be as the librettist of the musical *Houdini*, to come out in 2013–2014.

Acting Edition: Samuel French, Inc.

Awards and Honors: Aaron Sorkin won a 1999 Emmy for Writing, Drama Series—*The West Wing*; a Peabody Award in 2000 for *The West Wing*; a National Society of Film Critics Award, a Golden Globe Award, a BAFTA Award, and an Academy Award for Best Adapted Screenplay—*The Social Network* (2010); a New York Film Critics Circle Award for Best Screenplay, in collaboration with Steven Zaillian, and a nomination for an Oscar—*Moneyball* (2011).

NOTES

1. *New York Post*, November 16, 1989.

2. *New York Newsday*, November 16, 1989.

3. *Wall Street Journal*, November 17, 1989.

4. *Time*, November 27, 1989.

5. *New York Times*, November 16, 1989.

6. Otis L. Guernsey Jr., ed., *The Best Plays of 1989–1990* (New York: Applause, 1990), 23.

7. Thomas Fahy, *Considering Aaron Sorkin* (Jefferson, N.C.: McFarland, 2005), 1.

8. A detailed analysis of the television series *The West Wing* is provided in *Mr. Sorkin Goes to Washington* by Melissa Crawley (Jefferson, N.C.: McFarland, 2006).

9. *Los Angeles Times*, December 9, 2010.

City of Angels (1989)

Book by Larry Gelbart (United States, 1928–2009), Music by Cy Coleman (United States, 1929–2004), Lyrics by David Zippel (United States, 1954–)

The hardboiled territory of Dashiell Hammett, Raymond Chandler, and the 1940s noir films based on their works serve as the springboard for the musical comedy *City of Angels*. There is also a pinch of Ross Macdonald in this double-decker spoof about screenwriter Stine and his creation, private eye Stone.

As Stine punches the keys of his Smith Corona typewriter, Stone comes to life, walking through the mean streets of Sam Spade, Philip Marlowe, and Lew Archer. Stine's reality and Stone's make-believe celluloid world are embodied by twin casts—a Hollywood Cast and a Movie Cast. Characters from Stine's existence emerge in the screenplay, and the same actors fulfill a double duty—Gabby, Stine's wife, and Bobbi, Stone's ex-fiancée were played on Broadway by Kay McClelland; Rene Auberjonois portrayed both Buddy Fiddler, a pompous director-producer who keeps tampering with Stine's script, and Irwin S. Irving, a movie mogul within the screenplay; Donna, Buddy's secretary, and Oolie, Stone's girl-Friday, were enacted by Randy Graff; Dee Hoty appeared as Carla, Buddy's fickle wife, as well as Alaura, the femme fatale of the movie-in-the-making.

Since the narrative has writer Stine gradually sacrificing his artistic integrity to the Hollywood machine while his alter ego Stone clings to a code of honor, two actors undertook these parts—Gregg Edelman as Stine, James Naughton as Stone. At some crucial point in their deteriorating relationship, Stine and Stone sing a duet: "You're nothing without me / Without me, you're nothing at all."

Treading on the path blazed by *The Maltese Falcon* and its clones, the movie-within-the-play begins with the arrival of a client—the double-dealing Alaura Kingsley—to the gray office of Shamus Stone.

Stone's voice (over) relates that Alaura "had the kind of face a man could hang a dream on, a body that made the Venus de Milo look all thumbs, and only the floor kept her legs from going on forever."

Alaura engages Stone—with a much-needed advance of $100—to find her runaway stepdaughter, Mallory. The detective's Chandleresque voice-over continues: "One more for the rule of thumb department: Poor girls run away from home looking for something better, rich girls can't wait to find anything worse. With ten thousand and one new reasons to look for Mallory Kingsley, I started at the top, by going right to the bottom of the barrel."

The search for Mallory is over when she emerges, unexpectedly, beneath Stone's bed sheets, naked, inviting, and crooning:

> "Mr. Detective, you've been looking too hard,
> You should have started looking in your own back yard."

City of Angels parodies another hallmark of the hardboiled school—the sleuth's faithful, efficient, wisecracking secretary. We are first introduced to Oollie at her desk, answering the phone; "Stone Investigations, Miss Oolie speaking. . . . It's a flat rate. Twenty-five dollars a day plus eight cents a mile. . . . I'm sorry your wife's cheating on you, mister, but there's no discount for veterans." (She hangs up and begins to read her newspaper.)

Oolie represents the Della Streets, Effie Perrines, and Lucy Hamiltons of detective literature when she laments about having fallen in love with an unfeeling, hard-boiled boss.

The inevitable physical punishment scene occurs when Stone is administered a terrible beating by a pair of thugs—Big Six, "a mountain of a man," and his partner Sonny, "small but just as menacing," a Mike Mazurki-Elisha Cook Jr. combination.

Stone's voice (over) rasps, "It was as though I'd been hit by a wrecking ball wearing a pinkie ring."

Then there is the traditional adversarial relationship with the police. In a city morgue sequence, Lt. Munoz of the LAPD confronts Stone about his fatal shooting of Irwin S. Irving, whom the dick had caught in the act of making love with scantily clad Bobbi: "You're getting away with it, you son-of-a-bitch. Getting away with murder." Munoz assures Stone that given one more chance he will personally strap the detective into the gas chamber chair.

Following the murder of the Kingsleys' family doctor, Munoz orders his officer, Pasco, to "put the cuffs" on Stone. Munoz sings, "You're headed for a cell, Then to die and rot in hell."

As concocted by writer Stine, it turns out that Alaura has planned to get rid of her husband, stepdaughter, and stepson in order to inherit the Kingsley fortune. During a climactic struggle between Alaura and Stone, her revolver is pressed between them, three shots ring out, and "a red stain appears beneath Alaura's heart."

Screenwriter Stine pounds on his typewriter day and night to mold the chronicle of gumshoe Stone. When director Buddy Fiddler savages the manuscript to the point of complete mutilation, the exasperated Stine finally stops the shooting by calling out "Cut!"

Stine snatches the screenplay from Fiddler and throws it into the air. He and Stone change places: Stine smacks and kicks the studio cops that converge on him while Stone sits at the desk and pecks at the keys of the typewriter. The company freezes as Stine and Stone reprise "I'm nothing without you, without you I'm nothing at all."

* * *

City of Angels opened at New York's Virginia Theatre on December 11, 1989 to mostly rave reviews. Frank Rich joyfully remarked, "This is an evening in which even a throwaway wisecrack spreads laughter like wildfire through the house, until finally the roars from the balcony merge with those from the orchestra and the pandemonium takes a life of its own."[1] Clive Barnes wrote, "Gelbart's dialogue and, with their sincerest form of flattery, Zippel's lyrics, are so hard-boiled they are almost cracked, and the wit is as light-handed as a machine-gun. Yet all this is still backed with that taste, resonance and imagination which was all super-evident from the start of the show and never actually flags."[2]

"There's a miracle on Broadway," exclaimed Jack Kroll.[3] "The most brilliant of musical comedies," gushed Douglas Watt.[4] "The show pays honest homage to the pop-culture traditions of stage, cinema, radio and recording studio, yet brings them together in a fashion that feels fresh and new," chirped William A. Henry III.[5] David Patrick Stearns lauded "Robin Wagner's tropical deco sets, Michael Blakemore's stylish direction and Cy Coleman's jaunty score."[6]

Conversely, *New York Newsday*'s Linda Winer complained that "this show runs almost three hours, which turns out to be at least a half-hour too long for its slim material."[7] Howard Kissel found the characters "paper-thin" and expressed his concern that neither one of the actors, James Naughton ("as the gumshoe") and Gregg Edelman ("as the writer"), "will capture your sympathies."[8] John Beaufort stated tersely, "*City of Angels* has lots of just about everything except charm and heart."[9]

The yea-sayers won. *City of Angels* had a hefty run of 878 performances. The musical was revived off-Broadway by The Gallery Players and ran May 1–23, 2010.

* * *

The son of Jewish immigrants, Larry Simon Gelbart was born in Chicago in 1928. The family moved to Beverly Hills, California, and the elder Gelbart, a barber, made it a point to tell his clients, including Danny

Thomas, what a funny fifteen-year-old son he had. As a result, Larry was engaged to write gags for the Danny Thomas radio show during the 1940s. This was followed by contributions for Joan Davis, Jack Paar, Jack Carson, and Bob Hope. He served with Armed Forces Radio Service, and in the 1950s wrote for the television programs of Red Buttons, Sid Caesar, Art Carney, Dinah Shore, and Danny Kaye.

In the 1960s Gelbart began writing for the theatre. His initial Broadway effort, the book for the musical *The Conquering Hero* (1961), an adaptation of the Preston Sturges movie *Hail the Conquering Hero*, played for only eight performances,[10] but his book collaboration with Burt Shevelove, rewriting Plautus, with music and lyrics by Stephen Sondheim, on *A Funny Thing Happened on the Way to the Forum* (1962), yielded a major hit, running for 964 showings. A film version was released in 1966 and *Forum* was revived on Broadway in 1972 (156 performances) and 1996 (715 performances). Gelbart's other successes in New York included 1976's *Sly Fox*, a modernization of Ben Jonson's comedy of greed, *Volpone* (495 performances), and his contribution to the 1989 musical revue, *Jerome Robbins' Broadway* (633 performances). Gelbart's 1989 political satire, *Mastergate*, closed after sixty-nine showings.

In 1972, Gelbart was a major force behind the creation of the television series *M*A*S*H*, writing the pilot, often producing and occasionally directing the series for its first four seasons (1972–1976). His movies-for-television include *Barbarians at the Gate* (1993), about the battle for control of the RJR Nabisco corporation; *Weapons of Mass Distraction* (1997), depicting the rivalry between media moguls; and *And Starring Pancho Villa as Himself* (2003), starring Antonio Banderas as the Mexican revolutionary leader. Gelbart's wide screen credits include *The Notorious Landlady* (1962), *The Wrong Box* (1966), based on a Robert Louis Stevenson story; *Not with My Wife, You Don't!* (1966); *Oh, God!* (1977); *Neighbors* (1981); *Movie, Movie* (1978), a parody of 1930s Hollywood; *Rough Cut* (1980), a caper adventure credited to the pseudonym Francis Burns; *Tootsie* (1982); *Blame It on Rio* (1984); and *Bedazzled* (2000).

Gelbart published a memoir, *Laughing Matters*, in 1997. He died of cancer on September 11, 2009, at his Beverly Hills home, at age eighty-one.

Cy Coleman was born in 1929 in New York City to Eastern European Jewish parents. He was a child prodigy who gave piano recitals at Steinway Hall, Town Hall, and Carnegie Hall before he turned ten. Early in his professional career he led the Cy Coleman Trio, a much-in-demand club attraction that made many recordings. Coleman's contributions to Broadway as a composer began when he collaborated with Carolyn Leigh on the musicals *Wildcat* (1960, a starring vehicle for Lucille Ball), and *Little Me* (1963, book by Neil Simon). Teamed with Dorothy Fields, Coleman scored *Sweet Charity* (1966, featuring Gwen Verdon) and *See-*

saw (1974, based on William Gibson's *Two for the Seesaw*). In the late 1970s, Coleman composed *I Love My Wife* (1977) and *On the Twentieth Century* (1978). He remained prolific during the 1980s with *Barnum* (1980, starring Jim Dale and Glenn Close), *Welcome to the Club* (1988, book by A. E. Hotchner), and *City of Angels* (1989). The 1990s brought more Coleman musicals to Broadway: *The Will Rogers Follies* (1991); *The Life* (1997, a gritty look at the lowlife in a metropolitan city); and a revised production of *Little Me* (1999).

Coleman died of cardiac arrest on November 18, 2004 at the age of seventy-five. It is reported that to the very end, he remained part of the Broadway scene—just prior to passing away, he had attended the premiere of Michael Frayn's play *Democracy*.

David Zippel was born in Easton, Pennsylvania in 1954. A 1976 graduate of the University of Pennsylvania, he had intended to go to Harvard Law School to become a theatrical lawyer, but when Barbara Cook needed a lyricist, he offered his services and then changed course. In addition to *City of Angels*, his theatrical credits include *The Goodbye Girl* (1993), a musical based on Neil Simon's 1977 screenplay; *Princess* (2003), inspired by Frances Hodgson Burnett's *A Little Princess*; and *The Woman in White* (2004), an adaptation of the novel by Wilkie Collins. For the silver screen, Zippel contributed lyrics to *Hercules* (the song "Go the Distance" received a 1997 Academy Award and Golden Globe nominations for Best Original Song), *Mulan* (a 1998 Academy Award nomination for Best Original Musical Score), and *Tarzan* (1999).

To honor his late associate, Zippel devised and directed *The Best Is Yet to Come: The Music of Cy Coleman*, featuring songs from fourteen Coleman musicals, performed at off-Broadway's 59E59 Theatre on May 20, 2011. "A fingers-snapping, hard-charging, small-scale but still shiny-looking revue," said critic Charles Isherwood in the *New York Times*.[11]

Awards and Honors: *City of Angels* was a top ten selection in *The Best Plays of 1989–1990*. It won the Mystery Writers of America Edgar Award as Best Play. It was also awarded six Tonys, including Best Musical, Best Book of a Musical, and Best Original Score; eight Drama Desk Awards, including Outstanding Musical, Book, Music, Lyrics; four Outer Circle prizes, including Outstanding Broadway Musical, Outstanding Director (Michael Blakemore), and a Special Award to Larry Gelbart for his contribution to comedy. The television series *Your Show of Shows* earned Gelbart the Sylvania Award and two Emmy Awards. *M*A*S*H* garnered a Peabody Award and an Emmy for Outstanding Comedy Series. In 1981 he received the Laurel Award for outstanding career achievement in television writing from the Writer's Guild of America. Gelbart was also nominated for an Academy Award for scripting *Oh, God!* (1977), and, with Murray Schisgal, *Tootsie* (1982).

In addition to *City of Angels*, Cy Coleman also won a Tony Award for *On the Twentieth Century* (1978) and *The Will Rogers Follies* (1991). Many of his original scores were nominated for Tony Awards: *Little Me* (1963), *Sweet Charity* (1966), *Seesaw* (1974), *I Love My Wife* (1977), *Barnum* (1980), and *The Life* (1997). Coleman was elected to the Songwriter's Hall of Fame in 1981, was the recipient of the Songwriter's Hall of Fame Johnny Mercer Award in 1995, and garnered the ASCAP Foundation Richard Rodgers Award for lifetime achievement in American musical theatre. He was elected to the American Theatre Hall of Fame and received an Honorary Doctorate from Hofstra University in 2000.

David Zippel's lyrics and Andrew Lloyd Webber's music received a Tony nomination for Best Original Score of *The Woman in White* (2004). The show was also nominated for five Laurence Olivier Awards, including Best Musical.

NOTES

1. *New York Times*, December 12, 1989.
2. *New York Post*, December 12, 1989.
3. *Newsweek*, January 8, 1990.
4. *Daily News*, December 12, 1989.
5. *Time*, December 25, 1989.
6. *USA Today*, December 12, 1989.
7. *New York Newsday*, December 12, 1989.
8. *Daily News*, December 12, 1989.
9. *Christian Science Monitor*, January 9, 1990.
10. During the troubled pre-Broadway development of 1961's *The Conquering Hero*, Larry Gelbart uttered the now-classic line, "If Hitler is alive, I hope he's out of town with a musical."
11. *New York Times*, May 27, 2011.

Assassins (1990)

Book by John Weidman
(United States, 1946–), Music and Lyrics by
Stephen Sondheim (United States, 1930–)

Assassins is an offbeat chamber musical that begins and ends with a cho-rus line of gun-slingers—seven men and two women—who have entered the underbelly of American history as the killers or would-be killers of the president.

Against the background of a surreal carnival, the nine assassins as-semble in a shooting gallery, purchase guns and ammunition from the proprietor, croon the signature song "Everybody's Got the Right," and go their separate ways to quench their frustrations by squeezing the trig-ger on the nation's leader. "All you have to do is move your little finger and—you can change the world," say the disgruntled misfits.

The anti-heroes of *Assassins* are: John Wilkes Booth (1838–1865), who shot President Abraham Lincoln at Ford's Theatre, Washington, D.C. on April 14, 1865; Charles Guiteau (1841–1882), who killed President James Garfield in the waiting room of the Baltimore & Potomac Railroad station, Washington, D.C. on July 2, 1881; Leon Czolgosz (1873–1901), who as-sassinated President William McKinley at the Pan-American Exposition, Buffalo, New York on September 6, 1901; Giuseppe Zangara (1900–1933), who attempted to kill President-elect Franklin D. Roosevelt in Bayfront Park, Miami, Florida on February 5, 1933; Samuel Byck (1930–1974), who hijacked a commercial jetliner at the Baltimore-Washington International Airport on February 22, 1974, with the intent of crashing into President Richard Nixon's White House; Lynette ("Squeaky") Fromme (1948–), who attempted to shoot President Gerald Ford as he left the Senator Hotel, Sac-ramento, California on September 5, 1975; Sara Jane Moore (1930–), who attempted to assassinate President Gerald Ford as he left the St. Francis Hotel, San Francisco, California on September 22, 1975; John Hinckley (1955–), who shot and wounded President Ronald Reagan as he left the Washington Hilton Hotel, Washington, D.C. on March 30, 1981; and Lee

Harvey Oswald (1939–1963), who killed President John F. Kennedy in Dallas, Texas on November 22, 1963.

John Weidman's libretto travels through time, linking the nine assassins who support and inspire one another in what William A. Henry III of *Time* magazine calls "a grand conspiracy."[1] *Assassins* unfolds in the form of an intimate revue, with blackout sketches, musical numbers, and popping background slides rapidly following one another.

In scene 2, the Balladeer, a folk singer, strums his guitar as he relates "The Ballad of Booth." The Shakespearean actor, "a handsome devil," is writing in a diary his rationale for murder, charging Lincoln with such "High Crimes and Misdemeanors" as "ruthlessly" provoking a war between the states and "silencing" his critics by "hurdling" them into prison. Concerned about his place in history, Booth urges the Balladeer to "Press on the truth. . . . What I did was to kill the man who killed my country."

Scene 3 takes place in a turn-of-the-twentieth-century saloon, where some of the conspirators exchange notes and toast the American Dream. Scene 4 opens with a radio report from Miami's Bayfront Park. Mid-broadcast, a gunshot is heard. The announcer declares that an attempt on the life of President Roosevelt has failed; the police have a suspect in custody: "an immigrant. Giuseppe Zangara." The lights come up on five bystanders, clustered around a microphone, each telling the listeners their version of the event, including how each of them personally saved the president ("How I Saved Roosevelt"). Zangara, strapped into the electric chair, sings of his wretched youth—"No luck, no girl, Zangara no smart, no school." He is peeved that as an "American Nothing," no photographs are taken at his execution.

Scene 5 takes place at a rally in Chicago, summer 1901. Leon Czolgosz, a scruffy laborer, listens raptly to a lecture by American anarchist leader Emma Goldman. He introduces himself to Goldman and passionately offers to follow her dictates. She tells him to redirect his zeal to the fight for social justice.

In scene 6, Sara Jane Moore and Lynette Fromme are sitting on a park bench. Fromme, smoking a joint, speaks with reverence about mass murderer Charles Manson. Moore, munching on Kentucky Fried Chicken, confides to being an informant for the FBI and says that she has been a CPA, had five husbands, and is suffering from amnesia. The sequence ends with both women laughingly emptying their guns on the bucket of chicken.

In scene 7, Leon Czolgosz examines an empty pistol and reflects in song that "It takes a lot of men to make a gun"—men in mines, steel mills, machine factories—and yet one move of "your little finger" has the power to change the world. In the following scene, the Balladeer sings "The Ballad of Czolgosz"—"a quiet, simple man" who joins the receiving line at the

Pan-American Exposition in Buffalo, New York, his gun wrapped in a handkerchief. He later shoots President McKinley.

In scene 9, Sam Byck is sitting on a park bench in a dirty Santa Claus suit. At his side are a picket sign and a beat-up shopping bag. He talks into a tape recorder, sending a message to Leonard Bernstein. In the recording, he introduces himself as "an out-of-work tire salesman," and urges the composer to write more love songs, for "love makes the world go round." Byck complains of "the world's vicious, stinking pit of emptiness and pain," and accuses Bernstein of ignoring him, just like other celebrities—Jonas Salk, Jack Anderson, Hank Aaron, among them.

Scene 10: Lynette Fromme visits John Hinckley at his parents' home. Hinckley strums on his guitar as they exchange reflections about their love objects, Jodie Foster and Charles Manson. Hinckley gazes at an eight-by-ten photograph of the actress and Fromme waves a tattered newspaper clipping as together they sing "Unworthy of Your Love" and vow to find a way to pull Foster's and Manson's heart strings. Hinckley draws his gun and shoots at a picture of Ronald Reagan, projected on the wall.

Lights fade up on scene 11, illuminating Sara Jane Moore at target practice. She stands pigeon-toed, holding her gun with two hands, aiming at the Kentucky Fried Chicken bucket. She jerks the trigger—Bang! The bucket doesn't move. Charles Guiteau enters behind her and puts his hand over her eyes. She is momentarily startled. He circles her, eyeing her appraisingly, gives her marksmanship tips and tries to kiss her. When he's rebuffed, we hear the sound of trains, and Guiteau emerges at the Baltimore & Potomac Railroad Station in Washington where on Track 6 he shoots President Garfield in the back.

Immediately following, Guiteau is revealed at the foot of the gallows. The Hangman is waiting at the top. Guiteau and the Balladeer walk up the stairs singing "The Ballad of Guiteau," cheerfully earmarking him as a winner who goes to heaven.

In scene 13, Sara Jane Moore and Lynette Fromme prepare to assassinate Gerald Ford. Moore has brought along her nine-year-old son and her small dog. She gets rid of the barking dog by shooting him and shoving the body into her purse. She then gives her wailing son money for bubble gum; he runs off. "Your kid is an asshole," says Fromme, and the two women get into a verbal clash. To make a point, Moore waves her gun and the cylinder falls open, scattering the bullets. Both drop to their knees and start picking them up. Gerald Ford strolls by, hovers, and helps Moore collect her bullets. When Ford turns to leave, Fromme aims her gun at his back and pulls the trigger—it fails to go off. Exasperated, the two inept assassins resort to throwing bullets at the departing president.

Lights go up on scene 14, pinpointing Sam Byck behind the wheel of a '67 Buick, driving down a highway late at night. He looks bleary-eyed and strung out. The jacket of his Santa suit is unbuttoned, revealing a dirty T-shirt and a grease-stained pair of suspenders. He is on the way to the airport to hijack a plane, which he plans to crash dive into the White House. He reaches into a Burger King bag, shoves a fistful of French fries into his mouth, takes a long swallow of beer, and records a message addressed to Richard Nixon, complaining about contemporary American life and concluding that killing the president is the only solution. He throws his hands in the air in a parody of Nixon's "V for Victory" sign.

In scene 15, crowd noises blend into a slow, wordless lamentation for the victims of assassination as the gaggle of assassins are pinpointed by spotlights, reiterating their motives. The Balladeer enters with his guitar and tells them that their actions "didn't mean a nickel" and didn't solve the country's problems. The assassins advance on the Balladeer, force him off the stage, turn front, and lustily croon, "Another National Anthem," a song to be cherished by all Americans dispossessed of their dreams.

Scene 16: Lee Harvey Oswald appears on the sixth floor of the Texas School Book Depository in Dallas, Texas. He is dressed in faded jeans and a tattered T-shirt. On the floor beside him is a long package wrapped in a blanket. John Wilkes Booth enters and tells the hesitant Oswald that "when you kill a President, it isn't murder. Murder is a tawdry little crime; it's born of greed, or lust, or liquor. Adulterers and shopkeepers get murdered. But when a President gets killed, when Julius Caesar got killed . . . he was assassinated." Booth points out that Brutus, who assassinated Caesar, is still remembered after two thousand years.

Booth unfolds the wrapped blanket, revealing a high-powered rifle, and summons the other assassins to emerge from the shadows. They implore Oswald to act; their voices overlap, mounting in intensity—"We admire you. . . . We're your family. . . . You are the future. . . . We're depending on you. . . . Make us proud." Oswald crouches at the window and shoots. Silently, the assassins exit. The Book Depository disappears. A slide is projected upstage. It is the famous photo of Jack Ruby shooting Oswald.

In the last scene, one by one the assassins reappear, now with Oswald in their ranks, for a reprise of their motto, "Everybody's Got the Right," at the end of which they fire their guns at the audience.

* * *

Directed by Jerry Zaks and choreographed by D. J. Giagni, *Assassins* opened off-Broadway at Playwrights Horizons on January 27, 1990. The ninety-minute musical was presented without an intermission. The cast included Victor Garber (John Wilkes Booth), Patrick Cassidy (Balladeer), Jace Alexander (Lee Harvey Oswald), Annie Golden (Lynette Fromme), and Debra Monk (Sara Jane Moore).

The reviews were mostly negative. Critic Frank Rich found *Assassins* "a daring work" though "slender and sketchy." Rich praised composer Stephen Sondheim: "In keeping with his past musicals animating the passions of the certifiably insane (*Anybody Can Whistle*) and mass murderers (*Sweeney Todd*), this songwriter gives genuine, not mocking, voice to the hopes, fears and rages of two centuries' worth of American losers, misfits, nuts, zombies and freaks. . . . These are the lost and underprivileged souls who, having been denied every American's dream of growing up to be President, try to achieve a warped, nightmarish inversion of that dream instead." Conversely, Rich sniffs at John Weidman's "jokey book" and "tired gags," and at Jerry Zaks's "strangely confused production. . . . Mr. Zaks seems to have lost control of this nasty musical rather than to have found a style for it."[2]

David Patrick Stearns lamented "a minor Sondheim,"[3] while Linda Winer felt that the entire venture "is a bad idea, fuzzy headed and despite a lovely cast, unremarkably executed. It is a pseudo-serious revue, with surprisingly predictable music, that cannot decide whether to be preachy and sociological or jauntily amoral, darkly satiric or just plain silly."[4] Clive Barnes believed that "It adds up to an odd, uncertain evening, its uncertainty made almost stylistic by the constant undercutting of the drama with massive doses of triviality and facetiousness."[5]

Assassins ran for twenty-five sold-out performances. On October 29, 1992, the musical opened in London at the Donmar Warehouse, running for seventy-six showings. Off-Broadway's Roundabout Theatre revived *Assassins* on April 22, 2004—for 101 performances—directed by Joe Mantello, featuring Neil Patrick Harris in the roles of the Balladeer and Lee Harvey Oswald. Michael Cerveris played John Wilkes Booth, for which he received a Tony Award. Londoners had a second chance to view *Assassins* in a 2008 production at the sixty-seat Landor Theatre.

* * *

The son of librettist Jerome Weidman,[6] John Weidman followed in his father's footsteps with the books for a wide variety of stage musicals. John was born in New York City in 1946. After graduating from Harvard with a BA in 1968, he went to Yale Law School. He passed the bar exam but decided not to pursue a career as an attorney. He began contributing articles to *The National Lampoon* instead.

In 1976, Weidman collaborated with Stephen Sondheim on the musical *Pacific Overtures*, the story of a culture clash sparked by America's mid-nineteenth century mission to open up Japan to the West. *Pacific Overtures* opened at Broadway's Winter Garden Theatre on January 11, 1976, was nominated for Tony Awards for Best Musical, Best Book of a

Musical (Weidman), and Best Original Score (Sondheim), and ran for 193 performances. A 2005 off-Broadway revival lasted sixty-nine showings.

In 1986, Weidman began writing for PBS's *Sesame Street*, winning several Daytime Emmy Awards. The following year he co-wrote (with Timothy Crouse) a revised book for a revival of *Anything Goes* at New York City's Lincoln Center. The Cole Porter musical, depicting madcap antics aboard an ocean liner traveling from New York to London, won the Tony Award as Best Revival and ran for 784 performances. A 2011 revival produced by off-Broadway's Roundabout Theatre garnered a Tony for Best Revival of a Musical. It closed on July 8, 2012, after 521 showings.

Weidman teamed again with Sondheim on 1991's *Assassins*. Five years later he received a Tony nomination for the book of the musical *Big*, based on the film starring Tom Hanks, about an awkward kid whose wish to become an adult is miraculously granted. *Big*, Weidman's first collaboration with choreographer Susan Stroman, closed after 193 performances. Weidman and Stroman teamed again on *The Dance Story*, a three-part musical, each segment emphasizing people's difficulties in making a meaningful connection. *The Dance Story* was offered at the Mitzi E. Newhouse Theatre, Lincoln Center, in September 1999, and moved to the Center's Vivian Beaumont Theatre in March 2000, winning a Best Musical Tony and Drama Desk Award, and playing for 1,010 performances. A West End production opened at the Queen's Theatre in October 2002 and closed in May 2003.

Road Show (previously titled both *Wise Guys* and *Bounce*), with book by Weidman and music by Sondheim, depicts the adventures of real-life Addison Mizner and his brother Wilson across America—from the beginning of the twentieth century during the Alaskan Gold Rush to the Florida real estate boom of the 1920s. The musical premiered at the New York Theatre Workshop in 1999 under the title *Wise Guys*, directed by Sam Mendes, starring Nathan Lane and Victor Garber as the brothers Mizner. Re-written and re-titled *Bounce*, the show came to Chicago's Goodman Theatre in 2003, now directed by Harold Prince. A new version, named *Road Show*, ran at off-Broadway's Public Theatre from November 18–December 28, 2008, winning an Obie Award for Sondheim.

The Flight, with book by Weidman and music by David Shire, was inspired by the early history of aviation. It opened at London's Menier Chocolate Factory in July 2007 and received its American premiere at McCarter Theatre Center in Princeton, New Jersey in April 2010. *Happiness*, a 2009 musical about a disparate group of New Yorkers trapped in a stalled subway car, reunited Weidman with choreographer Susan Stroman. *Happiness* was commissioned and developed by Lincoln Center Theatre in Manhattan.

From 1999 to 2009, Weidman served as president of the Dramatists Guild of America.

Acting Edition: Theatre Communications Group.

Awards and Honors: *Assassins* won the 2004 Tony Award and Drama Desk Award for Best Revival of a Musical. John Weidman was nominated for Tony Award's Best Book of a Musical three times: *Pacific Overtures* (1976), *Big* (1996), and *Contact* (2000). Weidman was also nominated for a Drama Desk Award for Outstanding Book of a Musical for *Pacific Overtures* (1976), *Assassins* (1991), and *Big* (1996). Since 1986, Weidman has been a writer for television's *Sesame Street*, winning more than a dozen Emmy Awards for Outstanding Writing for a Children's Program.

NOTES

1. *Time*, February 4, 1991.
2. *New York Times*, January 28, 1991.
3. *USA Today*, February 4, 1991.
4. *New York Newsday*, January 28, 1991.
5. *New York Post*, January 28, 1991.
6. Jerome Weidman (1913–1998) won the Pulitzer Prize for Drama and the Tony Award, both in 1960, for the book of *Fiorello!* (the story of New York Mayor Fiorello LaGuardia, played by Tom Bosley). Weidman's next musical, *Tenderloin* (1960), unfolds in the Tenderloin district of 1890s New York, where Reverend Brock (portrayed by Maurice Evans) attempts to clean the area of prostitution and sin. The protagonist of *I Can Get It for You Wholesale* (1962) is Harry Bogen (Elliott Gould), a garment industry employee who is determined to get to the top even if he has to lie and embezzle. The musical introduced Barbra Streisand, who was nominated for a Tony as Best Featured Actress in a Musical. *Pousse-Café* (1966), set in New Orleans to the tunes of Duke Ellington, closed its doors after five previews and three performances. Weidman inserted a touch of the macabre in *Asterisk!* (1969), a comedy about a Manhattan man who devises a number of hilariously diabolical ways to get rid of his mother, who is a drain on his budget. Also in 1969, Weidman collaborated with James Yaffe on *Ivory Tower*, a courtroom drama that played in various resident theatres but never reached New York. It is the story of Simon Otway, a famous American author who lived in Paris during World War II, now accused of treason for calling on the invading Allied Forces, in several radio broadcasts, to lay down their arms and stop the bloodshed.

Accomplice (1990)

Rupert Holmes
(England/United States, 1947–)

Twenty years after *Sleuth*, but without the elegance of its predecessor, *Accomplice* is another game-play of wheels-within-wheels-within-wheels. Here, too, the audience is introduced to the twisty maze when perusing the playbill; characters are not given names, and readers note that there are more biographies for understudies than there are roles. Here, too, hardly anything is what it seems, and here, too, there are scattered elements that spoof the genre.

The action takes place in the mid-1970s. During an autumn afternoon, two couples plan a weekend retreat at a cozy English country cottage, a converted water mill. We first meet Derek and Janet Taylor, the hosts. He is "affable and charming." She is "an attractive brunette, sophisticated, sharp-edged." As they chat over drinks talking in pronounced English accents, awaiting the arrival of Jon and Melinda Harley, we learn that in case Derek dies, Janet will get control of his successful brokerage company.

When Derek leaves to gather some wood for the fireplace, Janet quickly pulls a vial of brown liquid from her purse. She pours the mixture into Derek's whiskey and soda glass. Derek returns, places the logs in the fire, and gulps his drink. Janet cheerfully tells Derek that she poured nicotine in his drink, a devise she saw in a play. Derek collapses to the floor, convulses a bit, and becomes still. Janet takes his glass from the coffee table, wraps it in a hand towel, and exits into the kitchen. We hear the grinding of a garbage disposal.

Janet returns and places a blanket on Derek. An arm shoots out from behind the blanket and grabs her neck, pulling her down violently. The blanket falls away and exposes the two kissing in a passionate embrace. The man first called Derek now speaks in a rougher, more working-class British accent, and is revealed as Janet's lover, Jon Harley.

Janet and Jon cover themselves with the blanket. There is some fidgeting under the cover and fierce love making is implied. Between grunts the pair exchanges congratulations for getting rid of Derek and taking possession of his company.

The second scene unfolds the next evening; it is raining outside. The real Derek, very much alive, enters struggling with his umbrella. Janet appears from the kitchen carrying a bowl of salmon mousse, which she places on a table. Derek pulls a lever by the bar and the mill wheel revolves slowly, twenty-five degrees, exposing a honeycombed wine rack. Derek leaves to get some crisps from the pantry and Janet sprinkles the entire contents of a large salt shaker into the dip. Derek returns with a box of crackers. As they leisurely converse, we learn that Derek's doctor has ordered him to ease up on salt because of "awfully pushy" blood pressure.

The relentless Janet makes a third attempt on Derek's life when he washes his feet in a foot tub and she lets her hair dryer fall into the water, triggering crackling sparks. Derek's face and body contort in electrical paralysis.

Jon and Melinda knock on the front door. Janet screams, rushes to meet them and mumbles, "Something's happened to Derek!" Jon leaves hurriedly for help as Melinda removes her wet trench coat, revealing a miniskirt outfit over a striking figure. Janet and Melinda cover Derek's body with a blanket, and suddenly Melinda kisses Janet on the lips. Janet reciprocates. They hold the kiss as the lights fade.

In act 1, we are baffled: why do the characters don wigs and exaggerated accents? And how is it possible for a murdered husband to reappear? When the curtain goes up on the second act, it becomes clear that the proceedings so far have been a play within a play. The action stops, the actors shed their characters, and the playwright, Rupert Holmes, moves down the aisle of the auditorium and steps onto the stage. He rebukes the cast for exaggerated performances, discusses the convoluted plot, and offers on-the-spot rewrites. "At first, this seems like a tiresome digression," said David Patrick Stearns of *USA Today*, "but Holmes (who also authored *The Mystery of Edwin Drood*) gets good mileage out of the technique. By breaking the whodunit artifice, he brings each successive murder plot closer to the audience."[1]

Other critics disagreed: "It's too clever by half, especially the second half," scoffed Doug Watt. "The script would have defeated even a Hitchcock in the end as well as the middle and beginning. It's unfair to have to sit through a play with our appetite continually aroused and then left unsatisfied."[2]

Frank Rich concurred: "In Rupert Holmes's last Broadway whodunit, *The Mystery of Edwin Drood*, the audience was invited to vote on the murderer at the end of the second act. In *Accomplice*, Mr. Holmes's new whodunit at the Richard Rodgers Theatre, the audience should be allowed to vote on the beginning, middle and end of the second act. The winner, in a landslide, would surely be None of the Above. . . . I found *Accomplice* incomprehensible after intermission, even though much of Act II is given over to extended round-table discussions among the characters as to what has happened or might happen or won't happen or can't happen. These verbose yet unilluminating explanations extend right through the curtain call, which itself is somewhat gabbier than any denouement in Agatha Christie."[3]

Following a description of the sexual shenanigans splattered around ("a pair of homosexual kisses, one each for male and female couples. . . . [The actress] Ms. Brill finds herself at the center of a dispute as to whether she will bare her breasts on stage. . . . For her part, [the actress] Ms. Nogulich is required to writhe on the floor with [the actor] Mr. McKean in an exceptionally noisy carnal romp"), Rich concluded that "It's enough to make one long for those predictable old whodunits in which the butlers always did it but at least had the common courtesy to do it quickly with their clothes and mouths both firmly zippered shut."[4]

Still, reviewer Linda Winer found *Accomplice* "a lightweight but harmless and amusingly crafted trifle that should entertain audiences who want a night out with nothing more to do than trying to guess the next plot twist. There are many, many twists and you probably won't be able to guess any of the important ones."[5]

What the critics missed is that the best parts of *Accomplice* are not the plot contortions (they are too mind-boggling), or the character delineations (they are all cardboard pawns at the hand of the playwright), but the good-natured satirical darts aimed at the world of the theatre. One of the foursome, Jon, complains that it is impossible to be one step ahead of an audience groomed on *Dial M for Murder*, *Write Me a Murder*, *Mousetrap*, and *Deathtrap*, while the actress enacting the role of Melinda laments that the shift from off-Broadway to Broadway is not much different—she is still portraying the nude, murdered prostitute.

Accomplice opened at Broadway's Richard Rodgers Theatre on April 26, 1990 and ran for fifty-two performances.

Acting Edition: Samuel French, Inc.

Awards and Honors: *Accomplice* won a Best Play Edgar in 1991 from the Mystery Writers of America.

NOTES

1. *USA Today*, April 30, 1990.
2. *Daily Mirror*, May 4, 1990.
3. *New York Times*, April 27, 1990.
4. *New York Times*, April 27, 1990.
5. *New York Newsday*, April 27, 1990.

Earth and Sky (1991)

Douglas Post (United States, 1958–)

At the dawn of the 1990s, off-Broadway's highly respected Second Stage attempted to resuscitate an almost forgotten genre, the whodunit, with the world premiere of *Earth and Sky*, subtitled "A Poetic Thriller" by its author, Douglas Post.

Mel Gussow of the *New York Times* called *Earth and Sky* "a case of film noir on stage."[1] The play unfolds in twenty-eight quick, intermissionless scenes, the action bleeding from one sequence to another via lights and sound. The metaphoric title refers to the incongruity in having nice, naïve Sara McKeon, part-time librarian and would-be poet, enter the dark netherland of Chicago when the body of her lover, David Ames, is found in an alley dumpster with a bullet in the back of his head.

Two hard-boiled homicide detectives, Horace Weber and Al Kersnowski, inform Sara that David, a restaurateur with pressing debts, was involved in the kidnapping-for-ransom and murder of the wife and child of a real estate tycoon. "Emily Lapointe and her little girl were found dead . . . severely beaten, raped, and dead," Weber tells Sara, who retorts with anguish: "David Ames was not a killer!"

Outraged that the police seem to have closed the book on the case, Sara undertakes her own private investigation of the events that led to David's death. She interviews various unsavory characters in the seedy town. Soon Sara finds herself in mortal danger, stalked by professional hit men Carl Eisenstadt and Julius Gatz, who themselves end up meeting the grim reaper prematurely. Despite police warnings, Sara pursues her quest relentlessly, fueled by the memory of the man she loved. Through flashbacks, Sara recalls their short-lived but passionate romance, tracing it, in reverse chronology, to their first meeting. Was she wrong about David? Following a succession of rapid plot jolts, perhaps one too many, Sara establishes David's innocence and uncovers the real culprit, who turns out to be none other than Police Detective Weber.

*   *   *

Earth and Sky was originally presented as a staged reading at the 1989 National Playwrights Conference at the Eugene O'Neill Theatre Center in Waterford, Connecticut, on July 20, 1989. The play went through eight drafts before it opened at off-Broadway's Second Stage Theatre on February 4, 1991. Andre Emotte directed. William Barclay designed the scenery.

The critics adopted the juxtaposition of the title: "It is thoroughly engrossing," beamed Clive Barnes, "a thoroughly genuine cop thriller, with devious plot turns, tough, corner-of-the-mouth, Chandler/Hammett-style dialogue,"[2] while Jan Stuart was caustic: "As crime stories go, *Earth and Sky* is fairly conventional, even in its not-so-surprising surprise windup. What it really wants is an ounce of the oddball unpredictability of *The Grifters* or the dreamy stylization of Mabou Mines' Philip Dick deconstruction *Flow My Tears, the Policeman Said.*"[3] A friendly rivalry was ignited behind the scenes at the *New York Daily News*: "There is nothing solid about *Earth and Sky*," lamented Howard Kissel;[4] "*Earth and Sky* is a twisty thriller guaranteed to keep you alert for its 100 minute length," countered David Watt.[5]

Subsequent productions of *Earth and Sky* were mounted by Victory Gardens Theatre, Chicago, Illinois (1992); Actors Forum Theatre (1995) and Copperview Theatre Company (1997), Los Angeles, California; Nuffield Theatre, Southampton, England (1999); Circle Theatre, Chicago, Illinois (1999); and Second Thought Theatre, Dallas, Texas (2005).

Douglas Post penned seven screenplay drafts of *Earth and Sky* between June 1991 and June 1998, but it has not yet been filmed. In 2009, a radio adaptation of *Earth and Sky* was presented by L.A. Theatre Works featuring Annette Bening, John Mahoney, Ed Begley Jr., and Steven Weber.

*   *   *

Another criminous play by Douglas Post, *Murder in Green Meadows*, was aired on December 4, 1986 as part of the NBC Chicago Playwrights Festival, a cooperative venture between WMAQ-TV and the Steppenwolf Theatre Company. The production received six Emmy Award nominations. Post expanded the television playlet into a full-length "Psychological Thriller for the Stage" and after several drafts it was presented in 1992 by Nuffield Theatre of Southampton, England. Follow-up productions took place at Stamford Theatre Works, Stamford, Connecticut (1993); Victory Gardens Theatre (1995) and Circle Theatre (1998), Chicago; the English Theatre of Hamburg, Germany (1999); Contemporary American Theatre Company, Columbus, Ohio (2001); Horse Cave Theatre, Horse Cave, Kentucky (2001); Totem Pole Playhouse, Fayetteville, Pennsylvania (2002); the English Theatre of Vienna, Austria (2003);

Studio Arena Theatre, Buffalo, New York (2004); and Vertigo Theatre, Calgary, Canada (2007).

Murder in Green Meadows begins with an idyllic friendship between two yuppie suburban couples—Joan and Thomas Devereaux and Carolyn and Jeffrey Symons. Soon a few ominous signs rear their ugly heads. Joan confides to Carolyn that at the age of twenty-three she set her doll collection on fire—"I didn't want them anymore, and I didn't want anyone else to have them." Thomas tells his wife how he killed a young student, Bradley, with a shovel for playing around with her, and now insists that she murder Jeff for the same reason. The twisty plot has Joan telling Jeff, "Thomas wanted me to kill you. . . . There's just something about him. Wicked as sin. We don't want to believe that such people exist. But they do. They're like black holes. No souls. (She points to a bloodied knife on the floor.) I killed him. I did it." Jeff finds the dead man in the next room and carries him to his car, planning to throw the body in the river. Joan begins to scream. Jeff returns, discovers the door locked, breaks in, and Joan shoots him twice. Thomas appears, bloody and covered with mud. "Nicely done," he says.

During the second act, Carolyn arrives, and Joan explains the shooting: "I thought he was a burglar." In a suspenseful scene, Jeff, dying, reveals the truth to Carolyn. Thomas and Joan seem to have perpetrated the perfect crime, but Carolyn manages to turn the tables, tricking them into a confession.

The main interest of *Murder in Green Meadows*, not unlike *Earth and Sky*, lies in the delineation of character and the relationship between two disturbed, evil people, rather than the "crime-doesn't-pay" motif. The two plays were presented simultaneously in Chicago in 1999—*Earth and Sky* at the Circle Theatre, *Murder in Green Meadows* at the Attic Playhouse. Reviewer Jack Helbig found *Earth and Sky* "a beautiful, evocative work that can be read either as a nourish thriller or as a journey through Sara's soul." Helbig, however, believed that in *Murder in Green Meadows*, playwright Post "became too wrapped up in producing a play full of twists."[6]

Among Post's two dozen plays there are several more tinged with elements of suspense. *Detective Sketches*, first produced at Chicago's Organic Lab Theatre in 1987, is a comic spoof of the hard-boiled detective story. *Drowning Sorrows* (Victory Gardens Theatre, Chicago, 1996) is the twisty yarn of a Manhattan heiress who has spent twenty years searching for the man who left her at the altar and mysteriously disappeared. In *Blissfield* (Victory Gardens Theatre, Chicago, 2000), a foreign correspondent returns to his midwest hometown to investigate the suicide of his best friend. In *Personal Effects* (Circle Theatre, Chicago, 2003), a successful tax attorney lands on the streets of Los Angeles and attempts to figure out why his life has been dismantled and by whom. The protagonist of *Somebody Foreign*

(City Lit Theatre, Chicago, 2006) is a Chicago woman with ties to the human rights movement in the Gaza strip who finds herself the target of an investigation by the FBI.

Post wrote the librettos of the pop operas *Prospero's Saxophone* (based on Shakespeare's *The Tempest*, Leo A. Lerner Theatre, Chicago, 1981); *Everyman* (from a medieval morality play, Free Shakespeare Company, Chicago, 1984); and *God and Country* (inspired by Sophocles's *Antigone*, Victory Gardens Theatre, Chicago, 2002).

* * *

Douglas Post received a BA from Trinity University, San Antonio, Texas, majoring in English, Speech, and Drama. He was teacher of playwriting at Northwest University, DePaul University, Victory Gardens Theatre, Chicago Dramatists, and O'Neill National Theatre Institute. His plays have been produced in Chicago, New York, Los Angeles, Canada, England, Wales, Germany, Austria, Russia, and China. He has been commissioned to write screenplays for Warner Brothers and NBC as well as radio adaptations of his plays. In addition, Post composed songs and incidental music for more than twenty-five productions in Chicago, where he lives and is resident playwright at the Victory Gardens Theatre. Post is the Chicago Regional Representative for the Dramatists Guild of America. His manuscripts are housed at the DePaul University Library Special Collection and Archives.

Acting Edition: *Earth and Sky* and *Murder in Green Meadows*: Dramatists Play Service.

Awards and Honors: Douglas Post won the 1991 Arnold L. Weissberger Playwriting Competition sponsored by New Dramatists for *Earth and Sky*. He was the recipient of the Midwestern Playwrights Festival Award in 1995 for *Personal Effects* and the Cunningham Commission for Youth Theatre Award in 2003. Post was nominated for a 1984 Joseph Jefferson Award for Original Incidental Music for *The Tempest* and for a 1986 Emmy Award for Individual Achievement in Writing for *Murder in Green Meadows*. He also garnered three Playwriting Fellowship Awards from the Illinois Arts Council in 1990, 1997, and 2006.

NOTES

1. *New York Times*, February 5, 1991.
2. *New York Post*, February 5, 1991.
3. *New York Newsday*, February 5, 1991.
4. *Daily News*, February 5, 1991.
5. *Daily News*, February 15, 1991.
6. *Chicago Reader*, September 23, 1999.

Death and the Maiden (1991)

Ariel Dorfman (United States, Argentina-born, 1942–)

Born in Buenos Aires, Argentina, Ariel Dorfman is a Chilean novelist and playwright persecuted by the regime of Augusto Pinochet and forced into exile in the United States. In 1991, Dorfman composed a play carved from his experiences, set in "a country that is probably Chile but could be any country that has given itself a democratic government just after a long period of dictatorship."

Death and the Maiden is the story of Paulina Salas, a South American married to a prominent lawyer, Gerardo Escobar, who has recently been appointed by the new president of the republic to head a commission investigating human rights violations.

On his way to their beach home, Gerardo has a flat tire. Doctor Roberto Miranda stops to help. Gerardo invites the Good Samaritan to spend the night. Upon hearing the doctor's voice, Paulina believes that he is the man who raped and tortured her fifteen years earlier as she lay blindfolded in a military detention center. While the household is asleep, Paulina slips into Roberto's bedroom, hits him with a blunt instrument, binds him to a chair, and gags him with her panties. Then, at gunpoint, she orders her shocked husband to serve as the doctor's defense attorney in "a trial."

Roberto vehemently denies that he was the doctor-torturer: "I'm a quiet man. Anyone can see that I'm incapable of violence." But Paulina draws from him a few tidbits of information—"small lies, small variations"—that could only have been known to her true torturer. She also finds in his car a cassette of Schubert's "Death and the Maiden," the quartet that played in the background when she was degraded.

Just as Paulina aims her gun at Roberto, a giant mirror descends, forcing the members of the audience to look at themselves. A final scene, occurring several months later, has Paulina and Gerardo attending a concert. Roberto enters, and, based on a stage instruction, he may or may not be an illusion in Paulina's head. The instruments are tested and tuned.

Then "Death and the Maiden" begins. Paulina and Roberto lock eyes for a moment. The music plays as the curtain falls.

* * *

In an afterword to the acting edition of *Death and the Maiden*, playwright Dorfman enumerates the "sort of questions" that triggered the writing of his play: "How can those who tortured and those who were tortured coexist in the same land? How to heal a country that has been traumatized by repression if the fear to speak out is still omnipresent everywhere? And how do you reach the truth if lying has become a habit? . . . I felt that *Death and the Maiden* touched upon a tragedy in an almost Aristotelian sense, a work of art that might help a collective to purge itself, through pity and terror, in other words to force the spectators to confront those predicaments that, if not brought into the light of day, could lead to their ruin."[1]

Death and the Maiden began as a reading at the Institute for Contemporary Art in London on November 30, 1990. A workshop production was staged in Santiago, Chile, on March 10, 1991. The play had an acclaimed world premiere at London's Royal Court Upstairs on July 9, 1991. Later that year, on November 4, it moved to the Mainstage at the Royal Court with the same cast (Juliet Stevenson, Bill Paterson, Michael Byrne) and director (Lindsay Posner), winning the Sir Laurence Olivier Award for Best Play of the season.

The American opening of *Death and the Maiden* took place at the Brooks Atkinson Theatre in New York on March 17, 1992 under the direction of Mike Nichols, featuring Glenn Close as Paulina, Richard Dreyfuss as Geraldo, and Gene Hackman as Roberto. The reception by the critics was split. "A good strong mainstream melodrama," wrote Clive Barnes. "[A] play that on its own modest terms possesses thrills, spills and passion."[2] Edwin Wilson believed that "Mr. Dorfman's challenging play is both a political document and a psychological thriller."[3] Linda Winer found *Death and the Maiden* "engrossing, moderately suspenseful, meticulously produced."[4]

On the other hand, Jack Roll complained that by concentrating on the problem, whether Paulina has the right man, the play turned into a whodunit, undercutting "what should be its most agonizing question: how could a civilized human being become an evil monster in an oppressive regime?"[5] Two *Daily News* reviewers pointed accusing fingers at *Death and the Maiden*: Howard Kissel wrote, "I had trouble taking what happened on stage seriously. I kept imagining I was watching parlor games in Beverly Hills."[6] Likewise, Doug Watt stated, "There's precious little intellectual content in this disappointing evening."[7]

The production elements, too, earned A's and F's. "Under Mike Nichols' riveting direction, the superb cast maintains the piano-string tautness and menacing situation," applauded John Beaufort.[8] "Mike Nichols' staging, alas, is too ornate and stately, its pace slowed by pregnant pauses and suspense-draining scene changes. Moreover, the actors seem weirdly naturalistic for so polemic a text," lamented William A. Henry III.[9] Nonetheless, Glenn Close won the 1991–1992 Tony Award for Best Actress; years later, in a televised Actor's Studio session, she said that the role of Paulina was "the hardest thing I ever had to do."[10]

Star power kept *Death and the Maiden* on the boards for 159 performances. The Mark Taper Forum of Los Angeles presented *Death and the Maiden* in 1994, starring Jimmy Smits, Wanda de Jesus, and Tomas Milian. That same year, a movie version, co-written by Dorfman, directed by Roman Polanski and starring Sigourney Weaver as Paulina, Ben Kingsley as Roberto, and Stuart Wilson as Gerardo, kept the tense proceedings confined to a secluded beach house. Dorfman also penned the libretto for an opera version that had its world premiere at Sweden's Malmo Opera House in September 2008.

* * *

Vladimiro Ariel Dorfman was born in Buenos Aires on May 6, 1942, the son of a prominent Argentine professor of economics and a literature teacher. At the age of two, his family was forced to flee to the United States because of his father's opposition to the Argentine government of Juan Peron. In 1954, during the McCarthy era, the Dorfmans moved to Chile. Dorfman was determined to become a writer as a youth. He attended the University of Chile and became a Chilean citizen in 1967. From 1968 to 1969, he attended graduate school at the University of California at Berkeley. His thesis on the absurd in plays by Harold Pinter, who he befriended years later, was published in 1968.

During 1970–1973, Dorfman served as a cultural advisor to president Salvador Allende. After the 1973 coup by Chilean General Augusto Pinochet, Dorfman was forced to leave the country and moved between Paris, Amsterdam, and Washington, D.C. Since 1985 he has taught at Duke University in Durham, North Carolina, where he is currently a professor of literature and Latin American Studies. Since the restoration of democracy in Chile in 1990, he has divided his time between Santiago and the United States, where he became a citizen in 2004.

Dorfman has been a human rights activist for many years, and has addressed the General Assembly of the United Nations and other forums on social issues. His plays, novels, short stories, essays, and poems often deal with the horrors of tyranny. His plays have been translated into more than forty languages and performed in more than 100 countries. *Widows*, a political allegory that Dorfman adapted from his 1983 novel, is the poignant story of a group of black-clad peasant women whose husbands "disappeared" into the maw of a military junta. While washing laundry by the river, the women discover a man's faceless corpse floating to the surface. A struggle ensues: each of the women believes the man to be her missing husband. *Widows* first played at the Mark Taper Forum, Los Angeles, in 1991 and reached New York's 59E59 Theatre in 2008. Critic Charles Isherwood pointed out that "Mr. Dorfman's compassion for the suffering of the women is palpable, as is his contempt for the brutal tactics of the military men." But, added Isherwood, "He has failed to translate his moral and emotional responses to these historically inspired events into compelling or even convincingly truthful drama."[11]

In Dorfman's *Reader*, a dedicated censor, Daniel Lucas, receives an unfinished novel and finds in it a description of his own past crimes. The play received its world premiere at the Traverse Theatre during 1995's Edinburgh Fringe Festival. Atypical of other Dorfman works, *Who's Who* is a murder mystery farce that unfolds in Hollywood during a terrorist plot. It premiered at Germany's Frankfurt Schauspielhaus in 1998. That same year, also in Germany, *Mascara* opened at the Bonn Schauspielhaus. A psychological thriller about a man whose invisibility allows him to take incriminating photographs, *Mascara* was dramatized by Dorfman from his 1988 novel in collaboration with his son Rodrigo.

Speak Truth to Power: Voices from Beyond the Dark is based on a book written by Kerry Kennedy, featuring interviews with human rights champions who overcame overwhelming odds against authoritarian rulers. The play was first presented at the Kennedy Center in Washington, D.C., in 2000 and subsequently aired on PBS as part of its Great Performances series. Directed by Gregory Mosher, it starred Sigourney Weaver, Kevin Kline, Alec Baldwin, and John Malkovich. Since then *Speak Truth to Power* has been performed across America and around the world. On November 2, 2006 the play was presented in the Middle East for the first time as part of a red-carpet gala dinner charity event at the Qatar National Theatre.

The Other Side, an antiwar play first shown at the New National Theatre in Tokyo, Japan, in 2004, reached New York's City Center Stage on December 13, 2005. It tells of an old couple residing near the border of two fighting countries, passing their days confirming the identity of dead bodies and burying them. "In *The Other Side*, Mr. Dorfman has set out to denounce the cruelty of global feuds fired by nationalism and ethnic prejudice," wrote critic Charles Isherwood. "But he expresses this unexceptional sentiment in the form of a ponderous comedy-drama that could itself be accused of a human-right violation, albeit a minor one: the wholesale waste of two first-rate actors [John Cullum and Rosemary Harris]."[12]

Inspired by Dante's epic poem *The Divine Comedy* and reminiscent of Jean-Paul Sartre's *No Exit*, Dorfman's *Purgatorio* features a man and a woman who, in their afterlife, interrogate one another while groping for forgiveness and contrition. The play had a workshop production at the

Theatre Studies Department of Duke University in February 2005 and later that year was produced by the Seattle Rep. Arcola Theatre in London's West End presented *Purgatorio* in 2008. The Hoy Polloy Theatre of Brunswick, Australia, mounted it in 2009.

Picasso's Closet, a counterfactual history in which the influential artist is murdered by the Nazis, had its premiere at Theatre J in Washington, D.C. in 2006. Dorfman wrote the book and Eric Woolfson the music of *Dancing Shadows*, wherein an imaginary village is devastated during a war. The musical was first presented at the Seoul Center Opera House, South Korea, in 2007.

For England's BBC-TV, Dorfman and his son Rodrigo scripted *Prisoners in Time* (1995), in which a tormented ex-prisoner of war and the mea-culpa Japanese man who tortured him meet face to face, each hoping to find redemption and peace. Dorfman's 1998 *Heading South, Looking North: A Bilingual Journey*, an account of his life of exile and bicultural roots, was the source of a feature-length documentary, *A Promise to the Dead*, which had its world premiere at the 2007 Toronto International Film Festival. The footage included glimpses of Salvador Allende, Hugo Chávez, Augusto Pinochet, Henry Kissinger, Richard Nixon—and Ariel Dorfman himself. Dorfman borrowed elements from the old classic *The Hands of Orlac*[13] when concocting the feature *Blood and Honey* (2010), a surreal murder thriller: a Taiwanese concert pianist, who had a heart transplant, is experiencing terrifying nightmares and decides to track down the identity of the donor. She discovers that she was given the heart of a murderer.

Acting Edition: Penguin Plays; Samuel French, Inc.

Awards and Honors: *Death and the Maiden* won the 1992 Laurence Olivier Theatre Award for Best Play. Ariel Dorfman's first novel, *Hard Rain* (1973), won the Sudamericana Award. Dorfman received the Lowell Thomas Award for his travel book, *Desert Memories* (2004). Dorfman and his son, Rodrigo, garnered a Writer's Guild of Great Britain Award for *Prisoners in Time* (1996). *Dancing Shadows*, Dorfman's musical in collaboration with composer Eric Woolfson, won five Korean "Tony" awards (2007). Dorfman won two Kennedy Center Theatre Awards for his plays *Reader* and *Widows*. In July 2010 he had the honor of delivering the Nelson Mandela Lecture in South Africa. He is a member of *L'Académie Universelle des Cultures* in Paris, and the American Academy of Arts and Sciences.

NOTES

1. Ariel Dorfman, *Death and the Maiden* (New York: Penguin, 1992), 73–74.
2. *New York Post*, March 18, 1992.
3. *Wall Street Journal*, March 24, 1992.

4. *New York Newsday*, March 18, 1992.

5. *Newsweek*, March 30, 1992.

6. *Daily News*, March 18, 1992.

7. *Daily News*, March 27, 1992.

8. *Christian Science Monitor*, March 27, 1992.

9. *Time*, March 30, 1992.

10. *Inside the Actor's Studio*, June 29, 1997.

11. *New York Times*, January 21, 2008.

12. *New York Times*, December 14, 2005.

13. *Les Mains d'Orlac* (*The Hands of Orlac*), a 1927 French novel by Maurice Renard, is the story of a famous pianist whose hands are crushed in a train wreck. A Parisian surgeon attaches the limbs of a murderer—with fatal results. *The Hands of Orlac* was the basis for a German expressionistic film in 1924, with Conrad Veidt in the role of Paul Orlac, and a 1935 American remake, titled *Mad Love*, featuring Colin Clive as the injured pianist and Peter Lorre as a deranged surgeon.

The Manchurian Candidate (1991)

John Lahr (United States, 1941–)

Richard Condon's 1959 novel, *The Manchurian Candidate*, was immensely successful and is still considered "the definitive psychological thriller."[1] Its protagonist, Sergeant Raymond Shaw, was secretly brainwashed by the enemy during the Korean War and sent back to the United States as a human time bomb to inflict havoc on an unsuspecting nation.

The strange saga of Raymond Shaw, who as the result of his indoctrination unwittingly strangles and shoots people, was filmed in 1962 by United Artists, scripted by George Axelrod and directed by John Frankenheimer with Laurence Harvey as Shaw; Angela Lansbury as his monstrously ambitious mother, Eleanor Iselin, called "quite possibly the worst human being ever portrayed on celluloid";[2] James Gregory as his demagogic politician stepfather, Johnny Iselin; and Frank Sinatra as an army buddy, Ben Marco, who realizes that all is not as it appears.[3]

The 1991 play version by John Lahr updates the proceedings to 1999. In place of the Korean conflict, Shaw, Marco, and their platoon are tackling Shiite Muslims on the border of Kuwait.

A London production, premiering at the Poole Arts Centre in Poole, Dorset, England, on June 6, 1991, directed by Robert Midgeley and Jonathan Myerson, designed by Tim Goodchild, utilized six kabuki-style screens, moved visibly by stagehands, to allow for quick shifts from one scene to another. Minimal props and furniture pieces are supplied by stagehands dressed in black. At the rear of the stage are two large video screens onto which images are occasionally projected. A percussionist seated at the back observes and underscores the action with eerie accompanying music.

The proceedings unfold in thirty-one kaleidoscopic scenes, zigzagging back and forth in time, beginning with the capture of a U.N. peacekeeping patrol in the Middle East, then tracing the return of the soldiers to America; Shaw's receiving the Congressional Medal of Honor; Marco's recurring nightmare pooh-poohed by his girlfriend, Eugenie; the hatching of a right-wing scheme by the Iselins to reach the White House and drop a nuclear bomb on the Persian Gulf—"the Arabs have been holdin' us over an oil barrel for too long"; Shaw's test killing of Holborn Gaines, editor of the *Daily Press*; the marriage of Shaw and Jocie Jordan, daughter of an influential senator; Shaw's somnambulistic killing of his wife and father-in-law by using a revolver equipped with a silencer; Marco's discovery that Shaw's manipulation was triggered by the vision of the Queen of Diamonds during a game of solitaire; Marco's confrontation with Shaw, "neutralizing" and "smashing" the unholy domination over him by shuffling a deck of cards: "Seven Queens. Seven commands. My authority is seven times greater than theirs. Look at them, Raymond. This is an order. I am giving you an order. I am telling you it's over. They don't control you any more"; Mrs. Iselin's delivering to Shaw a satchel containing a two-piece Kalashnikov sniper's rifle with a Lytton Aim Laser Sight: "The bullet will go where the dot is. And I want the dot *square* in the forehead of the President of the United States. . . . Johnny will be President. I will be First Lady. And the Lobbyists, who love to sniff the hem of power, baby, will be sniffin' mine. And then, sweetheart . . . then . . . the fun begins"; the convention rally in Madison Square Garden, during which Shaw shoots not the president but his mother and stepfather, then himself.

The *London Times* commented, "John Lahr's ingenious updating substitutes Japan-bashing for the red-baiting of Richard Condon's original, producing a wonderfully preposterous scenario."[4] The schizophrenic drama is tinged with incest, tension, and satire.

* * *

Richard Thomas Condon (1915–1996) was born in New York City, where he was educated in public schools. He served in the U.S. Merchant Marine and began his writing career working briefly in advertising. Condon was publicist in the American film industry for Walt Disney Productions (1936–1941), 20th Century Fox (1941–1945), Paramount (1948–1953), and United Artists (1953–1957). He became a theatrical producer on Broadway in the 1951–1952 season.

During 1958–1994, Condon penned eighteen complex novels of intrigue, of which the better known ones are *The Oldest Profession* (*The Happy Thieves*), 1958; *Winter Kills*, 1974; and *Prizzi's Honor*, 1982—all adapted to the screen. Condon co-scripted, with Janet Roach, the film *Prizzi's Honor*, a black comedy directed by John Huston, about a Mafia hit man (Jack Nicholson) who falls in love with his female counterpart (Kathleen Turner).

"At his strongest, Richard Condon can deliver chilling reality and thoughtfulness to his offbeat, antic descriptions of the labyrinth of human connivance," writes Shelly Lowenkopf.[5]

Condon's sole attempt on Broadway, *Men of Distinction* (48th Street Theatre, April 30, 1953), is a comedy that centers on a vice-infested New York society—including crooked politicians, public-relations shysters, idle playboys; it lasted only four performances.

Born in Los Angeles, California in 1941, and the son of famed actor Bert Lahr, John Lahr holds a BA from Yale University and a master's degree from Worcester College, Oxford. Lahr paid tribute to his father in *Notes on a Cowardly Lion* (1969), then continued to write nonfiction books about the theatre, notably *Astonish Me* (1973), a collection of essays examining contemporary "Pageants," "Playwrights," and "Performances," and *Light Fantastic* (1996), a wide-ranging analysis of "Adventurers in Theatre" with emphasis on the Who's Who among American and English playwrights. Lahr also penned a few novels with show business settings, including *The Autobiography Hound* (1973).

Fascinated with the life and works of the *enfant terrible* of British theatre, playwright Joe Orton, Lahr wrote a biography of Orton, *Prick Up Your Ears* (1978); coproduced a film version of *Prick Up Your Ears* (1987), scripted by Alan Bennett and directed by Stephen Frears; and, also in 1987, penned the play *Diary of a Somebody*, about Orton's amazing life and violent death, first produced at Kings Head Theatre, London.[6]

Since 1992, Lahr has written about theatre and popular culture in the *New Yorker*, now serving as the magazine's senior drama critic.

Acting Edition: Dramatists Play Service.

Awards and Honors: Richard Condon was the recipient of a Writers Guild Award (U.S.) and a BAFTA Award (UK), both in 1986. John Lahr has twice won the George Jean Nathan Award for Dramatic Criticism. In 2002, Lahr garnered a Best Special Theatrical Event Tony Award for "constructing" the one-woman show, *Elaine Stritch at Liberty*; he and actress Elaine Stritch also won the Drama Desk Award for the Best Book to a Musical.[7]

NOTES

1. John M. Reilly, ed., *Twentieth Century Crime and Mystery Writers* (New York: St. Martin's, 1980), 345.

2. William L. DeAndrea, *Encyclopedia Mysteriosa* (New York: Prentice Hall, 1994), 229.

3. A 2004 motion picture remake of *The Manchurian Candidate* was directed by Jonathan Demme, starring Denzel Washington (Major Ben Marco), Liev Schreiber (Raymond Shaw), and Meryl Streep (name changed to Eleanor Prentiss Shaw).

4. Quoted in *Dramatists Play Service Catalogue 95/96* (New York: Dramatists Play Service, 1996), 93.

5. Jay P. Pederson, ed., *St James Guide to Crime and Mystery Writers* (Detroit: St. James Press, 1996), 224.

6. Joe Orton's black comedy *Loot* (1966) and his other controversial plays are described in Amnon Kabatchnik's *Blood on the Stage, 1950–1975* (Lanham, Md.: Scarecrow Press, 2011), 488–97.

7. In June 2009, John Lahr filed a lawsuit in a Manhattan Supreme Court against Elaine Stritch for money he claims is owed him for work he did on *Elaine Stritch at Liberty*, the actress's one-woman biographical show that played off-Broadway, on Broadway, and beyond, and was also recorded on a cast album. Reportedly, Lahr was seeking unspecified damages, restitution, and 20 percent of the box-office grosses.

The Invisible Man (1991)

Ken Hill (England, 1937–1995)

H. G. Wells got the idea for his "Scientific Romance," *The Invisible Man*, from a snatch of a verse entitled "The Perils of Invisibility," published in 1869 under the authorship of "Bab" in *Fan* magazine. "Bab" was the pseudonym of W. S. Gilbert (1836–1911), the parodist and librettist who became world-famous when he teamed with composer Arthur Sullivan on a series of popular light operas. "The Perils of Invisibility" is the story of Old Peter, a fat man who is offered the gift of invisibility to escape a cantankerous wife.

Wells's novella was originally serialized in *Pearson's* magazine in 1897 and published in book form the same year. Wells discarded Gilbert's far-cical tone and treated the theme with a more realistic and menacing aura. Peter Haining, an authority on popular culture, writes in *The H. G. Wells Scrapbook*: "Mr. Wells's method is in its essentials much more realistic. He does not posit his invisible man; he tells us how he became invisible as a result of a discovery in physiology based upon actual scientific data, for Mr. Wells is no dabbler but deeply versed in these studies. It is char-acteristic, again, of his method that his invisible man should be neither a buffoon nor a humorist, but a moody, irritable egotist, with a violent and vindictive temper. Griffin, in short, is really a tragic figure."[1]

Wells's *The Invisible Man* has spawned a clutch of motion picture treat-ments beginning with *The Invisible Thief*, made in 1909 by Charles Pathé, the French pioneer of the film industry, and most notably in the classic 1933 Universal version directed by James Whale, starring Claude Rains in the title role.[2] Conversely, *The Invisible Man* was only adapted to the stage several times with Ken Hill's 1991 dramatization leading the pack.

The curtain rises on a Master of Ceremonies who mingles with the audi-ence as it arrives and establishes the music-hall style of the production. The MC announces that the proceedings will unfold "in the illustrious year of 1904" and introduces the Follies—a troupe of actors-singers-dancers who will perform the "main event, which tonight takes the form of a chilling dramatic presentation entitled 'The Terrible Tale of the Awful Events at the Village of Iping.'"

The MC calls upon "the only living survivor prepared to stand up and tell his tale—Mr. Thomas Marvel." Marvel, a tramp who sports a frock coat and waistcoat, raises his top hat, tells the musical director, "mood, Maestro, please," and instructs the backstage crew to project falling snow and emit the sound of howling wind. Marvel exits into the auditorium, where he stations himself in the back and watches as the lights come up on the saloon bar in the village of Iping.

Mrs. Hall, the innkeeper, is behind the bar, serving constable Jaffers, who is sitting on a high stool. Millie, a young maid, feeds the fireplace with logs while Teddy, a waiter, sits at the piano and tickles the keys. Miss Statchell, the new Scottish schoolmistress, puts her bag down, takes off her coat, and shakes the snowflakes off. The town's squire, Burdock, twirls his moustache and orders his footman, Wicksteed, to offer Miss Statchell a "Glen McCraggie." Burdock sits down at Statchell's table beaming but is soon taken aback when she puts a pipe in her mouth, lights it, and then takes a flask out of her bag and pours its contents into her drink.

The door opens with a loud gust of wind and a big sting of music as Griffin enters, carrying a doctor's bag. Every inch of him is bandaged, including his face, and there are dark goggles over his eyes. All react.

In a low, harsh voice, Griffin addresses Mrs. Hall, requesting a room. Millie is afraid to lead the newcomer to his room. Mrs. Hall gingerly takes his bag and leads him off.

JAFFERS (awe-struck, looking off after Griffin): Peculiar-looking beggar, ain't he?
TEDDY: Accident, I suppose.
MISS STATCHELL: To his whole face?
WICKSTEED: Could be a war wound, miss.

A hand appears at the top edge of the door. Millie notices it and makes gurgling noises. All stare at her, turn to look, and converge on the door. As they open it, a man is found hanging; he is totally nude. Millie screams, "It's Dr. Cuss! And not a stitch on him!" Blackout, scene change music, and the lights fade up on the village green, a few days later. Villagers are milling about.

Fearenside, a railroad employee, enters pulling a laden cart, a small dog nodding over a corner. He goes through the crowd, announcing, "Coming through! Delivery from the station!" Mrs. Hall and Miss Statchell are curious about a large box that came for the new lodger, Griffin. Fearenside takes the top off the box to reveal rows of bottles. "Looks like chemicals," he says. Miss Statchell holds up several bottles and mutters, "Queer selection, I must say. This one's lead monoxide, but this green one's got me baffled." They poke and prod the cart as Griffin comes out of the inn. He approaches them angrily and the dog, Mafeking, grabs his sleeve growling. Griffin struggles to free himself, and in the process knocks off his dark glasses. There are two black holes where his eyes should be. Griffin claps a hand over them, kneels, and searches for the glasses blindly. Miss Statchell moves forward, finds the glasses, and presses them into his hand. Griffin puts them back on, and hurries into the pub.

In the vicarage, Reverend Bunting and sexton Wadgers clean dusty busts while Miss Statchell plays her harmonica with flourish, a pipe in her mouth. "According to this new science fiction by Mr. Wells," she chats, "we'll soon be fighting a war with Martians, and flying to the moon." Bunting and Wadgers dismiss the notion that man will go to the moon. The topic shifts to the new movement of suffragists, and Bunting says, "If God had intended women to be equal, He would have created them so."

Wadgers and Miss Statchell go to their quarters. Bunting hides a cash box containing the church funds in the organ, picks up a candle, turns off the lamp, and exits. There's a tapping at the window, then a crash, and bits of glass fall to the floor. A tall stool shifts aside, papers are moved on the table, drawers are opened, and books are thrown out. Reverend Bunting re-appears, wearing a nightshirt and nightcap, carrying a candle. He sees the mess, mumbles, "Oh my word," and hurries to the organ. He brings out the cash box when suddenly his candle blows out. Bunting is thrown against the wall and he watches in horror as the cash box floats in the air. The curtains are flung aside and Bunting hears the sound of running feet crunching the gravel.

In the village green, constable Jaffers, squire Burdock, and Mrs. Hall discuss the vicarage robbery. Jaffers relates that strange footprints were found outside the window—of bare feet on a freezing cold night. "Some people think we've got a ghost," says Mrs. Hall. Behind them, the pub door opens and closes softly. They don't notice a bike straightening and wheeling off.

Burdock confesses to Miss Statchell that he is smitten with her. Before the schoolteacher can react, a scream is heard from the road. Constable Jaffers appears dragging a manacled Marvel. Jaffers tells the squire that the post office has been robbed and a lot of money is missing—a hundred quid in five-pound notes. He found the tramp lying in the road, pretending to groan and complaining that he has been beaten up; no doubt he's the thief.

The bicycle rides across the back and crashes. Jaffers recognizes his bike and wonders what happened to it. Marvel exclaims that "this bloke" ran right into him but he couldn't see him in the dark. Jaffers uncuffs him.

From the pub comes a terrible scream. They all rush in. Millie is standing by the staircase, clutching her broom. She stutters that when she was sweeping the landing she saw the new lodger's door open, thought it was empty, and went in to clean it. Suddenly the window "sort of blows open all of its own, and in floats this funny-looking white shape! . . . It was money! A bundle of five-pound notes! . . . Hanging in the air right in front of my eyes!"

Led by Jaffers, they all cross cautiously to the stranger's door. Fearfully, the constable knocks. "Go away!" calls Griffin from within. Miss Statchell pushes through the protesting group. She reminds Griffin that they met outside when she retrieved his glasses and he consents to see her. Jaffers tells Miss Statchell that she has five minutes and then "we're coming after you." The lights fade up on Griffin's room. Miss Statchell enters and looks around. There is bubbling equipment on the table, books and an oil lamp on the floor, general disorder elsewhere. A swivel chair turns and facing her is Griffin, wearing a dressing gown, scarf, gloves, and the usual bandages and glasses. He tells the schoolteacher that he had an accident with an experiment and a process that was to be reversible went wrong. He is searching for the cure.

Griffin also confides that an associate doctor, Gerald Kemp, wanted to steal the idea and was instrumental in a fire that engulfed the laboratory and everything went up in smoke, including crucial notebooks. Now he has to re-create the whole experiment from scratch. Agitated, Griffin sweeps objects off the table and buries his head in his hands.

Miss Statchell attempts to comfort Griffin and he is touched. "You could share with me—power," he says. "We could order a whole new world—the shape of things to come." The intimate moment is broken by a pounding on the door and Jaffers shouting, "Time's up, Miss! We're coming in!" Griffin feverishly collects his notebooks as Jaffers, Burdock, and Wicksteed crash the door. "What do you mean by bursting into a man's private rooms?" roars Griffin. Mrs. Hall points out that he hasn't paid rent for weeks. He tosses a bundle of notes in front of her and jeers, "Help yourself." Mrs. Hall says significantly, "*Fivers*, Mr. Jaffers."

To the accompaniment of sinister musical chords, Griffin throws his glasses at them, takes the bandages off the top of his head, and puts a cigarette to the space where his mouth is. The tip glows; smoke is expelled. Though dumbfounded, Jaffers waves a pair of handcuffs and orders, "Take off your gloves and hold out your hands." Griffin puts down the cigarette, pulls off his gloves, and tosses them at the constable who, horrified, stares at the empty sleeves. "The fact is," says Griffin, "*All* of me is like this. . . . I'm invisible."

Burdock and Wicksteed slip around the table and prepare to pounce on Griffin from behind. "Look out!" Miss Statchell shouts, and blows out the lamp. In the dim light, the headless Griffin throws his scarf at Mrs. Hall and slips out of the dressing gown. The nightshirt cavorts. Jaffers grapples with it but when the maid Millie dashes in with another lamp and light is restored, Jaffers is seen fighting with an empty shirt. All begin to feel the air around them. Suddenly, Millie shrieks and jumps; Burdock cries out, feeling his cheek; in rapid succession, Bunting, Jaffers, and Mrs. Hall are poked and prodded.

The door opens. Jaffers aims a mighty blow with his truncheon and there is a clonk and a cry from Griffin, "You stupid policeman! You'll die for that!" The truncheon flies from Jaffers's hand and invisible hands throttle him. Jaffers forces the hands apart, snatches a knife from the table and slashes around the room. His knife-holding hand is apparently grabbed, the knife begins to turn toward him, and after a strenuous struggle, the knife eventually pierces his neck. Jaffers collapses and dies.

Mrs. Hall kneels by the body. Miss Statchell utters a sudden gasp as Griffin holds her, turns her upstage, and says, "Thank you for trying to help. We'll meet again one day." She is kissed and released. The curtains bulge outward and there is a huge smash of broken glass. Burdock and Bunting run to the window and pull down the black curtains. There is a gaping hole in the window in the shape of a man.

Act 2 begins with the chorus crooning a warning song:

> "Who's there? What was that? It's him! He's very near!
> You never see him coming but you always know he's here."

In a forest glade, the tramp Marvel is accosted by the Invisible Man—he is thumped, pinched, pulled by the nose, and is ordered by a commanding voice to become a disciple, an assistant, as his new master grows in power. Marvel's first assignment is to go to Dr. Gerald Kemp's study and unlatch the back door. Griffin confronts Kemp and reminds the doctor that he caught him red-handed stealing his notes and that during an ensuing physical tussle, the laboratory caught fire. He had to rebuild the experiment, used it on himself, and the results were catastrophic: after a night of anguish, he stood before the mirror and saw his body "turn milky, then glassy, then became a mist and fade until all that was left was—space." So far he hasn't found a way of restoring his appearance.

Growing more and more intense, Griffin tells Kemp that he has decided to use his invisibility to establish a reign of terror, bring the country to its knees! He needs Kemp as a "skilled accomplice with a hideout." Impassioned, Griffin declares: "There's no end to what we can achieve! Train smashes! Munitions exploding! Leading figures assassinated! Government buildings destroyed! A new kind of warfare from a new kind of man! And the reward? *World domination!*"

Griffin, elated, dances a waltz with Marvel while Kemp crosses stealth-ily to the windows and throws them open to let in Colonel Adye, armed, followed by three moustached police officers. Griffin stares at Kemp ven-omously. "Invisible man, you're under arrest," announces Adye; but he is kicked in the groin and writhes downstage. Kemp and Marvel are thrust aside and the door swings open. Shouts and whistles are heard from the outside. Adye and the officers run out. "Charge!" cries the Colonel.

The citizens of Iping meet at the Village Hall. Reverend Bunting asks all to stay calm and elicits the information that the Invisible Man, in a tantrum, cut all the telephone wires, set fire to the police station, turned over everybody's dustbins, kicked a cat over a haystack, threw Mrs. Mof-fatt into the pond, and terrorized Miss Batchett in her bath.

Bunting waves a wooden bat, smashes it down on the table with rel-ish, and promises that "the viper that little Iping took to her bosom and who repaid our trust with wholesale mayhem—shall be destroyed!" All he needs, says Bunting, are some volunteers. Behind the reverend a cane carpet-beater floats into the air and smacks him soundly. Then Bunting's long scarf wraps itself around his throat and begins to tighten. Marvel and Adye run toward the reverend, who is released. Squire Burdock yells, "He must still be on stage," and people begin to feel around. Griffin wrestles Adye's gun. The gun fires, blowing Wicksteed's hat off. Feet are heard banging down the steps into the auditorium. Burdock addresses the audience: "Don't panic, everyone. Keep calm. There's absolutely no cause for alarm." The men rush into the auditorium, searching for the Invisible Man in the dress circle, the rear stalls, the gallery, and the boxes. They soon return dejected to the stage and inform Miss Statchell, Mrs. Hall, and Millie, "Not a sign of life. . . . Quiet as the grave."

Griffin's voice booms from the gallery: "In one week, I'll bring this class-ridden society to its knees. . . . And you, Kemp, in one week's time—at *noon* precisely—wherever you hide—the revenger of all ills shall seek you out." The auditorium door bangs.

ADYE: Do you think he meant all that?
MARVEL: Oh, yes. He's off his rocker, and he thinks he's God. He ought to be in politics, really.

They hear a loud whistle of an approaching train followed by a huge crash.

Spotlights pinpoint six newsboys as they announce blazing headlines while in the background are heard shots, explosions, screams, and crack-ling flames. Newsboy one proclaims, "Massive Train Crash! Hundreds Killed!" Newsboy two raises a placard, "Huge Explosion Rocks Capital!"

Newsboy three bellows, "State of Emergency Declared! All Police Leave Cancelled!" Newsboy four yells, "Acid Poured into House of Lords' Bath-Water! Big Invisible Man Hunt!" Newsboy five: "Lions Released from London Zoo Eat War Cabinet!" Newsboy six: "All Troops Mobilized! House of Parliament Razed! Buckingham Palace Destroyed!"

Marvel confides to the audience that "England was on her knees" but there was one glimmer of hope: The Invisible Man had sworn to kill Dr. Kemp; was it possible to set a trap? Dr. Kemp is placed in the Iping police station, surrounded by 300 uniformed officers—all handcuffed together. When the noon hour approaches, they cock their pistols. A church clock starts to strike twelve. Kemp groans and falls to his knees. The last chime echoes. All relax. Suddenly a massive explosion occurs nearby—the headquarters of the Imperial General Staff was blown up. Colonel Adye now believes that the threat on Kemp's life was only a decoy, a trick, in order to demolish the last center of organized resistance. The colonel orders the men to follow him toward the big cloud of smoke.

Dr. Kemp and Miss Statchell confess their attachment to one another when the door opens and Griffin's voice is heard: "I said I'd be back in a week, Gerald." Kemp is yanked to his knees. Miss Statchell intercedes, begging for Kemp's life, calling Griffin "a monster." Squire Burdock runs in but is hit in the stomach, punched in the face, thrown to the floor, and kicked several times. Griffin's voice moves to the door and fades as he threatens, "I'm coming for you, Kemp! And that damned village! They'll all *die*!"

The last scene unfolds in the village green, where Kemp, a hammer in hand, faces Griffin. Soon the hammer flies from the doctor's hand and he is thrown to the ground. First one leg, then the other, then one arm, then the other, are twisted back. He gasps, helpless. Slowly, the villagers appear, one at a time, Fearenside carrying a spade, Bunting carrying his stick, Mrs. Hall waving a broom, Millie a rolling pin. They circle around Kemp and aim blows at the space around the struggling doctor. The spade seems to hit its target. Griffin emits a terrible cry.

Miss Statchell kneels, finds Griffin's hand, and holds it. The Invisible Man sighs and dies. They cover him with a blanket. Colonel Adye calls for an army nurse. When they lift the blanket, the dead man is visible.

Miss Statchell: He's become visible in death.
Mrs Hall: Funny. He looks the same as anybody else.

Marvel waves to the audience and leads the company of players in a curtain-call song, in which the "dead" Jaffers and Griffin partake enthusiastically.

* * *

Directed by its author, Ken Hill, *The Invisible Man* was first presented at the Theatre Royal, Stratford East, on October 18, 1991. Brian Murphy portrayed Thomas Marvel and Jon Finch played Jack Griffin. Robin Don designed the set, utilizing revolving towers, gauze curtains, mobile trucks, and flown-in backings to achieve fluidity when the action shifted locales. The illusions were designed and built under the supervision of Paul Kieve.[3]

The reviews were ecstatic. Jeremy Kingston wrote, "The evening contains amazing stage tricks in plenty. . . . All criticism fails before the comical wonder of watching inanimate objects sport around in the air."[4] Andrew St. George hailed "a vastly enjoyable and rollicking version of the original spine-tingler . . . it manages to balance comedy and mystery without sacrificing either."[5] Jane Edwardes admired the "mind-boggling effects" and reported that "the audience, ranging from babes in arms to asthmatic grans, revelled in the gruesome events."[6] Michael Darvell complimented playwright Ken Hill for creating "a surprisingly deft version which has some truly inspired touches of magic" and actor Jon Finch who, "despite his frequent non appearances, manages to make the character fairly charismatic anyway."[7] John Peter lauded the "music-hall framework, complete with "ripe, grotty jokes and broad comic acting: a poncy vicar with a feather duster, a dim village constable, silly-ass village squire, lecherous village doctor, bustling village landlady and chirpy village tramp."[8] Michael Coveney enjoyed an evening that "radiates much warmth and pleasure,"[9] while Maureen Paton admired a "wonderfully enjoyable and imaginative production staged in Edwardian style."[10] Michael Arditti opined that "the humor is broad but always in character, and a splendid cast does each of those characters proud."[11] Rick Jones gushed about "a series of brilliant and very funny stage effects master-minded by illusionist Paul Kieve."[12]

A return engagement of *The Invisible Man* at the same Stratford East Theatre and with the participation of most of the original cast members took place on September 12–October 17, 1992. The show moved to West End's Vaudeville Theatre on February 6, 1993 with Michael N. Harbour in the title role. Paul Kieve's magical illusions were rekindled seventeen years later in a revival mounted by London's Menier Chocolate Factory; it previewed from November 12, 2010, opened officially on November 24, and ran through February 13, 2011.

* * *

In addition to Ken Hill, other playwrights have dramatized the H. G. Wells novella, each with his own conceit. Tim Kelly, the prolific American playwright, treated *The Invisible Man* as a farce. His 1977 one-act adaptation confines the action to the dining room of the Coach and Horses Inn and unfolds continuously during a winter afternoon. When the curtain rises, Jack Griffin has already been a lodger for several weeks and a series of burglaries nearby has bamboozled the villagers. In this version, Dr. Kemp is a woman. The maid, Millie, identifies the bandaged stranger as an invisible man but Mr. and Mrs. Hall, the innkeepers, and the vicar and his wife, who are residents at the inn, pooh-pooh the notion, calling Millie "silly," "lazy," "stupid," sloppy," and "ungrateful."

Griffin's mood changes from one extreme to another—violent outbursts are followed by tearful apologies. He often emits insane laughter and tends to grab Millie, Mrs. Hall, and Dr. Kemp by the throat, choking the women, then releasing them. The local law is represented by Colonel Adye, "a blustering sort with a whistle around his neck and a badge on his coat."

Lady Cynthia Tearjerk, Griffin's fiancée, arrives for a visit and throws her arms around him. He tosses her out. She weeps and wails as he exclaims, "I am not only invisible! I am invincible!" A Circus Lady shows up and offers Griffin a job. He rips up the contract and begins to strangle her. A fierce struggle ensues. At some point a dummy is thrown onstage and Griffin picks it up, punches it and kicks it, all the time laughing dementedly. The villagers form a semi-circle in an attempt to create a barricade. Griffin's voice is heard singing, "Here we go 'round the mulberry bush, the mulberry bush, the mulberry bush." All are caught up in the spirit of the tune and begin to croon and skip around the table holding hands like innocent children.

Suddenly the door opens, indicating that Griffin has made his exit. The villagers gather and stare offstage. We learn by their comments that Griffin was identified by his footsteps in the snow and wrestled to the ground. "What a relief to see the last of such a creature," says Mrs. Hall. They hear laughter from Griffin's room and turn around. Millie emerges wearing Griffin's long coat, hat, gloves, and goggles, her face concealed by bandages. Holding a jar of fluid she announces, "I drank what Griffin drank. I'm going to make you pay for the bad time you gave me! I'm going to take over the village! Ha, ha, ha!"

* * *

Playwright Eddie Cope, best known for his 1975 mystery spoof *Agatha Christie Made Me Do It*, concocted in 1980 "a comedy thriller" loosely based on H. G. Wells's *The Invisible Man*. Cope's play takes place in the rundown lobby of Rainbow Lodge, an isolated old hotel in the Colorado Rockies. Six college girls from Denver arrive on the scene in a wintry December and take over the hotel as a Christmas recess project.

Led by Linda Scott, a spunky drama student, the coeds soon learn that a previous owner stashed a sack of gold somewhere in the hotel.

The search for "the pot of gold at the end of the rainbow" pits the students against a scowling, limping caretaker, Hamilton; a young, snoopy deputy sheriff, Danny Thompson; a pair of mysterious lodgers, Fuller and Jane Beasley; and Jack Griffin, the invisible man. In this adaptation, he is a former British actor who played at the Old Vic in London, came to New York in a revival of a Bernard Shaw comedy, and at the conclusion of the engagement decided to stay in the United States. He took a part-time position at the Three Mile Island nuclear power plant, was eventually assigned to an unshielded area, and his body's chemistry counter-reacted. He became invisible. As a devotee of the American West, he came to this ghostly town.

The plot becomes more ominous when the four tires of the girls' bus are slashed and the hotel's telephone goes dead. Caretaker Hamilton is revealed as a Treasury Department employee and his body is found strangled in the linen closet. Soon thereafter, Fuller Beasley, an undercover government agent, is discovered dead in his bed with an ape-man glove wrapped around his neck. A third victim is Deputy Sheriff Thompson, who dies of a broken neck after he is pushed down the basement stairs.

In the final scene, Linda unearths a canvas bag filled with gold nuggets behind a stuffed fish hanging on the wall. The villain of the piece turns out to be Jane Beasley, who used to be a strong lady in the circus and is determined to get rid of anyone who stands between her and the hidden treasure. Jane forces Linda into a chair, binds and gags her, places a glove around Linda's neck and tightens it. Griffin tiptoes through the open door and says, "Tally ho! This is the end of your murder spree, old girl." He grabs Jane by the arms and ties her hands with the glove. He kisses Linda's hand and goes out to call the police from the deputy's car. Linda sighs and puts to her cheek the hand that Griffin kissed as the curtain descends.

Eddie Cope's *The Invisible Man* premiered at the Theatre Suburbia in Houston, Texas, in June–July, 1980. Harry Booker directed and played Jack Griffin. Catherine Dickerson portrayed Linda Scott.

* * *

Two rooms at Iping's Coach and Horses Inn—the bar and a bedroom—serve to delineate much of the action of *The Invisible Man* (1990) by Craig Sodaro. The curtain rises on a stormy spring night. A Gypsy woman, Miranda, gingerly reads cards on one of the tables and predicts with relish that "the joker means death." The door opens and a stranger enters, wearing an overcoat, gloves, a hat, and dark glasses. A white mask conceals his face. Although frightened by his odd appearance, the landlady, Mrs. Hall, rents Jack Griffin a room. Griffin claims to be a scientist, and indeed, soon his experiments keep the other lodgers up all night.

In this version, Adye is not an army colonel but an inept police constable, and Millie is not a maid but Mr. and Mrs. Hall's eighteen-year-old daughter who is betrothed to young, handsome Dr. Kemp. An added character is Jenny Jeffries, an inquisitive *London Times* reporter.

Soon the peace and calm of the sleepy town of Iping is shattered. Patrons of the local general store claim to have seen a vest and a pair of trousers walking about. A basket, an apple, and a hat are seen floating through the air. Barefoot footprints are found in the mud of the barnyard. And someone purloined the vicarage of yesterday's collection plate, seventeen pounds in all. "How *could* we have been robbed when we sat in the very next room and heard every sound?" puzzles Reverend Purdy.

In a moment of confrontation with Mrs. Hall, Griffin rips off his glasses and raises the mask. Those in the room, including the vicar and the constable, are horrified. Mrs. Hall jumps, for the invisible man has pinched her. Mr. Hall's head jerks back as if someone has slapped him. The vicar's hat flips off and the constable is jabbed in the stomach. Dr. Kemp enters and is tossed to the floor.

That evening in a small marsh a few miles outside of Iping, Thomas Marvel, a hobo, is accosted by Griffin. Marvel stares in disbelief as Griffin takes off his glove and there is nothing there.[13] Griffin recruits the astonished Marvel to fetch food, clothes, and his notes from the Coach and Horses. At the inn, Dr. Kemp peruses Griffin's journals and tells a skeptical Mrs. Hall that her mysterious lodger was a student at University College where he discovered the process of turning invisible. After experimenting with a cat, he tried it on himself.

Kemp catches Marvel sneaking into Griffin's room and sends him back to his master with a scribbled note. Constable Adye arrives with the news that farmer Wickem has been robbed and stabbed to death. A notation was found pinned to the victim's coat: "The reign of terror has begun!"

Later that night, Griffin stealthily enters his room and begins to search for his papers. Kemp confronts him. Griffin maintains that because of "the wickedness of the common man" he intends to flex his "invisible muscles" to "bring the masses to their knees." Kemp suggests that he give himself up for the murder of Mr. Wickem but Griffin furiously exclaims, "Never! It is by the shedding of blood that the reign of terror will be planted and bear fruit!"

The door opens by itself. On his way out, Griffin collides with an old boarder, Mrs. Henfrey. We see her struggling as if someone has her by the throat and she falls lifeless next to the bar. Mr. and Mrs. Hall enter in nightshirts, followed by several lodgers. Millie covers Mrs. Henfrey's corpse with a tablecloth. Jenny, the reporter, points at the window, "It's snowing. His footprints will be easy to follow." She sits and begins to write in a notepad. "He's the story of the century," she says.

Unexpectedly, the invisible man returns. He slaps Mrs. Hall, pulls Jenny by the hair, and attacks Millie, backing her against the bar. The three women call for help. Dr. Kemp bursts in, draws his gun, and fires three shots into the air around Millie. We hear a thud behind a screen. When they remove the screen, the actor playing Griffin is revealed. "Look! He's . . . he's becoming visible," says Jenny. Kemp drops to his side. "Take my journals," mumbles Griffin. "It's all in there. . . . Try again. Try . . . " He dies.

Jenny tells Kemp that her editor "would surely pay a good price" for Griffin's notes but the doctor tosses them into the fireplace.

* * *

The Aquila Theatre, a Professional Company in Residence at New York University, launched a workshop production of *The Invisible Man* in 2003, followed it with a tour, and, with the collaboration of choreographer Doug Varone, brought a movement-dance interpretation of the novel to Manhattan's Baruch Performing Arts Center for a limited run, October 21–November 6, 2005. Image and movement pushed the momentum of the narrative with only a few lines of dialogue from the novel itself. The entire action unfolds without an intermission on a bare stage representing a doctor's office and a patient's room. The nurses panic as the mad doctor experiments, dresses in black clothes and goggles, and spasms on the floor. A program note by Peter Meineck, the artistic director of Aquila, states that "a brilliant young English scientist, Griffin, renders himself invisible and in so doing isolates himself totally from human society. Griffin's journey is one of obsession, desperation and ultimately madness as Wells presents an image of the English countryside terrorized by an invisible man."

Anglo-Canadian playwright Michael O'Brien added wrinkles of his own when dramatizing *The Invisible Man* in 2006. A flashback reveals that when in medical school Griffin was jilted by a girl in favor of his more successful friend and that setback turned him sour on humanity. Canada's Shaw Festival presented the O'Brien version in October of 2006, eliciting a disparaging review in *The Playgoer*:

This script, sorry to say, sees an object lesson in where literary adaptation can go wrong. With all the wandering episodic sprawl of a screenplay but little of the thrills a movie thriller can offer, it was thoroughly untheatrical. The production by Neil Munro magnifies these weaknesses by crowding the stage with way too many characters cramped into tiny "rooms" in an awkward and dimly lit two-level set for much of the show. The whole project suffered from being both overliteral and "faithful" in this regard and also needlessly meddling in O'Brien's "improvements" to the plot. . . . The limitation with this material ends up being quite literally "now you see him, now you don't." O'Brien and Munro seemed to settle on making it into some adventure-romance, but the play was weighted down with too much plotting and stage traffic for us to enjoy the ride.[14]

* * *

Born in Birmingham, England in 1937, Kenneth Hill was educated at King Edward's School. He was a clerk, a basket weaver, and a television interviewer before dedicating his life to writing. His first play, *Night Season*, was mounted by the repertory Alexandra Theatre in his hometown. In 1970 he was invited to join Joan Littlewood's famed Theatre Workshop at the Theatre Royal, Stratford East, London. He appeared there in several productions, including Brendan Behan's *The Hostage* and served as resident writer. From 1973 to 1975, Hill took over as the artistic director of the Theatre Workshop. During this time he staged many plays, including his own adaptations of Alexandre Dumas's *The Count of Monte Cristo* and Bram Stoker's *Dracula*, both in 1974.

Hill proved to have an affinity for themes of horror and the supernatural. In addition to *Dracula* and *The Invisible Man* he penned *The Curse of the Werewolf* (1976), *The Mummy's Tomb* (1981), and *Phantom of the Opera* (1984), two years before Andrew Lloyd Webber's blockbuster opened in the West End. Hill's swashbuckling plays, after *The Count of Monte Cristo*, include *Sinbad the Sailor* (1981) and a musicalization of *Zorro*, which he was working on prior to his death of cancer in 1995. The show went ahead as a tribute to the critically acclaimed playwright and director.

Acting Edition: *The Invisible Man* by Ken Hill—Samuel French, Ltd.; *The Invisible Man* by Tim Kelly—Pioneer Drama Service; *The Invisible Man* by Eddie Cope—I. E. Clark, Inc.; *The Invisible Man* by Craig Sodaro—Eldridge Publishing Company.

Awards and Honors: The Ken Hill Memorial Trust was set up after Hill passed away in 1995 to aid the Theatre Royal Stratford East in supporting new talent in musical theatre. One of the theatre bars inside the Theatre Royal is named "The Ken Hill Bar" as a further tribute.

NOTES

1. Peter Haining, ed., *The H. G. Wells Scrapbook* (London: New English Library, 1978), 60.

2. James Whale (1889–1957), British born, was a cobbler before demonstrating talent for signwriting and enrolling at the Dudley School of Arts and Crafts. During World War I he was taken prisoner, and it is reported that while incarcerated, he continued to embellish his talent in drawing and sketching. After the armistice, Whale embarked on a stage career. His breakthrough came when directing a fringe production of R. C. Sherriff's *Journey's End*, starring a young, unknown

Laurence Olivier. The play transferred to the West End, with Colin Clive taking over the lead role, and ran for 593 performances. Whale also directed the ensuing Broadway production of *Journey's End* (485 performances) and its film version. In Hollywood, Whale left an indelible mark with his horror masterpieces *Franken-stein* (1931), *The Old Dark House* (1932), *The Invisible Man* (1933), and *Bride of Fran-kenstein* (1935). Among his major movies are the original *Waterloo Bridge* (1931), *Show Boat* (1936), *The Great Garrick* (1937), and *The Man in the Iron Mask* (1939). After a debilitating stroke, Whale, openly gay, became lonely and depressed. In 1957, at the age of sixty-seven, he committed suicide by drowning himself in his swimming pool. The film *Gods and Monsters* (1998), starring Ian McKellen, is a fictionalized character study of Whale. London-born William Claude Rains (1889–1967) appeared in West End plays and was a teacher at the Royal Academy of Dramatic Arts (where his best known students were Laurence Olivier and John Gielgud), before emigrating to America and becoming a renowned character ac-tor. His silky, polished voice was a major asset for his "criminal" career in the movies: mad scientist Jack Griffin in *The Invisible Man* (1933); jealous, murderous lawyer Lee Gentry in *Crime without Passion* (1934); villainous uncle John Jasper in *The Mystery of Edwin Drood* (1935); Maximus, a phony music-hall mind-reader in *The Clairvoyant* (1935); malicious Marquis Don Luis in *Anthony Adverse* (1936); power-hungry Earl of Hertford in *The Prince and the Pauper* (1937); Prince John in *The Adventures of Robin Hood* (1938); Don Jose Alvarez de Cordoba in *The Sea Hawk* (1940); corrupt Senator Joseph Harrison Payne in *Mr. Smith Goes to Washington* (1939); the title role in *The Phantom of the Opera* (1943); Alexander Sebastian, mem-ber of a Nazi spy ring, in *Notorious* (1946); sadistic composer Alexander Hollenius in *Deception* (1946); Victor Grandison, a radio personality with blood on his hands in *The Unsuspected* (1947); Arthur Martinage, the Machiavellian director of a South African mining company, in *Rope of Sand* (1949); Frederic Lannington, a sneering spouse who is done away with in *Where Danger Lives* (1950); Skalder, the captain of a Nazi supply ship in *Sealed Cargo* (1951); Kees Popinga, an embezzling clerk, in *The Paris Express*, aka *The Man Who Watched Trains Go By* (1953); an international thief, Aristides Mavros, in *Lisbon* (1956). Rains was nominated four times for a Best Supporting Actor Oscar, notably for the role of Inspector Louis Renault in *Casablanca* (1942), but won none. Detailed information about Claude Rains's ca-reer on stage and in the cinema can be found in *Claude Rains: An Actor's Voice* by David J. Skal (Lexington: University Press of Kentucky, 2008).

3. The acting edition of *The Invisible Man*, published by Samuel French Ltd., carries descriptions of the effects of the illusions but does not attempt to describe the methods of achieving them; some of the tricks involved are closely guarded secrets protected by the Magic Circle and may not be revealed to the general pub-lic. The acting edition provides detailed information about the furniture, props, lighting plot, and soundtrack.

4. *London Times*, October 25, 1991.

5. *Financial Times*, October 29, 1991.

6. *Time Out*, October 30, 1991.

7. *What's On*, October 30, 1991.

8. *Sunday Times*, October 27, 1991.

9. *Observer*, October 27, 1991.

10. *Daily Express*, October 28, 1991.

11. *Evening Standard*, October 24, 1991.

12. *Guardian*, October 29, 1991.

13. A production note explains the phenomenon: Beneath the glove, the actor has on another tight black glove; held up against the dark section of the background, the hand will disappear.

14. Playgoer.blogspot.com, October 11, 2006.

Sweet Revenge (1993)

Francis Durbridge (England, 1912–1998)

During an annual charity regatta, the famous conductor and notorious womanizer Julian Kane is found dead, the victim of a heart attack caused by Zarabell Four, a controversial tranquilizer with potentially lethal side effects.

Kane's host is Dr. Ross Marquand, a successful cardiac consultant. Ross's assistant, Judy Hilton, discovers that two vials of Zarabell Four are missing from their stock. When Inspector Norman Sanders finds out that Ross's much younger wife, Fay, had fallen in love with Kane, all fingers point to Ross. But as the Inspector widens his investigation, he realizes that each one of the regatta guests had a motive for Kane's demise.

Marian Palmer, Fay's best friend, had been Kane's lover, but he soon tired of her, ignored her phone calls, and during a face-to-face confrontation cruelly told her, "I despise your worst qualities, and your best, such as they are, bore me to distraction."

Fay's brother, Alan Wells, a compulsive gambler, had borrowed 18,000 pounds from Kane and had recently received an ultimatum to pay it back—or else.

Bill Yorke, Ross Marquand's old friend, bore an animosity to the victim for leading his twenty-one-year-old fiancée astray. She ultimately broke her engagement, went abroad with Kane, was jilted, and committed suicide.

But it turns out that another good friend of Ross, Sam Kennedy, a hard-working, conscientious general practitioner, fed Julian Kane the fateful drug to punish him for playing around with Liz, his daughter, and persuading her to try heroin. Liz became a drug addict and, given Kane's Don Juan treatment, has been on the verge of killing herself. "Julian Kane was a monster!" says Kennedy to Ross when he confesses that he deliberately gave Kane a drink laced with Zarabell. Ross agrees and decides not to report Kennedy to Inspector Sanders.

* * *

Sweet Revenge premiered at the Thorndike Theatre in Leatherhead, England, on January 12, 1993, directed by Val May and designed by Geoffrey Scott. Movie star Richard Todd portrayed Ross Marquand. The back cover of the play's acting edition includes several laudatory press quotes: "In *Sweet Revenge*, Francis Durbridge has included every element of the classic stage thriller"—*Hull Daily Mail*. "Just the right amount of twist and turn. . . . The packed theatre contained an audience riveted by what was happening"—*West Sussex Times*.

* * *

Francis Henry Durbridge was born in Hull, Yorkshire, England but lived most of his life in London. He was educated at a small private school in the Midlands and at Birmingham University where he studied Economics and English Literature.

Durbridge worked briefly as a stockbroker's clerk before dedicating himself to full-time writing. Called "The king of the British broadcast mystery"[1] by *Encyclopedia Mysteriosa*, Durbridge penned more than thirty radio plays between 1938 and 1968, featuring novelist-detective Paul Temple, arguably the most famous of all BBC radio sleuths. Assisted by his journalist wife Steve, Temple solved crimes in the milieu of the upper middle-class. Simultaneously, beginning in 1938 and for the next four decades, Durbridge published thirty-some novels, many highlighting the cases of Paul Temple, with some focusing on another series hero, Tim Frazer, an undercover man who gets involved in international intrigue.

The indefatigable author contributed to British television a dozen or so serials, all notable for suspenseful cliffhangers, and if that was not enough, added to his name four film scripts[2] and eight stage thrillers.

The Durbridge plays include *Suddenly at Home* (1971), a wheels-within-wheels thriller that relates the scheme of an opportunistic husband to murder his wife with the help of his mistress, whom he in turn betrays with a third woman. *The Gentle Hook* (1974) begins with a career woman killing a man in self-defense, but soon more blood is spilled. In *Murder with Love* (1976), a much-hated womanizer is presumably bludgeoned to death by an irate husband only to reappear alive and well in a tantalizing climax twist. *House Guest* (1976) is the story of a kidnapping, while *Deadly Nightcap* (1983) depicts a greedy husband who plots to kill his wife and make it look like she committed suicide.

In *Touch of Danger* (1987), the mistaken identity of a man found dead in Munich triggers a series of events involving the CID, the CIA, and a terrorist organization. *The Small Hours* (1991) begins with the hijacking of an aircraft and develops into a complex adventure of relentless pursuit and attempted murder.

"Durbridge has no special message, no mission to examine the springs of violence or the motivation which leads a man to murder," says Melvyn Barnes in *Twentieth-Century Crime and Mystery Writers*, "and seemingly no purpose other than to present to his audience one piece of craftsmanship after another. Nevertheless . . . Durbridge's ability as a skillful weaver of webs and a typically British exponent of the guessing-game has maintained his position as one of the most consistently entertaining crime writers."[3]

Acting Edition: Samuel French, Inc.

NOTES

1. William L. DeAndrea, *Encylopedia Mysteriosa* (New York: Prentice Hall, 1994), 104.

2. Francis Durbridge's films are *Send for Paul Temple*, featuring Anthony Hulme (1946); *Calling Paul Temple*, with John Bentley (1948); *Paul Temple's Triumph*, with Bentley (1950); and *Paul Temple Returns*, with Bentley (1952).

3. John M. Reilly, ed., *Twentieth-Century Crime and Mystery Writers* (New York: St. Martin's, 1980), 523.

Murder Is Easy (1993)

Clive Exton (England, 1930–2007)

More than half a century after its publication in 1939, an unheralded novel by Agatha Christie, *Murder Is Easy* (*Easy to Kill*), was adapted to the stage by Clive Exton.

It is the tale of a young former police officer, Luke Fitzwilliam, who has returned to England after years in the Far East. On the train from Dover to London, Fitzwilliam shares a compartment with a talkative "nice old lady," Lavinia Fullerton, who is on her way to report to Scotland Yard her suspicion of foul play in the village of Wychwood. Fullerton babbles about a series of murders committed in this otherwise sleepy village and speculates that the good Dr. Humbleby will be the next victim.

The next day, Fitzwilliam reads in the *Times* that Fullerton has been killed by a hit-and-run driver. It seems a coincidence until several days later the papers announce the unexpected death of Dr. John Ward Humbleby of Wychwood.

Fitzwilliam decides to look into the matter and sets off for Wychwood. He pretends to be researching a book on folklore. While interviewing an array of quirky rural characters, he unearths many possible motives for murder. Honoria Waynflete, a friend of the late Ms. Fullerton, joins Fitzwilliam in his quest to solve the case. Prior to fingering the culprit, Fitzwilliam manages to prevent another homicide and win the heart of Bridget Conway, the village beauty. Agatha Christie's sleight of hand is evident when Honoria Waynflete turns out to be the mad serial killer.

Exton's dramatization premiered at the Duke of York's Theatre in London, on February 23, 1993 and closed April 10. A made-for-television movie was broadcast on CBS *Saturday Night at the Movies* on January 2, 1982, with a cast headed by Bill Bixby (Luke Fitzwilliam), Olivia de Havilland (Honoria Waynflete), and Lesley-Anne Down (Bridget Conway). Helen Hayes had a cameo role as Lavinia Fullerton.

* * *

Born in London, Clive Jack Montague Brooks borrowed his pseudonym Clive Exton from Shakespeare's *Richard II*, dabbled in acting and playwriting, and became a prolific television and film scriptwriter. Several of Exton's early TV scripts were censored and held for years before their broadcast. *The Trial of Dr. Fancy* (1964) tells the story of a doctor shortening the legs of tall men embarrassed by their height. *The Big Fat* (1965) exposes shady practices in the advertising industry. *The Boneyard* (1966) deals with police corruption.

Between 1960 and 1964, Exton wrote eight scripts for ITV's *Armchair Theatre*. He continued his contributions to British television with episodes of *Out of This World*, *Out of the Unknown*, *Survivors*, *Dick Barton—Special Agent*, *Shades of Greene*, and *The Crezz*.

Exton collaborated with famed English playwright Tom Stoppard on the half-hour teleplay *The Boundary*, which aired live on the BBC series *The Eleventh Hour* on July 19, 1975. *The Boundary* was later converted to a one-act play, published by Samuel French, London, in 1991. The teleplay reveals a murder at a lexicographer's library with a touch of comic absurdity. The body of a woman is buried under disorderly piles of paper. It is Brenda, the wife of librarian Johnson and mistress of librarian Bunyans. Was she murdered by one of them? And why is the pane of glass in the French windows broken? What is the connection between the white-flannelled cricketer outside and the hidden corpse inside?

For the silver screen, Exton co-wrote *Isadora* (1968), a study of the dancer Isadora Duncan; *Entertaining Mr. Sloane* (1969), from the play by Joe Orton; *10 Rillington Place* (1970), based on the sensational John Christie-Timothy Evans murder case in 1940's England; *Doomwatch* (1972), depicting the hazardous effects of radioactivity; *Crazy House* (1973), called *Night of the Laughing Dead* in the United States, a horror spoof; *The Awakening* (1980), an Egyptian tomb saga adapted from Bram Stoker's novel *The Jewel of Seven Stars*; and *Red Sonja* (1985), a sword-and-sorcery adventure, inspired by the writings of Robert E. Howard, starring Arnold Schwarzenegger.

After ten years in Hollywood, Exton returned to London and to television. He dramatized the first episode on *The Ruth Rendell Mysteries*, and, during the late 1980s, 1990s, and early 2000s, penned many episodes for London Weekend Television's *Poirot*, including the two-hour *One, Two, Buckle My Shoe*; *Peril at End House*; *The Mysterious Affair at Styles*; *The ABC Murders*; *Hercule Poirot's Christmas*; *The Murder of Roger Ackroyd*; and *Murder in Mesopotamia*. The enormously successful series starred David Suchet in what many believe is the definitive portrayal of the Belgian detective.

Killer Joe (1993)

Tracy Letts (United States, 1965–)

Echoing Sam Shepard's *Buried Child* (1978), Tracy Lett's *Killer Joe* is a gritty, lurid drama about a dysfunctional rural family. Twenty-two-year-old Chris Smith, his twenty-year-old sister Dottie, his thirty-eight-year-old father Ansel, and his early-thirtyish stepmother Sharla live in a trailer on the outskirts of Dallas, Texas. The set is composed of a living room and kitchen. The ceiling is low. The walls are covered with ugly wood paneling. The furnishings are seedy and cheap. Tattered, smoke-stained shades cover the windows. A coffee table is covered with fast-food debris, empty beer cans, and filled ashtrays. Dirty, unmatched cups and utensils are scattered throughout the kitchen. A grimy refrigerator contains little more than beer, Coca-Cola, and a dribble of milk. An intricate antenna made of coat hangers and tin foil tops a monstrous television.

The curtain rises on a stormy night. T-Bone, a neighbor's pit bull with a bad attitude and a long chain, barks ferociously outside. There is a tap on the window and Chris's voice is heard swearing at the dog and demanding that someone open the door and let him in. Sharla, his stepmother, appears from the hallway, wearing only a man's sweat-stained T-shirt. She opens the door and Chris bursts inside. He runs to an off-stage bathroom and we hear urine splash into the toilet. Sharla gets a soda from the fridge, finds a cigarette, and lights it. Chris returns and asks Sharla to put some clothes on.

> SHARLA: Just relax, it's nothin' you haven't seen before, I'm sure.
> CHRIS: Nothin' half of Dallas County hasn't seen before, Sharla.

Ansel Smith, Chris's father, enters from the hallway, wearing only his underwear. Chris grabs a beer from the fridge, rolls a joint, and tells Ansel that his mother, Adele, threw him out—"No, goddamn it, I didn't hit her"—and he needs a place to stay. Sharla objects, insisting that Chris can stay only for the night, and stalks out.

Chris and Ansel pass the joint back and forth as Chris tells his father that he needs six thousand dollars. He can hold "these guys" off with a thousand. Adele stole two and a half ounces of coke from him and sold it, or gave it away, to her goddamn lover, Rex. Now he, Chris, doesn't have the drug he was planning to sell and pay "these guys" back. They're threatening to kill him.

Ansel says that he cannot loan the money to Chris; he never had a thousand dollars in his life. Chris asks his father if he would like to have fifteen thousand dollars. Adele has a fifty-thousand-dollar life insurance policy, he tells his dad, and the sole beneficiary is Dottie. They can hire Joe Cooper, a police detective who has a little business on the side—killing people. He charges twenty thousand but is a professional—"He'll do this right." They'll give him his cut out of the insurance money.

Ansel and Chris figure that after paying Killer Joe, they'll have thirty thousand. Chris projects splitting the money three ways—"you, me, and Dottie"—but Ansel insists that Sharla get a share. Reluctantly, Chris agrees. The two conspirators decide that Sharla and Dottie will never know of the plan.

Dottie appears, wearing a nightgown and robe; she passes them and strolls out the same way she entered. Chris shudders: "That sleep-walkin' gives me the creeps." Dottie reenters, gets a comic book, and says, "I heard y'all talkin' about killin' Momma. I think it's a good idea." She exits.

Two days later, Dottie is alone, exercising in the living room, matching moves with an action sequence from a karate movie that is playing on TV, when the trailer door opens and Killer Joe Cooper enters, wearing a raincoat and cowboy hat. He tells Dottie that he's supposed to meet Chris here at 10:30 and introduces himself as a detective in the Dallas Police Department. Dottie asks whether he has ever drawn his gun and shot anybody. He says yes, many times, "but it doesn't keep me up nights." She asks point-blank, "Are you gonna kill my mother?" and confides that her mother tried to smother her with a pillow when she was "real little."

T-Bone barks outside and Chris and Ansel enter. Both are soaking wet. They send Dottie to her room. Over beers, Joe asks for "particulars" about Adele's whereabouts, her schedule and habits. He warns that if they're caught in this crime, his participation must never be revealed. If they break this rule, they'll be killed. His payment is $25,000, in cash, in advance. Chris explains that they have a problem with the advance for they expect the money to come from his mother's large insurance policy.

Joe turns to leave but stops at the door. He will accept "a retainer," he says. "Call me if she's interested." Joe exits. Chris explains to his father, "We can forget about the whole thing, or we can—give him Dottie." Ansel curses furiously, fusses with the television antenna, and mellows: "Y'know, it might just do her some good."

Wearing a double-breasted suit, a new cowboy hat, and a pair of lizard-skin boots, Killer Joe arrives to court Dottie, carrying a bouquet of spring flowers. She emerges from her bedroom, wearing jeans and a sweatshirt. He gets a beer from the refrigerator and she sets the table for two. As they chat, Dottie tells Joe that she's twenty years old and Chris twenty-two; her dad was sixteen when Chris was born, Momma was fifteen. Joe confides that he has never been married "because women are deceitful, and lying, and manipulative, and vicious, and vituperative, and black-hearted, and evil, and old."

Dottie lights a candle, turns off the lights, and takes a casserole out of the oven. They begin eating and Dottie asks, "How are you gonna kill Momma?" Joe relates that he has assistants—operatives who will take care of it, unless he decides to do it himself. He may be the detective assigned to the case. Joe turns his back to her and asks Dottie to remove her jeans, tennis shoes, socks, bra, and underwear. She does. He unfastens his belt and opens his pants.

Thunder, lightning, and T-Bone's barks open the second act. Chris kicks the front door open and staggers inside. His shirt is soaked with blood. One eye is blackened and blood streams from his nose and mouth. Killer Joe, naked and holding a gun, enters from Dottie's bedroom. He grabs Chris from behind, forces him to the floor, and exits only to reemerge wearing a pair of slacks. Sharla and Ansel run in from the hallway. Dottie, wearing a robe, rushes to Chris. She gently wipes the blood from his face with a dishrag. Chris explains that the "old boys" caught up with him and jumped him in Wild Bill's parking lot. Moaning with pain, Chris asks Joe when he'll be carrying out the murder. "Tomorrow," says Joe. He suggests that Chris make himself scarce the next day.

In the morning, Killer Joe sits at the kitchen table, listening to an evangelist on the radio and fondling a gun. Chris enters hurriedly, his head and hand bandaged, and stammers that he would rather take a chance with Digger Soames, to whom he owes six thousand dollars; let Joe forget the killing scheme and give up Dottie, "who never did nothin' to nobody." Joe tells him that it's too late to change plans and points at a large, overstuffed garbage bag sitting by the kitchen door. Joe asks Chris to help him move the bag to the car.

Wearing mourning clothes, Chris paces nervously in the living room while Dottie watches a Road Runner cartoon on television. Chris tells his sister that he never meant to hurt her and that as soon as Killer Joe gets paid, he intends to go away. With the inheritance money, says Chris, Dottie will finally be able to go to a modeling school. T-Bone barks. Ansel and Sharla enter, wearing mourning attire. They are livid. Confronting Chris, they call him "you little bastard" and "you little son-of-a-bitch." They've just met the lawyer, Kilpatrick, and were told that Dottie is not the beneficiary. Rex, Adele's boyfriend, gets the fifty thousand dollars. Chris is exasperated: it was Rex who told him that Dottie was the sole inheritor, and it was Rex who told him about Killer Joe Cooper. "He played you like an accordion fish," says Ansel.

Ansel and Sharla leave for the funeral. Chris tells Dottie that he'll be leaving for Mexico or Peru, and he wants her to come with him—now, immediately. Dottie insists that she first has to see Joe.

The last scene unfolds later that day and is again punctuated by thunder and lightning. Sharla and Ansel enter, still wearing their funeral clothes. Sharla carries a bucket of fried chicken. Joe emerges from Dottie's bedroom. "She's asleep," he says and the three of them begin to munch on chicken and swig beer. Ansel keeps complaining about Chris's "stupidity" but Joe eventually gets Sharla to confess that she was Rex's lover and coconspirator. Joe reveals that he has already seen Rex and Sharla has lost a boyfriend. Joe grabs Sharla by the throat and takes a cashier's check from her pocket. The check was for $100,000, which Sharla had intended to share with Rex. The check is now worthless, as it was payable to Rex.

Joe punches Sharla squarely in the face. She falls to her knees. He holds a chicken leg in front of his crotch and orders Sharla to suck it. She objects and he slams her head onto the floor. Ansel rockets off the couch, about to attack, but Joe spins to face him and Ansel quickly retreats. Shaking, crying, Sharla takes the end of the chicken leg in her mouth. Joe bobs her head back and forth on the chicken leg. Obviously aroused, he jams the bone further into Sharla's mouth and eventually rams it to its hilt. He groans, gasps, and lets her go. Sharla gags, coughs out the leg, runs to the kitchen sink, and vomits.

T-Bone barks. Chris enters the trailer and Dottie comes out of the bedroom. Joe announces that Dottie has accepted his proposal of marriage. Chris says that he's leaving town, taking his sister with him. Joe reminds him that Dottie is his retainer. A violent, nightmarish scene ensues. Chris draws a gun and aims it at Joe's head. Sharla snatches a knife from the kitchen counter, screams, and buries it in Chris's upper chest. Chris reels and the gun fires, striking the floor. Joe charges Chris, buries his shoulder in Chris's stomach, and drives him into the wall. The gun flips out of Chris's hand. Dottie picks it up. Joe grabs the lamp cord, wraps it around Chris's neck, and heaves. Choked, dazed, Chris has what looks like a seizure. Dottie yells, "Stop it, Joe! Stop it!" However, Ansel falls on Chris's kicking legs, holds them tight under his arm, and Sharla seizes a potato peeler, sticking its blade into Chris's side, one, two, three times.

In a horrific development that would have made Sam Peckinpah proud, Chris flails, kicks Ansel, and backs up suddenly, smashing Joe against the wall. Joe loosens his grip momentarily and Chris elbows him sharply in the ribs. Joe gasps, lets go of the cord, falls to the floor. Chris approaches Dottie, his hand out, and asks for the gun. Ansel grabs him from behind and throws him all the way to the kitchen. Sharla smashes a beer bottle over Chris's head and Ansel shoves him into the refrigerator. Dottie keeps shouting "Stop it!" as Chris flails inside the refrigerator. Shelves and beer tumble out.

Chris tries to struggle out of the refrigerator, but Joe joins Ansel and Sharla, the three of them pummeling Chris, screaming, "Die, die, die!" Dottie fires the gun, striking the radio. Joe, Ansel, and Sharla roll out of the way and Chris pulls himself out of the refrigerator. They all look at Dottie.

She fires, striking Chris squarely in the chest, which rockets him back into the refrigerator. Dottie pivots and shoots Ansel in the stomach. Her father falls to his knees, blood spilling from his mouth. Sharla screams, scrambles behind Ansel, and wraps her arms around him. Joe starts toward Dottie. She turns and points the gun at his head. He advances. She cocks the gun. "I'm gonna have a baby," she says. Joe looks at her, uncertain, then smiles broadly, proudly—"A baby!"

Chris is dead in the refrigerator. Ansel is holding his stomach. Sharla is crying behind him. Joe is smiling. Dottie keeps her finger tensed on the trigger. On this final silhouette, the lights fade out.

* * *

Killer Joe was originally produced by the Next Lab Theatre in Evanston, Illinois, on August 3, 1993, directed by Wilson Milam and designed by Robert G. Smith. The cast consisted of Michael Shannon (Chris Smith), Marc A. Nelson (Ansel Smith), Holly Wantuch (Sharla Smith), Shawna Franks (Dottie Smith), and Paul Dillon (Killer Joe Cooper).

Killer Joe played at Scotland's Edinburgh Festival and London's West End before receiving its New York City premiere on September 29, 1994 at the 29th Street Repertory Theatre, where it ran for five weeks. Wilson Milam reprised his directorial assignment but the cast was replaced with Thomas Wehrle (Chris), Leo Farley (Ansel), Linda Jane Larsen (Sharla), Danna Lyons (Dottie), and David Mogentale (Killer Joe). The reviews were enticing. Clive Barnes coined *Killer Joe* "a play noir" and added: "Its graphic horrors out-grand the old Grand Guignol . . . and if this were a movie it would, with its nudity, rough language and raunchy sex scenes, rate what used to be an 'X' certificate."[1] Wilson Hampton wrote, "One watches the Smiths prey on one another with the same horrid fascination one might have watching a snake devour a rat. *Killer Joe* is not for everyone. Audiences should know there is full nudity, female and male, simulated fellatio, guns, knives and raw language."[2] Vincent Canby praised director Milam for his "authority and invention" and believed that "though *Killer Joe* is not always easy to watch, it is shock theatre of consistent style."[3]

Staged again by Milam, *Killer Joe* was revived at off-Broadway's Soho Playhouse on October 18, 1998, with two cast members of the original 1993 production—Michael Shannon and Marc A. Nelson—and the high-power contributions of Amanda Plummer (Sharla), Sarah Paulson (Dottie), and Scott Glenn (Killer Joe). The show ran for 283 performances. Since then, *Killer Joe* has been performed in at least fifteen countries in twelve languages.

The published acting edition of *Killer Joe* incorporates production notes. In adherence to strict realism, the playwright's instructions include: "No pre-show music. Only static from the TV"; "No 'incidental' or 'atmospheric' music within scenes"; "All music and sound should be sourced"; "Lighting should appear to be sourced"; "Scene changes should be as quick and quiet as possible."

In 2011, Tracy Letts scripted a movie version of *Killer Joe*. It was directed by William Friedkin and featured Matthew McConaughey (Killer Joe Cooper), Emile Hirsch (Chris Smith), Thomas Haden Church (Ansel Smith), Gina Gershon (Sharla Smith), and Juno Temple (Dottie Smith). Two behind-the-scenes characters of the play appear in the film: the victim, Adele, portrayed by Julia Adams, and drug pusher Digger Soames, enacted by Marc Macaulay. The movie was released in June 2012, NC-17.

* * *

Tracy Letts was born in Tulsa, Oklahoma in 1965 to best-selling author Billie Letts and professor-actor Dennis Letts. Letts was raised in Durant, Oklahoma and graduated from Durant High School in the early 1980s. He moved to Dallas, where he was waiting tables while launching his career as an actor in productions staged by Southern Methodist University. Letts moved to Chicago at the age of twenty and in 2002 joined the Steppenwolf Theatre Company where he appeared in *Betrayal*, *The Pillowman*, *The Dresser*, and *Glengarry Glen Ross*; he is still an active member of the company. He was also a founding member of Bang Bang Spontaneous Theatre.

Inspired by the plays of Tennessee Williams, the novels of William Faulkner, and the hard-boiled works of Jim Thompson, Letts wrote his first play, *Killer Joe*, in 1991. His second play, *Bug*, is a psycho-thriller set in a seedy Oklahoma City motel room. It centers on a meeting between Agnes White, a middle-aged divorced waitress with a fondness for cocaine, and Peter Evans, a young, soft-spoken AWOL Gulf War veteran. They become lovers but complications arise when Agnes's physically abusive ex-husband, Jerry Goss, is released from prison and arrives on the scene eagerly expecting to resume their relationship. On top of the triangle dilemma, there's a hidden bug infestation problem that causes scathing welts and festering sores, escalating to paranoia, conspiracy theories, and twisted psychological motives.

Bug received its world premiere at the Gate Theatre in London, opening in September 1996. The play came to off-Broadway's Barrow Street Theatre on February 29, 2004 and won the Lucille Lortel Award for Outstanding Play. Michael Shannon (Academy Award nominee for *Revolutionary Road*) played Peter Evans in both productions as well as in a 2007 motion picture version scripted by Letts and directed by William Friedkin.

Letts's *Man from Nebraska* is the story of Ken Carpenter, a church-going middle-aged man, who awakens one night to find that he no longer believes in God. This crisis of faith propels Carpenter into an extraordinary journey of self-discovery. The play was produced at Steppenwolf in 2003 and was a finalist for the Pulitzer Prize.

The dark comedy *August: Osage County* is a portrait of a dysfunctional American family. When the patriarch of the Weston clan disappears one summer night, the family reunites at the Oklahoma homestead, where three generations' long-held secrets are unflinchingly and uproariously revealed. Not one of the reunion's thirteen characters remains unscathed.

August: Osage County premiered in June 2007 at the Steppenwolf. Subsequently, the play opened at Broadway's Imperial Theatre on December 4, 2007, garnered rave reviews, ran for 648 performances, and won the 2008 Pulitzer Prize for Drama, the Tony Award for Best Play, and the Drama Desk Award for Outstanding Play. *August* also enjoyed sold-out engagements at London's National Theatre and San Diego's Old Globe Theatre.

Letts's follow-up at the Steppenwolf, *Superior Donuts*, was less fortunate. A bittersweet play about the relationship between the white owner of a small donut shop in the uptown neighborhood of Chicago and a black teenager who is his only employee, *Superior Donuts* was transferred to New York's Music Box Theatre on October 1, 2009, received mixed reviews, and lasted for 109 showings at a loss for its investors.

In 2009, Letts was commissioned by Artists Repertory Theatre of Portland, Oregon to modernize Anton Chekhov's masterpiece, *Three Sisters*. Simultaneously he won kudos for his performances in Herman Wouk's *The Caine Mutiny Court-Martial* (at Chicago's Red Orchid Theatre), David Mamet's *American Buffalo* (Princeton's McCarter Theatre Center), Edward Albee's *Who's Afraid of Virginia Woolf?* (Atlanta's Alliance Theatre Company), and Austin Pendleton's *Orson's Shadow* (off-Broadway's Barrow Street Theatre). On television, Letts appeared in *The District* (CBS), *Seinfeld* (NBC), and *Home Improvement* (ABC), among other shows. In the movies, he had supporting roles in *Straight Talk* (1992), *U.S. Marshals* (1998), and *Guinevere* (1999).

Acting Edition: Samuel French, Inc.

Awards and Honors: *Killer Joe*, produced at the Profiles Theatre in Chicago, garnered the 2010 Joseph Jefferson Award (Non-Equity Division). Tracy Letts received the 2005 21st Century Award from the Chicago Public Library Foundation. Letts won the 2008 Pulitzer Prize for Drama and the Tony Award for Best Original Play for *August: Osage County*. He was nominated for a Joseph Jefferson Award as Actor in a Principal Role in a Play for his performances at Chicago's Steppenwolf Theatre Company in *The Dresser* (2005), *American Buffalo* (2010), and *Who's Afraid of Virginia Woolf?* (2011).

NOTES

1. *New York Post*, October 12, 1994.
2. *New York Times*, October 21, 1994.
3. *New York Sunday Times*, October 23, 1994.

Murder in Play (1993)

Simon Brett (England, 1945–)

"In the Charles Paris books I am able to combine two of my major interests, the theatre and crime, together I hope, with a dash of humor," comments Simon Brett in *Twentieth Century Crime and Mystery Writers* about his series of detective stories featuring a sleuth-actor who gets entangled, behind the scenes of play production, in escapades of mayhem, mischief, and murder.[1] Brett blended his double interest into the mystery-comedy *Murder in Play*.

Unfolding during the early 1930s, *Murder in Play* takes place in a shabby-looking box-set representing the library of Priorswell Manor. A prompt book suggests, "The impression of the whole set is that it comes from a cost-conscious repertory production of a stage thriller at almost any time during the last forty years." The lights go up on Triggs, sashaying in a neat housemaid's uniform, serving cocktails to Lady Dorothy Cholmondley, a dowager in her sixties; her daughter, Virginia, an ingénue in evening gown; and Major Rodney Pirbright, about thirty, wearing a military dinner jacket. They are awaiting Mr. Papadopoulos, who is unusually late for his drink. Banter between Lady Dorothy and Major Pirbright suggests that they both look down upon Mr. Papadopoulos, calling him "a bounder," "a cad," "thimble-rigger," and "one who only understands the language of horsewhip."

Suddenly the household cook, Mrs. Puttock, rushes in, agitated, announcing in stage Cockney that the carving knife has gone missing. Mrs. Puttock is on edge because Sergeant Bovis from the village police station called to warn that there's a dangerous escaped prisoner on the loose.

VIRGINIA: An escaped prisoner—oh how ghastly!

RODNEY: Don't worry yourself, my angel. I'll be here to protect you. . . . (He draws a revolver from his trouser pocket.) Well, just let him try any of his little schemes at Priorswell Manor. He'll find that Major Rodney Pirbright is more than ready for him.

VIRGINIA: Oh, Rodney, you are brave.

Through an open French window, Rodney notices movement in the shrubbery. "Take that, you delinquent scum," blurts Rodney as he pulls the trigger. He is clearly surprised that it doesn't fire and pulls the trigger again, and again nothing happens. The Major improvises a line about "a sophisticated silencer," when Mr. Papadopoulos, looking very foreign and wearing an obvious wig, totters in from the garden, gasps feebly "I've been murdered!" and falls forward, face down. The handle of a carving knife protrudes from his back. A voice is heard from the rear of the auditorium, "And . . . curtain. End of Act One." We realize that heretofore, the melodramatic proceedings encompassed a play-within-a play.

With his tongue deep in cheek, Simon Brett relates an insider's view of the backstage machinations of little theatre, where a troupe of up-and-comers and has-beens are dress rehearsing *Murder at Priorswell Manor* under the direction of a non-talented, enormously egotistical, power-hungry director, Boris Smolensky. Lady Dorothy Cholmondley is played by Boris's wife, Renee Savage, "a classically trained actress in her forties" who surprise, surprise tends to get leading roles in many of her husband's productions. Virginia is enacted by Ginette Vincent, "extremely young, extremely pretty, and extremely brainless." Major Rodney Pirbright is played by Tim Fermor, "a slightly petulant, self-obsessed actor in his thirties." The actress performing Mrs. Puttock is Christa d'Amato, in her fifties, who, as she tells everyone within seconds of meeting them, "used to be one of the regular characters in the television soap opera, *Harley's Hotel*." Sophie Lawton, "an intelligent and attractive actress in her late twenties," appears as Triggs. The part of Mr. Papadopoulos is taken by Harrison Bracewell, "in his sixties and an actor of the old school. He has a bit of a drink problem and is not great about memorizing lines." The final component of the production team is Boris's regular stage manager, Pat, who "is not particularly attractive and her permanent uniform of paint-spattered t-shirt, jeans and trainers doesn't add much to her physical charms."

Following the rehearsal, Renee accuses Harrison of upstaging her and admonishes Pat for failing to fill the decanter with sherry—"How the hell am I supposed to act when I haven't even got the right props?" Sophie bemoans attending three years at drama school for the one line, "Yes, milady." Harrison relates that when his good friend Ralph Richardson faced a similar situation in which his stage gun wouldn't go off, "He just moved forward and gave his supposed victim a great kick in the bum. The other actor staggered downstage, clutching his hindquarters and dropped to the ground gasping, 'the boot, the boot was poisoned.'" Boris, the director, cries, "That was terrible! Terrible! You've all forgotten all the notes I gave you!" He then proceeds to lambast Pat for missing props, the gun's mishap, and a cupboard door opening at the wrong moment; rebukes Sophie, "Your Triggs is looking bored"; warns Harrison, "If I find another bottle in your dressing room, you'll be out of this production"; and berates the entire company, "Where's the life? Where's the energy?"

During a break, Pat goes into the cupboard with a toolbox and starts fixing an inside door latch. Tim confides to Sophie bitterly that within the first week of rehearsals "bloody Boris" took his girlfriend Ginette under his wing, "and I was out." Renee confronts Ginette: "I am fully aware of what's going on between you and Boris. . . . I just hope you don't get hurt too much when he drops you. . . . Other women to Boris are like so many Kleenex. He picks them up, he snuffles around in them for a little while, and then he drops them." Ginette insists: "It's different with Boris and me," but Renee retorts, "No, it's not . . . he always comes back to me in the end. No other woman stands the remotest chance with Boris so long as I'm alive." When the dress rehearsal resumes and Mr. Papadopoulos staggers in "knifed," life imitates art as Lady Dorothy, having gulped her glass of sherry, clutches at her throat choking, and slips from the chaise longue onto the floor. The cast members, suddenly out of character, surround her. Renee is dead.

Ginette finds herself accused of poisoning her married rival and is arrested. Adjusting to the new circumstances, Boris shifts Christa from the role of the cook to that of her Lady, Sophie to that of Virginia, and assigns Pat to the part of Mrs. Puttock. "I've never claimed to be able to act. I hate doing it," says the stage manager. The character of Triggs is eliminated. At an opportune moment, Boris corners Sophie and asks her to dinner, "Tonight maybe." Sophie cuts him off: "Boris, I cannot believe I'm hearing this. . . . Less than a week ago your wife was murdered by your mistress, and here you are, coming on to me. . . . Forget it, Boris." Theorizing that Ginette is "too stupid" and "couldn't plan her way out of a paper bag," Sophie and Tim undertake to unearth the guilty party. Since Boris does not project "the traditional image of a bereaved husband," the two amateur sleuths suspect the Russian director.

SOPHIE: You ever been in *Hamlet*, Tim?
TIM: Gave my Rosencrantz once in Chelmsford. Or was it my Guildenstern?
SOPHIE: Reason why I asked was . . . you remember?

> I have heard
> That guilty creatures sitting at a play
> Have by the very cunning of the scene
> Been struck so to the souls that presently
> They have proclaimed their malefactions,
> For murder, though it have no tongue, will speak
> With most miraculous organ.

SOPHIE: Do you get my drift?
TIM: I get your drift, but I don't see how.

SOPHIE: We still haven't had that rewritten scene, have we? If we were to substitute something we'd written specially.

TIM: You think our murderer might rise to a confession?

SOPHIE: Might. . . . "The play's the thing
That will the answer to 'whodunit' bring!"

The *Hamlet* trap succeeds. The rewritten lines in *Murder at Priorswell Manor* yield a confession. It is not Boris who turns out to be the murderer but Pat, the drab stage manager, who, quietly in love with Boris, and having taken all kinds of abuse from him for many years, has at long last gotten rid of his wife by poisoning the backstage decanter of sherry, while ensnaring his latest lover.

Murder in Play was commissioned for the 1993 Cheltenham Festival of Literature and first produced, under the title *Dead Bodies Everywhere*, in the Shaftsbury Hall Theatre, Cheltenham, on October 10, 1993. Chris Haslam, Anthony Lyons, and Kerstin Jarman directed the thriller. The play program listed the cast of *Murder at Priorswell Manor*, in order to suspend the audience's disbelief until the play-within-a-play formula is revealed.

* * *

Born in Worcester Park, Surrey, England in 1945, Simon Anthony Lee Brett was educated at Dulwich College, London, 1956–1964, and at Wadham College, Oxford, where he was president of the Oxford University Dramatic Society, graduating in 1967 with a BA (with honors) in English. Brett served as a radio producer for BBC, London, from 1967 to 1977, and as producer for London Weekend Television from 1977 to 1979. Also in the 1970s, he penned half a dozen plays, produced in London. In the 1980s, Brett wrote radio and television scripts, including an adaptation of his debut novel, *Cast, In Order of Disappearance*, as well as short stories published in *Ellery Queen's Mystery Magazine*.

Returning to the legitimate stage in the 1990s, Brett came up with *Mr. Quigley's Revenge*, commissioned for the Chichester Festival Youth Theatre and premiering on March 17, 1994—a rollicking comedy in which the hub of community life is captured through the activities taking place in Frinsley Village Hall; and *Silhouette*, opening at the Yvonne Amaud Theatre, Guilford, on August 19, 1997—an ingeniously structured whodunit depicting, in act 1, the murder investigation of a famous, pompous actor, with act 2 unfolding *before* the murder, turning plot and characters on their heads. A surprising denouement has Detective Inspector Bruton, the traditional policeman—dour, humorless, a bit slow—revealed as the murderer in cahoots with the victim's wife, an actress who before the final curtain raises her glass to the blood spattered body of her husband and says, "Cheers, Martin. Remember nobody upstages Celia Wallis and gets away with it!"

Commenting about Simon Brett's fifteen Charles Paris books, T. R. Steiner, in *St. James Guide to Crime and Mystery Writers*, asserts that "Brett's representation of contemporary British Boz Arts from the high West End to the desert of television sitcoms and game shows is acid and ceaselessly fascinating. The seedy rehearsal room in London's warehouse district, the desperate artiness of provincial amateur companies, the barracudas of TV production, the compulsory hard-boiled argot of the young, the untiring inventive bitchiness of British theater people. Of this world, Brett has given us a vivid fictional encyclopedia."[2]

Since 1999, Bill Nighy has starred as Charles Paris in a series of BBC Radio dramatizations. The latest is *Murder in the Title*, aired in February 2012.

Brett, a former chair of the British Crime Writers' Association, created another series sleuth, the widow Melita Pargeter, and concocted a few non-series suspense novels, one of which, *A Shock to the System*, he adapted to the screen in 1990. Brett also wrote detective stories for children, several nonfiction works on topics ranging from engraving to ill health, and edited the Faber Books of Parodies, Diaries, and Useful Verse. A Simon Brett manuscript collection is housed at Mugar Memorial Library, Boston University.

Author and critic Jon L. Breen salutes Simon Brett in the magazine *Mystery Scene*: "Among the avenues, side streets, and dark alleys in the crime fiction community, where is Main Street? If it's the pure whodunit, centered on a mysterious crime (usually murder) with a variety of possible suspects and solved by a detective (amateur or professional, brilliant or just persistent), a form that allows for any amount of lively prose, intriguing characters, specialized background, social observation, humor, and at least occasionally fair-play clues, Simon Brett is one of the best merchants currently doing business there."[3]

Acting Edition: Samuel French, Inc.

Awards and Honors: Simon Brett was the recipient of the Writers Guild of Great Britain Radio Award, 1973, the Broadcasting Press Guild Award, 1987, and the Malice Domestic Lifetime Achievement Award, 2012. He is currently president of the prestigious Detection Club in the United Kingdom.

NOTES

1. John M. Reilly, ed., *St. James Guide to Crime and Mystery Writers*, 2nd ed. (New York: St. Martin's, 1985), 103.

2. Jay P. Pederson, ed., *St. James Guide to Crime and Mystery Writers*, 4th ed. (Detroit: St. James Press, 1996), 107.

3. Jon L. Breen, *Mystery Scene* 123 (Winter 2012): 24.

Dracula (1995)

Steven Dietz (United States, 1958–)

Dracula by Steven Dietz is arguably the most faithful—and darkest—stage adaptation derived from Bram Stoker's novel. Unlike other theatrical versions, Dietz sets the vampire tale in 1897 but allows the action to move back and forth through time travel. Dietz captures the aura of the original book in which the saga of Count Dracula unfolds through letters and diaries.

In Dietz's rendition, the setting is composed of numerous environments, among them Lucy's bedroom, Renfield's cell, a guest room at Seward's asylum, and Dracula's castle in Transylvania. Both Mina Murray and her friend Lucy Westenra appear. Mina is Jonathan Harker's fiancée; Lucy loves Dr. Seward. As Mina bemoans Jonathan's lengthy trip abroad, the action shifts to Castle Dracula where two slithering, deadly pale vixens wrap their limbs around the solicitor's legs. Images of a coffin-sized wooden box opening slowly, creakily, and a ship's wheel, weathered, attached to a few battered planks, precede the count's arrival in England.

The proceedings are awash in blood. Drops of red liquid are spilled when Dracula bites Lucy's neck. Van Helsing, the vampire hunter, produces "the ghastly paraphernalia" of a blood transfusion as he swabs Seward's arm with alcohol, inserts a device into his and Lucy's arms, and turns a lever on a small pump. We soon see a long, thin tube go from clear to blood red.

When Mina peruses Harker's journal, a flashback depicts Harker's arrival to Castle Dracula. The host, an old man, "with hair long, gray and wild, a pallid complexion to his face and long, yellowed fingernails," greets the solicitor cordially, offers him an elegant supper, and uncorks a dusty bottle—"A gift from Attila. The Huns were despicable, but they knew their wine."

That night Harker finds himself tied to his bed, surrounded by the pair of harpies, their arms and legs sliding around him erotically. They kiss him on the mouth, all over his body, and hover above his exposed neck with fanged teeth. Dracula appears and growls at them, claiming Harker for himself. To pacify them, he takes a tiny, crying baby from a cloth bag. Harker looks on, horrified, as the women plunge their faces into the bag. Blood soon drips onto Harker's cheeks and chest.

More blood is spilled when madman Renfield swings a curved sword at Seward, nicking his arm. Renfield kneels, licks the liquid from the rapier's blade and murmurs to himself, "The blood is the life . . . the blood is the life . . . the blood is the life." In his cell, Renfield is rewarded by his master with a large rat. Dracula snaps the rat's neck and squeezes it with his hand, forcing a stream of blood to gush towards Renfield's mouth.

Lucy succumbs to the Count's bites and joins his league of the Undead. Soon she is seen wearing a long, tattered white garment, streaked with the fresh blood of victimized children, red drops trickling from the corners of her mouth. When the sun rises, Van Helsing, Harker, and Seward corner Lucy into a coffin. Seward strikes the stake three times, each eliciting a scream and the thrusting of a palm toward the sky. At the end there is a long silence, as blood drips from Seward's hands.

Mina is found in the morning with two pinpoints on her neck. Van Helsing conducts a blood transfusion during which Renfield escapes from his cell and arrives on the scene. Dracula, too, suddenly emerges and snaps Renfield's neck in one quick move, killing him instantly. The count calls Mina "my beautiful flower" and sucks on the end of the blood tube. Mina goes limp. Dracula reveals his fanged teeth and slowly bites her neck. He opens his shirt, slashes a long fingernail across his chest, drawing blood—"Drink. And be mine." Mina looks into his eyes and licks the wound slowly with her tongue. When Seward and Van Helsing rush in, her mouth and face are wet with fresh blood.

In the final sequence of the play, as in Stoker's novel, the vampire hunters travel to Transylvania, "to the lair of the Count." Mina has now joined the fanged vixens. But she is saved when Harker drives a wooden stake into the heart of coffined Dracula and, unsurprisingly, a stream of blood shoots into the air. The ritual of blood continues as Mina plunges a knife into the box and in one long, arched movement, severs Dracula's (unseen) head, then steps back, exhausted, her hand crimson.

* * *

Not for the squeamish, Steven Dietz's *Dracula* was first presented by the Arizona Theatre Company at the Temple of Music and Art in Tucson, with previews commencing on March 25, 1995 and press viewings from

March 31 to April 15. The play was directed by David Goldstein and designed by Bill Forrester. Patrick Page appeared in the title role.

Commemorating the 100th anniversary of the publication of Stoker's novel, the Cleveland Playhouse in Ohio produced Dietz's *Dracula* from September 23 through November 8, 1997. Peter Hackett directed; Seth Kanor portrayed the vampire. According to a press release issued at the opening, "Dietz believes people love to be scared. That's why Dracula's fame has survived all these years. He says, 'We have a desire for the excitement of the dark, sensual and mysterious allure of the unknown.'"[1]

When presented simultaneously in November 2007, two regional productions of *Dracula* garnered contrasting reviews. Covering a performance at San Diego's North Coast Repertory, critic George Weinberg-Harter asserted that "Dietz's script artfully follows Stoker's novel, written to resemble a collection of documents (journals, letters, reports, even transcriptions of recording cylinders), in its fragmented presentation of multiple viewpoints and shifting chronology. A supremely theatrical moment, excellently done in this production, turns the small stage into a sort of three-ring circus, with simultaneous stormy scenes—right, left, and center—of Renfield raving in his cell, Lucy transfixed at her window, and Harker trapped in the Transylvania castle—all of them at once in thrall to that hideous strength of the vampire."[2]

Conversely, reviewer John Garcia lambasted a production of *Dracula* at the Irving Arts Center, Irving, Texas, sniffing at "Dietz's bloated script. The dialogue gets way too flowery and snooty for my tastes. There are endless monologues with so much grandstanding, but never really expressing raw, to-the-core honest emotions. . . . There is also the issue of Dietz going all over the place with scenes popping back and forth, all over London and Transylvania that you beg for a mapquest just to figure out where in the hell you are in the play."[3]

* * *

Born and raised in Denver, Colorado, Steven Dietz graduated in 1980 with a BA in Theatre Arts from the University of Northern Colorado. There he wrote his first one-act play as his senior thesis. Soon thereafter Dietz moved to Minneapolis, where he launched his career as a director of new plays at the Playwrights' Center and other local theatres. He also founded a small theatre company, Quicksilver Stage, and began to write plays of his own. Dietz subsequently directed more than twenty world premieres in such prestigious theatres as the Old Globe in San Diego, California, Actors Theatre of Louisville, Kentucky, the McCarter Theatre in Princeton, New Jersey, and the Kennedy Center in Washington, D.C. A commission from ACT Theatre to write *God's Country*, an account of the Order, a murderous white supremacist movement, brought Dietz to

Seattle, Washington, in 1988, where he lived and worked until 2006. He now divides his time between Seattle and Austin, Texas, where he teaches playwriting and directing at the University of Texas.

Dietz is one of the most prolific American playwrights, yet his plays have not been performed on Broadway but are constantly mounted by little theatre groups across the land.[4] Dietz's plays have been translated into ten languages and have been seen in England, Germany, Austria, France, Sweden, Russia, Japan, Singapore, Thailand, Argentina, Brazil, Peru, and South Africa.

Dietz's thirty-plus plays range from political dramas to domestic comedies to mystery thrillers. In *More Fun Than Bowling* (first produced in St. Paul, Minnesota, 1986), a bowling alley owner reminisces about the ladies in his life. *Foolin' Around with Infinity* (Los Angeles, 1987) takes place in and around a nuclear missile silo located a mile beneath Utah, and reflects on the rising angst of the nuclear age. *Ten November* (Chicago, 1987) is the story of the SS *Edmund Fitzgerald*, which sank on Lake Superior on November 10, 1975, with thirty officers and men aboard. In *After You* (Louisville, Kentucky, 1990), Ben and Amy broke up a year ago. What will it take to get them together again? The background of *Halcyon Days* (Seattle, Washington, 1991) is the 1983 U.S. invasion of Granada while *Trust* (Seattle, 1992) is set against the backdrop of the rock music scene. The protagonists of *Lonely Planet* (Seattle, 1992) are Jody and Carl, two gay men who live in an unnamed American city in the midst of the AIDS epidemic. *The Nina Variations* (Seattle, 1996) presents forty-three variations on a searing scene between the star-crossed lovers Nina, an aspiring actress, and Treplev, a young writer, in Anton Chekhov's *The Seagull*.

Private Eyes (Louisville, Kentucky, 1997), labeled by the author as "a comedy of suspicion," is a play-within-a-play in which nothing is ever quite what it seems. A British director uses his power to seduce a young, beautiful actress to the chagrin of her husband, a member of the company. Or perhaps the affair is part of the play being rehearsed. When the director's wife arrives on the scene, the actress turns out to be just another notch on his belt, and all go their separate ways. The second act retells the events from the beginning, taking several turns and twists. *Still Life with Iris* (Seattle, 1997) is a fantastical adventure unfolding in the magical land of Nocturno, where a lost little girl is searching for her home. *Fiction* (Princeton, New Jersey, 2002) spotlights a seemingly devoted couple, both writers, whose relationship deteriorates into suspicion, deceit, and betrayal. In *Last of the Boys* (Princeton, 2004), Ben and Jeeter, two Vietnam veterans, meet for a last hurrah of reminiscences. Ghosts of the past come flickering to life, and by dawn, the friendship ends. *The Spot* (Louisville, 2004) centers on a political campaign where it's hard to decipher who is telling the truth, who is playing a game, and who is dominating the polls.

Yankee Tavern (Manalapan, Florida, 2009) features an old gin joint in lower Manhattan set to be demolished that is taken over by Adam, a young grad student. Monumental secrets may be brought to light before the walls come down on the tavern. Or will the secrets be buried in the rubble? *Becky's New Car* (Annapolis, Maryland, 2011) is the story of a middle-aged clerk in a car dealership with no prospects for change. Then one night a socially inept and grief-stricken millionaire stumbles in and Becky is offered nothing short of a new life.

In addition to *Dracula*, Dietz adapted to the stage more than ten plays from other sources, including *The Rememberer* (1994), based on the memoirs of Joyce Simmons Cheeka, a young Squaxin Indian girl who was forcibly taken from her home and placed in a government-run school in 1911; *Silence* (1995), from Shusaku Endo's novel; *Force of Nature* (1999), after Goethe's *Elective Affinities*; *Go, Dog, Go* (2003), a musical based on the children's book by P. D. Eastman; *Over the Moon* (2003), from the novel *The Small Bachelor* by P. G. Wodehouse; *Paragon Springs* (2004), inspired by Ibsen's *An Enemy of the People*; and *Sherlock Holmes: The Final Adventure* (2006), based on the play by William Gillette and Arthur Conan Doyle, involving a kidnapped damsel, scandalous letters, London's seamy underworld, and the life-and-death clash between the Great Detective and Professor Moriarty.

Acting Edition: Dramatists Play Service.

Awards and Honors: Steven Dietz received the PEN-USA West Award in Drama for 1992's *Lonely Planet*. He also won the 1995 Yomiuri Shimbun Award (the Japanese "Tony") for his adaptation of Shusaku Endo's novel *Silence*, and the 2007 Edgar Award for Drama from the Mystery Writers of America for *Sherlock Holmes: The Final Adventure*. Dietz is a two-time winner of the Kennedy Center Fund for New American Plays (for *Still Life with Iris*, 1997, and *Fiction*, 2003), as well as a two-time finalist for the Steinberg New Play Award (for 2004's *Last of the Boys* and 2008's *Becky's New Car*), given by the American Theatre Critics Association. Dietz is most recently the 2011–2012 recipient of the Ingram New Works Fellowship from Tennessee Repertory Theatre.

NOTES

1. In conjunction with its production of *Dracula*, the Cleveland Playhouse hosted a lecture-visit by Leonard Wolf, a New York University professor "whose hobby has been to examine the various interpretations of the immortal vampire in literature, film and theatre, plus showing how a sadistic creature who feeds on blood worked his way into mainstream culture." The Art Gallery at the Playhouse exhibited vintage movie memorabilia, displaying images of Dracula from Bela Lugosi, Christopher Lee, Frank Langella, Andy Warhol, Francis Ford Coppola,

and more. Sponsored by the Red Cross, A Very Scary Blood Drive was held at the Playhouse, with donors receiving "two for one tickets to any available performance of *Dracula*."

2. http://local.sandiego.com/arts/dracula-at-north-coast-repertory, November 3, 2007.

3. http://pegasusnews.com/news/2007/nov/07/theater-review-dracula, November 7, 2007.

4. Other playwrights who share the same fate include Tim Kelly, James Reach, Wilbur Braun, Jack Sharkey, Jules Tasca, Don Nigro, Fred Carmichael, Wall Spence, and F. Andrew Leslie.

True Crimes (1995)

Romulus Linney (United States, 1930–2011)

Leo Tolstoy (1828–1910) used a real-life incident that occurred in Tula, Russia in the 19th century in his five-act drama *The Power of Darkness*. Tolstoy wrote the play in 1886 but it was banned because of its raw realism and a harrowing scene in which the head of a newborn baby is crushed with a wooden board. The central character, the peasant Nikita, impregnates his stepdaughter, then, under his wife's influence, murders the baby. With pangs of conscience, Nikita surrenders to the police and confesses his crime.

The great Russian director Constantine Stanislavski wanted to stage *The Power of Darkness* in 1895, but the production did not materialize. He eventually directed it for his Moscow Art Theatre in 1902. The actor Jacob Adler produced the play in New York in 1904 with his own Yiddish translation. In 1923, famed director Erwin Piscator presented *The Power of Darkness* in Berlin.

The American playwright Romulus Linney was inspired by Tolstoy's drama when penning his 1995 play, *True Crimes*. Linney shifted the proceedings to the Appalachian Mountains of 1900.

The setting reveals the porch of Soony Sparks's mountain house, surrounded by a sizable yard with a split-rail fence. On the porch are a rocking chair, two old slat chairs, and a chest holding whiskey and glasses. Behind the platform is a wall of shabby homemade quilts through which characters enter and exit from the inner rooms.

The curtain rises on Logan Lovel, a cocky, lazy youth, sitting in one of the chairs, perusing a copy of a penny dreadful pamphlet, *True Crimes*. He soon relates to Jennie Notree, his mistress, the contents of a story about a woman who is raped. A tramp is arrested for the crime, a judge instructs the jury to find him guilty, and the tramp is hanged. Years later, it turns out that the tramp was innocent; the judge's own son raped the woman.

Jennie rebukes Logan for devouring tales of violence, but Logan insists that by reading books he is grooming himself to become a lawyer or a judge. "I could be a detective at least," he says, "or a sheriff or something!" Their conversation turns into a lover's quarrel, with Logan questioning Jennie's relationship with the elderly farmer Anson Tate. Jennie then accuses Logan of a tryst with Mary Sparks, the wife of the estate owner. "Just take care what married woman you play with, hear? Husbands have shotguns," declares Jennie as she stalks out.

A sprightly music cue and change of light indicate passage of time. Logan enthusiastically describes another *True Crimes* story, this time to Mary Sparks. But Mary is hardly listening. With plain lust, she suddenly jumps on Logan. They grind passionately, hastily undoing buttons on each other's clothes.

Enter Vangey Lovel and Ab Lovel, Logan's parents. They stroll up to the writhing couple and stand by, smiling. Mary jumps up, turns away, and buttons up her dress. Soon Vangey, Ab, Logan, and Mary sit on a quilt in a sort of conference. Vangey brings up the topic of Mary's husband, Soony Sparks, who, says Vangey, "is sick fixing to die." With Sawdust, a migrant farmhand, being the only working man on the Sparks's property, Vangey suggests that there's a need for "another man around the place."

Soony Sparks, a man in his sixties, enters through the wall of quilts and sits in the rocking chair. Mary brings in a bowl of spoon bread. Nancy Sparks, Soony's feeble-minded young daughter from an earlier marriage, appears from the garden, followed by Sawdust, a weather-beaten farmhand, seemingly a simpleton. Mary and Nancy open the chest and produce cups and whiskey. All drink.

Soony has a sudden, terrible coughing fit. Vangey suggests that "herb doctoring might help." She holds out a folded kerchief, revealing what she calls "cherry bark bitters, ground up in some freshness." She puts some in Soony's whisky.

Vangey and Ab ask Soony to let their son Logan cultivate "that gulch land around Foster's Creek." He'll work for Soony without pay, just room and board; he can sleep in the barn loft. Soony agrees and Vangey exclaims, "Let's drink to it!" Brisk music. A change of light indicates that time is passing.

Logan sits on the edge of the porch reading his *True Crimes* pamphlet. Enter Sawdust, working on a lock. Logan relates the contents of the story he reads: Lumberjack Jakes chops a harlot with an axe. Then he cuts her in two, a breast on each side. When arrested and brought to trial, his lawyer claims that Lumberjack is a son-a-bu-list, and has committed the crime in his sleep. The jury considers that carefully, before they hang him. Sawdust shivers and mumbles, "At there is violence, I don't care for it."

Exit Sawdust. Exit Logan. Enter Mary, pacing back and forth. Vangey appears and Mary runs to her. "Trouble," she says. Soony knows of her liaison with Logan and has sent for his sister. The fool Nancy must have inadvertently told him. Vangey asks where Soony keeps his money. In a lock box, answers Mary, nearly $6,000. He also keeps the farm titles and abstracts there. He will surely give it all to his sister.

Yes, agrees Vangey. Mary will lose everything—the money goes to Soony's sister, the farm to "that half-wit daughter," unless . . . Vangey holds out a folded kerchief and exposes cherry bark bitters.

MARY: Won't it hurt him? Won't he yell and scream?
VANGEY: He'll sleep first. Then he'll get cold, but wake up too late. All there is to it.

Mary takes the kerchief. Vangey calls Soony to come out. He enters slowly, sits in his chair, and pulls the quilt around him. Vangey goes off. Mary and Soony stare at each other. He coughs. She gets him whisky in a cup and sets it on a table next to him. She offers Soony "them cherry bark bitters you like." He dumps the deadly powder into his whiskey, stirs it with a finger, and gulps it all. He soon breathes deeply, in relief, and closes his eyes, falling asleep.

Music. Change of light. Time passes. Logan sits in Soony's chair, draws the quilt up comfortably around his knees, and reads another *True Crimes* book. Enter Sawdust. Logan informs the farmhand that he and Mary Sparks will be married next week. "She's a healthy woman. He was a sick man for a long time," says Logan. Sawdust states that he'll willingly accept Logan as his new boss. Logan consents to keep him on.

Music. Change of light. Nancy takes off her overalls, stands naked, and from a cardboard box, takes a flour sack dress and slowly puts it on. Logan is watching. She sits with Logan and he lays the quilt over both their knees. He reads aloud from *True Crimes* the story of Lydia Sherman, the Arsenic Fiend, who poisoned her three husbands—a carpenter ("arsenic in his oatmeal"), a dentist ("arsenic in the baking soda"), and a banker ("arsenic in his Brandy Slings").

Music. Change of light. Mary, grim, confronts Nancy, who is obviously pregnant. Nancy insists, "I want this baby!" Mary suggests that they claim Sawdust as the father, but Nancy shrugs, "Who'd believe you?" Vangey and Ab join the conversation. They remark that a neighbor, Bob Stoneman, will be willing to marry Nancy if given a considerable settlement—twenty-five acres. Mary expresses doubt, "Who'll take a wife with another man's baby in her?" Vangey proposes to be the midwife and suggests that the child be given to an orphanage. Nancy objects, "Babies die there."

Slow music. Time passes. Moonlight. From behind the wall quilts Nancy's labor screams are heard. On the porch, Sawdust and Logan share a jar of whiskey. Enter Ab, carrying a large shovel. He puts it at Logan's feet. Mary appears from the house and says, "The baby's born." She turns to Logan, "Take the shovel and dig the hole." Logan walks away: "It's a living soul." Vangey enters and states, "No, it ain't. Born dead."

Mary exits momentarily and returns carrying the newborn baby, wrapped in rags. "Was it a boy or a girl?" asks Logan. "Girl," answers Mary. Vangey takes the baby from Mary and shoves it into Logan's arms. Logan objects. Vangey, Ab, and Mary surround Logan and cajole him to bury the baby in the barn, under the pens. Logan starts off, baby in one arm, shovel under another. Suddenly, he exclaims, "Jesus God, she's moving! She's alive!" He sets the baby down on the edge of the porch.

The wily Vangey and Ab press Logan to kill the baby. Otherwise, they claim, they will remain "dire poor" all their lives. Logan howls, and brings the hilt of the shovel smashing down on the baby three savage times.

After a long, deadly pause, Logan whispers, "I heard her bones crack." Vangey gives him the covered baby, and Ab pushes him off. "Dig," says Mary.

The lights change. It is windy. Nancy, wrapped in the quilt, sits in the rocking chair, sipping tea. Vangey, Mary, and Logan stand by her. She tells them, stonily, that she consents to marry Fred Stoneman. Enter Sawdust, carrying a thick walking stick, and surprisingly proves to be a sly blackmailer. He announces that he is aware of the killing of the baby. He can tell the Stonemans to dig up the barn. When Ab takes a threatening step toward him, Sawdust pulls from its sheath a danger-ous-looking knife. Vangey slaps a brown envelope into Sawdust's hand and says, "You'll never see that much money in one place." Sawdust glances at the packet, sticks his knife into the porch, and makes clear that he's not content with the $500 offered. He knows that Soony kept "ten times this" off a string around his throat. Mary and Ab exit to get more money and soon return with a leather bag. Sawdust opens it, looks in, and saunters away.

In the last scene, the family awaits the Stonemans' arrival. Logan sud-denly declares that he intends to confess "and hang, like a man." Vangey calmly says, "That is a fine sentiment," helps Logan with his coat, and asks that he join the reception line of the family as they welcome the visi-tors. For a suspenseful moment, Logan wavers. He stares at Nancy, Mary, Vangey, and Ab. Will he leave and go to the police? After a pregnant pause, he takes his place among them. They freeze for a final tableau as the lights fade.

Thus, while Tolstoy's Nikita yields to pangs of conscience, confesses to the horrible crime, and seeks God's forgiveness, Linney's Logan has no redemption and leaves the audience with a sense of dread and foreboding.

* * *

Romulus Linney directed his own play when *True Crimes* opened on December 31, 1995 at off-Broadway's Theatre for the New City. The play ran without an intermission. Greg Evans, *Variety*'s critic, wrote, "Best described as an amorality play, Romulus Linney's *True Crimes* details the seduction of a dimwitted youth into an act of violent, vicious crime, . . . *True Crimes* certainly intrigues with its down-home depiction of spiraling evil."[1] Vincent Canby of the *New York Times* stated: "Romulus Linney may be the only dramatist today who can write about those rural Americans of the Southeast, sometimes called hillbillies, without turning them into either caricatures or picturesque mementos from another time and place."[2] John Istel of the *Village Voice* admired Christine Parks in the role of Vangey Lovel: "She plays the herbalist Lady Macbeth with a slow dangerous smile that communicates more about what evil really looks like than anything that Linney has written in the text."[3] Otis L. Guernsey Jr., editor of *The Best Plays of 1995–1996*, coined the play "a gnarled Gothic country tale about evil—greed, revenge, and murder. . . . The characters are unsavory, the writing assured and the acting earthily in tune with the subject."[4]

* * *

Romulus Zachariah Linney (called "Rom" by his friends) was born in Philadelphia, Pennsylvania in 1930. He was raised in Boone, North Carolina and Madison, Tennessee. When his father, a doctor, died in 1943, young Romulus moved with his mother to Washington.

Linney earned a BA from Oberlin College and an MFA in directing in 1958 at the Yale School of Drama. In between he spent two years in the army, stationed in Japan. He began his career writing two novels in the early 1960s but soon shifted gears to his true calling, penning plays. He wrote more than thirty dramas and comedies, many of them one-acts, wide-ranging in theme, content, and style. In addition to *True Crimes*, Linney's better known works include *The Sorrows of Frederick*, first performed at the Mark Taper Forum, Los Angeles, California in 1966, the story of Frederick the Great, the eighteenth-century King of Prussia, who, aged 73, leaves the battlefield to go home to bury his dog. Riding home, the king meditates on forsaking his love for music, poetry, and philosophy to pursue the military tradition of his family. *The Love Suicide at Schofield Barracks* depicts a ritual double suicide committed unexpectedly by an army general and his wife. A succession of witnesses testify at an official court of inquiry, and step by step a remarkable and compassionate portrait of the dead couple emerges. The suicide is finally revealed as an act of self-sacrifice in opposition to the horrors of war. Incubated by the Herbert Berghof Playwrights' Foundation in April 1971, and the only play by Linney to be produced on Broadway, *The Love Suicide at Schofield Barracks* came to the ANTA Theatre on February 9, 1972, fared poorly, and closed after five performances.

Childe Byron imagines a confrontation between Lord Byron and Ada, the Countess of Lovelace, who was the poet's estranged and only legitimate daughter. In sharp, sarcastic exchanges, the life and art of Byron unfold: his tempestuous youth; his incestuous relationship with his sister; his homosexual escapades; the scandal surrounding his brief marriage; and his castigation by the society of his day. *Childe Byron* was first produced by the Virginia Museum Theatre, Richmond, Virginia in February 1977, with Lindsay Crouse as the countess and William Hurt as the poet.

The Death of King Philip, presented at Boston's New England Chamber Opera in 1979, is set in Colonial America and tells the story of Mary Rowlandson, who is abducted with her baby during an Indian uprising that left many New England settlements in ruin. Mary's minister husband, Joseph Rowlandson, and other settlers relentlessly pursue the Indian leader, King Philip. After a series of savage acts committed by both sides, King Philip accepts the inevitable, lays down his arms and surrenders to his fate. But there is no victory here, says the playwright, only the sowing of the seeds of white racism that will bear bitter fruit in succeeding generations.

Another play depicting a clash of cultures is *El Hermano,* a one-act that debuted by off-Broadway's Ensemble Studio Theatre in 1981. In a seedy bar in 1954 San Francisco, two soldiers, looking for a good time before being shipped overseas, try to ingratiate themselves with two attractive Hispanic women. When the girls' brother attempts to explain that his sisters are ladies of good breeding, the GIs are convinced that he is their pimp, haggling over price. Tensions rise.

Hermann Goering, Hitler's second-in-command, is the main character in 2, a courtroom drama unfolding during the Nuremberg war crimes trials of 1945–1946. "Linney lets Goering examine Nazi prejudices and compare them with those existing in every country," said Otis L. Guernsey Jr. "2 forces us to study ourselves more deeply."[5] 2 was commissioned and first produced by the Actors Theatre of Louisville, Kentucky on March 8, 1990. It was cited by American Theatre Critics among the Outstanding New Plays of 1989–1990.

Two other courtroom dramas penned by Linney are *Mock Trial,* presented by off-Broadway's Theatre for the New City in 1988, in which law students simulate the People's Court of Montana in the case of a patriotic American named John Adams Jones being tried for treason;

and *A Lesson before Dying*, premiering at off-Broadway's Signature Theatre in 2000. Adapted from Ernest J. Gaines's celebrated novel, it is the story of Jefferson, an innocent young man who is condemned to death in backwoods Louisiana in 1948. At the trial, his lawyer, trying to save his life, called him no more a human being than a hog. In prison, he acts like one, insisting that he will be dragged like a hog to his death in the electric chair. Jefferson's godmother asks a schoolteacher to teach him to die like a man.

In addition to *True Crimes*, Linney set many of his plays in the rural South of his childhood, including *Holy Ghosts* (1971), *Appalachia Sounding* (1975), *Tennessee* (1979), *Laughing Stock* (1984), *Heathen Valley* (1986), *Sand Mountain* (1986), *Unchanging Love* (1991), *Gint* (1998), and *Love Drunk* (2009).

The tireless Linney adapted, updated, and relocated Henrik Ibsen's dramas *Ghosts* (1988) and *Peer Gynt* (1999); Anton Chekhov's short story "In the Ravine" to the play *Unchanging Love* aka *Precious Memories* (1991); Matthew Lewis's eighteenth-century Gothic novel *The Monk* to the play *Ambrosio* (1992); Willa Cather's novel *Lark* (2002); Charles Dickens's fable *A Christmas Carol* (1997); and August Strindberg's dramas *Miss Julia* and *The Ghost Sonata* (2010). He also wrote plays about Oscar Wilde, Delmore Schwartz, and the poet Anna Akhmatova.

Off-Broadway's prestigious Signature Theatre Company, which devotes full seasons to presenting the work of a single playwright, in 1991 chose Linney to be the first writer it would spotlight.

Linney was a member of off-Broadway's Ensemble Studio Theatre, chair of the MFA playwriting program at Columbia University's School of the Arts, and Professor of Playwriting in the Actors Studio MFA program at the New School in New York City. He also taught writing at Princeton University, the University of Pennsylvania, Hunter College, and Brooklyn College. "But commercial success eluded him," laments Jacob Gallagher-Ross, a DFA student, in the 2011–2012 *Alumni Magazine of Yale School of Drama*. "He never had a Broadway hit or a West End success. . . . The playwright was simply too uncompromising to bend his vision to suit the demands of the marketplace. . . . Romulus remained true to his own, more stringent, criteria: reaching across chasms between myth and reality, past and present, and the more concrete divisions between stage and auditorium or teacher and student, always aiming for that elusive point of intersection."[6]

Linney died of lung cancer on January 15, 2011 at his home in Germantown, New York. He was married three times and was the father of actress Laura Linney.

Acting Edition: Dramatists Play Service.

Awards and Honors: Romulus Linney was the recipient of two Obie Awards, one for Sustained Excellence in Playwriting; two National

Critics Awards; three Drama-Logue Awards; and many fellowships, including grants from the Guggenheim and Rockefeller Foundations. He was a member of the American Academy of Arts and Letters, which gave him its Award in Literature and the Gold Medal for Drama. In February 2012, Off-Broadway's Signature Theatre Company named a 199-seat performance space the Romulus Linney Courtyard Theatre on West 42nd Street in Manhattan.

NOTES

1. *Variety*, January 15, 1996.
2. *New York Times*, January 1, 1996.
3. *Village Voice*, January 16, 1996.
4. Otis L. Guernsey Jr., ed., *The Best Plays of 1995–1996* (New York: Dodd, Mead, 1996), 363.
5. Otis L. Guernsey Jr., ed., *The Best Plays of 1989–1990* (New York: Dodd, Mead, 1990), 485.
6. *Annual Magazine of Yale School of Drama, 2011–2012,* 51.

The Turn of the Screw (1996)

Jeffrey Hatcher (United States, 1958–)

Over the years there have been many attempts to dramatize Henry James's 1898 horror novella *The Turn of the Screw*, including a short-lived play by Allan Turpin performed in London in 1946, and an ill-fated effort to make it into a film by Mel Dinelli. An adaptation by singer-dancer William Archibald, who undertook the task through eight complete revisions, became the first to reach the New York stage under the title *The Innocents*.

The Innocents, staged by Peter Glenville and designed by Jo Mielziner, opened at Broadway's Playhouse on February 1, 1950 to mostly ecstatic reviews. The play ran for 141 performances and subsequently chilled the spines of West End critics when it opened at London's Majesty's Theatre on July 3, 1952. An MFA thesis production of *The Innocents* was performed at the Yale University School of Drama in 1958. The following year, on April 20, 1959, the play was revived for thirty-two performances at off-Broadway's Gramercy Arts Theatre. *The Innocents* was incarnated at Broadway's Morosco Theatre on October 1, 1976, directed by Harold Pinter. A quarter of a century after the initial production, the critics now declared the play "A haunting drama which doesn't haunt" (Leonard Probt),[1] "A pedestrian stage adaptation of a great novel" (Clive Barnes),[2] and "A ghost of a play" (Jack Kroll).[3] The show had to throw in the towel after twelve performances.

William Archibald, Truman Capote, and John Mortimer scripted an affecting motion picture version of *The Innocents* in 1961, moving from the confinement of a Victorian living room to the surrounding Gothic garden. In 1982, a dramatization by Ken Whitmore was first presented at the Coliseum Theatre, Oldham, England. Rusty Lemorande adapted and directed a lackluster 1992 British-French film version. In 1954, Benjamin Britten composed *The Turn of the Screw*, one of his finest operas.

Still titillated by the Henry James story, Jeffrey Hatcher penned a new theatrical rendition in 1996. Unlike previous adaptations, Hatcher's tells the dark, brooding tale on a spare set, in which one Victorian chair is placed in a void of shadows, and two actors—The Man, British, thirties to early fifties, who plays many male and female characters, and The Woman, who portrays the Governess (her name, Miss Giddens, is not mentioned in this adaptation).

The lights come up on The Man sitting in a chair and, as a nameless Narrator, presumably Henry James himself, introduces "a very agreeable, very worthy" governess who will tell the audience "a story of terror . . . and horror . . . and death."

The Governess steps forward and relates how, in 1872, as a twenty-year-old daughter of a poor country parson, she came to London to answer a job advertisement, and met with a gentleman "of great wealth and stature" at his "imposing house" on Harley Street. The Man, now playing The Uncle, interviews the girl and tells her that several years ago his brother and his wife died and he became the guardian of their two "delightful" children, eight-year-old Flora and twelve-year-old Miles. He is a bachelor, says the Uncle, and has no experience with children; his business affairs take up all his time so he needs a governess who will take "supreme authority" of Miles and Flora and never bother him with complaints, appeals, or anything.

The Governess continues her story and reports that the next morning, with her "heart beating with expectations," she boarded a coach on the road to Essex. She spent long hours in the "bumping, swinging coach" and finally arrived at a house called Bly, a sumptuous mansion surrounded by "a great lawn" and "a sparkling blue lake." A striking feature was a looming Gothic tower over which "rooks circled and cawed in the golden sky."

The Man moves to meet her, a hand at his side as if he is clutching a small child. He introduces himself as Mrs. Grose, the housekeeper. The Governess kneels, faces the unseen child, and expresses her joy at meeting Flora: "You are an angel. . . . Such a pretty frock and such a beautiful locket around your neck! Oh, we shall be *such* good friends, Flora."

Mrs. Grose explains that Flora doesn't speak, presumably because she is shy. The Governess, elated by the beautiful surroundings and delighted to meet such a pretty girl, babbles cheerfully that "silence is a virtue" and asks Flora to guide her through the garden. When they return, Mrs. Grose hands her a letter. The Governess reads that Miles has been dismissed from school for "behaviors of a nature injurious to the other children" and that he's on his way back to Bly.

The Man becomes the boy Miles, who, upon arrival, proves to be very polite and well mannered. He surprises the Governess by playing at the piano Saint-Saens's "Introduction Et Marche Royale Du Lion." Suddenly, Miles changes the music to Saint Saens's "Danse Macabre."

The Governess gazes for a moment at the rain-streaked panes of the nursery's window and sees a face. "He is staring at the fingers on the keys," narrates the Governess. "He has not come for me. He has come for someone else. *Miles!*"

The Man/Miles stops playing. The Governess sends the children to bed and asks Mrs. Grose if she has seen a redheaded man who has "a pale face, long, good features, and rather queer whiskers." Mrs. Grose recognizes the description as that of Peter Quint, the master's former valet, who had great power over Miles. When the master left, Quint remained the boy's tutor and had a cryptic hold of him. Miss Jessel, the former governess, also fell under Quint's spell. "She and Quint, they *did* things," says Grose in disdain.

Concerned, the Governess declares that in the morning they'll scour the grounds and send the trespasser packing. Better still, they'll call the constable and have Quint in irons. But, says Mrs. Grose, Peter Quint is dead! The housekeeper relates to the astounded Governess that at some point during Quint and Jessel's "infamous" relationship, the house "was filled with Jessel's weeping." She drowned herself in the lake when she became pregnant by the sadistic valet. They found her Bible floating in the reeds. And when she drowned, recounts Mrs. Grose, something happened to Quint: he abandoned Miles and Flora, got drunk every night, and then one winter night he dressed in his master's silks and went off from the house. He was found at the bottom of the tower, not a stone's throw from the lake. His head was split in two from the fall.

The Governess braces herself to encounter Quint's ghost face to face. She tells Mrs. Grose that she knows how to stop the "villain" Quint for good. She holds Flora's locket up and declares, "This is what we are fighting for, Mrs. Grose. Innocence. Beautiful, untouched innocence."

The two women realize that Flora is not in the house. They rush to the lake and are startled by the image of Jessel on the opposite side of the bank. They see Flora standing in an old rowboat, plucking at the mooring rope. "We watch as the knot unfurls and the coil snakes around her feet," shudders the Governess, "and the boat slides off across the dark waters." She continues to relate how Mrs. Grose pitched into the lake, tearing against the reeds, managing to get hold of Flora and bring her back to shore.

The Governess sends Mrs. Grose and Flora by carriage to the home of the girl's uncle. She is determined to exorcise Miles from Quint's demonic spell and believes that the boy can be saved if he divulges his relationship with the valet. The Governess pounces on Miles and forces a confession from him. In short order he admits that he conspired to deliver his sister into the hands of the *creatures*. The Governess climaxes her attack by demanding that he name his "villainous tutor." Miles shrieks, "Help!" but eventually yields to the Governess's relentless interrogation and whispers, "Peter Quint." He collapses to the floor. The Governess cradles him in her arms and begins to hum a lullaby. After the song is finished, she kisses Miles' lips and announces sadly, "his little heart—dispossessed—stopped." The lights fade out momentarily, leaving unresolved the question of whether the ghosts were literal or figments of the mind.

The lights rise on The Man now seated in the chair, as at the start of the play. He looks out front and informs the audience that Mrs. Grose died within the year, little Flora was sent to a madhouse, and the Governess moved on, taking care of children, from one house to another, "like a Flying Dutchman, an ancient mariner upon the sea."

* * *

Jeffrey Hatcher's adaptation of *The Turn of the Screw* was developed in workshops at the Portland Stage Company for its 6th Annual Little Festival of the Unexpected. The play premiered officially on January 11, 1996. It was directed by Greg Leaming, with set and costume designs by Judy Gailen. Joey L. Golden played The Man, and Susan Appel The Woman.

The published text of the play is preceded by author's notes in which Hatcher reports that when Greg Leaming, the artistic director of Portland Stage Company, commissioned him to dramatize *The Turn of the Screw*, they had three specific goals in mind: first, to create a dramatic piece that was true to the essence of Henry James's story and themes; second, to preserve the ambiguity of the story's point of view; and third, to provide an opportunity for two bravura performances. "Our goal was to create something rich and theatrical out of something spare and austere, so that by play's end, when the Governess and her demons battle to the death, the audience could be awed not only by what we had done, but what they had imagined."[4]

Hatcher's *The Turn of the Screw* made the rounds of regional theatres. Stage West of Springfield, Massachusetts booked the Portland production on February 10, 1996. Off-Broadway's Primary Stages, a company dedicated to new American plays by new American playwrights, produced *The Turn of the Screw* on March 24, 1999 under the direction of Melia Bensussen, featuring Rocco Sito and Enid Graham.

The back cover of the play's acting edition quotes two review blurbs: "It is both wonderful and terrifying. . . . Hatcher, as he sculpts James' fiction for the stage, provides a multi-faceted penetrating drama. . . . *The Turn of the Screw* is a suggesting, haunting piece"—*Springfield Union-News*. "In his thoughtful adaptation of Henry James' spooky tale, Jeffrey Hatcher does away with the supernatural flummery, exchanging the story's balanced ambiguities about the nature of reality for a portrait of psychological vampirism."—*Boston Globe*.

* * *

Jeffrey Hatcher spent his youth in Steubenville, Ohio, which is, according to Wikipedia, "a gritty Ohio River town better known for its mob connections, houses of ill repute and industrial detritus than for its literary sons and daughters."[5] Hatcher participated in high school dramatics, attended Denison University in Granville, Ohio, migrated to New York City, and ultimately settled in Minneapolis, Minnesota. He yearned initially to become an actor, but since 1987 has sought fulfillment as an author. He continues to draw on his home turf for inspiration.

Hatcher's sole contribution to Broadway is the book for the musical comedy *Never Gonna Dance*, which opened at the Broadhurst Theatre on December 4, 2003 and ran for eighty-four performances. It is based on the 1936 classic Fred Astaire-Ginger Rogers film *Swing Time*. A prolific playwright, Hatcher's more than forty thrillers, comedies, and dramas have been performed off-Broadway and regionally across the United States.

Elements of crime are interwoven in many of Hatcher's plays. *Scotland Road* (originally produced by Cincinnati Playhouse in the Park, 1993), was inspired by a tabloid story about a Titanic survivor found alive on an iceberg in 1990. The proceedings take place in a sanitarium, where a compassionate doctor and her malicious employer interrogate a woman found adrift at sea. She is dressed in turn-of-the-twentieth-century garb. Apparently in her twenties, she utters only one word: "Titanic." Her interrogators are determined to crack the woman's story, get her to confess that she's a fake, and reveal her true identity. By the play's end, all three characters' identities have been questioned and unexpected secrets are revealed.

Three Viewings (developed by Illusion Theater in Minneapolis, Minnesota, 1994, and subsequently produced by off-Broadway's Manhattan Theatre Club, 1995), presents several monologues set in a Midwestern funeral parlor. "Tell-Tale" depicts a mild-mannered undertaker whose unspoken passion for a local real estate woman leads him to commit crimes. "The Thief of Tears" is the story of a beautiful Los Angeles drifter who makes her living stealing jewelry from corpses. The heroine of "Thirteen Things about Ed Carpolotti" is the widow of a wheeler-dealer contractor who discovers that her husband has left her in debt to the banks, her family, and the mob. She has two days to come up with one million dollars.

The title character of *Miss Nelson Is Missing!* (The Children's Theatre Company in Minneapolis, Minnesota, 1997) is a nice, sympathetic schoolteacher who suddenly disappears. Her replacement is a hard-as-nails, detention-loving, recess-canceling, homework-overloading substitute teacher. With the Big Test approaching, the kids realize how much they miss Miss Nelson and they'll do anything—including hiring a private eye—to solve the mystery of her disappearance and bring her back.

In *Good 'N' Plenty* (Illusion Theatre, Minneapolis, Minnesota, 2001), a social studies instructor teaches students about the U.S. criminal justice system by staging a "drug game" where the students play pushers, buyers, and narcs. Most of the school lands in an actual jail.

Murder by Poe (The Acting Company, New York, 2004) adapts several Edgar Allan Poe stories into a haunting Grand Guignol presentation that takes place in 1840. A fragile woman in white, lost in the woods, finds shelter in a house full of characters from "The Black Cat," "The Tell-Tale Heart," "August Wilson," "The Mystery of Marie Roget," and "The Fall of the House of Usher." The French detective C. Auguste Dupin dominates the proceedings with his deductive prowess, solving the baffling case of "The Murders in the Rue Morgue" and the strange disappearance, in plain sight, of "The Purloined Letter."[6]

Hatcher's adaptation of Robert Louis Stevenson's 1886 novella *Dr. Jekyll and Mr. Hyde* (Arizona Theatre Company, Phoenix, Arizona, 2008) unfolds on the foggy streets in Victorian-era London. Dr. Henry Jekyll's experiments with powders and chemicals have brought forth his other self—Edward Hyde, a base, sadistic sensualist. The two sides battle each other in a deadly game of cat-and-mouse to determine who shall be master. In this complex interpretation, four actors portray the role of Hyde. The action unrolls in multiple locales, including a laboratory, a private surgery, a morgue, a dissecting theatre, a park, a hotel room, and various streets and alleys.

Sherlock Holmes and the Adventure of the Suicide Club (Arizona Theatre Company, Phoenix, Arizona, 2011) is loosely based on three Robert Louis Stevenson stories published in 1878 under the title *The Suicide Club*. Hatcher's play is set on the eve of World War I, "in the heart of London." Some of Europe's most powerful men gather to play a game—a game of murder. The club has a new member: Sherlock Holmes. Does the world's foremost consulting detective want to die?

In addition to his adaptations of the writings of Henry James, Edgar Allan Poe, and Robert Louis Stevenson, Hatcher has also tackled works by George Bernard Shaw (*Smash*, 1997), Georges Feydeau (*One Foot on the Floor*, 1997), Herman Melville (*Pierre*, 1998), Carlo Goldoni (*The Servant of Two Masters*, 1999), Jean Anouilh (*To Fool the Eye*, 2000), Nikolai Gogol (*The Government Inspector*, 2008), and Honoré de Balzac (*Cousin Bette*, 2009).

Hatcher scripted for television *Columbo: Ashes to Ashes* (1998) and *Murder at the Cannes Film Festival* (2000). For the movies he penned the period screenplays of *Stage Beauty* (2004), a backstage comedy unfolding in seventeenth-century England; *Casanova* (2005), a romp about the legendary lover of eighteenth-century Venice; and *The Duchess* (2008), focusing on the domestic dilemmas of the Duchess of Devonshire in the late 1700s.

* * *

Henry James (1843–1916) sought a career in the theatre—with disastrous results. His stage adaptation of the 1877 novel *The American* was given a trial performance in London on January 3, 1891, followed by a formal opening night on September 26. It was a misfire: "a mass of bald melodrama has been pitchforked into it, with a painfully incongruous effect," lamented the *New York Times* correspondent.[7] James's *Guy Domville* was hissed, hooted, and booed at its London bow on January 5, 1895.

The High Bid (1909), *Disengaged* (1909), and *The Saloon* (1911), fared somewhat better but fell short of expectations. It is ironic that posthumous adaptations of James's stories have triumphed on stage and screen. In addition to *The Innocents* there are *Berkeley Square* (1926) by John L. Balderston and J. C. Squire, based on James's unfinished 1917 novel, *The Sense of the Past*; *The Comic Artist* (1928), a conversion by Hubert Griffith of 1890's *The Tragic Muse*; *The Heiress* (1947), the Ruth and Augustus Goetz dramatization of 1881's *Washington Square*; *Letters from Paris* (1952), an adaptation by Dodie Smith of 1888's *The Reverberator*; *Child of Fortune* (1956), which Guy Bolton transformed from 1920's *The Wings of the Dove*; *Eugenia* (1957) by Randolph Carter, based on 1878's *The Europeans*; *The Aspern Papers* (1957), a Michael Redgrave stage treatment of the 1888 novelette; an operatic version of *The Wings of the Dove*, with libretto by Ethan Ayer, music by Douglas Moore (1961); *The Summer of Daisy Miller* (1963), a play by Bertram Greene based on 1879's *Daisy Miller*; *The Wings of the Dove* (1963), still another stage adaptation, by Christopher Taylor of James's longest, most complex novel; and Ronald Gow's *A Boston Story* (1968), suggested by the 1871 novella, *Watch the Ward*.

A 1990s tidal wave of renewed interest in James has triggered a lavish New York revival of *The Heiress* (1995), and a major biography, *Henry James, the Young Master*, by Sheldon M. Novick (Random House, 1996). Novick came up with a sequel, *Henry James, the Mature Master*, eleven years later (Random House, 2007). The University of Nebraska Press plans to publish all 12,000 of James's surviving letters. The filming of *The Aspern Papers, Portrait of a Lady, Washington Square, The Wings of the Dove*, and *The Golden Bowl*, as well as a Masterpiece Theatre-PBS television production of *The American*, indicate that Henry James, a failed playwright, has returned—with a vengeance.

Acting Edition: Dramatists Play Service.

Awards and Honors: Jeffrey Hatcher's *Scotland Road* won the 1993 Lois and Richard Rosenthal New Play Prize in Cincinnati, Ohio. Hatcher's dramatization of Robert Louis Stevenson's novella *Dr. Jekyll and Mr. Hyde* was nominated for a 2008 Edgar Award by the Mystery Writers of America. *Sherlock Holmes and the Adventure of the Suicide Club*, adapted from Stevenson's *The Suicide Club*, has been nominated for a 2012 Edgar.

NOTES

1. *WNBC-TV4*, New York, October 22, 1976.

2. *New York Times*, October 22, 1976.

3. *Newsweek*, November 1, 1976.

4. Jeffrey Hatcher, *The Turn of the Screw* (New York: Dramatists Play Service, 1997), 6.

5. http://en.wikipedia.org/wiki/jeffrey-hatcher.

6. Edgar Allan Poe (1809–1849), the father of the detective story, launched the genre with "The Murders in the Rue Morgue," a tale that appeared in April 1841 in *Graham's Magazine*, Philadelphia, Pennsylvania. Within the next three years Poe wrote three more detective stories—"The Mystery of Marie Roget," "The Purloined Letter," and "Thou Art the Man." "The Gold-Bug," with its deciphering of a coded message that leads to a buried treasure, is often compared to Poe's "tales of ratiocination." Poe's *Tales*, published by Wiley and Putnam (New York) in 1845, is one of the rarities in the field. Also desired by collectors is *Monsieur Dupin*, a compilation of all five stories mentioned above, published by McClure, Phillips (New York) in 1904.

7. *New York Times*, September 27, 1891.

Getting Away with Murder (1996)

Stephen Sondheim (United States, 1930–) and George Furth (United States, 1932–2008)

The mystery comedy, by now an endangered species, may have received its kiss of death in *Getting Away with Murder*, a surprisingly graceless effort by the distinguished collaborators of *Company* and *Merrily We Roll Along*, Stephen Sondheim and George Furth. Sondheim exhibited his knack for the macabre in *Sweeney Todd*, *Assassins*, and the movie *The Last of Sheila*; Furth demonstrated a fertile sense of humor in *Twigs*, *The Act*, and *The Supporting Cast*. *Getting Away with Murder* fails in both categories.

The core idea is vintage Agatha Christie. In the penthouse suite of a dilapidated Upper West Side building in Manhattan, seven patients are waiting for a group session with their therapist, Dr. Conrad Bering. They soon discover the doctor's pulped body in his inner office. Since "no one can get in or out the front door without signing in downstairs," and no one can "get onto this floor without the elevator key, which only *we* have," the patients conclude that one of them must be the murderer.

Under the leadership of Dan Gerard, a former cop, they commence to question one another regarding their movement and alibis.

The assorted characters represent an exemplary cross-section of the city—real estate, education, personal services, the arts, the law, and the idle rich. Dr. Bering meticulously selected the patients for personifying the Seven Deadly Sins: Dossie Lustig, a "lusty" restaurant hostess; Nan-Jun Vuong, an "envious" academic; Pamela Prideaux, an overly "proud" society matron; Gregory Reed, a "greedy" real estate tycoon; Vassili Laimorgos, a compulsive "glutton"; Dan Gerard, an "angry" police detective; and a newcomer to the group, Martin Chisolm, who has taken over the spot vacated by "lazy" Lila.

The three women and three of the men die twice in the course of the action, the first time as imagined by central character Martin Chisolm, who is revealed as the murderer by the end of act 1, and then for real, when Martin eliminates all evidence of his crime and leaves a slew of corpses in a building slated for demolition. Martin himself ends up falling down the shaft of a doorless elevator, joining two previous victims of this lackluster modus operandi.

Via flashbacks we learn the motive for Dr. Bering's murder. Martin inadvertently kills his drug-addicted son, giving him a sedative that reacted with the array of other drugs in his system. In his dying moments, Junior calls Dr. Bering for help. Martin—a political consultant, front-runner to succeed the mayor—comes to the doctor, pleading with him to hush the matter. When Bering refuses and picks up the phone to call the police, Martin bashes his head with a statuette. Murder begets murder, leading to slaughter by the ambitious politician whose Eighth Sin is that "of Control. Of Power. The sin of Manipulation, the sin of playing God."

* * *

The world premiere of *Getting Away with Murder* took place on September 10, 1995 at the Old Globe Theatre in San Diego, California, under the title *The Doctor Is Out*. Jack O'Brien directed and Douglas W. Schmidt designed the set. The reviews were mixed. "You won't miss the songs from this Sondheim show, but you might just miss the powerful human insight and emotional power of his best shows," wrote critic Jonathan Taylor.[1] "Overall, it's an odd amalgam of whodunit, thriller, comedy thriller, murder mystery—everything, practically," opined Michael Phillips. "But the play attempts a slippery blend of laughs and chills, and it doesn't always hold."[2] Paul Hodgins found *The Doctor Is Out* "an unapologetically old-fashioned pot-boiler, the kind of elaborate, plot-driven trifle that used to be the standard fare on Broadway and in London's West End."[3] Several other reviewers expressed their approval. "Should be a winner," declared Frances L. Bardacke.[4] "*The Doctor* is written with a nod to the grand tradition of *And Then There Were None* and *Diabolique*, with a little *Dallas* thrown in," stated Laurie Winer. "In the end, *The Doctor Is Out* is a thriller that enjoys riffing on the old."[5]

Getting Away with Murder opened, with a few cast changes, at New York's Broadhurst Theatre on March 17, 1996. Most critics greeted the play with hostility. Donald Lyons called it "a jaw-droppingly witless, endless, thrill-less nuisance next to which such elegant Christie artifacts as the play *Witness for the Prosecution* look like *Oedipus Rex*."[6]

Michael Feingold found *Getting Away with Murder* "all plot business and no fun whatever."[7] Jeremy Gerard bemoaned a mystery comedy "utterly thrill-free and almost utterly laugh-free."[8] Clive Barnes concluded, "*Getting Away with Murder* is not so much a whodunit as perhaps a whydoit, and definitely a whyseeit."[9] A qualified positive reaction came from Phil Roura: "But your heart is going to skip several beats and your neck is going to tingle before the night is over. And that hasn't happened since *Deathtrap*."[10] Sondheim and Furth got away with murder for seventeen performances.

* * *

Born in New York City in 1930, Stephen Sondheim was educated at Williams College, where he won the Hutchinson Prize for musical composition. He began his professional career writing scripts for TV's *Topper* series. For his first Broadway credit, Sondheim composed the theme song of N. Richard Nash's 1956 drama, *Girls of Summer*. In 1957, Sondheim collaborated with composer Leonard Bernstein and librettist Arthur Laurents on the milestone musical *West Side Story*. He then continued to provide the scores for many Broadway hits, making his name as one of the giants of the modern American musical.

Among his early successes were *Gypsy* (1959) and *A Funny Thing Happened on the Way to the Forum* (1962). In the 1970s he peaked with *Company* (1970), *Follies* (1971), *A Little Night Music* (1973), *Pacific Overtures* (1976), and *Sweeney Todd, the Demon Barber of Fleet Street* (1979). Along the way he provided additional lyrics for a revival of *Candide* (1973), wrote the music and lyrics for Aristophanes's *The Frogs* (1974), provided the lyrics for the musical cabaret *By Bernstein* (1975), and spawned a show dedicated to his work, *Side by Side by Sondheim* (1977).

The indefatigable composer-lyricist continued to score mightily during the 1980s: *Sunday in the Park with George* (1984), *Into the Woods* (1987), and *Jerome Robbins' Broadway* (1989), which included Sondheim's "You Gotta Have a Gimmick" from *Gypsy* and "Comedy Tonight" from *A Funny Thing Happened on the Way to the Forum*. Less spectacular were *Merrily We Roll Along* (1981) and *A Little Like Magic* (1986), a puppet show that included "Send in the Clowns." Sondheim also contributed to various revues: *Barbara Cook: A Concert for the Theatre* (1987), *Liliane Montevecchi on the Boulevard* (1988), and *Together Again for the First Time* (1989).

In 1991, Sondheim composed *Assassins* (1991), an experimental musical that probes the minds of the men and women who had attempted to assassinate U.S. presidents. Three years later he collaborated with James Lapine on *Passion*, the tale of a triangular love affair in 1863 Milan. In 2010, Lapine conceived and directed *Sondheim on Sondheim*, a portrait of the composer in his own words. That same year, eighty-five-year-old Elaine Stritch interpreted the composer's lyrics in *Elaine Stritch Singin' Sondheim . . . One Song at a Time*, at Manhattan's Café Carlyle.

For the silver screen, Sondheim coauthored the mystery *The Last of Sheila* (1973) with Anthony Perkins and composed the music for the epic *Reds* (1981).

Sondheim's lyrics were collected in two volumes, published by Knopf: *Finishing the Hat, 1954–1981* (2010) and *Look, I Made a Hat, 1981–2011* (2011).

* * *

Born George Schweinfurth in Chicago, George Furth majored in drama at Northwestern University and received his MFA from Columbia University in 1956. He began his acting career on Broadway in the early 1960s, but his main contribution lies in his playwriting. Furth teamed with Stephen Sondheim on the milestone musical *Company* (1970) and on *Merrily We Roll Along* (1981), a failed show that eventually drew a cult following.

Furth's *Twigs* (1971; televised 1974, 1975, 1978) contains four connected vignettes. *The Act* (1977), with music by John Kander and lyrics by Fred Ebb, was a Liza Minnelli vehicle about a Las Vegas performer, a has-been movie star now trying to make a comeback. *The Supporting Cast* (1981) is a comedy about the Malibu wife of a famous author writing a book that exposes her friends, all celebrity spouses, warts and all. *Precious Sons* (1986) is an autobiographical drama about a struggling Chicago family in the late 1940s. A son is caught between his desire to be an actor and his father's determination that he finish high school and go to college.

Frequently cast as a nerdy, ineffectual, seemingly nervous type, Furth participated in more than eighty-five films and television episodes from the early 1960s to the late 1990s. Perhaps his best remembered role is that of Woodcock, a loyal railroad clerk who refuses to open the train car containing the safe for outlaws *Butch Cassidy and the Sundance Kid*. His other movies include *The Best Man, A Rage to Live, The Cool Ones, The Boston Strangler, Myra Breckinridge, Blazing Saddles, Shampoo, Airport '77, Hooper, The Cannonball Run, Doctor Detroit, The Man with Two Brains*, and *Bulworth*.

Furth's appearances in criminous television shows occurred in *The Defenders, The Alfred Hitchcock Hour, Batman, The Girl from U.N.C.L.E., Felony Squad, Night Gallery, Archer, Ellery Queen, L.A. Law*, and *Murder, She Wrote*.

Never married, Furth died on August 11, 2008 at the age of 75.

Acting Edition: Dramatists Play Service.

Awards and Honors: Stephen Sondheim received seven Tony Awards, more than any other composer, winning Best Score for *Company* (1971), *Follies* (1972), *A Little Night Music* (1973), *Sweeney Todd, the Demon Barber of Fleet Street* (1979), *Into the Woods* (1988), and *Passion* (1994), and a special Tony for Lifetime Achievement in the Theatre (2008). Sondheim won the Pulitzer Prize for *Sunday in the Park with George* (1985) and an Oscar for Original Song, "Sooner or Later," in *Dick Tracy* (1991). With coauthor Anthony Perkins, Sondheim received the Mystery Writers of America 1974 Edgar Allan Poe Award for Best Motion Picture Screenplay for *The Last of Sheila*. Sondheim served as president of the Dramatists Guild, the professional association of playwrights, composers, lyricists, and librettists, from 1973 to 1981. In 1982 he was elected into the Theatre Hall of Fame and a year later into the American Academy of Arts and Letters.

He was an honoree at the 1993 Kennedy Center Celebration of the Performing Arts. In 1996 Sondheim was presented by President Clinton the National Medal of the Arts. In 2010, the 1,055-seat venue on Manhattan's West 43rd Street that had been named after actor-producer Henry Miller was renamed to honor Stephen Sondheim. In 2011, Sondheim received New York City's highest prize for achievement in the arts, the Handel Medallion. George Furth won both the Tony and Drama Desk Awards for Outstanding Book of a Musical for *Company* (1970) and was nominated for Drama Desk Award's Outstanding New Play for *Precious Sons* (1986).

NOTES

1. *Variety*, October 1, 1995.
2. *San Diego Union-Tribune*, September 18, 1995.
3. *Orange County Register*, September 19, 1995.
4. *San Diego Magazine*, September 1995.
5. *Los Angeles Times*, September 18, 1995.
6. *Wall Street Journal*, March 20, 1996.
7. *Village Voice*, March 26, 1996.
8. *Variety*, March 18, 1996.
9. *New York Post*, March 18, 1996.
10. *Daily News*, March 18, 1996.

Jane Eyre (1997)

Polly Teale (England, 1962–)

The pseudonymous publication of *Jane Eyre* in 1847 by "Currer Bell" proved a sensational success, selling out within three months. The public clamored for any information on the identity of the mysterious author, and speculation was rampant. Charlotte Brontë was identified only after the gothic novel had gone through several editions. By that time, it was already clear that she had written a classic of English literature.[1]

Through the years, *Jane Eyre* has been dramatized repeatedly. No adaptation has been as revolutionary as Polly Teale's 1997 version. "Returning to *Jane Eyre* fifteen years after I read it as a teenager I found not the horror story I remembered, but a psychological drama of the most powerful kind," wrote Teale, a co-artistic director of London's Shared Experience Theatre, in the published edition of her adaptation of Charlotte Brontë's novel. "Everything and everyone in the story is seen, larger than life, through the magnifying glass of Jane's psyche. Why though, I asked myself, did she invent a madwoman locked in an attic to torment her heroine? Why is Jane Eyre, a supremely rational young woman, haunted by a vengeful she-devil? Why do these two women exist in the same story?"[2]

In a sharp departure from the original novel and previous stage versions, Teale concluded that Jane, the plain, frustrated governess, and Bertha, the madwoman trapped in the attic of Thornfield Hall, are contrasting inner and outer forces of the same woman. A production note states, "Central to the adaptation is the idea that hidden inside the sensible, frozen Jane exists another self who is passionate and sensual. Bertha embodies the fire and longing which Jane must lock away in order to survive in Victorian England."[3] The roles of Jane and Bertha should be played by two dexterous actresses.

The curtain rises on a ten-year-old orphan, Jane Eyre, reading a book about foreign lands, and Bertha playing out Jane's secret imaginings. Their limbs are entangled as if they were one person. Bertha becomes unruly and wild as Jane allows her inner world to take over. This is only possible when she is alone and can let down her guard. When John Reed, a cocky cousin, enters the room, Jane attempts to control Bertha. John taunts Jane, calls her "a plain little girl," and roars with laughter at her rage. Bertha breaks free, springs forward, and attacks John. From this moment on, there is sort of a Jekyll-and-Hyde struggle for control between the girl's inner and outer selves. Bertha will continue to express the feelings that Jane is trying to conceal. A production note suggests that "there should be a strong sexual element in Bertha's movements."

Upset with Jane's recent tantrums, aunt Sarah Reed sends the "naughty" girl to Lowood School, a charity institution run by Mr. Brocklehurst, a stingy, insensitive minister. Young Jane goes through a series of abuses instigated by the headmaster, who asks the other students to shun her.

The action next catapults to "seven years later." Jane thrives on academic success and, upon completing her studies, serves two years as a teacher. When she decides to move on to another position, she advertises in the *Herald*. There is one reply—from Mrs. Alice Fairfax of Thornfield Hall. There is a position available for governess of the master's ward.

The following scene begins with the sound of horses' hooves and carriage wheels. Jane has arrived at Thornfield Hall where Mrs. Fairfax, the housekeeper, awaits. Jane's luggage is carried away by a servant as Mrs. Fairfax relates that the master of the house, Mr. Edward Rochester, is away in the Continent—his visits to England are rare—and introduces Jane to Adèle, "a ten-year-old with ringlets and perfect deportment. She looks like a doll." Jane and Adèle converse in French and establish an immediate rapport. Fairfax explains that the master, out of the goodness of his heart, has taken in the poor little waif. Adèle's mother, a French dancer, abandoned her, and there were rumors that she and Mr. Rochester—

Grace Poole, a maid, descends the staircase, picks up Jane's suitcase, and leads her to her room.[4] While Jane and Adèle embroider samplers, we hear Bertha kicking against the floor in a distant room. It is the sound of a caged animal, and this restlessness registers in Jane's body as she throws the sampler down and gets up.

The sound of hooves on a rocky road can be heard and a vague image of Rochester on a horse, galloping toward us in the mist, appears in the background. His dog, Pilot, runs ahead. Suddenly the horse rears up, slipping on the ice. Rochester falls in front of Jane. The dog snarls violently at Jane. Rochester struggles to his feet and orders Pilot to "Shut up." Unaware of the identity of the stranger, Jane helps him hobble toward his horse. He mounts with difficulty.

The following day, Jane meets Rochester as he sits in the drawing room's armchair with Pilot at his side. The dog licks Jane's fingers. Adèle looks for a box of presents, and Rochester tells her that "they will be delivered next week." Rochester interrogates Jane and learns that her parents are dead and that she has no brothers or sisters. Dismissed abruptly by the master, Jane meets Mrs. Fairfax in the hallway and expresses concern: "He blows hot and then cold in the space of a moment." The housekeeper says hesitatingly that Mr. Rochester "has painful thoughts . . . family trouble, I believe." From upstairs they hear a stifled laugh. It is Bertha, but Mrs. Fairfax tells Jane that the maid Grace Poole sleeps in the attic and has a weakness for drinking.

Adèle's presents arrive. She runs to Rochester, kisses him, and takes the large box to a corner. Rochester attempts to converse with Jane but she responds in monosyllables. He asks whether she thinks him handsome, and she answers, "No." He queries if she has ever been in love, and she remains silent. During the short encounter we see Bertha lying on the attic floor, rolling over and stretching like a cat, singing snatches of a West Indian rain song.

Jane lies down to sleep but begins to heave and murmur. She is having a sexual dream. Bertha steals across the attic carrying a lit candle. Carefully, she eases the keys from Grace's pocket, unlocks the door, enters Rochester's chamber, and straddles his sleeping body. Grace follows Bertha, grasps her, and wrestles her backward. The candle drops. While Bertha is forced back up the stairs, Jane awakes with a start and comes out into the passageway. She smells fire and runs to Rochester's room, beating back the smoke. She grabs a pitcher of water and throws it onto Rochester, drenching him. He wakes confused, accusing Jane of plotting to drown him.

The next day, over lunch, Mrs. Fairfax informs Jane that Mr. Rochester has gone to South Leas to visit "a certain young lady he will no doubt be pleased to see." As Blanche Ingram is mentioned—"very tall with a long graceful neck and beautiful dark eyes"—she appears in the background, running, laughing and fanning herself. "Talented too," adds Mrs. Fairfax. "She plays the piano and sings."

Jane picks up a mirror and forces herself to look at her reflection. She is unhappy with "that tired, uneven, charmless face," and Bertha, upstairs, becomes gradually more violent and contorted.

Lord Ingram and his daughter Blanche arrive for a weekend party. Blanche sings and Rochester joins her. Jane is transfixed in the hallway while Bertha listens and drinks in the sound, her ear to the floorboard. Blanche chatters flirtatiously about her ideal man—mature, not necessarily handsome, action driven, a hunter. She flutters around her host but Rochester abruptly announces that he has to leave for a day on business.

The next day, Blanche flops in an armchair, listless and irritable. Lord Ingram and little Adèle play cards. The doorbell rings. Mrs. Fairfax ushers in a tanned man of about forty-five, Richard Mason, a friend of Rochester's from his time in Spanish Town, Jamaica. With a trace of a foreign accent, Mason says that he is half frozen and sits by the fire. Soon another visitor arrives on the scene—a fortune-telling gypsy. Blanche is excited about meeting "a real sorceress" and rushes to the library. She returns pale, walks swiftly to her seat, murmurs, "She is a charlatan" and picks up a book. Adèle skips out to have her fortune told and returns in a fit of giggles. The action shifts to the library, where Jane takes her turn.

An old gypsy woman, hunched and swaddled in shawls, her face hidden from view, confides to Jane that she told Blanche Ingram that Rochester's fortune was not half of what she believed it to be. As the gypsy woman continues to talk, her voice becomes more and more familiar. Jane is shocked: "Mr. Rochester!"

Meanwhile, Mason walks upstairs and opens the attic room. He sees his sister for the first time in twelve years. The beautiful young woman he once knew is haggard and filthy. She suddenly jumps at Mason and bites his arm deeply. He staggers down the steps and falls to the ground. Rochester springs to his feet and runs into the hallway, his disguise falling away. Jane follows. She fetches a basin of water and presses a handkerchief to the wound. Rochester leaves to fetch a surgeon. Jane continues to dip the bloody handkerchief into the water and places the dressing back on Mason's wound. Upstairs, Bertha snarls wildly.

In the garden, at sunset, Rochester confesses that he had invited Blanche Ingram to Thornfield to provoke Jane's jealousy. He proposes to Jane and, taken aback, she accepts.

On the eve of the wedding, Jane is trying on a veil and Mrs. Fairfax is packing a trunk for a honeymoon trip to Venice. That night, Jane sleeps fitfully. Bertha enters her bedroom; her wrists, which Grace Poole tied after a convulsive rage, are bound across her chest, resembling a straitjacket. Bertha seizes the wedding veil, tries to put it on, looks at her reflection in the mirror, and, using her teeth, rips the veil to shreds.

A clergyman officiates at the wedding ceremony but the ritual is interrupted by Richard Mason, who makes a sudden entrance and declares that Rochester is already married to his sister Bertha. Mason produces a record of the marriage—it took place in October of 1934 in Spanish Town, Jamaica. Rochester admits that he wed Bertha Mason fifteen years ago and adds that he has kept his wife under lock and key because she's insane and dangerous. He motions to the wedding guests to follow him, leads them to the Thornfield attic, and unlocks the door. Bertha scurries back and forth like a wild animal. Rochester offers his hand. Bertha advances toward him, tries to kiss him on the mouth, and suddenly grapples with Rochester as if trying to strangle him and bites his shoulder. Grace pulls Bertha off and once again ties her wrists.

Jane runs from the attic into her room, pulls off her wedding dress, and puts on an old grey frock. She exits the room and finds Rochester waiting outside. She tells him that Adèle must have a new governess and, despite his pleadings, leaves Thornfield.

The action shifts, perhaps for too long, to Jane in the care of a village minister, Saint John Rivers, who falls in love with her and wants to take her to India as a missionary's wife. Jane agrees to go to India, but not as his wife. Meanwhile, in the attic, Bertha bites at the rope on her wrists. Her hands free, she lights a torch, opens the door, and descends the stairs. Soon Thornfield is on fire, with people running in all directions. Bertha stands on the roof carrying a flame. Rochester begins to climb to rescue her. He reaches the roof and holds his arms for her. Bertha cries out for Jane, who at Saint John's home hears the cry, looks up to the heavens and shouts, "I am coming! Wait for me!"

Jane stares at the wreckage of Thornfield Hall. She picks her way through the debris, then climbs the staircase, enters the attic, and sits down on Bertha's lap. It is as if by returning to Thornfield and following her true desires, Jane can reunite with her secret self.

Jane runs down the stairs. Bertha follows very slowly. A woman who scavenges in the debris tells Jane that a lunatic woman, who was kept in the attic and who turned out to be none other than Mr. Rochester's lawful wife, started the fire and climbed up onto the roof. Mr. Rochester attempted to save her but the woman sprang forward. The next minute she lay smashed to pieces—dead. Mr. Rochester remained alive but one hand was crushed and his eyesight gone. He resides now at Ferndean, in a desolate farmhouse.

Jane and Bertha arrive in Ferndean on a misty evening. Mrs. Fairfax starts as she sees Jane. Pilot leaps up from beside his master and bounds toward Jane, excited. Jane strokes his head and tells Rochester that she came back to stay—"I will be your eyes and your hands. I will be your nurse, your housekeeper, your companion."

* * *

Adapted and directed by Polly Teale, *Jane Eyre* was first performed by Shared Experience Theatre Company at the Wolsey Theatre Ipswich on September 4, 1997. Subsequent productions took place at the Cambridge Arts Theatre, Oxford Playhouse, Poole Arts Centre, London's Young Vic Theatre, Warwick Arts Centre, Richmond Theatre, and the Chichester Festival Theatre. The leading roles were played by Monica Dolan (Jane), Pooky Quesnel (Bertha), and James Clyde (Rochester).

The published edition of Teale's adaptation includes several review quotes: "Polly Teale has liberated *Jane Eyre* in a way that Charlotte Brontë could not. . . . Her most inspired idea is to fuse the mad woman in the attic with Jane's younger self. . . . Seeing the show is like an amazing speedread"—*Observer*.

"Puts the interior life of the book on stage as well as its narrative. Adaptations of this quality can't be dismissed as a poor second to reading the book"—*Time Out*.

"Polly Teale's fine production (she is also responsible for the adaptation) offers a satisfyingly meaty dramatic experience"—*Daily Telegraph*.

Featuring a different cast, *Jane Eyre* crossed the Atlantic and came to the Brooklyn Academy of Music on February 8, 2000 for six performances. Penny Laden portrayed the title role, Harriette Ashcroft was Bertha, and Sean Murray played Edward Rochester.

* * *

Polly Teale was born in East Grinstead, Sussex, England in 1962. In the 1980s, she authored a number of original plays and stage adaptations. Since 1995, Teale has been a joint artistic director (with Nancy Meckler) of Shared Experience Theatre in London, the company that commissioned and produced her adaptation of *Jane Eyre* in 1997. Previously, Teale directed Shared Experience's productions of Eugene O'Neill's *Desire under the Elms*, Helen Edmundson's dramatizations of Leo Tolstoy's *Anna Karenina*, and George Eliot's *The Mill and the Floss*. Other plays staged by Teale include Tennessee Williams's *The Glass Menagerie* at the Royal Lyceum in Edinburgh; August Strindberg's *Miss Julie* at London's Young Vic; Sheila Delaney's *A Taste of Honey* for English Touring Theatre; and Fay Weldon's translation of Gustav Flaubert's novel *Madame Bovary* at the Lyric Theatre in Hammersmith, London.

As a writer, Teale's work includes *Afters* (BBC Screen on Two) and *Fallen* (Traverse Theatre, Edinburgh). In addition to her adaptation of *Jane Eyre*, Teale's fascination with Charlotte Brontë is evident by her 2003 adaptation of Jean Rhys's *Wide Sargasso Sea* (a prequel to *Jane Eyre*) under the title *After Mrs. Rochester*, and penning *Brontë*, a play exploring the lives of Charlotte and her family, in 2005.

* * *

An early stage version of *Jane Eyre*, by John Brougham (1814–1880), a pioneering, prolific Irish-American actor-playwright, was presented by New York's Laura Keene's Varieties in 1856, with Laura Keene in the title role and George Jordan as Edward Rochester. Faithful to the Brontë novel, the five acts take place in various locales, beginning at the Lowood Academy, where the windows are barred "prison like" and orphan Jane Eyre is maltreated by the mean, miserly minister, Mr. Brocklehurst. Eight years pass, and Jane advertises in the *Herald* for a position. On her way to a job interview, she causes a rider to sharply rein his horse, fall to the ground, and hurt his foot (this scene is skipped in most adaptations of the novel). The man, gruff and cursing, turns out to be Jane's prospective employer, Edward Rochester, who is looking for a governess for his six-year-old ward, Adèle.

The action shifts to the interior of Rochester's manor where a group of pompous aristocrats await him. All are after Rochester's money and together they concoct a plan to have the host marry the beautiful, haughty Blanche Ingram. Brougham's version, more than others, throws satirical, savage darts at the Ingram family and their society friends.

From the very first production, many dramatizations of *Jane Eyre* were flawed. The drama critic of the *New York Times* said in 1870 that to try "to copy" the classic novel on the stage "is something like painting the color of the dying dolphin or clutching a fallen star. We may praise the daring of the attempt, but not often the results." While rejecting an adaptation by Charlotte Birch-Pfeiffer, the reviewer found Mme. Seebach's *Jane Eyre* "a bold and stirring piece of art. The changes of age and idiosyncrasy between the acts are admirably denoted, and many passages are worked up with an energy and a pathos that win plaudits from the coldest of judges."[5]

Four years later, the *New York Times* welcomed another "reproduction" of *Jane Eyre*, an "excellent dramatization of Charlotte Brontë's famous novel" by an anonymous writer, mounted at the Union Square Theatre with "elegance and completeness. . . . Miss Charlotte Thompson gave her usual portraiture of the heroine."[6] In 1876, Thompson reprised the role at the Brooklyn Theatre "and proved that she had lost none of the fervor with which she formerly delineated the personage of the orphan girl."[7]

The next actress to triumph in the role of Jane Eyre was Maggie Mitchell, who, according to the *New York Times*, demonstrated "power over an audience" in an adaptation by Clifton W. Tayleure, which played at New York's Grand Opera House in 1885. "Miss Mitchell is well supported by Mr. Charles Abbott, who invests the character of Rochester with interest and sympathy. The supporting company is better than is usually found in a star combination, and the scenery is good."[8]

An adaptation of *Jane Eyre*, written and directed by Phyllis Birkett, opened at the Theatre Royal in Huddersfield, England on September 12, 1929, and two years later made it to London's Kingsway Theatre, running twenty performances. Helen Jerome penned a more notable dramatization of the Brontë novel in 1936. Jerome had made a name for herself a year earlier with a stage version of Jane Austen's *Pride and Prejudice*, which debuted at New York's Plymouth Theatre on November 5, 1935 to critical acclaim, ran for 219 showings, and leaped across the Atlantic to London, where it opened at the St. James Theatre for a lengthy engagement.[9]

Jerome's *Jane Eyre* premiered at the Queen's Theatre, London, on October 13, 1936 with Curigwen Lewis (Jane) and Reginald Tate (Rochester). It ran for 299 performances. The play's success instigated the Theatre Guild to option it for a Broadway production. Katharine Hepburn (1907–2003), not quite yet the star she was destined to be, was cast in the lead with an assurance of a long tryout tour to ready the show for New York. *Jane Eyre* played to full houses and smashed all road-show records by pulling in $340,000 by the end of its run. In December 1937, following a performance at Boston's Colonial Theatre, the *New York Times* praised Helen Jerome for deriving "from the 89-year-old novel, a play with pleasantly Victorian atmosphere, considerable quaint humor, a large measure of charm, and a mingling of sentiment and melodrama."[10]

The provincial reviewers showered Hepburn with personal accolades. However, perhaps not confident enough to risk the slings and arrows of New York critics, Hepburn left the show and went to Hollywood; this caused the production to close its doors.[11] In 1938, Hepburn felt obliged to return to the Guild in *The Philadelphia Story*, as socialite Tracy Lord, and rejuvenated her then-tottering career.

A dramatization of *Jane Eyre* by Marjorie Carleton[12] confines the action to a single box-set depicting a reception room in the country home of Edward Rochester. A short flight of stairs leads to a door centered up stage, and arches up-right and up-left serve as exits to the rest of the house. Candles on the mantelpiece supply the illumination for night scenes. This version begins with Jane arriving for an interview for the position of governess in which the child does not appear. The Carleton adaptation was published by the Walter H. Baker Company in 1936. That same year, the Northwestern Press published *Jane Eyre, A Romantic Play in Three Acts* by Wall Spence.[13] Here, too, the entire action unfolds in one setting—a spacious drawing room at Thornfield Hall. This adaptation is more melodramatic than most, punctuating the action with frequent appearances by mad Bertha, who laughs maniacally and threatens Jane, "You will never marry him—never, never!" She also attacks her brother Mason and sets the place on fire. A unique character is that of an old, wrinkled gypsy woman, Zita, who in a cracked voice predicts that Blanche Ingram's plan to marry Rochester will go "poof" while Jane Eyre's "clouds" will give way to "a rainbow" of happiness.

Mesmerized playwrights kept adapting *Jane Eyre* to the stage throughout the twentieth century, generally faithful to the Brontë original novel but inserting nuances and wrinkles of their own. Notable dramatizations were by Pauline Phelps (published by Wetmore Declamation Bureau, 1941); Jane Kendall (first produced by The Canterbury Players, Chicago, on April 26 and 29, 1945 and published that year by the Dramatic Publishing Company); Constance Cox (adapted from a highly successful television serial broadcast by the BBC during February and March, 1956 and first produced on stage on July 9, 1956 at Her Majesty's Theatre in Carlisle, England, and published by J. Garnet Miller, Ltd., 1959); Huntington Hartford (presented at New York's Belasco Theatre on May 1, 1958, starring Eric Portman as Rochester, Jan Brooks as Jane, and Blanche Yurka as Mrs. Fairfax, garnering mixed reviews, running for fifty-two performances. The production lost the entire investment of nearly $500,000, making it the costliest non-musical to reach Broadway until that date); Peter Coe (who directed his version for the Chichester Festival Theatre, July 23–September 26, 1986); Fay Weldon (produced by the Birmingham Repertory, September 30–October 29, 1986); Willis Hall (presented at the Crucible Theatre, Sheffield, England, November 5–28, 1992 and published by Samuel French, Ltd., 1994); Charles Vance (first presented at the Forum Theatre, Billingham, England, on February 20, 1996 and published by Samuel French, Ltd., later that year); and Robert Johanson (first produced at the Paper Mill Playhouse, Millburn, New Jersey in February 1997 and published by Dramatic Publishing, 1998).

A two-act ballet based on *Jane Eyre* was created by the London Children's Ballet in 1994, and a ballet named *Jane* premiered at the Civic Auditorium, Kalamazoo, Michigan in 2007. An opera inspired by Brontë's novel was composed by John Joubert between 1987 and 1997, with libretto by Kenneth Birkin. Another opera, created by English composer Michael Berkeley with a libretto by David Malouf, was first presented by Music Theatre Wales at the Cheltenham Festival in 2000.

A musical version of *Jane Eyre,* with book by John Caird, music and lyrics by Paul Gordon, bounced around the regional circuit for several years before opening at Broadway's Brooks Atkinson Theatre on December 3, 2000. Marla Schaffel and James Barbour played Jane and Rochester. The *New York Times* critic Bruce Weber paid tribute to the original novel, "a magnificent melodrama, a horrid Gothic romance set in dark chambers," but found the musical "gloomy and mundane," capturing only "few of the richly available nuances." Weber appreciated the "very handsome, if very dark" physical aspects of the show, notably "a techno-sleek beauty" provided by British scene designer John Napier, but scoffed at "a tepid score" and "a fitful and hurried pace . . . an overall gallop through Brontë's significant plot that has the teasing quality of a movie trailer. . . . It's a failing that the directors have used the Brontë story for mere stage directions. The result is that a great adult fable has been attenuated to the thinness of a children's story."[14] The $7.3 million musical ran for 209 performances. It emerged in 2003 at the Mountain View Center for the Performing Arts in Mountain View, California. Another musical version, with book by Jana Smith and Wayne R. Scott, score by Jana Smith and Brad Roseborough, premiered in 2008 at the Lifehouse Theatre, Redlands,

California. A Jane Eyre–inspired symphony by Michel Bose premiered in Bandol, France on October 11, 2009.

Jane Eyre has been transferred to the screen many times. Silent film versions were made in 1910, 1914, 1915 (two films, one released as *The Castle of Thornfield*), 1918 (called *Woman and Wife*), 1921, and 1926 (German, *Orphan of Lowood*). *Jane Eyre* talkies include a 1934 version featuring Colin Clive and Virginia Bruce; 1943's *I Walked with a Zombie*, a classic horror film loosely based on Brontë's novel; 1944's much-admired rendition, scripted by John Houseman and Aldous Huxley, starring Orson Welles and Joan Fontaine; a 1956 version made in Hong Kong; and one shot in Mexico in 1963 called *The Secret*. George C. Scott and Susannah York played Rochester and Jane in a 1970 made-for-TV movie that was released theatrically in Europe, while William Hurt and Charlotte Gainsborough undertook the roles in a 1996 Franco Zeffirelli film. A new motion picture version of *Jane Eyre*, featuring Mia Wasikowska in the title role, Michael Fassbender as Edward Rochester, and Judi Dench as housekeeper Mrs. Fairfax, was released in March 2011.

A live television broadcast of *Jane Eyre* was produced by Westinghouse Studio One in 1952. Additional TV adaptations, on British and American television, took place in 1956 and 1961. BBC aired dramatizations of *Jane Eyre* in 1963, 1973, 1982, 1983, and 2006.

A graphic version of *Jane Eyre* was published by UK's Classical Comics in 2008.[15]

Acting Edition: Nick Hern Books.

Awards and Honors: Polly Teale won the Sydney Edward Award for Best Director and was nominated for a 2003 London Evening Standard Theatre Award for Best Play for *After Mrs. Rochester*, performed at the Duke of York's Theatre.

NOTES

1. In September 2010, Bauman Rare Books in New York City offered a first edition of *Jane Eyre*, three volumes bound in calf-gilt, for $36,000.

2. Polly Teale, *Jane Eyre* (London: Nick Hern Books, 1998), vi.

3. Teale, *Jane Eyre*, 3.

4. This adaptation relinquishes the mounting suspense and climactic surprise of discovering Poole's real function as guard of mad Bertha locked upstairs in the attic.

5. *New York Times*, October 6, 1870.

6. *New York Times*, November 17, 1874.

7. *New York Times*, February 8, 1876.

8. *New York Times*, November 17, 1885.

9. Helen Jerome's adaptation of *Pride and Prejudice* served as the basis for MGM's celebrated 1940 picture, starring Greer Garson and Laurence Olivier, and for the 1959 Broadway musical, *First Impressions*, with book by Abe Burrows, featuring Polly Bergen, Hermione Gingold, and Farley Granger (Alvin Theatre, March 19, 1959—eighty-four performances). Jerome's third costume drama, *Maria Walewska*, was adapted to the screen under the title *Conquest* (1937), with Greta Garbo as the Polish countess who had a passionate but doomed affair with Napoleon Bonaparte, played by Charles Boyer.

10. *New York Times*, January 3, 1937.

11. Katharine Hepburn's costar in the tryout run of *Jane Eyre* was British actor Dennis Hoey (1893–1960), who played Edward Rochester. Hoey was best known for the role of Inspector Lestrade in Universal's Sherlock Holmes films. Hoey adapted to the stage Anthony Gilbert's whodunit *Something Nasty in the Woodshed* (aka *Mystery in the Woodshed*) under the title *The Haven*, and starred in the play as series sleuth Arthur Crook. *The Haven* opened at Broadway's Playhouse Theatre on November 13, 1946, was lambasted by the critics, and closed after five performances.

12. Marjorie Carleton (1897–1964) was the American author of half a dozen suspense novels published between 1947 and 1963. Detective literature scholars Jacques Barzun and Wendell Hertig Taylor, in *A Catalogue of Crime*, find exceptional merit in Carleton's novels *A Bride Regrets* (1950) and *Vanished* (1955).

13. Inspired, no doubt, by old-dark-house classics like *Seven Keys to Baldpate*, *The Bat*, and *The Cat and the Canary*, Wall Spence specialized in wild melodramas unleashed in Gothic, isolated manors, situated over steep cliffs, complete with shadowy nooks, secret panels, and underground passages. The proceedings always unravel during a thunder and lightning storm or on the night of the full moon. The telephone line is cut, the lights flicker and go out at critical moments, heavy footsteps emanate from above, ghastly faces peer through windows, long arms reach out from corners, bodies fall out of closets, and eerie voices seem to issue from nowhere. Often, the plot hinges on a will read at midnight or a treasure chest hidden in a fireplace compartment. Villains nicknamed "The Phoenix" (*Whispering Walls*, 1935) or "The Owl" (*Mystery in Blue*, 1942) stalk beautiful women. Suspicious characters turn out to be masquerading detectives. Denouements reveal the identity of the blackguard with little surprise. Broad comedy is provided by frightened maids, scatter-brained spinsters, and buffoonish sheriffs. While Spence's plays were generally produced by community theatres and summer-stock companies, one burlesque mystery, *The House of Fear*, made it to Broadway's Republic Theatre on October 7, 1929. It is the tale of a psychic, Mme. Zita, who conducts a séance to frighten a murderer into a confession of the crime for which her son has been imprisoned in Sing Sing. The play ran for forty-eight performances, during which Wall Spence appeared across the street in the whodunit *Subway Express* as one of the suspects in a baffling murder case.

14. *New York Times*, December 11, 2000.

15. The Brontë sisters—Charlotte, Emily, and Anne—are the heroines of *The Brontës* by Alfred Sangster, a popular venture that premiered at the Repertory Theatre in Sheffield, England in May 1932 and moved to London's Royalty

Theatre a year later, running 238 performances. The three sisters and their brother Branwell are spotlighted in *Wild Dreamers* by Clemence Dane, a biographical drama that opened at West End's Apollo Theatre on May 26, 1933 with Diana Wynyard as Charlotte and Emlyn Williams as Branwell. In 1934, the Birmingham Repertory Theatre produced John Davison's *The Brontës of Haworth Parsonage*, which focuses on the decline and fall of Branwell Brontë and the rise and triumph of Charlotte Brontë. *Branwell*, a play by Martyn Richard about the sisters' lesser-known brother, was published by Longmans Ltd. in 1948. Margaret Webster arranged, adapted, and performed excerpts from works by and about Charlotte, Emily, and Anne Brontë, under the title *The Brontës*, shown at off-Broadway's Theatre de Lys in October 1963 (two performances) and at the Phoenix Theatre two months later (twenty performances). The one-woman show traveled to London's New Arts Theatre in January 1964 for a limited run. *Wide Sargasso Sea*, a 1966 novel by Jean Rhys, a prequel to *Jane Eyre* set in Jamaica and focusing on Rochester's deranged, Creole wife, was filmed in 1993, made into an opera in 1997, and adapted by BBC Wales for television in 2006. William Luce wrote *Currer Bell, Esq.* (Charlotte Brontë's nom de plume) as a radio play for the actress Julie Harris to perform on WGBH's *Masterpiece Radio Theatre*. It was subsequently filmed with Harris under the direction of Delbert Mann. Luce then turned the work into a stage play, retitled *Brontë: A Solo Portrait of Charlotte Brontë*, which Harris performed at benefits, colleges, and universities. With Charles Nelson Reilly as director, *Brontë* formally opened at the Marines Memorial Theatre in San Francisco on January 20, 1988. Similarly, actress Jill Alexander toured with a one-woman show about Charlotte Brontë in 2003. Warner Brothers filmed a strong drama about the lives, loves, and literary triumphs of the Brontë family, *Devotion* (1946), with Olivia de Havilland (Charlotte), Ida Lupino (Emily), Nancy Coleman (Anne), and Arthur Kennedy (Branwell). An imagined tale about the Brontë sisters, *Becoming Jane Eyre*, was penned by Sheila Kohler in 2009. At its center are Charlotte and the writing of *Jane Eyre*. Laura Joh Rowland launched a Victorian-era mystery series with *The Secret Adventures of Charlotte Brontë* (2008), in which Charlotte travels to London to clear her name of the false accusation of plagiarism, unintentionally witnesses a murder, and finds herself embroiled in a dangerous chain of events. A 2010 sequel, *Bedlam: The Further Secret Adventures of Charlotte Brontë*, begins with Charlotte's tour of the most sinister institution in London, the Bedlam Insane Asylum, and continues with a dangerous quest to unravel a secret that high-powered conspirators will kill to protect.

A Red Death (1997)

David Barr (United States, 1963–)

A Red Death is a play one imagines Raymond Chandler or Ross Macdonald would have written. Adapted by David Barr from a Walter Mosley novel of the same name, the protagonist is Ezekiel "Easy" Rawlins, a black private eye created by African-American writer Walter Mosley in a series of stylish hard-boiled detective stories that unfold in inner-city Los Angeles. Told in the first person by Rawlins, each of the novels swings with the complex rhythms of modern urban life. *Devil in a Blue Dress* (1990) takes place in 1948. Easy's assignment is to find the whereabouts of a blonde femme fatale known to frequent black jazz joints. With his gleefully homicidal sidekick Raymond "Mouse" Alexander as guide, Easy's quest takes the twosome on a vivid tour of L.A. in the forties and into the territory of race relations. *White Butterfly* (1992) sends Easy and Mouse on another odyssey, this time in 1956, among the seedy nightclubs of Watts and the dingy furnished rooms of Hollywood, in pursuit of a serial killer—a combination of crackling high tension and moral issues. The year is 1961 in *Black Betty* (1940), about a search for the missing housekeeper of an immensely rich Beverly Hills family. It, too, grapples with the big dilemmas that haunt American life. *A Little Yellow Dog* (1996) finds Easy taking on a job as supervising custodian of a Watts high school, leading a respectable, though somewhat boring, life—but not for long. When a corpse turns up in the school garden, Easy is the suspect and on the trail again—another brew of nerve-wracking suspense and shrewd social observations. *Gone Fishin'* (1997) takes Easy and Mouse back to their youth—Houston, 1939—when Easy has yet to develop his talent for unraveling riddles and Mouse has yet to kill his first man. Traveling in a "borrowed" old Ford, the two embark upon a journey to retrieve money from Mouse's stepfather, only to find themselves engulfed in a bayou world of voodoo, sex, and death that changes their lives and forever entwines their destinies.

A Red Death (1991), the second in a series, plunges Easy deep into the political, legal, and moral tar pits of Los Angeles during the early fifties. David Barr's stage adaptation peppers the proceedings with background testimony given to the Senate Committee for Control of Subversive Activities and utilizes excerpts from addresses by Senator Joseph McCarthy. The first person form is preserved by Easy as he sporadically addresses the audience directly; the action is revealed entirely from his point of view.

The play begins with Easy pretending to be the owner of a Magnolia Street apartment house, assigning his manager, Mofass, to collect rent from the tenants. Poinsettia Jackson, a tall black woman with a desperate disposition, pleads, "I ain't got it, and I'm sick," but Mofass insists, "I be back on Saturday, and if you ain't got the money, then you better be gone!" Later, when Poinsettia is found hanging in her room, Easy blames himself for being callous.

An investigating agent for the Internal Revenue Service, Reginald Arnold Lawrence, a wiry thin white male, calls Easy into his office regarding unpaid taxes from 1948–1952. "Tax evasion is a felony," says Lawrence. "You people—make an awful lot of noise about equality and freedom, but when it comes to paying your debt, you all sing a different song." Easy is offered a way out by Special Agent Darryl T. Craxton of the FBI: Infiltrate the First African Baptist Church and spy on former Polish resistance fighter, Chaim Wenzler, suspected of joining the Communist Party and stealing defense plans. "I figure the Reds to be one step worse than the Nazis," says Craxton.

Easy joins the congregation, befriends Wenzler and his daughter Shirley—then the murders begin. Reverend Towne, the minister of First African, and a young, beautiful black woman are found shot to death, half naked, in an inner chamber, obviously killed while making love. Wenzler, too, is plugged with a spray of bullets through his front door. It is next revealed that Poinsettia had not committed suicide but had been slain. The LAPD suspects Easy. A sadistic white cop, Andrew Reedy, interrogates Easy, punching, kicking, and brutally beating him with a billy club.

In order to clear his name, Easy sets out to nail the real culprit. Soliciting the help of his buddy Mouse, they confront Mofass. The manager points the finger at Reginald Lawrence, the IRS man: "Lawrence pulled me down a tax charge over a year ago. . . . I called Poinsettia, she hadn't paid no rent even way back then. She told me she'd be nice to me if I let her slide. I told her—if she was nice to my friend I'd let her slip by the summer." Mofass describes Lawrence as a heavy drinker who can't hold his liquor and once complained that Poinsettia was an anchor "on his neck." Mofass confesses that in an attempt to break out of Lawrence's clutches he fingered various "rich Negroes," including Easy Rawlins, as potential tax fraud victims to be blackmailed. When the FBI got Easy involved in the First African Church, Lawrence became concerned that his underhanded tactics would be discovered. He went to the church for information, had a squabble with Reverend Towne, and in a crazed fit returned to kill him.

Easy arranges to meet Lawrence in Griffith Park. The two men wrestle, with Lawrence getting the better of the exchange. He points a revolver at Easy's head. A gunshot is heard and Lawrence flies forward, dead. Mouse enters holding his long-barreled pistol, grinning at the body. "You damn fool, Easy Rawlins," he says. "You like some stupid cowboy. . . . Boy, I outta slap your silly ass."

* * *

Douglas Alan-Mann, artistic director of Chicago Theatre Company, the Windy City's only African-American equity troupe, approached Walter Mosley at a book signing and requested the stage rights to *A Red Death*. "Let me think about it," said Mosley. After kicking it back and forth for about a year, Mosley granted CTC permission to go ahead, preserving script approval. Playwright in Residence David Barr toiled through numerous stage readings and revisions. Finally, the world premiere of *A Red Death* took place on September 12, 1997, playing to sold-out houses through November 9. "The characters who populate Mosley's early 1950s Los Angeles setting form something of a cross between Charles Dickens and Richard Wright," wrote reviewer Sid Smith in the *Chicago Tribune*. "The fun, and ultimately the memorable lessons, come from the tapestry of characters."[1] Douglas Alan-Mann played the role of Easy Rawlins, supported by Daniel Bryant (Mouse); Steve Broussard (Mofass); Kimberly Hebert (Poinsettia); Martin Bedoian (Lawrence); Anthony Rodriguez (Craxton); and Tom Lentz (Wenzler).

The title color refers not only to the blood of murder but also to the political scare of the time. Director Delia Jolly Gray preserved the motif throughout the production with Lawrence's red silk tie, Craxton's red handkerchief, Mofass's red napkin tucked under his chin when gobbling pork chops, a neighbor's crimson apron, a prostitute's red gardenia, and Shirley Wenzler's red sash.

* * *

David Barr has been visible in Chicago theatre circles since 1986 and has received a number of acting citations and awards. His first writing effort, *The Death of Black Jesus*, was initially produced at the Unicorn Theatre in 1995. It made its professional premiere in 1996 with the Chicago Theatre Company. Later that year, the Dramatic Publishing Company released the play. Following *A Red Death*, Barr penned *Black Caesar*, a finalist in the 1997 Theodore Ward New Playwrights Contest sponsored by Chicago's Columbia College. Barr is also a lead writer for the syndicated cable TV talk show *Take Two*.

Walter Mosley was born in Los Angeles, California in 1952 to a father who was an African American custodian at a public school and a Polish Jewish mother who worked as a clerk. Both parents inspired young Walter to read the classics. He was educated at Goddard College, Plainfield, Vermont; John State College, where he received his BA in 1977; University of Minnesota graduate school; and City College, City University of New York, graduate writing program. He worked as a painter, potter, caterer, and computer programmer before dedicating himself to full-time writing at the age of thirty-four. He has written more than thirty books in a variety of genres—mysteries, science fiction, and nonfiction.

Heralded by President Clinton as his favorite mystery writer, Mosley scripted the film adaptation of his debut novel *Devil in a Blue Dress*, with Denzel Washington portraying Easy Rawlins. "Rawlins is a detective in the tradition of Chandler's Philip Marlowe and somewhat of Chester Himes's Coffin Ed and Grave Digger," states Jeffrey M. Wallmann, "a knight in tarnished armor who, defying all reason, seeks the truth that solves the crime even though the solution frequently leaves things unexplained and unresolved. . . . The main character aside from Rawlins is black Los Angeles whose Main Streets are really gray areas where moral and ethical certainties are hard to decipher and all the more perilous because of their ambiguity."[2]

In 1997, Mosley created another offbeat character—Socrates Fortlow, a deeply compassionate middle-aged ex-con. *Always Outnumbered, Always Outgunned* depicts a series of events in which Socrates, a fortress of a man with "rock-breaking" hands, utilizes his physical strength to rid the Watts neighborhood of arsonists and crack dealers. Leonid McGill, a hard drinking ex-boxer, now a New York private eye, solved his first case in 2009's *The Long Fall*, and has continued to put his life on the line in four successive novels. Mosley's non-genre books include *RL's Dream* (1995), recounting the cancer-ridden last days of a Mississippi Delta bluesman, and *Blue Light* (1998), an allegory triggered by the appearance of a mysterious blue radiance that critically affects the fate of San Francisco residents.

Mosley's first play, *The Fall of Heaven*, based on his novel *The Tempest Tales*, was initially produced at Playhouse in the Park, Cincinnati, Ohio, on January 21, 2010, and a year later, on January 7, 2011, staged by the Repertory Theatre in St. Louis, Missouri. The protagonist is Tempest Landry, a street-wise, quick-witted young man living in Harlem who unexpectedly finds himself at the Pearly Gates and is ordered to hell. In lieu of a technicality, Tempest is sent back to Earth with an angel as watchdog. A metaphorical good versus evil scenario ensues.

Mosley founded the Open Book Committee to promote racial integration in the publishing industry. He is a member of the executive board of PEN American Center, on the board of directors of the National Book Awards, and is a past president of the Mystery Writers of America.

Awards and Honors: Mystery Writers of America Edgar Allan Poe Award—Best Play, 1998. Walter Mosley—Private Eye Writers of America Shamus Award, 1990; Crime Writers' Association John Creasey Award, 1991; Black Caucus of the American Library Association's Literary Award and O. Henry Award, both in 1996.

NOTES

1. *Chicago Tribune*, September 23, 1997.
2. Jay P. Pederson, ed., *St. James Guide to Crime and Mystery Writers* (Detroit: St. James Press, 1996), 771.

The Scarlet Pimpernel (1997)

Book and Lyrics by Nan Knighton (United States), Music by Frank Wildhorn (United States, 1959–)

> They seek him here, they seek him there.
> Those Frenchies seek him everywhere.
> Is he in heaven?—Is he in hell?
> That demmed elusive Pimpernel?

This verse about the Scarlet Pimpernel, an enigmatic, mysterious person who helped Parisian aristocrats escape the guillotine during the French Revolution, was first used in a 1903 stage production, *The Scarlet Pimpernel*, written by the Hungarian-British Baroness Emmuska Orczy and her husband, Montagu Barstow.

It is 1792. France is saturated with the blood of decapitated nobles during the Reign of Terror. Many are in prison awaiting execution. An anonymous Englishman, called "The Scarlet Pimpernel" after the small flower crest with which he signs his messages, has assembled a band of daredevil followers to rescue these aristocrats from Madame la Guillotine and smuggle them to England. Among the Scarlet Pimpernel's lieutenants are Lord Anthony Dewhurst and Sir Andrew Ffoulkes. They and other members of the League of the Scarlet Pimpernel jealously guard the identity of their chief. The exploits of the Scarlet Pimpernel and his men are the talk of London society.

The first scene takes place at the Paris gates where the Scarlet Pimpernel, disguised as an old hag, manages to pass the sentries in a ramshackle horse-cart carrying the Comtesse de Tournai and her daughter.

The action shifts to a ball hosted by Lord Grenville, in London. The Prince of Wales, the guest of honor, is introduced to Citizen Chauvelin, an accredited agent of the French government. Among the elite of London society are Sir Percy and Lady Blakeney. The tall, dandyish Sir Percy, an authority on fashion and style, is universally acknowledged as "stupid" and "dull witted." No one understands why the French actress Marguerite St. Just, renowned for her beauty and arguably "the cleverest woman

496

in Europe," married the "demmed idiot." Their relationship is strained, for Sir Percy suspects, wrongly, that his wife has betrayed a family of French nobles to the bloodthirsty mob.

Chauvelin corners Marguerite. "Have you heard of the Scarlet Pimpernel, Citoyenne St. Just?" he asks. "Heard of the Scarlet Pimpernel?" she retorts. "Faith, man. We talk of nothing else. . . . We have hats 'à la Scarlet Pimpernel'; our horses are called 'Scarlet Pimpernel'; at the Prince of Wales' supper party the other night we had a 'soufflé à la Scarlet Pimpernel.'"[1]

Chauvelin reveals to Marguerite that her brother Armand has been arrested in Paris. Armand will be executed unless Marguerite helps unmask the Scarlet Pimpernel. Desperate, she consents.

During a minuet, Marguerite notices a scrap of paper passing from one hand to another and catches a glimpse before Sir Andrew Ffoulkes destroys it. She then confides to Chauvelin that the Scarlet Pimpernel will be in the ballroom at midnight, when the other guests are at supper.

As the clock chimes twelve, Chauvelin expects to confront the shadowy leader. To his chagrin, he only finds the lazy Sir Percy asleep, snoring, on the sofa.

In the next act, during a party given by Sir Percy and Lady Blakeney at their sumptuous home in Richmond, we learn that the daring Pimpernel is none other than Sir Percy himself.[2] Sir Percy leaves for France to effect the rescue of the Comte de Tournai, a friend, and of Armand St. Just, Marguerite's brother. Chauvelin, convinced now that the seemingly inept baronet is the Scarlet Pimpernel, follows. It is only after they are gone that Marguerite realizes her husband's true calling, and that she unwittingly betrayed him and sent him to his death. Marguerite relates her fears to Sir Andrew Ffoulkes and they cross over to France in a hired boat.

A battle of wits ensues between Sir Percy and Chauvelin, during which the Englishman dons various disguises, notably that of an elderly, stooped Jew, and that of a Republican captain of the guards. In a wayside inn near Calais, he sends Chauvelin's men on a false chase, then blinds his foe with a squirt of pepper and locks him in the cellar. Sir Percy not only rescues the Comte de Tournai and Armand, but also extracts Marguerite from a perilous position. They all board his schooner and set sail for England. Before reaching the white cliffs of Dover, a full reconciliation takes place between Sir Percy and his wife.

The Scarlet Pimpernel premiered unsuccessfully at the Theatre Royal, Nottingham, England, on October 15, 1903. With a rewritten last act it came to London's New Theatre on January 5, 1905, featuring Fred Terry, who also directed, in the title role. Julia Neilson played Lady Blakeney and Horace Hodges was Chauvelin. The reviews were hostile. In an interview with *The Bookman* magazine a decade later, Baroness Orczy recalls that "with the exception of one or two papers, the play received from the dramatic critics the soundest round of abuse that any play, to my knowledge, has ever had. It was 'melodramatic,' 'incoherent,' 'stagy,' 'the audience was made of friends who tried to cheer the actors and loudly condemned the authors' . . . 'we cannot help thinking that the Baroness Orczy and her husband would have been better advised had they allowed their own particular little pimpernel to blush and die unseen."[3] Still, the play won the affection of the public, ran for 122 performances, and Terry continued to masquerade as the Scarlet Pimpernel in revivals that took place in 1905, 1907, 1908, 1910, 1911, 1915, 1928, and 1929, with Neilson or Hodges often at his side. Along the way, the *New York Times* condemned *The Scarlet Pimpernel* as "the worst play in London,"[4] but the show kept playing to cheering spectators for more than 2000 performances.

The English company of *The Scarlet Pimpernel* came to New York's Knickerbocker Theater on October 24, 1910. The *New York Times* sniffed at the leading character as "a man who may yawn and yawn and be a hero still."[5] The run lasted forty performances.

More than half a century later, on January 6, 1964, a musical based on *The Scarlet Pimpernel*, opened at off-Broadway's Gramercy Arts Theatre, called *Pimpernel!* It featured David Daniels as Sir Percy Blakeney, Leila Martin as Lady Marguerite Blakeney, and William Larsen as Chauvelin. "Whatever the intent," scowled the *New York Times*, "the result is as flat as a drum head."[6] *Pimpernel* closed after three performances.

In England, an adaptation of *The Scarlet Pimpernel* by Beverly Cross, directed by Nicholas Hytner, was launched at the Chichester Festival and transferred to London's Her Majesty's Theatre on December 11, 1985. Cross follows the structure of the Orczy play but adds a few innovations. The curtain rises on a public square where several aristocrats are being led to the guillotine. A wild crowd jeers at the condemned as they mount the scaffold and cheers when the executioner holds up severed heads. In this version, Percy and his men disguise themselves as Carmelite nuns in order to rescue Armand St. Just and the Comte de Tournai. During the climactic sequences, Percy bamboozles Chauvelin by masquerading as his moustached henchman, Lambert. Donald Silden portrayed Sir Percy and Charles Kay appeared as Chauvelin, both receiving high praise from the critics, as did the entire production. "Its balance between thrills and laughter is now judged to perfection," wrote the *Sunday Telegraph*.[7] "It is a long time since the theatre saw an adventure so joyous and so preposterous as *The Scarlet Pimpernel*," chirped the *Daily Telegraph*.[8]

A decade passed, and on November 9, 1997, a lavish, $10 million musical adaptation of the play premiered at the Minskoff Theater in New York City, with book and lyrics by Nan Knighton, music by Frank Wildhorn. The action begins on stage of the Comedie Francaise in Paris, where the leading lady of the company, Marguerite St. Just, addresses her audience and relates that this will be her last performance before marrying "a tall and handsome English prince," Sir Percival Blakeney. In her heart, says Marguerite, she'll never leave Paris.

The actress's emotional farewell is interrupted by the noisy entrance of Chauvelin and his aides, Mercier and Coupeau, accompanied by a squadron of soldiers. Chauvelin announces that "by order of The Revolutionary Tribunal, this theatre is now declared closed." The confused troupe of actors and dancers disperse. Marguerite elicits from Chauvelin a promise that her friends, the Marquis de St. Cyr and his family, will only be deported with no harm coming to them, and hands Chauvelin a note indicating their whereabouts. Marguerite leaves for a waiting carriage and Chauvelin sings an ode to "Madame Guillotine" during which the scene changes into the interior of a prison.

Gloating about "glorious days" and "bloody bouquets," soldiers lead the imprisoned aristocrats to the guillotine. At the Place de la Bastille, the Marquis de St. Cyr, his hands tied, mourns humanity's loss of reason. His head is placed in the yoke and as Chauvelin exclaims, "Hail her majesty, Madame Guillotine," the blade falls. Blackout.

In England, at the Blakeney estate, Sir Percy and Marguerite enter from opposite sides of the stage for their wedding ceremony. The couple, supported by an ensemble of guests, sings "You Are My Home," and promise to cherish and hold one another for the rest of their lives. A wedding dance ensues. While the men take turns swirling with Marguerite, Lord Dewhurst enters and whispers to Percy that the Marquis de St. Cyr and his family were guillotined. Someone betrayed the St. Cyrs by delivering a note with the exact location of their hideaway. Dewhurst takes the note from his pocket, written with Marguerite's handwriting and signed with her seal.

Following the wedding feast, when Marguerite and Percy are left alone, she senses in him a change of attitude. Percy remarks, "You are such a demned remarkable—actress," and she leaves, confused. Percy sings "Prayer," castigating himself for being "a fool, a man deluded by his wife." The next morning, he assembles his friends—Ozzy, Dewhurst, Elton, Farleigh, Hal, and Ben—and proposes that they join forces to fight against the inhumane, bloodthirsty French revolutionists. He believes that they can "outwit the bastards" by the use of "diversions and disguise." While at home, says Percy, they should pretend to be unlikely heroes, "la crème of fancy fops," a breed of ninnies.

Armand St. Just, who has eavesdropped the conversation, enters and asks to join the group. Percy warns him that his sister, Marguerite, must know nothing of their conspiracy. The men gather around Percy's desk as he opens his ring and tells them that he will send instructions sealed by a family crest—The Scarlet Pimpernel. Fired up, they all belt "Into the Fire," comparing themselves to David against Goliath and vowing to knock down any obstacles that "block the way." The men throw off their waistcoats, grab props and costume pieces, and practice dueling with swords while the scene shifts to Percy's schooner sailing in the English Channel toward France.

A Rescue Ballet ensues—a "Keystone Kops" dance composed of a series of choreographed vignettes in which Percy and his League rescue prisoners. Robespierre chides Chauvelin for "sitting like a lame idiot" while "this Englishman taunts us." Masquerading as Grappin, a Belgian spy, Percy offers Robespierre his services to track the Pimpernel. Robespierre orders Chauvelin henceforth to work hand in hand with Grappin. Chauvelin croons "Falcon in the Dive," bracing himself for a "final duel in which the fittest will survive." He instructs Grappin to travel to England, make contact with the French actress Marguerite St. Just, now Lady Blakeney, suggesting that she may be of use in unearthing the Scarlet Pimpernel.

In the drawing room of the Blakeney estate, the household servants sing "Who Is the Scarlet Pimpernel?" There are rumors that the elusive Pimpernel "swaggers on a heath—with several daggers in his teeth," and that "he travels with his 12-foot spear—hacking off a Frenchman's ear." Percy poses for a portrait sketched by Marie Grosholtz, a former set designer for the Comedie Francais and Marguerite's good friend. Stretching lazily, he pooh-poohs the heroics of the Pimpernel. Marguerite draws Armand aside and expresses concern over his constant traveling. She also bemoans the fact that Percy is "never here."

Marguerite sings "When I Look at You," befuddled by the change that came over her husband whose love and care are now but a memory. She reprises the song in the estate's garden when the butler Jessup escorts Chauvelin in. The Frenchman tells Marguerite that he tried to save the St. Cyr family, but was overruled by Robespierre. He asks Marguerite to serve her country by helping to discover the identity of the Scarlet Pimpernel. Marguerite orders him out, but Chauvelin threatens to reveal to her husband that they were once lovers. Marguerite retorts that she won't succumb to blackmail. Percy enters. He is delighted to make the acquaintance of Monsieur Shove-lynn. Is it true, he asks, that Parisians no longer wear lace on their jabots? He is looking forward to meeting Shove-lynn at the Royal Ball. He must leave now to see to his ruby satin attire. Chauvelin does not understand how Marguerite could replace him with such a simpleton and sings "Where's The Girl?" reminding Marguerite of the days when she had "blaze in her eyes" and was "burning for life."

Later that day, Percy stands in the library, wearing an outrageous outfit, and addresses the members of his League, all dressed in colorful, shimmering chiffon. In "The Creation of Man," they strut and practice to "bear the weight of well-tailored clothes," draw their breeches tight and perfume their plumes. Percy pulls a handkerchief from his sleeve and instructs the men to behave like fops. They break into dance, at the end of which the group declares, "Buttons, buckles, ruffles and lace—represent the human race!"

At the Royal Palace, the Prince of Wales queries Percy and his friends about their frequent trips to France and asks if they're hooked up with this—Pimpernel fellow. The men's reactions range from horror to hilarity. A sentry declares, "Citizen Chauvelin, Agent of the French Republic," and Chauvelin enters with two aides. Percy introduces him to the prince as "Shove-lynn, a most stimulating fellow." Chauvelin corners Marguerite and informs her that Armand has been arrested in Paris. Unless Marguerite uncovers the identity of the Scarlet Pimpernel, her brother will be guillotined. He is certain that the English rogue will attend the ball tonight and has no doubt that the "greatest actress in Europe" can locate him; if so, he swears that Armand will be released.

The act 2 curtain rises on a masked ball. Present are the Prince of Wales, Percy, Marguerite, Chauvelin, and assorted guests. The ensemble sings "Who Is the Scarlet Pimpernel?" Marguerite emotes that "the man's a hero" while Percy declares him "a drunk, a fiddling Nero, a lazy lout." When Marguerite dances a minuet with Farleigh, she tells him that she must speak with the Pimpernel about a matter of life and death. Both Chauvelin and Percy hear her say, "The footbridge. One o'clock."

At the footbridge, Percy hides in the shadows and addresses Marguerite from behind, careful never to let her see him. He identifies himself as the Scarlet Pimpernel. Marguerite tells the silhouetted figure that her brother, Armand St. Just, has been arrested and, according to Chauvelin, will be executed. Marguerite reveals to the stranger that in France she lived as "a free woman" and briefly became Chauvelin's lover. Chauvelin held it over her, threatening, "How would you like your husband to know what sort of woman you are?" She says that she is afraid that her husband will leave her. With a heavy heart, Marguerite relates that she'd exposed the whereabouts of Marquis de St. Cyr but only upon a promise by Chauvelin that the aristocrat and his family would go free. Percy assures Marguerite that he'll save Armand and bids her to go and find her husband. Left alone, Percy sings "She Was There," an ode to the woman who "turned my whole world around."

As Percy moves to exit, he collides with Chauvelin. "Shove-lynn! Demme, then you're the Scarlet Pimpernel!" exclaims Percy, playing the fool. "Merde! This man is a nincompoop!" mumbles Chauvelin and stalks out. Percy's men run in and their leader tells them to prepare to sail to France.

In Paris, Chauvelin confronts Marguerite, expressing his admiration for her courage to travel to France, despite danger, in search of her brother. Percy enters, disguised as Grappin, and offers to cut the throats of both Marguerite and Armand. Chauvelin has a better idea: He asks Grappin to spread the news that the St. Justs are to die—a lure to trap the Scarlet Pimpernel. Grappin suggests that they take the brother and sister to the seacoast, for surely the Pimpernel must use a secret harbor.

In a prison cell, Marguerite sings "I'll Forget You," assuring the far-away Percy that she'll remember him until she dies. Chauvelin's aides, Mercier and Coupeau, name the prisoners who are to be carted to the guillotine, a list that includes the St. Justs. Outside the prison walls, the prisoners are "allowed" to escape. They'll be followed, Chauvelin assures Robespierre, and "before a new day dawns, it shall be recorded that the Scarlet Pimpernel fell to Madame Guillotine!"

The scene shifts to an interior of a rumbling carriage, where Armand, by a slip of the tongue, reveals to a shocked Marguerite that her husband Percy is the Scarlet Pimpernel.

On the shore of Miquelon, a small fishing village, Armand and Marguerite stop in their tracks when they see a rough-hewn guillotine towering on the pier. Chauvelin emerges behind the contraption and informs the St. Justs that they have led their leader into "a tight little trap." Soldiers enter and line the seascape.

Percy, dressed as Grappin, runs in and tells Chauvelin that the Pimpernel is none other than Lord Percy Blakeney, and that the Lord, accompanied by two men, took off on his horse toward Calais. Chauvelin orders the squadron to Calais, leaving several soldiers. Grappin exhibits to Chauvelin the famous Pimpernel ring and removes the Grappin disguise. Chauvelin grabs a sword from one of the soldiers and swings at Percy, who ducks. A fierce duel ensues. Chauvelin proves to be the better swordsman and Percy is disarmed. Chauvelin orders his men to drag Percy to the guillotine. A hooded executioner enters and forces Percy's head into the yoke. The blade falls. Percy's head drops into a basket. Marguerite collapses.

Suddenly Percy appears, with the executioner behind him. Chauvelin is dumbfounded. Percy lifts the head from the basket and explains that it is the work of designer Marie Grosholtz, who recently married Monsieur Tussaud. "Now she is Madame Tussaud," says Percy, "and quite a clever artist, what?"

Chauvelin orders the remaining six soldiers to seize Lord Percy. Instead, they surround him and reveal themselves as Dewhurst, Ozzy, Elton, Farleigh, Hal, and Ben. They tie Chauvelin up and gag him. Percy slips his ring onto Chauvelin's hand. The men will deliver the French agent to the town square and announce that they have captured the Scarlet Pimpernel.

The last scene unfolds aboard Percy's schooner. Percy and Marguerite reprise "When I Look at You," and as they warmly kiss, the curtain descends.

* * *

Directed by Peter Hunt and choreographed by Adam Pelty, *The Scarlet Pimpernel* opened at New York's Minskoff Theatre on November 9, 1997. The leading roles were played by Douglas Sills (Percy Blakeney), Christine Andreas (Marguerite St. Just), and Terrence Mann (Chauvelin). The show was snubbed by the critics with such sarcastic comments as "Frankly, 'Scarlet,' we don't give a damn";[9] "the music seems as amorphous as a jellyfish in hot water";[10] and "if it's pulse-racing suspense and derring-do you're after, you would be better off watching tourists crossing against the light in Times Square."[11] Clive Barnes of the *New York Post* believed that "Wildhorn's score sounds synthetic, characterless and so instantly unmemorable that even the repeats have a wilted freshness to them. . . . [Nan Knighton's] lyrics reveal much the same lack of flair and imagination which bedevils the music."[12] Only Douglas Sills, in the title role, garnered positive nods.

The Scarlet Pimpernel was sinking fast, but the Cablevision Systems Corporation decided to acquire the show and back a reincarnation that included extensive rewrites of book and score, a new director and choreographer (Robert Longbottom), and a revamped cast. With Douglas Sills still at the helm, *The Scarlet Pimpernel* reopened on November 4, 1998, won the graces of the press, continued to be reconstructed and reshaped—sometimes bloated, sometimes trimmed—and managed to run until January 2, 2000, amassing 772 performances. A national tour commenced a month later and ran for two months.

* * *

The Scarlet Pimpernel has had a robust career in the cinema and on television. Dustin Farnum starred as Sir Percy in a 1917 fifty-minute silent feature made in the United States. Two silent British films followed: *The Elusive Pimpernel*, 1919, with Cecil Humphreys, and *The Triumph of the Scarlet Pimpernel*, 1928, with Matheson Lang. The first talkie version, 1935's *The Scarlet Pimpernel*, with Leslie Howard (Sir Percy), Merle Oberon (Marguerite), and Raymond Massey (Chauvelin) is considered the best of the lot. Later sequels include *Return of the Scarlet Pimpernel*, featuring Barry Barnes (1937) and *The Elusive Pimpernel* (aka *The Fighting Pimpernel*), starring David Niven (1950). Two modernizations of the theme are *Pimpernel Smith* (1941), with Leslie Howard enacting a Cambridge professor who during World War I leads a group of students into Germany to rescue Nazi victims; and *Pimpernel Swenson* (1950), a Swedish film about an uncle entering a Soviet-occupied city to save his nephew.

Television versions include a 1955–1956 British series, *The Adventures of the Scarlet Pimpernel*, starring Marius Goring; a 1960 Dupont Show of the Month, *The Scarlet Pimpernel*, starring Michael Rennie and Maureen O'Hara; a Studio Uno production on Italian television, *La Primula Rossa* (1964), with Tata Giacobetti; a 1973 segment, *Battle of Wits*, in the British *Great Mysteries*, featuring Ian Bannen; a 1982 CBS presentation of *The Scarlet Pimpernel* with Anthony Andrews (Sir Percy), Jane Seymour (Marguerite), and Ian McKellen (Chauvelin); and a 1999–2000 A&E series with Richard E. Grant, Elizabeth McGovern, and Martin Shaw. Almost a century after its inception, the *New York Times* said that *"The Scarlet Pimpernel* remains a tingling adventure."[13]

* * *

Hungarian born Emmuska Orczy (1865–1947) was the only child of Baron Felix Orczy, a celebrated composer and conductor. She lived and studied in Brussels and Paris, and after the family moved in 1880, in London. At an art school she met young illustrator Montagu Barstow, the son of an English clergyman, and they married. In the late 1890s she began writing short stories for popular magazines.

In her autobiography, *Links in the Chain of Life*, Orczy explains that the image of the Scarlet Pimpernel came to her in a flash, on the platform of a dreary underground station: "I give you my word that as I was sitting there I saw—yes, I saw—Sir Percy Blakeney as you know him now. I saw him in his exquisite clothes, his slender hands holding up his spy-glass; I heard his lazy drawling speech, his quaint laugh. . . . It was a mental vision, of course, and lasted but a few seconds—but it was the whole life-story of the Scarlet Pimpernel that was there and then revealed to me."[14]

Orczy novelized *The Scarlet Pimpernel* and it was published in 1905, launching her prolific and successful literary career. She followed the initial novel with a series of popular sequels about the deceptive Sir Percy Blakeney and other swashbuckling historical romances. Several of her books were transferred to the screen: *Beau Brocade*, a highwayman story of the eighteenth century (also adapted to the stage in 1908); *The Laughing Cavalier*, in which a daring adventurer rises against the expansive dominance of Spain; *A Spy of Napoleon*, wherein a French exile strives to warn the Emperor of the looming Franco-Prussian war; and *The Emperor's Candlesticks*, depicting a Russian spy and a Polish agent who clash and fall in love. Among Orczy's stage plays—none successful—were *The Sin of Wil-*

liam Jackson (1906), *The Duke's Wager* (1911), *The Legion of Honour* (1918), and *Leatherface* (1922), a dramatization of one of her favorite novels.

Orczy made an important contribution to the genre of detective literature when creating "The Old Man in the Corner," fiction's first armchair sleuth. The nameless old man sits in a London teashop, gets information from a young reporter about crimes of the day, and solves them by intuition and logic. The cases of the old man first appeared in *Royal Magazine* in 1901. They were collected in book form in *The Case of Miss Elliott* (1905), *The Old Man in the Corner* (1909), and *Unravelled Knots* (1925). In 1924, The Old Man in the Corner was portrayed by Rolf Leslie in a series of short British films.

In *Lady Molly of Scotland Yard* (1910), Orczy fashioned an early woman sleuth, Lady Molly Robertson-Kirk, head of the "Female Department of Scotland Yard." Molly proves the innocence of her husband, a convicted murderer, and continues to solve twelve complicated cases. Patrick Mulligan, the unscrupulous lawyer of *Skin o' My Tooth* (1928), will go to any length to unravel a crime and exonerate his client. Meshing historical adventure with ingredients of mystery are *The Man in Grey* (1918) and *Castles in the Air* (1922).

* * *

Frank Wildhorn was born to Jewish parents in New York City in 1959. The family moved to Hollywood, Florida when he was fourteen. Frank was more interested in sports than music, but started fiddling around with the family organ between football practices. He soon taught himself to play the piano and as a teen joined various bands, from rock and roll to jazz. Aspiring to compose, he attended nearby Miami University for one year, then transferred to the University of Southern California, playing gigs at night in Los Angeles. Still a student, he began writing *Jekyll and Hyde*, based on the 1886 novella by Robert Louis Stevenson. In 1990, an album of songs from the show appeared, and soon afterward, with Leslie Bricusse providing the book, *Jekyll & Hyde* premiered at the Alley Theatre in Houston, Texas. In 1995–1996, the musical went on a national tour, and, proving itself a cult favorite, landed at Broadway's Plymouth Theatre on April 28, 1997 with Robert Cuccioli in the double title role. Despite scathing reviews, *Jekyll & Hyde* ran for 1,543 performances during a four-year run, recouping about 75 percent of the $7 million investment.

Following *Jekyll and Hyde* came *The Scarlet Pimpernel*. Wildhorn's next venture was *The Civil War*, for which he set to music letters, diaries, and other documents from the era. *The Civil War* opened at Houston's Alley Theatre in the fall of 1998 and moved to Broadway's St. James Theatre on April 22, 1999 for sixty-one performances. It earned Wildhorn a Tony nomination for Best Original Musical Score. *Dracula*, with a book by Don Black and Christopher Hampton based on Bram Stoker's 1897 vampire novel, opened at the Belasco Theatre, New York, on August 19, 2004, featuring Tom Hewitt as the count. The musical was lambasted by the critics and struggled to run for 157 showings. *Wonderland*, a show Wildhorn developed with magician David Copperfield, premiered at the Marquis Theatre on April 17, 2011 and lasted thirty-three performances.

Wildhorn's latest Broadway offering is the score for *Bonnie and Clyde*, with a book by Ivan Menchell and lyrics by Don Black, a $6 million musical about the infamous Bonnie Parker and Clyde Barrow, Depression-era outlaws and lovebirds who paved a bloody trail across the Southwest before being killed by Louisiana sheriff's deputies. *Bonnie and Clyde* incubated at the La Jolla Playhouse in San Diego, California and the Asolo Repertory Theatre in Sarasota, Florida before arriving in New York's Schoenfeld Theatre on December 1, 2011, featuring Laura Osnes and Jeremy Jordan in the title roles. The show received unanimously negative reviews. Ben Brantley of the *New York Times* wrote: "Directed and (sort of) choreographed by Jeff Calhoun, *Bonnie and Clyde* manages to make that triple-threat lure of sex, youth and violence seem about as glamorous as—and a lot less dangerous than—Black Friday at Walmart."[15] *Bonnie and Clyde* closed after sixty-nine performances.

Wildhorn composed the score of several musicals that haven't made it to Broadway. *Svengali*, based on the 1894 novel *Trilby* by George du Maurier, about a possessive vocal coach who uses hypnotism to transform the tone-deaf title character into an acclaimed singer, premiered at the Alley Theatre in Houston, Texas in April 1991, and in October was mounted by the Asolo Repertory Theatre in Sarasota, Florida. *Camille Claudel*, a second collaboration with Nan Knighton, who provided the book and lyrics, is based on a real-life French sculptor and graphic artist who had a tempestuous relationship with Auguste Rodin, for whom she was the source of inspiration. Linda Eder, Wildhorn's ex-wife, originated the role when the musical was presented by the Goodspeed Theatre in East Haddam, Connecticut in 2003 and by the New York Workshop the following year. *Waiting for the Moon*, with book and lyrics by Jack Murphy, tells the love story of famed American author F. Scott Fitzgerald and his wife Zelda. The Lenape Regional Performing Arts Center in Marlton, New Jersey hosted the world premiere of the musical in 2005. *Rudolph*, conceived for the stage by Wildhorn and Steve Cuden, is about the Crown Prince of Austria and his liaison with Baroness Mary Vetsera. Their deaths in 1889 at his Mayerling hunting lodge apparently were the result of a murder-suicide pact. *Rudolph* was given a reading in New York City in 2005 but the official world premiere took place the following year in Budapest, Hungary. Since then, *Rudolph* has played in Vienna, Austria (2009) and Péces, Hungary (2010). *The Count of Monte Cristo*, another collaboration between Wildhorn and Jack Murphy, is based on the classic 1844 novel by Alexandre Dumas. The first performance of the musical commenced on March 14, 2009 in St. Gallen, Switzerland with Thomas Borchert starring as Edmond Dantès. On April 21, 2010 the show played in Seoul, South Korea. Wildhorn and Leslie Bricusse, who had teamed on *Jekyll and Hyde*, got together again on *Cyrano de Bergerac*, inspired by the 1897 verse play of the same title by Edmond Rostand, the story of a gifted cadet, poet, and duelist—with a very large nose. The world premiere took place at the Nissay Theatre in Tokyo on May 5, 2009, closing three weeks later, and transferring to Osaka, where it ran for several performances.

Nan Knighton is a native of Baltimore, Maryland, the daughter of a physician and an artist. She received an undergraduate degree from Sarah Lawrence College, where she acted, directed, and wrote student productions, and a master's degree in creative writing from Boston University. She taught English and ran a drama department in a girls' school in Massachusetts and, back in Baltimore, wrote for the Maryland Center for Public Broadcasting's *Consumer Survival Kit*. When she married her second husband, an entertainment lawyer, Knighton moved to New York. She submitted a tape that included the lyrics of a love ballad and a jocular song to Frank Wildhorn, and was hired as lyricist for *The Scarlet Pimpernel*. Following *The Scarlet Pimpernel*, Knighton contributed to the Broadway scene the book of the musical *Saturday Night Fever*, based on the 1977 screenplay by Norman Wexler, about a Brooklyn youth who finds meaning to his life when dancing at a local disco (Minskoff Theatre, October 21, 1999—501 performances).

Acting Edition: Tams-Witmark Music Library.

Awards and Honors: *The Scarlet Pimpernel* was nominated for 1998 Tony Awards in the categories of Best Musical, Best Book of a Musical (Nan Knighton), Best Actor in a Musical (Douglas Sills), and for a Drama Desk Award for Outstanding Music (Frank Wildhorn). Wildhorn's *The Civil War* was nominated for 1999 Tony Awards for Best Musical and Best Original Score. Baroness Orczy's *The Old Man in the Corner* (1909) is included in the Howard Haycraft–Ellery Queen Definitive Library of Detective-Crime-Mystery Fiction.

NOTES

1. Baroness Orczy, *The Scarlet Pimpernel* (New York: Triangle, 1944), 84.
2. Sir Percy Blakeney/the Scarlet Pimpernel is the first among the literary heroes who establish a counterpart persona to baffle their foes. Others include the

Duke of Charnerace/Arsene Lupin, Don Diego/Zorro, Clark Kent/Superman, Bruce Wayne/Batman, Selina Kyle/Catwoman.

3. *Bookman*, August 1913.
4. *New York Times*, August 4, 1907.
5. *New York Times*, October 25, 1910.
6. *New York Times*, January 7, 1964.
7. *Sunday Telegraph*, London, December 15, 1985.
8. *Daily Telegraph*, London, December 13, 1985.
9. *Daily News*, November 10, 1997.
10. *New York Post*, November 10, 1997.
11. *New York Times*, November 10, 1997.
12. *New York Post*, November 10, 1997.
13. *New York Times*, March 5, 1999.
14. Baroness Orczy, *Links in the Chain of Life* (London: Hutchinson, 1944), 97.
15. *New York Times*, December 2, 2011.

Not About Nightingales (1998)

Tennessee Williams
(United States, 1911–1983)

In the 1930s, a young Tennessee Williams wrote several full-length plays, apprentice exercises that contained the seeds of his later masterworks. Inspired by a newspaper story about four inmates who went on a hunger strike and were murdered in a Philadelphia County prison, he penned *Not About Nightingales* in 1938. Dramaturge Michael Fuller writes in *Williams in an Hour* that *Not About Nightingales* "exemplifies one of the primary themes of Williams' mature work: the desire to flee a confining situation. It could not be more starkly expressed than it is in the setting of this play: a penitentiary in which prisoners are tortured in the 'Klondike,' a cell where the temperature reaches over 125 degrees."[1]

Initially titled *The Rest Is Silence*, Williams submitted the manuscript to the politically minded Group Theatre in New York, but it was summarily rejected. "Why was the play never produced?" asks Allean Hale rhetorically in his introduction to the printed version of the drama. "In 1939, a Broadway agent may have found a play with murder, violent death, a sympathetic black character, a drag queen, and syphilis difficult to market."[2] Sixty years later, actress Vanessa Redgrave tracked down *Not About Nightingales* in the archives of the University of Texas at Austin. Her brother, Corin Redgrave, portrayed the sadistic warden of "a large American prison" in the world premiere performance on March 5, 1998, at the Royal National Theatre, London, where it played in repertory through April 30. It was subsequently performed at the Alley Theatre in Houston, Texas, opening on June 5, 1998 for a one-month run. Corin Redgrave and *Nightingales* went to Broadway's Circle in the Square on February 25, 1999.

Not About Nightingales is a three-act play, with each act divided into several episodes. The curtain rises on a hallway outside the warden's office where two women sit on a bench: Mrs. Bristol, a worn matron holding a napkin-covered basket, and Eva Crane, a good-looking, somewhat nervous girl. Mrs. Bristol is here to give her son, Jack, some baked goods. Eva has come for a job interview and is hoping to become the warden's secretary. Eva tells Mrs. Bristol that she read in the *Sunday Supplement* that this is a model institution run by experts in psychology and sociology. She assures Mrs. Bristol that Jack will probably come out better and stronger than before he went in.

Jim Allison, a handsome inmate, walks in and informs the women that the warden is inspecting the grounds and may not be back for a while. Mrs. Bristol can't stay and leaves the food on the warden's desk. Jim tells Eva that he's a convict assigned to assist the warden during the day. He is also the editor of the *Prison Monthly*. At night, when he returns, his cellmates call him, "Canary Jim."

Warden Bert Whalen enters. He is described as "a powerful man, rather stout, but with coarse good looks." Eva introduces herself and pleads for the position. At first, the warden doesn't want to hear it, but in the end he reconsiders and gives her the job. Eva goes out, blind with joy, and Whalen tells Jim, "Dizzy as hell—but she's got a shape on her that would knock the bricks out of a Federal pen!"

In episode two, the guards march the convicts to their cells. Notable among the inmates of Hall C are Sailor Jack, Mrs. Bristol's son, who has the vacant look of a schizophrenic; Butch O'Fallon, a tough, domineering leader among the inmates; the Queen, gay, and not too smart; and Oliver (Ollie) Armsted, black, smart, religious, and respected by all. Schultz, a brutal guard, becomes furious at Sailor Jack for mumbling incoherently, and sends in guards to take him to "Klondike," a windowless boiler room lined with steam radiators that the prisoners call "a little suburb of hell."

The next morning, when Mrs. Bristol returns to see the warden, he tells her coarsely that her son had "violent delusions" and was transferred to the psychopathic ward. Jim informs Eva that the permanent, monotonous menu at the prison consists of stale spaghetti and meatballs. In order to put Jim back in line, the warden confides to Eva that when Jim first got to the prison, he had to whip him for fourteen straight days to break through his rebellious attitude. Since then, says Whalen, Jim has become a stool pigeon—"He keeps me posted on conditions among the men." The warden orders Jim to take off his shirt. Long scars across his shoulders down to the waist are visible; ten years have not obliterated them. The sight is too much for Eva and she faints.

Down in the cells, the inmates begin to get stomach pains. Butch suggests that they go on a hunger strike. Jim asks that they wait a bit longer. He's coming up for parole next month. Out of prison, he'll "sing so loud and so high that the echo will knock these walls down!" The men agree. Instead, they go to dinner and cause a small riot. The guards march them back to their cells. Schultz accuses a frail newcomer, Jeremy (Swifty) Trout, of "squawking" in the dining room and orders the guards to march him to Klondike. "Swifty won't make it," says Queen. "They'll kill him down there."

Eva discovers a discrepancy in the commissary report; six hundred dollars are unaccounted for. Warden Whalen pooh-poohs her concern, asks Eva to "drop that formality stuff" and come to his private chambers. He grips Eva in a firm embrace but releases her when Jim enters to report that Swifty, who has been confined to Klondike for five days in a straitjacket, is in a very bad shape. "I think he needs five more," says the warden. When Ollie Armsted is sent to the hole, the tortured black inmate, who was imprisoned for stealing a crate of canned food to feed his family, commits suicide by butting his head against the wall. The warden orders Jim to list the cause of death as "stomach ulcers, severe hemorrhages." Word spreads around the cells, and Butch declares, "Hunger strike!"

Act 2 begins with the prison chaplain resigning his post. Jim pleads with Eva to leave, arguing that it's not safe, but she refuses. She confesses her feelings for him; she'll wait till his parole hearing and depart with him. Jim is no longer optimistic about his release, but Eva assures him that she plans to go to the newspapers and reveal the true conditions in the prison. "You could tell that thirty-five hundred animals are being starved to death and threatened with torture," says Jim.

However, the warden tells Eva that she cannot leave because the prison is under quarantine—"a bad epidemic's broken out." Jim asks the warden about his parole: "I have been here ten years. . . . I'm due for a ticket-of-leave." The warden dismisses the notion. Desperate, Jim devises a plan to meet Eva in the southwest corner of the prison yard to attempt their escape.

Act 3 unfolds mostly in Klondike, where the prisoners from Hall C are beginning to feel the heat from the boiler room steam. Butch attempts to keep the morale up among the men by singing and dancing. The guard Schultz gleefully keeps raising the temperature—to 130, 140, 150. The loud, shrill hiss of steam emanates from the pipes. Soon the men are sprawled on the floor, breathing heavily. Swifty is the first to die. Queen staggers into a cloud of steam, screams, and falls. The bodies of the men quickly gather in the center. Butch is the only one still conscious.

Jim and Eva meet in the yard. The beam of a searchlight suddenly shines on them. Guards arrive and lead them to the warden's office. Warden Whalen flails Jim, who staggers to the floor, and orders the guards to drag him to Klondike. Schultz and his aide McBurney open the Klondike's door and survey the piled bodies. Butch jumps up and clutches Schultz's throat. Jim attacks McBurney and wrestles his revolver from him. Butch snatches a ring of keys from Schultz, tells Jim to open cells and let the prisoners out. He then pushes Schultz into the steaming cell and bolts its door. Schultz pounds and screams.

Jim enters the warden's office with the gun in hand, followed by other prisoners. Like a pack of wolves, they circle Whalen, who pleads with them to remember that he's a family man with a young daughter. Butch flays him with a rubber hose. The men converge from all sides, attack the warden with demonic fury, and throw his dead body out of the window into the surrounding water.

The siren of an approaching police boat is heard. Jim decides to jump into the river and swim to shore. He hands his shoes to Eva and tells her to look for him in the personal columns. It remains uncertain whether Jim makes it out.

* * *

When *Not About Nightingales* opened in London in March 1988, critic Benedict Nightingale dispatched to the *New York Times* his assessment of a "most exciting event. . . . Yes, *Not About Nightingales* can be callow, prolix, melodramatic. . . . Yet, isn't it ungrateful to admonish a bolt of lightning, fizzing down to earth, for not being quite subtle and measured enough? . . . As it is now staged by Trevor Nunn, the finished product cracks with dramatic electricity and infectious indignation."[3]

Upon the play's subsequent American premiere in June 1998 at the Alley Theatre in Houston, Texas, Ben Brantley of the *New York Times* found it "a fine, searing production. . . . *Not About Nightingales* is by no stretch of the imagination a mature piece of craftsmanship . . . but the emotional cloth of the drama, and much of its imagery, is pure Williams. As a cry of social protest for prison reform, it can be seen as much of an artifact as the 'big house' movies of the 1930's. As an anguished cry of empathy for fellow souls in captivity, it is a full-strength heartbreaker." The critic lauded Corin Redgrave for playing "the corrupt, lusty Boss Whalen with an outsize satanic gusto that is as unnerving as it is entertaining."[4]

Brantley reviewed *Not About Nightingales* again when the play opened at Broadway's Circle in the Square in February 1999: "A feverish full-strength compassion for people in cages makes *Nightingales* fly toward a realm of pain and beauty that is the province of greatness."[5] In a follow-up article in the *New York Times*, critic Vincent Canby wrote: "As staged by Trevor Nunn, the artistic director of the Royal National Theatre in London, the production is so spectacularly realized that it both serves the play and celebrates Williams' career. . . . The splendid production not only finds the work's theatrically vivid life, it also deepens our appreciation of the playwright: how he saw himself and how he dueled with his demons."[6]

Not About Nightingales ran for 125 performances.[7]

* * *

Thomas Lanier Williams III was born in Columbus, Mississippi in 1911. His father, Cornelius, a heavy-drinking traveling shoe salesman; his mother, Edwina, a snobbish, neurotic Southern belle; and his sister, Rose, shy, fragile, and mentally disturbed—all served as inspiration for the dysfunctional families in Williams's plays. A sickly child, "Tom," as he was called in his youth, spent his time hammering out stories on a typewriter. He attended Soldan High School and later studied at University City High School. At age sixteen he published an essay in *Smart Set*, and a year later, in 1928, his short story "The Vengeance of Nitocris," set in ancient Greece, was bought by the pulp magazine *Weird Tales*.

From 1929 to 1931, Williams attended the University of Missouri, in Columbia, where he enrolled in journalism classes. At the university he was a loner and in his junior year, he failed military training. His father pulled him out of school and put him to work at the International Shoe Factory. He disliked the nine-to-five routine and immersed himself in writing at night and on weekends. In the mid-1930s, Williams successively enrolled in Washington University in St. Louis, at the University of Iowa, and at the Dramatic Workshop of the New School in New York City. During that period he penned his early plays: *Candles in the Sun* (1936), about impoverished coal miners in Alabama; *Me, Vashya!* (1937), focusing on a munitions maker who sold arms to both sides during World War I; *The Fugitive Kind* (1937), set in a St. Louis flop house populated by hobos and mobsters; and *Spring Storm* (1937–1938), the story of a young man who yearns to escape the Mississippi Delta, and a young woman who is left behind, single with no prospects. "The plays he had written in the three colleges he attended up until the late age of twenty-seven were routine imitations of the then popular successes, also on subjects he knew nothing about, Hollywood producers, Pennsylvania prisoners, Alabama coal miners," writes Williams's friend Donald Windham in *As If . . .*[8] Conversely, Richard F. Leavitt, editor of *The World of Tennessee Williams*, theorizes that "If these early plays lacked unity, they also revealed many of the strengths which would later become characteristic of his work: flashes of poetic writing, realistic dialogue, memorable characterization, and several well-rounded individual scenes."[9]

In 1939, when *Story Magazine* published Williams's short tale "A Field of Blue Children," he adopted "Tennessee" as *nom de guerre*, a nickname given to him by university classmates because of his thick Southern drawl.

The poets, writers, and dramatists who influenced Williams included Emily Dickinson, Hart Crane, D. H. Lawrence, William Faulkner, Thomas

Wolfe, James Joyce, Ernest Hemingway, Anton Chekhov, August Strindberg, Eugene O'Neill, and William Inge. While struggling to have his work accepted, he was awarded a $1,000 grant from the Rockefeller Foundation and used the funds to move to New Orleans in 1939 to write for the Works Progress Administration (WPA), a federal program created to help needy artists, musicians, and authors during the Great Depression and subsequent years.

Williams held various jobs, including clerical worker, manual laborer, waiter, usher, and elevator operator, before a top talent agent, Audrey Wood, took him under her wing. *The Glass Menagerie*, his first Broadway play, opened at the Playhouse Theatre on March 31, 1945, received glowing reviews, won the New York Drama Critics Circle Award, and ran for 561 performances. A four-character "memory play," *The Glass Menagerie* is thought to be an autobiographical work, picturing Williams's own family: Amanda Wingfield is a faded Southern belle abandoned by her husband who is trying to raise two children under difficult financial conditions. Laura, her daughter, is slightly crippled and has an extra-sensitive mental condition. Tom, Amanda's son and Laura's younger brother, works at a shoe warehouse to support the family but is unhappy with his job, aspires to be a poet, and escapes from reality through constant trips to the movies and local bars. The original Broadway cast featured Laurette Taylor (Amanda), a performance considered a defining moment for American acting, Julie Haydon (Laura), and Eddie Dowling (Tom), who also codirected the production with Margo Jones. *The Glass Menagerie* was filmed in 1950, starring Gertrude Lawrence, Jane Wyman, and Kirk Douglas, and in 1987, featuring Joanne Woodward, Karen Allen, and John Malkovich. There were two television versions: a 1966 CBS Playhouse production with Shirley Booth as Amanda, and a 1973 ABC broadcast starring Katharine Hepburn.

A Streetcar Named Desire (Barrymore Theatre, December 3, 1947—855 performances) received the Pulitzer Prize for Drama in 1948 and cemented Williams's reputation as one of the most accomplished playwrights in the history of the American theatre. Unfolding in the French Quarter of New Orleans, the play deals with the clash between Blanche DuBois, a gentle, fading relic of the Old South, and Stanley Kowalski, an earthy, brutal member of the working class who is married to Blanche's sister, Stella. In their final confrontation, Stanley rapes Blanche, which results in a nervous breakdown. Stanley has her committed to a mental institution, and, at the closing curtain, Blanche utters her signature line to the doctor who leads the way: "Whoever you are, I have always depended on the kindness of strangers." The original Broadway cast, directed by Elia Kazan and designed by Jo Mielziner, featured Jessica Tandy (Blanche DuBois), Marlon Brando (Stanley Kowalski), and Kim Hunter (Stella Kowalski).

Vivien Leigh starred in a 1949 London production and in a 1951 film adaptation, which won several Academy Awards. Television versions were broadcast in 1955, with Jessica Tandy repeating her original role as Blanche; in 1984, with Ann-Margret; and in 1995, with Jessica Lange. A *Streetcar* opera, composed by André Previn with a libretto by Philip Littell, premiered at the San Francisco Opera during the 1988–1989 season, featuring Renée Fleming as Blanche.

Summer and Smoke (Music Box Theatre, October 6, 1948—102 performances) is set in Glorious Hill, Mississippi, at the turn of the twentieth century. The plot centers on Alma Winemiller, a prim minister's daughter who lets romance pass by but finally changes drastically; in the last scene she accosts a young traveling salesman in the town park and goes off with him to enjoy "after-dark entertainment" at Moon Lake Casino. The play was staged by Margo Jones and designed by Jo Mielziner, with Margaret Phillips appearing in the role of Alma. A successful 1952 revival at off-Broadway's Circle in the Square was directed by Jose Quintero and featured Geraldine Page as Alma, and put both Quintero and Page on the map. Page reprised the part in a 1961 film version. A television adaptation was produced in 1972, starring Lee Remick. A revised version of the play, titled *The Eccentricities of a Nightingale*, was presented in 1976, with Betsy Palmer as Alma, running for twenty-four showings at the Morosco Theatre. Blythe Danner starred in a 1976 television version of *Eccentricities*. An operatic treatment of the play, composed by Lee Hoiby, was produced by the Manhattan School of Music in December, 2010.

The protagonist of *The Rose Tattoo* (Martin Beck Theatre, February 3, 1951—306 performances) is Serafina Delle Rose, an Italian-American widow in a Louisiana Gulf Coast town who, mourning her husband, has withdrawn from the world and expects her daughter Rosa to do the same. Alvaro Mangiacavallo, a traveling trucker, arrives on the scene and reawakens Serafina through love and sex. Staged by Daniel Mann, designed by Boris Aronson, and featuring Maureen Stapleton (Serafina), Phyllis Love (Rosa), and Eli Wallach (Alvaro), *The Rose Tattoo* won the 1951 Tony Award for Best Play. A film adaptation was released in 1954, starring Anna Magnani, Marisa Pavan, and Burt Lancaster.

Williams's dramas directed by Elia Kazan include *Camino Real* (National Theatre, March 19, 1953—sixty performances), a morality play, expressionistic in form, set in a walled town bordering a desert and dealing with abstract ideas, including a symbolic use of time and place, and employs a large cast of romantic literary characters, among them Don Quixote, Margaret "Camille" Gautier, Casanova, and Esmeralda, the Gypsy girl from *The Hunchback of Notre Dame; Cat on a Hot Tin Roof* (Morosco Theatre, March 24, 1955—694 performances), which takes place in a plantation home in the Mississippi Delta, where Maggie (played by Barbara Bel Geddes) and

Brick (Ben Gazzara) are trying to solve their marriage problems while surrounded by vulturous relatives; and *Sweet Bird of Youth* (Martin Beck Theatre, March 10, 1959—375 performances), the story of a young, ambitious gigolo, Chance Wayne (Paul Newman) who befriends a faded movie star, Princess Kosmonopolis (Geraldine Page). Richard Brooks scripted and directed the film versions of both *Cat on a Hot Tin Roof* (1958), starring Elizabeth Taylor and Paul Newman, and *Sweet Bird of Youth* (1962), with Newman and Geraldine Page reprising their stage roles.

Harold Clurman staged and Boris Aronson designed *Orpheus Descending* (Martin Beck Theatre, March 21, 1957—sixty-eight performances), another Williams semi-poetic drama that takes place in a small Southern town marked by conformity, narrowness, racism, and sexual frustration. The story is set in a dry goods store run by a repressed middle-aged woman, Lady Torrance, whose elderly husband is dying. Into this scene steps Val Xavier, a strolling guitar player with a checkered past. Val serves as an antidote to Lady's loveless marriage and mundane small-town life. The leading roles were played by Maureen Stapleton (Lady) and Cliff Roberson (Val). A 1959 screen adaptation, under the title *The Fugitive Kind*, was directed by Sidney Lumet and starred Anna Magnani and Marlon Brando. A 1990 made-for-television movie, featuring Vanessa Redgrave, reverted to the title *Orpheus Descending*. The play was also adapted as a two-act opera by Bruce Saylor and J. D. McClatchy in 1994.

Garden District, opening at off-Broadway's York Playhouse on January 7, 1958, is the overall title of two of Williams's starkest one-act plays, *Suddenly Last Summer* and *Something Unspoken*. *Suddenly Last Summer*, the longer piece, is the story of Catharine Holly, a young woman who seems to go insane after her cousin Sebastian dies under mysterious circumstances on a trip to Europe. Sebastian's mother, Violet Venable, a wealthy Southern matriarch jealously guarding her son's memory, is searching for the truth about Sebastian's demise. Under the influence of a truth serum, Catherine reveals the harrowing event of Sebastian's death by cannibalism at the hand of naked, starving Spanish boys whose sexual favors he sought. Anne Meacham won an Obie Award for her performance of Catharine. A 1959 movie version, scripted by Gore Vidal and directed by Joseph L. Mankiewicz, added characters and sub-plots. Katharine Hepburn and Elizabeth Taylor, as aunt and niece, were both nominated for an Academy Award for Best Actress in a Leading Role. In 1993, Maggie Smith and Natasha Richardson appeared in a BBC television adaptation. Two years later *Suddenly Last Summer* finally made its Broadway debut, performed again with *Something Unspoken*, presented by uptown's Circle in the Square Theatre. The cast included Elizabeth Ashley as Mrs. Venable and Jordan Baker as Catharine. A 2004 London revival featured Diana Rigg and Victoria Hamilton, while a 2006 off-Broadway production by the Roundabout Theatre Company starred Blythe Danner and Carla Gugino.

Something Unspoken tells the story of Cornelia Scott, an elderly, wealthy Southern spinster who, despite an imperious facade, is vulnerable and eager for approval. Cornelia desires to be president of the local chapter of Daughters of the Confederacy, and is anxiously sitting at home, awaiting a call from the saloon where the voting is taking place. She is accompanied by her meek secretary, Grace Lancaster, who is in her forties. As the two women haltingly converse, it soon becomes clear that there's tension between them—"something unspoken"—related to an incident that happened long ago, perhaps an awkward sexual encounter. The issue remains unresolved when Cornelia is informed over the phone that she hasn't been elected.

A gentler, light-hearted Williams is revealed in *Period of Adjustment* (Helen Hayes Theatre, November 10, 1960—132 performances), a heartwarming comedy about two couples who go through marital problems but reconcile on Christmas Eve. The play was adapted to the screen in 1962 under the direction of George Roy Hill.

Williams returned to his heavier themes in *The Night of the Iguana* (Royale Theatre, December 28, 1961—316 performances), in which defrocked Reverend Lawrence Shannon obtains employment as a tour guide on the west coast of Mexico, establishes a relationship with the owner of a backwoods hotel, the lusty widow Maxine Faulk, and enters into a sexual liaison with sixteen-year-old Charlotte Goodall. The unmarried Hannah Jelkes arrives on the scene and the play's main axis is the development of a deep human bond between Jelkes and Shannon. At the end, the Reverend tears a gold cross from his neck as if to free himself from its constraints. The Broadway production starred Patrick O'Neal (Shannon), Bette Davis (Maxine), and Margaret Leighton (Hannah), who won the Tony Award for Best Actress in a Play. Reportedly, backstage was chaotic and Davis banned director Frank Corsaro from rehearsals shortly before the opening. A 1964 movie version was directed by John Huston and starred Richard Burton, Ava Gardner, and Deborah Kerr. Circle in the Square Theatre hosted two revivals of *The Night of the Iguana*: in 1976, directed by Joseph Hardy, with Richard Chamberlain, Sylvia Miles, and Dorothy McGuire, and in 1988, with Nicolas Surovy, Maria Tucci, and Jane Alexander. Robert Fallis staged a 1996 Broadway revival featuring William Petersen, Marsha Mason, and Cherry Jones. London theatregoers flocked to a 1992 production at the Royal National Theatre, directed by Richard Eyre, featuring Alfred Molina as Reverend Shannon and Eileen Atkins as Hannah, and a 2005 offering at the Lyric Theatre, staged by Anthony Page, starring Woody Harrelson in the role of Shannon and Jenny Seagrove as Hannah.

The Milk Train Doesn't Stop Here Anymore (Morosco Theatre, January 16, 1963—sixty-nine performances), staged by Herbert Machiz and designed by Jo Mielziner, is set in a villa on Italy's Divina Costiera, where the fabulously rich but terminally ill Mrs. Flora Goforth (Hermione Baddeley) feverishly dictates the memoirs of her life to a secretary. A young poet, Christopher Flanders (Paul Roebling), trespasses on her estate and Mrs. Goforth takes him as her companion so that she may end her days in his "peaceful presence." A revised version of the play was mounted at the Brooks Atkinson Theatre on January 1, 1964, directed by Tony Richardson, designed by Rouben Ter-Arutunian, and featuring Tallulah Bankhead and Tab Hunter. Despite the array of talent, it received poor notices and lasted for only five showings. However, *The Milk Train Doesn't Stop Here Anymore* was selected as one of the top ten in the Best Plays annual, and was filmed in 1968, starring Elizabeth Taylor and Richard Burton, under the title *Boom!*

For the cinema, Williams adapted, with associates, his dramas *The Glass Menagerie, A Streetcar Named Desire, The Rose Tattoo, Baby Doll* (from his one-act *27 Wagons Full of Cotton*), and *The Fugitive Kind*. He wrote more than seventy one-act plays during his lifetime. The most frequently produced by little theatres and colleges are *The Lady of Larkspur Lotion* (written in 1941), which depicts the conflict between a dreamy, gentle tenant and her brusque, practical landlady; *Moony's Kid Don't Cry* (1941, the first of Williams's plays to be published), about a young married couple who get into an argument over their child and their relationship; *The Case of the Crushed Petunias* (1941), the story of an unhappy Massachusetts salesgirl who escapes her mundane existence when she meets a visitor from the big city; *This Property Is Condemned* (1946), the study of a thirteen-year-old girl who clings to the memory of her dead prostitute sister, expanded into the film of the same name, starring Natalie Wood and Robert Redford; *Hello from Bertha* (1946), recounting the life and death of a low-class prostitute; *Lord Byron's Love Letter* (1946), in which an old New Orleans spinster claims that she has one of Lord Byron's love letters, given to her when she romanced the poet in Greece shortly before his death; and *I Rise in Flame, Cried the Phoenix* (1953), a fictionalized account of the death of English writer D. H. Lawrence on the French Riviera.

After the extraordinary successes of the 1940s and 1950s, the quality of Williams's work began to deteriorate due to turmoil with his male lovers as well as alcohol and drug abuse. His one enduring romantic relationship was with Frank Phillip Merlo (1922–1963), an occasional actor of Sicilian heritage. Upon Merlo's death from lung cancer, Williams plunged into depression and his increasing drug use resulted in several hospitalizations and commitments to mental health institutions.[10] On February 25, 1983, he was found dead in his suite at the Elysee Hotel in New York

City. He was 71. The medical examiner's report indicated that Williams choked on the cap from a bottle of eyedrops. Prescription drugs, including barbiturates, were found in the room.

Acting Edition: Samuel French, Inc.; New Directions Books; *Not About Nightingales* is also included in *Tennessee Williams, Plays 1937–1955* (New York: Library of America, 2000).

Awards and Honors: *Not About Nightingales* was nominated for 1999 Tony and Drama Desk awards as Best Play. Tennessee Williams's *A Streetcar Named Desire* won the 1948 Pulitzer Prize for Drama, and *Cat on a Hot Tin Roof* garnered the same prize in 1955. *The Rose Tattoo* won the 1951 Tony Award for Best Play. Nominated for Best Play Tony Awards were *Cat on a Hot Tin Roof* (1956) and *The Night of the Iguana* (1962). In a survey conducted in 1999 by England's National Theatre, *A Streetcar Named Desire, Cat on a Hot Tin Roof,* and *The Glass Menagerie* ranked among the most important plays of the twentieth century. Tennessee Williams was the recipient of a Rockefeller Fellowship in 1940. He garnered a National Institute of Arts and Letters grant in 1944, and Gold Medal for Drama in 1969. He won a Brandeis University Creative Arts Award in 1965, anointed Doctor of Humanities by the University of Missouri in 1969, and Doctor of Literature, Honoris Causa, at the University of Hartford, Connecticut in 1972. He became a member of the American Academy of Arts and Letters in 1976. In 1980 President Jimmy Carter honored him with the Presidential Medal of Freedom. The U.S. Postal Service issued a stamp with his image in 1994. In 2009, he was inducted into the Poet's Corner at Manhattan's Cathedral Church of Saint John the Divine. In 2011, to commemorate the 100th anniversary of Williams's birth, the Harry Ransom Center at the University of Texas at Austin, the home of his archives, exhibited "Becoming Tennessee Williams," a collection of his manuscripts, correspondence, and photographs. The Tennessee Williams Theatre in Key West, Florida, is named after him.

NOTES

1. Michael Fuller, *Williams in an Hour* (Hanover, N.H.: Hour, 2010), 15.
2. Tennessee Williams, *Not About Nightingales* (New York: New Directions, 1998), xxii.
3. *New York Times*, April 5, 1998.
4. *New York Times*, June 17, 1998.
5. *New York Times*, February 26, 1999.
6. *New York Times*, March 7, 1999.
7. In addition to *Not About Nightingales*, other twentieth-century prison plays of note include *Justice* (1910) by John Galsworthy; *Chicago* (1926) by Maurine Watkins and its 1975 musical incarnation, book by Fred Ebb and Bob Fosse, lyrics

by Fred Ebb, music by John Kander; *The Criminal Code* (1929) by Martin Flavin; *Smoky Cell* (1930) by Edgar Wallace; *The Last Mile* (1930) by John Wexler; *Children of Darkness* (1930) by Edwin Justus Mayer; *Hoppla! Such Is Life!* (1935) by Ernst Toller; *Chalked Out* (1937) by Warden Lewis E. Lawes; *Darkness at Noon* (1951) by Sidney Kingsley, based on the 1940 novel by Arthur Koestler; *The Prisoner* (1954) by Bridget Boland; *Murder Story* (1954) by Ludovic Kennedy; *The Quare Fellow* (1954) by Brendan Behan; *Inquest* (1970) by Donald Freed; *Fortune and Men's Eyes* (1974) by John Herbert; *Short Eyes* (1974) by Miguel Piñero; and the musical *The Kiss of the Spider Woman* (1992), book by Terrence McNally, lyrics by Fred Ebb, music by John Kander. Incarcerations are also pictured in *Stalag 17* (1951) by Donald Bevan and Edmond Trzcinski—prisoners of war in a Nazi camp; *The Physicists* (1962) by Friedrich Dürrenmatt—scientists held forcefully in an asylum; and *The Brig* (1963) by Kenneth H. Brown—AWOL soldiers confined to an army barracks in dehumanizing conditions.

8. Donald Windham, *As If . . .* (Verona, Italy: Stamperia valdonega, 1985), 15.

9. Richard F. Leavitt, *The World of Tennessee Williams* (New York: Putnam, 1978), 16.

10. Tennessee Williams's homosexuality and its effect on his work is recounted in *Eminent Outlaws* by Christopher Bram, a study that also covers renowned gay men of letters Truman Capote, Gore Vidal, James Baldwin, Allen Ginsberg, Edward Albee, and Tony Kushner (New York: Twelve Books, 2012).

The Collector (1998)

Mark Healy (England)

"In *the Collector*, Mr. Fowles painted an early portrait of a plausible psychopath who kidnaps a young woman out of what he imagines is love, telling the story from the two characters' opposing points of view until, at the end, the narratives converge with a shocking immediacy," wrote Sarah Lyall in a *New York Times* obituary of John Fowles in 2005.[1]

The 1963 novel gained instant success. Two years later it was transferred effectively to the screen, directed by William Wyler, starring Terence Stamp and Samantha Eggar. Englishman David Parker adapted *The Collector* to the stage, first presenting it at the King's Head Theatre Club, Islington, London, England, on February 8, 1971. A more developed version, by compatriot Mark Healy, premiered at the Derby Playhouse, Derby, England on October 2, 1998.

The curtain rises on pitch darkness. Suddenly a video image flicks on. The film, shot from a distance and obviously homemade, shows a young girl (Miranda) in different areas of London. The camera follows her going to art college, coming out of a tube station, walking in a park, shopping, entering a pub. The lights come up on Frederick Clegg, a bland-looking man in his late twenties, soon to be revealed as repressed and introverted.

Clegg watches the video, then crosses to the footlights and, somewhat nervously, addresses the audience. "It's my chance to tell you what happened—from my side," he says. Clegg relates that he fell for Miranda Grey, a beautiful, privileged art student, at first sight. When he won a great deal of money in a lottery, he bought first-rate photography equipment and began taking pictures of her. An entomologist, an avid collector of butterflies and moths, he began to hatch a plan of adding Miranda to his collection and purchased an old, secluded cottage, located one hour by car from London, two miles from the nearest village.

Clegg pulls back a curtain to reveal a cellar neatly furnished with a bed, folding screen, wall mirror, wardrobe, table and chair, and a bookcase full of expensive art books. Lying on the bed is nineteen-year-old Miranda Grey. She is fully dressed, gagged, bound—and unconscious. While untying her and carefully taking off the gag, Clegg tells the spectators that he followed Miranda for a few days, learned her routine, and after a quick struggle, chloroformed her and got her into his van.

Miranda opens her eyes and gasps for air. She recognizes her captor as a former city hall clerk and remembers seeing his picture in the papers when he won the football lottery. She begs to be released, promising she won't tell anyone what he's done. Her father is not rich, so it can't be money he's after. Is it sex? Clegg is taken aback: "It's not like that at all. . . . I love you." Clegg agrees to release Miranda in a month if she talks to him daily and does not try to escape. He will supply her with food, a stereo, books, and drawing materials.

A battle of wits ensues. Miranda occupies Clegg with small talk, learns that his mother left home for another man, and that his father, a traveling salesman and habitual drunkard, was killed in a car crash. An aunt, Annie, and a cousin, Maggie, "a cripple, spastic," who "makes everything around her deformed too," brought him up. He believes that spastics should be put out of their misery.

Clegg shows Miranda his collection of butterflies—"all caught or bred by me and set and arranged by me." She is astonished by the obvious skill and patience that have gone into the collection but blames Clegg for killing so many butterflies, so much beauty.

During the next few weeks the relationship between Clegg and Miranda goes through a gamut of emotions. At some point, exasperated, she calls him "Bastard! Fucking little shithead! Pissing little son of a bitch!" At another moment she softens and lets him take photographs of her. When he gathers the courage to kiss her, she vehemently rejects him. On a ruse, one night she moans in the dark, writhes in bed, complains of a terrible pain—"My appendix"—and yells for a doctor. Clegg says that he cannot honor her request.

More and more Miranda becomes like a caged animal, throws a vase of flowers at him, scatters clothes and books around the room, and eventually accuses him of driving her insane.

Clegg agrees to mail a note to her parents. He reads and approves her message, which relates that she's safe and not in any danger. Unnoticed by Clegg, Miranda slips another, smaller piece of paper into the envelope, seals it, and hands it to him. Clegg goes to leave, stops by the door, and holds the letter up to the light. He rips the envelope open and finds the hidden note. He reads it aloud: "Kidnapped by madman. Frederick Clegg. Prisoner in cellar. Lonely, timbered cottage. . . . Hill country, two hours from London. . . . Frightened." Clegg is on the verge of tears. How could Miranda call him a "madman"? A madman would have killed her by now.

The end of the month is approaching. On Day 27, Miranda has changed into a dress that Clegg has bought for her, combs her hair up, and puts on makeup. The smell of perfume hangs in the air. The table is set for dinner, including a bottle of wine and flowers in a vase. Clegg presents Miranda with a present—a leather case with a diamond necklace inside. She raises her glass for a toast when Clegg says, "Marry me. Please." Miranda states that she does not love him, but then, sensing disaster, desperately tries to compose herself. She walks around the table to Clegg, crouches beside him, kisses him gently on the lips, takes off his jacket, stands back and takes off her dress, undoes her hair, and moves back to him. She undoes his tie, pulls off his shirt and kisses him, but Clegg pushes her away and exclaims, "Don't touch me!"

Miranda loses control and throws a drink in his face. Clegg, furious, lunges at her. They fight violently. Miranda hits Clegg hard over the head with a metal vase. He stumbles and falls. For a moment Miranda stands ready to deliver a final blow, perhaps even to kill him as he tries to get up. But she cannot do it, and as she hesitates, her fate is sealed. Clegg catches her and manages to smother her with a chloroformed pad. Miranda passes out. "You've ruined it all," he sobs. "You've killed the romance. I can't respect you now. You've made yourself like any woman."

In the final sequences of the play Miranda becomes physically ill. Clegg orders her out of bed, pulls the bedclothes off her, and as she stands weak, shivering, and breathing hard, he takes photographs with blinding flashes. They'll be part of his new collection. In the morning he finds her on the floor. "I don't want to die," she whispers. He takes her in his arms, confused. She has stopped breathing. He carries her to the bed and lays her down, holding her tight.

The video image of Miranda looking healthy and happy starts up. We are back in the present. Clegg addresses the audience and tells that it took him three days to dig a hole for the body in an adjacent orchard. For a while he considered suicide by swallowing sleeping pills—"it would be like Romeo and Juliet." On second thought it occurred to him that he chose the wrong girl, one who didn't respect him enough; next time he'll know better. He's already seen a girl in a neighboring village who will be the perfect guest. She isn't as pretty as Miranda, but she's the same size so the clothes will fit. Tomorrow he'll go down and clear the cellar, give it a good airing—make it look new.

* * *

Mark Healy's adaptation of *The Collector* premiered at the Derby Playhouse in 1998 under the direction of Mark Clements, with the participation of Mark Letheren (Frederick Clegg) and Danielle Tilley (Miranda Grey). Healy provides "adapter's notes" in the acting edition of the play, relating that designer Steven Armstrong "produced an extraordinary, operatic set with scene changes marked with huge butterflies lit up behind gauze walls."[2]

Healy's version was also performed at the Arcola Theatre in Hackney, London from August 26 to September 20, 2008, and by the Vivid Theatre at the 2009 Edinburgh International Fringe Festival. In 2010, the Ruskin Group Theatre of Santa Monica, California presented *The Collector* from January 29 to March 6; the Masque Theatre of Muizenberg, Cape Town, South Africa from July 16 to July 24; and That Theatre Company of Copenhagen, Denmark from October 27 to November 27.

In addition to its stage adaptations by David Parker (1973) and Mark Healy (1998) and the 1965 motion picture version directed by William Wyler, *The Collector* inspired several songs: "The Collector," written by Sonny Curtis and recorded by the Everly Brothers; "The Butterfly Collector" by The Jam; "Prosthetics" by metal band SlipKnot; and "The Collector" by Nine Inch Nails.

In Stephen King's Dark Tower series, Finli O'Tego, also known as the Weasel, reads *The Collector* (another character, Dinky, peruses John Fowles's *The Magus*). In King's book *Misery*, Paul Sheldon compares his situation to that of Miranda in *The Collector*. In Neil Gaiman's comic *The Doll's House*, an episode titled "Collectors" is about a convention of serial killers; one of the films shown at the convention is *The Collector*.

A kidnapper in a two-part episode of television's *Criminal Minds* titled "The Fisher King" uses the book *The Collector* to send a coded message. In a segment of *The Simpsons*, "Treehouse of Horrors X," Comic Book Guy uses the persona "The Collector" when kidnapping Lucy Lawless from a comic book convention and taking her to his lair. *Seven Days*, a UPN television series, had an episode called "The Collector," in which a serial killer chloroforms and abducts women.

The Collector was the source of inspiration for several real-life crimes. Christopher Wilder (1945–1984), a serial killer of young girls on a spree that took him across the United States, had *The Collector* in his possession when he killed himself during a struggle with police in New Hampshire. It is said that Leonard Lake (1945–1985) had been obsessed with *The Collector* when he abducted eighteen-year-old Kathy Allen and later nineteen-year-old Brenda O'Connor in 1985. Lake and his coconspirator Charles Chi-tat Ng (born 1960) locked the women in a bunker built into a hill near Wilseyville, California where they raped, tortured, and murdered them. Lake was arrested when linked to a car belonging to one of their victims and at that point committed suicide by taking a cyanide capsule. Ng escaped to Canada but was subsequently extradited back to California. He is currently on death row at San Quentin prison. A diary written by Lake revealed that the murderers named the plot Operation Miranda after the character in Fowles's book. Robert Berdella (1949–1992), known as "The Kansas City Butcher," held his victims captive and photographed their torture before killing them. He claimed that the movie version of *The Collector* had been his inspiration when he was a teenager.

* * *

Travelling back and forth between both sides of the Atlantic, Mark Healy specialized in adapting well-known novels to the stage. His dramatization of Bram Stoker's *Dracula* premiered at the Fulton Opera House, Lancaster, Pennsylvania in 2005. An adaptation of another work by John Fowles, *The French Lieutenant's Woman*, debuted in 2006 at the Yvonne Arnaud Theatre in Guildford, England and toured the United Kingdom. Healy's stage versions of Jane Austen's *Persuasion* (1999) and *Sense and Sensibility* (2000), and Thomas Hardy's *Far From the Madding Crowd* (2008) were first presented by the Northcott Theatre, Exeter, England.

Trained at the Welsh College of Music and Drama and at the University of Hull, Healy was also a busy actor, appearing in a variety of roles including the eponymous role in *Hamlet*, Jack Worthing in *The Importance of Being Earnest*, Benedick in *Much Ado About Nothing*, and Petruchio in *The Taming of the Shrew* (all at the Northcott Theatre, Exeter), Gerald Croft in *An Inspector Calls* (national and Australian tours), Jack Absolute in *The Rivals* (national tour), Darcy in *Pride and Prejudice* (national tour), Doctor Seward in *Dracula* (Derby Playhouse), The Actor in *The Woman in Black* (Fortune Theatre, London, and Australian tour), and the title roles of *Henry VIII* and *King Lear* in New York City.

* * *

Born in Leigh-on-Sea, Essex, England, in 1926, John Fowles felt alienated from his parents, a tobacconist and a schoolteacher, who did not have any literary interest and were always laughing at "the fellow who couldn't draw"—Picasso. Similarly, he recoiled from his role as head boy at Bedford School, his prep school. "By the age of 18, I had had dominion over 600 boys, and learned all about power, hierarchy and the manipulation of the law," he wrote. "Ever since I have had a violent hatred of leaders, organizers, bosses; of anyone who thinks it good to get or have arbitrary power over other people."[3]

After a brief period of military service, which he spent as a lieutenant in the Royal Marines, Fowles studied French at New College, Oxford. He earned his bachelor's degree in 1950, and then took teaching positions in France and Greece. He started writing in his early twenties, initially imitating writers he admired: Defoe, Flaubert, D. H. Lawrence, and Hemingway. After attending a performance of Bela Bartok's *Bluebeard's Castle*, an opera about imprisoned women, and later coming across a newspaper account of a young man who had kidnapped a girl and held her for more than three months, Fowles began work on *The Collector*. In 1962 he took the manuscript to Jonathan Cape and it was published the following year. Critiquing the novel in the *New York Times Book Review*, Alan Pryce-Jones opined that "the slow degrees" by which Clegg destroys Miranda "make one of the most agonizing chapters in the whole literary history of obsession."[4]

The Magus (1966) is the first novel Fowles wrote but the second to be published. It is the story of Nicholas Urfe, a young Oxford graduate who accepts a job as teacher on a small Greek island where he meets a mysterious, wealthy Greek recluse, Maurice Conchis. Conchis may have collaborated with the Nazis during World War II, and Urfe finds himself at the mercy of psychological games and elaborate fantasies concocted by this enigmatic man. Fowles wrote the screenplay of *The Magus* (1968), directed by Guy Green and starring Michael Caine as Urfe and Anthony Quinn as Conchis. It was a failed endeavor. Caine said that it was one of the worst films he had been involved in and Woody Allen declared, "If I had to live my life again, I'd do everything the same, except that I wouldn't see *The Magus*."

The French Lieutenant's Woman (1969) is the nickname of Sarah Woodruff, a governess who lives in the coastal town of Lyme Regis as a disgraced woman, supposedly wooed and abandoned by a French naval officer. A geologist, Charles Smithson, is smitten by her. Though engaged to a young woman of his class, the daughter of a wealthy tradesman, he meets Sarah clandestinely and a scandal ensues. Sarah is portrayed as a mysterious being: Is she a genuine, long-suffering woman or a sly manipulator? The novelist offers three different endings. Scripted by Harold Pinter and directed by Karel Reisz, *The French Lieutenant's Woman* was adapted to the screen in 1981 starring Meryl Streep and Jeremy Irons.

The Ebony Tower (1974) is a collection of five short novels with interlacing themes. The title story is about an elderly, retired painter, Henry Breasley, whose home is invaded by a brash young artist assigned to write a biography of the famous man. In 1984, *The Ebony Tower* was adapted to television with Laurence Olivier in the role of Breasley. Another novelette, *The Enigma*, contains criminous elements: A British Member of Parliament, John Fielding, disappears without a trace. The police investigate: was foul play involved, or did Fielding fake his own disappearance? *The Enigma* was adapted to television in 1980, produced by BBC2.

Daniel Martin (1977) is a semi-autobiographical novel about a Hollywood screenwriter who returns to his native England and reestablishes a relationship with the widow of a dead friend, a woman he has loved since attending Oxford University in the 1940s. *Mantissa* (1982) is composed of a dialogue between a bestselling author and his psychiatrist. *A Mag-*

got (1985), a historical novel tinged with elements of science fiction, tells the story of a group of five travelers who set out on a horseback journey through rural England during 1736–1737. They arrive at an inn in a small village and go through a series of weird experiences, including the rape of one of them, the prostitute Rebecca Lee, by a satanic figure in a remote cave. The leader of the group, "Mr. Bartholomew" (real name unknown), the son of a duke, mysteriously disappears, and his deaf-mute manservant, Dick Thurlow, is found hanged. The novel's narrative incorporates letters, documents, interviews, and news stories, and is heavy with symbolism and ambiguity.

Fowles's nonfiction works include *The Aristos: A Self-Portrait in Ideas* (1964), *The Enigma of Stonehenge* (1980), *A Short History of Lyme Regis* (1983), *Wormholes* (1998), *The Journals*—Volume 1 (2003), and *The Journals*—Volume 2 (2006). A 1979 essay, "The Tree," illustrating the author's reverence for woods and wilderness, was reissued in 2010.

Fowles suffered a stroke in the late 1980s and had been ill for some time prior to his death in 2005 at his home in Lyme Regis, England, at the age of 79.

Acting Edition: Samuel French, Ltd.

Awards and Honors: John Fowles's novel *The Magus* (1966) has been included in the Modern Library List of Best 20th-Century Novels. In 2005, his novel *The French Lieutenant's Woman* (1969) was chosen by *Time* magazine as one of the 100 best English-language novels from 1923 to the present. On January 5, 2008, the *London Times* included John Fowles among "The 50 greatest British writers since 1945."

NOTES

1. *New York Times*, November 8, 2005.
2. Mark Healy, *The Collector* (London: Samuel French, 2006), unpaginated.
3. Quoted in the obituary of John Fowles by Sarah Lyall, *New York Times*, November 8, 2005.
4. Fowles obituary, *New York Times*, November 8, 2005.

The Talented Mr. Ripley (1998)

Phyllis Nagy (United States/England, 1962–)

Tom Ripley, one of the most amoral rogues in modern literature, was introduced by thriller writer Patricia Highsmith in her 1955 novel *The Talented Mr. Ripley*. Young, suave, charming, and deadly, Ripley returned in the sequels *Ripley Underground* (1970), *Ripley's Game* (1974), *The Boy Who Followed Ripley* (1980), and *Ripley under Water* (1991).

Phyllis Nagy's play adaptation of *The Talented Mr. Ripley* faithfully follows the original novel. The action unfolds in the 1950s. The set suggests limitless open space. Suspended above the stage is an enormous ship's compass that sits amid many watercolor paintings done in different styles and of various sizes. Most of the watercolors are seascapes of a violent, storm-beaten ocean. A small table and two chairs are used in various ways and in various locales in order to achieve fluid and continuous action.

The curtain rises on New Yorker Tom Ripley breaking through the fourth wall, telling the audience of his recurring nightmare about a poisonous adder that slithers up his right leg, reaches his jugular, and prepares for the big bite—when he, Ripley, wakes up.

We soon see Ripley maneuvering a typical confidence scheme as he meets a cartoonist, Mr. Reddington, in a coffee shop. He presents the faked calling card of a Manhattan District Internal Revenue Supervisor, and frightens Reddington with charges of tax irregularities, ultimately conning him out of $200.

Herbert Greenleaf, a shipping magnate, approaches Ripley with an offer to travel to Italy, meet Greenleaf's errant son, Richard, and persuade him to return home and join the family business. Ripley is told that he will be paid for all travel expenses and receive a generous stipend for two months. The Greenleaf offer comes in an opportune time, because Ripley's monthly allowance, thirty dollars, was cut off by his aunt Dottie, who insists that her nephew should at long last get a job. Therefore,

* * *

Phyllis Nagy was born in 1962 in New York City. She attended New York University, where she studied poetry and musical composition, receiving her BFA in 1986. A struggling playwright in the United States, her fortunes changed dramatically when she moved to London in 1992. In the mid-1990s she served as writer-in-residence at the Royal Court Theatre and soon began to build a reputation as a significant, innovative playwright. Nagy's plays have been performed widely throughout Europe, Australia, and Canada but she continues to enjoy a stronger reputation in Britain than in the United States.

"Nagy's humour is sharp, biting and cynical, and there is a raw and refreshing honesty about her depictions of modern-day society," writes Elizabeth O'Reilly in *British Council/ Literature*.

> She is particularly attuned to the moral and spiritual apathy of modern life, especially in urban culture. . . . Many of Nagy's characters are frustrated, unfulfilled and seeking escape, new horizons and a new sense of identity— like their author. . . . As a gay writer and a transatlantic emigrant, Nagy is no stranger to the experience of challenging conventional expectations of gender, culture and nationhood. However, her work explores far beyond autobiographical, and her characters subvert boundaries and conventions in many different ways. This is often quite severe and dramatic, and Nagy does not flinch from exploring the gruesome and the hard-hitting.[1]

Nagy's *Weldon Rising* (first produced at the Royal Court Theatre Upstairs, London, 1992) is a dark comedy unfolding on the hottest night of the year in New York's meatpacking district. The plot centers around a hate crime: Natty Weldon, a timid closeted sales clerk, witnesses the fatal stabbing of his lover Jimmy and runs away in terror. Other bystanders include a lesbian couple and a transvestite prostitute. No one intervenes. Posted on the back wall of the stage is a large-scale map of the district; in the final scene, Weldon steps right through it and disappears. *Butterfly Kiss* (Almeida Theatre, London, 1994), a multilayered play about matricide, is set in the actual and imagined past, present, and future. Lily Ross, molded and browbeaten by her parents, blows her mother's brains out in a violent burst of self-assertion. *Trip's Cinch* (Actors Theatre of Louisville, Kentucky, 1994) focuses on an alleged rape and, Rashomon-like, presents three perspectives about the case from the point of view of the suspect, a confident, rich man; the young woman; and a flashback to the night of the confrontation between them. The actual truth remains enigmatic. A dramatization of Nathaniel Hawthorne's *The Scarlet Letter* (Denver Center Theatre, 1994), highlights the elements of obsession and revenge.

The main characters of *The Strip* (Royal Court Theatre, London, 1995) are a female impersonator, a love-struck repo man, and a lesbian journalist who travel across America and land in Las Vegas, searching for fame and fortune. In *Disappeared* (Haymarket Studio Theatre, Leicester, UK, 1995), Sarah Casey, a young travel agent who has never been outside New York City, goes missing after leaving a seedy bar in Hell's Kitchen. Was Sarah killed, or did she merely "disappear" to escape her anonymous existence in a big, lonely city? *Never Land* (Royal Court Theatre, London, 1998) once again explores the yearning to escape from one's present reality and create a new existence. Henri Joubert and his family's one dream is to move from their remote, rain-swept village in southern France and settle in England. Nagy's colloquial version of Anton Chekhov's *The Seagull* was produced at Chichester, UK, Festival Theatre in the summer of 2003.

Nagy's first feature as writer-director was *Mrs. Harris*. It premiered at the Toronto International Film Festival in September 2005 before HBO broadcast it in February 2006. Based on a true story that shocked America, Annette Bening plays Jean Harris, the headmistress of an exclusive girls' school, who murders her former lover, noted cardiologist and diet expert Dr. Herman Tarnower (Ben Kingsley), after he spurned her in favor of his younger secretary-receptionist.

* * *

Patricia Highsmith was born Mary Patricia Plangman in Fort Worth, Texas in 1921. Her mother, an artist and fashion illustrator, divorced her father, a graphic artist, ten days before their daughter's birth, and Patricia was brought up by her adoptive father, Stanley Highsmith, also a graphic artist, in New York City. It is reported that Patricia had a complicated relationship with her mother and resented her stepfather. According to Highsmith, her mother once told her that she tried to abort her by drinking turpentine. Highsmith later fictionalized this love-hate relationship in her works. Upon visiting her grandmother in Fort Worth, Patricia made good use of her extensive library, wallowed in Arthur Conan Doyle's Sherlock Holmes stories, and from an early age was fascinated by case studies of pyromania and schizophrenia.

In 1938–1942, Highsmith attended Barnard College, where she studied English composition, playwriting, and logic, and served on the editorial board of the *Barnard Quarterly*. Answering an ad for "reporter/rewrite," she landed a job at the office of a comic book publisher. She soon became a freelance writer for comics, contributing to *Black Terror, Real Fact, Real Heroes,* and *True Crimes*. During 1943–1945 she wrote for Fawcett Publications, scripting for the comic characters Spy Smasher and Captain Midnight. From 1945 to 1947, she wrote for Western Comics.

Highsmith's first nationally published story, "The Heroine," which appeared in *Harper's Bazaar*, was included in the *O. Henry Memorial Award Prize Stories of 1946*. Other tales followed in *Cosmopolitan*, *Woman's Home Companion*, *Ellery Queen's Mystery Magazine*, and *The Saint Mystery Magazine*.

Highsmith's first novel was *Strangers on a Train*, presenting the unique premise that two young men—Guy Haines, an architect who hates his unfaithful wife, and Charles Bruno, a playboy chafing under his rich father's rule—would "exchange murders." Each would commit a killing that the other had a motive for, thus establishing a perfect alibi for both. The book had a modest success when published in 1950, but the following year it was filmed effectively by Alfred Hitchcock (with Farley Granger and Robert Walker), propelling Highsmith's career.[2]

Highsmith published her second novel, *The Price of Salt* (1952), under the pseudonym Claire Morgan. It made a splash as a lesbian novel with a rare happy ending and sold almost a million copies. Highsmith did not associate herself with this book until late in life, probably because of its autobiographical content, but she included homosexual undertones in many of her novels.

Most of Highsmith's output—twenty-two novels and eight collections of short stories—fall into the category of psychological thrillers. "Patricia Highsmith writes fiction that is intriguing, thought-provoking and sometimes hard to classify," writes Mary Ellen Becker in *Twentieth-Century Crime and Mystery Writers*. "Her psychological portraits and her refusal to employ the traditional formulas of suspense fiction—her originality and seriousness, in fact—are qualities which set her books apart from ordinary examples of the genre. Patricia Highsmith explores guilt—or its absence—in her characters. Often her protagonists are highly individual, even abnormal, but in her hands they take on life and are consistent and believable."[3] Bruce F. Murphy adds in *The Encyclopedia of Murder and Mystery*, "It has been said that Highsmith's work evokes horror, fear, and guilt, but the guilt is all in the mind of the reader; it is the *lack* of guilt that makes the stories horrifying."[4]

In 1966, Highsmith penned *Plotting and Writing Suspense Fiction*, in which she presents the essentials of creating stories in the genre and how a writer can use certain techniques. The 149-page book analyzes the vital elements of suspense in fiction—surprise, coincidence, speed, and the importance of stretching the reader's credulity almost to the breaking point. Always keeping in mind that the goal of suspense fiction is to excite and entertain the reader, Highsmith offers practical advice on shaping and developing ideas and demonstrates how to organize experience, record emotional reactions, and write with conviction. "The suspense writer can improve his lot and the reputation of the suspense novel," she asserts, "by putting into his books the qualities that have always made books good—insight, character, an opening of new horizons for the imagination of the reader."[5]

The Talented Mr. Ripley remains Highsmith's most celebrated novel. It was adapted to television in 1956 by Studio One and to the silver screen twice. In 1960, a French film, *Plein Soleil*, known as *Purple Noon*, was directed by René Clément and starred Alain Delon (Tom Ripley) and Maurice Ronet (Philippe Greenleaf). A highly regarded movie, its ending differs from the original story: When the murder yacht is being moved to dry dock, Philippe's decomposed body is found still attached to the boat because the anchor cable used to sink his corpse had become tangled around the propeller. Thus it is implied that Ripley will be arrested. A 1999 American version, directed by Anthony Minghella, starred Matt Damon and Jude Law.

Later Ripley novels were also filmed. *Ripley's Game* was directed by Wim Wenders as *The American Friend* (1977) with Dennis Hopper as Ripley, and, under its original title, was helmed by Liliana Cavani, with John Malkovich in the title role (2003). *Ripley Under Ground*, featuring Barry Pepper as Ripley, was shown at the 2005 AFI Film Festival but has not had a general release. In 2009, BBC Radio 4 aired adaptations of all five Ripley books with Ian Hart in the lead.

Stories by Highsmith were adapted to the television programs *77 Sunset Strip*, *The Alfred Hitchcock Hour*, *The Wednesday Thriller*, *ITV Play of the Week*, *Armchair Thriller*, *Tales of the Unexpected*, and *Chillers*. Highsmith's final novel, *Small g: a Summer Idyll*, was published posthumously, a month after her death in 1995. Much of its action unfolds in a Zurich bar that caters to gay and lesbian patrons. Rickie Markwelder, an HIV-positive artist, finds himself suspected of the murder of his lover.

Two hefty biographies, *Beautiful Shadow: The Life of Patricia Highsmith* by Andrew Wilson (2003, 534 pages) and Joan Schenkar's *The Talented Miss Highsmith* (2009, 684 pages) include troubling accounts of Highsmith's alcoholism, bisexuality, misanthropy, cruelty, racism, and anti-Semitism. Otto Penzler, who published six of Highsmith's books under his Mysterious Press imprint in Manhattan during the 1980s, said, "Two points should immediately be stated about Patricia Highsmith: She may have been one of the dozen best short-story writers of the 20th century, and she may have been one of the dozen most disagreeable and mean-spirited as well."[6]

Highsmith was highly critical of American culture and foreign policy; beginning in 1963, she resided exclusively in Europe. She died of aplastic anemia and cancer in Locarno, Switzerland, aged 74, and was cremated at the cemetery in Bellinzona.

Acting Edition: Methuen Publishing Ltd.

Awards and Honors: Patricia Highsmith's *The Talented Mr. Ripley* was nominated for an Edgar Allan Poe Award by the Mystery Writers of America in 1956 and a year later won the Grand Prix de Littérature Policière as best international crime novel. In 1999, the American film *The Talented Mr. Ripley* was nominated for five Academy Awards and five Golden Globe Awards, including Best Motion Picture Drama. In 1962, *Purple Noon,* based on the Ripley novel, won an MWA Edgar as Best Foreign Film. In 1963, Highsmith's short story, "The Terrapin" (published in *Ellery Queen Mystery Magazine*), was nominated for MWA's Edgar. In 1965, her novel *The Two Faces of January* won the Crime Writers Association of England's Silver Dagger Award for best foreign crime novel of the previous year. Phyllis Nagy was the recipient of a National Endowment for the Arts grant (1989, 1993), a McKnight Fellowship (1991), a Writers Guild Award for Best Play, *Disappeared* (1995), and a Drama-Logue Playwriting Award for *Weldon Rising* (1996). Nagy was nominated for Emmy Awards for both writing and directing the teleplay, *Mrs. Harris* (2005).

NOTES

1. http://literature.britishcouncil.org/phyllis-nagy.

2. Adapted to the stage by Craig Warner, *Strangers on a Train* premiered at the Gateway Theatre, Chester, England, on March 29, 1996, with Dominic McHale as Charles Bruno and Gerard Logan as Guy Haines. The thriller was produced subsequently at the Mercury Theatre, Colchester, England, on August 31, 2000, featuring Alan Cox (Bruno) and Stephen Billington (Haines).

3. John M. Reilly, ed., *Twentieth-Century Crime and Mystery Writers* (New York: St. Martin's, 1980), 766.

4. Bruce F. Murphy, *The Encyclopedia of Murder and Mystery* (New York: St. Martin's Minotaur, 1999), 243.

5. Patricia Highsmith, *Plotting and Writing Suspense Fiction* (Boston: The Writer, 1966), 144.

6. Andrew Wilson, *Beautiful Shadow: The Life of Patricia Highsmith* (New York: Bloomsbury, 2003), 406.

Art of Murder (1999)

Joe DiPietro (United States, c.1960–)

Born in Teaneck, New Jersey, and a graduate of Rutgers University with a bachelor's degree in English, playwright Joe DiPietro found fame and fortune in the field of musical comedy. He wrote the book and lyrics for the off-Broadway show *I Love You, You're Perfect, Now Change*—a series of vignettes about love and relationships—which ran for 5,003 performances between August 1, 1996 and July 27, 2008, making it the longest-running musical revue in off-Broadway history. He revised the librettos of Gershwin's *Oh, Kay!*—a 1926 musical that focused on bootleggers in the prohibition era; Rodgers and Hart's *Babes in Arms*—a 1937 musical concerning teenagers who put on a show; and Rodgers and Hammerstein's 1947 musical *Allegro*—centering on a doctor who is tempted by big money and celebrity status.

Additional credits by DiPietro include the book and lyrics for 2003's mega-hit *Memphis*, loosely based on Memphis disc jockey Dewey Phillips; 2005's *All Shook Up*, a jukebox musical with Elvis Presley music, inspired by William Shakespeare's *Twelfth Night*; 2008's *The Toxic Avenger*, a rock musical about a superhero; and the book for *Nice Work If You Can Get It*, resuscitating music and lyrics by George and Ira Gershwin, 2012.

In 1999, DiPietro detoured to the suspense genre with *Art of Murder*, a one-set thriller with four characters. The action unfolds during a single autumn evening in the living room of Jack and Annie Brooks's remote country house in Connecticut. Prominent in the room is a large, coffin-like isolation tank. Jack Brooks is one of the most accomplished and renowned painters of his generation.

The curtain rises on Annie, carrying paint supplies and crossing to an easel. Suddenly the isolation tank springs open and Jack, dripping wet in swim trunks, rises from it. He closes the tank, nods to Annie, and begins to dress. She continues to work on the canvas, which faces away from the audience.

Jack picks up a revolver and flips open the chamber. He inadvertently points it at Annie when the Irish maid, Kate, enters and utters a scream. The phone rings and Annie exits to an adjacent room. Jack moves toward Kate, but the maid says, "No, not tonight," and runs off.

Annie tells Jack that the caller was Vincent Cummings, a high-powered art dealer, who is on his way to their home. Soon Cummings arrives. Over scotch, Cumming tells the Brooks that a mutual friend, the young postmodernistic artist Nicole Erickson, has committed suicide. It may have been because Cummings recently looked at Erickson's work and realized that she wasn't ready for public attention just yet. Ironically, Erickson's death has caused a surge of interest in her work, and the prices have mushroomed, Cummings reports.

Jack exits to the kitchen and Annie, crying, relates to Vincent, "It's all over between Jack and me. . . . My husband is psychotic! . . . He's a monster." Annie startles Vincent by asking him to help her kill Jack. "Tonight, within the hour. . . . You and I—let's kill the colossal asshole."

Jack returns. He tells Vincent that the death of Nicole Erickson has given him an idea: what if his dead body is found on the floor tonight? Vincent, hesitatingly, says that the price of Jack's paintings will double within thirty days. He can create "a posthumous publicity machine." He would sell not only Jack's works but also his image—his rugged face, his piercing eyes—on T-shirts, posters, pillowcases. "I would make you mythic," concludes Vincent, then bursts out laughing—it was all harmless speculation, just for fun.

Annie asks Jack to get into the water tank and let her speak with Vincent. Jack sings "Que sera, sera" and disappears into the tank. Annie tells Vincent that she's figured "a foolproof way" to kill Jack without raising any suspicion. "It wouldn't be murder, Vincent, it would be suicide," she pronounces and exhibits a stack of notes written by Jack during his worst manic-depressive moments. "My career is dead. And so am I," reads one.

Annie pursues her point. Jack's tank can serve as a coffin. Right now, a lever controls the water flow, set to automatically cut off at the float level. She can rig it so that in one turn of the lever, the tank will fill to the brim. With a magnet, they can slide the inside metal bolt shut, so that it is unreachable from outside. She and Vincent would go out for dinner. Upon their return, they would find Jack's note and try to pry open the tank, but because it was locked from inside their frantic efforts to claw the lid open would be in vain.

Furthermore, says Annie, she was the one who for the last five years has actually painted the pictures that Jack signed. In awe of her husband, she agreed to put his name on her first painting, then the second, and soon gave away her artistic identity. She can keep creating pictures, and every few months they can tell the world that yet another "new" Jack Brooks work has been found hidden somewhere deep in the great artist's house.

Vincent agrees to participate in Annie's scheme. They knot the tank's handles; Annie exits to rig the water valve, returns, and puts on a glove before grabbing the lever and turning it. They hear the water gushing and Jack's pounding on the lid. After a few moments, the water stops. Jack bangs a few more times—then silence. Annie takes the magnet, goes to the tank, and slowly runs it along the side. A grating noise from inside indicates that the interior bolt has moved into place.

Annie places Jack's suicide note on the table, then jumps into Vincent's arms, and they kiss fiercely. "That's it, all done," Annie whispers. "And it's foolproof, I think."[1]

They hurry out. "I'm hungry," says Annie as she closes the door.

When act 2 begins, it is an hour later. The front door opens. Annie enters and turns on the lights. Vincent follows, carrying an open champagne bottle. As he's announcing that it's time to make their "tragic" discovery, the maid Kate enters from the kitchen. She has been back for about an hour and had assumed that her employers went out together. Kate exits and Vincent, concerned, declares, "This is the last murder I'm ever committing!" Annie notices that the suicide note is missing and sighs, "They do say that something goes wrong with every murder plan."

Annie retrieves the magnet and grabs the tank's handle. A gunshot sounds. The lights flash out. In the dark, another shot is heard and Annie lets out a terrified scream. Dim lights come on. Vincent rushes to the front door and pulls it open. On the other side is Jack, who jumps Vincent and begins to pummel him. Jack demands that Vincent confess to the murder of Nicole Erickson; if it wasn't for him taking the troubled young woman as a client, building her up, and then tearing her to shreds, she would not have committed suicide and would still be alive today.

Jack opens a side door. Perched on a hook is Annie's bloody body. Fearful, Vincent agrees to sign a letter in which he admits responsibility for Erickson's death. He is then shocked again as Annie steps down from the hook. Jack tells Vincent that it was all "the little woman's idea." They never filled the tank with water, the suicide note was a fake, and the shots were blanks. They now expect Vincent to sell each of their paintings for at least "one million big ones," or else they'll send his confession to the newspapers.

Vincent prepares to leave, but he makes a fatal mistake. He confronts Jack and tells him that he's not a true artist but an "ego-driven no-talent"; he, Vincent, created him and fed him "to a gullible public." Jack fires twice and Vincent falls. Jack realizes to his horror that the revolver was now loaded with real bullets and Vincent is actually dead. "I didn't mean to kill him," cries Jack. "I knew him for twenty years. . . . Someone put real bullets in there."

In another surprising plot maneuver, Annie tells Jack that Vincent wasn't the only one being set up tonight. She cannot allow Jack to continue to sign his name to her work. She mixed his drink with selenine. It's not fatal; it'll just immobilize him for a while. She'll then place him in the water tank and fill it to the brim. "I'm about to drown you," says Annie. "There's a monster in all of us."

Kate, the maid, enters. Jack tells her to phone the police, but soon realizes that she is in cahoots with his wife. The two women lift Jack into the tank. Annie closes the lid and runs the magnet along the side of the tank. The sound of the bolt closing is heard. Annie puts on a glove, then hesitates. "Oh, my God," she says. "Can I really do this to him, Kate?" The maid assures her that by the turn of the lever, she'll be free forever to live her life "as yourself." Annie turns the lever and the water gurgles.

Before calling the police, Annie crosses to the easel and signs the painting, "Annie Brooks."

* * *

Art of Murder was originally produced by the American Stage Company in Teaneck, New Jersey, opening on March 3, 1999. It was directed by John Rando with a set designed by Loren Sherman. The cast included Gregory Salata (Jack Brooks), Erika Rolfsrud (Annie Brooks), John Tillotson (Vincent Cummings), and Kate Stoutenborough (Kate).

The twisty thriller has not yet reached New York but has been presented by various resident companies, most recently at Thunder Bay Theatre in Alpena, Michigan, directed by Mark Butterfuss (March 4–15, 2009). Reviewer Diane Speer of the *Alpena News* wrote: "Filled with twists and turns, this hilarious whodunit keeps the audience engaged and waiting until the final moments to find out just who is going to survive all the inter related machinations."[2]

The back cover of the play's acting edition quotes several additional endorsing reviews: "A scintillating hit with thrills and chills and some wonderful humor"—*The Suburban News*; "It is hilarious, suspenseful, surprising and dazzling in every way"—*The Equinox News*; "Mr. DiPietro has created an insular world in which greed and vengeance and personal recognition are free to play with the sanity and the lives of everyone involved. *Art of Murder* takes the audience on a funhouse roller coaster ride"—*The Press-Journal*.

Acting Edition: Dramatists Play Service.

Awards and Honors: *Art of Murder* won the 2000 Mystery Writers of America's Edgar Award in the category of Best Play. Joe DiPietro garnered 2010 Tony Awards for Best Original Score and Best Book of a Musical for *Memphis. I Love You, You're Perfect, Now Change* was nominated for the Outer Critics Circle Award as Outstanding off-Broadway Musical in 1997. *The Toxic Avenger* won the 2009 Outer Critics Circle Award for Best New off-Broadway Musical.

NOTES

1. The "impossible" situation in a crime scene was invented by the father of the detective story, Edgar Allan Poe, in *The Murders in the Rue Morgue*, 1841 (throttled bodies found in the chimney of a locked room). The technique was utilized by Israel Zangwill in *The Big Bow Mystery*, 1892 (a victim with a cut throat is discovered in a shuttered bedroom), by Arthur Conan Doyle in *The Story of the Lost Special*, 1898 (the disappearance of a train from a railroad line guarded at both ends), and by Gaston Leroux in *The Mystery of the Yellow Room*, 1912 (a woman found mortally wounded in a sealed room surrounded by witnesses who claim that no one has entered or left the space). Among the better-known, and fiendishly ingenious, practitioners of the hermetically sealed puzzles were English authors Edgar Wallace, Margery Allingham, E. C. Bentley, Anthony Berkeley, G. K. Chesterton, and Agatha Christie. American writers who concocted impossible predicaments include Melville Davisson Post, Ellery Queen, S. S. Van Dine, and John Dickson Carr/Carter Dickson, the foremost exponent of the "locked room" mystery. On stage, locked-room murders were depicted in *In the Next Room* (1923), dramatized by Eleanor Robson and Harriet Ford from Burton E. Stevenson's 1912 novel, *The Mystery of the Boule Cabinet*; *The Canary Murder Case* (1928), adapted by Walton Butterfield and Lee Morrison from S. S. Van Dine's 1927 novel of the same name; *Alibi*, aka *The Fatal Alibi* (1932) by Michael Morton, based on Agatha Christie's 1926 novel *The Murder of Roger Ackroyd*; *The Locked Room* (1933) by Herbert Ashton Jr.; *Busman's Honeymoon* (1936) by Dorothy L. Sayers and Muriel St. Clare Byrne; and *Dragnet* (1956), an adaptation by James Reach of the popular NBC radio-television series, depicting hard-boiled Sergeant Joe Friday of the LAPD and his sidekick, Officer Frank Smith, on the case of a locked-room murder. Here, the victim is found shot in a study with the door bolted on the inside and the windows shuttered.

2. *Alpena News*, March 6, 2009.

Sherlock Holmes — The Last Act! (1999)

David Stuart Davies (England, 1946–)

British dramatist David Stuart Davies states that *Sherlock Holmes—The Last Act!* "is designed as a one man show which explores the character and some aspects of the career of Sherlock Holmes, the world's first consulting detective. It also places under scrutiny the friendship and feelings he had for his friend Watson."[1]

The year is 1916 and Holmes is sixty-two. He has just returned from Watson's funeral. In a reflective mood, he salutes his old friend: "You stimulated my thought processes, you provided the obvious which let me seek the unusual, pushing me nearer the truth."

Holmes conjures in his mind a kaleidoscope of past images: his shooting practice, forming VR—Victoria Regina—in bullet holes over the mantelpiece; the smoke bomb thrown by Watson into Irene Adler's room to reveal the whereabouts of an incriminating picture; the bludgeoned body of Sir Eustace Brackenstall at the Abbey Grange in Kent; a hypodermic syringe containing a 7 percent solution; dastardly Grimesby Roylott retrieving a poker from the hearth and proceeding to bend it; the struggle with Professor Moriarty on the edge of Reichenbach Falls.

The second act begins with Holmes, his eyes moist, addressing the dead Watson to explain why he disappeared for three years after the Reichenbach encounter. "If the world was convinced I was dead, that I too had perished with the Professor, it would remove my shackles—I could take a rest from crime." Holmes apologizes: "Watson, my dear Watson, I had no idea that you would be so affected."

Playwright Davies now strays away from the Canon and lets Holmes reveal an invented personal history of a childhood spent in North Yorkshire, "on the edge of the black North York Moors, where the wind sweeps across the terrain with a steady, wearing wail." It seems that young Sherlock grew up in the shadow of his brother Mycroft—"Not only was his frame stouter than mine but his sensitivities were more robust."

Their father was an army major general who beat his wife until she finally left home. One night, flushed with drink, the father tried to force the child Sherlock to enjoy "the beauty of the grape" and a struggle ensued. "I pushed him from me and he staggered backwards crashing to the floor, his head hitting the stone hearth of the fireplace. It smashed like an eggshell. . . . I am no doubt indirectly responsible for my father's death. . . . I am glad I have told you at last, my dear Watson."

Holmes slumps in his chair. He pulls a newspaper cutting from his pocket and reads it. "John H. Watson, the companion to Sherlock Holmes, whose accounts of the famous detective in the *Strand Magazine* thrilled a generation, was found dead yesterday by his housekeeper. He had suffered a sudden heart attack and died quietly in his sleep." Holmes smiles sadly—"Died in your bed, while sleeping. Typical. Never one to make a fuss, were you?"

The old detective picks up a cocaine bottle and a syringe, rolls up his sleeve, and injects himself. He returns to his chair and falls into a drug-induced sleep, dying. A spotlight intensifies on the door as it shuts with a slam. Holmes jerks up, his face aglow. "Watson? Is that you?" he asks, as violin music plays and the curtain descends.

* * *

David Stuart Davies devised *Sherlock Holmes—The Last Act!* for English actor Roger Llewellyn. Trained at the Royal Academy of Dramatic Art, Llewellyn has appeared in regional theatres throughout England, winning kudos for his portrayal of villainous Jack Stapleton in *The Hound of the Baskervilles. The Last Act* premiered at the Salisbury Playhouse, Wiltshire, England in May 1999 and has been touring ever since, performing in Edinburgh, London, New York, Canada, France, Saudi Arabia, and the Far East. The play was published by Calabash Press, British Columbia, in 1999.

Britain's David Stuart Davies (1946–) was a teacher of English for twenty years before becoming a full-time writer. Immersed in all matters Sherlockian, Davies founded the Northern Musgraves Sherlock Holmes Society, based in Yorkshire, and is the editor of *Sherlock* magazine.

Davies penned the studies *Holmes of the Movies* (1976), *Bending the Willow: Jeremy Brett as Sherlock Holmes* (1996), and *Starring Sherlock Holmes* (2001). Davies's novels, all featuring the Great Detective, include *Sherlock Holmes and the Hentzau Affair* (1991), in which the sleuth and Watson travel to the Kingdom of Ruritania (created in Anthony Hope's *The Prisoner of Zenda*), thwarting a throne takeover; *The Tangled Skein* (1992), picturing Holmes versus Count Dracula; *Scroll of the Dead* (1998), involving a fraudulent séance and secrets contained on an Egyptian papyrus; *The Shadow of the Rat* (1999), where the catalyst of horrifying events is a body recovered from the Thames—dead of bubonic plague; and *The Veiled Detective* (2004), presenting the outrageously intriguing premise that the man we know as Dr. John Watson, Holmes' faithful friend and chronicler, is a spy planted at 221B Baker Street by Professor Moriarty!

Acting Edition: Calabash Press, Ashcroft, British Columbia, Canada.

NOTE

1. David Stuart Davies, *Sherlock Holmes: The Last Act!* (Ashcroft, B.C.: Calabash, 1999), 14.

The Laramie Project (2000)

Moisés Kaufman (United States, Venezuela-born, 1963–) and the Members of Tectonic Theatre Project

A new dramatic form arose during the 1950s and 1960s: the political docudrama. Playwrights in various countries took it upon themselves to examine official documents and court records of historical events and incorporated their findings, sometimes verbatim, into theatrical fare. In England, Ludovic Kennedy wrote *Murder Story* (1954), dramatizing the real-life case known as the Croydon Rooftop Murder: Nineteen-year-old Derek Bentley and sixteen-year-old Christopher Craig exchanged bullets with the police on the premises of a Croydon factory. Craig shot and killed a police officer while trying to escape over a rooftop. The two boys were tried and convicted of murder. Craig, being underage, was sentenced to prison. Bentley was sentenced to death. Playwright Kennedy was deeply affected by the notion that the murderer should survive while his accomplice, who was not carrying a gun that fateful night, would be executed. The case inspired Kennedy to write *Murder Story* as a protest against capital punishment.

In the United States, Saul Levitt based his play *The Andersonville Trial* (1959) on the official records of the 1865 trial of Henry Wirz, commandant of the most notorious Confederate prison-of-war stockade. The courtroom drama raises the issue of passive moral conviction among military men who blindly obey the inhuman orders of their superiors. *Sequel to a Verdict* (1962) by Philip Dunning conjures up a case reminiscent of the Charles Lindbergh kidnapping tragedy.

In Germany, Rolf Hochhuth's *The Deputy* (1963) questions the failure of Pope Pius XII to speak out against the Nazi slaughter of Jews; Peter Weiss re-creates the horrific events at the Auschwitz concentration camp in *The Investigation* (1965); and Heinar Kipphardt's *In the Matter of J. Robert Oppenheimer* (1964) reexamines the hysterical era of McCarthyism when in 1954, Dr. Oppenheimer, "the father of the atomic bomb," was summoned to a congressional hearing regarding his security clearance.

Donald Freed's *Inquest* (1970) is concerned with the controversial Cold War trial and execution of Julius and Ethel Rosenberg, who were found guilty of delivering atomic secrets to the Soviet Union. *The Trial of the Catonsville Nine* (1971) was penned by Daniel Berrigan, a Catholic priest who was one of the seven men and two women who, at the height of the Vietnam War, entered the draft board in Catonsville, Maryland, and set 378 recruitment files on fire with homemade napalm. The nine were arrested, convicted, and sentenced to prison terms ranging from two to three and a half years.[1] Eric Bentley's *Are You Now or Have You Ever Been?* (1972) is centered on the 1950s House Un-American Activities Committee hearings, in which figures from the world of show business were subpoenaed to testify about their loyalty as Americans and asked to name any and all communists in the industry. Assembled directly from the transcripts of the hearings, the play uses the actual words spoken by Lillian Hellman, Elia Kazan, and Jerome Robbins, among others.

The Biko Inquest (1978), by Englishmen Norman Felton and Jon Blair, dramatizes the transcripts of the inquest into the 1977 death of South African activist Stephen Biko in a jail cell on September 12, 1977. Five police officers were accused of killing Biko. Emily Mann based *Execution of Justice* (1984) on the court records and her own investigation regarding the 1978 double-barreled killing of San Francisco's Mayor George Moscone and gay Supervisor Harvey Milk by Dan White, a former member of the city's Board of Supervisors.

New York's Tectonic Theatre Project, dedicated to experimentation with form and structure in contemporary drama, went a step further. With Artistic Director Moisés Kaufman at the helm, in 1998 company members traveled to Laramie, Wyoming, to interview townspeople regarding the murder of Matthew Shepard. On October 7, 1998, after midnight, Shepard, a gay student at the University of Wyoming in Laramie, met two local men, Aaron McKinney and Russell Henderson, at the popular Fireside Lounge and agreed to join them for a car ride. The duo robbed, pistol-whipped, and tortured Shepard, tied him to a fence in a remote, rural area, and left him to die. Shepard was discovered eighteen hours later by a cyclist. He never regained consciousness and remained on full life support at the Poudre Valley Hospital in Fort Collins, Colorado until he was pronounced dead at 12:53 a.m. on October 12, 1998. McKinney and Russell were arrested shortly thereafter. The police found a bloody gun and Shepard's shoes and wallet in their truck. Both were sentenced to two consecutive life terms. The Shepard murder brought national and international attention to hate crimes motivated by homophobia and affected legislation at the state and federal levels.

"The idea of *The Laramie Project* originated in my desire to learn more about why Matthew Shepard was murdered," wrote Moisés Kaufman in an introduction to the acting edition of the play, "about what happened that night, about the town of Laramie. The idea of listening to the citizens talk really interested me. How is Laramie different from the rest of the country, and how is it similar?"[2]

Four weeks after the homicide of Matthew Shepard, nine members of the Tectonic Theatre Project descended on Laramie. They returned to the town many times over the course of the next year and a half and conducted more than 200 interviews. By editing their copious notes, a play emerged. "The experience of working on *The Laramie Project*," stated Kaufman, "has been one of great sadness, great beauty, and, perhaps most important, great revelations—about our nation, about our ideas, about ourselves."[3]

The Laramie Project is divided into three acts; each in turn is divided into episodic "moments." The curtain rises on a Narrator introducing members of Tectonic Theatre as they begin a series of interviews with Laramie residents. Detective Sergeant Hing of the local police department relates that Wyoming is "one of the largest states in the country, and the least populated." Eileen Engen, a rancher, and Doc O'Connor, a limousine driver, speak of the pleasant environment. Philip Dubois, President of the University of Wyoming; Rebecca Hilliker, head of the theatre department; Zackie Salmon, a college administrator; and student Jedadiah Schultz are united in praising Laramie—population 26,687—as "a beautiful town, secluded enough that you can have your own identity. . . . A town with a personality that most larger cities are stripped of."

"As far as the gay issue," says seventy-year-old Marge Murray, "Laramie is live and let live." Doc O'Connor agrees: "There's more gay people in Wyoming than meets the eye. . . . And I don't think Wyoming people give a damn one way or another if you're gay or straight." Catherine Connolly, a professor at the university, reveals that she was "the first 'out' lesbian or gay faculty member on campus. And that was in 1992."

After absorbing the background information, the actor-interviewers visited the Fireside Lounge, the last place Shepard was seen alive. The Fireside had several pool tables and a stage area for karaoke. The owner, Matt Mickelson, and the bartender, Matt Galloway, relate that on the fateful night, at 10:30 p.m., Matthew Shepard showed up, alone, sat down and ordered his usual beer, Heineken. He did not seem to be looking for anyone; he just enjoyed his drink and the atmosphere. At approximately 11:45 p.m., Aaron McKinney and Russell Henderson came in, "stone-faced, dirty, grungy, rude." They walked up to the bar and paid for a pitcher with dimes and quarters. They took the pitcher into the pool room and kept to themselves. After a while, they returned to the main room and were seen talking to Shepard. Soon Aaron, Russell, and Matthew left together. Shadow, an African-American musician who was the establishment's DJ, saw them enter a small black truck. The three sat in the front seat with Matthew in the middle.

Aaron Kreifels, a university student, tells the interviewers that on Wednesday at 5:00 p.m. he left his dorm for a relaxing bicycle ride. "God wanted me to find him," says Kreifels, "because there's no way that I was going to go that way." He found himself in "deep-ass sand" and suddenly noticed something lying by a fence. At first he thought it was a scarecrow but getting closer noticed the hair and realized that the chest was going up and down. He ran to the nearest house as fast as he could and dialed 911 for the police.

Officer Reggie Fluty found Matthew tied to a fence with a thin white rope, covered in dried blood and barely breathing. His head was distorted and there was "a real harsh head wound." Matthew's shoes were missing.

Dr. Cantway, who worked the emergency room at Laramie's Ivinson Memorial Hospital the night Shepard was brought in, said that he was horrified by the fact that such severe injuries, "the kind that come from a car going down a hill at eighty miles an hour," were inflicted "from someone doing this to another person." Dr. Cantway added that "strangely," twenty minutes before Matthew was carried in, Aaron McKinney arrived with his girlfriend. Two days later Dr. Cantway found out the connection between Matthew and Aaron. "I was very struck!" exclaimed the doctor. "They were two kids! They were both my patients and they were two kids. I took care of both of them. . . . For a brief moment I wondered if this is how God feels when he looks down at us. How we are all his kids. . . . And I felt a great deal of compassion—for both of them."

The second act deals with the reactions of the Laramie residents as word spread about what was generally perceived as "a hate crime." During an arraignment, the judge summarized the essential facts of the case: The defendants, Aaron James McKinney and Russell Arthur Henderson, met Matthew Shepard at the Fireside Bar. After Mr. Shepard confided that he was gay, the subjects lured him into leaving with them in their vehicle and drove to a remote area. Both subjects tied their victim to a fence, robbed him, tortured him, and beat him. Later, officers of the Laramie Police Department found Shepard's credit card and shoes inside the pickup. "Said defendants left the victim begging for his life," said the judge.

Newspersons announced that McKinney and Henderson came from the poor side of town. Both were from broken homes and as teenagers had had run-ins with the law. They lived in trailer parks and scratched out a living working at fast-food restaurants and fixing roofs. Both pleaded not guilty to the charges.

On Monday, October 12, 1998, at 12:53 a.m., Matthew Shepard died. His family was at his bedside.

The third act begins on the day of the funeral. Matt Galloway, the bartender at the Fireside, tells the interviewers that despite a heavy snowstorm, thousands of people dressed in black, carrying umbrellas, attended the local churches and joined in prayer.

In court, Russell Henderson changed his "not guilty" plea to "guilty." He was sentenced "to serve a period of imprisonment for the term of your natural life" for the felony of murder with robbery, and a second period of life imprisonment for kidnapping—both to run consecutively.

The trial of Aaron McKinney commenced a year later. The prosecution played a tape recording of his confession during a police interrogation. "Some kid wanted a ride," said McKinney. "[A] queer dude . . . we drove out past Wal-Mart . . . he starts grabbing my leg and grabbing my genitals. . . . I beat him up pretty bad . . . with my fist. My pistol. The butt of the gun. . . . I had a few beers and I don't know . . . it was like somebody else doing it." The jury found McKinney guilty of kidnapping, aggravated robbery, and second-degree murder; not guilty of premeditated first-degree murder.

McKinney's defense team approached Matthew Shepard's parents, Dennis and Judy Shepard, and pled for their client's life. Dennis Shepard made a statement in court, announcing that he's been comforted by the fact that "Matt's beating, hospitalization, and funeral focused world-wide attention on hate. Good is coming out of evil. . . . This is the time to begin the healing process. To show mercy to someone who refused to show any mercy, Mr. McKinney, I am going to grant you life, as hard as it is for me to do so, because of Matthew. . . . May you have a long life, and may you thank Matthew every day for it."

* * *

The Laramie Project premiered at the Denver Center Theatre on February 26, 2000, ran for sixteen performances, and on May 18 moved to New York's Union Square Theatre, where it ran for 126 more. Critic Ben Brantley of the *New York Times* asserted that "while running two and a half hours with two intermissions, *The Laramie Project* sustains its emotional hold. As Mr. Kaufman demonstrated with *Gross Indecency*,[4] he has a remarkable gift for giving a compelling theatrical flow to journalistic and historical material. . . . The evening itself has the feeling of those candlelight vigils. There is the same sense of a stately procession through which swims a stirring medley of emotions: anger, sorrow, bewilderment and, most poignantly, a defiant glimmer of hope."[5]

In November 2000, Kaufman took his company to Laramie, Wyoming to perform the play there. In March 2002 Kaufman directed a television adaptation of *The Laramie Project* for HBO, remaining faithful to the interview format of the play, but the casting of many well-known actors (including Steve Buscemi, Peter Fonda, and Laura Linney) in the cameo roles of Laramie townspeople, conflicted with the documentary, real-life aura of the material.

Since then the play has been mounted more than 2,000 times by high schools, colleges, and community theatres across the United States, and by professional theatres in Canada, England, Ireland, Australia, and New Zealand. A recent revival was presented by the Promenade Players of Santa Monica, California, March 4–March 19, 2011. Several high school productions, in cities such as Yakima, Washington, Burbank, California, and Surrey, British Columbia, have been banned. Amid concerns from parents, who argued that the play's content was inappropriate for high school students, the Catholic Notre Dame High School in Lawrenceville, New Jersey, cancelled its production of *The Laramie Project* in March 2012, a decision that led to even more controversy among some of the students, staff members, and alumni.

Ten years after Matthew Shepard's murder, members of the Tectonic Theatre Project returned to Laramie and conducted follow-up interviews with local residents to explore the long-term impact of the case. According to Moisés Kaufman, "Laramie has changed in some ways. The city council passed a bias crime ordinance that tracks such crimes, though it does not include penalties for them. . . . Several residents say they came out publicly as gay. . . . The university hosts a four-day Shepard Symposium for local justice each spring. . . . And yet, to the bewilderment of some people here, there is no memorial to Mr. Shepard in Laramie. The long fence has been torn down where he lay dying for 18 hours on October 7, 1998. There is no marker. Wild grass blows in the wind. The Fireside tavern is also gone. . . . There is no longer a bar in town where gays, jocks, foreign students and cowboys mix together."[6]

The interviews were collated into an eighty-minute companion piece, *The Laramie Project: Ten Years Later*, which debuted as a stage reading at more than forty theatres across the nation—including La Jolla Playhouse in San Diego, California; Broad Stage in Santa Monica, California; Arena Stage in Washington, D.C.; Seattle Repertory Theatre; Berkeley Repertory Theatre; Alice Tully Hall at Lincoln Center, Manhattan; University of Arizona in Tucson; and University of Wyoming in Laramie—on October 12, 2009, the eleventh anniversary of Shepard's death. The sequel was also staged overseas in Spain, Australia, and Hong Kong.

Boston's Emerson College produced both *The Laramie Project* and *The Laramie Project: Ten Years Later* in its 2010–2011 season.[7]

* * *

Born and raised in Caracas, Venezuela, Moisés Kaufman is of Romanian and Ukrainian Jewish descent. He moved to New York in 1987, was awarded a Guggenheim Fellowship in 2002, and shortly thereafter founded the Tectonic Theatre Project, a company dedicated to experimentation with language and form in contemporary drama.

Among the plays that Kaufman wrote and developed at the Tectonic was *33 Variations*, which focuses on the latter period of Ludwig van Beethoven's life. It premiered at the Arena Stage in Washington, D.C. in 2007, ran at San Diego's La Jolla Playhouse in 2008, and presented on Broadway at the Eugene O'Neill Theatre, with Jane Fonda, in 2009. Kaufman's *Gross Indecency* covers the 1890s trials of Oscar Wilde, accused of homosexual sodomy with Lord Alfred Douglas. It debuted at off-Broadway's Greenwich House in February 1997, subsequently moved to the Minetta Lane Theatre, and had two stagings in Los Angeles, one at Mark Taper Forum in 1998, the other at the Electric Theatre in 2009.

Doug Wright's *I Am My Own Wife*, a one-man play that explores the life of Charlotte von Mahlsdorf, a transvestite who survived both the Nazi and communist governments in East Berlin, was directed by Kaufman for off-Broadway's Playwrights Horizons in 2003. It transferred to the Lyceum Theatre later that year, making this Kaufman's Broadway directorial debut, and was one of *Time* magazine's Ten Best Plays of the Year. Kaufman's next major assignment was the staging of *Bengal Tiger at the Baghdad Zoo*, an allegorical drama by Rajiv Joseph about a tiger that haunts the streets of present-day Baghdad seeking the meaning of life. Living characters interact with the dead as the war explodes around them. The play debuted at the Kirk Douglas Theatre in Culver City, California in 2009, and subsequently ran at the Mark Forum in Los Angeles. A Pulitzer Prize finalist, it came to Broadway's Richard Rodgers Theatre in 2011, starring Robin Williams in the title role. Critic Charles Isherwood of the *New York Times* wrote that the production was "directed with gorgeous finesse by Moisés Kaufman."[8]

Other plays staged by Kaufman include *One Arm* (2004), based on an unproduced screenplay by Tennessee Williams; *Master Class* (2004), with Rita Moreno; Oscar Wilde's *Lady Windermere's Fan* (2005); and *Macbeth* (2006), featuring Liev Schreiber.

Acting Edition: Vintage Books.

Awards and Honors: The 2000 off-Broadway production of *The Laramie Project* was nominated for the Drama Desk Award as a Unique Theatrical Experience. It won the Lucille Lortel Award for Best Play, the Outer Critics Circle Award for Best off-Broadway Play, the Los Angeles Garland Award for Best Play, the Florida Carbonell Award for Best Play, the Bay Area Theatre Critics Circle Award for direction, and the Joe A. Callaway Award for Direction—endorsed by Kaufman's peers in the Society of Stage Directors and Choreographers. Kaufman's 2002 television adaptation of *The Laramie Project* for HBO won the National Board of Review

Award, the Humanities Prize, and a Special Mention for Best First Film at the Berlin Film Festival. The film also earned Kaufman two Emmy Award nominations for Best Writer and Best Director. In 1997, Kaufman received a Tony Award nomination for Best Direction of the play *I Am My Own Wife*. In 1999, he was named Artist of the Year by Venezuela's Casa del Artista. Ten years later, Kaufman's play *33 Variations* was nominated for a Tony Award for Best Play.

NOTES

1. A plot synopsis, production data, and critics' evaluations of Ludovic Kennedy's *Murder Story* (1954), Saul Levitt's *The Andersonville Trial* (1959), Philip Dunning's *Sequel to a Verdict* (1962), Heinar Kipphardt's *In the Matter of J. Robert Openheimer* (1964), Donald Freed's *Inquest* (1970), and Daniel Berrigan's *The Trial of the Catonsville Nine* (1971) are covered in *Blood on the Stage, 1950–1975* by Amnon Kabatchnik (Lanham, Md.: Scarecrow Press, 2011).

2. Moisés Kaufman, *The Laramie Project* (New York: Vintage, 2001), vi.

3. Kaufman, *The Laramie Project*, vii.

4. The play *Gross Indecency* (1997) by Moisés Kaufman focuses on the trials of Oscar Wilde at the end of the nineteenth century. The famed author was prosecuted under Section 11 of the Criminal Law Amendment Act of 1886, which had made "acts of gross indecency" between men a criminal offense.

5. *New York Times*, May 19, 2000.

6. *New York Times*, September 17, 2008.

7. The Matthew Shepard and James Byrd Jr. Hate Crime Prevention Act, also known as the Matthew Shepard Act, is an American Act of Congress, passed on October 22, 2009, and signed into law by President Barack Obama on October 28, 2009. The measure expands the 1969 U.S. federal hate-crime law to include crimes motivated by a victim's actual or perceived gender, sexual orientation, gender identity, or disability.

8. *New York Times*, March 31, 2011.

Appendix A

Deadly Poison

Poison has claimed victims on the stage since Medea sent a robe smeared with a lethal concoction to her husband's lover, Creusa, who died painfully engulfed in flames (*Medea*, 431 BC, by Euripides). Heracles mortally wounds the centaur Nessus with a poisonous dart for having attempted to ravish his wife, the beautiful Deianira (*Trachiniae* aka *Maidens of Trachis*, 413 BC, by Sophocles). Ironically, the mythological Greek hero suffers a horrible death after donning a garment dipped in poisoned blood, dispatched to him by Deianira, who was jealous of a liaison between her husband and the princess Ione (*Hercules on Oeta*, first century AD, by Seneca). Hamlet was killed by a poisoned rapier in the bloody denouement of Shakespeare's 1601–1602 masterpiece. Various venoms were served and swallowed in seventeenth-century Jacobean horror tragedies and nineteenth-century blood-and-thunder melodramas.

Setting aside the blowpipe darts in several dramatizations of Arthur Conan Doyle's *The Sign of Four* (1901, 1903), Leo Tolstoy's *The Power of Darkness* (1902) is the first bona fide "poison play" of the twentieth century. A young wife poisons her considerably older, rich peasant husband, inherits his estate, and marries his virile servant. Snakebite is the cause of death in Conan Doyle's *The Speckled Band* (dramatized in 1910). In the end of Horace Annesley Vachell's *The Case of Lady Camber* (1915) it turns out that the lethal talin was not the cause of Lady Camber's demise. Yet the lingering suspicion that a jealous nurse poisoned her is the chief ingredient of suspense in the drama.

The 1920s and 1930s are considered the golden age of detective literature. Characters sip poison in the works of Agatha Christie, Dorothy L. Sayers, Georgette Heyer, Ellery Queen, and John Dickson Carr, and Anthony Berkeley's *The Poisoned Chocolate Case* (1929) led the pack. Simultaneously, poisoned concoctions became the hallmark of stage thrillers. A venomous mechanism that "strikes like a rattlesnake" is the instrument of death in *In the Next Room* (1923), dramatized by Eleanor Robson and Harriet Ford from the 1912 novel *The Mystery of the Boule Cabinet* by Burton E. Stevenson. Tondeleyo, a bored, greedy West African woman of mixed race, attempts to poison her English husband in Leon Gordon's *White Cargo* (1923), but is forced to swallow the lethal "quinine" herself. A poisoned drink is served to an alcoholic, drug-taking, and abusive husband in *The Fake* (1924) by Frederick Lonsdale. Darts dipped in curare and shot from a blowgun are fatal in *The Call of the Banshee*, aka *The Banshee* (1927) by W. D. Hepenstall and Ralph Culliman. Playwright Roland Pertwee used prussic acid in *Interference* (1927), cyanide of potassium in *To Kill a Cat* (1939), and crystals of strychnine in *Pink String and Sealing Wax* (1944) as deadly catalysts. In A. E. W. Mason's *The House of the Arrow* (1928), a wealthy French widow is murdered at home by an arrow dipped in poison. In Mason's *No Other Tiger* (1928), a money-hungry dancer exchanges her friend's medicine with poisonous disinfectant to kill her, because she wants to keep an envelope stuffed with 40,000 pounds, which the friend had given her for safekeeping. In Somerset Maugham's *The Sacred Flame* (1928), a mother feeds a lethal overdose of pills to her helpless paralytic son to end his suffering. A murderous doctor prescribes a moneyed widow an overdose of veronal in *Alibi* (1928), a dramatization by Michael Morton of Agatha Christie's 1926 novel, *The Murder of Roger Ackroyd*.

In Emlyn Williams's *Murder Has Been Arranged* (1930), a smiling villain, dressed as Caesar Borgia, poisons his uncle's drink during a costume party and inherits two million pounds. One of the many victims in Owen Davis's *The 9th Guest* (1930) swallows prussic acid. *Dishonored Lady* (1930), co-written by Edward Sheldon and Margaret Ayer Barnes, is a fictional Americanization of the notorious Madeleine Smith case in 1857 Glasgow, Scotland. A society butterfly inserts pellets of strychnine into the coffee of her show business lover to clear the way for marrying a titled, wealthy suitor. In *How to Be Healthy Though Married* (1930), by F. Tennyson Jesse and H. M. Harwood, a fickle Frenchwoman attempts to dispose of her elderly husband with doses of arsenic, only to discover that her cowardly lover supplied her with harmless bicarbonate of soda. When the in-debt bank clerk of Jeffrey Dell's *Payment Deferred* (1931) decides to murder a visiting nephew for pocket money, he mixes his drink with cyanide.

Clytemnestra used an axe to murder Agamemnon in Aeschylus' *Oresteia* (458 BC), but her modern incarnation, Christine Mannon, in Eugene O'Neill's *Mourning Becomes Electra* (1931), gets rid of her husband Ezra with a vial of deadly poison. In Patrick Hamilton's *John Brown's Body* (1931), a renowned scientist has an affair with an underage girl, kills her brother during a fierce struggle, and decides to end his life "the Socrates way" by swallowing the contents of a little green bottle. His toothpaste mixed with potassium cyanide, a hoodlum comes to a sorry end in *Whistling in the Dark* (1932) by Laurence Gross and Edward Childs Carpenter. In John Van Druten's *Diversion* (1932), a jealous lover strangles a fickle actress and pleads with his father, a physician, for poison to commit suicide. A dastardly blackmailer is shot and poisoned simultaneously in Arnold Ridley's *Recipe for Murder* (1932). In *The Locked Room* (1933) by Herbert Ashton Jr., the coroner finds small traces of arsenic in the stomach of a dead man, but it turns out that the victim was also shot in the heart and stabbed in the back!

The innocent wife of a brutal, alcoholic businessman is suspected of feeding him an overdose of sleeping potion in *Without Witness* (1933) by Anthony Armstrong and Harold Simpson. *Crime on the Hill* (1933), by Jack de Leon and Jack Celestin, is a prussic acid case. Bernard J. McOwen's *The Scorpion* (1933) portrays a femme fatale poisoned by a jealous native woman in the barracks of El Garah, a British outpost in the Sudan. The household maid is sent to her maker by a pinch of poison while a pet bird is fed a toxic grape in *Invitation to a Murder* (1934) by Rufus King. *The Eldest* (1935), by Carlton Miles and Eugenie Courtright, focuses on a woman who is sentenced to life imprisonment for poisoning her husband, but is wrongfully acquitted in a new trial. The artist Geoffrey Carroll, the blackguard of Martin Vale's *The Two Mrs. Carrolls* (1935), attempted to poison his first wife and, having fallen in love with a younger, more attractive neighbor, is now mixing the medicine for the sickly second Mrs. Carroll with poisonous tablets. Another dastardly husband is Bruce Lovell in *Love from a Stranger* (1936), adapted by Frank Vosper from Agatha Christie's short story *Philomel Cottage*. Lovell's young bride Cecily discovers to her horror that she has married a serial killer, and saves her life by telling him that she had sprinkled arsenic in his coffee.

The title character of Barré Lyndon's *The Amazing Dr. Clitterhouse* (1936) empties a vial of heroin tablets into the drink of a blackmailer. Eva Raydon, the heroine of Marie Belloc Lowndes's *What Really Happened* (1936), almost pays with her life for the poisoning—via fourteen grains of arsenic—of her husband by another woman. In Lowndes's *Her Last Adventure* (1936), a murderer, when arrested, attempts to commit suicide with a concealed dose of strychnine. In *Blind Man's Buff* (1936) by Ernst Toller, an innocent man is accused of murdering his wife when the postmortem reveals the effect of sinacidic acid. A disturbed, vengeful student pricks a classmate with a syringe filled with allopine and morphine, paralyzing him, in *Trunk Crime*, aka *The Last Straw* (1937) by Edward Percy and Reginald Denham. In James Reach's *The Case of the Squealing Cat* (1937), a tyrannical old millionaire is poisoned before he can alter his will. A parrot at the German consulate in New York dies after ingesting a poisonous grape in *Margin for Error* (1939) by Clare Boothe (Luce), and the consul himself soon follows suit after drinking a glass of drugged whiskey.

Two endearing sisters from Brooklyn spike their elderberry wine with a pinch of arsenic when serving lonely men in the macabre comedy *Arsenic and Old Lace* (1941) by Joseph Kesselring. In James Reach's *Mr. Snoop Is Murdered* (1941), a chain-smoking radio gossip columnist, while on the air, suddenly keels over—poisoned by a cigarette doped with arsenic. One of four people must have killed him, but who? Meek Harry Quincy schemes to get rid of his domineering siblings by having one of them poisoned and the other convicted of the crime in *Uncle Harry* (1942) by Thomas Job. In *Murder Without Crime* (1942) by J. Lee Thompson, sorrowful Stephen, taunted mercilessly by his landlord Matthew, intends to commit suicide by spraying poison in his whiskey, but Matthew, ever suspicious, switches glasses. In order to facilitate the escape of the Duke of Latteraine from prison, the rescuers dispatch the Duke's incapacitated servant with a poisoned jug of wine in *The Duke of Darkness* (1942) by Patrick Hamilton. The title character of Robert St. Clare's *Who Killed Ann Gage?* (1943) is poisoned by cyanide ingested through the smeared pages of a book she was reading. A young wife spikes the eggnog of her wealthy, elderly spouse with liquefied heads of sulfur matches in *Dark Hammock* (1944) by Reginald Denham and Mary Orr. An antique dealer tries to get rid of a nasty blackmailer with a poisonous dart shot from a blowpipe in Edward Percy's *The Shop at Sly Corner* (1945). Before Mary Hayley Bell's *Duet for Two Hands* (1945) even raises its curtain, a prominent surgeon has prescribed lethal tablets for his lover, an actress who is pregnant with his child and makes demands upon him.

Caligula, the Roman emperor, forces a vial of poison into the throat of a rebellious patrician in Albert Camus's *Caligula* (1945). In Arnold Ridley's *Murder Happens* (1945), the proprietor of a seaside hotel, henpecked by a sickly but abusive wife, pours poison into her medicine bottle. *Portrait in Black* (1946), by Ivan Goff and Ben Roberts, depicts the wife of an invalid shipping tycoon teaming up with her lover, the family doctor, to dispose of her spouse via a lethal hypodermic. A youthful lover takes poison and stabs the queen in the double-death climax of *The Eagle Has Two Heads* (1946) by Jean Cocteau. The title characters of Jean Genet's *The Maids* (1947), the sisters Lemercier, insert ten pills of phenobarbital in their hated mistress's tea. In Aldous Huxley's *The Giaconda Smile* (1948), a woman in love with the husband of her "best friend," poisons the wife, only to learn that the husband is in love with another, younger woman—and marries her. In *The Hawk and the Handsaw* (1948), author Michael Innes nixes Hamlet's suspicion that his uncle Claudius poisoned his father, the King of Denmark. Postmortem reveals that the title character of *The Late Edwina Black* (1949), by William Dinner and William Morum died of a lethal dose of arsenic. In *The Four of Hearts Mystery* (1949), adapted by William Rand from Ellery Queen's 1931 novel, the double murder of a newlywed couple takes place—off stage—in an airplane after morphine is planted in vintage wine bottles. An artist is condemned to prison for providing her sadistic brother with a lethal dose of tablets, but the sleuth of Charlotte Hastings' *Bonaventure* (1949), a nun, proves her innocence. With pangs of conscience for seducing the wife of his best friend and subsequently killing him, the protagonist of Ugo Betti's *Struggle Till Dawn* (1949) takes a deadly dose of poison. Private eye Nick Sherlock encounters a giant spider, whose bite is fatal, and escapes arsenic poisoning in the melodramatic *The Mystery of Mouldy Manor* (1950) by Ted Westgate. For monetary reasons, a doctor kills his wealthy patient with an overdose of insulin in *Remains to Be Seen* (1951) by Howard Lindsay and Russel Crouse. Socrates is condemned to death by poison in Maxwell Anderson's *Barefoot in Athens* (1951). In Friedrich Dürrenmatt's *The Marriage of Mr. Mississippi* (1952), a public prosecutor, mistakenly suspecting his wife of infidelity, poisons her coffee. Did Sir Francis Brittain, of Raymond Massey's *Hanging Judge* (1952), spike a blackmailer's drink with cyanide, or was it a suicide committed with the purpose of incriminating the judge? Upon losing a fortune in cards, a young Italian woman, who is the title character in Ugo Betti's *The Fugitive* (1953), pours rat poison into the winner's wine. James Reach's *The Girl in the Rain* (1953) is found unconscious on the road and seems to be suffering from amnesia—but is her malady only a sham? Could she be the notorious murderess sought by the police for the poisoning of several wealthy husbands? In David Campton's *The Laboratory* (1954), an apothecary in Renaissance Italy is visited by a court official, his wife, and his mistress, each asking for poison to dispose of the others. In *Deadly Poison* (1955) by Roland and Michael Pertwee, ten-year-old Lennie Grove finds a lost doctor's bag on the street and, on a lark, mixes tea that is served to his dad, mom, and grandma with potentially fatal pills. In Philip Mackie's *The Key of the Door* (1958), someone laces the medicine bottle of a much-hated actress with an overdose of sleeping pills. In Michael Gilbert's sardonically titled *A Clean Kill* (1959), the Other Woman, a chemist, does away with the wife of her beloved by tainting whiskey with grains of chlorazolidene, a newly invented cleaning fluid. In Robert Brome's The *Unsuspected* (1962), the title character is a playwright who serves a lethal overdose of sleeping pills to everyone who impedes his quest for fame and fortune. In Michael Gilbert's *The Shot in Question* (1963), the medical examiner finds morphine residue in the victim's body. But who injected her with the fatal dose?

In Peter Barnes's *The Time of the Barracudas* (1963), a man poisons his wife for insurance money and later marries a widow who has killed several previous husbands for the same reason. The moustached villain of Brian J. Burton's melodrama *The Murder of Maria Marten, or The Red Barn* (1964), substitutes medicine with rat poison to kill his illegitimate child.

Philip Mackie dramatized the George Simenon novel *Maigret and the Lady* (1965), in which Inspector Jules Maigret investigates the poisoning of a maid. In Hugh Wheeler's 1966 adaptation of Shirley Jackson's *We Have Always Lived in the Castle*, a disturbed young girl decimates almost an entire family by sprinkling sugar mixed with arsenic on their blackberries. One of the leading characters in Joe Orton's black comedy *Loot* (1966) is a nurse who, within seven years, poisoned seven husbands and is now anxious for one more conquest. In William McCleery's *A Case for Mason* (1967), the devoted housekeeper of a bestselling author poisons his two domineering wives so that he will be free to write "his beautiful books." The title character of Ira Levin's *Dr. Cook's Garden* (1967) is a Vermont small-town physician who poisoned thirty people he deemed undesirable in order to maintain the purity of his community. In Tim Kelly's 1970 one-act *The Last of Sherlock Holmes*, the world's foremost consulting detective succumbs to a poisonous pill that a jealous Dr. Watson inserted into a glass of brandy. A venomous blowgun dart pierces the neck of an army colonel in the musical spoof *Something's Afoot* (1972). In Jean-Claude van Itallie's satire on the mystery genre, *Murder Play* (1973), cocktail party revelers are murdered by a variety of methods, with one victim drinking poisoned coffee. In Charles Marowitz's *Sherlock's Last Case* (1974), Dr. Watson, angry about always playing second fiddle to the Great Detective, lures Holmes to a dark cellar, binds him to a chair, sprays him with acid, and leaves him for dead. A dotty old lady chokes to death on a slice of poisonous cake in Leslie Darbon's 1977 dramatization of Agatha Christie's 1950 novel, *A Murder Is Announced*. Sherlock Holmes fails to save the life of a client, who is murdered by a blowpipe's poison dart, in Paul Giovanni's *The Crucifer of Blood* (1978). Ravaged by a judge during a masquerade ball, the young, pretty wife of a London barber commits suicide by taking arsenic. This act triggers a quest for revenge by her husband, in *Sweeney Todd* (1979), "A Musical Thriller" with music and lyrics by Stephen Sondheim, book by Hugh Wheeler. Peter Shaffer's *Amadeus* (1979) poses the question, did the jealous composer Antonio Salieri attempt to murder Wolfgang Amadeus Mozart with arsenic?

In *My Cousin Rachel* (1980), adapted by Diana Morgan from Daphne du Maurier's 1951 novel, suspense is achieved through lingering doubt: is the charming young wife gradually poisoning the elderly master of the house? Young, handsome Harold Benton, the lead character of John Mattera's *An Open and Shut Case* (1981), aims to poison his rich, disabled, and elderly wife Elizabeth, but his plan goes awry in an unexpected way. Shirley Holmes, the heroine of Tim Kelly's *If Sherlock Holmes Were a Woman* (1982), attempts to solve the case of a dorm housemother found prostrate, seemingly dead, in her armchair. Was the victim's tea brewed with cyanide? Was the saccharine tinged with arsenic? Or was the instrument of death a poisonous blow-dart? In the climax of Tim Kelly's 1982 adaptation of Edgar Wallace's *The Mystery of the Black Abbot*, the mad, villainous Lord Harry Alford commits suicide by drinking poisonous liquid from a small antique flask. In Arthur Bicknell's *Moose Murders* (1983), a cold-blooded matriarch serves her twelve-year-old daughter a poison-laced vodka martini and chuckles joyfully, "Now I've got the whole Holloway fortune to myself." It is not until the shocking climax of *A Rose for Emily* (1983), adapted by Joseph Robinette from a short story by William Faulkner, that we understand why the title character had purchased arsenic from a local drug store. Xanax, a popular brand of alprazolam, an antianxiety medication, is utilized for murder in *Over My Dead Body* (1984) by Michael Sutton and Anthony Fingleton, suggested by the 1968 novel *The Murder League* by Robert L. Fish. A simple-minded maid is murdered by a poisoned lozenge in Hugh Leonard's *The Mask of Moriarty* (1985) while a cantankerous colonel is dispatched by strychnine in Charles Marowitz's *Clever Dick* (1986). In Jeffrey Archer's *Beyond Reasonable Doubt* (1987), a prominent Queen's Counsel is accused of mixing his wife's medicine with a lethal dose of the drug Cyclotoxelix. In *The Adventure of the Sussex Vampire* (1988), adapted by Peter Buckley from a Conan Doyle story, a Peruvian mother is suspected of biting the neck of her baby, drawing blood. Sherlock Holmes deduces that the mother was actually sucking the neck to draw venom out, saving the child's life.

In Rupert Holmes's spoof, *Accomplice* (1990), a determined wife pours a vial of nicotine into her husband's whiskey and soda, sprinkles the entire contents of a large salt shaker into the dip of salmon mousse to fatally affect his low blood pressure, and stabs him with a poisonous syringe—but miraculously the poor man survives. In Simon Brett's *Murder in Play* (1993), the lovesick stage manager of a community theatre drops poisonous tablets into a backstage decanter of sherry, disposing of the leading lady and snagging her husband. The victim of Francis Durbridge's *Sweet Revenge* (1993), a notorious womanizer, is fed Zarabell Four, a controversial tranquilizer known to have potentially lethal side effects. In Seth Greenland's political satire *Jungle Rot* (1995), Congolese Prime Minister Patrice Lumumba escapes an assassination attempt by the CIA that uses a lipstick that becomes poisonous only when combined with wine, because he doesn't drink alcohol. Wishing to dispose of her rich old husband, a farmer's wife mixes his whiskey with poisonous herbs in Romulus Linney's *True Crimes* (1995). In Robert Sheppard's spoof, *Agatha Christie's Greatest Case* (1997), the famous author investigates the murder of an English lord by rat poison. In Charles Busch's *Shanghai Moon* (1999), a waterfront madam does not realize that the tea offered by General Gong Fei is mixed with poison. A doctor is accused of poisoning his wife in Jeffrey Archer's courtroom drama *The Accused* (2000). The finger of suspicion keeps moving from suspect to suspect in *Who Poisoned His Meatball?* (2002) by Craig Sodaro. One of six diners at Luigi's Italian Restaurant mixed the spaghetti sauce with nicotine poisoning, killing the richest man in town. Who? Maura and Scott, the protagonists of Sam Bobrick's *The Stanway Case* (2003), meet when jurors in a murder trial and establish a romantic, albeit stormy, relationship. They eventually kill one another—she empties a vial of poison into his glass of wine; he strangles her.

Cyanide potassium, hyoscine, coniine, poisonous herbs, and overdoses of strong medicine are among the homicidal means introduced, respectively, in Agatha Christie's *Black Coffee* (1931), *Akhnaton* (1937), *Ten Little Indians* (1943), *Appointment with Death* (1945), *Verdict* (1958), *Go Back to Murder* (1960), *The Patient* (1962), and *Fiddlers Three* (1971).

Appendix B

Twentieth-Century Courtroom Dramas

1. Plays that unfold in a courtroom—civil, religious, military—or contain a pivotal courtroom scene:

Mrs. Dane's Defense (1900) by Henry Arthur Jones
The Living Corpse (1900) by Leo Tolstoy
Danton (1900) by Romain Rolland
Old Sleuth (1902) by Hal Reid
Sam Hill Jones (1902) by Hal Reid
Resurrection (1903) by Henri Bataille and Michael Morton, adapted from
   Leo Tolstoy's 1899 novel
The Silver Box (1906) by John Galsworthy
Madame X (1908) by Alexandre Bisson
Justice (1910) by John Galsworthy
The Confession (1911) by James Halleck Reid
The Boss (1911) by Edward Sheldon (1911)
The Mystery of the Yellow Room (1912) by Gaston Leroux
The Adored One aka *The Legend of Leonora* (1913) by J. M. Barrie
On Trial (1914) by Elmer Rice
The Ware Case (1915) by George Pleydell
The Man on the Box (1915) by Grace Livingston Furniss
Young America (1915) by Fred Ballard
The Guilty One (1916) by Charles Klein and Ruth Helen Davis
Lightnin' (1918) by Winchell Smith and Frank Bacon
For the Defense (1919) by Elmer Rice
Daddy Dumplins (1920) by Rufus King and George Barr McCutcheon
In the Night Watch (1921) by Michael Morton
Saint Joan (1923) by George Bernard Shaw
The Adding Machine (1923) by Elmer Rice
The Mongrel (1924) by Elmer Rice, adapted from the German of Herman
   Bahr

Beggar on Horseback (1924) by George S. Kaufman and Marc Connelly

The Trial of Jesus (1925) by John Masefield

A Holy Terror (1925) by Winchell Smith and George Abbott

The Enchanted Christmas Tree (1925) by Percival Wilde

An American Tragedy (1926) by Patrick Kearney, based upon the novel by Theodore Dreiser

Caponsacchi (1926) by Arthur Goodrich, based upon the poem "The Ring and the Book" by Robert Browning

Chicago (1926) by Maureen Dallas Watkins

The Pearl of Great Price (1926) by Robert McLaughlin

The Trial of Mary Dugan (1927) by Bayard Veiller

The Bellamy Trial (1928) by Frances Noyes Hart and Frank E. Carstarphen

Machinal (1928) by Sophie Treadwell

A Free Soul (1928) by Willard Mack

No Other Tiger (1928) by A. E. W. Mason

The Trial of You (1928) by Vere Bennett

Potiphar's Wife (1928) by Edgar C. Middleton

Scarlet Pages (1929) by Samuel Shipman and John B. Hymer

The Exception and the Rule (1929/1930) by Bertolt Brecht

The Silent Witness (1930) by Jack de Leon and Jack Celestin

Draw the Fires! (1930) by Ernst Toller

That's the Woman (1930) by Bayard Veiller

Cynara (1930) by H. M. Harwood and R. Gore Browne

Room 349 (1930) by Mark Linder

Precedent (1931) by I. J. Golden

Landslide (1932) by Ugo Betti

Nine Pine Street (1933) by John Colton and Carlton Miles

We, the People (1933) by Elmer Rice

Judgment Day (1934) by Elmer Rice

Legal Murder (1934) by Dennis Donoghue

They Shall Not Die (1934) by John Wexley

Libel! (1934) by Edward Wooll

Murder Trial (1934) by Sidney Bax

Night of January 16th (1935) by Ayn Rand

The Unguarded Hour (1935) by Bernard Merivale

Old Bailey (1935) by Campbell Dixon

For the Defence (1935) by John Hastings Turner

What Really Happened (1936) by Marie Belloc Lowndes

The Missing Witness (1936) by James Reach

Law and Order (1936) by Frederick Burtwell

Laughter in Court (1936) by Hugh Mills

Murder on Account (1936) by Hayden Talbot and Kathlyn Hayden

Blind Man's Buff (1936) by Ernst Toller and Denis Johnston

Young Madame Conti (1936) by Hubert Griffith and Benn W. Levy
Oscar Wilde (1936) by Leslie and Sewell Stokes
The Devil and Daniel Webster (1939) by Stephen Vincent Benét
Johnny Belinda (1940) by Elmer Harris
Native Son (1941) by Paul Green and Richard Wright
The Good Woman of Setzuan (1943) by Bertolt Brecht
Pick-Up Girl (1944) by Elsa Shelley
The Purification (1944) by Tennessee Williams
Signature (1945) by Elizabeth McFadden
Angel (1945) by Mary Hayley Bell
Christopher Blake (1946) by Moss Hart
The Story of Mary Surratt (1947) by John Parick
The Trial (1947) by Andre Gide and Jean Louis Barrault, based upon the
    novel by Franz Kafka
Blind Goddess (1947) by Patrick Hastings
The Exception and the Rule (1947) by Bertolt Brecht
The Caucasian Chalk Circle (1948) by Bertolt Brecht
Anne of the Thousand Days (1948) by Maxwell Anderson
The Vigil (1948) by Laszlo (Ladislaus) Fodor
Lost in the Stars (1949), book and lyrics by Maxwell Anderson, music
    by Kurt Weill, based upon the novel *Cry, the Beloved Country* by
    Alan Paton
A Pin to See the Peepshow (1951) by F. Tennyson Jesse and Harold Marsh
    Harwood, adapted from Jesse's novel
Barefoot in Athens (1951) by Maxwell Anderson
Billy Budd (1951) by Louis O. Coxe and Robert Chapman, adapted from
    the novella by Herman Melville
The Trial of Mr. Pickwick (1952) by Stanley Young, based on Charles
    Dickens's *The Pickwick Papers*
Witness for the Prosecution (1953) by Agatha Christie
The Crucible (1953) by Arthur Miller
The Caine Mutiny Court-Martial (1953), dramatized by Herman Wouk
    from his Pulitzer Prize novel
Carrington, V.C. (1953) by Dorothy Christie and Campbell Christie
Can-Can (1953), book by Abe Burrows, music and lyrics by Cole Porter
His and Hers (1954) by Fay Kanin and Michael Kanin
Inherit the Wind (1955) by Jerome Lawrence and Robert E. Lee
The Lark (1955) by Jean Anouilh
Man on Trial (1955) by Diego Fabbri
The Remarkable Incident at Carson Corners (c 1955) by Reginald Rose and
    Kristin Sergel
Time Limit! (1956) by Henry Denker and Ralph Berkey
The Ponder Heart (1956) by Joseph Fields and Jerome Chodorov, adapted
    from the story by Eudora Welty

Compulsion (1957), dramatized by Meyer Levin from his novel

The Defenders (1957), dramatized by Reginald Rose from his television show

Brothers in Law (1957) by Ted Willis and Henry Cecil

The Blacks (1958) by Jean Genet

The Resistible Rise of Arturo Ui (1958) by Bertolt Brecht

The Man Who Never Died (1958) by Barrie Stavis

You, the Jury (1958) by James Reach

The Trial of Dimitri Karamazov (1958) by Norman Rose, extracted from *The Brothers Karamazov* by Fyodor Mikhailovich Dostoyevsky

The Legend of Lizzie (1959) by Reginald Lawrence

Anatomy of a Murder (1959) by Elihu Winer, adapted from the novel by Robert Traver

Rashomon (1959) by Fay Kanin and Michael Kanin, based upon the stories by Ryunosake Akutagawa

Becket (1959) by Jean Anouilh

The Andersonville Trial (1959) by Saul Levitt

The Trial of Cob and Leach (1959) by Christopher Logue

One Way Pendulum (1959) by N. F. Simpson

Lock Up Your Daughters (1959), book by Bernard Miles, lyrics by Lionel Bart, music by Laurie Johnson, based upon the novel *Rape upon Rape* by Henry Fielding

The Trial of Joan of Arc at Rouen (1959) by Bertolt Brecht

Between Two Thieves (1960) by Warner Le Roy, adapted from the Italian of Diego Fabbri

The Deadly Game (1960) by James Yaffe, adapted from the novel *Traps* by Friedrich Dürrenmatt

A Man for All Seasons (1960) by Robert Bolt

Settled out of Court (1960) by William Saroyan and Henry Cecil, based on the novel by Cecil

Daughter of Silence (1961), dramatized by Morris L. West from his novel

We're All Guilty (1962) by James Reach

Sequel to a Verdict (1962) by Philip Dunning

The General's Dog (1962) by Heinar Kipphardt

Sweeney Todd the Barber (1962) by Brian J. Burton

The Advocate (1963) by Robert Noah

The Savage Parade (1963) by Anthony Shaffer

License to Murder (1963) by Elaine Morgan

A Case of Libel (1963) by Henry Denker, adapted from the book *My Life in Court* by Louis Nizer

A Darker Flower (1963) by Tim Kelly

Blues for Mr. Charlie (1964) by James Baldwin

Inadmissible Evidence (1964) by John Osborne

Hostile Witness (1964) by Jack Roffey

Hamp (1964) by John Wilson

The Investigation (1965) by Peter Weiss

Alibi for a Judge (1965) by Felicity Douglas, Henry Cecil, and Basil Dawson, adapted from the book by Cecil

Drat! The Cat! (1965), book and lyrics by Ira Levin, music by Milton Schafer

Justice Is a Woman (1966) by Jack Roffey and Ronald Kinnoch

The Man in the Glass Booth (1967) by Robert Shaw

For the Defense (1967) by James Reach

The Rimers of Eldritch (1967) by Lanford Wilson

According to the Evidence (1967) by Felicity Douglas, Henry Cecil, and Basil Dawson, adapted from the book by Cecil

The Trial of Lee Harvey Oswald (1967) by Amram Ducovny and Leon Friedman

The People vs. Ranchman (1968) by Megan Terry

Ivory Tower (1969) by Jerome Weidman and James Yaffe

The Lyons Mail (1969), adapted by George Rowell from *The Courier of Lyons* (1854) by Charles Reade

Conduct Unbecoming (1969) by Barry England

A Woman Named Anne (1969), adapted by Henry Cecil from his own novel

The Court Martial of Billy Budd (1969) by James M. Salem

Inquest (1970) by Donald Freed (aka *The U.S. vs. Julius and Ethel Rosenberg*)

The Trial (1970) by Steven Berkoff, based on the novel by Franz Kafka

A Voyage Round My Father (1970) by John Mortimer

Scratch (1971) by Archibald MacLeish, suggested by Stephen Vincent Benét's short story, "The Devil and Daniel Webster"

The Trial of the Catonsville Nine (1971) by David Berrigan

The Love Suicides at Schofield Barracks (1972) by Romulus Linney

The Remarkable Susan (1973) by Tim Kelly

The Trials of Oscar Wilde (1974) by Gyles Brandreth

Chicago (1975), book by Fred Ebb and Bob Fosse, lyrics by Fred Ebb, music by John Kander, based on the play by Maurine Dallas Watkins

The Runner Stumbles (1976) by Milan Stitt

Cause Célèbre (1977) by Terence Ratigan

The Biko Inquest (1978) by Norman Fenton and Jon Blair

Breaker Morant (1978) by Kenneth G. Ross

Zoot Suit (1978) by Luis Valdez

Esmeralda and the Hunchback of Notre Dame (1978) by Andrew Piotrowski

Nuts (1980) by Tom Topor

Salt Lake City Skyline (1980) by Thomas Babe

The New Trial (1982) by Peter Weiss

Execution of Justice (1984) by Emily Mann

The Mystery of Edwin Drood (1985), book, lyrics and music by Rupert
   Holmes, based on the unfinished novel by Charles Dickens
Never the Sinner (1985) by John Logan
The Boys of Winter (1985) by John Pielmeier
To Kill a Mockingbird (1987) by Christopher Sergel, adapted from the
   novel by Harper Lee
Les Misérables (1987), book by Alain Boublil and Claude-Michel Schön-
   berg, music by Schönberg, lyrics by Herbert Kretzmer, based on the
   novel by Victor Hugo
Beyond Reasonable Doubt (1987) by Jeffrey Archer
M. Butterfly (1988) by David Henry Hwang
Mock Trial (1988) by Romulus Linney
A Few Good Men (1989) by Aaron Sorkin
The Background (1989) by Jules Tasca, adapted from a story by "Saki"
2 (1990) by Romulus Linney
Green Fingers (1990) by Michael Wilcox
Slaughter on Second Street (1991) by David Kent
The Anastasia Trials in the Court of Women (1992) by Carolyn Gage
Hauptmann (1992) by John Logan
Empty Hearts (1992) by John Bishop
The Trial of Dr. Jekyll (1993) by William L. Slout
Starcrossed: The Trial of Galileo (1994), book and lyrics by Keith Levenson
   and Alexa Junge, music by Jeanine Tesori
The Boys in the Basement (1995) by Karen Houppert and Stephen Nunns
K: Impressions of a Trial (1995) by Garland Wright, adapted from Franz
   Kafka's novel *The Trial*
Greensboro: A Requiem (1996) by Emily Mann
Ragtime (1997) by E. L. Doctorow
Gross Indecency (1997) by Moisés Kaufman
Aftermath of a Murder (1997) by George Singer
Juris Prudence (1997) by Jason Milligan
*The Trial of One Short-sighted Black Woman vs. Mammy Louise and Safreeta
   Mae* (1998) by Marcia L. Leslie
Parade (1998), book by Alfred Uhry, lyrics and music by Jason Robert
   Brown
Shanghai Moon (1999) by Charles Busch
To Meet Oscar Wilde (1999) by Norman Holland
Everybody's Ruby (1999) by Thulani Davis

* * *

The Accused (2000) by Jeffrey Archer
The Perfect Murder (2000) by Hugh Janes
The Laramie Project (2000) by Moisés Kaufman

Comedy Court aka *Contempt of Court* (2000), book by David Landau, music and lyrics by Nikki Stern

Judgment at Nuremberg (2001) by Abby Mann

Romance (2005) by David Mamet

Direct from Death Row The Scottsboro Boys (2005), book by Mark Stein, music and lyrics by Harley White Jr.

The People vs. Mona (2007), book by Patricia Miller and Jim Wann, music and lyrics by Jim Wann

The Last Days of Judas Iscariot (2007) by Stephen Adly Guirgis

Court-Martial at Fort Devens (2007) by Jeffrey Sweet

The Big Bad Musical (2007), book by Alec Strum, music and lyrics by Bill Francoeur

The Lifeblood (2008) by Glyn Maxwell

Prisoner of the Crown (2008) by Richard F. Stockton

Thurgood (2008) by George Stevens Jr.

The Deep Throat Sex Scandal (2010) by David Bertolino

Sand in the Air (2011) by Brian Raine

South of Delancey (2011) by Karen Sommers

8 (2011) by Dustin Lance Black

A Time to Kill (2011) by Rupert Holmes, adapted from the novel by John Grisham

2. A trial looms in the background of the proceedings:

The Red Robe (1900) by Eugene Brieux

The House of Judges (1907) by Gaston Leroux

The Witness for the Defense (1911) by A. E. W. Mason

The Woman Who Was Acquitted (1919) by André de Lorde

The Attorney for the Defense (1924) by Eugene G. Hafer

The Letter (1927) by W. Somerset Maugham

Coquette (1927) by George Abbott and Ann Preston Bridgers

The Front Page (1928) by Ben Hecht and Charles MacArthur

Gods of the Lightning (1928) by Maxwell Anderson

Midnight (1930) by Claire Sifton and Paul Sifton

The Children's Hour (1934) by Lillian Hellman

Winterset (1935) by Maxwell Anderson

The Devil on Stilts (1937) by Florence Ryerson and Colin Clements

The Winslow Boy (1946) by Terence Rattigan

The Gioconda Smile (1948) by Aldous Huxley

Requiem for a Nun (1951) by William Faulkner

A Shot in the Dark (1961), adapted by Harry Kurnitz from *L'Idiote* by Marcel Achard

Lizzie! (1993) by Owen Haskell

Butterfly Kiss (1994) by Phyllis Nagy

* * *

The Stanway Case (2003) by Sam Bobrick
For All Time (2008) by K. J. Sanchez
Race (2009) by David Mamet
When We Go upon the Sea (2010) by Lee Blessing
Compulsion (2010) by Rinne Groff

3. Interrogations:

Interview (1904) by Octave Mirbeau
Enemies (1906) by Maxim Gorky
The Witch (1910), adapted by John Masefield from the Norwegian of H. Wiers-Jenssen
Hoppla! Such Is life! (1927) by Ernst Toller
Life of Galileo (1943) by Bertolt Brecht
Men without Shadows (1946) by Jean-Paul Sartre
Montserrat (1949), adapted by Lillian Hellman from a drama by Emmanuel Robles
The Queen and the Rebels (1949) by Ugo Betti
Darkness at Noon (1951) by Sidney Kingsley
The Prisoner (1954) by Bridget Boland
The Lark (1955), adapted by Lillian Hellman from Jean Anouilh's *L'Alouette*
The Dock Brief (1958) by John Mortimer
The Devils (1961) by John Whiting, adapted from the novel *The Devils of Loudun* by Aldous Huxley
In the Matter of J. Robert Oppenheimer (1968) by Heinar Kipphardt
The Trial (1972) by Anthony Booth
Answers (1972) by Tom Topor
Are You Now or Have You Ever Been (1972) by Eric Bentley
The Recantation of Galileo Galilei (1973) by Eric Bentley
From the Memoirs of Pontius Pilate (1976) by Eric Bentley
Time to Kill (1979) by Leslie Darbon
Agnes of God (1980) by John Pielmeier
Mastergate (1989) by Larry Gelbart
Death and the Maiden (1991) by Ariel Dorfman
Spain (1993) by Romulus Linney
Scotland Road (1993) by Jeffrey Hatcher
An Interview (1995) by David Mamet
The Interrogation of Nathan Hale (1995) by David Stanley Ford

* * *

Red Death (2001) by Lisa D'Amour
The Pillowman (2003) by Martin McDonagh

Security (2004) by Israel Horovitz
New Jerusalem (2008) by David Ives
The White Crow: Eichmann in Jerusalem (2009) by Donald Freed
Conviction (2010) by Oren Neeman
Jane Fonda in the Court of Public Opinion (2011) by Terry Jastrow
Oswald: The Actual Interrogation (2012) by Dennis Richard

4. Jury Room:

Resurrection (1903) by Michael Morton, adapted from the novel by Leo
    Tolstoy
The Woman on the Jury (1923) by Bernard K. Burns
The Jury of Her Peers (1925) by Edward Harry Peple
Ladies of the Jury (1929) by Fred Ballard
Good Men and True (1935) by Brian Marlow and Frank Merlin
Jury's Evidence (1936) by Jack de Leon and Jack Celestin
Ladies and Gentlemen (1939) by Ben Hecht and Charles MacArthur
Hanging Judge (1952) by Raymond Massey
Twelve Angry Men (teleplay aired on CBS's *Studio One* in 1954; play ver-
    sion published by Samuel French in 1955; Broadway debut, 2004) by
    Reginald Rose
Jury Room (1961) by C. B. Gilford
Twelve Angry Women (1984) by Sherman L. Sergel, adapted from a tele-
    play by Reginald Rose
Judge and Jury (1994) by Mark Dunn

* * *

Prisoner of the Crown (2008) by Richard F. Stockton

5. Lawyers and Judges out of Court:

The Lion and the Mouse (1905) by Charles Klein
At Bay (1913) by George Scarborough
The Last Resort (1914) by George Scarborough
At 9:45 (1919) by Owen Davis
Counsellor-at-Law (1931) by Elmer Rice
Counsel's Opinion (1932) by Roland Pertwee
The Judge (1938) by Jill Craigie and Jeffrey Dell
See My Lawyer (1939) by Richard Maibaum and Harry Clork
Corruption in the Palace of Justice (1945) by Ugo Betti
The Magnificent Yankee (1946) by Emmet Lavery
The Cocktail Party (1949) by T. S. Eliot
The Deep Blue Sea (1952) by Terence Rattigan

Hanging Judge (1952) by Raymond Massey

Can-Can (1953), book by Abe Burrows, music and lyrics by Cole Porter

Brothers in Law (1957) by Ted Willis and Henry Cecil

The Bargain (1961) by Michael Gilbert

Sweeney Todd The Barber (1962), book, music, and lyrics by Brian J. Burton

Time of Hope (1963) by Arthur Ketels and Violet Ketels, adapted from the novel by C. P. Snow

Feathertop (1963) by Maurice Valency, after a story by Nathaniel Hawthorne

After the Fall (1964) by Arthur Miller

Inadmissible Evidence (1964) by John Osborne

East Lynne (1965) by Brian J. Burton, adapted from the novel by Mrs. Henry Wood

Alibi for a Judge (1965) by Felicity Douglas and Henry Cecil, from the book by Cecil

The Judge (1967) by John Mortimer

A Case for Mason (1967) by William McCleary, based upon characters created by Erle Stanley Gardner

Sweeney Todd, the Demon Barber of Fleet Street (1969) by Austin Rosser

Jeremy Troy (1969) by Jack Sharkey

A Voyage Round My Father (1971) by John Mortimer

Sweeney Todd, the Demon Barber of Fleet Street (1973) by Christopher G. Bond

Clarence Darrow (1974) by David W. Rintels, adapted from the book *Clarence Darrow for the Defense* by Irving Stone

Curtains (1975) by Gloria Gonzalez

First Monday in October (1978) by Jerome Lawrence and Robert E. Lee

Aristocrats (1979) by Brian Friel

Sweeney Todd, the Demon Barber of Fleet Street (1979), book by Hugh Wheeler, music and lyrics by Stephen Sondheim

Guilty Conscience (1980) by Richard Levinson and William Link

Scales of Justice (1988) by William Kovacsik

The Perfect Murder (1989) by Mike Johnson

Lawyers (1998) by Henry G. Miller

Clarence Darrow Tonight (1999) by Laurence Luckinbill

* * *

Don't Go Gentle (2012) by Stephen Belber

Appendix C

Twentieth-Century Death-Row Plays

Throughout the twentieth century, quite a few plays climaxed on death row in European and American prisons. The vaults of Newgate, the scaffoldings of the Tower of London, the batteries of the Bastille, and the cells of Sing Sing were captured on the stage with nerve-wracking effect.

Among the dramas that boasted last-minute hanging, garroting, or electrocution are *Danton's Death* by George Büchner (written 1835; first produced 1902); *The Campden Wonder* by John Masefield (1907); *Man and the Masses* by Ernst Toller (1924); *An American Tragedy* by Patrick Kearney, based on Theodore Dreiser's 1925 novel (1926); *Spellbound* by Frank Vosper (1927); *Machinal* by Sophie Treadwell (1928); *Gods of the Lightning* by Maxwell Anderson (1928); *The Criminal Code* by Martin Flavin (1929); *The Last Mile* by John Wexley (1930); *Smoky Cell* by Edgar Wallace (1930); *Children of Darkness* by Edwin Justus Mayer (1930); *Draw the Fires!* by Ernst Toller (1930); *Midnight* by Claire Sifton and Paul Sifton (1930); *Elizabeth the Queen* by Maxwell Anderson (1930); *Two Seconds* by Elliott Lester (1931); *Mary of Scotland* by Maxwell Anderson (1933); *End and Beginning* by John Masefield (1933); *They Shall Not Die* by John Wexley (1934); *The Postman Always Rings Twice* by James M. Cain, dramatized from his 1934 novel (1936); *Leave Her to Heaven* by John Van Druten (1940); *Native Son* by Paul Green and Richard Wright (1941); *Uncle Harry* by Thomas Job (1942); *Antigone* by Jean Anouilh (1943); *Joan of Lorraine* by Maxwell Anderson (1946); *The Trial* by Andre Gide and Jean-Louis Barrault, based on Franz Kafka's 1925 novel (1947); *Anne of the Thousand Days* by Maxwell Anderson (1948); *Lost in the Stars* by Maxwell Anderson and Kurt Weill, based on the 1948 novel *Cry, the Beloved Country* by Alan Paton (1949); *Deathwatch* by Jean Genet (1949); *Song at the Scaffold* by Emmet Lavery, from the 1933 novel by Baroness Gertrud von le Fort (1949); *Darkness at Noon* by Sidney Kingsley, from the 1940 novel by Arthur Koestler (1951); *Requiem for a Nun* by William Faulkner (1951); *Billy Budd* by Louise O. Coxe and

Robert Chapman, from the 1886–1891 novel by Herman Melville (1951); *A Pin to See the Peepshow* by F. Tennyson Jesse and Harold Marsh Harwood, adapted from Jesse's 1934 novel (1951); *Murder Story* by Ludovic Kennedy (1954); *The Quare Fellow* by Brendan Behan (1954); *Compulsion* by Meyer Levin, dramatized from his 1956 novel (1957); *The Man Who Never Died* by Barrie Stavis (1958); *Channa Senesh* by Aharon Megged (1958); *Frankenstein* by David Campton (1959); *A Man for All Seasons* by Robert Bolt (1960); *Gallows Humor* by Jack Richardson (1961); *The Devils* by John Whiting (1961); *The Advocate* by Robert Noah (1963); *The Murder of Maria Marten, or The Red Barn* by Brian J. Burton (1964); *The People vs. Ranchman* by Megan Terry (1967); *The Disposal* (1968) by William Inge; *Inquest* by Donald Freed (1970); *The Runner Stumbles* by Milan Stitt (1976); *From the Memoirs of Pontius Pilate* by Eric Bentley (1976); *Breaker Morant* by Kenneth G. Ross (1978); *Hauptmann* by John Logan (1992).

Last-minute reprieves occur in *If I Were King* by Justin Huntly McCarthy (1901); *The Cardinal* by Louis N. Parker (1902); *A Working Girl's Wrongs* by Hal Reid (1903); *The Woman in the Case* by Clyde Fitch (1905); *How Hearts Are Broken* by Langdon McCormick (1905); *For a Human Life* by Hal Reid (1906); *The Confession* by James Halleck Reid (1911); *Silence* by Max Marcin (1924); *Beggar on Horseback* by George S. Kaufman and Marc Connelly (1924); *The Threepenny Opera* by Bertold Brecht and Kurt Weill (1928); *Fast Life* by Samuel Shipman and John B. Hymer (1928); *The Front Page* by Ben Hecht and Charles MacArthur (1928); *Midnight* by Claire and Paul Sifton (1930); *Precedent* by I. J. Golden (1931); *Riddle Me This!* by Daniel N. Rubin (1932); *Chalked Out* by Warden Lewis E. Lawes and Jonathan Finn (1937); *The Gioconda Smile* by Aldous Huxley (1948); *Dial "M" for Murder* by Frederick Knott (1952); *Hanging Judge* by Raymond Massey (1952); *The Prisoner* by Bridget Boland (1964); *Amazing Grace* by Michael Cristofer (1995); *Parade*, book by Alfred Uhry, music and lyrics by Jason Robert Brown (1998).

* * *

Dead Man Walking, opera, libretto by Terrence McNally, music by Jake Heggie (2000); *Direct from Death Row The Scottsboro Boys* by Mark Stein (2007); *Terre Haute* by Edmund White (2007); *The Exonerated* by Jessica Blank and Erik Jensen (2008); *When I Come to Die* by Nathan Louis Jackson (2011).

Last-minute reprieves: *The People vs. Friar Laurence*, book by Ron West, music and lyrics by Phil Swann and Ron West (2004); *The Exonerated*, by Jessica Blank and Erik Jensen (2002).

Appendix D
Children in Peril

Children have come to a sorry end on stage ever since a vengeful Medea presented her philandering husband Jason with the bodies of their infants in Euripides's *Medea* (431 BC), and the king's assassins stabbed Banquo's children in Shakespeare's *Macbeth* (c 1605).

Children have faced the Grim Reaper in many modern dramas. A grisly infanticide play, highlighted by a harrowing scene of a mother prodding her son to crush the skull of his newborn child, is Leo Tolstoy's *The Power of Darkness* (written in 1886; first produced 1902). In the climax of *At the Telephone*, a 1902 Grand Guignol playlet by André de Lorde, a countryside businessman, upon a visit to Paris, hears on the telephone the tortured screams of his six-year-old child as the little one and his mother are being strangled by a gang of tramps. An innocent mother is accused of killing her child in *How Hearts Are Broken* (1905) by Langdon McCormick. The villains of Hal Reid's *Lured from Home* (1905) kidnap little Helen Lindsay and plan to hurl her into a freshly dug excavation; the blackguards of Reid's *A Child Shall Lead Them* (1907) tie young Rita Lyle to a red-hot stove and place a powder-keg next to her; both girls are saved in the nick of time. A little girl is locked in an airtight bank vault in the climax of Paul Armstrong's *Alias Jimmy Valentine* (1910). *The Child* (1913), by Elizabeth McFadden, depicts a childless Midwestern couple who kidnap a baby.

A mother strangles her illegitimate baby in John Galsworthy's *Windows* (1922) while another mother smothers her baby with a pillow in Eugene O'Neill's *Desire under the Elms* (1924). A murderous monk stabs a little boy to death as part of a blood-libel against the Jews of Prague in H. Leivick's *The Golem* (1925). *Post Road* (1934) by Wilbur Daniel Steele is centered on the kidnapping of an infant for ransom. Lillian de la Torre's *Remember Constance Kent* (1949) spotlights the English murderess who in 1860 cut the throat of her four-year-old half-brother with a razor. A six-month-old baby is suffocated in his cradle (off stage) by the nanny in *Requiem for a*

Nun (1951) by William Faulkner. In Maxwell Anderson's *Bad Seed* (1954), little Rhoda Penmark drowns classmate Claude in the pond, jealous that he won the penmanship medal she desired. In David Campton's *Frankenstein: The Gift of Fire* (1959), the monster kills the boy William, Victor Frankenstein's younger brother.

Inspired by a real-life homicide in Victorian England, Brian J. Burton's melodrama *The Murder of Maria Marten, or The Red Barn* (1964) spotlights a dastardly villain who substitutes medicine with rat poison to kill his illegitimate child. Edward Bond's controversial *Saved* (1965) depicts a baby stoned to death by a gang of cockney toughs (on stage). A group of spoiled, malevolent teenagers kidnap a ten-year-old girl and plan to eliminate her via an overdose of sleeping pills in *The Playroom* (1965) by Mary Drayton. The disturbed kid sister of *We Have Always Lived in the Castle* (adapted by Hugh Wheeler in 1966 from the 1962 novel by Shirley Jackson) drops an African-American orphan, Jonas, to the bottom of a dumbwaiter shaft as an eerie "sacrifice." Three children in an attic play vicious games of predator and prey, accuser and accused, killer and victim in Jose Triana's *The Criminals*. (1970). The heroine of Charlotte Hasting's *The Enquiry* (1972) is sent to prison for killing her brain-dead child, a crime actually committed by her husband. One of the lingering questions in Ira Levin's *Veronica's Room* (1973) is why did fifteen-year-old Veronica kill her kid sister Cissie?

In the musical *Annie* (1977), based on Harold Gray's comic strip "Little Orphan Annie," a hard-drinking orphanage matron mistreats the eleven-year-old, redheaded title character and her young friends. In Sam Shepard's *Buried Child* (1978), an infant boy born of an incestuous relationship between a mother and her son is drowned by the woman's husband, a farmer, and buried in an arid courtyard. A black Philadelphia teenager senselessly shoots to death a twelve-year-old girl in *Zooman and the Sign* (1980) by Charles Fuller. In Arthur Bicknell's "mystery farce" *Moose Murders* (1983), an autocratic matriarch serves her twelve-year-old daughter a poison-laced vodka martini and squeals, "Now I've got the whole Holloway fortune to myself." A child named Victor is drowned by a mad maid in *The Mystery of Irma Vep* (1984) by Charles Ludlam. In Stephen Mallatratt's *The Woman in Black*, subtitled "A Ghost Story" (1987), the specter of an old woman seeking revenge for the death of her child unleashes a macabre sequence of events that culminates in the demise of other children. A jealous brother pricks a baby with a poisonous arrow in *The Adventure of the Sussex Vampire* (1988) by Peter Buckley, based on a short story by Arthur Conan Doyle. A little girl is kidnapped for ransom and murdered in the dark netherland of Chicago in *Earth and Sky* (1991) by Douglas Post.

In Steven Dietz's *Dracula* (1995), the count hands over a bag containing a tiny, crying baby to a pair of vixens who then proceed to plunge their teeth into the bag. In Dominique Dibbell's *Buried* (1995), a depraved father claims to have sexually abused, killed, and secretly buried as many as seventy-one of his infant daughters—or is it a fantasy abetted by alcohol and drugs? A rural, dysfunctional family conspires to smash the skull of an unwanted baby girl in *True Crimes* (1995) by Romulus Linney. Another baby girl is devoured by a cave man at the fade-out of one of the vignettes in *Apparition* (2005) by Anne Washburn. In *Coram Boy* (2007), adapted by Helen Edmundson from Jamila Gavin's novel, a nefarious "Coram Man" buries babies alive in eighteenth-century England. The focal point of Chad Beckim's *'nami* (2007) is the abduction of a little girl who was a survivor of the Indian Ocean tsunami. The title character of Howard Barker's short, poetic *Gary the Thief* (2010) is a ferocious working-class hoodlum who kills a baby and goes to prison; the title character of *Matilda* (2012), a musical based on Roald Dahl's 1988 children's novel, is a five-year-old girl who revolts against an extremely domineering schoolmistress.

Appendix E
Notable One-Acts of Mayhem, Mischief, and Murder

Albee, Edward

The Zoo Story

Albert, Ned

Dora, the Beautiful Dishwasher
Fireman, Save My Child!

Allen, Woody

Death
Death Knocks
Riverside Drive

Anderson, Kenneth

The "Admiral Benbow" (adapted from
 Robert Louis Stevenson's *Treasure
 Island*)

Anderson, Maxwell

Second Overture

Anderson, Robert

Solitaire

Anouilh, Jean

Medea

Anthony, Trent

The Masque of the Red Death (adapted
 from a story by Edgar Allan Poe)

Arrabal, Fernando

The Labyrinth
Picnic on the Battlefield
The Two Executioners

Austin, Harry

The Chinese Pendant
Maria Marten

Ayckbourn, Alan

A Cut in the Rates
Gizmo

Barker, Clive

Frankenstein in Love (inspired by
 William Shakespeare's *Titus
 Andronicus*)

Beach, Lewis

The Clod

Beim, Norman

The Hit
A Queen's Revenge

Bell, Neal

Drive

Benét, Stephen Vincent

The Devil and Daniel Webster

Bennett, Alan

A Question of Attribution

Berkoff, Steven

The Fall of the House of Usher (adapted
     from a story by Edgar Allan Poe)
The Penal Colony (from a story by
     Franz Kafka)
Tell-Tale Heart (from a story by Edgar
     Allan Poe)

Bishop, John

Borderlines: Borderline and *Keepin' an
     Eye on Louie*

Blankenship, Catherine

Murder Is Fun!

Booth, Anthony

None the Wiser
The Trial

Booth, Richard

The Horror Zone

Boyle, Viki

The Whole Truth

Bradbury, Ray

Kaleidoscope
The Pedestrian
Touched with Fire

Braun, Wilbur

Curse You, Jack Dalton
Her Fatal Beauty
The White Phantom

Bray, James L.

To Burn a Witch

Brecht, Bertolt

The Exception and the Rule
In Search of Justice
The Measures Taken

Brenner, Marlene

The Roof

Bromberg, Conrad

Transfers

Brome, Robert

Markheim (adapted from a story by
     Robert Louis Stevenson)
The Minister's Black Veil (from a story
     by Nathaniel Hawthorne)
One Day in the Life of Ivan Denisovich
     (from Alexander Solzhenitsyn)
The Suicide Club (from a story by
     Robert Louis Stevenson)
The Tell-Tale Heart (from a story by
     Edgar Allan Poe)

Brooke, Rupert

Lithuania

Burton, Brian J.

Foiled Again!
Ghost of a Chance
Murder Play
Three Hisses for Villainy!!!

Busch, Charles

Vampire Lesbians of Sodom

Calderon, George

The Little Stone House

Campton, David

After Midnight—Before Dawn
The Do-It-Yourself Frankenstein Outfit
Little Brother, Little Sister
Our Branch in Brussels
Who Calls?

Carlino, Lewis John

Junk Yard

Carmichael, Fred

Damsel of the Desert
Foiled by an Innocent Maid

Carroll, John R.

Murder Well Rehearsed

Carter, Lincoln J.

The Bride Special

Chekhov, Anton

On the High Road

Childress, Alice

String

Christie, Agatha

Rule of Three (*The Rats; Afternoon at the Seaside; The Patient*)

Churchill, Caryl

Blue Kettle
Hot Fudge
The Judge's Wife

Coble, Eric

Nightfall with Edgar Allan Poe

Coen, Ethan

Four Benches
Homeland Security

Connelly, Marc

Little David

Coward, Noel

Ways and Means

Cox, Constance

Lady Audley's Secret (based on a novel by Mary Elizabeth Braddon)

Maria Marten or The Murder in the Red Barn

Cucci, Frank

The Ofay Watcher

Dane, Clemence

Mr. Fox
Shivering Shocks or, The Hiding Place
A Traveller Returns

Darby, Edward

Two Bottles of Relish (based on a short story by Lord Dunsany)

Davies, David Stuart

Fixed Point (*The Life and Death of Sherlock Holmes; Sherlock Holmes through the Magnifying Glass; Sherlock Holmes—The Last Act*) [all three based on stories by Arthur Conan Doyle]

Daviot, Gordon

The Pen of My Aunt

Davis, Richard Harding

Peace Maneuvers

De Lorde, André

At the Telephone
The Cabinet of Dr. Caligari (based on the 1919 German movie)
The System of Dr. Tarr and Prof. Fether (from a short story by Edgar Alan Poe)

De Mille, William C.

Food

Dennis, Richard

Maria Marten

Dizenzo, Charles

The Metamorphosis (from a story by
    Franz Kafka)

Dorfman, Ariel

Widows

Downing, Martin

The Demon
Frankenstein's Guests
Out for the Count

Duffield, Brainerd

The Lottery (based on a story by
    Shirley Jackson)
The Summer People (based on a story
    by Shirley Jackson)

Dunsany, Lord

The Gods of the Mountain
A Night in an Inn
The Queen's Enemies

Durang, Christopher

*The Hardy Boys and the Mystery of
    Where Babies Come From*
A Stye of the Eye (part of *Durang/
    Durang*)

Dürrenmatt, Friedrich

*Conversation at Night with a Despised
    Character*
Episode on an Autumn Evening aka
    Incident at Twilight

Edwards, Mark R.

Wanted . . . Dead or Alive

Edwards, Perry

The Outcasts of Poker Flat (from a story
    by Bret Harte)

Eyen, Tom

Aretha in the Ice Palace
My Next Husband Will Be a Beauty

Falk, Lee

Home at Six

Feiffer, Jules

The Dicks

Feydeau, Georges

Fit to Be Tried
I Want You to Go to Sleep

Fletcher, Lucille

The Hitch-Hiker
Sorry, Wrong Number

Fo, Dario

An Ordinary Day
Medea
The Virtuous Burglar

Foote, Horton

The One-Armed Man

Fratti, Mario

Brothel
Her Voice
Porno
The Return

Fuller, Clark

The Rocking-Horse Winner (from a story
    by D. H. Lawrence)

Fuller, James

The Open Window (from a story by
    "Saki")

Gagliano, Frank

Paradise Gardens East

Gardner, Herbert

The Elevator

Genet, Jean

Deathwatch
The Maids

George, Charles

Bertha, the Bartender's Beautiful Baby
The Darkest Hour

Giffen, Sidney

Crime Conscious

Gillette, William

Among Thieves
The Red Owl

Glaspell, Susan

Trifles

Gogol, Nikolai

Gamblers

Gonzalez, Gloria

Curtains

Goodman, Jules Eckert

Back to Your Knitting

Goodman, Kenneth Sawyer

The Game of Chess

Gray, Virginia H.

Willie's Lie Detector

Green, George MacEwan

Sequence of Events

Green, Paul

Hymn to the Rising Sun
In Abraham's Bosom
Unto Such Glory

Greenberg, Richard

The Author's Voice
Vanishing Act

Gregg, Andy

The Family Jewels

Griscom, Bert, and John Ledru

The Shrieking Owl
The Song of Death

Guare, John

Cop-Out
The Loveliest Afternoon of the Year

Gurney, A. R.

The Golden Fleece

Hall, Holworthy, and Robert Middlemass

The Valiant

Hardwick, Michael, and Mollie Hardwick

The Blue Carbuncle; Charles Augustus Milverton; The Mazarin Stone; The Speckled Band (all four adapted from stories by Arthur Conan Doyle)

Harnick, Sheldon, and Jerry Bock

The Lady or the Tiger? (from a story by Frank R. Stockton)

Harrison, Neil

Whodidit?

Hartinian, Linda

Flow My Tears, the Policeman Said (from a novel by Phillip K. Dick)

Hatcher, Jeffrey

Murder by Poe (adapted from stories by Edgar Allan Poe)
The Thief of Tears

Havel, Vaclav

Audience
The Mistake

Hay, Ian

The Fourpenny Box

Henley, Beth

Control Freaks

Herlihy, James Leo

Bad-Bad Jo-Jo
Terrible Jim Fitch

Hershey, John

The Sign of Four (adapted from the novel by Arthur Conan Doyle)

Hischak, Thomas

Twice the Usual Number of Suspects

Holloway, Jonathan

The Dark
The Monkey's Paw (adapted from a short story by W. W. Jacobs)

Horovitz, Israel

The Indian Wants the Bronx
A Mother's Love

Rats
Security

Hwang, David Henry

Bondage
The House of Sleeping Beauties

Inge, William

The Disposal
A Murder
The Tiny Closet

Ionesco, Eugene

The Lesson

Jacobs, W. W.

The Boatswain's Mate
A Distant Relative
The Ghost of Jerry Bundler
In the Library

Jakes, John

Stranger with Roses
Violence

**Jesse, F. Tennyson,
and H. M. Harwood**

The Black Mask

Jones, Henry Arthur

The Knife

Jones, LeRoi

Dutchman

Kelly, Tim

The Adventure of the Clouded Crystal
Dog Eat Dog
Fog on the Mountain
The Hound of the Baskervilles (adapted from the novel by Arthur Conan Doyle)

Mason, Robert

An Evening with Edgar Allan Poe (based
    on stories by Edgar Allan Poe)

Mastrosimone, William

A Tantalizing

Mattera, John

Abra-Cadaver
An Open and Shut Case

Mattera, John, and Stephen Barrows

Frankenstein

May, Elaine

The Way of All Fish

McGreevey, John

Seeds of Suspicion (adapted from
    Dorothy L. Sayers's story, *Suspicion*)

McLellan, C. M. S.

The Shirkers

McNally, Terrence

Sweet Eros
Witness

**McOwen, J. B., and
Harry E. Humphrey**

The Skull

McPherson, Conor

The Good Thief
St. Nicholas
This Lime Tree Bower

Melfi, Leonard

Birdbath
Charity

Halloween
Mr. Tucker's Taxi
Rusty and Rico

Merivale, Bernard

Mystery Cottage
Robin-a-Tiptoe

Méténier, Oscar

Mademoiselle Fifi (adapted from a short
    story by Guy de Maupassant)

Miller, Arthur

Clara (part of *Danger: Memory!*)
Some Kind of Love Story

Miller, Kathryn Schultz

Poe! Poe! Poe! (adapted from writings
    by Edgar Allan Poe)

Milligan, Jason

Juris Prudence

Milne, A. A.

The Man in the Bowler Hat

Morlock, Frank J.

Clash of the Vampires

Mortimer, John

The Dock Brief

Mrozek, Slawomir

The Policeman

Nigro, Don

The Dead Wife
The Last of the Dutch Hotel
The Malefactor's Bloody Register
Mulberry Street
The Rooky Wood

Queirolo, Jose Martinez

R.I.P.

Rattigan, Terence

Before Dawn

Reach, James

Mr. Snoop Is Murdered

Reakes, Paul

Bang, You're Dead!
Mantrap

Redgrave, Michael

The Seventh Man

Ribman, Ronald

The Son Who Hunted Tigers in Jakarta

Richardson, Jack

Gallows Humor

Richmond, Susan

Treasure Island (from the novel by
    Robert Louis Stevenson)

Riggs, Lynn

Knives from Syria
Reckless

Robinette, Joseph

A Rose for Emily (based on a short
    story by William Faulkner)

Rubinstein, H. F.

Grand Guignol

**Ryerson, Florence, and
Colin Clements**

The Willow Plate

St. Clair, Robert

Who Killed Ann Gage?

St. Vincent Millay, Edna

Aria da Capo

Salem, James M.

The Court Martial of Billy Budd (from
    the novel by Herman Melville)

Saroyan, William

Hello out There

Sartène, Jean

The Claw

Sartre, Jean-Paul

No Exit

Saunders, James

Alas, Poor Fred
Birdsong
A Slight Accident

Schisgal, Murray

The Tiger

Schnitzler, Arthur

The Green Cockatoo

Sergel, Christopher

An Occurrence at Owl Creek Bridge
    (based on a short story by
    Ambrose Bierce)

Shaffer, Peter

The Public Eye
White Liars

Shanley, John Patrick

Out West

Shaw, George Bernard

Augustus Does His Bit
Cymbeline Refinished
Passion, Poison and Petrifaction
The Shewing-Up of Blanco Posnet
The Six of Calais

Shepard, Sam

Action
Killer's Head
Melodrama Play

Spence, Wall

The Case of the Weird Sisters
Four Frightened Sisters
The Locked Room

Sperinck, Jim

Jekyll in Hiding

Steele, Wilbur Daniel

The Giant's Stair

Stone, Joel

Horrors of Doctor Moreau (based on
     H. G. Wells's novel *The Island of
     Doctor Moreau*)

Stoppard, Tom

After Margritte
The Fifteen Minute Hamlet
The Real Inspector Hound

Stoppard, Tom, and Clive Exton

The Boundary

Stoppel, Frederick

Soulmates

Strindberg, August

Pariah

Strong, Austin

The Drums of Oude

Synge, J. M.

Deirdre of the Sorrows

Tait, Lance

The Fall of the House of Usher (inspired
     by an Edgar Allan Poe story)
The Imp of the Perverse (inspired by an
     Edgar Allan Poe story)

Tasca, Jules

The Background (from a tale by "Saki")
Blind Spot (from a tale by "Saki")
Hardstuff
The Macduff Tragedy
The Necklace (from a tale by Guy de
     Maupassant)

Taylor, Douglas

Five in Judgment

Taylor, Markland J.

The Inexperienced Ghost (based on a
     short story by H. G. Wells)

Topor, Tom

Answers

Totheroh, Dan

The Breaking of the Calm

Tristram, David

Brenton Versus Brenton

Twain, Mark

Down the River

Valency, Maurice

Conversation with a Sphinx

Feathertop (after a story by Nathaniel
   Hawthorne)

Van Itallie, Jean-Claude

Final Orders
Motel (part of *America Hurrah*)

Wallace, Edgar

The Forest of Happy Dreams

Walsh, Norman

Number One

Wasserman, Dale

Boy on Blacktop Road

Wells, John S.

The Ladykiller

Westgate, Ted

The Mystery of Mouldy Manor

Whiting, John

No Why

Wilde, Oscar

Salome

Wilde, Percival

Blood of the Martyrs
The Dyspeptic Ogre
The Finger of God
In the Net
The Luck-Piece
Pawns
The Traitor
World without End

Wilder, Thornton

Childhood
The Drunken Sisters
Mozart and the Gray Steward
Queens of France

Williams, Tennessee

The Dark Room
Something Unspoken
Suddenly Last Summer

Wilson, Lanford

A Poster of the Cosmos

Witney, Frederick

Coals of Fire

Yeats, William Butler

Purgatory

Index

Note: Bold page ranges refer to the entry for that particular play in the book.

About the Author

Amnon Kabatchnik holds a B.S. in theatre and journalism from Boston University, where he won the Rodgers & Hammerstein Award, and an M.F.A. from the Yale School of Drama. He has been a member of the director's unit with the Actors Studio in New York and has been appointed professor of theatre at the State University of New York at Binghamton, Stanford University, Ohio State University, Florida State University, and Elmira College.

Off Broadway, Kabatchnik has directed, among other plays, the American premiere of Anton Chekhov's A *Country Scandal* (Platonov); *Evenings with Chekhov*; *Vincent*, a drama about Van Gogh; and revivals of Maxwell Anderson's *Winterset*, John Willard's *The Cat and the Canary*, and Reginald Denham's *Ladies in Retirement*. At the Phoenix Theatre, he served as assistant to Tyrone Guthrie on Friedrich Schiller's *Mary Stuart* and Karl Capek's *The Makropulos Secret*, and to Tony Richardson on Eugène Ionesco's *The Chairs* and *The Lesson*. Kabatchnik's work in New York earned him the Lola D'Annunzio Honorary Citation for Outstanding Contribution to the Off-Broadway Theatre.

Kabatchnik has directed numerous dramas, comedies, thrillers, and musicals for national road companies, resident theatres, and summer stock and staged many crime-tinged plays including *Arsenic and Old Lace*, *Angel Street*, *The Mousetrap*, *Ten Little Indians*, *Dracula*, *Sleuth*, *Wait until Dark*, *Dial M for Murder*, and *A Shot in the Dark*. He has also directed productions in Israel and Canada.

Kabatchnik has written a weekly column of book reviews for the *Tallahassee Democrat*, *Corning Leader*, *Star-Gazette* of Elmira, N.Y., and *Chemung Valley Reporter*. He also contributed articles and reviews to *The Armchair Detective*, *Mystery News*, *Clues*, and other journals in the field of suspense.

He is the author of *Blood on the Stage: Milestone Plays of Crime, Mystery, and Detection: An Annotated Repertoire, 1900–1925* (2008), *Sherlock Holmes on the Stage: A Chronological Encyclopedia of Plays Featuring the Great Detective* (2008), *Blood on the Stage: Milestone Plays of Crime, Mystery, and Detection: An Annotated Repertoire, 1925–1950* (2009), and *Blood on the Stage: Milestone Plays of Crime, Mystery, and Detection: An Annotated Repertoire, 1950–1975* (2011), all published by Scarecrow Press.